Best-Loved Short Stories of Nineteenth-Century America

Edited by STEFAN DZIEMIANOWICZ

BARNES
&NOBLE
BOOKS
NEW YORK

Publisher's Note

All footnotes appearing herein are from the original editions of the works.

2003 Barnes & Noble Books

ISBN 0-7607-3479-8

Text design by Rhea Braunstein

Printed and bound in the United States of America

03 04 05 06 07 08 09 MP 9 8 7 6 5 4 3 2 1

BVG

Contents

Introduction

You and I tell stories by the dozens: accounts of our time in military service or in the supermarket checkout line, reminiscences of grandparents and dogs and beach vacations, reports of amatory triumph or disappointment. But we don't tell *short stories* like the ones in *Best-Loved Short Stories of Nineteenth-Century America*. Ours are likely to begin at random and trail off when we lose the thread of discourse; we touch on various topics and leave it to our listeners to make proper connections. Literary short stories, in contrast, possess beginnings, middles, and endings; they present situations with defined contours and characters who cast shadows; they offer themes—that is, they have something to say about how people live their lives, think their thoughts, and feel their emotions.

Such firm design was not always the case. People have always enjoyed brief narratives. The Bible abounds with story episodes, and other ancient literature is rife with them. Campfire and hearth fire transformed into strange masks the faces of those who sat by them, telling popular myths, legends, fables, and fairy tales. In our time, we recall those tales and retell them at the dinner table or to our children at bedtime. They comprise some of the chief mainstays of the human spirit.

Yet these myths and legends are not short stories as we now understand that term. The short story did not come into being until the nineteenth century in America, when one writer, Edgar Allan Poe, devised it as a conscious art literary form. While he was at it, he also invented many of the different kinds of stories that are still vivaciously with us: the detective story, the puzzle story, the study of abnormal psychology, the science fiction story, the symbolic character study, and a colorful number of others. Poe was the most conscious and purposeful of writers. He aimed to design stories that would create a single, overwhelming effect, and he succeeded in this ambition as often and as powerfully as anyone has done since his time.

It was neither possible nor desirable that this new literary form should entirely supplant the older tradition of oral storytelling. Tales such as Washington Irving's "The Legend of Sleepy Hollow" and Mark Twain's "The Celebrated Jumping Frog of Calaveras County" derive from the pipe smoker's musing and the porch whittler's yarning; they continue to be popular, but they no longer make up our literary mainstream. The ingenuity and flexibility of Poe's invention ensured that writers would employ this new resource in richly individual ways that the inventor could not have foreseen.

Missing from Poe's gallery of eccentric characters and from his array of extreme situations, however, was any depiction of the ordinary, workaday world in which most of us live and in which we find a drama that Poe's type of exaggerated expression would falsify. For some writers, the ingenuity of that master of the macabre was a limiting rather than a liberating factor because it omitted too many aspects of the world we recognize.

The recognizable world would soon claim its large place in literature. The mode that came to be called *realism* was introduced into the short story by such practitioners as George Washington Cable and Harriet Beecher Stowe, finding a hospitable home there and making possible powerful, down-to-earth studies such as Hamlin Garland's "Under the Lion's Paw" and muted, gravely observant sketches such as Mary E. Wilkins-Freeman's "A New England Nun."

These two particular stories are also known as *local color* stories because the element of place is so prominent in them. Certain narratives could take place only in the locales their authors provided and nowhere else. Cable's "Jean-ah Poquelin" had to be set in Louisiana; Mary N. Murfree's "The Dancin' Party at Harrison's Cove" requires the mountains of southern Appalachia for its backdrop; the incidents of "John's Trial," by Philander Deming, might be probable in any wilderness setting, but the Champlain Valley in the Adirondacks provides so pronounced a flavor for the story that to transplant it elsewhere would be injurious if not fatal.

The advent of the well-made short story was like the development of a new musical instrument with the range and pliability of the piano. It admitted brighter and deeper tones: the warm sentiment of Bret Harte's "The Luck of Roaring Camp," the whimsical entertainment of Thomas Bailey Aldrich's "Marjorie Daw," the political satire of John W. De Forest's "An Inspired Lobbyist," and the teasing impudence of Frank R. Stockton's "The Lady, or the Tiger?"

And soon an even grittier strain of realism developed: *naturalism*. This kind of writing sought to bring to light some of the most oppressed and depressed aspects of social life, from which our literature thus far had averted its gaze. The followers of naturalism thought it time for us to take a good, hard look at certain themes and subject matter: "This is what I want you to do. I want you to hide your disgust, take no heed to your clean clothes, and come right down with me—here, into the thickest of the fog and mud and foul effluvia." So says the narrator of Rebecca Harding Davis's "Life in the Iron Mills or The Korl Woman," and she delivers on her promise, showing "lanes and alleys and back-yards where the mill-hands lodged . . . the filth and drunkenness, the pig-pens, the ash-heaps covered with potato-skins, the bloated, pimpled woman at the door." She discovers not only "a new disgust," but also "a new sense of sudden triumph, and, under all, a new, vague dread, unknown before, smothered down."

Brave authors such as Stephen Crane marched boldly into this vast, rarely explored territory, exposing the harrowing underside of society. But naturalism, too, had its limitations, confining itself almost entirely to the life of a single social class and too often exhibiting that life in an unrelieved monotone. Ambrose Bierce, who was a master of realism as well as of fantasy, mocked the outlook of the genre as "nature, as it is seen by toads." His story "An Occurrence at Owl Creek Bridge" meticulously describes a reality that turns out to be illusion, the fantasy of a desperate mind.

The short story proved to be a precise and adaptable means of expressing the conflict between the outer, "real" world and the internal, subjective one. Most of us live in both of these worlds, hoping and striving to strike a balance, trying to ascertain whether our perceptions are congruent with the facts. Charlotte Perkins Gilman in "The Yellow Wallpaper" follows the lead of Poe's "The Tell-Tale Heart" by immersing us in the private inner world of a character whose perceptions seem sorely at variance with reality. Yet in these distorted perceptions we recognize certain truths, dramatic revelations unavailable to the mode of strict realism. Nathaniel Hawthorne in "The Minister's Black Veil" and Herman Melville in "Bartleby the Scrivener" reverse the process: the private desires, compulsions, and secret guilt of their characters take place in the actual world; the inner and outer become unified.

Hawthorne and Melville belong to that species of writers we know as "fabulists" because their purposes and some of their methods hark back to forms as ancient as fairy tales and the animal fables of Aesop. For the fabulists, theme was the predominant feature of story, and they found it to be most economically delivered through means not strictly realistic. They used recognizable setting as convenience rather than as a thematic element, and their stories can take place anywhere in the world. Their characters can be eccentric in behavior and exotic in personal appearance, but what these writers had to say they desired to apply to every living person. The last two words of Melville's story are "Ah, humanity!"

As the short story developed, it increased its power to depict both the outer and inner worlds so that, in the most skillful hands, the distinction between the objective and the subjective became moot. In his or her nature, the short story writer had both a poet's fluid intuition and beauty of language and a scientist's driving curiosity and unpitying powers of observation and analysis.

That description obviously applies to such writers as Kate Chopin and Sarah Pratt McLean Greene. Without the finest of intuitive equipment, Chopin could not have observed the tints of emotion that color her "Athénaïse": without rational analysis, she could not have conveyed to us what those subtle feelings add up to. There is political passion behind Greene's "The Singular Vote of Aut Tilbox," but her reasoning skills make the story a hilarious satire.

The great nineteenth-century American short story writers emphasized the perceived analogies between the material world and the immaterial, and they made those analogies palpable and dramatic. The truths they found by balancing intuitive perceptions with factual observation have passed the only certain test to which artistic truths can be subjected: they have endured, vibrantly and vividly, the passing of the decades.

Fred Chappell
University of North Carolina at Greensboro
April 2003

How I Went Out to Service

Louisa May Alcott
(1832–1888)

When I was eighteen I wanted something to do. I had tried teaching for two years, and hated it; I had tried sewing, and could not earn my bread in that way, at the cost of health; I tried story-writing and got five dollars for stories which now bring a hundred; I had thought seriously of going upon the stage, but certain highly respectable relatives were so shocked at the mere idea that I relinquished my dramatic aspirations.

"What *shall* I do?" was still the question that perplexed me. I was ready to work, eager to be independent, and too proud to endure patronage. But the right task seemed hard to find, and my bottled energies were fermenting in a way that threatened an explosion before long.

My honored mother was a city missionary that winter, and not only served the clamorous poor, but often found it in her power to help the decayed gentlefolk by quietly placing them where they could earn their bread without the entire sacrifice of taste and talent which makes poverty so hard for such to bear. Knowing her tact and skill, people often came to her for companions, housekeepers, and that class of the needy who do not make their wants known through an intelligence office.

One day, as I sat dreaming splendid dreams, while I made a series of little petticoats out of the odds and ends sent in for the poor, a tall, ministerial gentleman appeared, in search of a companion for his sister. He possessed an impressive nose, a fine flow of language, and a pair of large hands, encased in black kid gloves. With much waving of these somber members, Mr. R. set forth the delights awaiting the happy soul who should secure this home. He described it as a sort of heaven on earth. "There are books, pictures, flowers, a piano, and the best of society," he said. "This person will be one of the family in all respects, and only required to help about the lighter work, which my sister has done herself hitherto, but is now a martyr to neuralgia and needs a gentle friend to assist her."

My mother, who never lost her faith in human nature, in spite of many impostures, believed every word, and quite beamed with benevolent interest as she listened and tried to recall some needy young woman to whom this charming home would be a blessing. I also innocently thought:

"That sounds inviting. I like housework and can do it well. I should have time to enjoy the books and things I love, and D— is not far away from home. Suppose I try it."

So, when my mother turned to me, asking if I could suggest any one, I became as red as a poppy and said abruptly:

"Only myself."

"Do you really mean it?" cried my astonished parent.

"I really do if Mr. R. thinks I should suit," was my steady reply, as I partially obscured my crimson countenance behind a little flannel skirt, still redder.

The Reverend Josephus gazed upon me with the benign regard which a bachelor of five and thirty may accord a bashful damsel of eighteen. A smile dawned upon his countenance, "sick-lied o'er with the pale cast of thought," or dyspepsia; and he softly folded the black gloves, as if about to bestow a blessing as he replied, with emphasis:

"I am sure you would, and we should think ourselves most fortunate if we could secure your society, and—ahem—services for my poor sister."

"Then I'll try it," responded the impetuous maid.

"We will talk it over a little first, and let you know to-morrow, sir," put in my prudent parent, adding, as Mr. R. arose: "What wages do you pay?"

"My dear madam, in a case like this let me not use such words as those. Anything you may think proper we shall gladly give. The labor is very light, for there are but three of us and our habits are of the simplest sort. I am a frail reed and may break at any mo-ment; so is my sister, and my aged father cannot long remain; therefore, money is little to us, and any one who comes to lend her youth and strength to our feeble household will not be forgotten in the end, I assure you." And, with another pensive smile, a farewell wave of the impressive gloves, the Reverend Josephus bowed like a well-sweep and departed.

"My dear, are you in earnest?" asked my mother.

"Of course, I am. Why not try this experiment? It can but fail, like all the others."

"I have no objection; only I fancied you were rather too proud for this sort of thing."

"I am too proud to be idle and dependent, ma'am. I'll scrub floors and take in washing first. I do housework at home for love; why not do it abroad for money? I like it better than teaching. It is healthier than sewing and surer than writing. So why not try it?"

"It is going out to service, you know, though you are called a companion. How does that suit?"

"I don't care. Every sort of work that is paid for is service; and I don't mind being a companion, if I can do it well. I may find it is my mission to take care of neuralgic old ladies and lackadaisical clergymen. It does not sound exciting, but it's better than nothing," I answered, with a sigh; for it *was* rather a sudden downfall to give up being a Siddons and become a Betcinder.

How my sisters laughed when they heard the new plan! But they soon resigned themselves, sure of fun, for Lu's adventures were the standing joke of the family. Of course, the highly respectable relatives held up their hands in holy horror at the idea of one of the clan degrading herself by going out to service. Teaching a private school was the proper thing for an indigent gentlewoman. Sewing even, if done in the seclusion of home and not mentioned in public, could be tolerated. Story-writing was a genteel accomplishment and reflected credit upon the name. But leaving the paternal roof to wash other people's teacups, nurse other people's ails, and obey other people's orders for hire—this, this was degradation; and headstrong Louisa would disgrace her name forever if she did it.

Opposition only fired the revolutionary blood in my veins, and I crowned my iniquity by the rebellious declaration:

"If doing this work hurts my respectability, I wouldn't give much for it. My aristocratic ancestors don't feed or clothe me and my democratic ideas of honesty and honor won't let me be idle or dependent. You need not know me if you are ashamed of me, and I won't ask you for a penny; so, if I never do succeed in anything, I shall have the immense satisfaction of knowing I am under no obligation to any one."

In spite of the laughter and the lamentation, I got ready my small wardrobe, consisting of two calico dresses and one delaine, made by myself, also several large and uncompromising blue aprons and three tidy little sweeping-caps; for I had some English notions about housework and felt that my muslin hair-protectors would be useful in some of the "light labors" I was to undertake. It is needless to say they were very becoming. Then, firmly embracing my family, I set forth, one cold January day, with my little trunk, a stout heart, and a five-dollar bill for my fortune.

"She will be back in a week," was my sister's prophecy, as she wiped her weeping eye.

"No, she won't, for she has promised to stay the month out and she will keep her word," answered my mother, who always defended the black sheep of her flock.

I heard both speeches, and registered a tremendous vow to keep that promise, if I died in the attempt—little dreaming, poor innocent, what lay before me.

Josephus meantime had written me several remarkable letters, describing the different members of the family I was about to enter. His account was peculiar, but I believed every word of it and my romantic fancy was much excited by the details he gave. The principal ones are as follows, condensed from the voluminous epistles which he evidently enjoyed writing:

"You will find a stately mansion, fast falling to decay, for my father will have nothing repaired, preferring that the old house and its master should crumble away together. I have, however, been permitted to rescue a few rooms from ruin; and here I pass my recluse life, surrounded by the things I love. This will naturally be more attractive to you than the gloomy apartments my father inhabits, and I hope you will here allow me to minister to your young and cheerful nature when your daily cares are over. I need such companionship and shall always welcome you to my abode.

"Eliza, my sister, is a child at forty, for she has lived alone with my father and an old servant all her life. She is a good creature, but not lively, and needs stirring up, as you will soon see. Also I hope by your means to rescue her from the evil influence of Puah, who, in my estimation, is a *wretch*. She has gained entire control over Eliza, and warps her mind with great skill, prejudicing her against *me* and thereby desolating my home. Puah hates *me* and always has. Why I know not, except I will not yield to her control. She ruled here for years while I was away, and my return upset all her nefarious plans. It will always be my firm opinion that she has tried to *poison me*, and may again. But even this dark suspicion will not deter me from my duty. I cannot send her away, for both my deluded father and my sister have entire faith in her, and I cannot shake it. She is faithful and kind to them, so I submit and remain to guard them, even at the risk of my life.

"I tell you these things because I wish you to know all and be warned, for this old hag has a specious tongue, and I should grieve to see you deceived by her lies. Say nothing, but watch her silently, and help me to thwart her evil plots; but do not trust her, or beware."

Now this was altogether romantic and sensational, and I felt as if about to enter one of those delightfully dangerous houses we read of in novels, where perils, mysteries, and sins freely disport themselves, till the newcomer sets all to rights, after unheard of trials and escapes.

I arrived at twilight, just the proper time for the heroine to appear; and, as no one answered my modest solo on the rusty knocker, I walked in and looked about me. Yes, here was the long, shadowy hall, where the ghosts doubtless walked at midnight. Peering in at an open door on the right, I saw a parlor full of ancient furniture, faded, dusty, and dilapidated. Old portraits stared at me from the walls and a damp chill froze the marrow of my bones in the most approved style.

"The romance opens well," I thought, and, peeping in at an opposite door, beheld a luxurious apartment, full of the warm glow of firelight, the balmy breath of hyacinths and roses, the white glimmer of piano keys, and tempting rows of books along the walls.

The contrast between the two rooms was striking, and, after an admiring survey, I continued my explorations, thinking that I should not mind being "ministered to" in that inviting place when my work was done.

A third door showed me a plain, dull sitting room, with an old man napping in his easy-chair. I heard voices in the kitchen beyond, and, entering there, beheld Puah the fiend. Unfortunately, for the dramatic effect of the tableaux, all I saw was a mild-faced old woman, buttering toast, while she conversed with her familiar, a comfortable gray cat.

The old lady greeted me kindly, but I fancied her faded blue eye had a weird expression and her amiable words were all a snare, though I own I was rather disappointed at the commonplace appearance of this humble Borgia.

She showed me to a tiny room, where I felt more like a young giantess than ever, and was obliged to stow away my possessions as snugly as in a ship's cabin. When I presently descended, armed with a blue apron and "a heart for any fate," I found the old man awake and received from him a welcome full of ancient courtesy and kindliness. Miss Eliza crept in like a timid mouse, looking so afraid of her buxom companion that I forgot my own shyness in trying to relieve hers. She was so enveloped in shawls that all I could discover was that my mistress was a very nervous little woman, with a small button of pale hair on the outside of her head and the vaguest notions of work inside. A few spasmodic remarks and many awkward pauses brought me to teatime, when Josephus appeared, as tall, thin, and cadaverous as ever. After his arrival there was no more silence, for he preached all suppertime something in this agreeable style.

"My young friend, our habits, as you see, are of the simplest.

We eat in the kitchen, and all together, in the primitive fashion; for it suits my father and saves labor. I could wish more order and elegance; but *my* wishes are not consulted and I submit. I live above these petty crosses, and, though my health suffers from bad cookery, I do not murmur. Only, I must say, in passing, that if you *will* make your battercakes green with saleratus, Puah, I shall feel it my duty to throw them out of the window. *I* am used to poison; but I cannot see the coals of this blooming girl's stomach destroyed, as mine have been. And, speaking of duties, I may as well mention to you, Louisa (I call you so in a truly fraternal spirit), that I like to find my study in order when I come down in the morning; for I often need a few moments of solitude before I face the daily annoyances of my life. I shall permit *you* to perform this light task, for *you* have some idea of order (I see it in the formation of your brow), and feel sure that *you* will respect the sanctuary of thought. Eliza is so blind she does not see dust, and Puah enjoys devastating the one poor refuge I can call my own this side the grave. We are all waiting for you, sir. My father keeps up the old formalities, you observe; and I endure them, though *my* views are more advanced."

The old gentleman hastily finished his tea and returned thanks, when his son stalked gloomily away, evidently oppressed with the burden of his wrongs, also, as I irreverently fancied, with the seven "green" flapjacks he had devoured during the sermon.

I helped wash up the cups, and during that domestic rite Puah chatted in what I should have considered a cheery, social way had I not been darkly warned against her wiles.

"You needn't mind half Josephus says, my dear. He likes to hear himself talk and always goes on so before folks. I sometimes thinks his books and new ideas have sort of muddled his wits, for he is as full of notions as a paper is of pins; and he gets dreadfully put out if we don't give in to 'em. But, gracious me! they are so redicklus

sometimes and so selfish I can't allow him to make a fool of himself or plague Lizy. She don't dare to say her soul is her own; so I
have to stand up for her. His pa don't know half his odd doings;
for I try to keep the old gentleman comfortable and have to manage 'em all, which is not an easy job I do assure you."

I had a secret conviction that she was right, but did not commit myself in any way, and we joined the social circle in the sitting
room. The prospect was not a lively one, for the old gentleman
nodded behind his newspaper; Eliza, with her head pinned up in a
little blanket, slumbered on the sofa, Puah fell to knitting silently;
and the plump cat dozed under the stove. Josephus was visible, ar-
tistically posed in the luxurious recesses of his cell, with the light
beaming on his thoughtful brow, as he pored over a large volume
or mused with upturned eye.

Having nothing else to do, I sat and stared at him, till, emerging from a deep reverie, with an effective start, he became conscious of my existence and beckoned me to approach the
"sanctuary of thought" with a dramatic waft of his large hand.

I went, took possession of an easy chair, and prepared myself
for elegant conversation. I was disappointed, however; for Josephus
showed me a list of his favorite dishes, sole fruit of all that absorbing thought, and, with an earnestness that flushed his saffron countenance, gave me hints as to the proper preparation of these
delicacies.

I mildly mentioned that I was not a cook; but was effectually
silenced by being reminded that I came to be generally useful, to
take his sister's place, and see that the flame of life which burned
so feebly in this earthly tabernacle was fed with proper fuel. Mince
pies, Welsh rarebits, sausages, and strong coffee did not strike me as
strictly spiritual fare; but I listened meekly and privately resolved
to shift this awful responsibility to Puah's shoulders.

Detecting me in gape, after an hour of this high converse, he presented me with an overblown rose, which fell to pieces before I got out of the room, pressed my hand, and dismissed me with a fervent "God bless you, child. Don't forget the dropped eggs for breakfast."

I was up betimes next morning and had the study in perfect order before the recluse appeared, enjoying a good prowl among the books as I worked and becoming so absorbed that I forgot the eggs, till a gusty sigh startled me, and I beheld Josephus, in dressing gown and slippers, languidly surveying the scene.

"Nay, do not fly," he said, as I grasped my duster in guilty haste. "It pleases me to see you here and lends a sweet, domestic charm to my solitary room. I like that graceful cap, that housewifely apron, and I beg you to wear them often; for it refreshes my eye to see something tasteful, young, and womanly about me. Eliza makes a bundle of herself and Puah is simply detestable."

He sank languidly into a chair and closed his eyes, as if the mere thought of his enemy was too much for him. I took advantage of this momentary prostration to slip away, convulsed with laughter at the looks and words of this bald-headed sentimentalist.

After breakfast I fell to work with a will, eager to show my powers and glad to put things to rights, for many hard jobs had evidently been waiting for a stronger arm than Puah's and a more methodical head than Eliza's.

Everything was dusty, moldy, shiftless, and neglected, except the domain of Josephus. Up-stairs the paper was dropping from the walls, the ancient furniture was all more or less dilapidated, and every hold and corner was full of relics tucked away by Puah, who was a regular old magpie. Rats and mice reveled in the empty rooms and spiders wove their tapestry undisturbed, for the old man would have nothing altered or repaired and his part of the house was fast going to ruin.

I longed to have a grand "clearing up"; but was forbidden to do more than to keep things in livable order. On the whole, it was fortunate, for I soon found that my hands would be kept busy with the realms of Josephus, whose ethereal being shrank from dust, shivered at a cold breath, and needed much cosseting with dainty food, hot fires, soft beds, and endless service, else, as he expressed it, the frail reed would break.

I regret to say that a time soon came when I felt supremely indifferent as to the breakage, and very skeptical as to the fragility of a reed that ate, slept, dawdled, and scolded so energetically. The rose that fell to pieces so suddenly was a good symbol of the rapid disappearance of all the romantic delusions I had indulged in for a time. A week's acquaintance with the inmates of this odd house quite settled my opinion, and further developments only confirmed it.

Miss Eliza was a nonentity and made no more impression on me than a fly. The old gentleman passed his days in a placid sort of doze and took no notice of what went on about him. Puah had been a faithful drudge for years, and, instead of being a "wretch," was, as I soon satisfied myself, a motherly old soul, with no malice in her. The secret of Josephus's dislike was that the reverend tyrant ruled the house, and all obeyed him but Puah, who had nursed him as a baby, boxed his ears as a boy, and was not afraid of him even when he became a man and a minister. I soon repented of my first suspicions, and grew fond of her, for without my old gossip I should have fared ill when my day of tribulation came.

At first I innocently accepted the fraternal invitations to visit the study, feeling that when my day's work was done I earned a right to rest and read. But I soon found that this was not the idea. I was not to read; but to be read to. I was not to enjoy the flowers, pictures, fire, and books; but to keep them in order for my lord to enjoy. I was also to be a passive bucket, into which he was to pour all manner of philosophic, metaphysical, and sentimental rubbish. I was to serve his needs, soothe his sufferings, and sympathize with all his sorrows—be a galley slave, in fact.

As soon as I clearly understood this, I tried to put an end to it by shunning the study and never lingering there an instant after my work was done. But it availed little, for Josephus demanded much sympathy and was bound to have it. So he came and read poems while I washed dishes, discussed his pet problems all mealtimes, and put reproachful notes under my door, in which were comically mingled complaints of neglect and orders for dinner.

I bore it as long as I could, and then freed my mind in a declaration of independence, delivered in the kitchen, where he found me scrubbing the hearth. It was not an impressive attitude for an orator, nor was the occupation one a girl would choose when receiving calls; but I have always felt grateful for the intense discomfort of that moment, since it gave me the courage to rebel outright. Stranded on a small island of mat, in a sea of soapsuds, I brandished a scrubbing brush, as I indignantly informed him that I came to be a companion to his sister, not to him, and I should keep that post or none. This I followed up by reproaching him with the delusive reports he had given me of the place and its duties, and assuring him that I should not stay long unless matters mended.

"But I offer you lighter tasks, and you refuse them," he began, still hovering in the doorway, whither he had hastily retired when I opened my batteries.

"But I don't like the tasks, and consider them much worse than hard work," was my ungrateful answer, as I sat upon my island, with the softsoap conveniently near.

"Do you mean to say you prefer to scrub the hearth to sitting in my charming room while I read Hegel to you?" he demanded, glaring down upon me.

"Infinitely," I responded promptly, and emphasized my words by beginning to scrub with a zeal that made the bricks white with foam.

"Is it possible!" and, with a groan at my depravity, Josephus retired, full of ungodly wrath.

I remember that I immediately burst into jocund song, so that no doubt might remain in his mind, and continued to warble cheerfully till my task was done. I also remember that I cried heartily when I got to my room, I was so vexed, disappointed, and tired. But my bower was so small I should soon have swamped the furniture if I had indulged copiously in tears; therefore I speedily dried them up, wrote a comic letter home, and waited with interest to see what would happen next.

Far be it from me to accuse one of the nobler sex of spite or the small revenge of underhand annoyances and slights to one who could not escape and would not retaliate; but after that day a curious change came over the spirit of that very unpleasant dream. Gradually all the work of the house had been slipping into my hands; for Eliza was too poorly to help and direct, and Puah too old to do much besides the cooking. About this time I found that even the roughest work was added to my share, for Josephus was unusually feeble and no one was hired to do his chores. Having made up my mind to go when the month was out, I said nothing, but dug paths, brought water from the well, split kindlings, made fires, and sifted ashes, like a true Cinderella.

There never had been any pretense of companionship with Eliza, who spent her days mulling over the fire, and seldom exerted herself except to find odd jobs for me to do—rusty knives to clean, sheets to turn, old stockings to mend, and, when all else failed, some paradise of moths and mice to be cleared up; for the house was full of such "glory holds."

If I remonstrated, Eliza at once dissolved into tears and said she must do as she was told; Puah begged me to hold on till spring, when things would be much better; and pity pleaded for the two poor souls. But I don't think I could have stood it if my promise had not bound me, for when the fiend said "Budge" honor said "Budge not" and I stayed.

But, being a mortal worm, I turned now and then when ireful Josephus trod upon me too hard, especially in the matter of boot-blacking. I really don't know why that is considered such humiliating work for a woman; but so it is, and there I drew the line. I would have cleaned the old man's shoes without a murmur; but he preferred to keep their native rustiness intact. Eliza never went out, and Puah affected carpet-slippers of the Chinese-junk pattern. Josephus, however, plumed himself upon his feet, which like his nose, were large, and never took his walks abroad without his boots in a high state of polish. He had brushed them himself at first; but soon after the explosion I discovered a pair of muddy boots in the shed, set suggestively near the blacking-box. I did not take the hint; feeling instinctively that this amiable being was trying how much I would bear for the sake of peace.

The boots remained untouched; and another pair soon came to keep them company, whereat I smiled wickedly as I chopped just kindlings enough for my own use. Day after day the collection grew, and neither party gave in. Boots were succeeded by shoes, then rubbers gave a pleasing variety to the long line, and then I knew the end was near.

"Why are not my boots attended to?" demanded Josephus, one evening, when obliged to go out.

"I'm sure I don't know," was Eliza's helpless answer.

"I told Louizy I guessed you'd want some of 'em before long," observed Puah with an exasperating twinkle in her old eye.

"And what did she say?" asked my lord with an ireful whack of his velvet slippers as he cast them down.

"Oh! she said she was so busy doing your other work you'd have to do that yourself; and I thought she was about right."

"Louizy" heard it all through the slide, and could have embraced the old woman for her words, but kept still till Josephus had resumed his slippers with a growl and retired to the shed, leaving Eliza in tears, Puah chuckling, and the rebellious handmaid exulting in the china-closet.

Alas! for romance and the Christian virtues, several pairs of boots were cleaned that night, and my sinful soul enjoyed the spectacle of the reverend bootblack at his task. I even found my "fancy work," as I called the evening job of paring a bucketful of hard russets with a dull knife, much cheered by the shoe-brush accompaniment played in the shed.

Thunder-clouds rested upon the martyr's brow at breakfast, and I was as much ignored as the cat. And what a relief that was! The piano was locked up, so were the bookcases, the newspapers mysteriously disappeared, and a solemn silence reigned at table, for no one dared to talk when that gifted tongue was mute. Eliza fled from the gathering storm and had a comfortable fit of neuralgia in her own room, where Puah nursed her, leaving me to skirmish with the enemy.

It was not a fair fight, and that experience lessened my respect for mankind immensely. I did my best, however—grubbed about all day and amused my dreary evenings as well as I could; too proud even to borrow a book, lest it should seem like a surrender. What a long month it was, and how eagerly I counted the hours of that last week, for my time was up Saturday and I hoped to be off at once. But when I announced my intention such dismay fell upon Eliza that my heart was touched, and Puah so urgently begged me to stay till they could get some one that I consented to remain a few days longer, and wrote posthaste to my mother, telling her to send a substitute quickly or I should do something desperate.

That blessed woman, little dreaming of all the woes I had endured, advised me to be patient, to do the generous thing, and be sure I should not regret it in the end. I groaned, submitted, and did regret it all the days of my life.

Three mortal weeks I waited; for, though two other victims came, I was implored to set them going, and tried to do it. But both fled after a day or two, condemning the place as a very hard one and calling me a fool to stand it another hour. I entirely agreed with them on both points, and, when I had cleared up after the second incapable lady, I tarried not for the coming of a third, but clutched my property and announced my departure by the next train.

Of course, Eliza wept, Puah moaned, the old man politely regretted, and the younger one washed his hands of the whole affair by shutting himself up in his room and forbidding me to say farewell because "he could not bear it." I laughed, and fancied it done for effect then; but I soon understood it better and did not laugh.

At the last moment, Eliza nervously tucked a sixpenny pocketbook into my hand and shrouded herself in the little blanket with a sob. But Puah kissed me kindly and whispered, with an odd look: "Don't blame us for anything. Some folks is liberal and some ain't." I thanked the poor old soul for her kindness to me and trudged gayly away to the station, whither my property had preceded me on a wheelbarrow, hired at my own expense.

I never shall forget that day. A bleak March afternoon, a sloppy, lonely road, and one hoarse crow stalking about a field, so like Josephus that I could not resist throwing a snowball at him. Behind me stood the dull old house, no longer either mysterious or romantic in my disenchanted eyes; before me rumbled the barrow, bearing my dilapidated wardrobe; and in my pocket reposed what I fondly hoped was, if not a liberal, at least an honest return for seven weeks of the hardest work I ever did.

Unable to resist the desire to see what my earnings were, I opened the purse and beheld *four dollars.*

I have had a good many bitter minutes in my life; but one of the bitterest came to me as I stood there in the windy road, with the sixpenny pocketbook open before me, and looked from my poor chapped, grimy, chill-blained hands to the paltry sum that was considered reward enough for all the hard and humble labor they had done.

A girl's heart is a sensitive thing. And mine had been very full lately; for it had suffered many of the trials that wound deeply yet cannot be told; so I think it was but natural that my first impulse was to go straight back to that sacred study and fling this insulting money at the feet of him who sent it. But I was so boiling over with indignation that I could not trust myself in his presence, lest I should be unable to resist the temptation to shake him, in spite of his cloth.

No, I would go home, show my honorable wounds, tell my pathetic tale, and leave my parents to avenge my wrongs. I did so; but over that harrowing scene I drop a veil, for my feeble pen refuses to depict the emotions of my outraged family. I will merely mention that the four dollars went back and the Reverend Josephus never heard the last of it in that neighborhood.

My experiment seemed a dire failure and I mourned it as such for years; but more than once in my life I have been grateful for that serio-comico experience, since it has taught me many lessons. One of the most useful of these has been the power of successfully making a companion, not a servant, of those whose aid I need, and helping to gild their honest wages with the sympathy and justice which can sweeten the humblest and lighten the hardest task.

Marjorie Daw

Thomas Bailey Aldrich
(1836–1907)

I

DR. DILLON TO EDWARD DELANEY, ESQ.,
AT THE PINES, NEAR RYE, N.H.
AUGUST 8, 187–.

My Dear Sir: I am happy to assure you that your anxiety is without reason. Flemming will be confined to the sofa for three or four weeks, and will have to be careful at first how he uses his leg. A fracture of this kind is always a tedious affair. Fortunately, the bone was very skilfully set by the surgeon who chanced to be in the drug-store where Flemming was brought after his fall, and I apprehend no permanent inconvenience from the accident. *Flemming is doing perfectly well physically;* but I must confess that the irritable and morbid state of mind into which he has fallen causes me a great deal of uneasiness. He is the last man in the world who ought to break his leg. You know how impetuous our friend is ordinarily, what a soul of restlessness and energy, never content unless he is rushing at some object, like a sportive bull at a red shawl; but amiable withal. He is no longer amiable. His temper has become something frightful. Miss Fanny Flemming came up from Newport, where the family are staying for the summer, to nurse him; but he packed her off the next morning in tears. He has a complete set of Balzac's works, twenty-seven volumes, piled up near his sofa, to throw at Watkins whenever that exemplary serving-man appears with his meals. Yesterday I very innocently brought Flemming a small basket of lemons. You know it was a strip of lemon-peel on the curbstone that caused our friend's mischance. Well, he no sooner set his eyes upon these lemons than he fell into such a rage as I cannot adequately describe. This is only one of his moods, and the least distressing. At other times he sits with bowed head regarding his splintered limb, silent, sullen, despairing. When this fit is on him—and it sometimes lasts all day—nothing can distract his melancholy. He refuses to eat, does not even read the newspapers; books, except as projectiles for Watkins, have no charms for him. His state is truly pitiable.

Now, if he were a poor man, with a family depending on his daily labor, this irritability and despondency would be natural enough. But in a young fellow of twenty-four, with plenty of money and seemingly not a care in the world, the thing is monstrous. If he continues to give way to his vagaries in this manner, he will end by bringing on an inflammation of the fibula. It was the fibula he broke. I am at my wits' end to know what to prescribe for him. I have anæsthetics and lotions, to make people sleep and to soothe pain; but I've no medicine that will make a man have a little common-sense. That is beyond my skill, but maybe it is not beyond yours. You are Flemming's intimate friend, his *fidus Achates*. Write to him, write to him frequently, distract his mind, cheer him up, and prevent him from becoming a confirmed case of melancholia. Perhaps he has some important plans disarranged by his present confinement. If he has you will know, and will know how to advise him judiciously. I trust your father finds the change beneficial? I am, my dear sir, with great respect, etc.

II

EDWARD DELANEY TO JOHN FLEMMING,
WEST 38TH STREET, NEW YORK
AUGUST 9, —.

My Dear Jack: I had a line from Dillon this morning, and was rejoiced to learn that your hurt is not so bad as reported. Like a certain personage, you are not so black and blue as you are painted. Dillon will put you on your pins again in two to three weeks, if you will only have patience and follow his counsels. Did you get my note of last Wednesday? I was greatly troubled when I heard of the accident.

I can imagine how tranquil and saintly you are with your leg in a trough! It is deuced awkward, to be sure, just as we had promised ourselves a glorious month together at the sea-side; but we must make the best of it. It is unfortunate, too, that my father's health renders it impossible for me to leave him. I think he has much improved; the sea air is his native element: but he still needs my arm to lean upon in his walks, and requires some one more careful than a servant to look after him. I cannot come to you, dear Jack, but I have hours of unemployed time on hand, and I will write you a whole post-office full of letters, if that will divert you. Heaven knows, I haven't anything to write about. It isn't as if we were living at one of the beach houses; then I could do you some character studies, and fill your imagination with groups of sea-goddesses, with their (or somebody else's) raven and blond manes hanging down their shoulders. You should have Aphrodite in morning wrapper, in evening costume, and in her prettiest bathing suit. But we are far from all that here. We have rooms in a farm-house, on a cross-road, two miles from the hotels, and lead the quietest of lives.

I wish I were a novelist. This old house, with its sanded floors and high wainscots, and its narrow windows looking out upon a cluster of pines that turn themselves into æolian-harps every time the wind blows, would be the place in which to write a summer romance. It should be a story with the odors of the forest and the breath of the sea in it. It should be a novel like one of that Russian fellow's—what's his name?—Tourguénieff, Turguenef, Turgenif, Toorguniff, Turgénjew—nobody knows how to spell him. Yet I wonder if even a Liza or an Alexandra Paulovna could stir the heart of a man who has constant twinges in his leg. I wonder if one of our own Yankee girls of the best type, haughty and *spirituelle,* would be of any comfort to you in your present deplorable condition. If I thought so, I would hasten down to the Surf House and catch one for you; or, better still, I would find you one over the way.

Picture to yourself a large white house just across the road, nearly opposite our cottage. It is not a house, but a mansion, built, perhaps, in the colonial period, with rambling extensions, and gambrel roof, and a wide piazza on three sides—a self-possessed, high-bred piece of architecture, with its nose in the air. It stands back from the road, and has an obsequious retinue of fringed elms and oaks and weeping willows. Sometimes in the morning, and of-tener in the afternoon, when the sun has withdrawn from that part of the mansion, a young woman appears on the piazza with some mysterious Penelope web of embroidery in her hand, or a book. There is a hammock over there—of pineapple fibre, it looks from here. A hammock is very becoming when one is eighteen, and has golden hair, and dark eyes, and an emerald-colored illusion dress looped up after the fashion of a Dresden china shepherdess, and is *chaussée* like a belle of the time of Louis Quatorze. All this splendor goes into that hammock, and sways there like a pond-lily in the golden afternoon. The window of my bedroom looks down on that piazza—and so do I.

But enough of this nonsense, which ill becomes a sedate young attorney taking his vacation with an invalid father. Drop me a line, dear Jack, and tell me how you really are. State your case. Write me a long, quiet letter. If you are violent or abusive, I'll take the law to you.

III

JOHN FLEMMING TO EDWARD DELANEY
AUGUST 11, —.

Your letter, dear Ned, was a godsend. Fancy what a fix I am in—I, who never had a day's sickness since I was born. My left leg weighs three tons. It is embalmed in spices and smothered in layers of fine linen, like a mummy. I can't move. I haven't moved for five thousand years. I'm of the time of Pharaoh.

I lie from morning till night on a lounge, staring into the hot street. Everybody is out of town enjoying himself. The brownstone-front houses across the street resemble a row of particularly ugly coffins set up on end. A green mould is settling on the names of the deceased, carved on the silver door-plates. Sardonic spiders have sewed up the key-holes. All is silence and dust and desolation.—I interrupt this a moment, to take a shy at Watkins with the second volume of César Birotteau. Missed him! I think I could bring him down with a copy of Sainte-Beuve or the Dictionnaire Universel, if I had it. These small Balzac books somehow don't quite fit my hand; but I shall fetch him yet. I've an idea Watkins is tapping the old gentleman's Château Yquem. Duplicate key of the wine-cellar. Hibernian swarries in the front basement. Young Cheops up stairs, snug in his cerements. Watkins glides into my chamber, with that colorless, hypocritical face of his drawn out long like an accordion; but I know he grins all the way down stairs, and is glad I have broken my leg. Was not my evil star in the very zenith when I ran up to town to attend that dinner at Delmonico's? I didn't come up altogether for that. It was partly to buy Frank Livingstone's roan mare Margot. And now I shall not be able to sit in the saddle these two months. I'll send the mare down to you at The Pines—is that the name of the place?

Old Dillon fancies that I have something on my mind. He drives me wild with lemons. Lemons for a mind diseased! Nonsense. I am only as restless as the devil under this confinement—a thing I'm not used to. Take a man who has never had so much as a headache or a toothache in his life, strap one of his legs in a section of water-spout, keep him in a room in the city for weeks, with the hot weather turned on, and then expect him to smile and purr and be happy! It is preposterous. I can't be cheerful or calm.

Your letter is the first consoling thing I have had since my disaster, ten days ago. It really cheered me up for half an hour. Send me a screed, Ned, as often as you can, if you love me. Anything will do. Write me more about that little girl in the hammock. That was very pretty, all that about the Dresden china shepherdess and the pond-lily; the imagery a little mixed, perhaps, but very pretty. I didn't suppose you had so much sentimental furniture in your upper story. It shows how one may be familiar for years with the reception-room of his neighbor, and never suspect what is directly under his mansard. I supposed your loft stuffed with dry legal parchments, mortgages and affidavits; you take down a package of manuscript, and lo! there are lyrics and sonnets and canzonettas.

You really have a graphic descriptive touch, Edward Delaney, and I suspect you of anonymous love-tales in the magazines.

I shall be a bear until I hear from you again. Tell me all about your pretty *inconnue* across the road. What is her name? Who is she? Who's her father? Where's her mother? Who's her lover? You cannot imagine how this will occupy me. The more trifling the better. My imprisonment has weakened me intellectually to such a degree that I find your epistolary gifts quite considerable. I am passing into my second childhood. In a week or two I shall take to India-rubber rings and prongs of coral. A silver cup, with an appropriate inscription, would be a delicate attention on your part. In the mean time, write!

IV

EDWARD DELANEY TO JOHN FLEMMING
AUGUST 12, —.

The sick pasha shall be amused. *Bismillah!* he wills it so. If the story-teller becomes prolix and tedious—the bow-string and the sack, and two Nubians to drop him into the Piscataqua! But, truly, Jack, I have a hard task. There is literally nothing here—except the little girl over the way. She is swinging in the hammock at this moment. It is to me compensation for many of the ills of life to see her now and then put out a small kid boot, which fits like a glove, and set herself going. Who is she, and what is her name? Her name is Daw. Only daughter of Mr. Richard W. Daw, ex-colonel and banker. Mother dead. One brother at Harvard, elder brother killed at the battle of Fair Oaks, nine years ago. Old, rich family, the Daws. This is the homestead, where father and daughter pass eight months of the twelve; the rest of the year in Baltimore and Washington. The New England winter too many for the old gentleman. The daughter is called Marjorie—Marjorie Daw. Sounds odd at first, doesn't it? But after you say it over to yourself half a dozen times, you like it. There's a pleasing quaintness to it, something prim and violet-like. Must be a nice sort of girl to be called Marjorie Daw.

I had mine host of The Pines in the witness-box last night, and drew the foregoing testimony from him. He has charge of Mr. Daw's vegetable-garden, and has known the family these thirty years. Of course I shall make the acquaintance of my neighbors before many days. It will be next to impossible for me not to meet Mr. Daw or Miss Daw in some of my walks. The young lady has a favorite path to the sea-beach. I shall intercept her some morning, and touch my hat to her. Then the princess will bend her fair head to me with courteous surprise not unmixed with haughtiness. Will snub me, in fact. All this for thy sake, O Pasha of the Snapt Axletree! . . . How oddly things fall out! Ten minutes ago I was called down to the parlor—you know the kind of parlors in farm-houses on the coast, a sort of amphibious parlor, with sea-shells on the mantel-piece and spruce branches in the chimney-place—where I found my father and Mr. Daw doing the antique polite to each other. He had come to pay his respects to his new neighbors. Mr. Daw is a tall, slim gentleman of about fifty-five, with a florid face and snow-white mustache and side-whiskers. Looks like Mr. Dombey, or as Mr. Dombey would have looked if he had served a few years in the British Army. Mr. Daw was a colonel in the late war, commanding the regiment in which his son was a lieutenant. Plucky old boy, backbone of New Hampshire granite. Before taking his leave, the colonel delivered himself of an invitation as if he were issuing a general order. Miss Daw has a few friends coming, at 4 P.M., to play croquet on the lawn (parade-ground) and have tea (cold rations) on the piazza. Will we honor them with our company? (or be sent to the guard-house.) My father declines on the plea of ill-health. My father's son bows with as much suavity as he knows, and accepts.

In my next I shall have something to tell you. I shall have seen the little beauty face to face. I have a presentiment, Jack, that this Daw is a *rara avis!* Keep up your spirits, my boy, until I write you another letter—and send me along word how's your leg.

V

EDWARD DELANEY TO JOHN FLEMMING
AUGUST 13, —.

The party, my dear Jack, was as dreary as possible. A lieutenant of the navy, the rector of the Episcopal Church at Stillwater, and a society swell from Nahant. The lieutenant looked as if he had swallowed a couple of his buttons, and found the bullion rather indigestible; the rector was a pensive youth, of the daffydowndilly sort; and the swell from Nahant was a very weak tidal wave indeed. The women were much better, as they always are; the two Miss Kingsburys of Philadelphia, staying at the Sea-shell House, two bright and engaging girls. But Marjorie Daw!

The company broke up soon after tea, and I remained to smoke a cigar with the colonel on the piazza. It was like seeing a picture to see Miss Marjorie hovering around the old soldier, and doing a hundred gracious little things for him. She brought the cigars and lighted the tapers with her own delicate fingers, in the most enchanting fashion. As we sat there, she came and went in the summer twilight, and seemed, with her white dress and pale gold hair, like some lovely phantom that had sprung into existence out of the smoke-wreaths. If she had melted into air, like the statue of Galatea in the play, I should have been more sorry than surprised.

It was easy to perceive that the old colonel worshipped her, and she him. I think the relation between an elderly father and a daughter just blooming into womanhood the most beautiful possible. There is in it a subtle sentiment that cannot exist in the case of mother and daughter, or that of son and mother. But this is getting into deep water.

I sat with the Daws until half past ten, and saw the moon rise on the sea. The ocean, that had stretched motionless and black against the horizon, was changed by magic into a broken field of glittering ice, interspersed with marvellous silvery fjords. In the far distance the Isles of Shoals loomed up like a group of huge bergs drifting down on us. The Polar Regions in a June thaw! It was exceedingly fine. What did we talk about? We talked about the weather—and *you!* The weather has been disagreeable for several days past—and so have you. I glided from one topic to the other very naturally. I told my friends of your accident; how it had frustrated all our summer plans, and what our plans were. I played quite a spirited solo on the fibula. Then I described you; or, rather, I didn't. I spoke of your amiability, of your patience under this severe affliction; of your touching gratitude when Dillon brings you little presents of fruit; of your tenderness to your sister Fanny, whom you would not allow to stay in town to nurse you, and how you heroically sent her back to Newport, preferring to remain alone with Mary, the cook, and your man Watkins, to whom, by the way, you were devotedly attached. If you had been there, Jack, you wouldn't have known yourself. I should have excelled as a criminal lawyer, if I had not turned my attention to a different branch of jurisprudence.

Miss Marjorie asked all manner of leading questions concerning you. It did not occur to me then, but it struck me forcibly afterwards, that she evinced a singular interest in the conversation. When I got back to my room, I recalled how eagerly she leaned forward, with her full, snowy throat in strong moonlight, listening to what I said. Positively, I think I made her like you!

Miss Daw is a girl whom you would like immensely, I can tell you that. A beauty without affectation, a high and tender nature— if one can read the soul in the face. And the old colonel is a noble character, too.

I am glad that the Daws are such pleasant people. The Pines is an isolated spot, and my resources are few. I fear I should have found life here somewhat monotonous before long, with no other society than that of my excellent sire. It is true, I might have made a target of the defenceless invalid; but I haven't a taste for artillery, *moi*.

VI

JOHN FLEMMING TO EDWARD DELANEY
AUGUST 17, —.

For a man who hasn't a taste for artillery, it occurs to me, my friend, you are keeping up a pretty lively fire on my inner works. But go on. Cynicism is a small brass field-piece that eventually bursts and kills the artilleryman.

You may abuse me as much as you like, and I'll not complain; for I don't know what I should do without your letters. They are curing me. I haven't hurled anything at Watkins since last Sunday, partly because I have grown more amiable under your teaching, and partly because Watkins captured my ammunition one night, and carried it off to the library. He is rapidly losing the habit he had acquired of dodging whenever I rub my ear, or make any slight motion with my right arm. He is still suggestive of the wine-cellar, however. You may break, you may shatter Watkins, if you will, but the scent of the Roederer will hang round him still.

Ned, that Miss Daw must be a charming person. I should certainly like her. I like her already. When you spoke in your first letter of seeing a young girl swinging in a hammock under your chamber window, I was somehow strangely drawn to her. I cannot account for it in the least. What you have subsequently written of Miss Daw has strengthened the impression. You seem to be describing a woman I have known in some previous state of existence, or dreamed of in this. Upon my word, if you were to send me her photograph, I believe I should recognize her at a glance. Her manner, that listening attitude, her traits of character, as you indicate them, the light hair and the dark eyes—they are all familiar things to me. Asked a lot of questions, did she? Curious about me? That is strange.

You would laugh in your sleeve, you wretched old cynic, if you knew how I lie awake nights, with my gas turned down to a star, thinking of The Pines and the house across the road. How cool it must be down there! I long for the salt smell in the air. I picture the colonel smoking his cheroot on the piazza. I send you and Miss Daw off on afternoon rambles along the beach. Sometimes I let you stroll with her under the elms in the moonlight, for you are great friends by this time, I take it, and see each other every day. I know your ways and your manners! Then I fall into a truculent mood, and would like to destroy somebody. Have you noticed anything in the shape of a lover hanging around the colonial Lares and Penates? Does that lieutenant of the horse-marines or that young Stillwater parson visit the house much? Not that I am pining for news of them, but any gossip of the kind would be in order. I wonder, Ned, you don't fall in love with Miss Daw. I am ripe to do it myself. Speaking of photographs, couldn't you manage to slip one of her *cartes-de-visite* from her album—she must have an album, you know—and send it to me? I will return it before it could be missed. That's a good fellow! Did the mare arrive safe and sound? It will be a capital animal this autumn for Central Park.

O—my leg? I forgot about my leg. It's better.

VII

EDWARD DELANEY TO JOHN FLEMMIMG
AUGUST 20, —.

You are correct in your surmises. I am on the most friendly terms with our neighbors. The colonel and my father smoke their afternoon cigar together in our sitting-room or on the piazza opposite, and I pass an hour or two of the day or the evening with the daughter. I am more and more struck by the beauty, modesty, and intelligence of Miss Daw.

You asked me why I do not fall in love with her. I will be frank, Jack: I have thought of that. She is young, rich, accomplished, uniting in herself more attractions, mental and personal, than I can recall in any girl of my acquaintance; but she lacks the something that would be necessary to inspire in me that kind of interest. Possessing this unknown quantity, a woman neither beautiful nor wealthy nor very young could bring me to her feet. But not Miss Daw. If we were shipwrecked together on an uninhabited island—let me suggest a tropical island, for it costs no more to be picturesque—I would build her a bamboo hut, I would fetch her bread-fruit and cocoanuts, I would fry yams for her, I would lure the ingenuous turtle and make her nourishing soups, but I wouldn't make love to her—not under eighteen months. I would like to have her for a sister, that I might shield her and counsel her, and spend half my income on thread-laces and camel's-hair shawls. (We are off the island now.) If such were not my feeling, there would still be an obstacle to my loving Miss Daw. A greater misfortune could scarcely befall me than to love her. Flemming, I am about to make a revelation that will astonish you. I may be all wrong in my premises and consequently in my conclusions; but you shall judge.

That night when I returned to my room after the croquet party at the Daw's, and was thinking over the trivial events of the evening, I was suddenly impressed by the air of eager attention with which Miss Daw had followed my account of your accident. I think I mentioned this to you. Well, the next morning, as I went to mail my letter, I overtook Miss Daw on the road to Rye, where the post-office is, and accompanied her thither and back, an hour's walk. The conversation again turned on you, and again I remarked that inexplicable look of interest which had lighted up her face the previous evening. Since then, I have seen Miss Daw perhaps ten times, perhaps oftener, and on each occasion I found that when I was not speaking of you, or your sister, or some person or place associated with you, I was not holding her attention. She would be absent-minded, her eyes would wander away from me to the sea, or to some distant object in the landscape; her fingers would play with the leaves of a book in a way that convinced me she was not listening. At these moments if I abruptly changed the theme—I did it several times as an experiment—and dropped some remark about my friend Flemming, then the sombre blue eyes would come back to me instantly.

Now, is not this the oddest thing in the world? No, not the oddest. The effect which you tell me was produced on you by my casual mention of an unknown girl swinging in a hammock is certainly as strange. You can conjecture how that passage in your letter of Friday startled me. Is it possible, then, that two people who have never met, and who are hundreds of miles apart, can exert a magnetic influence on each other? I have read of such psychological phenomena, but never credited them. I leave the solution of the problem to you. As for myself, all other things being favorable, it would be impossible for me to fall in love with a woman who listens to me only when I am talking of my friend!

I am not aware that any one is paying marked attention to my fair neighbor. The lieutenant of the navy—he is stationed at Rivermouth—sometimes drops in of an evening, and sometimes the rector from Stillwater; the lieutenant the oftener. He was there last night. I would not be surprised if he had an eye to the heiress; but he is not formidable. Mistress Daw carries a neat little spear of irony, and the honest lieutenant seems to have a particular facility for impaling himself on the point of it. He is not dangerous, I should say; though I have known a woman to satirize a man for years, and marry him after all. Decidedly, the lowly rector is not dangerous; yet, again, who has not seen Cloth of Frieze victorious in the lists where Cloth of Gold went down?

As to the photograph. There is an exquisite ivorytype of Marjorie, in passe-partout, on the drawing-room mantel-piece. It would be missed at once if taken. I would do anything reasonable for you, Jack; but I've no burning desire to be hauled up before the local justice of the peace, on a charge of petty larceny.

P.S.—Enclosed is a spray of mignonette, which I advise you to treat tenderly. Yes, we talked of you again last night, as usual. It is becoming a little dreary for me.

VIII

EDWARD DELANEY TO JOHN FLEMMING
AUGUST 22, —.

Your letter in reply to my last has occupied my thoughts all the morning. I do not know what to think. Do you mean to say that you are seriously half in love with a woman whom you have never seen—with a shadow, a chimera? for what else can Miss Daw be to you? I do not understand it at all. I understand neither you nor her. You are a couple of ethereal beings moving in finer air than I can breathe with my commonplace lungs. Such delicacy of sentiment is something that I admire without comprehending. I am bewildered. I am of the earth earthy, and I find myself in the incongruous position of having to do with mere souls, with natures so finely tempered that I run some risk of shattering them in my awkwardness. I am as Caliban among the spirits!

Reflecting on your letter, I am not sure it is wise in me to continue this correspondence. But no, Jack; I do wrong to doubt the good sense that forms the basis of your character. You are deeply interested in Miss Daw; you feel that she is a person whom you may perhaps greatly admire when you know her: at the same time you bear in mind that the chances are ten to five that, when you do come to know her, she will fall far short of your ideal, and you will not care for her in the least. Look at it in this sensible light, and I will hold back nothing from you.

Yesterday afternoon my father and myself rode over to Rivermouth with the Daws. A heavy rain in the morning had cooled the atmosphere and laid the dust. To Rivermouth is a drive of eight miles, along a winding road lined all the way with wild barberry-bushes. I never saw anything more brilliant than these bushes, the green of the foliage and the pink of the coral berries intensified by the rain. The colonel drove, with my father in front, Miss Daw and I on the back seat. I resolved that for the first five miles your name should not pass my lips. I was amused by the artful attempts she made, at the start, to break through my reticence. Then a silence fell upon her; and then she became suddenly gay. That keenness which I enjoyed so much when it was exercised on the lieutenant was not so satisfactory directed against myself. Miss Daw has great sweetness of disposition, but she can be disagreeable. She is like the young lady in the rhyme, with the curl on her forehead,

> *"When she is good,*
> *She is very, very good,*
> *And when she is bad, she is horrid!"*

I kept to my resolution, however; but on the return home I relented, and talked of your mare! Miss Daw is going to try a side-saddle on Margot some morning. The animal is a trifle too light for my weight. By the by, I nearly forgot to say that Miss Daw sat for a picture yesterday to a Rivermouth artist. If the negative turns out well, I am to have a copy. So our ends will be accomplished without crime. I wish, though, I could send you the ivorytype in the drawing-room; it is cleverly colored, and would give you an idea of her hair and eyes, which of course the other will not.

No, Jack, the spray of mignonette did not come from me. A man of twenty-eight doesn't enclose flowers in his letters—to another man. But don't attach too much significance to the circumstance. She gives sprays of mignonette to the rector, sprays to the lieutenant. She has even given a rose from her bosom to your slave. It is her jocund nature to scatter flowers, like Spring.

If my letters sometimes read disjointedly, you must understand that I never finish one at a sitting, but write at intervals, when the mood is on me.

The mood is not on me now.

IX

EDWARD DELANEY TO JOHN FLEMMING
AUGUST 23, —.

I have just returned from the strangest interview with Marjorie. She has all but confessed to me her interest in you. But with what modesty and dignity! Her words elude my pen as I attempt to put them on paper; and, indeed, it was not so much what she said as her manner; and that I cannot reproduce. Perhaps it was of a piece with the strangeness of this whole business, that she should tacitly acknowledge to a third party the love she feels for a man she has never beheld! But I have lost, through your aid, the faculty of being surprised. I accept things as people do in dreams. Now that I am again in my room, it all appears like an illusion—the black masses of Rembrandtish shadow under the trees, the fire-flies whirling in Pyrrhic dances among the shrubbery, the sea over there, Marjorie sitting on the hammock!

It is past midnight, and I am too sleepy to write more.

THURSDAY MORNING.

My father has suddenly taken it into his head to spend a few days at the Shoals. In the mean while you will not hear from me. I see Marjorie walking in the garden with the colonel. I wish I could speak to her alone, but shall probably not have an opportunity before we leave.

X

EDWARD DELANEY TO JOHN FLEMMING
AUGUST 28, —.

You were passing into your second childhood, were you? Your intellect was so reduced that my epistolary gifts seemed quite considerable to you, did they? I rise superior to the sarcasm in your favor of the 11th instant, when I notice that five days' silence on my part is sufficient to throw you into the depths of despondency.

We returned only this morning from Appledore, that enchanted island—at four dollars per day. I find on my desk three letters from you! Evidently there is no lingering doubt in *your* mind as to the pleasure I derive from your correspondence. These letters are undated, but in what I take to be the latest are two passages that require my consideration. You will pardon my candor, dear Flemming, but the conviction forces itself upon me that as your leg grows stronger your head becomes weaker. You ask my advice on a certain point. I will give it. In my opinion you could do nothing more unwise than to address a note to Miss Daw, thanking her for the flower. It would, I am sure, offend her delicacy beyond pardon. She knows you only through me; you are to her an abstraction, a figure in a dream—a dream from which the faintest shock would awaken her. Of course, if you enclose a note to me and insist on its delivery, I shall deliver it; but I advise you not to do so.

You say you are able, with the aid of a cane, to walk about your chamber, and that you purpose to come to The Pines the instant Dillon thinks you strong enough to stand the journey. Again I advise you not to. Do you not see that, every hour you remain away, Marjorie's glamour deepens, and your influence over her increases? You will ruin everything by precipitancy. Wait until you are entirely recovered; in any case, do not come without giving me warning. I fear the effect of your abrupt advent here—under the circumstances.

Miss Daw was evidently glad to see us back again, and gave me both hands in the frankest way. She stopped at the door a moment, this afternoon, in the carriage; she had been over to Rivermouth for her pictures. Unluckily the photographer had spilt some acid on the plate, and she was obliged to give him another sitting. I have an intuition that something is troubling Marjorie. She had an abstracted air not usual with her. However, it may be only my fancy.... I end this, leaving several things unsaid, to accompany my father on one of those long walks which are now his chief medicine—and mine!

XI

EDWARD DELANEY TO JOHN FLEMMING
AUGUST 29, —.

I write in great haste to tell you what has taken place here since my letter of last night. I am in the utmost perplexity. Only one thing is plain—*you* must not dream of coming to The Pines. Marjorie has told her father everything! I saw her for a few minutes, an hour ago, in the garden; and, as near as I could gather from her confused statement, the facts are these: Lieutenant Bradly—that's the naval officer stationed at Rivermouth—has been paying court to Miss Daw for some time past, but not so much to her liking as to that of the colonel, who it seems is an old friend of the young gentleman's father. Yesterday (I knew she was in some trouble when she drove up to our gate) the colonel spoke to Marjorie of Bradly—urged his suit, I infer. Marjorie expressed her dislike for the lieutenant with characteristic frankness, and finally confessed to her father—well, I really do not know what she confessed. It must have been the vaguest of confessions, and must have sufficiently puzzled the colonel. At any rate, it exasperated him. I suppose I am implicated in the matter, and that the colonel feels bitterly towards me. I do not see why: I have carried no messages between you and Miss Daw; I have behaved with the greatest discretion. I can find no flaw anywhere in my proceeding. I do not see that anybody has done anything—except the colonel himself.

It is probable, nevertheless, that the friendly relations between the two houses will be broken off. "A plague o' both your houses," say you. I will keep you informed, as well as I can, of what occurs over the way. We shall remain here until the second week in September. Stay where you are, or, at all events, do not dream of joining me. . . . Colonel Daw is sitting on the piazza looking rather wicked. I have not seen Marjorie since I parted with her in the garden.

XII

Edward Delaney to Thomas Dillon, M.D., Madison Square, New York

August 30, —.

My Dear Doctor: If you have any influence over Flemming, I beg of you to exert it to prevent his coming to this place at present. There are circumstances, which I will explain to you before long, that make it of the first importance that he should not come into this neighborhood. His appearance here, I speak advisedly, would be disastrous to him. In urging him to remain in New York, or to go to some inland resort, you will be doing him and me a real service. Of course you will not mention my name in this connection. You know me well enough, my dear doctor, to be assured that, in begging your secret co-operation, I have reasons that will meet your entire approval when they are made plain to you. We shall return to town on the 15th of next month, and my first duty will be to present myself at your hospitable door and satisfy your curiosity, if I have excited it. My father, I am glad to state, has so greatly improved that he can no longer be regarded as an invalid. With great esteem, I am, etc., etc.

XIII

EDWARD DELANEY TO JOHN FLEMMING
AUGUST 31, —.

Your letter, announcing your mad determination to come here, has just reached me. I beseech you to reflect a moment. The step would be fatal to your interests and hers. You would furnish just cause for irritation to R. W. D.; and, though he loves Marjorie tenderly, he is capable of going to any lengths if opposed. You would not like, I am convinced, to be the means of causing him to treat *her* with severity. That would be the result of your presence at The Pines at this juncture. I am annoyed to be obliged to point out these things to you. We are on very delicate ground, Jack; the situation is critical, and the slightest mistake in a move would cost us the game. If you consider it worth the winning, be patient. Trust a little to my sagacity. Wait and see what happens. Moreover, I understand from Dillon that you are in no condition to take so long a journey. He thinks the air of the coast would be the worst thing possible for you; that you ought to go inland, if anywhere. Be advised by me. Be advised by Dillon.

XIV

Telegrams

September 1, —.

1.—To Edward Delaney.

Letter received. Dillon be hanged. I think I ought to be on the ground.

J. F.

2.—To John Flemming.

Stay where you are. You would only complicate matters. Do not move until you hear from me.

E. D.

3.—To Edward Delaney.

My being at The Pines could be kept secret. I must see her.

J. F.

4.—To John Flemming.

Do not think of it. It would be useless. R. W. D. has locked M. in her room. You would not be able to effect an interview.

E. D.

5.—To Edward Delaney.

Locked her in her room. Good God. That settles the question. I shall leave by the twelve-fifteen express.

J. F.

XV

THE ARRIVAL

On the second day of September, 187-, as the down express due at 3.40 left the station at Hampton, a young man, leaning on the shoulder of a servant, whom he addressed as Watkins, stepped from the platform into a hack, and requested to be driven to "The Pines." On arriving at the gate of a modest farm-house, a few miles from the station, the young man descended with difficulty from the carriage, and, casting a hasty glance across the road, seemed much impressed by some peculiarity in the landscape. Again leaning on the shoulder of the person Watkins, he walked to the door of the farm-house and inquired for Mr. Edward Delaney. He was informed by the aged man who answered his knock, that Mr. Edward Delaney had gone to Boston the day before, but that Mr. Jonas Delaney was within. This information did not appear satisfactory to the stranger, who inquired if Mr. Edward Delaney had left any message for Mr. John Flemming. There *was* a letter for Mr. Flemming, if he were that person. After a brief absence the aged man reappeared with a Letter.

XVI

EDWARD DELANEY TO JOHN FLEMMING
SEPTEMBER 1, —.

I am horror-stricken at what I have done! When I began this correspondence I had no other purpose than to relieve the tedium of your sick-chamber. Dillon told me to cheer you up. I tried to.

I thought you entered into the spirit of the thing. I had no idea, until within a few days, that you were taking matters *au sérieux*.

What can I say? I am in sackcloth and ashes. I am a pariah, a dog of an outcast. I tried to make a little romance to interest you, something soothing and idyllic, and, by Jove! I have done it only too well! My father doesn't know a word of this, so don't jar the old gentleman any more than you can help. I fly from the wrath to come—when you arrive! For O, dear Jack, there isn't any colonial mansion on the other side of the road, there isn't any piazza, there isn't any hammock—there isn't any Marjorie Daw!!

An Occurrence at Owl Creek Bridge

Ambrose Bierce
(1842–1914?)

I

A man stood upon a railroad bridge in northern Alabama, looking down into the swift water twenty feet below. The man's hands were behind his back, the wrists bound with a cord. A rope closely encircled his neck. It was attached to a stout cross-timber above his head and the slack fell to the level of his knees. Some loose boards laid upon the sleepers supporting the metals of the railway supplied a footing for him and his executioners—two private soldiers of the Federal army, directed by a sergeant who in civil life may have been a deputy sheriff. At a short remove upon the same temporary platform was an officer in the uniform of his rank, armed. He was a captain. A sentinel at each end of the bridge stood with his rifle in the position known as "support," that is to say, vertical in front of the left shoulder, the hammer resting on the forearm thrown straight across the chest— a formal and unnatural position, enforcing an erect carriage of the body. It did not appear to be the duty of these two men to know what was occurring at the centre of the bridge; they merely block-aded the two ends of the foot planking that traversed it.

Beyond one of the sentinels nobody was in sight; the railroad ran straight away into a forest for a hundred yards, then, curving, was lost to view. Doubtless there was an outpost farther along. The other bank of the stream was open ground—a gentle acclivity topped with a stockade of vertical tree trunks, loopholed for rifles, with a single embrasure through which protruded the muzzle of a brass cannon commanding the bridge. Midway of the slope be-tween the bridge and fort were the spectators—a single company of infantry in line, at "parade rest," the butts of the rifles on the ground, the barrels inclining slightly backward against the right shoulder, the hands crossed upon the stock. A lieutenant stood at the right of the line, the point of his sword upon the ground, his left hand resting upon his right. Excepting the group of four at the centre of the bridge, not a man moved. The company faced the bridge, staring stonily, motionless. The sentinels, facing the banks of the stream, might have been statues to adorn the bridge. The captain stood with folded arms, silent, observing the work of his subordinates, but making no sign. Death is a dignitary who when he comes announced is to be received with formal manifestations of respect, even by those most familiar with him. In the code of military etiquette silence and fixity are forms of deference.

The man who was engaged in being hanged was apparently about thirty-five years of age. He was a civilian, if one might judge from his habit, which was that of a planter. His features were good—a straight nose, firm mouth, broad forehead, from which his long, dark hair was combed straight back, falling behind his ears to the collar of his well-fitting frock-coat. He wore a mustache and pointed beard, but no whiskers; his eyes were large and dark gray, and had a kindly expression which one would hardly have ex-pected in one whose neck was in the hemp. Evidently this was no vulgar assassin. The liberal military code makes provision for hanging many kinds of persons, and gentlemen are not excluded.

The preparations being complete, the two private soldiers stepped aside and each drew away the plank upon which he had been standing. The sergeant turned to the captain, saluted and placed himself immediately behind that officer, who in turn moved apart one pace. These movements left the condemned man and the sergeant standing on the two ends of the same plank, which spanned three of the cross-ties of the bridge. The end upon which the civilian stood almost, but not quite, reached a fourth. This plank had been held in place by the weight of the captain; it was now held by that of the sergeant. At a signal from the former the latter would step aside, the plank would tilt and the condemned man go down between two ties. The arrangement commended itself to his judgment as simple and effective. His face had not been covered nor his eyes bandaged. He looked a moment at his "unsteadfast footing," then let his gaze wander to the swirling water of the stream racing madly beneath his feet. A piece of dancing driftwood caught his attention and his eyes followed it down the current. How slowly it appeared to move! What a sluggish stream!

He closed his eyes in order to fix his last thoughts upon his wife and children. The water, touched to gold by the early sun, the brooding mists under the banks at some distance down the stream, the fort, the soldiers, the piece of drift—all had distracted him. And now he became conscious of a new disturbance. Striking through the thought of his dear ones was a sound which he could neither ignore nor understand, a sharp, distinct, metallic percussion like the stroke of a blacksmith's hammer upon the anvil; it had the same ringing quality. He wondered what it was, and whether immeasurably distant or near by—it seemed both. Its recurrence was regular, but as slow as the tolling of a death knell. He awaited each stroke with impatience and—he knew not why—apprehension. The intervals of silence grew progressively longer; the delays became maddening. With their greater infrequency the sounds increased in strength and sharpness. They hurt his ear like the thrust of a knife; he feared he would shriek. What he heard was the ticking of his watch.

He unclosed his eyes and saw again the water below him. "If I could free my hands," he thought, "I might throw off the noose and spring into the stream. By diving I could evade the bullets and, swimming vigorously, reach the bank, take to the woods and get away home. My home, thank God, is as yet outside their lines; my wife and little ones are still beyond the invader's farthest advance."

As these thoughts, which have here to be set down in words, were flashed into the doomed man's brain rather than evolved from it the captain nodded to the sergeant. The sergeant stepped aside.

II

Peyton Farquhar was a well-to-do planter, of an old and highly respected Alabama family. Being a slave owner and like other slave owners a politician he was naturally an original secessionist and ardently devoted to the Southern cause. Circumstances of an imperious nature, which it is unnecessary to relate here, had prevented him from taking service with the gallant army that had fought the disastrous campaigns ending with the fall of Corinth, and he chafed under the inglorious restraint, longing for the release of his energies, the larger life of the soldier, the opportunity for distinction. That opportunity, he felt, would come, as it comes to all in war time. Meanwhile he did what he could. No service was too humble for him to perform in aid of the South, no adventure too perilous for him to undertake if consistent with the character of a civilian who was at heart a soldier, and who in good faith and without too much qualification assented to at least a part of the frankly villainous dictum that all is fair in love and war.

One evening while Farquhar and his wife were sitting on a rustic bench near the entrance to his grounds, a gray-clad soldier rode up to the gate and asked for a drink of water. Mrs. Farquhar was only too happy to serve him with her own white hands. While she was fetching the water her husband approached the dusty horseman and inquired eagerly for news from the front.

"The Yanks are repairing the railroads," said the man, "and are getting ready for another advance. They have reached the Owl Creek bridge, put it in order and built a stockade on the north bank. The commandant has issued an order, which is posted everywhere, declaring that any civilian caught interfering with the railroad, its bridges, tunnels or trains will be summarily hanged. I saw the order."

"How far is it to the Owl Creek bridge?" Farquhar asked.

"About thirty miles."

"Is there no force on this side the creek?"

"Only a picket post half a mile out, on the railroad, and a single sentinel at this end of the bridge."

"Suppose a man—a civilian and student of hanging—should elude the picket post and perhaps get the better of the sentinel," said Farquhar, smiling, "what could he accomplish?"

The soldier reflected. "I was there a month ago," he replied. "I observed that the flood of last winter had lodged a great quantity of driftwood against the wooden pier at this end of the bridge. It is now dry and would burn like tow."

The lady had now brought the water, which the soldier drank. He thanked her ceremoniously, bowed to her husband and rode away. An hour later, after nightfall, he repassed the plantation, going northward in the direction from which he had come. He was a Federal scout.

III

As Peyton Farquhar fell straight downward through the bridge he lost consciousness and was as one already dead. From this state he was awakened—ages later, it seemed to him—by the pain of a sharp pressure upon his throat, followed by a sense of suffocation. Keen, poignant agonies seemed to shoot from his neck downward through every fibre of his body and limbs. These pains appeared to flash along well-defined lines of ramification and to beat with an inconceivably rapid periodicity. They seemed like streams of pulsating fire heating him to an intolerable temperature. As to his head, he was conscious of nothing but a feeling of fulness—of congestion. These sensations were unaccompanied by thought. The intellectual part of his nature was already effaced; he had power only to feel, and feeling was torment. He was conscious of motion. Encompassed in a luminous cloud, of which he was now merely the fiery heart, without material substance, he swung through unthinkable arcs of oscillation, like a vast pendulum. Then all at once, with terrible suddenness, the light about him shot upward with the noise of a loud splash; a frightful roaring was in his ears, and all was cold and dark. The power of thought was restored; he knew that the rope had broken and he had fallen into the stream. There was no additional strangulation; the noose about his neck was already suffocating him and kept the water from his lungs. To die of hanging at the bottom of a river!—the idea seemed to him ludicrous. He opened his eyes in the darkness and saw above him a gleam of light, but how distant, how inaccessible! He was still sinking, for the light became fainter and fainter until it was a mere glimmer.

Then it began to grow and brighten, and he knew that he was rising toward the surface—knew it with reluctance, for he was now very comfortable. "To be hanged and drowned," he thought, "that is not so bad; but I do not wish to be shot. No; I will not be shot; that is not fair."

He was not conscious of an effort, but a sharp pain in his wrist apprised him that he was trying to free his hands. He gave the struggle his attention, as an idler might observe the feat of a juggler, without interest in the outcome. What splendid effort!—what magnificent, what superhuman strength! Ah, that was a fine endeavor! Bravo! The cord fell away; his arms parted and floated upward, the hands dimly seen on each side in the growing light. He watched them with a new interest as first one and then the other pounced upon the noose at his neck. They tore it away and thrust it fiercely aside, its undulations resembling those of a water-snake. "Put it back, put it back!" He thought he shouted these words to his hands, for the undoing of the noose had been succeeded by the direst pang that he had yet experienced. His neck ached horribly; his brain was on fire; his heart, which had been fluttering faintly, gave a great leap, trying to force itself out at his mouth. His whole body was racked and wrenched with an insupportable anguish! But his disobedient hands gave no heed to the command. They beat the water vigorously with quick, downward strokes, forcing him to the surface. He felt his head emerge; his eyes were blinded by the sunlight; his chest expanded convulsively, and with a supreme and crowning agony his lungs engulfed a great draught of air, which instantly he expelled in a shriek!

He was now in full possession of his physical senses. They were, indeed, preternaturally keen and alert. Something in the awful disturbance of his organic system had so exalted and refined them that they made record of things never before perceived. He felt the ripples upon his face and heard their separate sounds as they struck. He looked at the forest on the bank of the stream, saw the individual trees, the leaves and the veining of each leaf—saw the very insects upon them: the locusts, the brilliant-bodied flies, the gray spiders stretching their webs from twig to twig. He noted the prismatic colors in all the dewdrops upon a million blades of grass. The humming of the gnats that danced above the eddies of the stream, the beating of the dragon-flies' wings, the strokes of the water-spiders' legs, like oars which had lifted their boat—all these made audible music. A fish slid along beneath his eyes and he heard the rush of its body parting the water.

He had come to the surface facing down the stream; in a moment the visible world seemed to wheel slowly round, himself the pivotal point, and he saw the bridge, the fort, the soldiers upon the bridge, the captain, the sergeant, the two privates, his executioners. They were in silhouette against the blue sky. They shouted and gesticulated, pointing at him. The captain had drawn his pistol, but did not fire; the others were unarmed. Their movements were grotesque and horrible, their forms gigantic.

Suddenly he heard a sharp report and something struck the water smartly within a few inches of his head, spattering his face with spray. He heard a second report, and saw one of the sentinels with his rifle at his shoulder, a light cloud of blue smoke rising from the muzzle. The man in the water saw the eye of the man on the bridge gazing into his own through the sights of the rifle. He observed that it was a gray eye and remembered having read that gray eyes were keenest, and that all famous marksmen had them. Nevertheless, this one had missed.

A counter-swirl had caught Farquhar and turned him half round; he was again looking into the forest on the bank opposite the fort. The sound of a clear, high voice in a monotonous singsong now rang out behind him and came across the water with a distinctness that pierced and subdued all other sounds, even the

beating of the ripples in his ears. Although no soldier, he had fre-
quented camps enough to know the dread significance of that deliberate, drawling, aspirated chant; the lieutenant on shore was
taking a part in the morning's work. How coldly and pitilessly—
with what an even, calm intonation, presaging, and enforcing tranquillity in the men—with what accurately measured intervals fell
those cruel words:

"Attention, company! . . . Shoulder arms! . . . Ready! . . .
Aim! . . . Fire!"

Farquhar dived—dived as deeply as he could. The water roared
in his ears like the voice of Niagara, yet he heard the dulled thunder of the volley and, rising again toward the surface, met shining
bits of metal, singularly flattened, oscillating slowly downward.
Some of them touched him on the face and hands, then fell away,
continuing their descent. One lodged between his collar and neck;
it was uncomfortably warm and he snatched it out.

As he rose to the surface, gasping for breath, he saw that he
had been a long time under water; he was perceptibly farther
down stream—nearer to safety. The soldiers had almost finished
reloading; the metal ramrods flashed all at once in the sunshine as
they were drawn from the barrels, turned in the air, and thrust
into their sockets. The two sentinels fired again, independently
and ineffectually.

The hunted man saw all this over his shoulder; he was now
swimming vigorously with the current. His brain was as energetic
as his arms and legs; he thought with the rapidity of lightning.

"The officer," he reasoned, "will not make that martinet's error
a second time. It is as easy to dodge a volley as a single shot. He
has probably already given the command to fire at will. God help
me, I cannot dodge them all!"

An appalling plash within two yards of him was followed by a
loud, rushing sound, *diminuendo,* which seemed to travel back

through the air to the fort and died in an explosion which stirred
the very river to its deeps! A rising sheet of water curved over him,
fell down upon him, blinded him, strangled him! The cannon had
taken a hand in the game. As he shook his head free from the commotion of the smitten water he heard the deflected shot humming
through the air ahead, and in an instant it was cracking and smash-
ing the branches in the forest beyond.

"They will not do that again," he thought; "the next time they
will use a charge of grape. I must keep my eye upon the gun; the
smoke will apprise me—the report arrives too late; it lags behind
the missile. That is a good gun."

Suddenly he felt himself whirled round and round—spinning
like a top. The water, the banks, the forests, the now distant bridge,
fort and men—all were commingled and blurred. Objects were
represented by their colors only; circular horizontal streaks of
color—that was all he saw. He had been caught in a vortex and was
being whirled on with a velocity of advance and gyration that
made him giddy and sick. In a few moments he was flung upon
the gravel at the foot of the left bank of the stream—the southern
bank—and behind a projecting point which concealed him from
his enemies. The sudden arrest of his motion, the abrasion of one
of his hands on the gravel, restored him, and he wept with delight.
He dug his fingers into the sand, threw it over himself in handfuls
and audibly blessed it. It looked like diamonds, rubies, emeralds; he
could think of nothing beautiful which it did not resemble. The
trees upon the bank were giant garden plants; he noted a definite
order in their arrangement, inhaled the fragrance of their blooms.
A strange, roseate light shone through the spaces among their
trunks and the wind made in their branches the music of æolian
harps. He had no wish to perfect his escape—was content to remain in that enchanting spot until retaken.

A whiz and rattle of grapeshot among the branches high above his head roused him from his dream. The baffled cannoneer had fired him a random farewell. He sprang to his feet, rushed up the sloping bank, and plunged into the forest.

All that day he traveled, laying his course by the rounding sun. The forest seemed interminable; nowhere did he discover a break in it, not even a woodman's road. He had not known that he lived in so wild a region. There was something uncanny in the revelation.

By night fall he was fatigued, footsore, famishing. The thought of his wife and children urged him on. At last he found a road which led him in what he knew to be the right direction. It was as wide and straight as a city street, yet it seemed untraveled. No fields bordered it, no dwelling anywhere. Not so much as the barking of a dog suggested human habitation. The black bodies of the trees formed a straight wall on both sides, terminating on the horizon in a point, like a diagram in a lesson in perspective. Overhead, as he looked up through this rift in the wood, shone great golden stars looking unfamiliar and grouped in strange constellations. He was sure they were arranged in some order which had a secret and malign significance. The wood on either side was full of singular noises, among which—once, twice, and again, he distinctly heard whispers in an unknown tongue.

His neck was in pain and lifting his hand to it he found it horribly swollen. He knew that it had a circle of black where the rope had bruised it. His eyes felt congested; he could no longer close them. His tongue was swollen with thirst; he relieved its fever by thrusting it forward from between his teeth into the cold air. How softly the turf had carpeted the untraveled avenue—he could no longer feel the roadway beneath his feet!

Doubtless, despite his suffering, he had fallen asleep while walking, for now he sees another scene—perhaps he has merely recovered from a delirium. He stands at the gate of his own home. All is as he left it, and all bright and beautiful in the morning sunshine. He must have traveled the entire night. As he pushes open the gate and passes up the wide white walk, he sees a flutter of female garments; his wife, looking fresh and cool and sweet, steps down from the veranda to meet him. At the bottom of the steps she stands waiting, with a smile of ineffable joy, an attitude of matchless grace and dignity. Ah, how beautiful she is! He springs forward with extended arms. As he is about to clasp her he feels a stunning blow upon the back of the neck; a blinding white light blazes all about him with a sound like the shock of a cannon— then all is darkness and silence!

Peyton Farquhar was dead; his body, with a broken neck, swung gently from side to side beneath the timbers of the Owl Creek bridge.

Jean-ah Poquelin

George Washington Cable
(1844–1925)

In the first decade of the present century, when the newly established American Government was the most hateful thing in
Louisiana—when the Creoles were still kicking at such vile in-
novations as the trial by jury, American dances, anti-smuggling
laws, and the printing of the Governor's proclamation in English—
when the Anglo-American flood that was presently to burst in a
crevasse of immigration upon the delta had thus far been felt only
as slippery seepage which made the Creole tremble for his footing—there stood, a short distance above what is now Canal Street,
and considerably back from the line of villas which fringed the
riverbank on Tchoupitoulas Road, an old colonial plantation
house half in ruin.

It stood aloof from civilization, the tracts that had once been
its indigo fields given over to their first noxious wildness, and
grown up into one of the horridest marshes within a circuit of
fifty miles.

The house was of heavy cypress, lifted up on pillars, grim,
solid, and spiritless, its massive build a strong reminder of days still

earlier, when every man had been his own peace officer and the insurrection of the blacks a daily contingency. Its dark, weather-beaten roof and sides were hoisted up above the jungly plain in a distracted way, like a gigantic ammunition wagon stuck in the mud and abandoned by some retreating army. Around it was a dense growth of low water willows, with half a hundred sorts of thorny or fetid bushes, savage strangers alike to the "language of flowers" and to the botanist's Greek. They were hung with countless strands of discolored and prickly smilax, and the impassable mud below bristled with *chevaux de frise* of the dwarf palmetto. Two lone forest trees, dead cypresses, stood in the center of the marsh, dotted with roosting vultures. The shallow strips of water were hid by myriads of aquatic plants, under whose coarse and spiritless flowers, could one have seen it, was a harbor of reptiles, great and small, to make one shudder to the end of his days.

The house was on a slightly raised spot, the levee of a draining canal. The waters of this canal did not run; they crawled, and were full of big, ravening fish and alligators that held it against all comers.

Such was the home of old Jean Marie Poquelin, once an opulent indigo planter, standing high in the esteem of his small, proud circle of exclusively male acquaintances in the old city; now a hermit, alike shunned by and shunning all who had ever known him. "The last of his line," said the gossips. His father lies under the floor of the St. Louis Cathedral, with the wife of his youth on one side, and the wife of his old age on the other. Old Jean visits the spot daily. His half brother—alas! there was a mystery; no one knew what had become of the gentle, young half brother, more than thirty years his junior, whom once he seemed so fondly to love, but who, seven years ago, had disappeared suddenly, once for all, and left no clue of his fate.

They had seemed to live so happily in each other's love. No father, mother, wife to either, no kindred upon earth. The elder a bold, frank, impetuous, chivalric adventurer; the younger a gentle, studious, book-loving recluse; they lived upon the ancestral estate like mated birds, one always on the wing, the other always in the nest.

There was no trait in Jean Marie Poquelin, said the old gossips, for which he was so well known among his few friends as his apparent fondness for his "little brother." "Jacques said this," and "Jacques said that"; he "would leave this or that, or any thing to Jacques," for Jacques was a scholar, and "Jacques was good," or "wise," or "just," or "farsighted," as the nature of the case required; and "he should ask Jacques as soon as he got home," since Jacques was never elsewhere to be seen.

It was between the roving character of the one brother, and the bookishness of the other, that the estate fell into decay. Jean Marie, generous gentleman, gambled the slaves away one by one, until none was left, man or woman, but one old African mute.

The indigo fields and vats of Louisiana had been generally abandoned as unremunerative. Certain enterprising men had substituted the culture of sugar; but while the recluse was too apathetic to take so active a course, the other saw larger, and, at that time, equally respectable profits, first in smuggling, and later in the African slave trade. What harm could he see in it? The whole people said it was vitally necessary, and to minister to a vital public necessity—good enough, certainly, and so he laid up many a doubloon, that made him none the worse in the public regard.

One day old Jean Marie was about to start upon a voyage that was to be longer, much longer, than any that he had yet made. Jacques had begged him hard for many days not to go, but he laughed him off, and finally said, kissing him:

"*Adieu, 'tit frère.*"

"No," said Jacques, "I shall go with you."

They left the old hulk of a house in the sole care of the African mute, and went away to the Guinea coast together.

Two years after, old Poquelin came home without his vessel. He must have arrived at his house by night. No one saw him come. No one saw "his little brother"; rumor whispered that he, too, had returned, but he had never been seen again.

A dark suspicion fell upon the old slave trader. No matter that the few kept the many reminded of the tenderness that had ever marked his bearing to the missing man. The many shook their heads. "You know he has a quick and fearful temper"; and "why does he cover his loss with mystery?" "Grief would out with the truth."

"But," said the charitable few, "look in his face; see that expression of true humanity." The many did look in his face, and, as he looked in theirs, he read the silent question: "Where is thy brother Abel?" The few were silenced, his former friends died off, and the name of Jean Marie Poquelin became a symbol of witchery, devilish crime, and hideous nursery fictions.

The man and his house were alike shunned. The snipe and duck hunters forsook the marsh, and the woodcutters abandoned the canal. Sometimes the hardier boys who ventured out there snake-shooting heard a low thumping of oarlocks on the canal. They would look at each other for a moment half in consternation, half in glee, then rush from their sport in wanton haste to assail with their gibes the unoffending, withered old man who, in rusty attire, sat in the stern of a skiff, rowed homeward by his white-headed African mute.

"O Jean-ah Poquelin! O Jean-ah! Jean-ah Poquelin!"

It was not necessary to utter more than that. No hint of wickedness, deformity, or any physical or moral demerit; merely the name and tone of mockery: "Oh, Jean-ah Poquelin!" and while they tumbled one over another in their needless haste to fly, he would rise carefully from his seat, while the aged mute, with downcast face, went on rowing, and, rolling up his brown fist and extending it toward the urchins, would pour forth such an unholy broadside of French imprecation and invective as would all but craze them with delight.

Among both blacks and whites the house was the object of a thousand superstitions. Every midnight, they affirmed, the *feu follet* came out of the marsh and ran in and out of the rooms, flashing from window to window. The story of some lads, whose word in ordinary statements was worthless, was generally credited, that the night they camped in the woods, rather than pass the place after dark, they saw, about sunset, every window blood-red, and on each of the four chimneys an owl sitting, which turned his head three times round, and moaned and laughed with a human voice. There was a bottomless well, everybody professed to know, beneath the sill of the big front door under the rotten veranda; whoever set his foot upon that threshold disappeared forever in the depth below.

What wonder the marsh grew as wild as Africa! Take all the Faubourg Ste. Marie, and half the ancient city, you would not find one graceless daredevil reckless enough to pass within a hundred yards of the house after midnight.

The alien races pouring into old New Orleans began to find the few streets named for the Bourbon princes too strait for them. The wheel of fortune, beginning to whirl, threw them off beyond the ancient corporation lines, and sowed civilization and even trade upon the lands of the Graviers and Girods. Fields became roads, roads streets. Everywhere the leveler was peering through his glass, rodsmen were whacking their way through willow brakes and rose hedges, and the sweating Irishmen tossed the blue clay up with their long-handled shovels.

"Ha! that is all very well," quoth the Jean-Baptistes, feeling the reproach of an enterprise that asked neither cooperation nor advice of them, "but wait till they come yonder to Jean Poquelin's marsh; ha! ha! ha!" The supposed predicament so delighted them, that they put on a mock terror and whirled about in an assumed stampede, then caught their clasped hands between their knees in excess of mirth, and laughed till the tears ran; for whether the streetmakers mired in the marsh, or contrived to cut through old "Jean-ah's" property, either event would be joyful. Meantime a line of tiny rods, with bits of white paper in their split tops, gradually extended its way straight through the haunted ground, and across the canal diagonally.

"We shall fill that ditch," said the men in mud boots, and brushed close along the chained and padlocked gate of the haunted mansion. Ah, Jean-ah Poquelin, those were not Creole boys, to be stampeded with a little hard swearing.

He went to the Governor. That official scanned the odd figure with no slight interest. Jean Poquelin was of short, broad frame, with a bronzed leonine face. His brow was ample and deeply furrowed. His eye, large and black, was bold and open like that of a war horse, and his jaws shut together with the firmness of iron. He was dressed in a suit of Attakapas cottonade, and his shirt unbuttoned and thrown back from the throat and bosom, sailorwise, showed a herculean breast, hard and grizzled. There was no fierceness or defiance in his look, no harsh ungentleness, no symptom of his unlawful life or violent temper; but rather a peaceful and peaceable fearlessness. Across the whole face, not marked in one or another feature, but as it were laid softly upon the countenance like an almost imperceptible veil, was the imprint of some great grief. A careless eye might easily overlook it, but, once seen, there it hung—faint, but unmistakable.

The Governor bowed.

"Parlez-vous français?" asked the figure.

"I would rather talk English, if you can do so," said the Governor.

"My name, Jean Poquelin."

"How can I serve you, Mr. Poquelin?"

"My 'ouse is yond'; *dans le marais là-bas.*"

The Governor bowed.

"Dat *marais* billong to me."

"Yes, sir."

"To me; Jean Poquelin; I hown 'im meself."

"Well, sir?"

"He don't billong to you; I get him from me father."

"That is perfectly true, Mr. Poquelin, as far as I am aware."

"You want to make strit pass yond'?"

"I do not know, sir; it is quite probable; but the city will in-demnify you for any loss you may suffer—you will get paid, you understand."

"Strit can't pass dare."

"You will have to see the municipal authorities about that, Mr. Poquelin."

A bitter smile came upon the old man's face.

"*Pardon, Monsieur,* you is not *le Gouverneur?*"

"Yes."

"*Mais,* yes. You har *le Gouverneur*—yes. Veh-well. I come to you. I tell you, strit can't pass at me 'ouse."

"But you will have to see—"

"I come to you. You is *le Gouverneur.* I know not the new laws. I ham a Fr-r-rench-a-man! Fr-rench-a-man have some-thing *aller au contraire*—he come at his *Gouverneur.* I come at you. If me not had been bought from me king like *bossals* in the hold time, ze king gof—France would-a-show *Monsieur le Gou-verneur* to take care his men to make strit in right places. *Mais,* I know; we billong to *Monsieur le Président.* I want you do somesin for me, eh?"

"What is it?" asked the patient Governor.

"I want you tell *Monsieur le Président,* strit—can't—pass—at— me—'ouse."

"Have a chair, Mr. Poquelin"; but the old man did not stir. The Governor took a quill and wrote a line to a city official, introducing Mr. Poquelin, and asking for him every possible courtesy. He handed it to him, instructing him where to present it.

"Mr. Poquelin," he said, with a conciliatory smile, "tell me, is it your house that our Creole citizens tell such odd stories about?"

The old man glared sternly upon the speaker, and with immovable features said:

"You don't see me trade some Guinea nigga'?"

"Oh, no."

"You don't see me make some smugglin'?"

"No, sir; not at all."

"But, I am Jean Marie Poquelin. I mine me hown bizniss. Dat all right? Adieu."

He put his hat on and withdrew. By and by he stood, letter in hand, before the person to whom it was addressed. This person employed an interpreter.

"He says," said the interpreter to the officer, "he come to make you the fair warning how you muz not make the street pas' at his 'ouse."

The officer remarked that "such impudence was refreshing"; but the experienced interpreter translated freely.

"He says: 'Why you don't want?' " said the interpreter.

The old slave trader answered at some length.

"He says," said the interpreter, again turning to the officer, "the morass is a too unhealth' for peopl' to live."

"But we expect to drain his old marsh; it's not going to be a marsh."

"Il dit"—the interpreter explained in French.

The old man answered tersely.

"He says the canal is a private," said the interpreter.

"Oh! *that* old ditch; that's to be filled up. Tell the old man we're going to fix him up nicely."

Translation being duly made, the man in power was amused to see a thundercloud gathering on the old man's face.

"Tell him," he added, "by the time we finish, there'll not be a ghost left in his shanty."

The interpreter began to translate, but—

"*J' comprends, j' comprends,*" said the old man, with an impatient gesture, and burst forth, pouring curses upon the United States, the President, the Territory of Orleans, Congress, the Governor and all his subordinates, striding out of the apartment as he cursed, while the object of his maledictions roared with merriment and rammed the floor with his foot.

"Why, it will make his old place worth ten dollars to one," said the official to the interpreter.

" 'Tis not for de worse of de property," said the interpreter.

"I should guess not," said the other, whittling his chair— "seems to me as if some of these old Creoles would liever live in a crawfish hole than to have a neighbor."

"You know what make old Jean Poquelin make like that? I will tell you. You know—"

The interpreter was rolling a cigarette, and paused to light his tinder; then, as the smoke poured in a thick double stream from his nostrils, he said, in a solemn whisper:

"He is a witch."

"Ho, ho, ho!" laughed the other.

"You don't believe it? What you want to bet?" cried the interpreter, jerking himself half up and thrusting out one arm while he bared it of its coat sleeve with the hand of the other. "What you want to bet?"

"How do you know?" asked the official.

"Dass what I goin' to tell you. You know, one evening I was shooting some *grosbec*. I killed three; but I had trouble to find them, it was becoming so dark. When I have them I start' to come home; then I got to pas' at Jean Poquelin's house."

"Ho, ho, ho!" laughed the other, throwing his leg over the arm of his chair.

"Wait," said the interpreter. "I come along slow, not making some noises; still, still—"

"And scared," said the smiling one.

"*Mais,* wait. I get all pas' the 'ouse. 'Ah!' I say; 'all right!' Then I see two thing' before! Hah! I get as cold and humide, and shake like a leaf. You think it was nothing? There I see, so plain as can be (though it was making nearly dark), I see Jean—Marie—Po-que-lin walkin' right in front, and right there beside of him was something like a man—but not a man—white like paint!—I dropp' on the grass from scared—they pass'; so sure as I live 'twas the ghos' of Jacques Poquelin, his brother!"

"Pooh!" said the listener.

"I'll put my han' in the fire," said the interpreter.

"But did you never think," asked the other, "that that might be Jack Poquelin, as you call him, alive and well, and for some cause hid away by his brother?"

"But there har' no cause!" said the other, and the entrance of third parties changed the subject.

Some months passed and the street was opened. A canal was first dug through the marsh, the small one which passed so close to Jean Poquelin's house was filled, and the street, or rather a sunny road, just touched a corner of the old mansion's dooryard. The morass ran dry. Its venomous denizens slipped away through the bulrushes; the cattle roaming freely upon its hardened surface trampled the superabundant undergrowth. The bellowing frogs croaked to westward. Lilies and the flower-de-luce sprang up in the place of reeds; smilax and poison oak gave way to the purple-plumed ironweed and pink spiderwort; the bindweeds ran every-where blooming as they ran, and on one of the dead cypresses a giant creeper hung its green burden of foliage and lifted its scarlet trumpets. Sparrows and red-birds flitted through the bushes, and dewberries grew ripe beneath. Over all these came a sweet, dry smell of salubrity which the place had not known since the sedi-ments of the Mississippi first lifted it from the sea.

But its owner did not build. Over the willow brakes, and down the vista of the open street, bright new houses, some singly, some by ranks, were prying in upon the old man's privacy. They even settled down toward his southern side. First a woodcutter's hut or two, then a market gardener's shanty, then a painted cottage, and all at once the *faubourg* had flanked and half surrounded him and his dried-up marsh.

Ah! then the common people began to hate him. "The old tyrant!" "You don't mean an old *tyrant?*" "Well, then, why don't he build when the public need demands it? What does he live in that unneighborly way for?" "The old pirate!" "The old kidnaper!" How easily even the most ultra Louisianians put on the imported virtues of the North when they could be brought to bear against the hermit. "There he goes, with the boys after him! Ah! ha! ha! Jean-ah Poquelin! Ah! Jean-ah! Aha! aha! Jean-ah Marie! Jean-ah Poquelin! The old villain!" How merrily the swarming *Américains* echo the spirit of persecution! "The old fraud," they say—"pre-tends to live in a haunted house, does he? We'll tar and feather him some day. Guess we can fix him."

He cannot be rowed home along the old canal now; he walks. He has broken sadly of late, and the street urchins are ever at his heels. It is like the days when they cried: "Go up, thou baldhead," and the old man now and then turns and delivers ineffectual curses.

To the Creoles—to the incoming lower class of superstitious

Germans, Irish, Sicilians, and others—he became an omen and embodiment of public and private ill fortune. Upon him all the vagaries
of their superstitions gathered and grew. If a house caught fire, it was
imputed to his machinations. Did a woman go off in a fit, he had
bewitched her. Did a child stray off for an hour, the mother shivered
with the apprehension that Jean Poquelin had offered him to strange
gods. The house was the subject of every bad boy's invention who
loved to contrive ghostly lies. "As long as that house stands we shall
have bad luck. Do you not see our pease and beans dying, our cab-
bages and lettuce going to seed and our gardens turning to dust,
while every day you can see it raining in the woods? The rain will
never pass old Poquelin's house. He keeps a fetich. He has conjured
the whole Faubourg St. Marie. And why, the old wretch? Simply because our playful and innocent children call after him as he passes."

A "Building and Improvement Company," which had not yet
got its charter, "but was going to," and which had not, indeed, any
tangible capital yet, but "was going to have some," joined the
"Jean-ah Poquelin" war. The haunted property would be such a
capital site for a market house! They sent a deputation to the old
mansion to ask its occupant to sell. The deputation never got beyond the chained gate and a very barren interview with the
African mute. The President of the Board was then empowered
(for he had studied French in Pennsylvania and was considered
qualified) to call and persuade M. Poquelin to subscribe to the
company's stock; but—

"Fact is, gentlemen," he said at the next meeting, "it would
take us at least twelve months to make Mr. Pokaleen understand
the rather original features of our system, and he wouldn't subscribe when we'd done; besides, the only way to see him is to stop
him on the street."

There was a great laugh from the Board; they couldn't help it.
"Better meet a bear robbed of her whelps," said one.

"You're mistaken as to that," said the President. "I did meet him, and stopped him, and found him quite polite. But I could get no satisfaction from him; the fellow wouldn't talk in French, and when I spoke in English he hoisted his old shoulders up, and gave the same answer to everything I said."

"And that was—?" asked one or two, impatient of the pause.

"That it 'don't worse w'ile?' "

One of the Board said: "Mr. President, this market-house project, as I take it, is not altogether a selfish one; the community is to be benefited by it. We may feel that we are working in the public interest [the Board smiled knowingly], if we employ all possible means to oust this old nuisance from among us. You may know that at the time the street was cut through, this old Poquelann did all he could to prevent it. It was owing to a certain connection which I had with that affair that I heard a ghost story [smiles, followed by a sudden dignified check]—ghost story, which, of course, I am not going to relate; but I *may* say that my profound conviction, arising from a prolonged study of that story, is, that this old villain, John Poquelann, has his brother locked up in that old house. Now, if this is so, and we can fix it on him, I merely *suggest* that we can make the matter highly useful. I don't know," he added, beginning to sit down, "but that it is an action we owe to the community—hem!"

"How do you propose to handle the subject?" asked the President.

"I was thinking," said the speaker, "that, as a Board of Directors, it would be unadvisable for us to authorize any action involving trespass; but if you, for instance, Mr. President, should, as it were, for mere curiosity, *request* someone, as, for instance, our excellent Secretary, simply as a personal favor, to look into the matter—this is merely a suggestion."

The Secretary smiled sufficiently to be understood that, while he certainly did not consider such preposterous service a part of his duties as secretary, he might, notwithstanding, accede to the President's request; and the Board adjourned.

Little White, as the Secretary was called, was a mild, kind-hearted little man, who, nevertheless, had no fear of anything, unless it was the fear of being unkind.

"I tell you frankly," he privately said to the President, "I go into this purely for reasons of my own."

The next day, a little after nightfall, one might have descried this little man slipping along the rear fence of the Poquelin place, preparatory to vaulting over into the rank, grass-grown yard, and bearing himself altogether more after the manner of a collector of rare chickens than according to the usage of secretaries.

The picture presented to his eye was not calculated to enliven his mind. The old mansion stood out against the western sky, black and silent. One long, lurid pencil stroke along a sky of slate was all that was left of daylight. No sign of life was apparent; no light at any window, unless it might have been on the side of the house hidden from view. No owls were on the chimneys, no dogs were in the yard.

He entered the place, and ventured up behind a small cabin which stood apart from the house. Through one of its many crannies he easily detected the African mute crouched before a flickering pine knot, his head on his knees, fast asleep.

He concluded to enter the mansion, and, with that view, stood and scanned it. The broad rear steps of the veranda would not serve him; he might meet someone midway. He was measuring, with his eye, the proportions of one of the pillars which supported it, and estimating the practicability of climbing it, when he heard a footstep. Someone dragged a chair out toward the railing, then seemed to change his mind and began to pace the veranda, his footfalls resounding on the dry boards with singular loudness. Little White drew a step backward, got the figure between himself and the sky, and at once recognized the short, broad-shouldered form of old Jean Poquelin.

He sat down upon a billet of wood, and, to escape the stings of a whining cloud of mosquitoes, shrouded his face and neck in his handkerchief, leaving his eyes uncovered.

He had sat there but a moment when he noticed a strange, sickening odor, faint, as if coming from a distance, but loathsome and horrid.

Whence could it come? Not from the cabin; not from the marsh, for it was as dry as powder. It was not in the air; it seemed to come from the ground.

Rising up, he noticed, for the first time, a few steps before him a narrow footpath leading toward the house. He glanced down it—ha! right there was someone coming—ghostly white!

Quick as thought, and as noiselessly, he lay down at full length against the cabin. It was bold strategy, and yet, there was no deny-ing it, little White felt that he was frightened. "It is not a ghost," he said to himself. "I *know* it cannot be a ghost"; but the perspiration burst out at every pore, and the air seemed to thicken with heat. "It is a living man," he said in his thoughts. "I hear his footstep, and I hear old Poquelin's footsteps, too, separately, over on the veranda. I am not discovered; the thing has passed; there is that odor again; what a smell of death! Is it coming back? Yes. It stops at the door of the cabin. Is it peering in at the sleeping mute? It moves away. It is in the path again. Now it is gone." He shuddered. "Now, if I dare venture, the mystery is solved." He rose cautiously, close against the cabin, and peered along the path.

The figure of a man, a presence if not a body—but whether clad in some white stuff or naked, the darkness would not allow him to determine—had turned, and now, with a seeming painful gait, moved slowly from him. "Great Heaven! can it be that the dead do walk?" He withdrew again the hands which had gone to his eyes. The dreadful object passed between two pillars and under the house. He listened. There was a faint sound as of feet within a staircase; then all was still except the measured tread of Jean Poquelin walking on the veranda, and the heavy respirations of the mute slumbering in the cabin.

The little Secretary was about to retreat; but as he looked once more toward the haunted house a dim light appeared in the crack of a closed window, and presently old Jean Poquelin came, dragging his chair, and sat down close against the shining cranny. He spoke in a low, tender tone in the French tongue, making some inquiry. An answer came from within. Was it the voice of a human? So unnatural was it—so hollow, so discordant, so unearthly—that the stealthy listener shuddered again from head to foot; and when something stirred in some bushes nearby—though it may have been nothing more than a rat—and came scuttling through the grass, the little Secretary actually turned and fled. As he left the enclosure he moved with bolder leisure through the bushes; yet now and then he spoke aloud: "Oh, oh! I see, I understand!" and shut his eyes in his hands.

How strange that henceforth little White was the champion of Jean Poquelin! In season and out of season—wherever a word was uttered against him—the Secretary, with a quiet, aggressive force that instantly arrested gossip, demanded upon what authority the statement or conjecture was made; but as he did not condescend to explain his own remarkable attitude, it was not long before the disrelish and suspicion which had followed Jean Poquelin so many years fell also upon him.

It was only the next evening but one after his adventure that he made himself a source of sullen amazement to one hundred and fifty boys, by ordering them to desist from their wanton hallooing. Old Jean Poquelin, standing and shaking his cane, rolling out his long-drawn maledictions, paused and stared, then gave the Secretary a courteous bow and started on. The boys, save one, from pure astonishment, ceased; but a ruffianly little Irish lad, more daring than any had yet been, threw a big hurtling clod that struck old Poquelin between the shoulders and burst like a shell. The enraged old man wheeled with uplifted staff to give chase to the scampering vagabond; and—he may have tripped, or he may not, but he fell full length. Little White hastened to help him up, but he waved him off with a fierce imprecation and, staggering to his feet, resumed his way homeward. His lips were reddened with blood.

Little White was on his way to the meeting of the Board. He would have given all he dared spend to have stayed away, for he felt both too fierce and too tremulous to brook the criticisms that were likely to be made.

"I can't help it, gentlemen; I can't help you to make a case against the old man, and I'm not going to."

"We did not expect this disappointment, Mr. White."

"I can't help that, sir. No, sir; you had better not appoint any more investigations. Somebody'll investigate himself into trouble. No, sir; it isn't a threat, it is only my advice, but I warn you that whoever takes the task in hand will rue it to his dying day—which may be hastened, too."

The President expressed himself surprised.

"I don't care a rush," answered little White, wildly and foolishly. "I don't care a rush if you are, sir. No, my nerves are not disordered; my head's as clear as a bell. No, I'm *not* excited."

A Director remarked that the Secretary looked as though he had waked from a nightmare.

"Well, sir, if you want to know the fact, I have; and if you choose to cultivate old Poquelin's society you can have one, too."

"White," called a facetious member, but White did not notice. "White," he called again.

"What?" demanded White, with a scowl.

"Did you see the ghost?"

"Yes, sir; I did," cried White, hitting the table, and handing the President a paper which brought the Board to other business.

The story got among the gossips that somebody (they were afraid to say little White) had been to the Poquelin mansion by night and beheld something appalling. The rumor was but a shadow of the truth, magnified and distorted as is the manner of shadows. He had seen skeletons walking, and had barely escaped the clutches of one by making the sign of the cross.

Some madcap boys with an appetite for the horrible plucked up courage to venture through the dried marsh by the cattle path, and come before the house at a spectral hour when the air was full of bats. Something which they but half saw—half a sight was enough— sent them tearing back through the willow brakes and acacia bushes to their homes, where they fairly dropped down, and cried:

"Was it white?" "No—yes—nearly so—we can't tell—but we saw it." And one could hardly doubt, to look at their ashen faces, that they had, whatever it was.

"If that old rascal lived in the country we come from," said certain *Américains,* "he'd have been tarred and feathered before now, wouldn't he, Sanders?"

"Well, now he just would."

"And we'd have rid him on a rail, wouldn't we?"

"That's what I allow."

"Tell you what you *could* do." They were talking to some rol- licking Creoles who had assumed an absolute necessity for doing *something.* "What is it you call this thing where an old man marries a young girl, and you come out with horns and—"

"Charivari?" asked the Creoles.

"Yes, that's it. Why don't you shivaree him?" Felicitous sugges- tion.

Little White, with his wife beside him, was sitting on their doorsteps on the sidewalk, as Creole custom had taught them, looking toward the sunset. They had moved into the lately opened street. The view was not attractive on the score of beauty. The houses were small and scattered, and across the flat commons, spite of the lofty tangle of weeds and bushes, and spite of the thickets of acacia, they needs must see the dismal old Poquelin mansion, tilted awry and shutting out the declining sun. The moon, white and slender, was hanging the tip of its horn over one of the chimneys.

"And you say," said the Secretary, "the old black man has been going by here alone? Patty, suppose old Poquelin should be concocting some mischief; he don't lack provocation; the way that clod hit him the other day was enough to have killed him. Why, Patty, he dropped as quick as *that!* No wonder you haven't seen him. I wonder if they haven't heard something about him up at the drugstore. Suppose I go and see."

"Do," said his wife.

She sat alone for half an hour, watching that sudden going out of the day peculiar to the latitude.

"That moon is ghost enough for one house," she said, as her husband returned. "It has gone right down the chimney."

"Patty," said little White, "the drug clerk says the boys are going to shivaree old Poquelin tonight. I'm going to try to stop it."

"Why, White," said his wife, "you'd better not. You'll get hurt."

"No, I'll not."

"Yes, you will."

"I'm going to sit out here until they come along. They're compelled to pass right by here."

"Why, White, it may be midnight before they start; you're not going to sit out here till then."

"Yes, I am."

"Well, you're very foolish," said Mrs. White in an undertone, looking anxious, and tapping one of the steps with her foot.

They sat a very long time talking over little family matters.

"What's that?" at last said Mrs. White.

"That's the nine-o'clock gun," said White, and they relapsed into a long-sustained, drowsy silence.

"Patty, you'd better go in and go to bed," said he at last.

"I'm not sleepy."

"Well, you're very foolish," quietly remarked little White, and again silence fell upon them.

"Patty, suppose I walk out to the old house and see if I can find out anything."

"Suppose," said she, "you don't do any such—listen!"

Down the street arose a great hubbub. Dogs and boys were howling and barking; men were laughing, shouting, groaning, and blowing horns, whooping, and clanking cowbells, whinnying, and howling, and rattling pots and pans.

"They are coming this way," said little White. "You had better go into the house, Patty."

"So had you."

"No. I'm going to see if I can't stop them."

"Why, White!"

"I'll be back in a minute," said White, and went toward the noise.

In a few moments the little Secretary met the mob. The pen hesitates on the word, for there is a respectable difference, measurable only on the scale of the half century, between a mob and a *charivari*. Little White lifted his ineffectual voice. He faced the head of the disorderly column, and cast himself about as if he were made of wood and moved by the jerk of a string. He rushed to one who seemed, from the size and clatter of his tin pan, to be a leader. *"Stop these fellows, Bienvenu, stop them just a minute, till I tell them something."*

Bienvenu turned and brandished his instruments of discord in an imploring way to the crowd. They slackened their pace, two or three hushed their horns and joined the prayer of little White and Bienvenu for silence. The throng halted. The hush was delicious.

"Bienvenu," said little White, "don't shivaree old Poquelin tonight; he's—"

"My fwang," said the swaying Bienvenu, "who tail you I goin' to chahivahi somebody, eh? You sink bickause I make a little play-fool wiz zis tin pan zat I am *dhonk?*"

"Oh, no, Bienvenu, old fellow, you're all right. I was afraid you might not know that old Poquelin was sick, you know, but you're not going there, are you?"

"My fwang, I vay soy to tail you zat you ah dhonk as de dev'. I am *shem* of you. I ham ze servan' of *ze publique.* Zese *citoyens* goin' to wickwest Jean Poquelin to give to the Ursuline' two hondred fifty dolla'—"

"*Hé quoi!*" cried a listener, "*Cinq cent piastres, oui!*"

"*Oui!*" said Bienvenu, "and if he wiffuse we make him some lit' *musique;* ta-ra-ta!" He hoisted a merry hand and foot, then frowning, added: "Old Poquelin got no bizniz dhink s'much w'isky."

"But, gentlemen," said little White, around whom a circle had gathered, "the old man is very sick."

"My faith!" cried a tiny Creole, "we did not make him to be sick. W'en we have say we going make *le charivari,* do you want that we hall tell a lie? My faith! 'sfools!"

"But you can shivaree somebody else," said desperate little White.

"*Oui!*" cried Bienvenu, "*et chahivahi* Jean-ah Poquelin tomo'w!"

"Let us go to Madame Schneider!" cried two or three, and amid huzzas and confused cries, among which was heard a stentorian Celtic call for drinks, the crowd again began to move.

"Cent piastres pour l'hôpital de charité!"

"Hurrah!"

"One hongred dolla' for Charity Hospital!"

"Hurrah!"

"Whang!" went a tin pan, the crowd yelled, and Pandemonium gaped again. They were off at a right angle.

Nodding, Mrs. White looked at the mantle clock.

"Well, if it isn't away after midnight."

The hideous noise downstreet was passing beyond earshot. She raised a sash and listened. For a moment there was silence. Someone came to the door.

"Is that you, White?"

"Yes. They've gone down to shivaree the old Dutchwoman who married her stepdaughter's sweetheart. They say she has got to pay a hundred dollars to the hospital before they stop."

The couple retired, and Mrs. White slumbered. She was awakened by her husband snapping the lid of his watch.

"What time?" she asked.

"Half past three. Patty, I haven't slept a wink. Those fellows are out yet. Don't you hear them?"

"Why, White, they're coming this way!"

"I know they are," said White, sliding out of bed and drawing on his clothes, "and they're coming fast. You'd better go away from that window, Patty. My! what a clatter!"

"Here they are," said Mrs. White, but her husband was gone. Two or three hundred men and boys pass the place at a rapid walk straight down the broad, new street, toward the hated house of ghosts. The din was terrific. She saw little White at the head of the rabble brandishing his arms and trying in vain to make himself heard; but they only shook their heads, laughing and hooting the louder, and so passed, bearing him on before them.

Swiftly they pass out from among the houses, away from the

dim oil lamps of the street, out into the broad starlit commons, and enter the willowy jungles of the haunted ground. Some hearts fail and their owners lag behind and turn back, suddenly remembering how near morning it is. But the most part push on, tearing the air with their clamor.

Down ahead of them in the long, thicket-darkened way there is—singularly enough—a faint dancing light. It must be very near the old house; it is. It has stopped now. It is a lantern, and is under a well-known sapling which has grown up on the wayside since the canal was filled. Now it swings mysteriously to and fro. A goodly number of the more ghost-fearing give up the sport; but a full hundred move forward at a run, doubling their devilish howling and banging.

Yes; it is a lantern, and there are two persons under the tree. The crowd draws near—drops into a walk; one of the two is the old African mute; he lifts the lantern up so that it shines on the other; the crowd recoils; there is a hush of all clangor, and all at once, with a cry of mingled fright and horror from every throat, the whole throng rushes back, dropping everything, sweeping past little White and hurrying on, never stopping until the jungle is left behind, and then to find that not one in ten has seen the cause of the stampede, and not one of the tenth is certain what it was.

There is one huge fellow among them who looks capable of any villainy. He finds something to mount on, and, in the Creole *patois,* calls a general halt. Bienvenu sinks down, and, vainly trying to recline gracefully, resigns the leadership. The herd gather round the speaker; he assures them that they have been outraged. Their right peaceably to traverse the public streets has been trampled upon. Shall such encroachments be endured? It is now daybreak. Let them go now by the open light of day and force a free passage of the public highway!

A scattering consent was the response, and the crowd, thinned now and drowsy, straggled quietly down toward the old house. Some drifted ahead, others sauntered behind, but everyone, as he again neared the tree, came to a standstill. Little White sat upon a bank of turf on the opposite side of the way looking very stern and sad. To each newcomer he put the same question:

"Did you come here to go to old Poquelin's?"

"Yes."

"He's dead." And if the shocked hearer started away he would say: "Don't go away."

"Why not?"

"I want you to go to the funeral presently."

If some Louisianian, too loyal to dear France or Spain to understand English, looked bewildered, someone would interpret for him; and presently they went. Little White led the van, the crowd trooping after him down the middle of the way. The gate, that had never been seen before unchained, was open. Stern little White stopped a short distance from it; the rabble stopped behind him. Something was moving out from under the veranda. The many whisperers stretched upward to see. The African mute came very slowly toward the gate, leading by a cord in the nose a small brown bull, which was harnessed to a rude cart. On the flat body of the cart, under a black cloth, were seen the outlines of a long box.

"Hats off, gentlemen," said little White, as the box came in view, and the crowd silently uncovered.

"Gentlemen," said little White, "here come the last remains of Jean Marie Poquelin, a better man, I'm afraid, with all his sins—yes, a better—a kinder man to his blood—a man of more self-forgetful goodness—than all of you put together will ever dare to be."

There was a profound hush as the vehicle came creaking through the gate; but when it turned away from them toward the forest, those in front started suddenly. There was a backward rush, then all stood still again staring one way; for there, behind the bier, with eyes cast down and labored step, walked the living remains—all that was left—of little Jacques Poquelin, the long-hidden brother—a leper, as white as snow.

Dumb with horror, the cringing crowd gazed upon the walking death. They watched, in silent awe, the slow *cortège* creep down the long, straight road and lessen on the view, until by and by it stopped where a wild, unfrequented path branched off into the undergrowth toward the rear of the ancient city.

"They are going to the *Terre aux Lépreux,*" said one in the crowd. The rest watched them in silence.

The little bull was set free; the mute, with the strength of an ape, lifted the long box to his shoulder. For a moment more the mute and the leper stood in sight, while the former adjusted his heavy burden; then, without one backward glance upon the unkind human world, turning their faces toward the ridge in the depths of the swamp known as the Leper's Land, they stepped into the jungle, disappeared, and were never seen again.

Athénaïse

A STORY OF TEMPERAMENT

Kate Chopin
(1851–1904)

I

Athénaïse went away in the morning to make a visit to her parents, ten miles back on rigolet de Bon Dieu. She did not return in the evening, and Cazeau, her husband, fretted not a little. He did not worry much about Athénaïse, who, he suspected, was resting only too content in the bosom of her family; his chief solicitude was manifestly for the pony she had ridden. He felt sure those "lazy pigs," her brothers, were capable of neglecting it seriously. This misgiving Cazeau communicated to his servant, old Félicité, who waited upon him at supper.

His voice was low pitched, and even softer than Félicité's. He was tall, sinewy, swarthy, and altogether severe looking. His thick black hair waved, and it gleamed like the breast of a crow. The sweep of his mustache, which was not so black, outlined the broad contour of the mouth. Beneath the under lip grew a small tuft which he was much given to twisting, and which he permitted to grow, apparently for no other purpose. Cazeau's eyes were dark blue, narrow and overshadowed. His hands were coarse and stiff from close acquaintance with farming tools and implements, and he handled his fork and knife clumsily. But he was distinguished looking, and succeeded in commanding a good deal of respect, and even fear sometimes.

He ate his supper alone, by the light of a single coal-oil lamp that but faintly illuminated the big room, with its bare floor and huge rafters, and its heavy pieces of furniture that loomed dimly in the gloom of the apartment. Félicité, ministering to his wants, hovered about the table like a little, bent, restless shadow.

She served him with a dish of sunfish fried crisp and brown. There was nothing else set before him beside the bread and butter and the bottle of red wine which she locked carefully in the buffet after he had poured his second glass. She was occupied with her mistress's absence, and kept reverting to it after he had expressed his solicitude about the pony.

"Dat beat me! on'y marry two mont', an' got de head turn' a'ready to go 'broad. C'est pas Chrétien, ténez!"

Cazeau shrugged his shoulders for answer, after he had drained his glass and pushed aside his plate. Félicité's opinion of the unchristianlike behavior of his wife in leaving him thus alone after two months of marriage weighed little with him. He was used to solitude, and did not mind a day or a night or two of it. He had lived alone ten years, since his first wife died, and Félicité might have known better than to suppose that he cared. He told her she was a fool. It sounded like a compliment in his modulated, caressing voice. She grumbled to herself as she set about clearing the table, and Cazeau arose and walked outside on the gallery; his spur, which he had not removed upon entering the house, jangled at every step.

The night was beginning to deepen, and to gather black about the clusters of trees and shrubs that were grouped in the yard. In the beam of light from the open kitchen door a black boy stood feeding a brace of snarling, hungry dogs; further away, on the steps of a cabin, some one was playing the accordion; and in still another direction a little negro baby was crying lustily. Cazeau walked around to the front of the house, which was square, squat and one-story.

A belated wagon was driving in at the gate, and the impatient driver was swearing hoarsely at his jaded oxen. Félicité stepped out on the gallery, glass and polishing towel in hand, to investigate, and to wonder, too, who could be singing out on the river. It was a party of young people paddling around, waiting for the moon to rise, and they were singing Juanita, their voices coming tempered and melodious through the distance and the night.

Cazeau's horse was waiting, saddled, ready to be mounted, for Cazeau had many things to attend to before bedtime; so many things that there was not left to him a moment in which to think of Athénaïse. He felt her absence, though, like a dull, insistent pain.

However, before he slept that night he was visited by the thought of her, and by a vision of her fair young face with its drop-ping lips and sullen and averted eyes. The marriage had been a blunder; he had only to look into her eyes to feel that, to discover her growing aversion. But it was a thing not by any possibility to be undone. He was quite prepared to make the best of it, and ex-pected no less than a like effort on her part. The less she revisited the rigolet, the better. He would find means to keep her at home hereafter.

These unpleasant reflections kept Cazeau awake far into the night, notwithstanding the craving of his whole body for rest and sleep. The moon was shining, and its pale effulgence reached dimly into the room, and with it a touch of the cool breath of the spring night. There was an unusual stillness abroad; no sound to be heard save the distant, tireless, plaintive note of the accordion.

II

Athénaïse did not return the following day, even though her husband sent her word to do so by her brother, Montéclin, who passed on his way to the village early in the morning.

On the third day Cazeau saddled his horse and went himself in search of her. She had sent no word, no message, explaining her absence, and he felt that he had good cause to be offended. It was rather awkward to have to leave his work, even though late in the afternoon—Cazeau had always so much to do; but among the many urgent calls upon him, the task of bringing his wife back to a sense of her duty seemed to him for the moment paramount.

The Michés, Athénaïse's parents, lived on the old Gotrain place. It did not belong to them; they were "running" it for a merchant in Alexandria. The house was far too big for their use. One of the lower rooms served for the storing of wood and tools; the person "occupying" the place before Miché having pulled up the flooring in despair of being able to patch it. Upstairs, the rooms were so large, so bare, that they offered a constant temptation to lovers of the dance, whose importunities Madame Miché was accustomed to meet with amiable indulgence. A dance at Miché's and a plate of Madame Miché's gumbo filé at midnight were pleasures not to be neglected or despised, unless by such serious souls as Cazeau.

Long before Cazeau reached the house his approach had been observed, for there was nothing to obstruct the view of the outer road; vegetation was not yet abundantly advanced, and there was but a patchy, straggling stand of cotton and corn in Miché's field.

Madame Miché, who had been seated on the gallery in a rocking-chair, stood up to greet him as he drew near. She was short and fat, and wore a black skirt and loose muslin sack fastened at the throat with a hair brooch. Her own hair, brown and glossy, showed but a few threads of silver. Her round pink face was cheery, and her eyes were bright and good humored. But she was plainly perturbed and ill at ease as Cazeau advanced.

Montéclin, who was there too, was not ill at ease, and made no attempt to disguise the dislike with which his brother-in-law inspired him. He was a slim, wiry fellow of twenty-five, short of stature like his mother, and resembling her in feature. He was in shirt-sleeves, half leaning, half sitting, on the insecure railing of the gallery, and fanning himself with his broad-rimmed felt hat.

"Cochon!" he muttered under his breath as Cazeau mounted the stairs, "sacré cochon!"

"Cochon" had sufficiently characterized the man who had once on a time declined to lend Montéclin money. But when this same man had had the presumption to propose marriage to his well-beloved sister, Athénaïse, and the honor to be accepted by her, Montéclin felt that a qualifying epithet was needed fully to express his estimate of Cazeau.

Miché and his oldest son were absent. They both esteemed Cazeau highly, and talked much of his qualities of head and heart, and thought much of his excellent standing with city merchants.

Athénaïse had shut herself up in her room. Cazeau had seen her rise and enter the house at perceiving him. He was a good deal mystified, but no one could have guessed it when he shook hands with Madame Miché. He had only nodded to Montéclin, with a muttered "Comment ça va?"

"Tiens! something tole me you were coming to-day!" exclaimed Madame Miché, with a little blustering appearance of being cordial and at ease, as she offered Cazeau a chair.

He ventured a short laugh as he seated himself.

"You know, nothing would do," she went on, with much gesture of her small, plump hands, "nothing would do but Athénaïse mus' stay las' night fo' a li'le dance. The boys wouldn' year to their sister leaving."

Cazeau shrugged his shoulders significantly, telling as plainly as words that he knew nothing about it.

"Comment! Montéclin didn' tell you we were going to keep Athénaïse?" Montéclin had evidently told nothing.

"An' how about the night befo'," questioned Cazeau, "an' las' night? It isn't possible you dance every night out yere on the Bon Dieu!"

Madame Miché laughed, with amiable appreciation of the sarcasm; and turning to her son, "Montéclin, my boy, go tell yo' sister that Monsieur Cazeau is yere."

Montéclin did not stir except to shift his position and settle himself more securely on the railing.

"Did you year me, Montéclin?"

"Oh yes, I yeard you plain enough," responded her son, "but you know as well as me it's no use to tell 'Thénaïse anything. You been talkin' to her yo'se'f since Monday, an' pa's preached himse'f hoa'se on the subject, an' you even had uncle Achille down yere yesterday to reason with her. W'en 'Thénaïse said she wasn' goin' to set her foot back in Cazeau's house, she meant it."

This speech, which Montéclin delivered with thorough unconcern, threw his mother into a condition of painful but dumb embarrassment. It brought two fiery red spots to Cazeau's cheeks, and for the space of a moment he looked wicked.

What Montéclin had spoken was quite true, though his taste in the manner and choice of time and place in saying it were not of the best. Athénaïse, upon the first day of her arrival, had announced that she came to stay, having no intention of returning under Cazeau's roof. The announcement had scattered consternation, as she knew it would. She had been implored, scolded, entreated, stormed at, until she felt herself like a dragging sail that all the winds of heaven had beaten upon. Why in the name of God had she married Cazeau? Her father had lashed her with the question a dozen times. Why indeed? It was difficult now for her to understand why, unless because she supposed it was customary for girls to marry when the right opportunity came. Cazeau, she knew, would make life more comfortable for her; and again, she had liked him, and had even been rather flustered when he pressed her hands and kissed them, and kissed her lips and cheeks and eyes, when she accepted him.

Montéclin himself had taken her aside to talk the thing over. The turn of affairs was delighting him.

"Come, now, 'Thénaïse, you mus' explain to me all about it, so we can settle on a good cause, an' secu' a separation fo' you. Has he been mistreating an' abusing you, the sacré cochon?" They were alone together in her room, whither she had taken refuge from the angry domestic elements.

"You please to reserve yo' disgusting expressions, Montéclin. No, he has not abused me in any way that I can think."

"Does he drink? Come 'Thénaïse, think well over it. Does he ever get drunk?"

"Drunk! Oh, mercy, no—Cazeau never gets drunk."

"I see; it's jus' simply you feel like me; you hate him."

"No, I don't hate him," she returned reflectively, adding with a sudden impulse, "It's jus' being married that I detes' an' despise. I hate being Mrs. Cazeau, an' would want to be Athénaïse Miché again. I can't stan' to live with a man, to have him always there, his coats an' pantaloons hanging in my room, his ugly bare feet— washing them in my tub, befo' my very eyes, ugh!" She shuddered with recollections, and resumed, with a sigh that was almost a sob: "Mon Dieu, mon Dieu! Sister Marie Angélique knew w'at she was saying; she knew me better than myse'f w'en she said God had sent me a vocation an' I was turning deaf ears. W'en I think of a

blessed life in the convent, at peace! Oh, w'at was I dreaming of!"
and then the tears came.

Montéclin felt disconcerted and greatly disappointed at having
obtained evidence that would carry no weight with a court of justice. The day had not come when a young woman might ask the
court's permission to return to her mamma on the sweeping
ground of a constitutional disinclination for marriage. But if there
was no way of untying this Gordian knot of marriage, there was
surely a way of cutting it.

"Well, 'Thénaïse, I'm mightly durn sorry you got no better
groun's 'an w'at you say. But you can count on me to stan' by you
w'atever you do. God knows I don' blame you fo' not wantin' to
live with Cazeau."

And now there was Cazeau himself, with the red spots flam-
ing in his swarthy cheeks, looking and feeling as if he wanted to
thrash Montéclin into some semblance of decency. He arose
abruptly, and approaching the room which he had seen his wife
enter, thrust open the door after a hasty preliminary knock.
Athénaïse, who was standing erect at a far window, turned at his
entrance.

She appeared neither angry nor frightened, but thoroughly
unhappy, with an appeal in her soft dark eyes and a tremor on her
lips that seemed to him expressions of unjust reproach, that
wounded and maddened him at once. But whatever he might feel,
Cazeau knew only one way to act toward a woman.

"Athénaïse, you are not ready?" he asked in his quiet tones. "It's
getting late; we havin' any time to lose."

She knew that Montéclin had spoken out, and she had hoped
for a wordy interview, a stormy scene, in which she might have
held her own as she had held it for the past three days against her
family, with Montéclin's aid. But she had no weapon with which
to combat subtlety. Her husband's looks, his tones, his mere pres-

ence, brought to her a sudden sense of hopelessness, and instinctive realization of the futility of rebellion against a social and sacred institution.

Cazeau said nothing further, but stood waiting in the doorway. Madame Miché had walked to the far end of the gallery, and pretended to be occupied with having a chicken driven from her parterre. Montéclin stood by, exasperated, fuming, ready to burst out.

Athénaïse went and reached for her riding skirt that hung against the wall. She was rather tall, with a figure which, though not robust, seemed perfect in its fine proportions. "La fille de son père," she was often called, which was a great compliment to Miché. Her brown hair was brushed all fluffily back from her temples and low forehead, and about her features and expression lurked a softness, a prettiness, a dewiness, that were perhaps too childlike, that savored of immaturity.

She slipped the riding skirt, which was of black alpaca, over her head, and with impatient fingers hooked it at the waist over her pink linenlawn. Then she fastened on her white sunbonnet and reached for her gloves on the mantel piece.

"If you don' wan' to go, you know w'at you got to do, 'Thénaïse," fumed Montéclin. "You don' set yo' feet back on Cane River, by God, unless you want to—not w'ile I'm alive."

Cazeau looked at him as if he were a monkey whose antics fell short of being amusing.

Athénaïse still made no reply, said not a word. She walked rapidly past her husband, past her brother, bidding good-by to no one, not even to her mother. She descended the stairs, and without assistance from any one mounted the pony, which Cazeau had ordered to be saddled upon his arrival. In this way she obtained a fair start of her husband, whose departure was far more leisurely, and for the greater part of the way she managed to keep an appreciable gap between them. She rode almost madly at first, with the wind inflating her skirt balloonlike about her knees, and her sun-bonnet falling back between her shoulders.

At no time did Cazeau make an effort to overtake her until traversing an old fallow meadow that was level and hard as a table. The sight of a great solitary oak tree, with its seemingly immutable outlines, that had been a landmark for ages—or was it the odor of elderberry stealing up from the gully to the south? or what was it that brought vividly back to Cazeau, by some association of ideas, a scene of many years ago? He had passed that old live-oak hundreds of times, but it was only now that the memory of one day came back to him. He was a very small boy that day, seated before his father on horseback. They were proceeding slowly, and Black Gabe was moving on before them at a little dogtrot. Black Gabe had run away, and had been discovered back in the Gotrain swamp. They had halted beneath this big oak to enable the negro to take breath; for Cazeau's father was a kind and considerate master, and every one had agreed at the time that Black Gabe was a fool, a great idiot indeed, for wanting to run away from him.

The whole impression was for some reason hideous, and to dispel it Cazeau spurred his horse to a swift gallop. Overtaking his wife, he rode the remainder of the way at her side in silence.

It was late when they reached home. Félicité was standing on the grassy edge of the road, in the moonlight, waiting for them.

Cazeau once more ate his supper alone, for Athénaïse went to her room, and there she was crying again.

III

Athénaïse was not one to accept the inevitable with patient resignation, a talent born in the souls of many women; neither was she the one to accept it with philosophical resignation, like her husband. Her sensibilities were alive and keen and responsive. She met the pleasurable things of life with frank, open appreciation, and against distasteful conditions she rebelled. Dissimulation was as foreign to her nature as guile to the breast of a babe, and her rebellious outbreaks, by no means rare, had hitherto been quite open and aboveboard. People often said that Athénaïse would know her own mind some day, which was equivalent to saying that she was at present unacquainted with it. If she ever came to such knowledge, it would be by no intellectual research, by no subtle analyses or tracing the motives of actions to their source. It would come to her as the song to the bird, the perfume and color to the flower.

Her parents had hoped—not without reason and justice—that marriage would bring the poise, the desirable pose, so glaringly lacking in Athénaïse's character. Marriage they knew to be a wonderful and powerful agent in the development and formation of a woman's character; they had seen its effect too often to doubt it.

"And if this marriage does nothing else," exclaimed Miché in an outburst of sudden exasperation, "it will rid us of Athénaïse, for I am at the end of my patience with her! You have never had the firmness to manage her"—he was speaking to his wife—"I have not had the time, the leisure, to devote to her training; and what good we might have accomplished, that maudit Montéclin—Well, Cazeau is the one! It takes just such a steady hand to guide a disposition like Athénaïse's, a master hand, a strong will that compels obedience."

And now, when they had hoped for so much, here was Athénaïse, with gathered and fierce vehemence, beside which her former outbursts appeared mild, declaring that she would not, and she would not, and she would not continue to enact the role of wife to Cazeau. If she had had a reason! as Madame Miché lamented; but it could not be discovered that she had any sane one.

He had never scolded, or called names, or deprived her of comforts, or been guilty of any of the many reprehensible acts commonly attributed to objectionable husbands. He did not slight nor
neglect her. Indeed, Cazeau's chief offense seemed to be that he
loved her, and Athénaïse was not the woman to be loved against
her will. She called marriage a trap set for the feet of unwary and
unsuspecting girls, and in round, unmeasured terms reproached her
mother with treachery and deceit.

"I told you Cazeau was the man," chuckled Miché, when his
wife had related the scene that had accompanied and influenced
Athénaïse's departure.

Athénaïse again hoped, in the morning, that Cazeau would
scold or make some sort of a scene, but he apparently did not dream
of it. It was exasperating that he should take her acquiescence so for
granted. It is true he had been up and over the fields and across the
river and back long before she was out of bed, and he may have
been thinking of something else, which was no excuse, which was
even in some sense an aggravation. But he did say to her at breakfast, "That brother of yo's, that Montéclin, is unbearable."

"Montéclin? Par exemple!"

Athénaïse, seated opposite to her husband, was attired in a
white morning wrapper. She wore a somewhat abused, long face,
it is true—an expression of countenance familiar to some husbands—
but the expression was not sufficiently pronounced to mar the
charm of her youthful freshness. She had little heart to eat, only
playing with the food before her, and she felt a pang of resentment
at her husband's healthy appetite.

"Yes, Montéclin," he reasserted. "He's developed into a firs'-
class nuisance; an' you better tell him, Athénaïse—unless you want
me to tell him—to confine his energies after this to matters that
concern him. I have no use fo' him or fo' his interference in w'at
regards you an' me alone."

This was said with unusual asperity. It was the little breach that Athénaïse had been watching for, and she charged rapidly: "It's strange, if you detes' Montéclin so heartily, that you would desire to marry his sister." She knew it was a silly thing to say, and was not surprised when he told her so. It gave her a little foothold for further attack, however. "I don't see, anyhow, w'at reason you had to marry me, w'en there were so many others," she complained, as if accusing him of persecution and injury. "There was Marianne running after you fo' the las' five years till it was disgraceful; an' any one of the Dortrand girls would have been glad to marry you. But no, nothing would do; you mus' come out on the rigolet fo' me." Her complaint was pathetic, and at the same time so amusing that Cazeau was forced to smile.

"I can't see w'at the Dortrand girls or Marianne have to do with it," he rejoined; adding, with no trace of amusement, "I married you because I loved you; because you were the woman I wanted to marry, an' the only one. I reckon I tole you that befo'. I thought—of co'se I was a fool fo' taking things fo' granted—but I did think that I might make you happy in making things easier an' mo' comfortable fo' you. I expected—I was even that big a fool—believed that yo' coming yere to me would be like the sun shining out of the clouds, an' that our days would be like w'at the story-books promise after the wedding. I was mistaken. But I can't imagine w'at induced you to marry me. W'atever it was, I reckon you foun' out you made a mistake, too. I don' see anything to do but make the best of a bad bargain, an' shake han's over it." He had arisen from the table, and, approaching, held out his hand to her. What he had said was commonplace enough, but it was significant, coming from Cazeau, who was not often so unreserved in expressing himself.

Athénaïse ignored the hand held out to her. She was resting her chin in her palm, and kept her eyes fixed moodily upon the table. He rested his hand, that she would not touch, upon her head for an instant, and walked away out of the room.

She heard him giving orders to workmen who had been waiting for him out on the gallery, and she heard him mount his horse and ride away. A hundred things would distract him and engage his attention during the day. She felt that he had perhaps put her and her grievance from his thoughts when he crossed the threshold; whilst she—

Old Félicité was standing there holding a shining tin pail, asking for flour and lard and eggs from the storeroom, and meal for the chicks.

Athénaïse seized the bunch of keys which hung from her belt and flung them at Félicité's feet.

"Tiens! tu vas les garder comme tu as jadis fait. Je ne veux plus de ce train là, moi!"

The old woman stooped and picked up the keys from the floor. It was really all one to her that her mistress returned them to her keeping, and refused to take further account of the ménage.

IV

It seemed now to Athénaïse that Montéclin was the only friend left to her in the world. Her father and mother had turned from her in what appeared to be her hour of need. Her friends laughed at her, and refused to take seriously the hints which she threw out—feeling her way to discover if marriage were as distasteful to other women as to herself. Montéclin alone understood her. He alone had always been ready to act for her and with her, to comfort and solace her with his sympathy and his support. Her only hope for rescue from her hateful surroundings lay in Montéclin. Of herself she felt powerless to plan, to act, even to conceive a way out of this pitfall into which the whole world seemed to have con-spired to push her.

She had a great desire to see her brother and wrote asking him to come to her. But it better suited Montéclin's spirit of adventure to appoint a meeting place at the turn of the lane, where Athénaïse might appear to be walking leisurely for health and recreation, and where he might seem to be riding along, bent on some errand of business or pleasure.

There had been a shower, a sudden downpour, short as it was sudden, that had laid the dust in the road. It had freshened the pointed leaves of the live oaks, and brightened up the big fields of cotton on either side of the lane till they seemed carpeted with green, glittering gems.

Athénaïse walked along the grassy edge of the road, lifting her crisp skirts with one hand, and with the other twirling a gay sun-shade over her bare head. The scent of the fields after the rain was delicious. She inhaled long breaths of their freshness and perfume, that soothed and quieted her for the moment. There were birds splashing and spluttering in the pools, pluming themselves on the fencerails, and sending out little sharp cries, twitters, and shrill rhapsodies of delight.

She saw Montéclin approaching from a great distance—almost as far away as the turn of the woods. But she could not feel sure it was he; it appeared too tall for Montéclin, but that was because he was riding a large horse. She waved her parasol to him; she was so glad to see him. She had never been so glad to see Montéclin be-fore; not even the day when he had taken her out of the convent, against her parents' wishes, because she had expressed a desire to remain there no longer. He seemed to her, as he drew near, the embodiment of kindness, of bravery, of chivalry, even of wisdom, for she had never known Montéclin at a loss to extricate himself from a disagreeable situation.

He dismounted, and, leading his horse by the bridle, started to walk beside her, after he had kissed her affectionately and asked her what she was crying about. She protested that she was not crying, for she was laughing, though drying her eyes at the same time on her handkerchief, rolled in a soft mop for the purpose.

She took Montéclin's arm, and they strolled slowly down the lane; they could not seat themselves for a comfortable chat, as they would have liked, with the grass all sparkling and bristling wet.

Yes, she was quite as wretched as ever, she told him. The week which had gone by since she saw him had in no wise lightened the burden of her discontent. There had even been some additional provocations laid upon her, and she told Montéclin all about them—about the keys, for instance, which in a fit of temper she had returned to Félicité's keeping; and she told how Cazeau had brought them back to her as if they were something she had accidentally lost, and he had recovered; and how he had said, in that aggravating tone of his, that it was not the custom on Cane River for the Negro servants to carry the keys, when there was a mistress at the head of the household.

But Athénaïse could not tell Montéclin anything to increase the disrespect which he already entertained for his brother-in-law; and it was then he unfolded to her a plan which he had conceived and worked out for her deliverance from this galling matrimonial yoke.

It was not a plan which met with instant favor, which she was at once ready to accept, for it involved secrecy and dissimulation, hateful alternatives, both of them. But she was filled with admiration for Montéclin's resources and wonderful talent for contrivance. She accepted the plan; not with the immediate determination to act upon it, rather with the intention to sleep and to dream upon it.

Three days later she wrote to Montéclin that she had aban-

doned herself to his counsel. Displeasing as it might be to her sense
of honesty, it would yet be less trying than to live on with a soul
full of bitterness and revolt, as she had done for the past two
months.

V

When Cazeau awoke, one morning at his usual very early hour, it
was to find the place at his side vacant. This did not surprise him
until he discovered that Athénaïse was not in the adjoining room,
where he had often found her sleeping in the morning on the
lounge. She had perhaps gone out for an early stroll, he reflected,
for her jacket and hat were not on the rack where she had hung
them the night before. But there were other things absent—a gown
or two from the armoire; and there was a great gap in the piles of
lingerie on the shelf; and her traveling-bag was missing, and so were
her bits of jewelry from the toilet tray—and Athénaïse was gone!

But the absurdity of going during the night, as if she had been
a prisoner, and he the keeper of a dungeon! So much secrecy and
mystery, to go sojourning out on the Bon Dieu! Well, the Michés
might keep their daughter after this. For the companionship of no
woman on earth would he again undergo the humiliating sensa-
tion of baseness that had overtaken him in passing the old oak-tree
in the fallow meadow.

But a terrible sense of loss overwhelmed Cazeau. It was not
new or sudden; he had felt it for weeks growing upon him, and it
seemed to culminate with Athénaïse's flight from home. He knew
that he could again compel her return as he had done once before—
compel her to return to the shelter of his roof, compel her cold and
unwilling submission to his love and passionate transports; but the
loss of self-respect seemed to him too dear a price to pay for a wife.

He could not comprehend why she had seemed to prefer him above others; why she had attracted him with eyes, with voice, with a hundred womanly ways, and finally distracted him with love which she seemed, in her timid, maidenly fashion, to return. The great sense of loss came from the realization of having missed a chance for happiness—a chance that would come his way again only through a miracle. He could not think of himself loving any other woman, and could not think of Athénaïse ever—even at some remote date—caring for him.

He wrote her a letter, in which he disclaimed any further intention of forcing his commands upon her. He did not desire her presence ever again in his home unless she came of her free will, uninfluenced by family or friends; unless she could be the companion he had hoped for in marrying her, and in some measure return affection and respect for the love which he continued and would always continue to feel for her. This letter he sent out to the rigolet by a messenger early in the day. But she was not out on the rigolet, and had not been there.

The family turned instinctively to Montéclin, and almost literally fell upon him for an explanation; he had been absent from home all night. There was much mystification in his answers, and a plain desire to mislead in his assurances of ignorance and innocence.

But with Cazeau there was no doubt or speculation when he accosted the young fellow. "Montéclin, w'at have you done with Athénaïse?" he questioned bluntly. They had met in the open road on horseback, just as Cazeau ascended the river bank before his house.

"W'at have you done to Athénaïse?" returned Montéclin for answer.

"I don't reckon you've considered yo' conduct by any light of decency an' propriety in encouraging yo' sister to such an action, but let me tell you—"

"Voyons! you can let me alone with yo' decency an' morality an' fiddlesticks. I know you mus' 'a' done Athénaïse pretty mean that she can't live with you; an' fo' my part, I'm mighty durn glad she had the spirit to quit you."

"I ain't in the humor to take any notice of yo' impertinence, Montéclin; but let me remine you that Athénaïse is nothing but a chile in character; besides that, she's my wife, an' I hole you responsible fo' her safety an' welfare. If any harm of any description happens to her, I'll strangle you, by God, like a rat, and fling you in Cane River, if I have to hang fo' it!" He had not lifted his voice. The only sign of anger was a savage gleam in his eyes.

"I reckon you better keep yo' big talk fo' the women, Cazeau," replied Montéclin, riding away.

But he went doubly armed after that, and intimated that the precaution was not needless, in view of the threats and menaces that were abroad touching his personal safety.

VI

Athénaïse reached her destination sound of skin and limb, but a good deal flustered, a little frightened, and altogether excited and interested by her unusual experiences.

Her destination was the house of Sylvie, on Dauphine Street, in New Orleans—a three-story gray brick, standing directly on the banquette, with three broad stone steps leading to the deep front entrance. From the second-story balcony swung a small sign, conveying to passers-by the intelligence that within were *"chambres garnies."*

It was one morning in the last week of April that Athénaïse presented herself at the Dauphine Street house. Sylvie was expecting her, and introduced her at once to her apartment, which was in the second story of the back ell, and accessible by an open, out-side gallery. There was a yard below, paved with broad stone flag-ging; many fragrant flowering shrubs and plants grew in a bed along the side of the opposite wall, and others were distributed about in tubs and green boxes.

It was a plain but large enough room into which Athénaïse was ushered, with matting on the floor, green shades and Nottingham lace curtains at the windows that looked out on the gallery, and fur-nished with a cheap walnut suit. But everything looked exquisitely clean, and the whole place smelled of cleanliness.

Athénaïse at once fell into the rocking-chair, with the air of exhaustion and intense relief of one who has come to the end of her troubles. Sylvie, entering behind her, laid the big traveling-bag on the floor and deposited the jacket on the bed.

She was a portly quadroon of fifty or thereabout, clad in an ample *volante* of the old-fashioned purple calico so much affected by her class. She wore large golden hoop-earrings, and her hair was combed plainly, with every appearance of effort to smooth out the kinks. She had broad, coarse features, with a nose that turned up, exposing the wide nostrils, and that seemed to emphasize the lofti-ness and command of her bearing—a dignity that in the presence of white people assumed a character of respectfulness, but never of obsequiousness. Sylvie believed firmly in maintaining the color-line, and would not suffer a white person, even a child, to call her "Madame Sylvie"—a title which she exacted religiously, however, from those of her own race.

"I hope you be please' wid yo' room, madame," she observed amiably. "Dat's de same room w'at yo' brother, M'sieur Miché, all time like w'en he come to New Orlean'. He well, M'sieur Miché? I receive' his letter las' week, an' dat same day a gent'man want I give 'im dat room. I say, 'No, dat room already ingage'.' Ev-body like dat room on 'count it so quite (quiet). M'sieur Gouvernail, dere in nax' room, you can't pay 'im! He been stay t'ree year' in dat room; but all fix' up fine wid his own furn'ture an' books, 'tel you can't see! I say to 'im plenty time', 'M'sieur Gouvernail, w'y you don't take dat t'ree-story front, now, long it's empty?' He tells me, 'Leave me 'lone, Sylvie; I know a good room w'en I fine it, me.' "

She had been moving slowly and majestically about the apartment, straightening and smoothing down bed and pillows, peering into ewer and basin, evidently casting an eye around to make sure that everything was as it should be.

"I sen' you some fresh water, Madame," she offered upon retiring from the room. "An' w'en you want an't'ing, you jus' go out on de gall'ry an' call Pousette: she year you plain—she right down dere in de kitchen."

Athénaïse was really not so exhausted as she had every reason to be after that interminable and circuitous way by which Montéclin had seen fit to have her conveyed to the city.

Would she ever forget that dark and truly dangerous midnight ride along the "coast" to the mouth of Cane River! There Montéclin had parted with her, after seeing her aboard the St. Louis and Shreveport packet which he knew would pass there before dawn. She had received instructions to disembark at the mouth of Red River, and there transfer to the first south-bound steamer for New Orleans, all of which instructions she had followed implicitly, even to making her way at once to Sylvie's upon her arrival in the city. Montéclin had enjoined secrecy and much caution; the clandestine nature of the affair gave it a savor of adventure which was highly pleasing to him. Eloping with his sister was only a little less engaging than eloping with some one else's sister.

But Montéclin did not do the *grand seigneur* by halves. He had paid Sylvie a whole month in advance for Athénaïse's board and lodging. Part of the sum he had been forced to borrow, it is true, but he was not niggardly.

Athénaïse was to take her meals in the house, which none of the other lodgers did; the one exception being that Mr. Gouvernail was served with breakfast on Sunday mornings.

Sylvie's clientèle came chiefly from the southern parishes; for the most part, people spending but a few days in the city. She prided herself upon the quality and highly respectable character of her patrons, who came and went unobtrusively.

The large parlor opening upon the front balcony was seldom used. Her guests were permitted to entertain in this sanctuary of elegance—but they never did. She often rented it for the night to parties of respectable and discreet gentlemen desiring to enjoy a quiet game of cards outside the bosom of their families. The second-story hall also led by a long window out on the balcony. And Sylvie advised Athénaïse, when she grew weary of her back room, to go and sit on the front balcony, which was shady in the afternoon, and where she might find diversion in the sounds and sights of the street below.

Athénaïse refreshed herself with a bath, and was soon unpacking her few belongings, which she ranged neatly away in the bureau drawers and the armoire.

She had revolved certain plans in her mind during the past hour or so. Her present intention was to live on indefinitely in this big, cool clean back room on Dauphine Street. She had thought seriously, for moments, of the convent, with all readiness to embrace the vows of poverty and chastity; but what about obedience? Later, she intended, in some roundabout way, to give her parents and her husband the assurance of her safety and welfare, reserving the right to remain unmolested and lost to them. To live on at the expense of Montéclin's generosity was wholly out of the question, and Athénaïse meant to look about for some suitable and agreeable employment.

The imperative thing to be done at present, however, was to go out in search of material for an inexpensive gown or two; for she found herself in the painful predicament of a young woman having almost literally nothing to wear. She decided upon pure white for one, and some sort of a sprigged muslin for the other.

VII

On Sunday morning, two days after Athénaïse's arrival in the city, she went in to breakfast somewhat later than usual, to find two covers laid at table instead of the one to which she was accustomed. She had been to mass, and did not remove her hat, but put her fan, parasol, and prayerbook aside. The dining-room was situated just beneath her own apartment, and, like all rooms of the house, was large and airy; the floor was covered with a glistening oilcloth.

The small, round table, immaculately set, was drawn near the open window. There were some tall plants in boxes on the gallery outside; and Pousette, a little, old, intensely black woman, was splashing and dashing buckets of water on the flagging, and talking loud in her Creole patois to no one in particular.

A dish piled with delicate river shrimps and crushed ice was on the table; a caraffe of crystal-clear water, a few *hors d'oeuvres,* beside a small golden-brown crusty loaf of French bread at each plate. A half-bottle of wine and the morning paper were set at the place opposite Athénaïse.

She had almost completed her breakfast when Gouvernail came in and seated himself at table. He felt annoyed at finding his cherished privacy invaded. Sylvie was removing the remains of a mutton chop from before Athénaïse, and serving her with a cup of café au lait.

"M'sieur Gouvernail," offered Sylvie in her most insinuating and impressive manner, "you please leave me make you acquaint' wid Madame Cazeau. Dat's M'sieur Miché's sister; you meet 'im two t'ree time', you rec'lec', an' been one day to de race wid 'im. Madame Cazeau, you please leave me make you acquaint' wid M'sieur Gouvernail."

Gouvernail expressed himself greatly pleased to meet the sister of Monsieur Miché, of whom he had not the slightest recollection. He inquired after Monsieur Miché's health, and politely offered Athénaïse a part of his newspaper—the part which contained the Woman's Page and the social gossip.

Athénaïse faintly remembered that Sylvie had spoken of a Monsieur Gouvernail occupying the room adjoining hers, living amid luxurious surroundings and a multitude of books. She had not thought of him further than to picture him a stout, middle-aged gentleman, with a bushy beard turning gray, wearing large gold-rimmed spectacles, and stooping somewhat from much bending over books and writing material. She had confused him in her mind with the likeness of some literary celebrity that she had run across in the advertising pages of a magazine.

Gouvernail's appearance was, in truth, in no sense striking. He looked older than thirty and younger than forty, was of medium height and weight, with a quiet, unobtrusive manner which seemed to ask that he be let alone. His hair was light brown, brushed carefully and parted in the middle. His mustache was brown, and so were his eyes, which had a mild, penetrating quality. He was neatly dressed in the fashion of the day; and his hands seemed to Athénaïse remarkably white and soft for a man's.

He had been buried in the contents of his newspaper, when he suddenly realized that some further little attention might be due to Miché's sister. He started to offer her a glass of wine, when he was surprised and relieved to find that she had quietly slipped away while he was absorbed in his own editorial on Corrupt Legislation.

Gouvernail finished his paper and smoked his cigar out on the gallery. He lounged about, gathered a rose for his buttonhole, and had his regular Sunday-morning confab with Pousette, to whom he paid a weekly stipend for brushing his shoes and clothing. He made a great pretense of haggling over the transaction, only to enjoy her uneasiness and garrulous excitement.

He worked or read in his room for a few hours, and when he quitted the house, at three in the afternoon, it was to return no more till late at night. It was his almost invariable custom to spend Sunday evenings out in the American quarter, among a congenial set of men and women—*des esprits forts,* all of them, whose lives were irreproachable, yet whose opinions would startle even the traditional "sapeur," for whom "nothing is sacred." But for all his "advanced" opinions, Gouvernail was a liberal-minded fellow; a man or woman lost nothing of his respect by being married.

When he left the house in the afternoon, Athénaïse had already ensconced herself on the front balcony. He could see her through the jalousies when he passed on his way to the front entrance. She had not yet grown lonesome or homesick; the newness of her surroundings made them sufficiently entertaining. She found it diverting to sit there on the front balcony watching people pass by, even though there was no one to talk to. And then the comforting, comfortable sense of not being married!

She watched Gouvernail walk down the street, and could find no fault with his bearing. He could hear the sound of her rockers for some little distance. He wondered what the "poor little thing" was doing in the city, and meant to ask Sylvie about her when he should happen to think of it.

VIII

The following morning, towards noon, when Gouvernail quitted
his room, he was confronted by Athénaïse, exhibiting some confusion and trepidation at being forced to request a favor of him at so
early a stage of their acquaintance. She stood in her doorway, and
had evidently been sewing, as the thimble on her finger testified,
as well as a long-threaded needle thrust in the bosom of her gown.
She held a stamped but unaddressed letter in her hand.

And would Mr. Gouvernail be so kind as to address the letter
to her brother, Mr. Montéclin Miché? She would hate to detain
him with explanations this morning—another time, perhaps—but
now she begged that he would give himself the trouble.

He assured her that it made no difference, that it was no trouble whatever; and he drew a fountain pen from his pocket and addressed the letter at her dictation, resting it on the inverted rim of
his straw hat. She wondered a little at a man of his supposed erudition stumbling over the spelling of "Montéclin" and "Miché."

She demurred at overwhelming him with the additional trouble of posting it, but he succeeded in convincing her that so simple a task as the posting of a letter would not add an iota to the
burden of the day. Moreover, he promised to carry it in his hand,
and thus avoid any possible risk of forgetting it in his pocket.

After that, and after a second repetition of the favor, when she
had told him that she had had a letter from Montéclin, and looked
as if she wanted to tell him more, he felt that he knew her better.
He felt that he knew her well enough to join her out on the balcony, one night, when he found her sitting there alone. He was not
one who deliberately sought the society of women, but he was not
wholly a bear. A little commiseration for Athénaïse's aloneness,
perhaps some curiosity to know further what manner of woman

she was, and the natural influence of her feminine charm were equal unconfessed factors in turning his steps towards the balcony when he discovered the shimmer of her white gown through the open hall window.

It was already quite late, but the day had been intensely hot, and neighboring balconies and doorways were occupied by chattering groups of humanity, loath to abandon the grateful freshness of the outer air. The voices about her served to reveal to Athénaïse the feeling of loneliness that was gradually coming over her. Notwithstanding certain dormant impulses, she craved human sympathy and companionship.

She shook hands impulsively with Gouvernail, and told him how glad she was to see him. He was not prepared for such an admission, but it pleased him immensely, detecting as he did that the expression was as sincere as it was outspoken. He drew a chair up within comfortable conversational distance of Athénaïse, though he had no intention of talking more than was barely necessary to encourage Madame—He had actually forgotten her name!

He leaned an elbow on the balcony rail, and would have offered an opening remark about the oppressive heat of the day, but Athénaïse did not give him the opportunity. How glad she was to talk to someone, and how she talked!

An hour later she had gone to her room, and Gouvernail stayed smoking on the balcony. He knew her quite well after that hour's talk. It was not so much what she had said as what her half saying had revealed to his quick intelligence. He knew that she adored Montéclin, and he suspected that she adored Cazeau without being herself aware of it. He had gathered that she was self-willed, impulsive, innocent, ignorant, unsatisfied, dissatisfied; for had she not complained that things seemed all wrongly arranged in this world, and no one was permitted to be happy in his own way? And he told her he was sorry she had discovered that primordial fact of existence so early in life.

He commiserated her loneliness, and scanned his bookshelves next morning for something to lend her to read, rejecting everything that offered itself to his view. Philosophy was out of the question, and so was poetry; that is, such poetry as he possessed. He had not sounded her literary tastes, and strongly suspected she had none; that she would have rejected The Duchess as readily as Mrs. Humphrey Ward. He compromised on a magazine.

It had entertained her passably, she admitted, upon returning it. A New England story had puzzled her, it was true, and a Creole tale had offended her, but the pictures had pleased her greatly, especially one which had reminded her so strongly of Montéclin after a hard day's ride that she was loath to give it up. It was one of Remington's Cowboys, and Gouvernail insisted upon her keeping it—keeping the magazine.

He spoke to her daily after that, and was always eager to render her some service or to do something towards her entertainment.

One afternoon he took her out to the lake end. She had been there once, some years before, but in winter, so the trip was comparatively new and strange to her. The large expanse of water studded with pleasure-boats, the sight of children playing merrily along the grassy palisades, the music, all enchanted her. Gouvernail thought her the most beautiful woman he had ever seen. Even her gown—the sprigged muslin—appeared to him the most charming one imaginable. Nor could anything be more becoming than the arrangement of her brown hair under the white sailor hat, all rolled back in a soft puff from her radiant face. And she carried her parasol and lifted her skirts and used her fan in ways that seemed quite unique and peculiar to herself, and which he considered almost worthy of study and imitation.

They did not dine out there at the water's edge, as they might have done, but returned early to the city to avoid the crowd. Athénaïse wanted to go home, for she said Sylvie would have dinner prepared and would be expecting her. But it was not difficult to persuade her to dine instead in the quiet little restaurant that he knew and liked, with its sanded floor, its secluded atmosphere, its delicious menu, and its obsequious waiter wanting to know what he might have the honor of serving to "monsieur et madame." No wonder he made the mistake, with Gouvernail assuming such an air of proprietorship! But Athénaïse was very tired after it all; the sparkle went out of her face, and she hung draggingly on his arm in walking home.

He was reluctant to part from her when she bade him good-night at her door and thanked him for the agreeable evening. He had hoped she would sit outside until it was time for him to regain the newspaper office. He knew that she would undress and get into her peignoir and lie upon her bed; and what he wanted to do, what he would have given much to do, was to go and sit beside her, read to her something restful, soothe her, do her bidding, whatever it might be. Of course there was no use in thinking of that. But he was surprised at his growing desire to be serving her. She gave him an opportunity sooner than he looked for.

"Mr. Gouvernail," she called from her room, "will you be so kine as to call Pousette an' tell her she fo'got to bring my ice water?"

He was indignant at Pousette's negligence, and called severely to her over the banisters. He was sitting before his own door, smoking. He knew that Athénaïse had gone to bed, for her room was dark, and she had opened the slats of the door and windows. Her bed was near a window.

Pousette came flopping up with the ice water, and with a hundred excuses: "Mo pa oua vou a tab c'te lanuite, mo cri vou pé gagni deja la-bas; parole! Vou pas cri conté ça Madame Sylvie?" She had not seen Athénaïse at table, and thought she was gone. She swore to this, and hoped Madame Sylvie would not be informed of her remissness.

A little later Athénaïse lifted her voice again: "Mr. Gouvernail, did you remark that young man sitting on the opposite side from us, coming in, with a gray coat an' a blue ban' aroun' his hat?"

Of course Gouvernail had not noticed any such individual, but he assured Athénaïse that he had observed the young fellow particularly.

"Don't you think he looked something—not very much, of co'se—but don't you think he had a little faux-air of Montéclin?"

"I think he looked strikingly like Montéclin," asserted Gouvernail, with the one idea of prolonging the conversation. "I meant to call your attention to the resemblance, and something drove it out of my head."

"The same with me," returned Athénaïse. "Ah, my dear Montéclin! I wonder w'at he is doing now?"

"Did you receive any news, any letter from him today?" asked Gouvernail, determined that if the conversation ceased it should not be through lack of effort on his part to sustain it.

"Not today, but yesterday. He tells me that maman was so distracted with uneasiness that finally, to pacify her, he was fo'ced to confess that he knew w'ere I was, but that he was boun' by a vow of secrecy not to reveal it. But Cazeau has not noticed him or spoken to him since he threaten' to throw po' Montéclin in Cane river. You know Cazeau wrote me a letter the morning I lef', thinking I had gone to the rigolet. An' maman opened it, an' said it was full of the mos' noble sentiments, an' she wanted Montéclin to sen' it to me; but Montéclin refuse' poin' blank, so he wrote to me."

Gouvernail preferred to talk of Montéclin. He pictured Cazeau as unbearable, and did not like to think of him.

A little later Athénaïse called out, "Good night, Mr. Gouvernail."

"Good night," he returned reluctantly. And when he thought that she was sleeping, he got up and went away to the midnight pandemonium of his newspaper office.

IX

Athénaïse could not have held out through the month had it not been for Gouvernail. With the need of caution and secrecy always uppermost in her mind, she made no new acquaintances, and she did not seek out persons already known to her; however, she knew so few, it required little effort to keep out of their way. As for Sylvie, almost every moment of her time was occupied in looking after her house; and, moreover, her deferential attitude towards her lodgers forbade anything like the gossipy chats in which Athénaïse might have condescended sometimes to indulge with her landlady. The transient lodgers, who came and went, she never had occasion to meet. Hence she was entirely dependent upon Gouvernail for company.

He appreciated the situation fully; and every moment that he could spare from his work he devoted to her entertainment. She liked to be out of doors, and they strolled together in the summer twilight through the mazes of the old French quarter. They went again to the lake end, and stayed for hours on the water; returning so late that the streets through which they passed were silent and deserted. On Sunday morning he arose at an unconscionable hour to take her to the French market, knowing that the sights and sounds there would interest her. And he did not join the intellectual coterie in the afternoon, as he usually did, but placed himself all day at the disposition and service of Athénaïse.

Notwithstanding all, his manner toward her was tactful, and evinced intelligence and a deep knowledge of her character, surprising upon so brief an acquaintance. For the time he was everything to her that she would have him; he replaced home and friends. Sometimes she wondered if he had ever loved a woman. She could not fancy him loving anyone passionately, rudely, offensively, as Cazeau loved her. Once she was so naïve as to ask him outright if he had ever been in love, and he assured her promptly that he had not. She thought it an admirable trait in his character, and esteemed him greatly therefor.

He found her crying one night, not openly or violently. She was leaning over the gallery rail, watching the toads that hopped about in the moonlight, down on the damp flagstones of the courtyard. There was an oppressively sweet odor rising from the cape jessamine. Pousette was down there, mumbling and quarreling with someone, and seeming to be having it all her own way— as well she might, when her companion was only a black cat that had come in from a neighboring yard to keep her company.

Athénaïse did admit feeling heartsick, body-sick, when he questioned her; she supposed it was nothing but homesick. A letter from Montéclin had stirred her all up. She longed for her mother, for Montéclin; she was sick for a sight of the cotton fields, the scent of the ploughed earth, for the dim, mysterious charm of the woods, and the old tumble-down home on the Bon Dieu.

As Gouvernail listened to her, a wave of pity and tenderness swept through him. He took her hands and pressed them against him. He wondered what would happen if he were to put his arms around her.

He was hardly prepared for what happened, but he stood it courageously. She twined her arms around his neck and wept outright on his shoulder; the hot tears scalding his cheek and neck, and her whole body shaken in his arms. The impulse was powerful to strain her to him; the temptation was fierce to seek her lips; but he did neither.

He understood a thousand times better than she herself understood it that he was acting as substitute for Montéclin. Bitter as the conviction was, he accepted it. He was patient; he could wait. He hoped some day to hold her with a lover's arms. That she was married made no particle of difference to Gouvernail. He could not conceive or dream of it making a difference. When the time came that she wanted him—as he hoped and believed it would come—he felt he would have a right to her. So long as she did not want him, he had no right to her—no more than her husband had. It was very hard to feel her warm breath and tears upon his cheek, and her struggling bosom pressed against him and her soft arms clinging to him and his whole body and soul aching for her, and yet to make no sign.

He tried to think what Montéclin would have said and done, and to act accordingly. He stroked her hair, and held her in a gentle embrace, until the tears dried and the sobs ended. Before releasing herself she kissed him against the neck; she had to love somebody in her own way! Even that he endured like a stoic. But it was well he left her, to plunge into the thick of rapid, breathless, exacting work till nearly dawn.

Athénaïse was greatly soothed, and slept well. The touch of friendly hands and caressing arms had been very grateful. Henceforward she would not be lonely and unhappy, with Gouvernail there to comfort her.

X

The fourth week of Athénaïse's stay in the city was drawing to a close. Keeping in view the intention which she had of finding some suitable and agreeable employment, she had made a few tentatives in that direction. But with the exception of two little girls who had promised to take piano lessons at a price that would be embarrassing to mention, these attempts had been fruitless. Moreover, the homesickness kept coming back, and Gouvernail was not always there to drive it away.

She spent much of her time weeding and pottering among the flowers down in the courtyard. She tried to take an interest in the black cat, and a mockingbird that hung in a cage outside the kitchen door, and a disreputable parrot that belonged to the cook next door, and swore hoarsely all day long in bad French.

Beside, she was not well; she was not herself, as she told Sylvie. The climate of New Orleans did not agree with her. Sylvie was distressed to learn this, as she felt in some measure responsible for the health and well-being of Monsieur Miché's sister; and she made it her duty to inquire closely into the nature and character of Athénaïse's malaise.

Sylvie was very wise, and Athénaïse was very ignorant. The extent of her ignorance and the depth of her subsequent enlightenment were bewildering. She stayed a long, long time quite still, quite stunned, after her interview with Sylvie, except for the short, uneven breathing that ruffled her bosom. Her whole being was steeped in a wave of ecstasy. When she finally arose from the chair in which she had been seated, and looked at herself in the mirror, a face met hers which she seemed to see for the first time, so transfigured was it with wonder and rapture.

One mood quickly followed another, in this new turmoil of her senses, and the need of action became uppermost. Her mother must know at once, and her mother must tell Montéclin. And Cazeau must know. As she thought of him, the first purely sensuous tremor of her life swept over her. She half whispered his name, and the sound of it brought red blotches into her cheeks. She spoke it over and over, as if it were some new, sweet sound born out of darkness and confusion, and reaching her for the first time. She was impatient to be with him. Her whole passionate nature was aroused as if by a miracle.

She seated herself to write to her husband. The letter he would get in the morning, and she would be with him at night. What would he say? How would he act? She knew that he would forgive her, for had he not written a letter?—and a pang of resentment toward Montéclin shot through her. What did he mean by withholding that letter? How dared he not have sent it?

Athénaïse attired herself for the street, and went out to post the letter which she had penned with a single thought, a spontaneous impulse. It would have seemed incoherent to most people, but Cazeau would understand.

She walked along the street as if she had fallen heir to some magnificent inheritance. On her face was a look of pride and satisfaction that passersby noticed and admired. She wanted to talk to some one, to tell some person; and she stopped at the corner and told the oyster-woman, who was Irish, and who God-blessed her, and wished prosperity to the race of Cazeaus for generations to come. She held the oyster-woman's fat, dirty little baby in her arms and scanned it curiously and observingly, as if a baby were a phenomenon that she encountered for the first time in life. She even kissed it!

Then what a relief it was to Athénaïse to walk the streets without dread of being seen and recognized by some chance acquaintance from Red River! No one could have said now that she did not know her own mind.

She went directly from the oyster-woman's to the office of Harding & Offdean, her husband's merchants; and it was with such an air of partnership, almost proprietorship, that she demanded a sum of money on her husband's account, they gave it to her as un-

hesitatingly as they would have handed it over to Cazeau himself.
When Mr. Harding, who knew her, asked politely after her health,
she turned so rosy and looked so conscious, he thought it a great
pity for so pretty a woman to be such a little goose.

Athénaïse entered a dry-goods store and bought all manner of
things—little presents for nearly everybody she knew. She bought
whole bolts of sheerest, softest, downiest white stuff; and when the
clerk, in trying to meet her wishes, asked if she intended it for infant's use, she could have sunk through the floor, and wondered
how he might have suspected it.

As it was Montéclin who had taken her away from her husband, she wanted it to be Montéclin who should take her back to
him. So she wrote him a very curt note—in fact it was a postal
card—asking that he meet her at the train on the evening following. She felt convinced that after what had gone before, Cazeau
would await her at their own home; and she preferred it so.

Then there was the agreeable excitement of getting ready to
leave, of packing up her things. Pousette kept coming and going,
coming and going; and each time that she quitted the room it was
with something that Athénaïse had given her—a handkerchief, a
petticoat, a pair of stockings with two tiny holes at the toes, some
broken prayer-beads, and finally a silver dollar.

Next it was Sylvie who came along bearing a gift of what she
called "a set of pattern' "—things of complicated design which
never could have been obtained in any newfangled bazaar or pattern store, that Sylvie had acquired of a foreign lady of distinction
whom she had nursed years before at the St. Charles hotel. Athénaïse accepted and handled them with reverence, fully sensible of
the great compliment and favor, and laid them religiously away in
the trunk which she had lately acquired.

She was greatly fatigued after the day of unusual exertion, and went early to bed and to sleep. All day long she had not once thought of Gouvernail, and only did think of him when aroused for a brief instant by the sound of his footfalls on the gallery, as he passed in going to his room. He had hoped to find her up, waiting for him.

But the next morning he knew. Some one must have told him. There was no subject known to her which Sylvie hesitated to discuss in detail with any man of suitable years and discretion.

Athénaïse found Gouvernail waiting with a carriage to convey her to the railway station. A momentary pang visited her for having forgotten him so completely, when he said to her, "Sylvie tells me you are going away this morning."

He was kind, attentive, and amiable, as usual, but respected to the utmost the new dignity and reserve that her manner had developed since yesterday. She kept looking from the carriage window, silent, and embarrassed as Eve after losing her ignorance. He talked of the muddy streets and the murky morning, and of Montéclin. He hoped she would find everything comfortable and pleasant in the country, and trusted she would inform him whenever she came to visit the city again. He talked as if afraid or mistrustful of silence and himself.

At the station she handed him her purse, and he bought her ticket, secured for her a comfortable section, checked her trunk, and got all the bundles and things safely aboard the train. She felt very grateful. He pressed her hand warmly, lifted his hat, and left her. He was a man of intelligence, and took defeat gracefully; that was all. But as he made his way back to the carriage, he was thinking, "By heaven, it hurts, it hurts!"

XI

Athénaïse spent a day of supreme happiness and expectancy. The fair sight of the country unfolding itself before her was balm to her vision and to her soul. She was charmed with the rather unfamiliar, broad, clean sweep of the sugar plantations, with their monster sugar houses, their rows of neat cabins like little villages of a single street, and their impressive homes standing apart amid clusters of trees. There were sudden glimpses of a bayou curling between sunny, grassy banks, or creeping sluggishly out from a tangled growth of wood, and brush, and fern, and poison-vines, and palmettos. And passing through the long stretches of monotonous woodlands, she would close her eyes and taste in anticipation the moment of her meeting with Cazeau. She could think of nothing but him.

It was night when she reached her station. There was Montéclin, as she had expected, waiting for her with a two-seated buggy, to which he had hitched his own swift-footed, spirited pony. It was good, he felt, to have her back on any terms; and he had no fault to find since she came of her own choice. He more than suspected the cause of her coming; her eyes and her voice and her foolish little manner went far in revealing the secret that was brimming over in her heart. But after he had deposited her at her own gate, and as he continued his way toward the rigolet, he could not help feeling that the affair had taken a very disappointing, an ordinary, a most commonplace turn, after all. He left her in Cazeau's keeping.

Her husband lifted her out of the buggy, and neither said a word until they stood together within the shelter of the gallery. Even then they did not speak at first. But Athénaïse turned to him with an appealing gesture. As he clasped her in his arms, he felt the yielding of her whole body against him. He felt her lips for the first time respond to the passion of his own.

The country night was dark and warm and still, save for the distant notes of an accordion which some one was playing in a cabin away off. A little Negro baby was crying somewhere. As Athénaïse withdrew from her husband's embrace, the sound arrested her.

"Listen, Cazeau! How Juliette's baby is crying! Pauvre ti chou, I wonder w'at is the matter with it?"

The Bride Comes to Yellow Sky

Stephen Crane
(1871–1900)

I

The great Pullman was whirling onward with such dignity of motion that a glance from the window seemed simply to prove that the plains of Texas were pouring eastward. Vast flats of green grass, dull-hued spaces of mesquit and cactus, little groups of frame houses, woods of light and tender trees, all were sweeping into the east, sweeping over the horizon, a precipice.

A newly married pair had boarded this coach at San Antonio. The man's face was reddened from many days in the wind and sun, and a direct result of his new black clothes was that his brick-coloured hands were constantly performing in a most conscious fashion. From time to time he looked down respectfully at his attire. He sat with a hand on each knee, like a man waiting in a barber's shop. The glances he devoted to other passengers were furtive and shy.

The bride was not pretty, nor was she very young. She wore a dress of blue cashmere, with small reservations of velvet here and there, and with steel buttons abounding. She continually twisted her head to regard her puff sleeves, very stiff, straight, and high. They embarrassed her. It was quite apparent that she had cooked, and that she expected to cook, dutifully. The blushes caused by the careless scrutiny of some passengers as she had entered the car were strange to see upon this plain, under-class countenance, which was drawn in placid, almost emotionless lines.

They were evidently very happy. "Ever been in a parlour-car before?" he asked, smiling with delight.

"No," she answered; "I never was. It's fine, ain't it?"

"Great! And then after a while we'll go forward to the diner, and get a big lay-out. Finest meal in the world. Charge a dollar."

"Oh, do they?" cried the bride. "Charge a dollar? Why, that's too much—for us—ain't it, Jack?"

"Not this trip, anyhow," he answered bravely. "We're going to go the whole thing."

Later he explained to her about the trains. "You see, it's a thousand miles from one end of Texas to the other; and this train runs right across it, and never stops but four times." He had the pride of an owner. He pointed out to her the dazzling fittings of the coach; and in truth her eyes opened wider as she contemplated the sea-green figured velvet, the shining brass, silver, and glass, the wood that gleamed as darkly brilliant as the surface of a pool of oil. At one end a bronze figure sturdily held a support for a separated chamber, and at convenient places on the ceiling were frescos in olive and silver.

To the minds of the pair, their surroundings reflected the glory of their marriage that morning in San Antonio; this was the environment of their new estate; and the man's face in particular beamed with an elation that made him appear ridiculous to the negro porter. This individual at times surveyed them from afar with an amused and superior grin. On other occasions he bullied them with skill in ways that did not make it exactly plain to them that they were being bullied. He subtly used all the manners of the most unconquerable kind of snobbery. He oppressed them; but of this oppression they had small knowledge, and they speedily forgot that infrequently a number of travellers covered them with stares of derisive enjoyment. Historically there was supposed to be something infinitely humorous in their situation.

"We are due in Yellow Sky at 3:42," he said, looking tenderly into her eyes.

"Oh, are we?" she said, as if she had not been aware of it. To evince surprise at her husband's statement was part of her wifely amiability. She took from a pocket a little silver watch; and as she held it before her, and stared at it with a frown of attention, the new husband's face shone.

"I bought it in San Anton' from a friend of mine," he told her gleefully.

"It's seventeen minutes past twelve," she said, looking up at him with a kind of shy and clumsy coquetry. A passenger, noting this play, grew excessively sardonic, and winked at himself in one of the numerous mirrors.

At last they went to the dining-car. Two rows of negro waiters, in glowing white suits, surveyed their entrance with the interest, and also the equanimity, of men who had been forewarned. The pair fell to the lot of a waiter who happened to feel pleasure in steering them through their meal. He viewed them with the manner of a fatherly pilot, his countenance radiant with benevolence. The patronage, entwined with the ordinary deference, was not plain to them. And yet, as they returned to their coach, they showed in their faces a sense of escape.

To the left, miles down a long purple slope, was a little ribbon of mist where moved the keening Rio Grande. The train was approaching it at an angle, and the apex was Yellow Sky. Presently it was apparent that, as the distance from Yellow Sky grew shorter, the husband became commensurately restless. His brick-red hands were more insistent in their prominence. Occasionally he was even rather absent-minded and far-away when the bride leaned forward and addressed him.

As a matter of truth, Jack Potter was beginning to find the shadow of a deed weigh upon him like a leaden slab. He, the town marshal of Yellow Sky, a man known, liked, and feared in his corner, a prominent person, had gone to San Antonio to meet a girl he believed he loved, and there, after the usual prayers, had actually induced her to marry him, without consulting Yellow Sky for any part of the transaction. He was now bringing his bride before an innocent and unsuspecting community.

Of course people in Yellow Sky married as it pleased them, in accordance with a general custom; but such was Potter's thought of his duty to his friends, or of their idea of his duty, or of an unspoken form which does not control men in these matters, that he felt he was heinous. He had committed an extraordinary crime. Face to face with this girl in San Antonio, and spurred by his sharp impulse, he had gone headlong over all the social hedges. At San Antonio he was like a man hidden in the dark. A knife to sever any friendly duty, any form, was easy to his hand in that remote city. But the hour of Yellow Sky—the hour of daylight—was approaching.

He knew full well that his marriage was an important thing to his town. It could only be exceeded by the burning of the new hotel. His friends could not forgive him. Frequently he had reflected on the advisability of telling them by telegraph, but a new cowardice had been upon him. He feared to do it. And now the train was hurrying him toward a scene of amazement, glee, and reproach. He glanced out of the window at the line of haze swinging slowly in toward the train.

Yellow Sky had a kind of brass band, which played painfully, to the delight of the populace. He laughed without heart as he thought of it. If the citizens could dream of his prospective arrival with his bride, they would parade the band at the station and escort them, amid cheers and laughing congratulations, to his adobe home.

He resolved that he would use all the devices of speed and plainscraft in making the journey from the station to his house. Once within that safe citadel, he could issue some sort of vocal bulletin, and then not go among the citizens until they had time to wear off a little of their enthusiasm.

The bride looked anxiously at him. "What's worrying you, Jack?"

He laughed again. "I'm not worrying, girl; I'm only thinking of Yellow Sky."

She flushed in comprehension.

A sense of mutual guilt invaded their minds and developed a finer tenderness. They looked at each other with eyes softly aglow. But Potter often laughed the same nervous laugh; the flush upon the bride's face seemed quite permanent.

The traitor to the feelings of Yellow Sky narrowly watched the speeding landscape. "We're nearly there," he said.

Presently the porter came and announced the proximity of Potter's home. He held a brush in his hand, and, with all his airy superiority gone, he brushed Potter's new clothes as the latter slowly turned this way and that way. Potter fumbled out a coin and gave it to the porter, as he had seen others do. It was a heavy and muscle-bound business, as that of a man shoeing his first horse.

The porter took their bag, and as the train began to slow they moved forward to the hooded platform of the car. Presently the two engines and their long string of coaches rushed into the station of Yellow Sky.

"They have to take water here," said Potter, from a constricted throat and in mournful cadence, as one announcing death. Before the train stopped his eye had swept the length of the platform, and he was glad and astonished to see there was none upon it but the station-agent, who, with a slightly hurried and anxious air, was walking toward the water-tanks. When the train had halted, the porter alighted first, and placed in position a little temporary step.

"Come on, girl," said Potter, hoarsely. As he helped her down they each laughed on a false note. He took the bag from the negro, and bade his wife cling to his arm. As they slunk rapidly away, his hang-dog glance perceived that they were unloading the two trunks, and also that the station-agent, far ahead near the baggage-car, had turned and was running toward him, making gestures. He laughed, and groaned as he laughed, when he noted the first effect of his marital bliss upon Yellow Sky. He gripped his wife's arm firmly to his side, and they fled. Behind them the porter stood, chuckling fatuously.

II

The California express on the Southern Railway was due at Yellow Sky in twenty-one minutes. There were six men at the bar of the Weary Gentleman saloon. One was a drummer who talked a great deal and rapidly; three were Texans who did not care to talk at that time; and two were Mexican sheep-herders, who did not talk as a general practice in the Weary Gentleman saloon. The bar-keeper's dog lay on the board walk that crossed in front of the door. His head was on his paws, and he glanced drowsily here and there with the constant vigilance of a dog that is kicked on occasion. Across the sandy street were some vivid green grass-plots, so wonderful in appearance, amid the sands that burned near them in a blazing sun, that they caused a doubt in the mind. They exactly resembled the grass mats used to represent lawns on the stage. At the cooler end of the railway station, a man without a coat sat in a tilted chair and smoked his pipe. The fresh-cut bank of the Rio Grande circled near the town, and there could be seen beyond it a great plum-coloured plain of mesquit.

Save for the busy drummer and his companions in the saloon, Yellow Sky was dozing. The new-comer leaned gracefully upon the bar, and recited many tales with the confidence of a bard who has come upon a new field.

"—and at the moment that the old man fell downstairs with the bureau in his arms, the old woman was coming up with two scuttles of coal, and of course——"

The drummer's tale was interrupted by a young man who suddenly appeared in the open door. He cried: "Scratchy Wilson's drunk, and has turned loose with both hands." The two Mexicans at once set down their glasses and faded out of the rear entrance of the saloon.

The drummer, innocent and jocular, answered: "All right, old man. S'pose he has? Come in and have a drink, anyhow."

But the information had made such an obvious cleft in every skull in the room that the drummer was obliged to see its importance. All had become instantly solemn. "Say," said he, mystified, "what is this?" His three companions made the introductory gesture of eloquent speech; but the young man at the door forestalled them.

"It means, my friend," he answered, as he came into the saloon, "that for the next two hours this town won't be a health resort."

The barkeeper went to the door, and locked and barred it; reaching out of the window, he pulled in heavy wooden shutters, and barred them. Immediately a solemn, chapel-like gloom was upon the place. The drummer was looking from one to another.

"But say," he cried, "what is this, anyhow? You don't mean there is going to be a gun-fight?"

"Don't know whether there'll be a fight or not," answered one man, grimly; "but there'll be some shootin'—some good shootin'."

The young man who had warned them waved his hand. "Oh, there'll be a fight fast enough, if any one wants it. Anybody can get a fight out there in the street. There's a fight just waiting."

The drummer seemed to be swayed between the interest of a foreigner and a perception of personal danger.

"What did you say his name was?" he asked.

"Scratchy Wilson," they answered in chorus.

"And will he kill anybody? What are you going to do? Does this happen often? Does he rampage around like this once a week or so? Can he break in that door?"

"No; he can't break down that door," replied the barkeeper. "He's tried it three times. But when he comes you'd better lay down on the floor, stranger. He's dead sure to shoot at it, and a bullet may come through."

Thereafter the drummer kept a strict eye upon the door. The time had not yet been called for him to hug the floor, but, as a minor precaution, he sidled near to the wall. "Will he kill anybody?" he said again.

The men laughed low and scornfully at the question.

"He's out to shoot, and he's out for trouble. Don't see any good in experimentin' with him."

"But what do you do in a case like this? What do you do?"

A man responded: "Why, he and Jack Potter——"

"But," in chorus the other men interrupted, "Jack Potter's in San Anton'."

"Well, who is he? What's he got to do with it?"

"Oh, he's the town marshal. He goes out and fights Scratchy when he gets on one of these tears."

"Wow!" said the drummer, mopping his brow. "Nice job he's got."

The voices had toned away to mere whisperings. The drummer wished to ask further questions, which were born of an increasing anxiety and bewilderment; but when he attempted them, the men merely looked at him in irritation and motioned him to remain silent. A tense waiting hush was upon them. In the deep shadows of the room their eyes shone as they listened for sounds from the street. One man made three gestures at the barkeeper; and the latter, moving like a ghost, handed him a glass and a bottle. The man poured a full glass of whisky, and set down the bottle noiselessly. He gulped the whisky in a swallow, and turned again toward the door in immovable silence. The drummer saw that the barkeeper, without a sound, had taken a Winchester from beneath the bar. Later he saw this individual beckoning to him, so he tiptoed across the room.

"You better come with me back of the bar."

"No, thanks," said the drummer, perspiring; "I'd rather be where I can make a break for the back door."

Whereupon the man of bottles made a kindly but peremptory gesture. The drummer obeyed it, and, finding himself seated on a box with his head below the level of the bar, balm was laid upon his soul at sight of various zinc and copper fittings that bore a resemblance to armour-plate. The barkeeper took a seat comfortably upon an adjacent box.

"You see," he whispered, "this here Scratchy Wilson is a wonder with a gun—a perfect wonder; and when he goes on the wartrail, we hunt our holes—naturally. He's about the last one of the old gang that used to hang out along the river here. He's a terror when he's drunk. When he's sober he's all right—kind of simple—wouldn't hurt a fly—nicest fellow in town. But when he's drunk—whoo!"

There were periods of stillness. "I wish Jack Potter was back from San Anton'," said the barkeeper. "He shot Wilson up once—in the leg—and he would sail in and pull out the kinks in this thing."

Presently they heard from a distance the sound of a shot, followed by three wild yowls. It instantly removed a bond from the men in the darkened saloon. There was a shuffling of feet. They looked at each other. "Herehecomes," they said.

III

A man in a maroon-coloured flannel shirt, which had been purchased for purposes of decoration, and made principally by some Jewish women on the East Side of New York, rounded a corner and walked into the middle of the main street of Yellow Sky. In either hand the man held a long, heavy, blue-black revolver. Often he yelled, and these cries rang through a semblance of a deserted village, shrilly flying over the roofs in a volume that seemed to have no relation to the ordinary vocal strength of a man. It was as if the surrounding stillness formed the arch of a tomb over him. These cries of ferocious challenge rang against walls of silence. And his boots had red tops with gilded imprints, of the kind beloved in winter by little sledding boys on the hillsides of New England.

The man's face flamed in a rage begot of whisky. His eyes, rolling, and yet keen for ambush, hunted the still doorways and windows. He walked with the creeping movement of the midnight cat. As it occurred to him, he roared menacing information. The long revolvers in his hands were as easy as straws; they were moved with an electric swiftness. The little fingers of each hand played sometimes in a musician's way. Plain from the low collar of the shirt, the cords of his neck straightened and sank, straightened and sank, as passion moved him. The only sounds were his terrible invitations. The calm adobes preserved their demeanour at the passing of this small thing in the middle of the street.

There was no offer of fight—no offer of fight. The man called to the sky. There were no attractions. He bellowed and fumed and swayed his revolvers here and everywhere.

The dog of the barkeeper of the Weary Gentleman saloon had not appreciated the advance of events. He yet lay dozing in front of his master's door. At sight of the dog, the man paused and raised his revolver humorously. At sight of the man, the dog sprang up and walked diagonally away, with a sullen head, and growling. The man yelled, and the dog broke into a gallop. As it was about to enter an alley, there was a loud noise, a whistling, and something spat the ground directly before it. The dog screamed, and, wheeling in terror, galloped headlong in a new direction. Again there was a noise, a whistling, and sand was kicked viciously before it. Fear-stricken, the dog turned and flurried like an animal in a pen. The man stood laughing, his weapons at his hips.

Ultimately the man was attracted by the closed door of the Weary Gentleman saloon. He went to it and, hammering with a revolver, demanded drink.

The door remaining imperturbable, he picked a bit of paper from the walk, and nailed it to the framework with a knife. He then turned his back contemptuously upon this popular resort and, walking to the opposite side of the street and spinning there on his heel quickly and lithely, fired at the bit of paper. He missed it by a half-inch. He swore at himself, and went away. Later he comfortably fusilladed the windows of his most intimate friend. The man was playing with this town; it was a toy for him.

But still there was no offer of fight. The name of Jack Potter, his ancient antagonist, entered his mind, and he concluded that it would be a glad thing if he should go to Potter's house, and by bombardment induce him to come out and fight. He moved in the direction of his desire, chanting Apache scalp-music.

When he arrived at it, Potter's house presented the same still front as had the other adobes. Taking up a strategic position, the man howled a challenge. But this house regarded him as might a great stone god. It gave no sign. After a decent wait, the man howled further challenges, mingling with them wonderful epithets.

Presently there came the spectacle of a man churning himself into deepest rage over the immobility of a house. He fumed at it as the winter wind attacks a prairie cabin in the North. To the distance there should have gone the sound of a tumult like the fighting of two hundred Mexicans. As necessity bade him, he paused for breath or to reload his revolvers.

IV

Potter and his bride walked sheepishly and with speed. Sometimes they laughed together shamefacedly and low.

"Next corner, dear," he said finally.

They put forth the efforts of a pair walking bowed against a strong wind. Potter was about to raise a finger to point the first appearance of the new home when, as they circled the corner, they came face to face with a man in a maroon-coloured shirt, who was feverishly pushing cartridges into a large revolver. Upon the instant the man dropped his revolver to the ground and, like lightning, whipped another from its holster. The second weapon was aimed at the bridegroom's chest.

There was a silence. Potter's mouth seemed to be merely a grave for his tongue. He exhibited an instinct to at once loosen his arm from the woman's grip, and he dropped the bag to the sand.

As for the bride, her face had gone as yellow as old cloth. She was a slave to hideous rites, gazing at the apparitional snake.

The two men faced each other at a distance of three paces. He of the revolver smiled with a new and quiet ferocity.

"Tried to sneak up on me," he said. "Tried to sneak up on me!" His eyes grew more baleful. As Potter made a slight movement, the man thrust his revolver venomously forward. "No; don't you do it, Jack Potter. Don't you move a finger toward a gun just yet. Don't you move an eyelash. The time has come for me to settle with you, and I'm goin' to do it my own way, and loaf along with no interferin'. So if you don't want a gun bent on you, just mind what I tell you."

Potter looked at his enemy. "I ain't got a gun on me, Scratchy," he said. "Honest, I ain't." He was stiffening and steadying, but yet somewhere at the back of his mind a vision of the Pullman floated: the sea-green figured velvet, the shining brass, silver, and glass, the wood that gleamed as darkly brilliant as the surface of a pool of oil—all the glory of the marriage, the environment of the new estate. "You know I fight when it comes to fighting, Scratchy Wilson; but I ain't got a gun on me. You'll have to do all the shootin' yourself."

His enemy's face went livid. He stepped forward, and lashed his weapon to and fro before Potter's chest. "Don't you tell me you ain't got no gun on you, you whelp. Don't tell me no lie like that. There ain't a man in Texas ever seen you without no gun. Don't take me for no kid." His eyes blazed with light, and his throat worked like a pump.

"I ain't takin' you for no kid," answered Potter. His heels had not moved an inch backward. "I'm takin' you for a damn fool. I tell you I ain't got a gun, and I ain't. If you're goin' to shoot me up, you better begin now; you'll never get a chance like this again."

So much enforced reasoning had told on Wilson's rage; he was calmer. "If you ain't got a gun, why ain't you got a gun?" he sneered. "Been to Sunday-school?"

"I ain't got a gun because I've just come from San Anton' with my wife. I'm married," said Potter. "And if I'd thought there was going to be any galoots like you prowling around when I brought my wife home, I'd had a gun, and don't you forget it."

"Married!" said Scratchy, not at all comprehending.

"Yes, married. I'm married," said Potter, distinctly.

"Married?" said Scratchy. Seemingly for the first time, he saw the drooping, drowning woman at the other man's side. "No!" he said. He was like a creature allowed a glimpse of another world. He moved a pace backward, and his arm, with the revolver, dropped to his side. "Is this the lady?" he asked.

"Yes; this is the lady," answered Potter.

There was another period of silence.

"Well," said Wilson at last, slowly, "I s'pose it's all off now."

"It's all off if you say so, Scratchy. You know I didn't make the trouble." Potter lifted his valise.

"Well, I 'low it's off, Jack," said Wilson. He was looking at the ground. "Married!" He was not a student of chivalry; it was merely that in the presence of this foreign condition he was a simple child of the earlier plains. He picked up his starboard revolver, and, placing both weapons in their holsters, he went away. His feet made funnel-shaped tracks in the heavy sand.

Life in the Iron Mills or The Korl Woman

Rebecca Harding Davis
(1831–1910)

"Is this the end?
O Life, as futile, then, as frail!
What hope of answer or redress?"

A cloudy day: do you know what that is in a town of iron-works? The sky sank down before dawn, muddy, flat, immovable. The air is thick, clammy with the breath of crowded human beings. It stifles me. I open the window, and, looking out, can scarcely see through the rain the grocer's shop opposite, where a crowd of drunken Irishmen are puffing Lynchburg tobacco in their pipes. I can detect the scent through all the foul smells ranging loose in the air.

The idiosyncrasy of this town is smoke. It rolls sullenly in slow folds from the great chimneys of the iron-foundries, and settles down in black, slimy pools on the muddy streets. Smoke on the wharves, smoke on the dingy boats, on the yellow river—clinging in a coating of greasy soot to the house-front, the two faded poplars, the faces of the passers-by. The long train of mules, dragging masses of pig-iron through the narrow street, have a foul vapor hanging to their reeking sides. Here, inside, is a little broken figure of an angel pointing upward from the mantel-shelf; but even its wings are covered with smoke, clotted and black. Smoke everywhere! A dirty canary chirps desolately in a cage beside me. Its dream of green fields and sunshine is a very old dream—almost worn out, I think.

From the back-window I can see a narrow brick-yard sloping down to the river-side, strewed with rain-butts and tubs. The river, dull and tawny-colored, *(la belle rivière!)* drags itself sluggishly along, tired of the heavy weight of boats and coal-barges. What wonder? When I was a child, I used to fancy a look of weary, dumb appeal upon the face of the negro-like river slavishly bearing its burden day after day. Something of the same idle notion comes to me to-day, when from the street-window I look on the slow stream of human life creeping past, night and morning, to the great mills. Masses of men, with dull, besotted faces bent to the ground, sharpened here and there by pain or cunning; skin and muscle and flesh begrimed with smoke and ashes; stooping all night over boiling caldrons of metal, laired by day in dens of drunkenness and infamy; breathing from infancy to death an air saturated with fog and grease and soot, vileness for soul and body. What do you make of a case like that, amateur psychologist? You call it an altogether serious thing to be alive: to these men it is a drunken jest, a joke—horrible to angels perhaps, to them commonplace enough. My fancy about the river was an idle one: it is no type of such a life. What if it be stagnant and slimy here? It knows that beyond there waits for it odorous sunlight—quaint old gardens, dusky with soft, green foliage of apple-trees, and flushing crimson with roses—air, and fields, and mountains. The future of the Welsh puddler passing just now is not so pleasant. To be stowed away, after his grimy work is done, in a hole in the muddy graveyard, and after that—*not* air, nor green fields, nor curious roses.

Can you see how foggy the day is? As I stand here, idly tapping the window-pane, and looking out through the rain at the dirty back-yard and the coal-boats below, fragments of an old story float up before me—a story of this house into which I happened to come to-day. You may think it a tiresome story enough, as foggy as the day, sharpened by no sudden flashes of pain or pleasure.—I know: only the outline of a dull life, that long since, with thousands of dull lives like its own, was vainly lived and lost: thousands of them—massed, vile, slimy lives, like those of the torpid lizards in yonder stagnant water-butt.—Lost? There is a curious point for you to settle, my friend, who study psychology in a lazy, *dilettante* way. Stop a moment. I am going to be honest. This is what I want you to do. I want you to hide your disgust, take no heed to your clean clothes, and come right down with me—here, into the thickest of the fog and mud and foul effluvia. I want you to hear this story. There is a secret down here, in this nightmare fog, that has lain dumb for centuries: I want to make it a real thing to you. You, Egoist, or Pantheist, or Arminian, busy in making straight paths for your feet on the hills, do not see it clearly—this terrible question which men here have gone mad and died trying to answer. I dare not put this secret into words. I told you it was dumb. These men, going by with drunken faces and brains full of unawakened power, do not ask it of Society or of God. Their lives ask it; their deaths ask it. There is no reply. I will tell you plainly that I have a great hope; and I bring it to you to be tested. It is this: that this terrible dumb question is its own reply; that it is not the sentence of death we think it, but, from the very extremity of its darkness, the most solemn prophecy which the world has known of the Hope to come. I dare make my meaning no clearer, but will only tell my story. It will, perhaps, seem to you as foul and dark as this thick vapor about us, and as pregnant with death; but if your eyes are free as mine are to look deeper, no perfume-tinted dawn will be so fair with promise of the day that shall surely come.

My story is very simple—only what I remember of the life of one of these men—a furnace-tender in one of Kirby & John's rolling-mills—Hugh Wolfe. You know the mills? They took the great order for the Lower Virginia railroads there last winter; run usually with about a thousand men. I cannot tell why I choose the half-forgotten story of this Wolfe more than that of myriads of these furnace-hands. Perhaps because there is a secret underlying sympathy between that story and this day with its impure fog and thwarted sunshine—or perhaps simply for the reason that this house is the one where the Wolfes lived. There were the father and son—both hands, as I said, in one of Kirby & John's mills for making railroad-iron—and Deborah, their cousin, a picker in some of the cotton-mills. The house was rented then to half a dozen families. The Wolfes had two of the cellar-rooms. The old man, like many of the puddlers and feeders of the mills, was Welsh—had spent half of his life in the Cornish tin-mines. You may pick the Welsh emigrants, Cornish miners, out of the throng passing the windows, any day. They are a trifle more filthy; their muscles are not so brawny; they stoop more. When they are drunk, they neither yell, nor shout, nor stagger, but skulk along like beaten hounds. A pure, unmixed blood, I fancy: shows itself in the slight angular bodies and sharply-cut facial lines. It is nearly thirty years since the Wolfes lived here. Their lives were like those of their class: incessant labor, sleeping in kennel-like rooms, eating rank pork and molasses, drinking—God and the distillers only know what; with an occasional night in jail, to atone for some drunken excess. Is that all of their lives?—of the portion given to them and these their duplicates swarming the streets to-day?—nothing beneath?— all? So many a political reformer will tell you—and many a private reformer, too, who has gone among them with a heart tender with Christ's charity, and come out outraged, hardened.

One rainy night, about eleven o'clock, a crowd of half-clothed women stopped outside of the cellar-door. They were going home from the cotton-mill.

"Good-night, Deb," said one, a mulatto, steadying herself against the gas-post. She needed the post to steady her. So did more than one of them.

"Dah's a ball to Miss Potts' to-night. Ye'd best come."

"Inteet, Deb, if hur'll come, hur'll hef fun," said a shrill Welsh voice in the crowd.

Two or three dirty hands were thrust out to catch the gown of the woman, who was groping for the latch of the door.

"No."

"No? Where's Kit Small, then?"

"Begorra! on the spools. Alleys behint, though we helped her, we dud. An wid ye! Let Deb alone! It's ondacent frettin' a quite body. Be the powers, an' we'll have a night of it! there'll be lashin's o' drink—the Vargent be blessed and praised for 't!"

They went on, the mulatto inclining for a moment to show fight, and drag the woman Wolfe off with them; but, being pacified, she staggered away.

Deborah groped her way into the cellar, and, after considerable stumbling, kindled a match, and lighted a tallow dip, that sent a yellow glimmer over the room. It was low, damp—the earthen floor covered with a green, slimy moss—a fetid air smothering the breath. Old Wolfe lay asleep on a heap of straw, wrapped in a torn horse-blanket. He was a pale, meek little man, with a white face and red rabbit-eyes. The woman Deborah was like him; only her face was even more ghastly, her lips bluer, her eyes more watery. She wore a faded cotton gown and a slouching bonnet. When she walked, one could see that she was deformed, almost a hunchback.

She trod softly, so as not to waken him, and went through into the room beyond. There she found by the half-extinguished fire an iron saucepan filled with cold boiled potatoes, which she put upon a broken chair with a pint-cup of ale. Placing the old candlestick beside this dainty repast, she untied her bonnet, which hung limp and wet over her face, and prepared to eat her supper. It was the first food that had touched her lips since morning. There was enough of it, however: there is not always. She was hungry—one could see that easily enough—and not drunk, as most of her companions would have been found at this hour. She did not drink, this woman—her face told that, too—nothing stronger than ale. Perhaps the weak, flaccid wretch had some stimulant in her pale life to keep her up—some love or hope, it might be, or urgent need. When that stimulant was gone, she would take to whiskey. Man cannot live by work alone. While she was skinning the potatoes, and munching them, a noise behind her made her stop.

"Janey!" she called, lifting the candle and peering into the darkness. "Janey, are you there?"

A heap of ragged coats was heaved up, and the face of a young girl emerged, staring sleepily at the woman.

"Deborah," she said, at last, "I'm here the night."

"Yes, child. Hur's welcome," she said, quietly eating on.

The girl's face was haggard and sickly; her eyes were heavy with sleep and hunger: real Milesian eyes they were, dark, delicate blue, glooming out from black shadows with a pitiful fright.

"I was alone," she said, timidly.

"Where's the father?" asked Deborah, holding out a potato, which the girl greedily seized.

"He's beyant—wid Haley—in the stone house." (Did you ever hear the word *jail* from an Irish mouth?) "I came here. Hugh told me never to stay me-lone."

"Hugh?"

"Yes."

A vexed frown crossed her face. The girl saw it, and added quickly—

"I have not seen Hugh the day, Deb. The old man says his watch lasts till the mornin'."

The woman sprang up, and hastily began to arrange some bread and flitch in a tin pail, and to pour her own measure of ale into a bottle. Tying on her bonnet, she blew out the candle.

"Lay ye down, Janey dear," she said, gently, covering her with the old rags. "Hur can eat the potatoes, if hur's hungry."

"Where are ye goin', Deb? The rain's sharp."

"To the mill, with Hugh's supper."

"Let him bide till th' morn. Sit ye down."

"No, no,"—sharply pushing her off. "The boy'll starve."

She hurried from the cellar, while the child wearily coiled herself up for sleep. The rain was falling heavily, as the woman, pail in hand, emerged from the mouth of the alley, and turned down the narrow street, that stretched out, long and black, miles before her. Here and there a flicker of gas lighted an uncertain space of muddy footwalk and gutter; the long rows of houses, except an occasional lager-bier shop, were closed; now and then she met a band of mill-hands skulking to or from their work.

Not many even of the inhabitants of a manufacturing town know the vast machinery of system by which the bodies of workmen are governed, that goes on unceasingly from year to year. The hands of each mill are divided into watches that relieve each other as regularly as the sentinels of an army. By night and day the work goes on, the unsleeping engines groan and shriek, the fiery pools of metal boil and surge. Only for a day in the week, in half-courtesy to public censure, the fires are partially veiled; but as soon as the clock strikes midnight, the great furnaces break forth with renewed fury, the clamor begins with fresh, breathless vigor, the engines sob and shriek like "gods in pain."

As Deborah hurried down through the heavy rain, the noise of these thousand engines sounded through the sleep and shadow of the city like far-off thunder. The mill to which she was going lay on the river, a mile below the city-limits. It was far, and she was weak, aching from standing twelve hours at the spools. Yet it was her almost nightly walk to take this man his supper, though at every square she sat down to rest, and she knew she should receive small word of thanks.

Perhaps, if she had possessed an artist's eye, the picturesque oddity of the scene might have made her step stagger less, and the path seem shorter; but to her the mills were only "summat deilish to look at by night."

The road leading to the mills had been quarried from the solid rock, which rose abrupt and bare on one side of the cinder-covered road, while the river, sluggish and black, crept past on the other. The mills for rolling iron are simply immense tent-like roofs, covering acres of ground, open on every side. Beneath these roofs Deborah looked in on a city of fires, that burned hot and fiercely in the night. Fire in every horrible form: pits of flame waving in the wind; liquid metal-flames writhing in tortuous streams through the sand; wide caldrons filled with boiling fire, over which bent ghastly wretches stirring the strange brewing; and through all, crowds of half-clad men, looking like revengeful ghosts in the red light, hurried, throwing masses of glittering fire. It was like a street in Hell. Even Deborah muttered, as she crept through, " 'T looks like t' Devil's place!" It did—in more ways than one.

She found the man she was looking for, at last, heaping coal on a furnace. He had not time to eat his supper; so she went behind the furnace, and waited. Only a few men were with him, and they noticed her only by a "Hyur comes t' hunchback, Wolfe."

Deborah was stupid with sleep; her back pained her sharply; and her teeth chattered with cold, with the rain that soaked her clothes and dripped from her at every step. She stood, however, patiently holding the pail, and waiting.

"Hout, woman! ye look like a drowned cat. Come near to the fire,"—said one of the men, approaching to scrape away the ashes.

She shook her head. Wolfe had forgotten her. He turned, hearing the man, and came closer.

"I did no' think; gi' me my supper, woman."

She watched him eat with a painful eagerness. With a woman's quick instinct, she saw that he was not hungry—was eating to please her. Her pale, watery eyes began to gather a strange light.

"Is't good, Hugh? T'ale was a bit sour, I feared."

"No, good enough." He hesitated a moment. "Ye're tired, poor lass! Bide here till I go. Lay down there on that heap of ash, and go to sleep."

He threw her an old coat for a pillow, and turned to his work. The heap was the refuse of the burnt iron, and was not a hard bed; the half-smothered warmth, too, penetrated her limbs, dulling their pain and cold shiver.

Miserable enough she looked, lying there on the ashes like a limp, dirty rag—yet not an unfitting figure to crown the scene of hopeless discomfort and veiled crime: more fitting, if one looked deeper into the heart of things—at her thwarted woman's form, her colorless life, her waking stupor that smothered pain and hunger—even more fit to be a type of her class. Deeper yet if one could look, was there nothing worth reading in this wet, faded thing, half-covered with ashes? no story of a soul filled with groping passionate love, heroic unselfishness, fierce jealousy? of years of weary trying to please the one human being whom she loved, to gain one look of real heart-kindness from him? If anything like this were hidden beneath the pale, bleared eyes, and dull, washed-out-looking face, no one had ever taken the trouble to read its faint signs: not the half-clothed furnace-tender, Wolfe, certainly. Yet he was kind to her: it was his nature to be kind, even to the very rats that swarmed in the cellar; kind to her in just the same way. She knew that. And it might be that very knowledge had given to her face its apathy and vacancy more than her low, torpid life. One sees that dead, vacant look steal sometimes over the rarest, finest of women's faces—in the very midst, it may be, of their warmest summer's day; and then one can guess at the secret of intolerable solitude that lies hid beneath the delicate laces and brilliant smile. There was no warmth, no brilliancy, no summer for this woman; so the stupor and vacancy had time to gnaw into her face perpetually. She was young, too, though no one guessed it; so the gnawing was the fiercer.

She lay quiet in the dark corner, listening, through the monotonous din and uncertain glare of the works, to the dull plash of the rain in the far distance—shrinking back whenever the man Wolfe happened to look towards her. She knew, in spite of all his kindness, that there was that in her face and form which made him loathe the sight of her. She felt by instinct, although she could not comprehend it, the finer nature of the man, which made him among his fellow-workmen something unique, set apart. She knew, that, down under all the vileness and coarseness of his life, there was a groping passion for whatever was beautiful and pure— that his soul sickened with disgust at her deformity, even when his words were kindest. Through this dull consciousness, which never left her, came, like a sting, the recollection of the dark blue eyes and lithe figure of the little Irish girl she had left in the cellar. The recollection struck through even her stupid intellect with a vivid glow of beauty and of grace. Little Janey, timid, helpless, clinging to Hugh as her only friend: that was the sharp thought, the bitter thought, that drove into the glazed eyes a fierce light of pain. You laugh at it? Are pain and jealousy less savage realities down here in this place I am taking you to than in your own house or your own heart—your heart, which they clutch at sometimes? The note is the same, I fancy, be the octave high or low.

If you could go into this mill where Deborah lay, and drag out from the hearts of these men the terrible tragedy of their lives, taking it as a symptom of the disease of their class, no ghost Horror would terrify you more. A reality of soul-starvation, of living death, that meets you every day under the besotted faces on the street—I can paint nothing of this, only give you the outside outlines of a night, a crisis in the life of one man: whatever muddy depth of soul-history lies beneath you can read according to the eyes God has given you.

Wolfe, while Deborah watched him as a spaniel its master, bent over the furnace with his iron pole, unconscious of her scrutiny, only stopping to receive orders. Physically, Nature had promised the man but little. He had already lost the strength and instinct vigor of a man, his muscles were thin, his nerves weak, his face (a meek, woman's face) haggard, yellow with consumption. In the mill he was known as one of the girl-men: "Molly Wolfe" was his *sobriquet*. He was never seen in the cockpit, did not own a terrier, drank but seldom; when he did, desperately. He fought sometimes, but was always thrashed, pommelled to a jelly. The man was game enough, when his blood was up: but he was no favorite in the mill; he had the taint of school-learning on him—not to a dangerous extent, only a quarter or so in the free-school in fact, but enough to ruin him as a good hand in a fight.

For other reasons, too, he was not popular. Not one of themselves, they felt that, though outwardly as filthy and ash-covered; silent, with foreign thoughts and longings breaking out through his quietness in innumerable curious ways: this one, for instance. In the neighboring furnace-buildings lay great heaps of the refuse from the ore after the pig-metal is run. *Korl* we call it here: a light, porous substance, of a delicate, waxen, flesh-colored tinge. Out of the blocks of this korl, Wolfe, in his off-hours from the furnace, had a habit of chipping and moulding figures—hideous, fantastic enough, but sometimes strangely beautiful: even the mill-men saw that, while they jeered at him. It was a curious fancy in the man, almost a passion. The few hours for rest he spent hewing and hacking with his blunt knife, never speaking, until his watch came again—working at one figure for months, and, when it was finished, breaking it to pieces perhaps, in a fit of disappointment. A morbid, gloomy man, untaught, unled, left to feed his soul in grossness and crime, and hard, grinding labor.

I want you to come down and look at this Wolfe, standing there among the lowest of his kind, and see him just as he is, that you may judge him justly when you hear the story of this night. I want you to look back, as he does every day, at his birth in vice, his starved infancy; to remember the heavy years he has groped through as boy and man—the slow, heavy years of constant, hot work. So long ago he began, that he thinks sometimes he has worked there for ages. There is no hope that it will ever end. Think that God put into this man's soul a fierce thirst for beauty—to know it, to create it; to *be*—something, he knows not what—other than he is. There are moments when a passing cloud, the sun glinting on the purple thistles, a kindly smile, a child's face, will rouse him to a passion of pain—when his nature starts up with a mad cry of rage against God, man, whoever it is that has forced this vile, slimy life upon him. With all this groping, this mad desire, a great blind intellect stumbling through wrong, a loving poet's heart, the man was by habit only a coarse, vulgar laborer, familiar with sights and words you would blush to name. Be just: when I tell you about this night, see him as he is. Be just—not like man's law, which seizes on one isolated fact, but like God's judging angel, whose clear, sad eye saw all the countless cankering days of this man's life, all the countless nights, when, sick with starving, his soul fainted in him, before it judged him for this night, the saddest of all.

I called this night the crisis of his life. If it was, it stole on him unawares. These great turning-days of life cast no shadow before, slip by unconsciously. Only a trifle, a little turn of the rudder, and the ship goes to heaven or hell.

Wolfe, while Deborah watched him, dug into the furnace of melting iron with his pole, dully thinking only how many rails the lump would yield. It was late—nearly Sunday morning; another hour, and the heavy work would be done—only the furnaces to replenish and cover for the next day. The workmen were growing more noisy, shouting, as they had to do, to be heard over the deep clamor of the mills. Suddenly they grew less boisterous—at the far end, entirely silent. Something unusual had happened. After a moment, the silence came nearer; the men stopped their jeers and drunken choruses. Deborah, stupidly lifting up her head, saw the cause of the quiet. A group of five or six men were slowly approaching, stopping to examine each furnace as they came. Visitors often came to see the mills after night: except by growing less noisy, the men took no notice of them. The furnace where Wolfe worked was near the bounds of the works; they halted there hot and tired: a walk over one of these great foundries is no trifling task. The woman, drawing out of sight, turned over to sleep. Wolfe, seeing them stop, suddenly roused from his indifferent stupor, and watched them keenly. He knew some of them: the overseer, Clarke—a son of Kirby, one of the mill-owners—and a Doctor May, one of the town-physicians. The other two were strangers. Wolfe came closer. He seized eagerly every chance that brought him into contact with this mysterious class that shone down on him perpetually with the glamour of another order of being. What made the difference between them? That was the mystery of his life. He had a vague notion that perhaps to-night he could find it out. One of the strangers sat down on a pile of bricks, and beckoned young Kirby to his side.

"This *is* hot, with a vengeance. A match, please?"—lighting his cigar. "But the walk is worth the trouble. If it were not that you must have heard it so often, Kirby, I would tell you that your works look like Dante's Inferno."

Kirby laughed.

"Yes. Yonder is Farinata himself in the burning tomb"—pointing to some figure in the shimmering shadows.

"Judging from some of the faces of your men," said the other, "they bid fair to try the reality of Dante's vision, some day."

Young Kirby looked curiously around, as if seeing the faces of his hands for the first time.

"They're bad enough, that's true. A desperate set, I fancy. Eh, Clarke?"

The overseer did not hear him. He was talking of net profits just then—giving, in fact, a schedule of the annual business of the firm to a sharp peering little Yankee, who jotted down notes on a paper laid on the crown of his hat: a reporter for one of the city-papers, getting up a series of reviews of the leading manufactories. The other gentlemen had accompanied them merely for amusement. They were silent until the notes were finished, drying their feet at the furnaces, and sheltering their faces from the intolerable heat. At last the overseer concluded with—

"I believe that is a pretty fair estimate, Captain."

"Here, some of you men!" said Kirby, "bring up those boards. We may as well sit down, gentlemen, until the rain is over. It cannot last much longer at this rate."

"Pig-metal"—mumbled the reporter—"um!—coal facilities—um!—hands employed, twelve hundred—bitumen—um!—all right, I believe, Mr. Clarke—sinking-fund—what did you say was your sinking-fund?"

"Twelve hundred hands?" said the stranger, the young man who had first spoken. "Do you control their votes, Kirby?"

"Control? No." The young man smiled complacently. "But my father brought seven hundred votes to the polls for his candidate last November. No force-work, you understand—only a speech or two, a hint to form themselves into a society, and a bit of red and blue bunting to make them a flag. The Invincible Roughs—I believe that is their name. I forget the motto: 'Our country's hope,' I think."

There was a laugh. The young man talking to Kirby sat with an amused light in his cool gray eye, surveying critically the half-clothed figures of the puddlers, and the slow swing of their brawny muscles. He was a stranger in the city—spending a couple of months in the borders of a Slave State, to study the institutions of the South—a brother-in-law of Kirby's—Mitchell. He was an amateur gymnast—hence his anatomical eye; a patron, in a *blasé* way, of the prize-ring; a man who sucked the essence out of a science or philosophy in an indifferent, gentlemanly way; who took Kant, Novalis, Humboldt, for what they were worth in his own scales; accepting all, despising nothing, in heaven, earth, or hell, but one-idead men; with a temper yielding and brilliant as summer water, until his Self was touched, when it was ice, though brilliant still. Such men are not rare in the States.

As he knocked the ashes from his cigar, Wolfe caught with a quick pleasure the contour of the white hand, the blood-glow of a red ring he wore. His voice, too, and that of Kirby's, touched him like music—low, even, with chording cadences. About this man Mitchell hung the impalpable atmosphere belonging to the thoroughbred gentleman. Wolfe, scraping away the ashes beside him, was conscious of it, did obeisance to it with his artist sense, unconscious that he did so.

The rain did not cease. Clarke and the reporter left the mills; the others, comfortably seated near the furnace, lingered, smoking and talking in a desultory way. Greek would not have been more unintelligible to the furnace-tenders, whose presence they soon forgot entirely. Kirby drew out a newspaper from his pocket and read aloud some article, which they discussed eagerly. At every sentence, Wolfe listened more and more like a dumb, hopeless animal, with a duller, more stolid look creeping over his face, glancing now and then at Mitchell, marking acutely every smallest sign of refinement, then back to himself, seeing as in a mirror his filthy body, his more stained soul.

Never! He had no words for such a thought, but he knew now, in all the sharpness of the bitter certainty, that between them there was a great gulf never to be passed. Never!

The bells of the mills rang for midnight. Sunday morning had dawned. Whatever hidden message lay in the tolling bells floated past these men unknown. Yet it was there. Veiled in the solemn music ushering the risen saviour was a key-note to solve the darkest secrets of a world gone wrong—even this social riddle which the brain of the grimy puddler grappled with madly to-night.

The men began to withdraw the metal from the caldrons. The mills were deserted on Sundays, except by the hands who fed the fires, and those who had no lodgings and slept usually on the ash-heaps. The three strangers sat still during the next hour, watching the men cover the furnaces, laughing now and then at some jest of Kirby's.

"Do you know," said Mitchell, "I like this view of the works better than when the glare was fiercest? These heavy shadows and the amphitheatre of smothered fires are ghostly, unreal. One could fancy these red smouldering lights to be the half-shut eyes of wild beasts, and the spectral figures their victims in the den."

Kirby laughed. "You are fanciful. Come, let us get out of the den. The spectral figures, as you call them, are a little too real for me to fancy a close proximity in the darkness—unarmed, too."

The others rose, buttoning their over-coats, and lighting cigars.

"Raining, still," said Doctor May, "and hard. Where did we leave the coach, Mitchell?"

"At the other side of the works.—Kirby, what's that?"

Mitchell started back, half-frightened, as, suddenly turning a corner, the white figure of a woman faced him in the darkness— a woman, white, of giant proportions, crouching on the ground, her arms flung out in some wild gesture of warning.

"Stop! Make that fire burn there!" cried Kirby, stopping short.

The flame burst out, flashing the gaunt figure into bold relief.

Mitchell drew a long breath.

"I thought it was alive," he said, going up curiously.

The others followed.

"Not marble, eh?" asked Kirby, touching it.

One of the lower overseers stopped.

"Korl, Sir."

"Who did it?"

"Can't say. Some of the hands; chipped it out in off-hours."

"Chipped to some purpose, I should say. What a flesh-tint the stuff has! Do you see, Mitchell?"

"I see."

He had stepped aside where the light fell boldest on the figure, looking at it in silence. There was not one line of beauty or grace in it: a nude woman's form, muscular, grown coarse with labor, the powerful limbs instinct with some one poignant longing. One idea: there it was in the tense, rigid muscles, the clutching hands, the wild, eager face, like that of a starving wolf's. Kirby and Doctor May walked around it, critical, curious. Mitchell stood aloof, silent. The figure touched him strangely.

"Not badly done," said Doctor May. "Where did the fellow learn that sweep of the muscles in the arm and hand? Look at them! They are groping—do you see?—clutching: the peculiar action of a man dying of thirst."

"They have ample facilities for studying anatomy," sneered Kirby, glancing at the half-naked figures.

"Look," continued the Doctor, "at this bony wrist, and the strained sinews of the instep! A working-woman—the very type of her class."

"God forbid!" muttered Mitchell.

"Why?" demanded May. "What does the fellow intend by the figure? I cannot catch the meaning."

"Ask him," said the other, dryly. "There he stands,"—pointing to Wolfe, who stood with a group of men, leaning on his ash-rake.

The Doctor beckoned him with the affable smile which kind-hearted men put on, when talking to these people.

"Mr. Mitchell has picked you out as the man who did this—I'm sure I don't know why. But what did you mean by it?"

"She be hungry."

Wolfe's eyes answered Mitchell, not the Doctor.

"Oh-h! But what a mistake you have made, my fine fellow! You have given no sign of starvation to the body. It is strong—terribly strong. It has the mad, half-despairing gesture of drowning."

Wolfe stammered, glanced appealingly at Mitchell, who saw the soul of the thing, he knew. But the cool, probing eyes were turned on himself now—mocking, cruel, relentless.

"Not hungry for meat," the furnace-tender said at last.

"What then? Whiskey?" jeered Kirby, with a coarse laugh.

Wolfe was silent a moment, thinking.

"I dunno," he said, with a bewildered look. "It mebbe. Summat to make her live, I think—like you. Whiskey ull do it, in a way."

The young man laughed again. Mitchell flashed a look of disgust somewhere—not at Wolfe.

"May," he broke out impatiently, "are you blind? Look at that woman's face! It asks questions of God, and says, 'I have a right to know.' Good God, how hungry it is!"

They looked a moment; then May turned to the mill-owner:—

"Have you many such hands as this? What are you going to do with them? Keep them at puddling iron?"

Kirby shrugged his shoulders. Mitchell's look had irritated him.

"*Ce n'est pas mon affaire.* I have no fancy for nursing infant geniuses. I suppose there are some stray gleams of mind and soul among these wretches. The Lord will take care of his own; or else they can work out their own salvation. I have heard you call our American system a ladder which any man can scale. Do you doubt it? Or perhaps you want to banish all social ladders, and put us all on a flat table-land—eh, May?"

The Doctor looked vexed, puzzled. Some terrible problem lay hid in this woman's face, and troubled these men. Kirby waited for an answer, and, receiving none, went on, warming with his subject.

"I tell you, there's something wrong that no talk of '*Liberté*' or '*Égalité*' will do away. If I had the making of men, these men who do the lowest part of the world's work should be machines—nothing more—hands. It would be kindness. God help them! What are taste, reason, to creatures who must live such lives as that?" He pointed to Deborah, sleeping on the ash-heap. "So many nerves to sting them to pain. What if God had put your brain, with all its agony of touch, into your fingers, and bid you work and strike with that?"

"You think you could govern the world better?" laughed the Doctor.

"I do not think at all."

"That is true philosophy. Drift with the stream, because you cannot dive deep enough to find bottom, eh?"

"Exactly," rejoined Kirby. "I do not think. I wash my hands of all social problems—slavery, caste, white or black. My duty to my operatives has a narrow limit—the pay-hour on Saturday night. Outside of that, if they cut korl, or cut each other's throats, (the more popular amusement of the two,) I am not responsible."

The Doctor sighed—a good honest sigh, from the depths of his stomach.

"God help us! Who is responsible?"

"Not I, I tell you," said Kirby, testily. "What has the man who pays them money to do with their souls' concerns, more than the grocer or butcher who takes it?"

"And yet," said Mitchell's cynical voice, "look at her! How hungry she is!"

Kirby tapped his boot with his cane. No one spoke. Only the dumb face of the rough image looking into their faces with the awful question, "What shall we do to be saved?" Only Wolfe's face, with its heavy weight of brain, its weak, uncertain mouth, its desperate eyes, out of which looked the soul of his class—only Wolfe's face turned towards Kirby's. Mitchell laughed—a cool, musical laugh.

"Money has spoken!" he said, seating himself lightly on a stone with the air of an amused spectator at a play. "Are you answered?"—turning to Wolfe his clear, magnetic face.

Bright and deep and cold as Arctic air, the soul of the man lay tranquil beneath. He looked at the furnace-tender as he had looked at a rare mosaic in the morning; only the man was the more amusing study of the two.

"Are you answered? Why, May, look at him! '*De profundis clamavi.*' Or, to quote in English, 'Hungry and thirsty, his soul faints in him.' And so Money sends back its answer into the depths through you, Kirby! Very clear the answer, too!—I think I remember reading the same words somewhere:—washing your hands in Eau de Cologne, and saying, 'I am innocent of the blood of this man. See ye to it!' "

Kirby flushed angrily.

"You quote Scripture freely."

"Do I not quote correctly? I think I remember another line, which may amend my meaning: 'Inasmuch as ye did it unto one of the least of these, ye did it unto me.' Deist? Bless you, man, I was raised on the milk of the Word. Now, Doctor, the pocket of the world having uttered its voice, what has the heart to say? You are a philanthropist, in a small way—*n'est ce pas?* Here, boy, this gentleman can show you how to cut korl better—or your destiny. Go on, May!"

"I think a mocking devil possesses you to-night," rejoined the Doctor, seriously.

He went to Wolfe and put his hand kindly on his arm. Something of a vague idea possessed the Doctor's brain that much good was to be done here by a friendly word or two: a latent genius to be warmed into life by a waited-for sun-beam. Here it was: he had brought it. So he went on complacently:—

"Do you know, boy, you have it in you to be a great sculptor, a great man?—do you understand?" (talking down to the capacity of his hearer: it is a way people have with children, and men like Wolfe,)—"to live a better, stronger life than I, or Mr. Kirby here? A man may make himself anything he chooses. God has given you stronger powers than many men—me, for instance."

May stopped, heated, glowing with his own magnanimity. And it was magnanimous. The puddler had drunk in every word, looking through the Doctor's flurry, and generous heat, and self-approval, into his will, with those slow, absorbing eyes of his.

"Make yourself what you will. It is your right."

"I know," quietly. "Will you help me?"

Mitchell laughed again. The Doctor turned now, in a passion—

"You know, Mitchell, I have not the means. You know, if I had, it is in my heart to take this boy and educate him for"—

"The glory of God, and the glory of John May."

May did not speak for a moment; then, controlled, he said—

"Why should one be raised, when myriads are left?—I have not the money, boy," to Wolfe, shortly.

"Money?" He said it over slowly, as one repeats the guessed answer to a riddle, doubtfully. "That is it? Money?"

"Yes, money—that is it," said Mitchell, rising, and drawing his furred coat about him. "You've found the cure for all the world's diseases.—Come, May, find your good-humor, and come home. This damp wind chills my very bones. Come and preach your Saint-Simonian doctrines to-morrow to Kirby's hands. Let them have a clear idea of the rights of the soul, and I'll venture next week they'll strike for higher wages. That will be the end of it."

"Will you send the coach-driver to this side of the mills?" asked Kirby, turning to Wolfe.

He spoke kindly: it was his habit to do so. Deborah, seeing the puddler go, crept after him. The three men waited outside. Doctor May walked up and down, chafed. Suddenly he stopped.

"Go back, Mitchell! You say the pocket and the heart of the world speak without meaning to these people. What has its head to say? Taste, culture, refinement? Go!"

Mitchell was leaning against a brick wall. He turned his head indolently, and looked into the mills. There hung about the place a thick, unclean odor. The slightest motion of his hand marked that he perceived it, and his insufferable disgust. That was all. May said nothing, only quickened his angry tramp.

"Besides," added Mitchell, giving a corollary to his answer, "it would be of no use. I am not one of them."

"You do not mean"—said May, facing him.

"Yes, I mean just that. Reform is born of need, not pity. No vital movement of the people's has worked down, for good or evil; fermented, instead, carried up the heaving, cloggy mass. Think back through history, and you will know it. What will this lowest deep—thieves, Magdalens, negroes—do with the light filtered through ponderous Church creeds, Baconian theories, Goethe schemes? Some day, out of their bitter need will be thrown up their own light-bringer—their Jean Paul, their Cromwell, their Messiah."

"Bah!" was the Doctor's inward criticism. However, in practice, he adopted the theory; for, when, night and morning, afterwards, he prayed that power might be given these degraded souls to rise, he glowed at heart, recognizing an accomplished duty.

Wolfe and the woman had stood in the shadow of the works as the coach drove off. The Doctor had held out his hand in a frank, generous way, telling him to "take care of himself, and to remember it was his right to rise." Mitchell had simply touched his hat, as to an equal, with a quiet look of thorough recognition. Kirby had thrown Deborah some money, which she found, and clutched eagerly enough. They were gone now, all of them. The man sat down on the cinder-road, looking up into the murky sky.

" 'T be late, Hugh. Wunnot hur come?"

He shook his head doggedly, and the woman crouched out of his sight against the wall. Do you remember rare moments when a sudden light flashed over yourself, your world, God? when you stood on a mountain-peak, seeing your life as it might have been, as it is? one quick instant, when custom lost its force and everyday usage? when your friend, wife, brother, stood in a new light?

your soul was bared, and the grave—a foretaste of the nakedness of the Judgment-Day? So it came before him, his life, that night. The slow tides of pain he had borne gathered themselves up and surged against his soul. His squalid daily life, the brutal coarseness eating into his brain, as the ashes into his skin: before, these things had been a dull aching into his consciousness; to-night, they were reality. He gripped the filthy red shirt that clung, stiff with soot, about him, and tore it savagely from his arm. The flesh beneath was muddy with grease and ashes—and the heart beneath that! And the soul? God knows.

Then flashed before his vivid poetic sense the man who had left him—the pure face, the delicate, sinewy limbs, in harmony with all he knew of beauty or truth. In his cloudy fancy he had pictured a Something like this. He had found it in this Mitchell, even when he idly scoffed at his pain: a Man all-knowing, all-seeing, crowned by Nature, reigning—the keen glance of his eye falling like a sceptre on other men. And yet his instinct taught him that he too—He! He looked at himself with sudden loathing, sick, wrung his hands with a cry, and then was silent. With all the phantoms of his heated, ignorant fancy, Wolfe had not been vague in his ambitions. They were practical, slowly built up before him out of his knowledge of what he could do. Through years he had day by day made this hope a real thing to himself—a clear, projected figure of himself, as he might become.

Able to speak, to know what was best, to raise these men and women working at his side up with him: sometimes he forgot this defined hope in the frantic anguish to escape—only to escape—out of the wet, the pain, the ashes, somewhere, anywhere—only for one moment of free air on a hill-side, to lie down and let his sick soul throb itself out in the sunshine. But to-night he panted for life. The savage strength of his nature was roused; his cry was fierce to God for justice.

"Look at me!" he said to Deborah, with a low, bitter laugh, striking his puny chest savagely. "What am I worth, Deb? Is it my fault that I am no better? My fault? My fault?"

He stopped, stung with a sudden remorse, seeing her hunchback shape writhing with sobs. For Deborah was crying thankless tears, according to the fashion of women.

"God forgi' me, woman! Things go harder wi' you nor me. It's a worse share."

He got up and helped her to rise; and they went doggedly down the muddy street, side by side.

"It's all wrong," he muttered, slowly—"all wrong! I dunnot understan'. But it'll end some day."

"Come home, Hugh!" she said, coaxingly; for he had stopped, looking around bewildered.

"Home—and back to the mill!" He went on saying this over to himself, as if he would mutter down every pain in this dull despair.

She followed him through the fog, her blue lips chattering with cold. They reached the cellar at last. Old Wolfe had been drinking since she went out, and had crept nearer the door. The girl Janey slept heavily in the corner. He went up to her, touching softly the worn white arm with his fingers. Some bitterer thought stung him, as he stood there. He wiped the drops from his forehead, and went into the room beyond, livid, trembling. A hope, trifling, perhaps, but very dear, had died just then out of the poor puddler's life, as he looked at the sleeping, innocent girl— some plan for the future, in which she had borne a part. He gave it up that moment, then and forever. Only a trifle, perhaps, to us: his face grew a shade paler—that was all. But, somehow, the man's soul, as God and the angels looked down on it, never was the same afterwards.

Deborah followed him into the inner room. She carried a

candle, which she placed on the floor, closing the door after her. She had seen the look on his face, as he turned away: her own grew deadly. Yet, as she came up to him, her eyes glowed. He was seated on an old chest, quiet, holding his face in his hands.

"Hugh!" she said, softly.

He did not speak.

"Hugh, did hur hear what the man said—him with the clear voice? Did hur hear? Money, money—that it wud do all?"

He pushed her away—gently, but he was worn out; her rasping tone fretted him.

"Hugh!"

The candle flared a pale yellow light over the cobwebbed brick walls, and the woman standing there. He looked at her. She was young, in deadly earnest; her faded eyes, and wet, ragged figure caught from their frantic eagerness a power akin to beauty.

"Hugh, it is true! Money ull do it! Oh, Hugh, boy, listen till me! He said it true! It is money!"

"I know. Go back! I do not want you here."

"Hugh, it is t' last time. I'll never worrit hur again."

There were tears in her voice now, but she choked them back.

"Hear till me only to-night! If one of t' witch people wud come, them we heard of t' home, and gif hur all hur wants, what then? Say, Hugh!"

"What do you mean?"

"I mean money."

Her whisper shrilled through his brain.

"If one of t' witch dwarfs wud come from t' lane moors to-night, and gif hur money, to go out—*out,* I say—out, lad, where t' sun shines, and t' heath grows, and t' ladies walk in silken gownds, and God stays all t' time—where t' man lives that talked to us to-night—Hugh knows—Hugh could walk there like a king!"

He thought the woman mad, tried to check her, but she went on, fierce in her eager haste.

"If *I* were t' witch dwarf, if I had t' money, wud hur thank me? Wud hur take me out o' this place wid hur and Janey? I wud not come into the gran' house hur wud build, to vex hur wid t' hunch—only at night, when t' shadows were dark, stand far off to see hur."

Mad? Yes! Are many of us mad in this way?

"Poor Deb! poor Deb!" he said, soothingly.

"It is here," she said, suddenly jerking into his hand a small roll. "I took it! I did it! Me, me!—not hur! I shall be hanged, I shall be burnt in hell, if anybody knows I took it! Out of his pocket, as he leaned against t' bricks. Hur knows?"

She thrust it into his hand, and then, her errand done, began to gather chips together to make a fire, choking down hysteric sobs.

"Has it come to this?"

That was all he said. The Welsh Wolfe blood was honest. The roll was a small green pocket-book containing one or two gold pieces, and a check for an incredible amount, as it seemed to the poor puddler. He laid it down, hiding his face again in his hands.

"Hugh, don't be angry wud me! It's only poor Deb—hur knows?"

He took the long skinny fingers kindly in his.

"Angry? God help me, no! Let me sleep. I am tired."

He threw himself heavily down on the wooden bench, stunned with pain and weariness. She brought some old rags to cover him.

It was late on Sunday evening before he awoke. I tell God's truth, when I say he had then no thought of keeping this money. Deborah had hid it in his pocket. He found it there. She watched him eagerly, as he took it out.

"I must gif it to him," he said, reading her face.

"Hur knows," she said with a bitter sigh of disappointment. "But it is hur right to keep it."

His right! The word struck him. Doctor May had used the same. He washed himself, and went out to find this man Mitchell. His right! Why did this chance word cling to him so obstinately? Do you hear the fierce devils whisper in his ear, as he went slowly down the darkening street?

The evening came on, slow and calm. He seated himself at the end of an alley leading into one of the larger streets. His brain was clear to-night, keen, intent, mastering. It would not start back, cowardly, from any hellish temptation, but meet it face to face. Therefore the great temptation of his life came to him veiled by no sophistry, but bold, defiant, owning its own vile name, trusting to one bold blow for victory.

He did not deceive himself. Theft! That was it. At first the word sickened him; then he grappled with it. Sitting there on a broken cart-wheel, the fading day, the noisy groups, the church-bells' tolling passed before him like a panorama, while the sharp struggle went on within. This money! He took it out, and looked at it. If he gave it back, what then? He was going to be cool about it.

People going by to church saw only a sickly mill-boy watching them quietly at the alley's mouth. They did not know that he was mad, or they would not have gone by so quietly: mad with hunger; stretching out his hands to the world, that had given so much to them, for leave to live the life God meant him to live. His soul within him was smothering to death; he wanted so much, thought so much, and *knew*—nothing. There was nothing of which he was certain, except the mill and things there. Of God and heaven he had heard so little, that they were to him what fairy-land is to a child: something real, but not here; very far off. His brain, greedy, dwarfed, full of thwarted energy and unused powers, questioned these men and women going by, coldly, bitterly, that night. Was it not his right to live as they—a pure life, a good, true-hearted life, full of beauty and kind words? He only wanted to know how to use the strength within him. His heart warmed, as he thought of it. He suffered himself to think of it longer. If he took the money?

Then he saw himself as he might be, strong, helpful, kindly. The night crept on, as this one image slowly evolved itself from the crowd of other thoughts and stood triumphant. He looked at it. As he might be! What wonder, if it blinded him to delirium—the madness that underlies all revolution, all progress, and all fall?

You laugh at the shallow temptation? You see the error under-lying its argument so clearly—that to him a true life was one of full development rather than self-restraint? that he was deaf to the higher tone in a cry of voluntary suffering for truth's sake than in the fullest flow of spontaneous harmony? I do not plead his cause. I only want to show you the mote in my brother's eye: then you can see clearly to take it out.

The money—there it lay on his knee, a little blotted slip of paper, nothing in itself; used to raise him out of the pit; something straight from God's hand. A thief! Well, what was it to be a thief? He met the question at last, face to face, wiping the clammy drops of sweat from his forehead. God made this money—the fresh air, too—for his children's use. He never made the difference between poor and rich. The Something who looked down on him that mo-ment through the cool gray sky had a kindly face, he knew—loved his children alike. Oh, he knew that!

There were times when the soft floods of color in the crim-son and purple flames, or the clear depth of amber in the water below the bridge, had somehow given him a glimpse of another world than this—of an infinite depth of beauty and of quiet somewhere—somewhere—a depth of quiet and rest and love.

Looking up now, it became strangely real. The sun had sunk quite below the hills, but his last rays struck upward, touching the zenith. The fog had risen, and the town and river were steeped in its thick, gray damp; but overhead, the sun-touched smoke-clouds opened like a cleft ocean—shifting, rolling seas of crimson mist, waves of billowy silver veined with blood-scarlet, inner depths unfathomable of glancing light. Wolfe's artist-eye grew drunk with color. The gates of that other world! Fading, flashing before him now! What, in that world of Beauty, Content, and Right, were the petty laws, the mine and thine, of mill-owners and mill-hands?

A consciousness of power stirred within him. He stood up. A man—he thought, stretching out his hands—free to work, to live, to love! Free! His right! He folded the scrap of paper in his hand. As his nervous fingers took it in, limp and blotted, so his soul took in the mean temptation, lapped it in fancied rights, in dreams of improved existences, drifting and endless as the cloud-seas of color. Clutching it, as if the tightness of his hold would strengthen his sense of possession, he went aimlessly down the street. It was his watch at the mill. He need not go, need never go again, thank God!—shaking off the thought with unspeakable loathing.

Shall I go over the history of the hours of that night? how the man wandered from one to another of his old haunts, with a half-consciousness of bidding them farewell—lanes and alleys and back-yards where the mill-hands lodged—noting, with a new eagerness, the filth and drunkenness, the pig-pens, the ash-heaps covered with potato-skins, the bloated, pimpled women at the doors—with a new disgust, a new sense of sudden triumph, and, under all, a new, vague dread, unknown before, smothered down, kept under, but still there? It left him but once during the night, when, for the second time in his life, he entered a church. It was a sombre Gothic pile, where the stained light lost itself in far-retreating arches; built to meet the requirements and sympathies of a far other class than Wolfe's. Yet it touched, moved him uncontrollably. The distances, the shadows, the still, marble figures, the mass of silent kneeling worshippers, the mysterious music, thrilled, lifted his soul with a wonderful pain. Wolfe forgot himself, forgot the new life he was going to live, the mean terror gnawing underneath. The voice of the speaker strengthened the charm; it was clear, feeling, full, strong. An old man, who had lived much, suffered much; whose brain was keenly alive, dominant; whose heart was summer-warm with charity. He taught it to-night. He held up Humanity in its grand total; showed the great world-cancer to his people. Who could show it better? He was a Christian reformer; he had studied the age thoroughly; his outlook at man had been free, world-wide, over all time. His faith stood sublime upon the Rock of Ages; his fiery zeal guided vast schemes by which the gospel was to be preached to all nations. How did he preach it to-night? In burning, light-laden words he painted the incarnate Life, Love, the universal Man: words that became reality in the lives of these people—that lived again in beautiful words and actions, trifling, but heroic. Sin, as he defined it, was a real foe to them; their trials, temptations, were his. His words passed far over the furnace-tender's grasp, toned to suit another class of culture; they sounded in his ears a very pleasant song in an unknown tongue. He meant to cure this world-cancer with a steady eye that had never glared with hunger, and a hand that neither poverty nor strychnine-whiskey had taught to shake. In this morbid, distorted heart of the Welsh puddler he had failed.

Wolfe rose at last, and turned from the church down the street. He looked up; the night had come on foggy, damp; the golden mists had vanished, and the sky lay dull and ash-colored. He wandered again aimlessly down the street, idly wondering what had become of the cloud-sea of crimson and scarlet. The trial-day of this man's life was over, and he had lost the victory. What followed was mere drifting circumstance—a quicker walking over the path—that was all. Do you want to hear the end of it? You wish me to make a tragic story out of it? Why, in the police-reports of the morning paper you can find a dozen such tragedies: hints of shipwrecks unlike any that ever befell on the high seas; hints that here a power was lost to heaven—that there a soul went down where no tide can ebb or flow. Commonplace enough the hints are—jocose sometimes, done up in rhyme.

Doctor May a month after the night I have told you of, was reading to his wife at breakfast from this fourth column of the morning-paper: an unusual thing—these police-reports not being, in general, choice reading for ladies; but it was only one item he read.

"Oh, my dear! You remember that man I told you of, that we saw at Kirby's mill?—that was arrested for robbing Mitchell? Here he is; just listen:—'Circuit Court. Judge Day. Hugh Wolfe, operative in Kirby & John's Loudon Mills. Charge, grand larceny. Sentence, nineteen years hard labor in penitentiary.'—Scoundrel! Serves him right! After all our kindness that night! Picking Mitchell's pocket at the very time!"

His wife said something about the ingratitude of that kind of people, and then they began to talk of something else.

Nineteen years! How easy that was to read! What a simple word for Judge Day to utter! Nineteen years! Half a lifetime!

Hugh Wolfe sat on the window-ledge of his cell, looking out. His ankles were ironed. Not usual in such cases; but he had made two desperate efforts to escape. "Well," as Haley, the jailer, said, "small blame to him! Nineteen years' imprisonment was not a pleasant thing to look forward to." Haley was very good-natured about it, though Wolfe had fought him savagely.

"When he was first caught," the jailer said afterwards, in telling the story, "before the trial, the fellow was cut down at once—laid there on that pallet like a dead man, with his hands over his eyes. Never saw a man so cut down in my life. Time of the trial, too, came the queerest dodge of any customer I ever had. Would choose no lawyer. Judge gave him one, of course. Gibson it was. He tried to prove the fellow crazy; but it wouldn't go. Thing was plain as daylight: money found on him. 'Twas a hard sentence—all the law allows; but it was for 'xample's sake. These mill-hands are gettin' onbearable. When the sentence was read, he just looked up, and said the money was his by rights, and that all the world had gone wrong. That night, after the trial, a gentleman came to see him here, name of Mitchell—him as he stole from. Talked to him for an hour. Thought he came for curiosity, like. After he was gone, thought Wolfe was remarkable quiet, and went into his cell. Found him very low; bed all bloody. Doctor said he had been bleeding at the lungs. He was as weak as a cat; yet, if ye'll b'lieve me, he tried to get a-past me and get out. I just carried him like a baby, and threw him on the pallet. Three days after, he tried it again: that time reached the wall. Lord help you! he fought like a tiger—giv' some terrible blows. Fightin' for life, you see; for he can't live long, shut up in the stone crib down yonder. Got a death-cough now. 'T took two of us to bring him down that day; so I just put the irons on his feet. There he sits, in there. Goin' to-morrow, with a batch more of 'em. That woman, hunchback, tried with him—you remember?—she's only got three years. 'Complice. But she's a woman, you know. He's been quiet ever since I put on irons: giv' up, I suppose. Looks white, sick-lookin'. It acts different on 'em, bein' sentenced. Most of 'em gets reckless, devilish-like. Some prays awful, and sings them vile songs of the mills, all in a breath. That woman, now, she's desper't'. Been beggin' to see Hugh, as she calls him, for three days. I'm a-goin' to let her in. She don't go with him. Here she is in this next cell. I'm a-goin' now to let her in."

He let her in. Wolfe did not see her. She crept into a corner of the cell, and stood watching him. He was scratching the iron bars of the window with a piece of tin which he had picked up, with an idle, uncertain, vacant stare, just as a child or idiot would do.

"Tryin' to get out, old boy?" laughed Haley. "Them irons will need a crow-bar beside your tin, before you can open 'em."

Wolfe laughed, too, in a senseless way.

"I think I'll get out," he said.

"I believe his brain's touched," said Haley, when he came out.

The puddler scraped away with the tin for half an hour. Still Deborah did not speak. At last she ventured nearer, and touched his arm.

"Blood?" she said, looking at some spots on his coat with a shudder.

He looked up at her, "Why, Deb!" he said, smiling—such a bright, boyish smile, that it went to poor Deborah's heart directly, and she sobbed and cried out loud.

"Oh, Hugh, lad! Hugh! dunnot look at me, when it wur my fault! To think I brought hur to it! And I loved hur so! Oh lad, I dud!"

The confession, even in this wretch, came with the woman's blush through the sharp cry.

He did not seem to hear her—scraping away diligently at the bars with the bit of tin.

Was he going mad? She peered closely into his face. Something she saw there made her draw suddenly back—something which Haley had not seen, that lay beneath the pinched, vacant look it had caught since the trial, or the curious gray shadow that rested on it. That gray shadow—yes, she knew what that meant. She had often seen it creeping over women's faces for months, who died at last of slow hunger or consumption. That meant death, distant, lingering: but this—Whatever it was the woman saw, or thought she saw, used as she was to crime and misery, seemed to make her sick with a new horror. Forgetting her fear of him, she caught his shoulders, and looked keenly, steadily, into his eyes.

"Hugh!" she cried, in a desperate whisper—"oh, boy, not that! for God's sake, not *that!*"

The vacant laugh went off his face, and he answered her in a muttered word or two that drove her away. Yet the words were kindly enough. Sitting there on his pallet, she cried silently a hopeless sort of tears, but did not speak again. The man looked up furtively at her now and then. Whatever his own trouble was, her distress vexed him with a momentary sting.

It was market-day. The narrow window of the jail looked down directly on the carts and wagons drawn up in a long line, where they had unloaded. He could see, too, and hear distinctly the clink of money as it changed hands, the busy crowd of whites and blacks shoving, pushing one another, and the chaffering and swearing at the stalls. Somehow, the sound, more than anything else had done, wakened him up—made the whole real to him. He was done with the world and the business of it. He let the tin fall, and looked out, pressing his face close to the rusty bars. How they crowded and pushed! And he—he should never walk that pavement again! There came Neff Sanders, one of the feeders at the mill, with a basket on his arm. Sure enough, Neff was married the other week. He whistled, hoping he would look up; but he did not. He wondered if Neff remembered he was there—if any of the boys thought of him up there, and thought that he never was to go down that old cinder-road again. Never again! He had not quite understood it before; but now he did. Not for days or years, but never!—that was it.

How clear the light fell on that stall in front of the market! and how like a picture it was, the dark-green heaps of corn, and the crimson beets, and golden melons! There was another with game: how the light flickered on that pheasant's breast, with the purplish blood dripping over the brown feathers! He could see the red shining of the drops, it was so near. In one minute he could be down there. It was just a step. So easy, as it seemed, so natural to go! Yet it could never be—not in all the thousands of years to come—that he should put his foot on that street again! He thought of himself with a sorrowful pity, as of some one else. There was a dog down in the market, walking after his master with such a stately, grave look!—only a dog, yet he could go backwards and forwards just as he pleased: he had good luck! Why, the very vilest cur, yelping there in the gutter, had not lived his life, had been free to act out whatever thought God had put into his brain; while he—No, he would not think of that! He tried to put the thought away, and to listen to a dispute between a countryman and a woman about some meat; but it would come back. He, what had he done to bear this?

Then came the sudden picture of what might have been, and now. He knew what it was to be in the penitentiary—how it went with men there. He knew how in these long years he should slowly die, but not until soul and body had become corrupt and rotten—how, when he came out, if he lived to come, even the lowest of the mill-hands would jeer him—how his hands would be weak, and his brain senseless and stupid. He believed he was almost that now. He put his hand to his head, with a puzzled, weary look. It ached, his head, with thinking. He tried to quiet himself. It was only right, perhaps; he had done wrong. But was there right or wrong for such as he? What was right? And who had ever taught him? He thrust the whole matter away. A dark, cold quiet crept through his brain. It was all wrong; but let it be! It was nothing to him more than the others. Let it be!

The door grated, as Haley opened it.

"Come, my woman! Must lock up for t' night. Come, stir yerself!"

She went up and took Hugh's hand.

"Good-night, Deb," he said, carelessly.

She had not hoped he would say more; but the tired pain on her mouth just then was bitterer than death. She took his passive hand and kissed it.

"Hur'll never see Deb again!" she ventured, her lips growing colder and more bloodless.

What did she say that for? Did he not know it? Yet he would not be impatient with poor old Deb. She had trouble of her own, as well as he.

"No, never again," he said, trying to be cheerful.

She stood just a moment, looking at him. Do you laugh at her, standing there, with her hunchback, her rags, her bleared, withered face, and the great despised love tugging at her heart?

"Come, you!" called Haley, impatiently.

She did not move.

"Hugh!" she whispered.

It was to be her last word. What was it?

"Hugh, boy, not *THAT!*"

He did not answer. She wrung her hands, trying to be silent, looking in his face in an agony of entreaty. He smiled again, kindly.

"It is best, Deb. I cannot bear to be hurted any more."

"Hur knows," she said, humbly.

"Tell my father good-bye; and—and kiss little Janey."

She nodded, saying nothing, looked in his face again, and went out of the door. As she went, she staggered.

"Drinkin' to-day?" broke out Haley, pushing her before him. "Where the Devil did you get it? Here, in with ye!" and he shoved her into her cell, next to Wolfe's, and shut the door.

Along the wall of her cell there was a crack low down by the floor, through which she could see the light from Wolfe's. She had discovered it days before. She hurried in now, and, kneeling down by it, listened, hoping to hear some sound. Nothing but the rasping of the tin on the bars. He was at his old amusement again. Something in the noise jarred on her ear, for she shivered as she heard it. Hugh rasped away at the bars. A dull old bit of tin, not fit to cut korl with.

He looked out of the window again. People were leaving the market now. A tall mulatto girl, following her mistress, her basket on her head, crossed the street just below, and looked up. She was laughing; but, when she caught sight of the haggard face peering out through the bars, suddenly grew grave, and hurried by. A free, firm step, a clear-cut olive face, with a scarlet turban tied on one side, dark, shining eyes, and on the head the basket poised, filled with fruit and flowers, under which the scarlet turban and bright eyes looked out half-shadowed. The picture caught his eye. It was good to see a face like that. He would try to-morrow, and cut one like it. *To-morrow!* He threw down the tin, trembling, and covered his face with his hands. When he looked up again, the daylight was gone.

Deborah, crouching near by on the other side of the wall, heard no noise. He sat on the side of the low pallet, thinking. Whatever was the mystery which the woman had seen on his face, it came out now slowly, in the dark there, and became fixed—a something never seen on his face before. The evening was darkening fast. The market had been over for an hour; the rumbling of the carts over the pavement grew more infrequent: he listened to each, as it passed, because he thought it was to be for the last time. For the same reason, it was, I suppose, that he strained his eyes to catch a glimpse of each passer-by, wondering who they were, what kind of homes they were going to, if they had children—listening eagerly to every chance word in the street, as if—(God be merciful to the man! what strange fancy was this?)—as if he never should hear human voices again.

It was quite dark at last. The street was a lonely one. The last passenger, he thought, was gone. No—there was a quick step: Joe Hill, lighting the lamps. Joe was a good old chap; never passed a fellow without some joke or other. He remembered once seeing the place where he lived with his wife. "Granny Hill" the boys called her. Bedridden she was; but so kind as Joe was to her! kept the room so clean!—and the old woman, when he was there, was laughing at "some of t' lad's foolishness." The step was far down the street; but he could see him place the ladder, run up, and light the gas. A longing seized him to be spoken to once more.

"Joe!" he called, out of the grating. "Good-bye, Joe!"

The old man stopped a moment, listening uncertainly; then hurried on. The prisoner thrust his hand out of the window, and called again, louder; but Joe was too far down the street. It was a little thing; but it hurt him—this disappointment.

"Good-bye, Joe!" he called, sorrowfully enough.

"Be quiet!" said one of the jailers, passing the door, striking on it with his club.

Oh, that was the last, was it?

There was an inexpressible bitterness on his face, as he lay down on the bed, taking the bit of tin, which he had rasped to a tolerable degree of sharpness, in his hand—to play with, it may be. He bared his arms, looking intently at their corded veins and sinews. Deborah, listening in the next cell, heard a slight clicking sound, often repeated. She shut her lips tightly, that she might not scream, the cold drops of sweat broke over her, in her dumb agony.

"Hur knows best," she muttered at last, fiercely clutching the boards where she lay.

If she could have seen Wolfe, there was nothing about him to frighten her. He lay quite still, his arms outstretched, looking at the pearly stream of moonlight coming into the window. I think in that one hour that came then he lived back over all the years that had gone before. I think that all the low, vile life, all his wrongs, all his starved hopes, came then, and stung him with a farewell poison that made him sick unto death. He made neither moan nor cry, only turned his worn face now and then to the pure light, that seemed so far off, as one that said, "How long, O Lord? how long?"

The hour was over at last. The moon, passing over her nightly path, slowly came nearer, and threw the light across his bed on his feet. He watched it steadily, as it crept up, inch by inch, slowly. It seemed to him to carry with it a great silence. He had been so hot and tired there always in the mills! The years had been so fierce and cruel! There was coming now quiet and coolness and sleep. His tense limbs relaxed, and settled in a calm languor. The blood ran fainter and slow from his heart. He did not think now with a savage anger of what might be and was not; he was conscious only of deep stillness creeping over him. At first he saw a sea of faces: the mill-men—women he had known, drunken and bloated—Janeys timid and pitiful—poor old Debs: then they floated together like a mist, and faded away, leaving only the clear, pearly moonlight.

Whether, as the pure light crept up the stretched-out figure, it brought with it calm and peace, who shall say? His dumb soul was alone with God in judgment. A Voice may have spoken for it from far-off Calvary, "Father, forgive them, for they know not what they do!" Who dare say? Fainter and fainter the heart rose and fell, slower and slower the moon floated from behind a cloud, until, when at last its full tide of white splendor swept over the cell, it seemed to wrap and fold into a deeper stillness the dead figure that never should move again. Silence deeper than the Night! Nothing that moved, save the black nauseous stream of blood dripping slowly from the pallet to the floor!

There was outcry and crowd enough in the cell the next day. The coroner and his jury, the local editors, Kirby himself, and boys with their hands thrust knowingly into their pockets and heads on one side, jammed into the corners. Coming and going all day. Only one woman. She came late, and outstayed them all. A Quaker, or Friend, as they call themselves. I think this woman was known by that name in heaven. A homely body, coarsely dressed in gray and white. Deborah (for Haley had let her in) took notice of her. She watched them all—sitting on the end of the pallet, holding his head in her arms—with the ferocity of a watch-dog, if any of them touched the body. There was no meekness, no sorrow, in her face; the stuff out of which murderers are made, instead. All the time Haley and the woman were laying straight the limbs and cleaning the cell, Deborah sat still, keenly watching the Quaker's face. Of all the crowd there that day, this woman alone had not spoken to her—only once or twice had put some cordial to her lips. After they all were gone, the woman, in the same still, gentle way, brought a vase of wood-leaves and berries, and placed it by the pallet, then opened the narrow window. The fresh air blew in, and swept the woody fragrance over the dead face. Deborah looked up with a quick wonder.

"Did hur know my boy wud like it? Did hur know Hugh?"

"I know Hugh now."

The white fingers passed in a slow, pitiful way over the dead, worn face. There was a heavy shadow in the quiet eyes.

"Did hur know where they'll bury Hugh?" said Deborah in a shrill tone, catching her arm.

This had been the question hanging on her lips all day.

"In t' town-yard? Under t' mud and ash? T' lad'll smother, woman! He wur born in t' lane moor, where t' air is frick and strong. Take hur out, for God's sake, take hur out where t' air blows!"

The Quaker hesitated, but only for a moment. She put her strong arm around Deborah and led her to the window.

"Thee sees the hills, friend, over the river? Thee sees how the light lies warm there, and the winds of God blow all the day? I live there—where the blue smoke is, by the trees. Look at me." She turned Deborah's face to her own, clear and earnest, "Thee will believe me? I will take Hugh and bury him there to-morrow."

Deborah did not doubt her. As the evening wore on, she leaned against the iron bars, looking at the hills that rose far off, through the thick sodden clouds, like a bright, unattainable calm. As she looked, a shadow of their solemn repose fell on her face: its fierce discontent faded into a pitiful, humble quiet. Slow, solemn tears gathered in her eyes: the poor weak eyes turned so hopelessly to the place where Hugh was to rest, the grave heights looking higher and brighter and more solemn than ever before. The Quaker watched her keenly. She came to her at last, and touched her arm.

"When thee comes back," she said, in a low, sorrowful tone, like one who speaks from a strong heart deeply moved with re-morse or pity, "thee shall begin thy life again—there on the hills. I came too late; but not for thee—by God's help, it may be."

Not too late. Three years after, the Quaker began her work. I end my story here. At evening-time it was light. There is no need to tire you with the long years of sunshine, and fresh air, and slow, patient Christ-love, needed to make healthy and hopeful this im-pure body and soul. There is a homely pine house, on one of these hills, whose windows overlook broad, wooded slopes and clover-crimsoned meadows—niched into the very place where the light is warmest, the air freest. It is the Friends' meeting-house. Once a week they sit there, in their grave, earnest way, waiting for the Spirit of Love to speak, opening their simple hearts to receive His words. There is a woman, old, deformed, who takes a humble place among them: waiting like them: in her gray dress, her worn face, pure and meek, turned now and then to the sky. A woman much loved by these silent, restful people; more silent than they, more humble, more loving. Waiting: with her eyes turned to hills higher and purer than these on which she lives—dim and far off now, but to be reached some day. There may be in her heart some latent hope to meet there the love denied her here—that she shall find him whom she lost, and that then she will not be all-unworthy. Who blames her? Something is lost in the passage of every soul from one eternity to the other—something pure and beautiful, which might have been and was not: a hope, a talent, a love, over which the soul mourns, like Esau deprived of his birthright. What blame to the meek Quaker, if she took her lost hope to make the hills of heaven more fair?

Nothing remains to tell that the poor Welsh puddler once lived, but this figure of the mill-woman cut in korl. I have it here in a corner of my library. I keep it hid behind a curtain—it is such a rough, ungainly thing. Yet there are about it touches, grand sweeps of outline, that show a master's hand. Sometimes—to-night, for instance—the curtain is accidentally drawn back, and I see a bare arm stretched out imploringly in the darkness, and an eager, wolfish face watching mine: a wan, woful face, through which the spirit of the dead korl-cutter looks out, with its thwarted life, its mighty hunger, its unfinished work. Its pale, vague lips seem to tremble with a terrible question. "Is this the End?" they say—"nothing beyond?—no more?" Why, you tell me you have seen that look in the eyes of dumb brutes—horses dying under the lash. I know.

The deep of the night is passing while I write. The gas-light wakens from the shadows here and there the objects which lie scattered through the room: only faintly, though; for they belong to the open sunlight. As I glance at them, they each recall some task or pleasure of the coming day. A half-moulded child's head; Aphrodite; a bough of forest-leaves; music; work; homely frag-ments, in which lie the secrets of all eternal truth and beauty.

Prophetic all! Only this dumb, woful face seems to belong to and end with the night. I turn to look at it. Has the power of its desperate need commanded the darkness away? While the room is yet steeped in heavy shadow, a cool, gray light suddenly touches its head like a blessing hand, and its groping arm points through the broken cloud to the far East, where, in the flickering, nebulous crimson, God has set the promise of the Dawn.

An Inspired Lobbyist

John W. De Forest
(1826–1906)

Acertain fallen angel (politeness toward his numerous and influential friends forbids me to mention his name abruptly) lately entered into the body of Mr. Ananias Pullwool, of Washington, D.C.

As the said body was a capacious one, having been greatly enlarged circumferentially since it acquired its full longitude, there was accommodation in it for both the soul of Pullwool himself (it was a very little one) and for his distinguished visitant. Indeed, there was so much room in it that they never crowded each other, and that Pullwool hardly knew, if he even so much as mistrusted, that there was a chap in with him. But other people must have been aware of this double tenantry, or at least must have been shrewdly suspicious of it, for it soon became quite common to hear fellows say, "Pullwool has got the Devil in him."

There was, indeed, a remarkable change—a change not so much moral as physical and mental—in this gentleman's ways of deporting and behaving himself. From being logy in movement and slow if not absolutely dull in mind, he became wonderfully agile and energetic. He had been a lobbyist, and he remained a lobbyist still, but such a different one, so much more vigorous, eager, clever, and impudent, that his best friends (if he could be said to have any friends) scarcely knew him for the same Pullwool. His fat fingers were in the buttonholes of congressmen from the time when they put those buttonholes on in the morning to the time when they took them off at night. He seemed to be at one and the same moment treating some honorable member in the bar-room of the Arlington, and running another honorable member to cover in the committee-rooms of the Capitol. He log-rolled bills which nobody else believed could be log-rolled, and he pocketed fees which absolutely and point-blank refused to go into other people's pockets. During this short period of his life he was the most successful and famous lobbyist in Washington, and the most sought after by the most rascally and desperate claimants of unlawful millions.

But, like many another man who has the Devil in him, Mr. Pullwool ran his luck until he ran himself into trouble. An investigating committee pounced upon him; he was put in confinement for refusing to answer questions; his filchings were held up to the execration of the envious both by virtuous members and a virtuous press; and when he at last got out of durance he found it good to quit the District of Columbia for a season. Thus it happened that Mr. Pullwool and his eminent lodger took the cars and went to and fro upon the earth seeking what they might devour.

In the course of their travels they arrived in a little State, which may have been Rhode Island, or may have been Connecticut, or may have been one of the Pleiades, but which at all events had two capitals. Without regard to Morse's Gazetteer, or to whatever other Gazetteer may now be in currency, we shall affirm that one of these capitals was called Slowburg and the other Fastburg. For some hundreds of years (let us say five hundred, in order to be sure and get it high enough) Slowburg and Fastburg had shared between them, turn and turn about, year on and year off, all the gubernatorial and legislative pomps and emoluments that the said State had to bestow. On the 1st of April of every odd year, the governor, preceded by citizen soldiers, straddling or curvetting through the mud—the governor, followed by twenty barouches full of eminent citizens, who were not known to be eminent at any other time, but who made a rush for a ride on this occasion as certain old ladies do at funerals—the governor, taking off his hat to pavements full of citizens of all ages, sizes, and colors, who did not pretend to be eminent—the governor, catching a fresh cold at every corner, and wishing the whole thing were passing at the equator—the governor triumphally entered Slowburg—observe, Slowburg—read his always enormously long message there, and convened the legislature there. On the 1st of April of every even year the same governor, or a better one who had succeeded him, went through the same ceremonies in Fastburg. Each of these capitals boasted, or rather blushed over, a shabby old barn of a State-House, and each of them maintained a company of foot-guards, and ditto of horse-guards, the latter very loose in their saddles. In each the hotels and boarding-houses had a full year and a lean year, according as the legislature sat in the one or in the other. In each there was a loud call for fresh shad and stewed oysters, or a comparatively feeble call for fresh shad and stewed oysters, under the same biennial conditions.

Such was the oscillation of grandeur and power between the two cities. It was an old-time arrangement, and like many other old-fashioned things, as for instance wood fires in open fireplaces, it had not only its substantial merits but its superficial inconveniences. Every year certain ancient officials were obliged to pack up hundreds of public documents and expedite them from Fastburg to Slowburg, or from Slowburg back to Fastburg. Every year there

was an expense of a few dollars on this account, which the State
treasurer figured up with agonies of terror, and which the opposition roared at as if the administration could have helped it. The
State-Houses were two mere deformities of patched plaster and
leprous whitewash; they were such shapeless, graceless, dilapidated
wigwams, that no sensitive patriot could look at them without
wanting to fly to the uttermost parts of the earth; and yet it was
not possible to build new ones, and hardly possible to obtain appropriations enough to shingle out the weather; for Fastburg
would vote no money to adorn Slowburg, and Slowburg was
equally niggardly towards Fastburg. The same jealousy produced
the same frugality in the management of other public institutions,
so that the patients of the lunatic asylum were not much better
lodged and fed than the average sane citizen, and the gallows-birds
in the State's prison were brought down to a temperance which
caused admirers of that species of fowl to tremble with indignation. In short, the two capitals were as much at odds as the two
poles of a magnet, and the results of this repulsion were not all of
them worthy of hysterical admiration.

But advantages seesawed with disadvantages. In this double-
ender of a State, political jobbery was at fault, because it had no
headquarters. It could not get together a ring; it could not raise a
corps of lobbyists. Such few axe-grinders as there were had to
dodge back and forth between the Fastburg grindstone and the
Slowburg grindstone, without ever fairly getting their tools sharpened. Legislature here and legislature there; it was like guessing at
a pea between two thimbles; you could hardly ever put your finger on the right one. Then what one capital favored the other dis-
favored; and between them appropriations were kicked and hustled
under the table; the grandest of railroad schemes shrunk into
waste-paper baskets; in short, the public treasury was next door to
the unapproachable. Such, indeed, was the desperate condition of

lobbyists in this State, that, had it contained a single philanthropist of the advanced radical stripe, he would surely have brought in a bill for their relief and encouragement.

Into the midst of this happily divided community dropped Mr. Ananias Pullwool with the Devil in him. It remains to be seen whether this pair could figure up anything worth pocketing out of the problem of two capitals.

It was one of the even years, and the legislature met in Fastburg, and the little city was brimful. Mr. Pullwool with difficulty found a place for himself without causing the population to slop over. Of course he went to a hotel, for he needed to make as many acquaintances as possible, and he knew that a bar was a perfect hothouse for ripening such friendships as he cared for. He took the best room he could get; and as soon as chance favored, he took a better one, with parlor attached; and on the sideboard in the parlor he always had cigars and decanters. The result was that in a week or so he was on jovial terms with several senators, numerous members of the lower house, and all the members of the "third house." But lobbying did not work in Fastburg as Mr. Pullwool had found it to work in other capitals. He exhibited the most dazzling double-edged axes, but nobody would grind them; he pointed out the most attractive and convenient of logs for rolling, but nobody would put a lever to them.

"What the doose does this mean?" he at last inquired of Mr. Josiah Dicker, a member who had smoked dozens of his cigars and drunk quarts out of his decanters. "I don't understand this little old legislature at all, Mr. Dicker. Nobody wants to make any money; at least, nobody has the spirit to try to make any. And yet the State is full; never been bled a drop; full as a tick. What does it mean?"

Mr. Dicker looked disconsolate. Perhaps it may be worth a moment's time to explain that he could not well look otherwise. Broken in fortune and broken in health, he was a failure and knew it. His large forehead showed power, and he was in fact a lawyer of some ability; and still he could not support his family, could not keep a mould of mortgages from creeping all over his house-lot, and had so many creditors that he could not walk the streets comfortably. The trouble lay in hard drinking, with its resultant waste of time, infidelity to trust, and impatience of application. Thin, haggard, duskily pallid, deeply wrinkled at forty, his black eyes watery and set in baggy circles of a dull brown, his lean dark hands shaky and dirty, his linen wrinkled and buttonless, his clothing frayed and unbrushed, he was an impersonation of failure. He had gone into the legislature with a desperate hope of somehow finding money in it, and as yet he had discovered nothing more than his beggarly three dollars a day, and he felt himself more than ever a failure. No wonder that he wore an air of profound depression, approaching to absolute wretchedness and threatening suicide.

He looked the more cast down by contrast with the successful Mr. Pullwool, gaudily alight with satin and jewelry, and shining with conceit. Pullwool, by the way, although a dandy (that is, such a dandy as one sees in gambling-saloons and behind liquor-bars), was far from being a thing of beauty. He was so obnoxiously gross and shapeless, that it seemed as if he did it on purpose and to be irritating. His fat head was big enough to make a dwarf of, hunchback and all. His mottled cheeks were vast and pendulous to that degree that they inspired the imaginative beholder with terror, as reminding him of avalanches and landslides which might slip their hold at the slightest shock, and plunge downward in a path of destruction. One puffy eyelid drooped in a sinister way; obviously that was the eye that the Devil had selected for his own; he kept it well curtained for purposes of concealment. Looking out of this peep-hole, the Satanic badger could see a short, thick nose, and by leaning forward a little, he could get a glimpse of a broad chin of several stories. Another unpleasing feature was a full set of false

teeth, which grinned in a ravenous fashion that was truly disqui-
eting, as if they were capable of devouring the whole internal revenue. Finally, this continent of a physiognomy was diversified by a
gigantic hairy wart, which sprouted defiantly from the temple
nearest the game eye, as though Lucifer had accidentally poked
one of his horns through. Mr. Dicker, who was a sensitive, squeam-
ish man (as drunkards sometimes are, through bad digestion and
shaky nerves), could hardly endure the sight of this wart, and always wanted to ask Pullwool why he didn't cut it off.

'What's the meaning of it all?" persisted the Washington wire-
puller with bland superiority, much as the city mouse may have
surveyed the country mouse.

"Two capitals," responded Dicker, withdrawing his nervous
glance from the wart, and locking his hands over one knee to quiet
their trembling.

Mr. Pullwool, having the Old Harry in him, and being consequently full of all malice and subtlety, perceived at once the full
scope and force of the explanation.

"I see," he said, dropping gently back into his arm-chair, with
the plethoric, soft movement of a subsiding pillow. The puckers of
his cumbrous eyelids drew a little closer together; his bilious eyes
peered out cautiously between them, like sallow assassins watching
through curtained windows; for a minute or so he kept up what
might without hyperbole be called a devil of a thinking.

"I've got it," he broke out at last. "Dicker, I want you to bring
in a bill to make Fastburg the only capital."

"What is the use?" asked the legislator, looking more disconsolate, more hopeless than ever. "Slowburg will oppose it and
beat it."

"Never you mind," persisted Mr. Pullwool. "You bring in your
little bill and stand up for it like a man. There's money in it. You
don't see it? Well, I do; I'm used to seeing money in things; and in

this case I see it plain. As sure as whiskey is whiskey, there's money in it."

Mr. Pullwool's usually dull and, so to speak, extinct countenance was fairly alight and flame with exultation. It was almost a wonder that his tallowy person did not gutter beneath the blaze, like an over-fat candle under the flaring of a wick too large for it.

"Well, I'll bring in the bill," agreed Mr. Dicker, catching the enthusiasm of his counsellor and shaking off his lethargy. He perceived a dim promise of fees, and at the sight his load of despondency dropped away from him, as Christian's burden loosened in presence of the cross. He looked a little like the confident, resolute Tom Dicker, who twenty years before had graduated from college, the brightest, bravest, most eloquent fellow in his class, and the one who seemed to have before him the finest future.

"Snacks!" said Mr. Pullwool.

At this brazen word Mr. Dicker's countenance fell again; he was ashamed to talk so frankly about plundering his fellow-citizens; "a little grain of conscience turned him sour."

"I will take pay for whatever I can do as a lawyer," he stammered.

"Get out!" laughed the Satanic one. "You just take all there is a going! You need it bad enough. I know when a man's hard up. I know the signs. I've been as bad off as you; had to look all ways for five dollars; had to play second fiddle and say thanky. But what I offer you ain't a second fiddle. It's as good a chance as my own. Even divides. One half to you, and one half to me. You know the people and I know the ropes. It's a fair bargain. What do you say?"

Mr. Dicker thought of his decayed practice and his unpaid bills; and, flipping overboard his little grain of conscience, he said, "Snacks."

"All right," grinned Pullwool, his teeth gleaming alarmingly. "Word of a gentleman," he added, extending his pulpy hand,

loaded with ostentatious rings, and grasping Dicker's recoiling fingers. "Harness up your little bill as quick as you can and drive it
like Jehu. Fastburg to be the only capital. Slowburg no claims at all,
historical, geographical, or economic. The old arrangement a
humbug; as inconvenient as a fifth wheel of a coach; costs the State
thousand of greenbacks every year. Figure it all up statistically and
dab it over with your shiniest rhetoric and make a big thing of it
every way. That's what you've got to do; that's your little biz. I'll
tend to the rest."

"I don't quite see where the money is to come from," observed
Mr. Dicker.

"Leave that to me," said the veteran of the lobbies; "my name
is Pullwool and I know how to pull the wool over men's eyes, and
then I know how to get at their britches-pockets. You bring in
your bill and make your speech. Will you do it?"

"Yes," answered Dicker, bolting all scruples in another half-
tumbler of brandy.

He kept his word. As promptly as parliamentary forms and
mysteries would allow, there was a bill under the astonished noses
of honorable lawgivers, removing the seat of legislation from
Slowburg and centering it in Fastburg. This bill Mr. Thomas
Dicker supported with that fluency and fiery enthusiasm of oratory which had for a time enabled him to show as the foremost
man of his State. Great was the excitement, great the rejoicing and
anger. The press of Fastburg sent forth shrieks of exultation, and
the press of Slowburg responded with growlings of disgust. The
two capitals and the two geographical sections which they represented were ready to fire Parrot guns at each other, without regard
to life and property in the adjoining regions of the earth. If there
was a citizen of the little Commonwealth who did not hear of this
bill and did not talk of it, it was because that citizen was as deaf as
a post and as dumb as an oyster. Ordinary political distinctions

were forgotten, and the old party-whips could not manage their
very wheel-horses, who went snorting and kicking over the traces
in all directions. In short, both in the legislature and out of it, nothing was thought of but the question of the removal of the capital.

Among the loudest of the agitators was Mr. Pullwool; not that
he cared one straw whether the capital went to Fastburg, or to
Slowburg, or to Ballyhack; but for the money which he thought
he saw in the agitation he did care mightily, and to get that money
he labored with a zeal which was not of this world alone. At the
table of his hotel and in the bar-room of the same institution and
in the lobbies of the legislative hall and in editorial sanctums and
barbers' shops and all other nooks of gossip, he trumpeted the
claims of Fastburg as if that little city were the New Jerusalem and
deserved to be the metropolis of the sidereal universe. All sorts of
trickeries, too; he sent spurious telegrams and got fictitious items
into the newspapers; he lied through every medium known to the
highest civilization. Great surely was his success, for the row which
he raised was tremendous. But a row alone was not enough; it was
the mere breeze upon the surface of the waters; the treasure-ship
below was still to be drawn up and gutted.

"It will cost money," he whispered confidentially to capitalists
and land-owners. "We must have the sinews of war, or we can't
carry it on. There's your city lots goin' to double in value, if this
bill goes through. What per cent will you pay on the advance?
That's the question. Put your hands in your pockets and pull 'em
out full, and put back ten times as much. It's a sure investment;
warranted to yield a hundred per cent; the safest and biggest thing
agoing."

Capitalists and land-owners and merchants harkened and believed and subscribed. The slyest old hunks in Fastburg put a flat-
tering fore-finger into his long pocket-book, touched a greenback
which had been laid away there as neatly as a corpse in its coffin,

and resurrected it for the use of Mr. Pullwool. By tens, by twenties, by fifties, and by hundreds the dollars of the ambitious citizens of the little metropolis were charmed into the porte monnaie of this rattlesnake of a lobbyist.

"I never saw a greener set," chuckled Pullwool. "By jiminy, I believe they'd shell out for a bill to make their town a seaport, if it was a hundred miles from a drop of water."

But he was not content with individual subscriptions, and conscientiously scorned himself until he had got at the city treasury.

"The corporation must pony up," he insisted, with the mayor. "This bill is just shaking in the wind for lack of money. Fastburg must come down with the dust. You ought to see to it. What are you chief magistrate for? Ain't it to tend to the welfare of the city? Look here, now; you call the common council together; secret session, you understand. You call 'em together and let me talk to 'em. I want to make the loons comprehend that it's their duty to vote something handsome for this measure."

The mayor hummed and hawed one way, and then he hawed and hummed the other way, and the result was that he granted the request. There was a secret session in the council-room, with his honor at the top of the long, green table, with a row of more or less respectable functionaries on either side of it, and with Mr. Pullwool and the Devil at the bottom. Of course, it is not to be supposed that this last-named personage was visible to the others, or that they had more than a vague suspicion of his presence. Had he fully revealed himself, had he plainly exhibited his horns and hoofs, or even so much as uncorked his perfume-bottle of brimstone, it is more than probable that the city authorities would have been exceedingly scandalized, and they might have adjourned the session. As it was, seeing nothing more disagreeable than the obese form of the lobbyist, they listened calmly while he unfolded his project.

Mr. Pullwool spoke at length, and to Fastburg ears eloquently, Fastburg must be the sole capital; it had every claim, historical and geographical, and commercial, to that distinction; it ought, could, would, and should be the sole capital; that was about the substance of his exordium.

"But, gentlemen, it will cost," he went on. "There is an unscrupulous and furious opposition to the measure. The other side—those fellows from Slowburg and vicinity—are putting their hands into their britches-pockets. You must put your hands into yours. The thing will be worth millions to Fastburg. But it will cost thousands. Are you ready to fork over? *Are* you ready?"

"What's the figure?" asked one of the councilmen. "What do you estimate?"

"Gentlemen, I shall astonish *some* of you," answered Mr. Pullwool, cunningly. It was well put; it was as much as to say, "I shall astonish the green ones; of course, the really strong heads among you won't be in the least bothered." "I estimate," he continued, "that the city treasury will have to put up a good round sum, say a hundred thousand dollars, be it more or less."

A murmur of surprise, of chagrin, and of something like indignation ran along the line of official mustaches. "Nonsense," "The dickens," "Can't be done," "We can't think of it," broke out several councilmen, in a distinctly unparliamentary manner.

"Gentlemen, one moment," pleaded Pullwool, passing his greasy smile around the company, as though it were some kind of refreshment. "Look at the whole job; it's a big job. We must have lawyers; we must have newspapers in all parts of the State; we must have writers to work up the historical claims of the city; we must have fellows to buttonhole honorable members; we must have fees for honorable members themselves. How can you do it for less?"

Then he showed a schedule; so much to this wire-puller and that and the other; so much apiece to so many able editors; so much for eminent legal counsel; finally, a trifle for himself. And one hundred thousand dollars or thereabouts was what the schedule footed up, turn it whichever way you would.

Of course, this common council of Fastburg did not dare to vote such a sum for such a purpose. Mr. Pullwool had not expected that it would; all that he had hoped for was the half of it; but that half he got.

"Did they do it?" breathlessly inquired Tom Dicker of him, when he returned to the hotel.

"They done it," calmly, yet triumphantly, responded Mr. Pullwool.

"Thunder!" exclaimed the amazed Dicker. "You are the most extraordinary man! You must have the very Devil in you!"

Instead of being startled by this alarming supposition, Mr. Pullwool looked gratified. People thus possessed generally do look gratified when the possession is alluded to.

But the inspired lobbyist did not pass his time in wearing an aspect of satisfaction. When there was money to get and to spend he could run his fat off almost as fast as if he were pouring it into candle-moulds. The ring—the famous capital ring of Fastburg—must be seen to, its fingers greased, and its energy quickened. Before he rolled his apple-dumpling of a figure into bed that night, he had interviewed Smith and Brown the editors, Jones and Robinson the lawyers, Smooth and Slow the literary characters, various lobbyists and various lawgivers.

"Work, gentlemen, and capitalize Fastburg and get your dividends, was his inspiring message to one and all. He promised Smith and Brown ten dollars for every editorial, and five dollars for every hum-bugging telegram, and two dollars for every telling item. Jones and Robinson were to have five hundred dollars apiece for concurrent legal statements of the claim of the city; Smooth and Slow, as being merely authors and so not accustomed to obtain much for their labor, got a hundred dollars between them for working up the case historically. To the lobbyists and members Pullwool was munificent; it seemed as if those gentlemen could not be paid enough for their "influence"; as if they alone had that kind of time which is money. Only, while dealing liberally with them, the inspired one did not forget himself. A thousand for Mr. Sly; yes, Mr. Sly was to receipt for a thousand; but he must let half of it stick to the Pullwool fingers. The same arrangement was made with Mr. Green and Mr. Sharp and Mr. Bummer and Mr. Pickpurse and Mr. Buncombe. It was a game of snacks, half to you and half to me; and sometimes it was more than snacks—a thousand for you two and a thousand for me too.

With such a greasing of the wheels, you may imagine that the machinery of the ring worked to a charm. In the city and in the legislature and throughout the State there was the liveliest buzzing and humming and clicking of political wheels and cranks and cogs that had ever been known in those hitherto pastoral localities. The case of Fastburg against Slowburg was put in a hundred ways and proved as sure as it was put. It really seemed to the eager burghers as if they already heard the clink of hammers on a new State-House and beheld a perpetual legislature sitting on their fences and curbstones until the edifice should be finished. The great wire-puller and his gang of stipendiaries were the objects of popular gratitude and adoration. The landlord of the hotel which Mr. Pullwool patronized actually would not take pay for that gentleman's board.

"No, sir!" declared this simple Boniface, turning crimson with enthusiasm. "You are going to put thousands of dollars into my purse, and I'll take nothing out of yours. And any little thing in the way of cigars and whiskey that you want, sir, why, call for it. It's my treat, sir."

"Thank you, sir," kindly smiled the great man. "That's what I call the square thing. Mr. Boniface, you are a gentleman and a scholar; and I'll mention your admirable house to my friends. By the way, I shall have to leave you for a few days."

"Going to leave us!" exclaimed Mr. Boniface, aghast. "I hope not till this job is put through."

"I must run about a bit," muttered Pullwool, confidentially. "A little turn through the State, you understand, to stir up the country districts. Some of the members ain't as hot as they should be, and I want to set their constituents after them. Nothing like getting on a few deputations."

"O, exactly!" chuckled Mr. Boniface, ramming his hands into his pockets and cheerfully jingling a bunch of keys and a penknife, for lack of silver. It was strange indeed that he should actually see the Devil in Mr. Pullwool's eye and should not have a suspicion that he was in danger of being humbugged by him. "And your rooms?" he suggested. "How about them?"

"I keep them," replied the lobbyist, grandly, as if blaspheming the expense—to Boniface. "Our friends must have a little hole to meet in. And while you are about it, Mr. Boniface, see that they get something to drink and smoke; and we'll settle it between us."

"Pre-cisely!" laughed the landlord, as much as to say, "My treat!"

And so Mr. Pullwool, that Pericles and Lorenzo de' Medici rolled in one, departed for a season from the city which he ruled and blessed. Did he run about the State and preach and crusade in behalf of Fastburg, and stir up the bucolic populations to stir up their representatives in its favor? Not a bit of it; the place that he went to and the only place that he went to was Slowburg; yes, covering up his tracks in his usual careful style, he made direct for the rival of Fastburg. What did he propose to do there? O, how can we reveal the whole duplicity and turpitude of Ananias Pullwool? The subject is too vast for a merely human pen; it requires the literary ability of a recording angel. Well, we must get our feeble lever under this boulder of wickedness as we can, and do our faint best to expose all the reptiles and slimy things beneath it.

The first person whom this apostle of lobbyism called upon in Slowburg was the mayor of that tottering capital.

"My name is Pullwool," he said to the official, and he said it with an almost enviable ease of impudence, for he was used to introducing himself to people who despised and detested him. "I want to see you confidentially about this capital ring which is making so much trouble."

"I thought you were in it," replied the mayor, turning very red in the face, for he had heard of Mr. Pullwool as the leader of said ring; and being an iracund man, he was ready to knock his head off.

"In it!" exclaimed the possessed one. "I wish I was. It's a fat thing. More than fifty thousand dollars paid out already!"

"Good gracious!" exclaimed the mayor, in despair.

"By the way, this is between ourselves," added Pullwool. "You take it so, I hope. Word of honor, eh?"

"Why, if you have anything to communicate that will help us, why, of course I promise secrecy," stammered the mayor. "Yes, certainly; word of honor."

"Well, I've been looking about among those fellows a little," continued Ananias. "I've kept my eyes and ears open. It's a way I have. And I've learned a thing or two that it will be to your advantage to know. Yes, sir! fifty thousand dollars!—the city has voted it and paid it, and the ring has got it. That's why they are all working so. And depend upon it, they'll carry the legislature and turn Slowburg out to grass, unless you wake up and do something."

"By heavens!" exclaimed the iracund mayor, turning red again. "It's a piece of confounded rascality. It ought to be exposed."

"No, don't expose it," put in Mr. Pullwool, somewhat alarmed. "That game never works. Of course they'd deny it and swear you down, for bribing witnesses is as easy as bribing members. I'll tell you what to do. Beat them at their own weapons. Raise a purse that will swamp theirs. That's the way the world goes. It's an auction. The highest bidder gets the article."

Well, the result of it all was that the city magnates of Slowburg did just what had been done by the city magnates of Fastburg, only, instead of voting fifty thousand dollars into the pockets of the ring, they voted sixty thousand. With a portion of this money about him, and with authority to draw for the rest on proper vouchers, Mr. Pullwool, his tongue in his cheek, bade farewell to his new allies. As a further proof of the ready wit and solid impudence of this sublime politician and model of American statesmen, let me here introduce a brief anecdote. Leaving Slowburg by the cars, he encountered a gentleman from Fastburg, who saluted him with tokens of amazement, and said, "What are you doing here, Mr. Pullwool?"

"O, just breaking up those fellows a little," whispered the man with the Devil in him. "They were making too strong a fight. I had to *see* some of them," putting one hand behind his back and rubbing his fingers together, to signify that there had been a taking of bribes. "But be shady about it. For the sake of the good cause, keep quiet. Mum's the word."

The reader can imagine how briskly the fight between the two capitals re-opened when Mr. Pullwool re-entered the lobby. Slowburg now had its adherents, and they struggled like men who saw money in their warfare, and they struggled not in vain. To cut a very long story very short, to sum the whole of an exciting drama in one sentence, the legislature kicked overboard the bill to make Fastburg the sole seat of government. Nothing had come of the whole row, except that the pair of simple little cities had spent over one hundred thousand dollars, and that the capital ring, fighting on both sides and drawing pay from both sides, had lined its pockets, while the great creator of the ring had crammed his to bursting.

"What does this mean, Mr. Pullwool?" demanded the partially honest and entirely puzzled Tom Dicker, when he had discovered by an unofficial count of noses how things were going. "Fastburg has spent all its money for nothing. It won't be sole capital after all."

"I never expected it would be," replied Pullwool, so tickled by the Devil that was in him that he could not help laughing. "I never wanted it to be. Why, it would spoil the little game. This is a trick that can be played every year."

"Oh!!" exclaimed Mr. Dicker, and was dumb with astonishment for a minute.

"Didn't you see through it before?" grinned the grand master of all guile and subtlety.

"I did not," confessed Mr. Dicker, with a mixture of shame and abhorrence. "Well," he presently added, recovering himself, "shall we settle?"

"O, certainly, if you are ready," smiled Pullwool, with the air of a man who has something coming to him.

"And what, exactly, will be my share?" asked Dicker, humbly.

"What do you mean?" stared Pullwool, apparently in the extremity of amazement.

"You said *snacks,* didn't you?" urged Dicker, trembling violently.

"Well, *snacks* it is," replied Pullwool. "Haven't you had a thousand?"

"Yes," admitted Dicker.

"Then you owe me five hundred?"

Mr. Dicker did not faint, though he came very near it, but he staggered out of the room as white as a sheet, for he was utterly crushed by this diabolical impudence.

That very day Mr. Pullwool left for Washington, and the Devil left for *his* place, each of them sure to find the other when he wanted him, if indeed their roads lay apart.

John's Trial

Philander Deming
(1829–1915)

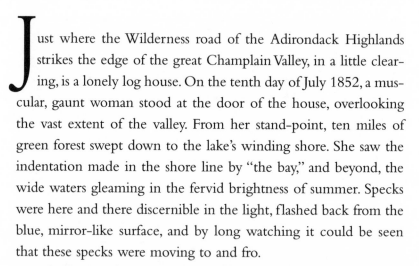

J ust where the Wilderness road of the Adirondack Highlands strikes the edge of the great Champlain Valley, in a little clearing, is a lonely log house. On the tenth day of July 1852, a muscular, gaunt woman stood at the door of the house, overlooking the vast extent of the valley. From her stand-point, ten miles of green forest swept down to the lake's winding shore. She saw the indentation made in the shore line by "the bay," and beyond, the wide waters gleaming in the fervid brightness of summer. Specks were here and there discernible in the light, flashed back from the blue, mirror-like surface, and by long watching it could be seen that these specks were moving to and fro.

The woman knew that these distant moving atoms were boats freighting lumber through Lake Champlain. She knew there was but one boat that would be likely to turn aside, and come into the little bay, and that this boat would be her son John's sloop.

That was why she watched so anxiously a speck that neared the bay, and at length entered it. To make doubly sure, she brought to bear an old spyglass, whose principal lens was cracked entirely through. It gave her a smoky view of the famous sloop, "The Dolly Ann," John's property; and then she was entirely certain that her son, who had been three weeks absent on his voyage, was coming home.

Jupiter the house-dog, who had been watching her, seemed to know it too, perfectly well; for, as she turned from her survey through the glass, his canine nature developed a degree of wriggling friskiness of which the grave old dog seemed half ashamed. He whined, and walked about the door-yard for a few moments, then gave his mistress a long, steady look, and, seeming satisfied with what he read in her face, jumped over the fence, and started down the road into the valley, at a full-run.

The woman knew that three or four hours must yet elapse before John and Jupiter would come along the path together, tired by their long tramp up the mountain-side. She thought and waited, as lonely mothers think and wait for absent sons.

At about four o'clock a young, dark-eyed man and the dog came up the road and to the house. "Heigho, mother, all well?" was the man's greeting. The woman's greeting was only, "How do you do, John?" There was no show of sentiment, not even a handshake; but a bright look in the man's face, and a tremor in the voice of the woman, conveyed the impression that these plain people felt a great deal more than they expressed.

Two hours passed away; and, after supper, the neighbors, who had seen John and the dog come up the road, dropped in for a talk with "the captain," as John was called by his friends.

Soon the inquiry was made, "Where did you leave your cousin William?"

John had taken his cousin William, who lived upon the lake-shore, with him upon this last trip, and hence the question.

But John did not answer the question directly. He seemed troubled and unhappy about it. He finally acknowledged that he and William had not agreed, and that high words and blows had passed between them, and added that his cousin had finally left the boat, and had gone away in a huff, he knew not where, but somewhere into the pineries of Canada. He declared, getting warm in his recollection of the quarrel, that he "didn't care a darn" where Will went, anyway.

A month passed away: it was August. Cousin Will did not return. But certain strange stories came up the lake from Canada, and reached the dwellers along the Adirondack Wilderness road. No cousin William had been seen in the pineries; but just across the Canada line, at the mouth of Fish River, where the sloops were moored to receive their lading of lumber, a bruised, swollen, festering corpse had risen, and floated in the glare of a hot, August day. The boatmen rescued it, and buried it upon the shore. They described it as the body of a hale, vigorous young man, agreeing in height, size, and appearance with cousin William.

And there was another story told by the captain of a sloop which had been moored at the mouth of Fish River, near by John's sloop, on the fatal voyage from which cousin William had not returned.

The captain said, that, upon the 4th of July, he had heard quarrelling upon John's sloop all the afternoon, and had noticed that only two men were there. He thought the men had been drinking. At nightfall there was a little lull; but soon after dark the noise broke out again. He could see nothing through the gloom; but he heard high and angry words, and at length blows, and then a dull, crushing thud, followed by a plunge into the water; and then there was entire silence. He listened for an hour, in the stillness of the summer night, but heard no further sound from the boat. In the early gray of the next morning, the captain, looking across the intervening space to John's sloop, which he described as hardly a stone's-throw from his own, saw a hat lying upon the deck, and, using his glass, was confident that he saw "spatters of blood." He thought it "none of his business," and, taking advantage of a light breeze, sailed away, and said nothing. But, when the floating corpse was found, he felt sure there had been a murder, and, as he expressed it, felt bound to tell his story like an honest man, and so told it.

Putting these things together, it soon grew to be the current opinion upon the lake, that Capt. John had murdered his cousin William. The dwellers upon the Wilderness road also came, by slow degrees, and unwillingly, to the same conclusion. It was felt and said that John ought to be arrested.

Accordingly, on a dreary day in November, two officers from the county town, twenty miles away down the lake-shore, came and climbed the steep road to the lonely log house, and arrested John. It was undoubtedly a dreadful blow to those two lonely people living isolated in the wilderness. Perhaps there ought to have been some crying and a scene; but there was no such thing. The officers testified that neither John nor his mother made any fuss about it. There was a slight twitching of the strong muscles of her face as she talked with the officers, but no other outward sign.

John gave more evidence of the wound he felt. He was white and quivering; yet he silently, and without objection, made ready to go with the officers. He was soon prepared, and they started. John, as he went out of the door, turned and said, "Good-by: it will all be made right, mother." She simply answered, "Yes, good-by: I know it, my son."

The trio went on foot down the road to the next house, where the officers had left their team. Jupiter, standing up with his fore-paws upon the top of the fence, gazed wistfully after them. When they passed around the bend of the road, out of sight, Jupiter went into the house. The strong woman was there about her work, as usual; but the heavy tears would now and then fall upon the hard pine floor. She knew that her own boy would spend the coming night in the county jail.

At twelve o'clock of that chill November night, the woman and the dog went out of the house: she fastened the door, and then they went together down the dark mountain-road, while the autumn winds swept dismally through the great wilderness, and the midnight voice of the pines mourned the dying year. The next day, at noon, a very weary woman on foot, with a small bundle and a large dog, put up at the little village hotel hard by the county jail.

Another day passed, and then the preliminary examination came on before a justice, to determine whether there was sufficient evidence to hold John in custody until a grand jury of the county should be assembled for the next Court of Oyer and Terminer.

Three days were spent in this examination before the justice; the captain of the sloop who had overheard the quarrel in the night told his story, and the boatmen who had found the body told theirs. Two men who had been the crew of John's little vessel were also called; but they could tell little more than that they were absent on shore upon the 4th of July, and, when they returned to the vessel, William had gone, they knew not where nor why.

The evidence against John seemed to the magistrate clear and conclusive. But the counsel for the accused (employed by John's mother) took the ground, that, as the offence was committed in Canada, a justice in the United States had no jurisdiction in the matter.

This view prevailed, and after five days the accused was set at liberty. But that voice of the people, which the ancient proverb says is like the voice of God, had decided that John was guilty. It was under this crushing condemnation that John and his mother left the county town on a cold December day, turning their steps homeward; and at evening they climbed the acclivity so familiar to them, and reached the lonely log house upon the mountain. Their neighbors were glad to see them back again, but were plain to say that "it appeared like as if John was guilty." These dwellers in the solitudes were accustomed to speak truly what they thought. John and his mother, too, spoke openly of this matter. It was only of showing affection and love that these people were ashamed and shy. They both admitted to their neighbors that the evidence was very strong; but John added quietly that he was not guilty, as if that settled the whole matter.

But the voice of the people, and a sense of justice, would not let this crime rest. It came to be very generally known that a man guilty of murder was living near the shore of Lake Champlain unmolested. Arrangements were effected by which it came to pass that the Canadian authorities made a formal application to the United States for the delivery of one John Wilson, believed to be guilty of the murder of his cousin William Wilson.

And so again two officers, this time United States officials, climbed up to the little log house upon the edge of the great valley. Through a drifting, blinding storm of snow they were piloted by a neighbor to the lonely house. They made known their errand; and, in the course of half an hour, the officers and their prisoner were out in the storm *en route* for the distant city of Montreal.

It was many days before the woman saw her son again. For four months John was imprisoned, awaiting his trial before the Canadian courts. Doubtless those four months seemed long to the solitary woman. She had not much opportunity to indulge in melancholy fancies: she spent much of her time in pulling brush and wood out of the snow, and breaking it up with an axe, so as to adapt it to the size of her stove.

The neighbors tried to be kind, and often took commissions from her to the store and the gristmill in the valley. "But after all," said Pete Searles, one of John's friends, in speaking of the matter afterward, "what could neighbors amount to, when the nearest of

them lived a mile away, and all of them were plain to say that they
believed she was the mother of a murderer?"

But the neighbors said the woman did not seem to mind the
solitude and the rough work. Morning, noon, and night she was
out in the snow or the storm at the little hovel of a barn back of
the house, taking care of two cows and a few sheep which were
hers and John's. At other times travellers upon the Wilderness road
would see her gaunt, angular figure clambering down a rocky
ridge, dragging poles to the house to be cut up for fuel.

She received two letters from John in the course of the winter. The first told her that he was imprisoned, and awaiting his trial
in Montreal; and the next one said that this trial had been set down
for an early day in March.

This correspondence was all the information the mother had
of her son; for the lake was frozen during the winter, so that the
boats did not run, and no news could come from Canada by the
boatmen.

When March came and passed away without intelligence from
John, it was taken by the dwellers upon the lake-shore and along
the Wilderness road as a sure indication that he had been convicted
of the crime. A letter or newspaper announcing the fact was con-
fidently looked for by the neighbors whenever they went to the
distant post-office for their weekly mail.

As March went out, and spring days and sunshine came, it was
noticed that the face of John's mother looked sharp and white; but
she went about the same daily duties as before, without seeming to
feel ill or weak.

On a plashy April day full of sunshine, she stood on the rocky
ridge back of the house, looking down upon the lake. A few early
birds had come back, and were twittering about the clearing. Although the snow still lingered in patches upon the highlands, the
valley looked warm below, and the first boats of the season were

dotting the wide, distant mirror of "old Champlain." A man came slowly up the muddy line of road, through the gate, and around the house; then first the woman saw him. A slight spasm passed over her face. There was a little pitiful quiver of the muscles about the mouth, and then she walked slowly down the ridge to where the man stood. She struggled a little with herself before she said, "Well, John, I am glad to see you back."

John tried to be cool also; but nature was too much for him. He could not raise his eyes to hers; and his simple response, "Yes, mother," was chokingly uttered.

The two walked into the house together in the old familiar way. The woman, without a word, began to spread the table; and her son went out and prepared fuel, and, bringing it in, replenished the fire. Then he sat down in his accustomed place by the stove, with a pleasant remark about how well the fire burned, and how good it seemed to be home again. And the woman spoke a few kind, motherly words.

It was the way they had always done when John came back; but now there was a great sadness in it, for he had come *"from prison."* Jupiter seemed fully to realize the situation. He exhibited none of that friskiness which characterized the welcome he had usually given; but, when John was seated, the old dog came slowly up to him, laid his fore-paws and his head in his master's lap, and looked sadly in his face.

As they sat down to supper, John began to tell of his fare in the jail at Montreal, and to speak freely of his life there. "Will you have to go back?" said his mother, with that quiver about the mouth again. "No, mother," said John: "it is finished, and I am discharged."

After supper the story was told over, how well John's counsel had worked for him, and how the judge had said there was not sufficient evidence to convict of so great a crime.

John continued from this time on, through the spring, to live

at home. He allowed his sloop to float idly in the bay, while, as he
said, he himself rested. The truth was, he saw, as others did not, that
his mother had carried a fearful weight, and now, when it was
lifted by his return, that the resources of her life were exhausted.
The change, not yet apparent to other eyes, was clear to his vision.
So it is that these silent spirits read each other.

As the warm weather advanced, the strong woman became
weak; and, as the June flowers began to bloom, she ceased to move
about much, and sat the most of each day in a chair by the open
door. John managed the house, and talked with his mother. Her
mind changed with the relaxation of her physical frame. She no
longer strove to hide her tears, but, like a tired infant, would weep,
without restraint or concealment, as she told her son of the early
loves and romance of her girlhood life in a warm valley of the
West. He learned more of his mother's heart in those June days
than he had surmised from all he had known of her before. And
he understood what this predicted. He felt that the heart nearest
his own was counting over the treasures of life ere it surrendered
them forever.

There was no great scene when the woman died. It was at
evening, just as the July fervors were coming on. She had wept
much in the morning. As the day grew warm she became very
weak and faint, and about noon was moved by her son from her
chair to her bed, and so died as the sun went down.

John was alone in the house when she died. Since his return
from Montreal, he had been made to feel that he had but one
friend besides his mother. Only one neighbor had called upon
him, and that was Pete Searles. *He* had ever proved true. But John
did not like to trouble his one friend, who lived two miles away,
to come and stay with him during the night: so he lighted a candle, took down from a shelf a little Bible and hymn-book that he
and his mother had carried on an average about four times a year

to a schoolhouse used as a church, some six miles away; and so, alone with the dead, he spent the hours in reading and tears and meditation.

In the morning he locked the door of his home, and walked "over to Pete's." As he met his friend, he said in a clear voice, but with eyes averted, "She has gone, Pete. If you will just take the key and go over there, I'll go down to the lake, and get the things, and tell Downer, and we'll have the funeral, say on Thursday."

Pete hesitated a moment, then took the key John offered him, and said, "Yes, John: I will tell my woman, and we will go over and fix it, and be there when you come back." And so John went on his way. "Downer" was the minister, and "the things" were a coffin and a shroud.

On Thursday was the funeral. Pete took care to have all the people of the neighborhood there, although it hardly seemed as if John desired it. The popular voice, having once decided it, still held John as a murderer, and claimed that he was cleared from the charge only by the tricks of his lawyer. John knew of this decision. At the funeral he was stern, cold, white, and statue-like. While others wept, but few tears fell from his eyes; and even these seemed wrung from him by an anguish, for the most part suppressed or concealed.

He chose that his mother should be buried, not in the "burying-ground" at the settlement, but upon their own little farm where she had lived. And so, in a spot below the rocky ridge, where wild violets grew, she was laid to rest.

John spent the night following the funeral at Pete's house, then returned to his own home, and from that time his *solitary* life began. He took his cattle and his sheep over to Pete's, made all fast about his home, and resumed his boating upon Lake Champlain. He fully realized that he was a marked man. He was advised, it was said even by his own legal counsel, to leave the country, and to leave his name behind him; but no words influenced him. Firm and steady in his course, strictly temperate and just, he won respect where he could not gain confidence.

The years rolled by. Capt. John still was a boatman, and still kept his home at the lonely log house on the edge of the great valley. From each voyage he returned, and spent a day and night alone at the old place; and it was noticed that a strong, high paling was built around his mother's grave, and a marble head-stone was placed there, and other flowers grew with the wild violets. Even in winter, when there was no boating, and he boarded down by the lake, he made many visits to the old homestead. His figure, which, though youthful, was now growing gaunt and thin, as his mother's had been, was often seen by Pete at nightfall upon the top of a certain rocky ridge, standing out clear and sharp against the cold blue steel of the winter sky.

John had no companions, and sought none. The young men and women of his set had married and settled in life: he was still the same.

But there came a change. Eleven years had passed since the mother died, and it was June again. John was spending a day at the old place once more. He sat in the door, looking out on the magnificent landscape—the broad lake, and the dim line of mountains away across the valley. The lovely day seemed to cheer this stern, lonely man.

Three persons came up the road: they advanced straight to where John was sitting. One of them stepped forward, looked John steadily in the face, held out his hand to him, and said, "John, do you know me?"

The voice seemed to strike him with a sharp, stunning shock. He quivered, held his breath, stared into the eyes of the questioner, and then, suddenly becoming unnaturally cool and collected, said, "Is it you, William?"

The two who stood back had once been John's warmest friends. They now came forward, and, with such words as they could command, told the story of William's sudden return, and sought for themselves forgiveness for the cruel and false suspicion which had so long estranged them from their friend.

John seemed to hear this as one in a dream. He talked with William and the men, in a manner that seemed strangely cold and indifferent, about where William had been voyaging so long in distant seas and of his strange absence. A quarter of an hour passed away. The men proposed that John should go with them to their homes, and said there would be a gathering of friends there. They pressed the invitation with warmth, and such true feelings as our voices express when a dear friend has been greatly wronged, and we humbly acknowledge it.

John said absently, in reply, that he did not know. He looked uneasily around as if in search of something—perhaps his hat. He essayed to rise from his chair, but could not, and in a moment he fell back, ashy pale, fainting, and breathless. The men had not looked for this; but, accustomed as they were to the rough life of the wilderness, they were not alarmed. They fanned the fainting man with their straw hats, and, as soon as water could be found, applied it to his hands and face. He soon partially recovered, and, looking up, said in a broken voice, "Give me a little time, boys." At this hint the two old friends, who were now crying, stepped out of the door, and cousin William sat down out upon the door-step.

John found that a *little* time was not enough. He had travelled too long and far in that fearful desert of loneliness easily or quickly to return. A nervous fever followed the shock he received, and for two months he did not leave the homestead, and was confined to his bed. But the old house was not lonely: the men and women came, both his old friends and some new-comers, and tried to make up to him in some degree the love and sympathy he had so long missed. But for many days it was evident that their kindness pained and oppressed him.

"It appears like," said Pete, "that a rough word don't hurt him; but a kind one he can't stand." And this was true. His soul was fortified against hatred and contempt; but a kind voice, or a gentle caress, seemed to wound him so that he would sob like an infant.

As he recovered from his illness, he continued gentle, kind, and shrinking to a fault. By the operation of some spiritual law that I do not fully comprehend, he was, after his recovery, one of those who win a strange affection from others. His influence seemed like a mild fascination. It was said of him in after-years that he was more truly loved, and by more people, than any other man or woman in all the settlements round. Children loved him with a passionate attachment, and the woman of childlike nature whom he made his wife is said to have died of grief at his death. He departed this life at the age of thirty-eight years; and he sleeps on the edge of the great valley, with his mother and his wife beside him.

The Lynching of Jube Benson

Paul Laurence Dunbar

(1872–1906)

Gordon Fairfax's library held but three men, but the air was dense with clouds of smoke. The talk had drifted from one topic to another much as the smoke wreaths had puffed, floated, and thinned away. Then Handon Gay, who was an ambitious young reporter, spoke of a lynching story in a recent magazine, and the matter of punishment without trial put new life into the conversation.

"I should like to see a real lynching," said Gay rather callously.

"Well, I should hardly express it that way," said Fairfax, "but if a real, live lynching were to come my way, I should not avoid it."

"I should," spoke the other from the depths of his chair, where he had been puffing in moody silence. Judged by his hair, which was freely sprinkled with gray, the speaker might have been a man of forty-five or fifty, but his face, though lined and serious, was youthful, the face of a man hardly past thirty.

"What! you, Dr. Melville? Why, I thought that you physicians wouldn't weaken at anything."

"I have seen one such affair," said the doctor gravely; "in fact, I took a prominent part in it."

"Tell us about it," said the reporter, feeling for his pencil and note-book, which he was, nevertheless, careful to hide from the speaker.

The men drew their chairs eagerly up to the doctor's, but for a minute he did not seem to see them, but sat gazing abstractedly into the fire; then he took a long draw upon his cigar and began:

"I can see it all very vividly now. It was in the summer time and about seven years ago. I was practicing at the time down in the little town of Bradford. It was a small and primitive place, just the location for an impecunious medical man, recently out of college.

"In lieu of a regular office, I attended to business in the first of two rooms which I rented from Hiram Daly, one of the more prosperous of the townsmen. Here I boarded and here also came my patients—white and black—whites from every section, and blacks from 'nigger town,' as the west portion of the place was called.

"The people about me were most of them coarse and rough, but they were simple and generous, and as time passed on I had about abandoned my intention of seeking distinction in wider fields and determined to settle into the place of a modest country doctor. This was rather a strange conclusion for a young man to arrive at, and I will not deny that the presence in the house of my host's beautiful young daughter, Annie, had something to do with my decision. She was a girl of seventeen or eighteen, and very far superior to her surroundings. She had a native grace and a pleasing way about her that made everybody that came under her spell her abject slave. White and black who knew her loved her, and none, I thought, more deeply and respectfully than Jube Benson, the black man of all work about the place.

"He was a fellow whom everybody trusted—an apparently steady-going, grinning sort, as we used to call him. Well, he was completely under Miss Annie's thumb, and as soon as he saw that I began to care for Annie, and anybody could see that, he transferred some of his allegiance to me and became my faithful servitor also. Never did a man have a more devoted adherent in his wooing than did I, and many a one of Annie's tasks which he volunteered to do gave her an extra hour with me. You can imagine that I liked the boy, and you need not wonder any more that, as both wooing and my practice waxed apace, I was content to give up my great ambitions and stay just where I was.

"It wasn't a very pleasant thing, then, to have an epidemic of typhoid break out in the town that kept me going so that I hardly had time for the courting that a fellow wants to carry on with his sweetheart while he is still young enough to call her his girl. I fumed, but duty was duty, and I kept to my work night and day. It was now that Jube proved how invaluable he was as a coadjutor. He not only took messages to Annie, but brought sometimes little ones from her to me, and he would tell me little secret things that he had overheard her say that made me throb with joy and swear at him for repeating his mistress's conversation. But, best of all, Jube was a perfect Cerberus, and no one on earth could have been more effective in keeping away or deluding the other young fellows who visited the Dalys. He would tell me of it afterwards, chuckling softly to himself, 'An', Doctah, I say to Mistah Hemp Stevens, " 'Scuse us, Mistah Stevens, but Miss Annie, she des gone out," an' den he go outer de gate lookin' moughty lonesome. When Sam Elkins come, I say, "Sh, Mistah Elkins, Miss Annie, she done tuk down," an' he say, "What, Jube, you don' reckon hit de—" Den he stop an' look skeert, an' I say, "I feared hit is, Mistah Elkins," an' sheks my haid ez solemn. He goes outer de gate lookin' lak his bes' frien' done daid, an' all de time Miss Annie behine de cu'tain ovah de po'ch des a-laffin' fit to kill.'

"Jube was a most admirable liar, but what could I do? He knew that I was a young fool of a hypocrite, and when I would rebuke him for these deceptions, he would give way and roll on the floor in an excess of delighted laughter until from very contagion I had to join him—and, well, there was no need of my preaching when there had been no beginning to his repentance and when there must ensue a continuance of his wrong-doing.

"This thing went on for over three months, and then, pouf! I was down like a shot. My patients were nearly all up, but the reaction from overwork made me an easy victim of the lurking germs. Then Jube loomed up as a nurse. He put everyone else aside, and with the doctor, a friend of mine from a neighboring town, took entire charge of me. Even Annie herself was put aside, and I was cared for as tenderly as a baby. Tom, that was my physician and friend, told me all about it afterward with tears in his eyes. Only he was a big, blunt man, and his expressions did not convey all that he meant. He told me how Jube had nursed me as if I were a sick kitten and he my mother. Of how fiercely he guarded his right to be the sole one to 'do' for me, as he called it, and how, when the crisis came, he hovered, weeping, but hopeful, at my bedside, until it was safely passed, when they drove him, weak and exhausted, from the room. As for me, I knew little about it at the time, and cared less. I was too busy in my fight with death. To my chimerical vision there was only a black but gentle demon that came and went, alternating with a white fairy, who would insist on coming in on her head, growing larger and larger and then dissolving. But the pathos and devotion in the story lost nothing in my blunt friend's telling.

"It was during the period of a long convalescence, however, that I came to know my humble ally as he really was, devoted to the point of abjectness. There were times when, for very shame at his goodness to me, I would beg him to go away, to do something else. He would go, but before I had time to realize that I was not being ministered to, he would be back at my side, grinning and puttering just the same. He manufactured duties for the joy of performing them. He pretended to see desires in me that I never had, because he liked to pander to them, and when I became entirely exasperated, and ripped out a good round oath, he chuckled with the remark, 'Dah, now, you sholy is gittin' well. Nevah did hyeah a man anywhaih nigh Jo'dan's sho' cuss lak dat.'

"Why, I grew to love him, love him, oh, yes, I loved him as well—oh, what am I saying? All human love and gratitude are damned poor things; excuse me, gentlemen, this isn't a pleasant story. The truth is usually a nasty thing to stand.

"It was not six months after that that my friendship to Jube, which he had been at such great pains to win, was put to too severe a test.

"It was in the summer time again, and, as business was slack, I had ridden over to see my friend, Dr. Tom. I had spent a good part of the day there, and it was past four o'clock when I rode leisurely into Bradford. I was in a particularly joyous mood and no premonition of the impending catastrophe oppressed me. No sense of sorrow, present or to come, forced itself upon me, even when I saw men hurrying through the almost deserted streets. When I got within sight of my home and saw a crowd surrounding it, I was only interested sufficiently to spur my horse into a jog trot, which brought me up to the throng, when something in the sullen, settled horror in the men's faces gave me a sudden, sick thrill. They whispered a word to me, and without a thought save for Annie, the girl who had been so surely growing into my heart, I leaped from the saddle and tore my way through the people to the house.

"It was Annie, poor girl, bruised and bleeding, her face and dress torn from struggling. They were gathered round her with white faces, and oh! with what terrible patience they were trying to gain from her fluttering lips the name of her murderer. They made way for me and I knelt at her side. She was beyond my skill, and my will merged with theirs. One thought was in our minds.

" 'Who?' I asked.

"Her eyes half opened. 'That black—' She fell back into my arms dead.

"We turned and looked at each other. The mother had broken down and was weeping, but the face of the father was like iron.

" 'It is enough,' he said; 'Jube has disappeared.' He went to the door and said to the expectant crowd, 'She is dead.'

"I heard the angry roar without swelling up like the noise of a flood, and then I heard the sudden movement of many feet as the men separated into searching parties, and, laying the dead girl back upon her couch, I took my rifle and went out to join them.

"As if by intuition the knowledge had passed among the men that Jube Benson had disappeared, and he, by common consent, was to be the object of our search. Fully a dozen of the citizens had seen him hastening toward the woods and noted his skulking air, but, as he had grinned in his old good-natured way, they had, at the time, thought nothing of it. Now, however, the diabolical reason of his slyness was apparent. He had been shrewd enough to disarm suspicion, and by now was far away. Even Mrs. Daly, who was visiting with a neighbor, had seen him stepping out by a back way, and had said with a laugh, 'I reckon that black rascal's a-running off somewhere.' Oh, if she had only known!

" 'To the woods! To the woods!' that was the cry; and away we went, each with the determination not to shoot, but to bring the culprit alive into town, and then to deal with him as his crime deserved.

"I cannot describe the feelings I experienced as I went out that night to beat the woods for this human tiger. My heart smoldered within me like a coal, and I went forward under the impulse of a will that was half my own, half some more malignant power's. My throat throbbed drily, but water nor whiskey would not have quenched my thirst. The thought has come to me since that now I could interpret the panther's desire for blood and sympathize with it, but then I thought nothing. I simply went forward, and watched, watched with burning eyes for a familiar form that I had looked for as often before with such different emotions.

"Luck or ill-luck, which you will, was with our party, and just as dawn was graying the sky, we came upon our quarry crouched in the corner of a fence. It was only half light, and we might have passed, but my eyes caught sight of him, and I raised the cry. We leveled our guns and he rose and came toward us.

" 'I t'ought you wa'n't gwine see me,' he said sullenly; 'I didn't mean no harm.'

" 'Harm!'

"Some of the men took the word up with oaths, others were ominously silent.

"We gathered around him like hungry beasts, and I began to see terror dawning in his eyes. He turned to me, 'I's moughty glad you's hyeah, Doc,' he said; 'you ain't gwine let 'em whup me.'

" 'Whip you, you hound,' I said, 'I'm going to see you hanged,' and in the excess of my passion I struck him full on the mouth. He made a motion as if to resent the blow against such great odds, but controlled himself.

" 'W'y, Doctah,' he exclaimed in the saddest voice I have ever heard, 'w'y, Doctah! I ain't stole nuffin' o' yo'n, an' I was comin' back. I only run off to see my gal, Lucy, ovah to de Centah.'

" 'You lie!' I said, and my hands were busy helping others bind him upon a horse. Why did I do it? I don't know. A false education, I reckon, one false from the beginning. I saw his black face glooming there in the half light, and I could only think of him as a monster. It's tradition. At first I was told that the black man would catch me, and when I got over that, they taught me that the devil was black, and when I had recovered from the sickness of that belief, here were Jube and his fellows with faces of menacing blackness. There was only one conclusion: This black man stood for all the powers of evil, the result of whose machinations had been gathering in my mind from childhood up. But this has nothing to do with what happened.

"After firing a few shots to announce our capture, we rode back into town with Jube. The ingathering parties from all directions met us as we made our way up to the house. All was very quiet and orderly. There was no doubt that it was, as the papers would have said, a gathering of the best citizens. It was a gathering of stern, determined men, bent on a terrible vengeance.

"We took Jube into the house, into the room where the corpse lay. At sight of it he gave a scream like an animal's, and his face went the color of storm-blown water. This was enough to condemn him. We divined rather than heard his cry of 'Miss Ann, Miss Ann; oh, my God! Doc, you don't t'ink I done it?'

"Hungry hands were ready. We hurried him out into the yard. A rope was ready. A tree was at hand. Well, that part was the least of it, save that Hiram Daly stepped aside to let me be the first to pull upon the rope. It was lax at first. Then it tightened, and I felt the quivering soft weight resist my muscles. Other hands joined, and Jube swung off his feet.

"No one was masked. We knew each other. Not even the culprit's face was covered, and the last I remember of him as he went into the air was a look of sad reproach that will remain with me until I meet him face to face again.

"We were tying the end of the rope to a tree, where the dead man might hang as a warning to his fellows, when a terrible cry chilled us to the marrow.

" 'Cut 'im down, cut 'im down; he ain't guilty. We got de one.

Cut him down, fu' Gawd's sake. Here's de man; we foun' him hidin' in de barn!'

"Jube's brother, Ben, and another Negro came rushing toward us, half dragging, half carrying a miserable-looking wretch between them. Someone cut the rope and Jube dropped lifeless to the ground.

" 'Oh, my Gawd, he's daid, he's daid!' wailed the brother, but with blazing eyes he brought his captive into the center of the group, and we saw in the full light the scratched face of Tom Skinner, the worst white ruffian in town; but the face we saw was not as we were accustomed to see it, merely smeared with dirt. It was blackened to imitate a Negro's.

"God forgive me; I could not wait to try to resuscitate Jube. I knew he was already past help; so I rushed into the house and to the dead girl's side. In the excitement they had not yet washed or laid her out. Carefully, carefully, I searched underneath her broken finger nails. There was skin there. I took it out, the little curled pieces, and went with it to my office.

"There, determinedly, I examined it under a powerful glass, and read my own doom. It was the skin of a white man, and in it were embedded strands of short, brown hair or beard.

"How I went out to tell the waiting crowd I do not know, for something kept crying in my ears, 'Blood guilty! Blood guilty!'

"The men went away stricken into silence and awe. The new prisoner attempted neither denial nor plea. When they were gone I would have helped Ben carry his brother in, but he waved me away fiercely, 'You he'ped murder my brothah, you dat was *his* frien'; go 'way, go 'way! I'll tek him home myse'f.' I could only respect his wish, and he and his comrade took up the dead man and between them bore him up the street on which the sun was now shining full.

"I saw the few men who had not skulked indoors uncover as

they passed, and I—I—stood there between the two murdered ones, while all the while something in my ears kept crying, 'Blood guilty! Blood guilty!' "

The doctor's head dropped into his hands and he sat for some time in silence, which was broken by neither of the men; then he rose, saying, "Gentlemen, that was my last lynching."

Sister Josepha

Alice Dunbar-Nelson
(1875–1935)

S ister Josepha told her beads mechanically, her fingers numb with the accustomed exercise. The little organ creaked a dismal "O Salutaris," and she still knelt on the floor, her white-bonneted head nodding suspiciously. The Mother Superior gave a sharp glance at the tired figure; then, as a sudden lurch forward brought the little sister back to consciousness, Mother's eyes relaxed into a genuine smile.

The bell tolled the end of vespers, and the sombre-robed nuns filed out of the chapel to go about their evening duties. Little Sister Josepha's work was to attend to the household lamps, but there must have been as much oil spilled upon the table to-night as was put in the vessels. The small brown hands trembled so that most of the wicks were trimmed with points at one corner which caused them to smoke that night.

"Oh, cher Seigneur," she sighed, giving an impatient polish to a refractory chimney, "it is wicked and sinful, I know, but I am so tired. I can't be happy and sing any more. It doesn't seem right for le bon Dieu to have me all cooped up here with nothing to see but stray visitors, and always the same old work, teaching those mean little girls to sew, and washing and filling the same old lamps. Pah!" And she polished the chimney with a sudden vigorous jerk which threatened destruction.

They were rebellious prayers that the red mouth murmured that night, and a restless figure that tossed on the hard dormitory bed. Sister Dominica called from her couch to know if Sister Josepha were ill.

"No," was the somewhat short response; then a muttered, "Why can't they let me alone for a minute? That pale-eyed Sister Dominica never sleeps; that's why she is so ugly."

About fifteen years before this night some one had brought to the orphan asylum connected with this convent, du Sacré Cœur, a round, dimpled bit of three-year-old humanity, who regarded the world from a pair of gravely twinkling black eyes, and only took a chubby thumb out of a rosy mouth long enough to answer in monosyllabic French. It was a child without an identity; there was but one name that any one seemed to know, and that, too, was vague—Camille.

She grew up with the rest of the waifs; scraps of French and American civilization thrown together to develop a seemingly inconsistent miniature world. Mademoiselle Camille was a queen among them, a pretty little tyrant who ruled the children and dominated the more timid sisters in charge.

One day an awakening came. When she was fifteen, and almost fully ripened into a glorious tropical beauty of the type that matures early, some visitors to the convent were fascinated by her and asked the Mother Superior to give the girl into their keeping.

Camille fled like a frightened fawn into the yard, and was only unearthed with some difficulty from behind a group of palms. Sulky and pouting, she was led into the parlour, picking at her blue pinafore like a spoiled infant.

"The lady and gentleman wish you to go home with them, Camille," said the Mother Superior, in the language of the convent. Her voice was kind and gentle apparently; but the child, accustomed to its various inflections, detected a steely ring behind its softness, like the proverbial iron hand in the velvet glove.

"You must understand, madame," continued Mother, in stilted English, "that we never force children from us. We are ever glad to place them in comfortable—how you say that?—quarters—maisons—homes—bien! But we will not make them go if they do not wish."

Camille stole a glance at her would-be guardians, and decided instantly, impulsively, finally. The woman suited her; but the man! It was doubtless intuition of the quick, vivacious sort which belonged to her blood that served her. Untutored in worldly knowledge, she could not divine the meaning of the pronounced leers and admiration of her physical charms which gleamed in the man's face, but she knew it made her feel creepy, and stoutly refused to go.

Next day Camille was summoned from a task to the Mother Superior's parlour. The other girls gazed with envy upon her as she dashed down the courtyard with impetuous movement. Camille, they decided crossly, received too much notice. It was Camille this, Camille that; she was pretty, it was to be expected. Even Father Ray lingered longer in his blessing when his hands pressed her silky black hair.

As she entered the parlour, a strange chill swept over the girl. The room was not an unaccustomed one, for she had swept it many times, but to-day the stiff black chairs, the dismal crucifixes, the gleaming whiteness of the walls, even the cheap lithograph of the Madonna which Camille had always regarded as a perfect specimen of art, seemed cold and mean.

"Camille, ma chère," said Mother, "I am extremely displeased with you. Why did you not wish to go with Monsieur and Madame Lafayé yesterday?"

The girl uncrossed her hands from her bosom, and spread them out in a deprecating gesture.

"Mais, ma mère, I was afraid."

Mother's face grew stern. "No foolishness now," she exclaimed.

"It is not foolishness, ma mère; I could not help it, but that man looked at me so funny, I felt all cold chills down my back. Oh, dear Mother, I love the convent and the sisters so, I just want to stay and be a sister too, may I?"

And thus it was that Camille took the white veil at sixteen years. Now that the period of novitiate was over, it was just beginning to dawn upon her that she had made a mistake.

"Maybe it would have been better had I gone with the funny-looking lady and gentleman," she mused bitterly one night. "Oh, Seigneur, I'm so tired and impatient; it's so dull here, and, dear God, I'm so young."

There was no help for it. One must arise in the morning, and help in the refectory with the stupid Sister Francesca, and go about one's duties with a prayerful mien, and not even let a sigh escape when one's head ached with the eternal telling of beads.

A great fête day was coming, and an atmosphere of preparation and mild excitement pervaded the brown walls of the convent like a delicate aroma. The old Cathedral around the corner had stood a hundred years, and all the city was rising to do honour to its age and time-softened beauty. There would be a service, oh, but such a one! with two Cardinals, and Archbishops and Bishops, and all the accompanying glitter of soldiers and orchestras. The little sisters of the Convent du Sacré Cœur clasped their hands in anticipation of the holy joy. Sister Josepha curled her lip, she was so tired of churchly pleasures.

The day came, a gold and blue spring day, when the air hung heavy with the scent of roses and magnolias, and the sunbeams fairly laughed as they kissed the houses. The old Cathedral stood gray and solemn, and the flowers in Jackson Square smiled cheery birthday greetings across the way. The crowd around the door surged and pressed and pushed in its eagerness to get within. Ribbons stretched across the banquette were of no avail to repress it, and important ushers with cardinal colours could do little more.

The Sacred Heart sisters filed slowly in at the side door, creating a momentary flutter as they paced reverently to their seats, guarding the blue-bonneted orphans. Sister Josepha, determined to see as much of the world as she could, kept her big black eyes opened wide, as the church rapidly filled with the fashionably dressed, perfumed, rustling, and self-conscious throng.

Her heart beat quickly. The rebellious thoughts that will arise in the most philosophical of us surged in her small heavily gowned bosom. For her were the gray things, the neutral-tinted skies, the ugly garb, the coarse meats; for them the rainbow, the ethereal airiness of earthly joys, the bonbons and glacés of the world. Sister Josepha did not know that the rainbow is elusive, and its colours but the illumination of tears; she had never been told that earthly ethereality is necessarily ephemeral, nor that bonbons and glacés, whether of the palate or of the soul, nauseate and pall upon the taste. Dear God, forgive her, for she bent with contrite tears over her worn rosary, and glanced no more at the worldly glitter of femininity.

The sunbeams streamed through the high windows in purple and crimson lights upon a veritable fugue of colour. Within the seats, crush upon crush of spring millinery; within the aisles erect lines of gold-braided, gold-buttoned military. Upon the altar, broad sweeps of golden robes, great dashes of crimson skirts, mitres and gleaming crosses, the soft neutral hue of rich lace vestments; the tender heads of childhood in picturesque attire; the proud, golden magnificence of the domed altar with its weighting mass of lilies and wide-eyed roses, and the long candles that sparkled their yellow star points above the reverent throng within the altar rails.

The soft baritone of the Cardinal intoned a single phrase in the suspended silence. The censer took up the note in its delicate clink clink, as it swung to and fro in the hands of a fair-haired child. Then the organ, pausing an instant in a deep, mellow, long-drawn note, burst suddenly into a magnificent strain, and the choir sang forth, "Kyrie Eleïson, Christe Eleïson." One voice, flute-like, piercing, sweet, rang high over the rest. Sister Josepha heard and trembled, as she buried her face in her hands, and let her tears fall, like other beads, through her rosary.

It was when the final word of the service had been intoned, the last peal of the exit march had died away, that she looked up meekly, to encounter a pair of youthful brown eyes gazing pityingly upon her. That was all she remembered for a moment, that the eyes were youthful and handsome and tender. Later, she saw that they were placed in a rather beautiful boyish face, surmounted by waves of brown hair, curling and soft, and that the head was set on a pair of shoulders decked in military uniform. Then the brown eyes marched away with the rest of the rear guard, and the white-bonneted sisters filed out the side door, through the narrow court, back into the brown convent.

That night Sister Josepha tossed more than usual on her hard bed, and clasped her fingers often in prayer to quell the wickedness in her heart. Turn where she would, pray as she might, there was ever a pair of tender, pitying brown eyes, haunting her persistently. The squeaky organ at vespers intoned the clank of military accoutrements to her ears, the white bonnets of the sisters about her faded into mists of curling brown hair. Briefly, Sister Josepha was in love.

The days went on pretty much as before, save for the one little heart that beat rebelliously now and then, though it tried so hard to be submissive. There was the morning work in the refectory, the stupid little girls to teach sewing, and the insatiable lamps that were so greedy for oil. And always the tender, boyish brown eyes, that looked so sorrowfully at the fragile, beautiful little sister, haunting, following, pleading.

Perchance, had Sister Josepha been in the world, the eyes would have been an incident. But in this home of self-repression and retrospection, it was a life-story. The eyes had gone their way, doubtless forgetting the little sister they pitied; but the little sister?

The days glided into weeks, the weeks into months. Thoughts of escape had come to Sister Josepha, to flee into the world, to merge in the great city where recognition was impossible, and, working her way like the rest of humanity, perchance encounter the eyes again.

It was all planned and ready. She would wait until some morning when the little band of black-robed sisters wended their way to mass at the Cathedral. When it was time to file out the side-door into the courtway, she would linger at prayers, then slip out another door, and unseen glide up Chartres Street to Canal, and once there, mingle in the throng that filled the wide thoroughfare. Beyond this first plan she could think no further. Penniless, garbed, and shaven though she would be, other difficulties never presented themselves to her. She would rely on the mercies of the world to help her escape from this torturing life of inertia. It seemed easy now that the first step of decision had been taken.

The Saturday night before the final day had come, and she lay feverishly nervous in her narrow little bed, wondering with wide-eyed fear at the morrow. Pale-eyed Sister Dominica and Sister Francesca were whispering together in the dark silence, and Sister Josepha's ears pricked up as she heard her name.

"She is not well, poor child," said Francesca. "I fear the life is too confining."

"It is best for her," was the reply. "You know, sister, how hard it would be for her in the world, with no name but Camille, no friends, and her beauty; and then—"

Sister Josepha heard no more, for her heart beating tumultuously in her bosom drowned the rest. Like the rush of the bitter salt tide over a drowning man clinging to a spar, came the complete submerging of her hopes of another life. No name but Camille, that was true; no nationality, for she could never tell from whom or whence she came; no friends, and a beauty that not even an ungainly bonnet and shaven head could hide. In a flash she realised the deception of the life she would lead, and the cruel self-torture of wonder at her own identity. Already, as if in anticipation of the world's questionings, she was asking herself, "Who am I? What am I?"

The next morning the sisters du Sacré Cœur filed into the Cathedral at High Mass, and bent devout knees at the general confession. "Confiteor Deo omnipotenti," murmured the priest; and tremblingly one little sister followed the words, "Je confesse à Dieu, tout puissant—que j'ai beaucoup péché par pensées—c'est ma faute—c'est ma faute—c'est ma très grande faute."

The organ pealed forth as mass ended, the throng slowly filed out, and the sisters paced through the courtway back into the brown convent walls. One paused at the entrance, and gazed with swift longing eyes in the direction of narrow, squalid Chartres Street, then, with a gulping sob, followed the rest, and vanished behind the heavy door.

Maverick

Mary Hallock Foote
(1847–1938)

Traveling Buttes is a lone stage-station on the road, largely speaking, from Blackfoot to Boise. I do not know whether the stages take that road now, but ten years ago they did, and the man who kept the stage-house was a person of primitive habits and corresponding appearances named Gilroy.

The stage-house is perhaps half a mile from the foot of the largest butte, one of three that loom on the horizon, and appear to "travel" from you, as you approach them from the plains. A day's ride with the Buttes as a landmark is like a stern chase, in that you seem never to gain upon them.

From the stage-house the plain slopes up to the foot of the Big Butte, which rises suddenly in the form of an enormous tepee, as if Gitche Manito, the mighty, had here descended and pitched his tent for a council of the nations.

The country is destitute of water. To say that it is "thirsty" is to mock with vain imagery that dead and mummied land on the borders of the Black Lava. The people at the stage-house had located a precious spring, four miles up, in a cleft near the top of the Big

Butte; they piped the water down to the house and they sold it to travelers on that Jericho road at so much per horse. The man was thrown in, but the man usually drank whisky.

Our guide commented unfavorably on this species of husbandry, which is common enough in the arid West, and as legitimate as selling oats or hay; but he chose to resent it in the case of Gilroy, and to look upon it as an instance of individual and exceptional meanness.

"Any man that will jump God's water in a place like this, and sell it the same as drinks—he'd sell water to his own father in hell!"

This was our guide's opinion of Gilroy. He was equally frank, and much more explicit, in regard to Gilroy's sons. "But," he concluded, with a philosopher's acceptance of existing facts, "it ain't likely that any of that outfit will ever git into trouble, so long as Maverick is sheriff of Lemhi County."

We were about to ask why, when we drove up to the stagehouse, and Maverick himself stepped out and took our horses.

"What the—infernal has happened to the man?" my companion, Ferris, exclaimed; and our guide answered indifferently, as if he were speaking of the weather—

"Some Injuns caught him alone in an out-o'-the-way ranch, when he was a kid, and took a notion to play with him. This is what was left when they got through. I never see but one worse-looking man," he added, speaking low, as Maverick passed us with the team: "him a bear wiped over the head with its paw. 'Twas quicker over with, I expect, but he lived, and *he* looked worse than Maverick."

"Then I hope to the Lord I may never see him!" Ferris ejaculated; and I noticed that he left his dinner untasted, though he had boasted of a hunter's appetite.

We were college friends on a hunting trip, but we had not got into the country of game. In two days more we expected to make

Jackson's Hole, and I may mention that "hole," in this region, signifies any small, deep valley, well hidden amidst high mountains,
where moisture is perennial, and grass abounds. In these pockets of
plenty, herds of elk gather and feed as tame as park pets; and other
hunted creatures, as wild but less innocent, often find sanctuary
here, and cache their stolen stock and other spoil of the road and
the range.

We did not forget to put our question concerning Maverick,
that unhappy man, in his character of legalized protector of the
Gilroy gang. What did our free-spoken guide mean by that insin-
uation?

We were told that Gilroy, in his rough-handed way, had been
as a father to the lad, after the savages wreaked their pleasure on
him: and his people being dead or scattered, Maverick had made
himself useful in various humble capacities at the stage-house,
and had finally become a sort of factotum there and a member
of the family. And though perfectly square himself, and much respected on account of his personal courage and singular misfortunes, he could never see the old man's crookedness, nor the
more than crookedness of his sons. He was like a son of the
house, himself; but most persons agreed that it was not as a
brother he felt toward Rose Gilroy. And a tough lookout it was
for the girl; for Maverick was one whom no man would lightly
cross, and in her case he was acting as "general dog around the
place," as our guide called it. The young fellows were shy of the
house, notwithstanding the attraction it held. It was likely to be
Maverick or nobody for Rose.

We did not see Rose Gilroy, but we heard her step in the stage-
house kitchen, and her voice, as clear as a lark's, giving orders to
the tall, stooping, fair young Swede, who waited on us at table, and
did other work of a menial character in that singular establishment.

"How is it the watch-dog allows such a pretty sprig as that

around the place?" Ferris questioned, eyeing our knight of the trencher, who blushed to feel himself remarked.

"He won't stay," our guide pronounced; "they don't none of 'em stay when they're good-lookin'. The old man he's failin' considerable these days—gettin' kind o' silly—and the boys are away the heft of the time. Maverick pretty much runs the place. I don't justly blame the critter. He's watched that little Rose grow up from a baby. How's he goin' to quit being fond of her now she's a woman? I dare say he'd a heap sooner she'd stayed a little girl. And these yere boys around here they're a triflin' set, not half so able to take care of her as Maverick. He's got the sense and he's got the sand; but there's that awful head on him! I don't blame him much, lookin' the way he does, and feelin' the same as any other man."

We left Traveling Buttes and its cruel little love-story, but we had not gone a mile when a horseman overtook us with a message for Ferris from his new foreman at the ranch, a summons which called him back for a day at the least. Ferris was exceedingly annoyed: a day at the ranch meant four days on the road; but the business was imperative. We held a brief council, and decided that, with Ferris returning, our guide should push on with the animals and camp outfit into a country of grass, and look up a good camping-spot (which might not be the first place he struck) this side of Jackson's Hole. It remained for me to choose between going with the stuff, or staying for a longer look at the phenomenal Black Lava fields at Arco; Arco being another name for desolation on the very edge of that weird stone sea. This was my ostensible reason for choosing to remain at Arco; but I will not say the reflection did not cross me that Arco is only sixteen miles from Traveling Buttes—not an insurmountable distance between geology and a pretty girl, when one is five and twenty, and has not seen a pretty face for a month of Sundays.

Arco, at that time, consisted of the stage-house, a store, and one or two cabins—a poor little seed of civilization dropped by the wayside, between the Black Lava and the hills where Lost River comes down and "sinks" on the edge of the lava. The station is somewhat back from the road, with its face—a very grimy, unwashed countenance—to the lava. Quaking asps and mountain birches follow the water, pausing a little way up the gulch behind the house, but the eager grass tracks it all the way till it vanishes; and the dry bed of the stream goes on and spreads in a mass of coarse sand and gravel, beaten flat, flailed by the feet of countless driven sheep that have gathered here. For this road is on the great overland sheep-trail from Oregon eastward—the march of the million mouths, and what the mouths do not devour the feet tramp down.

The staple topic of conversation at Arco was one very common in the far West, when a tenderfoot is of the company. The poorest place can boast of some distinction, and Arco, though hardly on the highroad of fashion and commerce, had frequently been named in print in connection with crime of a highly sensational and picturesque character. Scarcely another fifty miles of stage-road could boast of so many and such successful road-jobs; and although these affairs were of almost monthly occurrence, and might be looked for to come off always within that noted danger-limit, yet it was a fact that the law had never yet laid finger on a man of the gang, nor gained the smallest clew to their hide-out. It was a difficult country around Arco, one that lent itself to secrecy. The road-agents came, and took, and vanished as if the hills were their co-partners as well as the receivers of their goods. As for the lava, which was its front dooryard, so to speak, for a hundred miles, the man did not live who could say he had crossed it. What it held or was capable of hiding, in life or in death, no man knew.

The day after Ferris left me I rode out upon that arrested tide—those silent breakers which for ages have threatened, but never reached, the shore. I tried to fancy it as it must once have been, a sluggish, vitreous flood, filling the great valley, and stiffening as it slowly pushed toward the bases of the hills. It climbed and spread, as dough rises and crawls over the edge of the pan. The Black Lava is always called a sea—that image is inevitable; yet its movement had never in the least the character of water. "This is where hell pops," an old plainsman feelingly described it, and the suggestion is perfect. The colors of the rock are those produced by fire: its texture is that of slag from a furnace. One sees how the lava hardened into a crust, which cracked and sank in places, mingling its tumbled edges with the creeping flood not cooled beneath. After all movement had ceased and the mass was still, time began upon its tortured configurations, crumbled and wore and broke, and sifted a little earth here and there, and sealed the burnt rock with fairy print of lichens, serpent-green and orange and rust-red. The spring rains left shallow pools which the summer dried. Across it, a few dim trails wander a little way and give out, like the water.

For a hundred miles to the Snake River this Plutonian gulf obliterates the land—holds it against occupation or travel. The shoes of a marching army would be cut from their feet before they had gone a dozen miles across it; horses would have no feet left; and water would have to be packed as on an ocean, or a desert, cruise.

I rode over places where the rock rang beneath my horse's hoofs like the iron cover of a manhole. I followed the hollow ridges that mounted often forty feet above my head, but always with that gruesome effect of thickening movement—that sluggish, atomic crawl; and I thought how one man pursuing another into this frozen hell might lose himself, but never find the object of his quest. If he took the wrong furrow, he could not cross from one blind gut into another, nor hope to meet the fugitive at any future turning.

I don't know why the fancy of a flight and pursuit should so have haunted me, in connection with the Black Lava; probably the desperate and lawless character of our conversation at the stage-house gave rise to it.

I had fallen completely under the spell of that skeleton flood. I watched the sun sink, as it sinks at sea, beyond its utmost ragged ridges; I sat on the borders of it, and stared across it in the gray moonlight; I rode out upon it when the Buttes, in their delusive nearness, were as blue as the gates of amethyst, and the morning was as fair as one great pearl; but no peace or radiance of heaven or earth could change its aspect more than that of a mound of skulls. When I began to dream about it, I thought I must be getting morbid. This is worse than Gilroy's, I said; and I promised myself I would ride up there next day and see if by chance one might get a peep at the Rose that all were praising, but none dared put forth a hand to pluck. Was it indeed so hard a case for the Rose? There are women who can love a man for the perils he has passed. Alas, Maverick! could any one get used to a face like that?

Here, surely, was the story of Beauty and her poor Beast humbly awaiting, in the mask of a brutish deformity, the recognition of Love pure enough to divine the soul beneath, and unselfish enough to deliver it. Was there such love as that at Gilroy's? However, I did not make that ride.

It was the fourth night of clear, desert moonlight since Ferris had left me: I was sleepless, and so I heard the first faint throb of a horse's feet approaching from the east, coming on at a great pace, and making the turn to the stage-house. I looked out, and on the trodden space in front I saw Maverick dismounting from a badly blown horse.

"Halloo! what's up?" I called from the open window of my bedroom on the ground-floor.

"Did two men pass here on horseback since dark?"

"Yes," I said; "about twelve o'clock: a tall man and a little short fellow."

"Did they stop to water?"

"No, they did not; and they seemed in such a tearing hurry that I watched them down the road"—

"I am after those men, and I want a fresh horse," he cut in. "Call up somebody quick!"

"Shall you take one of the boys along?" I inquired, with half an eye to myself, after I had obeyed his command.

He shook his head. "Only one horse here that's good for anything: I want that myself."

"There is my horse," I suggested; "but I'd rather be the one who rides her. She belongs to a friend."

"Take her, and come on, then, but understand—this ain't a Sunday-school picnic."

"I'm with you, if you'll have me."

"I'd sooner have your horse," he remarked, shifting the quid of tobacco in his cheek.

"You can't have her without me, unless you steal her," I said.

"Git your gun, then, and shove some grub into your pockets: I can't wait for nobody."

He swung himself into the saddle.

"What road do you take?"

"There ain't but one," he shouted, and pointed straight ahead.

I overtook him easily within the hour; he was saving his horse, for this was his last chance to change until Champagne Station, fifty miles away.

He gave me rather a cynical smile of recognition as I ranged alongside, as if to say, "You'll probably get enough of this before we are through." The horses settled down to their work, and they "humped theirselves," as Maverick put it, in the cool hours before sunrise.

At daybreak his awful face struck me all afresh, as inscrutable in its strange distortion as some stone god in the desert, from whose graven hideousness a thousand years of mornings have silently drawn the veil.

"What do you want those fellows for?" I asked, as we rode. I had taken for granted that we were hunting suspects of the road-agent persuasion.

"I want 'em on general principles," he answered shortly.

"Do you think you know them?"

"I think they'll know me. All depends on how they act when we get within range. If they don't pay no attention to us, we'll send a shot across their bows. But more likely they'll speak first."

He was very gloomy, and would keep silence for an hour at a time. Once he turned on me as with a sudden misgiving.

"See here, don't you git excited; and whatever happens, don't you meddle with the little one. If the big fellow cuts up rough, he'll take his chances, but you leave the little one to me. I want him—I want him for State's evidence," he finished hoarsely.

"The little one must be the Benjamin of the family," I thought—"one of the bad young Gilroys, whose time has come at last; and Sheriff Maverick finds his duty hard."

I could not say whether I really wished the men to be over-taken, but the spirit of the chase had undoubtedly entered into my blood. I felt as most men do, who are not saints or cowards, when such work as this is to be done. But I knew I had no business to be along. It was one thing for Maverick, but the part of an amateur in a man-hunt is not one to boast of.

The sun was now high, and the fresh tracks ahead of us were plain in the dust. Once they left the road and strayed off into the lava, incomprehensibly to me; but Maverick understood, and pressed forward. "We'll strike them again further on. D—— fool!" he muttered, and I observed that he alluded but to one, "huntin' waterholes in the lava in the tail end of August!"

They could not have found water, for at Belgian Flat they had stopped and dug for it in the gravel, where a little stream in freshet time comes down the gulch from the snow-fields higher up, and sinks, as at Arco, on the lip of the lava. They had dug, and found it, and saved us the trouble, as Maverick remarked.

Considerable water had gathered since the flight had paused here and lost precious time. We drank our fill, refreshed our horses, and shifted the saddle-girths; and I managed to stow away my lunch during the next mile or so, after offering to share it with Maverick, who refused it as if the notion of food made him sick. He had considerable whisky aboard, but he was, I judged, one of those men on whom drink has little effect; else some counter-flame of excitement was fighting it in his blood.

I looked for the development of the personal complication whenever we should come up with the chase, for the man's eye burned, and had his branded countenance been capable of any expression that was not cruelly travestied, he would have looked the impersonation of wild justice.

It was now high noon, and our horses were beginning to feel the steady work; yet we had not ridden as they brought the good news from Ghent: that is the pace of a great lyric; but it's not the pace at which justice, or even vengeance, travels in the far West. Even the furies take it coolly when they pursue a man over these roads, and on these poor brutes of horses, in fifty-mile stages, with drought thrown in.

Maverick had had no mercy on the pony that brought him sixteen miles; but this piece of horse-flesh he now bestrode must last him through at least to Champagne Station, should we not overhaul our men before. He knew well when to press and when to spare the pace, a species of purely practical consideration which seemed habitual with him; he rode like an automaton, his baleful face borne straight before him—the Gorgon's head.

Beyond Belgian Flat—how far beyond I do not remember, for I was beginning to feel the work, too, and the country looked all alike to me as we made it, mile by mile—the road follows close along by the lava, but the hills recede, and a little trail cuts across, meeting the road again at Deadman's Flat. Here we could not trust to the track, which from the nature of the ground was indistinct. So we divided our forces, Maverick taking the trail—which I was quite willing he should do, for it had a look of most sinister invitation—while I continued by the longer road. Our little discussion, or some atmospheric change—some breath of coolness from the hills—had brought me up out of my stupor of weariness. I began to feel both alert and nervous; my heart was beating fast. The still sunshine lay all around us, but where Maverick's white horse was climbing, the shadows were turning eastward, and the deep gulches, with their patches of aspen, were purple instead of brown. The aspens were left shaking where he broke through them and passed out of sight.

I kept on at a good pace, and about three o'clock I, being then as much as half a mile away, saw the spot which I knew must be Deadman's Flat; and there were our men, the tall one and his boyish mate, standing quietly by their horses in broad sunlight, as if there were no one within a hundred miles. Their horses had drunk, and were cropping the thin grass, which had set its tooth in the gravel where, as at the other places, a living stream had perished. I spurred forward, with my heart thumping, but before they saw me I saw Maverick coming down the little gulch; and from the way he came I knew that he had seen them.

The scene was awful in its treacherous peacefulness. Their shadows slept on the broad bed of sunlight, and the gulch was as cool and still as a lady's chamber. The great dead desert received the silence like a secret.

Tenderfoot as I was, I knew quite well what must happen now;

yet I was not prepared—could not realize it—even when the tall one put his hand quickly behind him and stepped ahead of his horse. There was the flash of his pistol, and the loud crack echoing in the hill; a second shot, and then Maverick replied deliberately, and the tall one was down, with his face in the grass.

I heard a scream that sounded strangely like a woman's; but there were only the three, the little one, acting wildly, and Maverick bending over him who lay with his face in the grass. I saw him turn the body over, and the little fellow seemed to protest, and to try to push him away. I thought it strange he made no more of a fight, but I was not near enough to hear what those two said to each other.

Still, the tragedy did not come home to me. It was all like a scene, and I was without feeling in it except for that nervous trembling which I could not control.

Maverick stood up at length, and came slowly toward me, wiping his face. He kept his hat in his hand, and, looking down at it, said huskily:—

"I gave that man his life when I found him last spring runnin' loose like a wild thing in the mountains, and now I've took it; and God above knows I had no grudge ag'in' him, if he had stayed in his place. But he would have it so."

"Maverick, I saw it all, and I can swear it was self-defense."

His face drew into the tortured grimace which was his smile. "This here will never come before a jury," he said. "It's a family affair. Did ye see how he acted? Steppin' up to me like he was a first-class shot, or else a fool. He ain't nary one; he's a poor silly tool, the whip-hand of a girl that's boltin' from her friends like they was her mortal enemies. Go and take a look at him; then maybe you'll understand."

He paused, and uttered the name of Jesus Christ, but not as such men often use it, with an inconsequence dreadful to hear: he was not idly swearing, but calling that name to witness solemnly in a case that would never come before a jury.

I began to understand.

"Is it—is the girl"—

"Yes; it's our poor little Rose—that's the little one, in the gray hat. She'll give herself away if I don't. She don't care for nothin' nor nobody. She was runnin' away with that fellow—that dish-washin' Swede what I found in the mountings eatin' roots like a ground-hog, with the ends of his feet froze off. Now you know all I know—and more than she knows, for she thinks she was fond of him. She wa'n't, never—for I watched 'em, and I know. She was crazy to git away, and she took him for the chance."

His excitement passed, and we sat apart and watched the pair at a distance. She—the little one—sat as passively by her dead as Maverick pondering his cruel deed; but with both it was a hope-less quiet.

"Come," he said at length, "I've got to bury him. You look after her, and keep her with you till I git through. I'm givin' you the hardest part," he added wistfully, as if he fully realized how he had cut himself off from all such duties, henceforth, to the girl he was consigning to a stranger's care.

I told him I thought that the funeral had more need of me than the mourner, and I shrank from intruding myself.

"I dassent leave her by herself—see? I don't know what notion she may take next, and she won't let me come within a rope's len'th of her."

I will not go over again that miserable hour in the willows, where I made her stay with me, out of sight of what Maverick was doing. Ours were the tender mercies of the wicked, I fear; but she must have felt that sympathy at least was near her, if not help. I will not say that her youth and distressful loveliness did not sharpen my perception of a sweet life wasted, gone utterly astray, which might have brought God's blessing into some man's home—perhaps Maverick's, had he not been so hardly dealt with. She was not of that great disposition of heart which can love best that which has sorest need of love; but she was all woman, and helpless and distraught with her tangle of grief and despair, the nature of which I could only half comprehend.

We sat there by the sunken stream, on the hot gravel where the sun had lain, the willows sifting their inconstant shadows over us; and I thought how other things as precious as "God's water" go astray on the Jericho road, or are captured and sold for a price, while dry hearts ache with the thirst that asks a "draught divine."

The man's felt hat she wore, pulled down over her face, was pinned to her coil of braids which had slipped from the crown of her head. The hat was no longer even a protection; she cast it off, and the blond braids, that had not been smoothed for a day and night, fell like ropes down her back. The sun had burned her cheeks and neck to a clear crimson; her blue eyes were as wild with weeping as a child's. She was a rose, but a rose that had been trampled in the dust; and her prayer was to be left there, rather than that we should take her home.

I suppose I must have had some influence over her, for she allowed me to help her to arrange her forlorn disguise, and put her on her horse, which was more than could have been expected from the way she had received me. And so, about four o'clock, we started back.

There was a scene when we headed the horses to the west; she protesting with wild sobs that she would not, could not, go home, that she would rather die, that we should never get her back alive, and so on. Maverick stood aside bitterly, and left her to me, and I was aware of a grotesque touch of jealousy—which, after all, was perhaps natural—in his dour face whenever he looked back at us. He kept some distance ahead, and waited for us when we fell too far in the rear.

This would happen when from time to time her situation seemed to overpower her, and she would stop in the road, and wring her hands, and try to throw herself out of the saddle, and pray me to let her go.

"Go where?" I would ask. "Where do you wish to go? Have you any plan, or suggestion, that I could help you to carry out?" But I said it only to show her how hopeless her resistance was. This she would own piteously, and say: "Nobody can help me. There ain't nowhere for me to go. But I can't go back. You won't let him make me, will you?"

"Why cannot you go back to your father and your brothers?"

This would usually silence her, and, setting her teeth upon her trouble, she would ride on, while I reproached myself, I knew not why.

After one of these struggles—when she had given in to the force of circumstances, but still unconsenting and rebellious— Maverick fell back, and ranged his horse by her other side.

"I know partly what's troubling you, and I'd rid you of that part quick enough," he said, with a kind of dogged patience in his hard voice; "but you can't get on there without me. You know that, don't you? You don't blame me for staying?"

"I don't blame you for anything but what you've done to-day. You've broke my heart, and ruined me, and took away my last chance, and I don't care what becomes of me, so I don't have to go back."

"You don't have to any more than you have to live. Dyin' is a good deal easier, but we can't always die when we want to. Suppose I found a little lost child on the road, and it cried to go home, and I didn't know where 'home' was, would I leave it there just because it cried and hung back? I'd take you to a better home if I knew of one; but I don't. And there's the old man. I suppose we could get some doctor to certify that he's out of his mind, and get him sent up to Blackfoot; but I guess we'd have to buy the doctor first."

"Oh, hush, do, and leave me alone," she said.

Maverick dug his spurs into his horse, and plunged ahead.

"There," she cried, "now you know part of it; but it's the least part—the least, the least! Poor father, he's awful queer. He don't more than half the time know who I am," she whispered "But it ain't him I'm running away from. It's myself—my own life."

"What is it—can't you tell me?"

She shook her head, but she kept on telling, as if she were talking to herself.

"Father he's like I told you, and the boys—oh, that's worse! I can't get a decent woman to come there and live, and the women at Arco won't speak to me because I'm livin' there alone. They say—they think I ought to get married—to Maverick or somebody. I'll die first. I *will* die, if there's any way to, before I'll marry him!"

This may not sound like tragedy as I tell it, but I think it was tragedy to her. I tried to persuade her that it must be her imagination about the women at Arco; or, if some of them did talk—as indeed I myself had heard, to my shame and disgust—I told her I had never known that place where there was not one woman, at least, who could understand and help another in her trouble.

"*I* don't know of any," she said simply.

There was no more to do but ride on, feeling like her executioner; but

> "Ride hooly, ride hooly, now, gentlemen,
>   Ride hooly now wi' me,"

came into my mind; and no man ever kept beside a "wearier burd," on a sadder journey.

At dusk we came to Belgian Flat, and here Maverick, dismounting, mixed a little whisky in his flask with water which he dipped from the pool. She must have recalled who dug the well, and with whom she had drunk in the morning. He held it to her lips. She rejected it with a strong shudder of disgust.

"Drink it!" he commanded. "You'll kill yourself, carryin' on like this." He pressed it on her, but she turned away her face like a sick and rebellious child.

"Maybe she'll drink it for you," said Maverick, with bitter patience, handing me the cup.

"Will you?" I asked her gently. She shook her head, but at the same time she let me take her hand, and put it down from her face, and I held the cup to her lips. She drank it, every drop. It made her deathly sick, and I took her off her horse, and made a pillow of my coat, so that she could lie down. In ten minutes she was asleep. Maverick covered her with his coat after she was no longer conscious.

We built a fire on the edge of the lava, for we were both chilled and both miserable, each for his own part in that day's work.

The flat is a little cup-shaped valley formed by high hills, like dark walls, shutting it in. The lava creeps up to it in front.

We hovered over the fire, and Maverick fed it, savagely, in silence. He did not recognize my presence by a word—not so much as if I had been a strange dog. I relieved him of it after a while, and went out a little way on the lava. At first all was blackness after the strong glare of the fire; but gradually the desolation took shape, and I stumbled about in it, with my shadow mocking me in derisive beckonings, or crouching close at my heels, as the red flames towered or fell. I stayed out there till I was chilled to the bone, and then went back defiantly. Maverick sat as if he had not moved, his elbows on his knees, his face in his hands. I wondered if he were thinking of that other sleeper under the birches of Deadman's Gulch, victim of an unhappy girl's revolt. Had she loved him? Had she deceived him as well as herself? It seemed to me they were all like children who had lost their way home.

By midnight the moon had risen high enough to look at us coldly over the tops of the great hills. Their shadows crept forth upon the lava. The fire had died down. Maverick rose, and scattered the winking brands with his boot-heel.

"We must pull out," he said. "I'll saddle up, if you will"—The hoarseness in his voice choked him, and he nodded toward the sleeper.

I dreaded to waken the poor Rose. She was very meek and quiet after the brief respite sleep had given her. She sat quite still, and watched me while I shook the sand from my coat, put it on, and buttoned it to the chin, and drew my hat down more firmly. There was a kind of magnetism in her gaze; I felt it creep over me like the touch of a soft hand.

When her horse was ready, Maverick brought it, and left it standing near, and went back to his own, without looking toward us.

"Come, you poor, tired little girl," I said, holding out my hand. She could not find her way at first in the uncertain light, and she seemed half asleep still, so I kept her hand in mine, and guided her to her horse. "Now, once more up," I encouraged her; and suddenly she was clinging to me, and whispering passionately:

"Can't you take me somewhere? Where are those women that you know?" she cried, shaking from head to foot.

"Dear little soul, all the women I know are two thousand miles away," I answered.

"But can't you take me *somewhere*? There must be some place. I know you would be good to me; and you could go away afterward, and I wouldn't trouble you any more."

"My child, there is not a place under the heavens where I

could take you. You must go on like a brave girl, and trust to your friends. Keep up your heart, and the way will open. God will not forget you," I said, and may He forgive me for talking cant to that poor soul in her bitter extremity.

She stood perfectly still one moment while I held her by the hands. I think she could have heard my heart beat; but there was nothing I could do. Even now I wake in the night, and wonder if there was any other way—but one; the way that for one wild moment I was half tempted to take.

"Yes; the way will open," she said very low. She cast off my hands, and in a second she was in the saddle, and off up the road, riding for her life. And we two men knew no better than to follow her.

I knew better, or I think, now, that I did. I told Maverick we had pushed her far enough. I begged him to hold up and at least not to let her see us on her track. He never answered a word, but kept straight on, as if possessed. I don't think he knew what he was doing. At least there was only one thing *he* was capable of doing— following that girl till he dropped.

Two miles beyond the Flat there is another turn, where the shoulder of a hill comes down and crowds the road, which passes out of sight. She saw us hard upon her, as she reached this bend. Maverick was ahead. Her horse was doing all he could, but it was plain he could not do much more. She looked back, and flung out her hand in the man's sleeve that half covered it. She gave a little whimpering cry, the most dreadful sound I ever heard from any hunted thing.

We made the turn after her; and there lay the road white in the moonlight, and as bare as my hand. She had escaped us.

We pulled up the horses, and listened. Not a sound came from the hills or the dark gulches, where the wind was stirring the quaking asps; the lonesome hush-sh made the silence deeper. But we heard a horse's step go clink, clinking—a loose, uncertain step wandering away in the lava.

"Look! Look there! My God!" groaned Maverick.

There was her horse limping along one of the hollow ridges, but the saddle was empty.

"She has taken to the lava!"

I had no need to be told what that meant; but if I had needed, I learned what it meant before the night was through. I think that if I were a poet, I could add another "dolorous circle" to the wailing-place for lost souls.

But she had found a way. Somewhere in that stony-hearted wilderness she is at rest. We shall see her again when the sea—the stupid, cruel sea that crawls upon the land—gives up its dead.

Under the Lion's Paw

Hamlin Garland
(1860–1940)

It was the last of autumn and first day of winter coming together. All day long the ploughmen on their prairie farms
had moved to and fro in their wide level fields through the
falling snow, which melted as it fell, wetting them to the skin—
all day, notwithstanding the frequent squalls of snow, the dripping, desolate clouds, and the muck of the furrows, black and
tenacious as tar.

Under their dripping harness the horses swung to and fro
silently, with that marvellous uncomplaining patience which marks
the horse. All day the wild geese, honking wildly, as they sprawled
sidewise down the wind, seemed to be fleeing from an enemy behind, and with neck outthrust and wings extended, sailed down
the wind, soon lost to sight.

Yet the ploughman behind his plough, though the snow lay on
his ragged great-coat, and the cold clinging mud rose on his heavy
boots, fettering him like gyves, whistled in the very beard of the
gale. As day passed, the snow, ceasing to melt, lay along the
ploughed land, and lodged in the depth of the stubble, till on each

slow round the last furrow stood out black and shining as jet between the ploughed land and the gray stubble.

When night began to fall, and the geese, flying low, began to alight invisibly in the near corn-field, Stephen Council was still at work "finishing a land." He rode on his sulky plough when going with the wind, but walked when facing it. Sitting bent and cold but cheery under his slouch hat, he talked encouragingly to his four-in-hand.

"Come round there, boys!—Round agin! We got t' finish this land. Come in there, Dan! *Stiddy,* Kate—stiddy! None o' y'r tantrums, Kittie. It's purty tuff, but got a be did. *Tchk! tchk!* Step along, Pete! Don't let Kate git y'r single-tree on the wheel. *Once more!*"

They seemed to know what he meant, and that this was the last round, for they worked with greater vigor than before.

"Once more, boys, an' then, sez I, oats an' a nice warm stall, an' sleep f'r all."

By the time the last furrow was turned on the land it was too dark to see the house, and the snow was changing to rain again. The tired and hungry man could see the light from the kitchen shining through the leafless hedge, and lifting a great shout, "Supper f'r a half a dozen!"

It was nearly eight o'clock by the time he had finished his chores and started for supper. He was picking his way carefully through the mud, when the tall form of a man loomed up before him with a premonitory cough.

"Waddy ye want?" was the rather startled question of the farmer.

"Well, ye see," began the stranger, in a deprecating tone, "we'd like t' git in f'r the night. We've tried every house f'r the last two miles, but they hadn't any room f'r us. My wife's jest about sick, 'n' the children are cold and hungry——"

"Oh, y' want a stay all night, eh?"

"Yes, sir; it 'ud be a great accom———"

"Waal, I don't make it a practice t' turn anybody way hungry, not on sech nights as this. Drive right in. We ain't got much, but sech as it is———"

But the stranger had disappeared. And soon his steaming, weary team, with drooping heads and swinging single-trees, moved past the well to the block beside the path. Council stood at the side of the "schooner" and helped the children out—two little half-sleeping children—and then a small woman with a babe in her arms.

"There ye go!" he shouted jovially, to the children. "*Now* we're all right! Run right along to the house there, an' tell Mam' Council you wants sumpthin' t' eat. Right this way, Mis'—keep right off t' the right there. I'll go an' git a lantern. Come," he said to the dazed and silent group at his side.

"Mother," he shouted, as he neared the fragrant and warmly lighted kitchen, "here are some wayfarers an' folks who need sumpin' t' eat an' a place t' snooze." He ended by pushing them all in.

Mrs. Council, a large, jolly, rather coarse-looking woman, took the children in her arms. "Come right in, you little rabbits. 'Most asleep, hey? Now here's a drink o' milk f'r each o' ye. I'll have s'm tea in a minute. Take off y'r things and set up t' the fire."

While she set the children to drinking milk, Council got out his lantern and went out to the barn to help the stranger about his team, where his loud, hearty voice could be heard as it came and went between the haymow and the stalls.

The woman came to light as a small, timid, and discouraged-looking woman, but still pretty, in a thin and sorrowful way.

"Land sakes! An' you've travelled all the way from Clear Lake t'-day in this mud! Waal! waal! No wonder you're all tired out.

Don't wait f'r the men, Mis'——" She hesitated, waiting for the name.

"Haskins."

"Mis' Haskins, set right up to the table an' take a good swig o' tea whilst I make y' s'm toast. It's green tea, an' it's good. I tell Council as I git older I don't seem to enjoy Young Hyson n'r Gunpowder. I want the reel green tea, jest as it comes off'n the vines. Seems t' have more heart in it, some way. Don't s'pose it has. Council says it's all in m' eye."

Going on in this easy way, she soon had the children filled with bread and milk and the woman thoroughly at home, eating some toast and sweet-melon pickles, and sipping the tea.

"See the little rats!" she laughed at the children. "They're full as they can stick now, and they want to go to bed. Now, don't git up, Mis' Haskins; set right where you are an' let me look after 'em. I know all about young ones, though I'm all alone now. Jane went an' married last fall. But, as I tell Council, it's lucky we keep our health. Set right there, Mis' Haskins; I won't have you stir a finger."

It was an unmeasured pleasure to sit there in the warm, homely kitchen, the jovial chatter of the housewife driving out and holding at bay the growl of the impotent, cheated wind.

The little woman's eyes filled with tears which fell down upon the sleeping baby in her arms. The world was not so desolate and cold and hopeless, after all.

"Now I hope Council won't stop out there and talk politics all night. He's the greatest man to talk politics an' read the *Tribune*. How old is it?"

She broke off and peered down at the face of the babe.

"Two months 'n' five days," said the mother, with a mother's exactness.

"Ye don't say! I want 'o know! The dear little pudzy-wudzy!"

she went on, stirring it up in the neighborhood of the ribs with her fat forefinger.

"Pooty tough on 'oo to go gallivant'n' 'cross lots this way——"

"Yes, that's so; a man can't lift a mountain," said Council, entering the door. "Mother, this is Mr. Haskins, from Kansas. He's been eat up 'n' drove out by grasshoppers."

"Glad t' see yeh!—Pa, empty that wash-basin 'n' give him a chance t' wash."

Haskins was a tall man, with a thin, gloomy face. His hair was a reddish brown, like his coat, and seemed equally faded by the wind and sun. And his sallow face, though hard and set, was pathetic somehow. You would have felt that he had suffered much by the line of his mouth showing under his thin, yellow mustache.

"Hain't Ike got home yet, Sairy?"

"Hain't seen 'im."

"W-a-a-l, set right up, Mr. Haskins; wade right into what we've got; 'taint much, but we manage to live on it—she gits fat on it," laughed Council, pointing his thumb at his wife.

After supper, while the women put the children to bed, Haskins and Council talked on, seated near the huge cooking-stove, the steam rising from their wet clothing. In the Western fashion Council told as much of his own life as he drew from his guest. He asked but few questions; but by and by the story of Haskins' struggles and defeat came out. The story was a terrible one, but he told it quietly, seated with his elbows on his knees, gazing most of the time at the hearth.

"I didn't like the looks of the country, anyhow," Haskins said, partly rising and glancing at his wife. "I was ust t' northern Ingyannie, where we have lots o' timber 'n' lots o' rain, 'n' I didn't like the looks o' that dry prairie. What galled me the worst was goin' s' far away acrosst so much fine land layin' all through here vacant."

"And the 'hoppers eat ye four years hand runnin', did they?"

"Eat! They wiped us out. They chawed everything that was green. They jest set around waitin' f'r us to die t' eat us, too. My God! I ust t' dream of 'em sittin' 'round on the bedpost, six feet long, workin' their jaws. They eet the fork-handles. They got worse 'n' worse till they jest rolled on one another, piled up like snow in winter. Well, it ain't no use. If I was t' talk all winter I couldn't tell nawthin'. But all the while I couldn't help thinkin' of all that land back here that nobuddy was usin' that I ought 'o had 'stead o' bein' out there in that cussed country."

"Wall, why didn't ye stop an' settle here?" asked Ike, who had come in and was eating his supper.

"Fer the simple reason that you fellers wantid ten 'r fifteen dollars an acre fer the bare land, and I hadn't no money fer that kind o' thing."

"Yes, I do my own work," Mrs. Council was heard to say in the pause which followed. "I'm a gettin' purty heavy t' be on m' laigs all day, but we can't afford t' hire, so I keep rackin' around somehow, like a foundered horse. S' lame—I tell Council he can't tell how lame I am, f'r I'm jest as lame in one laig as t' other." And the good soul laughed at the joke on herself as she took a handful of flour and dusted the biscuit-board to keep the dough from sticking.

"Well, I hain't never been very strong," said Mrs. Haskins. "Our folks was Canadians an' small-boned, and then since my last child I hadn't got up again fairly. I don't like t' complain. Tim has about all he can bear now—but they was days this week when I jest wanted to lay right down an' die."

"Waal, now, I'll tell ye," said Council, from his side of the stove, silencing everybody with his good-natured roar, "I'd go down and see Butler, anyway, if I was you. I guess he'd let you have his place purty cheap; the farm's all run down. He's ben anxious t' let t' somebuddy next year. It 'ud be a good chance fer you. Anyhow, you go to bed and sleep like a babe. I've got some ploughing t' do, anyhow, an' we'll see if somethin' can't be done about your case. Ike, you go out an' see if the horses is all right, an' I'll show the folks t' bed."

When the tired husband and wife were lying under the generous quilts of the spare bed, Haskins listened a moment to the wind in the eaves, and then said with a slow and solemn tone:

"There are people in this world who are good enough t' be angels, an' only haff t' die to *be* angels."

II

Jim Butler was one of those men called in the West "land poor." Early in the history of Rock River he had come into the town and started in the grocery business in a small way, occupying a small building in a mean part of the town. At this period of his life he earned all he got, and was up early and late sorting beans, working over butter, and carting his goods to and from the station. But a change came over him at the end of the second year, when he sold a lot of land for four times what he paid for it. From that time forward he believed in land speculation as the surest way of getting rich. Every cent he could save or spare from his trade he put into land at forced sale, or mortgages on land, which were "just as good as the wheat," he was accustomed to say.

Farm after farm fell into his hands, until he was recognized as one of the leading landowners of the county. His mortgages were scattered all over Cedar County, and as they slowly but surely fell in he sought usually to retain the former owner as tenant.

He was not ready to foreclose; indeed, he had the name of being one of the "easiest" men in the town. He let the debtor off again and again, extending the time whenever possible.

"I don't want y'r land," he said. "All I'm after is the int'rest on my money—that's all. Now, if y' want 'o stay on the farm, why, I'll give y' a good chance. I can't have the land layin' vacant." And in many cases the owner remained as tenant.

In the meantime he had sold his store; he couldn't spend time in it; he was mainly occupied now with sitting around town on rainy days smoking and "gassin' with the boys," or in riding to and from his farms. In fishing-time he fished a good deal. Doc Grimes, Ben Ashley, and Cal Cheatham were his cronies on these fishing excursions or hunting trips in the time of chickens or partridges. In winter they went to Northern Wisconsin to shoot deer.

In spite of all these signs of easy life Butler persisted in saying he "hadn't enough money to pay taxes on his land," and was careful to convey the impression that he was poor in spite of his twenty farms. At one time he was said to be worth fifty thousand dollars, but land had been a little slow of sale of late, so that he was not worth so much. A fine farm, known as the Higley place, had fallen into his hands in the usual way the previous year, and he had not been able to find a tenant for it. Poor Higley, after working himself nearly to death on it in the attempt to lift the mortgage, had gone off to Dakota, leaving the farm and his curse to Butler.

This was the farm which Council advised Haskins to apply for; and the next day Council hitched up his team and drove down to see Butler.

"You jest let *me* do the talkin'," he said. "We'll find him wearin' out his pants on some salt barrel somew'ers; and if he thought you *wanted* the place he'd sock it to you hot and heavy. You jest keep quiet; I'll fix 'im."

Butler was seated in Ben Ashley's store telling fish yarns when Council sauntered in casually.

"Hello, But; lyin' agin, hey?"

"Hello, Steve! How goes it?"

"Oh, so-so. Too dang much rain these days. I thought it was

gon' t' freeze up f'r good last night. Tight squeak if I get m' ploughin' done. How's farmin' with *you* these days?"

"Bad. Ploughin' ain't half done."

"It 'ud be a religious idee f'r you t' go out an' take a hand y'rself."

"I don't haff to," said Butler, with a wink.

"Got anybody on the Higley place?"

"No. Know of anybody?"

"Waal, no; not eggsackly. I've got a relation back t' Michigan who's ben hot an' cold on the idea o' comin' West f'r some time. *Might* come if he could get a good lay-out. What do you talk on the farm?"

"Well, I d' know. I'll rent it on shares or I'll rent it money rent."

"Wall, how much money, say?"

"Well, say ten per cent, on the price—two-fifty."

"Wall, that ain't bad. Wait on 'im till 'e thrashes?"

Haskins listened eagerly to this important question, but Council was coolly eating a dried apple which he had speared out of a barrel with his knife. Butler studied him carefully.

"Well, knocks me out of twenty-five dollars interest."

"My relation'll need all he's got t' git his crops in," said Council, in the same, indifferent way.

"Well, all right; *say* wait," concluded Butler.

"All right; this is the man. Haskins, this is Mr. Butler—no relation to Ben—the hardest-working man in Cedar County."

On the way home Haskins said: "I ain't much better off. I'd like that farm; it's a good farm, but it's all run down, an' so 'm I. I could make a good farm of it if I had half a show. But I can't stock it n'r seed it."

"Waal, now, don't you worry," roared Council in his ear. "We'll pull y' through somehow till next harvest. He's agreed t' hire it ploughed, an' you can earn a hundred dollars ploughin' an' y' c'n git the seed o' me, an' pay me back when y' can."

Haskins was silent with emotion, but at last he said, "I ain't got nothin' t' live on."

"Now, don't you worry 'bout that. You jest make your headquarters at ol' Steve Council's. Mother'll take a pile o' comfort in havin' y'r wife an' children 'round. Y' see, Jane's married off lately, an' Ike's away a good 'eal, so we'll be darn glad t' have y' stop with us this winter. Nex' spring we'll see if y' can't git a start agin." And he chirruped to the team, which sprang forward with the rumbling, clattering wagon.

"Say, looky here, Council, you can't do this. I never saw——" shouted Haskins in his neighbor's ear.

Council moved about uneasily in his seat and stopped his stammering gratitude by saying: "Hold on, now; don't make such a fuss over a little thing. When I see a man down, an' things all on top of 'm, I jest like t' kick 'em off an' help 'm up. That's the kind of religion I got, an' it's about the *only* kind."

They rode the rest of the way home in silence. And when the red light of the lamp shone out into the darkness of the cold and windy night, and he thought of this refuge for his children and wife, Haskins could have put his arm around the neck of his burly companion and squeezed him like a lover. But he contented himself with saying, "Steve Council, you'll git y'r pay f'r this some day."

"Don't want any pay. My religion ain't run on such business principles."

The wind was growing colder, and the ground was covered with a white frost, as they turned into the gate of the Council farm, and the children came rushing out, shouting, "Papa's come!" They hardly looked like the same children who had sat at the table the night before. Their torpidity, under the influence of sunshine and Mother Council, had given way to a sort of spasmodic cheerfulness, as insects in winter revive when laid on the hearth.

III

Haskins worked like a fiend, and his wife, like the heroic woman that she was, bore also uncomplainingly the most terrible burdens. They rose early and toiled without intermission till the darkness fell on the plain, then tumbled into bed, every bone and muscle aching with fatigue, to rise with the sun next morning to the same round of the same ferocity of labor.

The eldest boy, now nine years old, drove a team all through the spring, ploughing and seeding, milked the cows, and did chores innumerable, in most ways taking the place of a man; an infinitely pathetic but common figure—this boy—on the American farm, where there is no law against child labor. To see him in his coarse clothing, his huge boots, and his ragged cap, as he staggered with a pail of water from the well, or trudged in the cold and cheerless dawn out into the frosty field behind his team, gave the city-bred visitor a sharp pang of sympathetic pain. Yet Haskins loved his boy, and would have saved him from this if he could, but he could not.

By June the first year the result of such Herculean toil began to show on the farm. The yard was cleaned up and sown to grass, the garden ploughed and planted, and the house mended. Council had given them four of his cows.

"Take 'em an' run 'em on shares. I don't want a milk s' many. Ike's away s' much now, Sat'd'ys an' Sund'ys, I can't stand the bother anyhow."

Other men, seeing the confidence of Council in the newcomer, had sold him tools on time; and as he was really an able farmer, he soon had round him many evidences of his care and thrift. At the advice of Council he had taken the farm for three years, with the privilege of re-renting or buying at the end of the term.

"It's a good bargain, an' y' want 'o nail it," said Council. "If you have any kind ov a crop, you c'n pay y'r debts, an' keep seed an' bread."

The new hope which now sprang up in the heart of Haskins and his wife grew almost as a pain by the time the wide field of wheat began to wave and rustle and swirl in the winds of July. Day after day he would snatch a few moments after supper to go and look at it.

"Have ye seen the wheat t'-day, Nettie?" he asked one night as he rose from supper.

"No, Tim, I ain't had time."

"Well, take time now. Le's go look at it."

She threw an old hat on her head—Tommy's hat—and look-ing almost pretty in her thin, sad way, went out with her husband to the hedge.

"Ain't it grand, Nettie? Just look at it."

It was grand. Level, russet here and there, heavy-headed, wide as a lake, and full of multitudinous whispers and gleams of wealth, it stretched away before the gazers like the fabled field of the cloth of gold.

"Oh, I think—I *hope* we'll have a good crop, Tim; and oh, how good the people have been to us!"

"Yes; I don't know where we'd be t'-day if it hadn't ben f'r Council and his wife."

"They're the best people in the world," said the little woman, with a great sob of gratitude.

"We'll be in the field on Monday, sure," said Haskins, gripping the rail on the fences as if already at the work of the harvest.

The harvest came, bounteous, glorious, but the winds came and blew it into tangles, and the rain matted it here and there close to the ground, increasing the work of gathering it threefold.

Oh, how they toiled in those glorious days! Clothing dripping with sweat, arms aching, filled with briers, fingers raw and bleeding, backs broken with the weight of heavy bundles, Haskins and his man toiled on. Tommy drove the harvester, while his father and a hired man bound on the machine. In this way they cut ten acres every day, and almost every night after supper, when the hand went to bed, Haskins returned to the field shocking the bound grain in the light of the moon. Many a night he worked till his anxious wife came out at ten o'clock to call him in to rest and lunch.

At the same time she cooked for the men, took care of the children, washed and ironed, milked the cows at night, made the butter, and sometimes fed the horses and watered them while her husband kept at the shocking. No slave in the Roman galleys could have toiled so frightfully and lived, for this man thought himself a free man, and that he was working for his wife and babes.

When he sank into his bed with a deep groan of relief, too tired to change his grimy, dripping clothing, he felt that he was getting nearer and nearer to a home of his own, and pushing the wolf of want a little farther from his door.

There is no despair so deep as the despair of a homeless man or woman. To roam the roads of the country or the streets of the city, to feel there is no rood of ground on which the feet can rest, to halt weary and hungry outside lighted windows and hear laughter and song within—these are the hungers and rebellions that drive men to crime and women to shame.

It was the memory of this homelessness, and the fear of its coming again, that spurred Timothy Haskins and Nettie, his wife, to such ferocious labor during that first year.

IV

" 'M, yes; 'm, yes; first-rate," said Butler, as his eye took in the neat garden, the pig-pen, and the well-filled barnyard. "You're gitt'n quite a stock around yeh. Done well, eh?"

Haskins was showing Butler around the place. He had not seen it for a year, having spent the year in Washington and Boston with Ashley, his brother-in-law, who had been elected to Congress.

"Yes, I've laid out a good deal of money durin' the last three years. I've paid out three hundred dollars f'r fencin'."

"Um—h'm! I see, I see," said Butler, while Haskins went on.

"The kitchen there cost two hundred; the barn ain't cost much in money, but I've put a lot o' time on it. I've dug a new well, and I——"

"Yes, yes, I see. You've done well. Stock worth a thousand dollars," said Butler, picking his teeth with a straw.

"About that," said Haskins, modestly. "We begin to feel's if we was gitt'n' a home f'r ourselves; but we've worked hard. I tell ye we begin to feel it, Mr. Butler, and we're goin' t' begin to ease up purty soon. We've been kine o' plannin' a trip back t' *her* folks after the fall ploughin's done."

"*Eggs*-actly!" said Butler, who was evidently thinking of something else. "I suppose you've kine o' kalklated on stayin' here three years more?"

"Well, yes. Fact is, I think I c'n buy the farm this fall, if you'll give me a reasonable show."

"Um—m! What do you call a reasonable show?"

"Waal; say a quarter down and three years' time."

Butler looked at the huge stacks of wheat which filled the yard, over which the chickens were fluttering and crawling, catching grasshoppers, and out of which the crickets were singing innumerably. He smiled in a peculiar way as he said, "Oh, I won't be hard on yer. But what did you expect to pay f'r the place?"

"Why, about what you offered it for before, two thousand five hundred, or *possibly* three thousand dollars," he added quickly, as he saw the owner shake his head.

"This farm is worth five thousand and five hundred dollars," said Butler, in a careless and decided voice.

"*What!*" almost shrieked the astounded Haskins. "What's that? Five thousand? Why, that's double what you offered it for three years ago."

"Of course, and it's worth it. It was all run down then, now it's in good shape. You've laid out fifteen hundred dollars in improvements, according to your own story."

"But *you* had nothin' t' do about that. It's my work an' my money."

"You bet it was; but it's my land."

"But what's to pay me for all my—"

"Ain't you had the use of 'em?" replied Butler, smiling calmly into his face.

Haskins was like a man struck on the head with a sandbag; he couldn't think; he stammered as he tried to say: "But—I never'd git the use— You'd rob me! More'n that: you agreed—you promised that I could buy or rent at the end of three years at——"

"That's all right. But I didn't say I'd let you carry off the improvements, nor that I'd go on renting the farm at two-fifty. The land is doubled in value, it don't matter how; it don't enter into the question; an' now you can pay me five hundred dollars a year rent, or take it on your own terms at fifty-five hundred, or—git out."

He was turning away when Haskins, the sweat pouring from his face, fronted him, saying again:

"But *you've* done nothing to make it so. You hain't added a cent. I put it all there myself, expectin' to buy. I worked an' sweat to improve it. I was workin' for myself an' babes——"

"Well, why didn't you buy when I offered to sell? What y' kickin' about?"

"I'm kickin' about payin' you twice f'r my own things—my own fences, my own kitchen, my own garden."

Butler laughed. "You're too green t' eat, young feller. *Your* improvements! The law will sing another tune."

"But I trusted your word."

"Never trust anybody, my friend. Besides, I didn't promise not to do this thing. Why, man, don't look at me like that. Don't take me for a thief. It's the law. The reg'lar thing. Everybody does it."

"I don't care if they do. It's stealin' jest the same. You take three thousand dollars of my money. The work o' my hands and my wife's." He broke down at this point. He was not a strong man mentally. He could face hardship, ceaseless toil, but he could not face the cold and sneering face of Butler.

"But I don't take it," said Butler, coolly "All you've got to do is to go on jest as you've been a-doin', or give me a thousand dollars down, and a mortgage at ten per cent on the rest."

Haskins sat down blindly on a bundle of oats near by, and with staring eyes and drooping head went over the situation. He was under the lion's paw. He felt a horrible numbness in his heart and limbs. He was hid in a mist, and there was no path out.

Butler walked about, looking at the huge stacks of grain, and pulling now and again a few handfuls out, shelling the heads in his hands and blowing the chaff away. He hummed a little tune as he did so. He had an accommodating air of waiting.

Haskins was in the midst of the terrible toil of the last year. He was walking again in the rain and the mud behind his plough; he felt the dust and dirt of the threshing. The ferocious husking-time, with its cutting wind and biting, clinging snows, lay hard upon him. Then he thought of his wife, how she had cheerfully cooked and baked, without holiday and without rest.

"Well, what do you think of it?" inquired the cool, mocking, insinuating voice of Butler.

"I think you're a thief and a liar!" shouted Haskins, leaping up. "A black-hearted houn'!" Butler's smile maddened him; with a sudden leap he caught a fork in his hands, and whirled it in the air. "You'll never rob another man, damn ye!" he grated through his teeth, a look of pitiless ferocity in his accusing eyes.

Butler shrank and quivered, expecting the blow; stood, held hypnotized by the eyes of the man he had a moment before despised—a man transformed into an avenging demon. But in the deadly hush between the lift of the weapon and its fall there came a gush of faint, childish laughter and then across the range of his vision, far away and dim, he saw the sun-bright head of his baby girl, as, with the pretty, tottering run of a two-year-old, she moved across the grass of the dooryard. His hands relaxed; the fork fell to the ground; his head lowered.

"Make out y'r deed an' morgige, an' git off'n my land, an' don't ye never cross my line agin; if y' do, I'll kill ye."

Butler backed away from the man in wild haste, and climbing into his buggy with trembling limbs drove off down the road, leaving Haskins seated dumbly on the sunny pile of sheaves, his head sunk into his hands.

The Yellow Wallpaper

Charlotte Perkins Gilman
(1860–1935)

It is very seldom that mere ordinary people like John and myself secure ancestral halls for the summer.

A colonial mansion, a hereditary estate, I would say a haunted house, and reach the height of romantic felicity—but that would be asking too much of fate!

Still I will proudly declare that there is something queer about it.

Else, why should it be let so cheaply? And why have stood so long untenanted?

John laughs at me, of course, but one expects that in marriage.

John is practical in the extreme. He has no patience with faith, an intense horror of superstition, and he scoffs openly at any talk of things not to be felt and seen and put down in figures.

John is a physician, and *perhaps*—(I would not say it to a living soul, of course, but this is dead paper and a great relief to my mind—) *perhaps* that is one reason I do not get well faster.

You see, he does not believe I am sick!

And what can one do?

If a physician of high standing, and one's own husband, assures friends and relatives that there is really nothing the matter with one but temporary nervous depression—a slight hysterical tendency—what is one to do?

My brother is also a physician, and also of high standing, and he says the same thing.

So I take phosphates or phosphites—whichever it is, and tonics, and journeys, and air, and exercise, and am absolutely forbidden to "work" until I am well again.

Personally, I disagree with their ideas.

Personally, I believe that congenial work, with excitement and change, would do me good.

But what is one to do?

I did write for a while in spite of them; but it *does* exhaust me a good deal—having to be so sly about it, or else meet with heavy opposition.

I sometimes fancy that in my condition if I had less opposition and more society and stimulus—but John says the very worst thing I can do is to think about my condition, and I confess it always makes me feel bad.

So I will let it alone and talk about the house.

The most beautiful place! It is quite alone, standing well back from the road, quite three miles from the village. It makes me think of English places that you read about, for there are hedges and walls and gates that lock, and lots of separate little houses for the gardeners and people.

There is a *delicious* garden! I never saw such a garden—large and shady, full of box-bordered paths, and lined with long grape-covered arbors with seats under them.

There were greenhouses, too, but they are all broken now.

There was some legal trouble, I believe, something about the heirs and co-heirs; anyhow, the place has been empty for years.

That spoils my ghostliness, I am afraid, but I don't care—there is something strange about the house—I can feel it.

I even said so to John one moonlight evening, but he said what I felt was a *draught,* and shut the window.

I get unreasonably angry with John sometimes. I'm sure I never used to be so sensitive. I think it is due to this nervous condition.

But John says if I feel so, I shall neglect proper self-control; so I take pains to control myself—before him, at least, and that makes me very tired.

I don't like our room a bit. I wanted one downstairs that opened on the piazza and had roses all over the window, and such pretty old-fashioned chintz hangings! but John would not hear of it.

He said there was only one window and not room for two beds, and no near room for him if he took another.

He is very careful and loving, and hardly lets me stir without special direction.

I have a schedule prescription for each hour in the day; he takes all care from me, and so I feel basely ungrateful not to value it more.

He said we came here solely on my account, that I was to have perfect rest and all the air I could get. "Your exercise depends on your strength, my dear," said he, "and your food somewhat on your appetite; but air you can absorb all the time." So we took the nursery at the top of the house.

It is a big, airy room, the whole floor nearly, with windows that look all ways, and air and sunshine galore. It was nursery first and then playroom and gymnasium, I should judge; for the windows are barred for little children, and there are rings and things in the walls.

The paint and paper look as if a boys' school had used it. It is stripped off—the paper—in great patches all around the head of my bed, about as far as I can reach, and in a great place on the other side of the room low down. I never saw a worse paper in my life.

One of those sprawling flamboyant patterns committing every artistic sin.

It is dull enough to confuse the eye in following, pronounced enough to constantly irritate and provoke study, and when you follow the lame uncertain curves for a little distance they suddenly commit suicide—plunge off at outrageous angles, destroy themselves in unheard of contradictions.

The color is repellant, almost revolting; a smouldering unclean yellow, strangely faded by the slow-turning sunlight.

It is a dull yet lurid orange in some places, a sickly sulphur tint in others.

No wonder the children hated it! I should hate it myself if I had to live in this room long.

There comes John, and I must put this away—he hates to have me write a word.

We have been here two weeks, and I haven't felt like writing before, since that first day.

I am sitting by the window now, up in this atrocious nursery, and there is nothing to hinder my writing as much as I please, save lack of strength.

John is away all day, and even some nights when his cases are serious.

I am glad my case is not serious!

But these nervous troubles are dreadfully depressing.

John does not know how much I really suffer. He knows there is no *reason* to suffer, and that satisfies him.

Of course it is only nervousness. It does weigh on me so not to do my duty in any way!

I meant to be such a help to John, such a real rest and comfort, and here I am a comparative burden already!

Nobody would believe what an effort it is to do what little I am able—to dress and entertain, and other things.

It is fortunate Mary is so good with the baby. Such a dear baby!

And yet I *cannot* be with him, it makes me so nervous.

I suppose John never was nervous in his life. He laughs at me so about this wallpaper!

At first he meant to repaper the room, but afterwards he said that I was letting it get the better of me, and that nothing was worse for a nervous patient than to give way to such fancies.

He said that after the wallpaper was changed it would be the heavy bedstead, and then the barred windows, and then that gate at the head of the stairs, and so on.

"You know the place is doing you good," he said, "and really, dear, I don't care to renovate the house just for a three months' rental."

"Then do let us go downstairs," I said, "there are such pretty rooms there."

Then he took me in his arms and called me a blessed little goose, and said he would go down to the cellar, if I wished, and have it whitewashed into the bargain.

But he is right enough about the beds and windows and things.

It is an airy and comfortable room as any one need wish, and, of course, I would not be so silly as to make him uncomfortable just for a whim.

I'm really getting quite fond of the big room, all but that horrid paper.

Out of one window I can see the garden, those mysterious deep-shaded arbors, the riotous old-fashioned flowers, and bushes and gnarly trees.

Out of another I get a lovely view of the bay and a little private wharf belonging to the estate. There is a beautiful shaded lane that runs down there from the house. I always fancy I see people walking in these numerous paths and arbors, but John has cautioned me not to give way to fancy in the least. He says that with my imaginative power and habit of story-making, a nervous weakness like mine is sure to lead to all manner of excited fancies, and that I ought to use my will and good sense to check the tendency. So I try.

I think sometimes that if I were only well enough to write a little it would relieve the press of ideas and rest me.

But I find I get pretty tired when I try.

It is so discouraging not to have any advice and companionship about my work. When I get really well, John says we will ask Cousin Henry and Julia down for a long visit; but he says he would as soon put fireworks in my pillow-case as to let me have those stimulating people about now.

I wish I could get well faster.

But I must not think about that. This paper looks to me as if it *knew* what a vicious influence it had!

There is a recurrent spot where the pattern lolls like a broken neck and two bulbous eyes stare at you upside down.

I get positively angry with the impertinence of it and the everlastingness. Up and down and sideways they crawl, and those absurd, unblinking eyes are everywhere. There is one place where two breadths didn't match, and the eyes go all up and down the line, one a little higher than the other.

I never saw so much expression in an inanimate thing before, and we all know how much expression they have! I used to lie awake as a child and get more entertainment and terror out of blank walls and plain furniture than most children could find in a toy-store.

I remember what a kindly wink the knobs of our big, old bureau used to have, and there was one chair that always seemed like a strong friend.

I used to feel that if any of the other things looked too fierce I could always hop into that chair and be safe.

The furniture in this room is no worse than inharmonious, however, for we had to bring it all from downstairs. I suppose when this was used as a playroom they had to take the nursery things out, and no wonder! I never saw such ravages as the children have made here.

The wallpaper, as I said before, is torn off in spots, and it sticketh closer than a brother—they must have had perseverance as well as hatred.

Then the floor is scratched and gouged and splintered, the plaster itself is dug out here and there, and this great heavy bed which is all we found in the room, looks as if it had been through the wars.

But I don't mind it a bit—only the paper.

There comes John's sister. Such a dear girl as she is, and so careful of me! I must not let her find me writing.

She is a perfect and enthusiastic housekeeper, and hopes for no better profession. I verily believe she thinks it is the writing which made me sick!

But I can write when she is out, and see her a long way off from these windows.

There is one that commands the road, a lovely shaded winding road, and one that just looks off over the country. A lovely country, too, full of great elms and velvet meadows.

This wallpaper has a kind of subpattern in a different shade, a particularly irritating one, for you can only see it in certain lights, and not clearly then.

But in the places where it isn't faded and where the sun is

just so—I can see a strange, provoking, formless sort of figure, that seems to skulk about behind that silly and conspicuous front design.

There's sister on the stairs!

Well, the Fourth of July is over! The people are gone and I am tired out. John thought it might do me good to see a little company, so we just had mother and Nellie and the children down for a week.

Of course I didn't do a thing. Jennie sees to everything now.

But it tired me all the same.

John says if I don't pick up faster he shall send me to Weir Mitchell in the fall.

But I don't want to go there at all. I had a friend who was in his hands once, and she says he is just like John and my brother, only more so!

Besides, it is such an undertaking to go so far.

I don't feel as if it was worth while to turn my hand over for anything, and I'm getting dreadfully fretful and querulous.

I cry at nothing, and cry most of the time.

Of course I don't when John is here, or anybody else, but when I am alone.

And I am alone a good deal just now. John is kept in town very often by serious cases, and Jennie is good and lets me alone when I want her to.

So I walk a little in the garden or down that lovely lane, sit on the porch under the roses, and lie down up here a good deal.

I'm getting really fond of the room in spite of the wallpaper. Perhaps *because* of the wallpaper.

It dwells in my mind so!

I lie here on this great immovable bed—it is nailed down, I believe—and follow that pattern about by the hour. It is as good as gymnastics, I assure you. I start, we'll say, at the bottom, down in the corner over there where it has not been touched, and I determine for the thousandth time that I *will* follow that pointless pattern to some sort of a conclusion.

I know a little of the principle of design, and I know this thing was not arranged on any laws of radiation, or alternation, or repetition, or symmetry, or anything else that I ever heard of.

It is repeated, of course, by the breadths, but not otherwise.

Looked at in one way each breadth stands alone, the bloated curves and flourishes—a kind of "debased Romanesque" with *delirium tremens*—go waddling up and down in isolated columns of fatuity.

But, on the other hand, they connect diagonally, and the sprawling outlines run off in great slanting waves of optic horror, like a lot of wallowing seaweeds in full chase.

The whole thing goes horizontally, too, at least it seems so, and I exhaust myself in trying to distinguish the order of its going in that direction.

They have used a horizontal breadth for a frieze, and that adds wonderfully to the confusion.

There is one end of the room where it is almost intact, and there, when the crosslights fade and the low sun shines directly upon it, I can almost fancy radiation after all—the interminable grotesque seem to form around a common centre and rush off in headlong plunges of equal distraction.

It makes me tired to follow it. I will take a nap I guess.

I don't know why I should write this.

I don't want to.

I don't feel able.

And I know John would think it absurd. But I *must* say what I feel and think in some way—it is such a relief!

But the effort is getting to be greater than the relief.

Half the time now I am awfully lazy, and lie down ever so much.

John says I musn't lose my strength, and has me take cod liver oil and lots of tonics and things, to say nothing of ale and wine and rare meat.

Dear John! He loves me very dearly, and hates to have me sick. I tried to have a real earnest reasonable talk with him the other day, and tell him how I wish he would let me go and make a visit to Cousin Henry and Julia.

But he said I wasn't able to go, nor able to stand it after I got there; and I did not make out a very good case for myself, for I was crying before I had finished.

It is getting to be a great effort for me to think straight. Just this nervous weakness I suppose.

And dear John gathered me up in his arms, and just carried me upstairs and laid me on the bed, and sat by me and read to me till it tired my head.

He said I was his darling and his comfort and all he had, and that I must take care of myself for his sake, and keep well.

He says no one but myself can help me out of it, that I must use my will and self-control and not let any silly fancies run away with me.

There's one comfort, the baby is well and happy, and does not have to occupy this nursery with the horrid wallpaper.

If we had not used it, that blessed child would have! What a fortunate escape! Why, I wouldn't have a child of mine, an impressionable little thing, live in such a room for worlds.

I never thought of it before, but it is lucky that John kept me here after all, I can stand it so much easier than a baby, you see.

Of course I never mention it to them any more—I am too wise—but I keep watch of it all the same.

There are things in that paper that nobody knows but me, or ever will.

Behind that outside pattern the dim shapes get clearer every day.

It is always the same shape, only very numerous.

And it is like a woman stooping down and creeping about behind that pattern. I don't like it a bit. I wonder—I begin to think—I wish John would take me away from here!

It is so hard to talk with John about my case, because he is so wise, and because he loves me so.

But I tried it last night.

It was moonlight. The moon shines in all around just as the sun does.

I hate to see it sometimes, it creeps so slowly, and always comes in by one window or another.

John was asleep and I hated to waken him, so I kept still and watched the moonlight on that undulating wallpaper till I felt creepy.

The faint figure behind seemed to shake the pattern, just as if she wanted to get out.

I got up softly and went to feel and see if the paper *did* move, and when I came back John was awake.

"What is it, little girl?" he said. "Don't go walking about like that—you'll get cold."

I thought it was a good time to talk, so I told him that I really was not gaining here, and that I wished he would take me away.

"Why, darling!" said he, "our lease will be up in three weeks, and I can't see how to leave before.

"The repairs are not done at home, and I cannot possibly leave town just now. Of course if you were in any danger, I could and would, but you really are better, dear, whether you can see it or not. I am a doctor, dear, and I know. You are gaining flesh and color, your appetite is better, I feel really much easier about you."

"I don't weigh a bit more," said I, "nor as much; and my appetite may be better in the evening when you are here, but it is worse in the morning when you are away!"

"Bless her little heart!" said he with a big hug, "she shall be as sick as she pleases! But now let's improve the shining hours by going to sleep, and talk about it in the morning!"

"And you won't go away?" I asked gloomily.

"Why, how can I, dear? It is only three weeks more and then we will take a nice little trip of a few days while Jennie is getting the house ready. Really dear you are better!"

"Better in body perhaps—" I began, and stopped short, for he sat up straight and looked at me with such a stern, reproachful look that I could not say another word.

"My darling," said he, "I beg of you, for my sake and for our child's sake, as well as for your own, that you will never for one instant let that idea enter your mind! There is nothing so dangerous, so fascinating, to a temperament like yours. It is a false and foolish fancy. Can you not trust me as a physician when I tell you so?"

So of course I said no more on that score, and we went to sleep before long. He thought I was asleep first, but I wasn't, and lay there for hours trying to decide whether that front pattern and the back pattern really did move together or separately.

On a pattern like this, by daylight, there is a lack of sequence, a defiance of law, that is a constant irritant to a normal mind.

The color is hideous enough, and unreliable enough, and infuriating enough, but the pattern is torturing.

You think you have mastered it, but just as you get well underway in following, it turns a back-somersault and there you are. It slaps you in the face, knocks you down, and tramples upon you. It is like a bad dream.

The outside pattern is a florid arabesque, reminding one of a fungus. If you can imagine a toadstool in joints, an interminable string of toadstools, budding and sprouting in endless convolutions—why, that is something like it.

That is, sometimes!

There is one marked peculiarity about this paper, a thing nobody seems to notice but myself, and that is that it changes as the light changes.

When the sun shoots in through the east window—I always watch for that first long, straight ray—it changes so quickly that I never can quite believe it.

That is why I watch it always.

By moonlight—the moon shines in all night when there is a moon—I wouldn't know it was the same paper.

At night in any kind of light, in twilight, candlelight, lamplight, and worst of all by moonlight, it becomes bars! The outside pattern I mean, and the woman behind it is as plain as can be.

I didn't realize for a long time what the thing was that showed behind, that dim subpattern, but now I am quite sure it is a woman.

By daylight she is subdued, quiet. I fancy it is the pattern that keeps her so still. It is so puzzling. It keeps me quiet by the hour.

I lie down ever so much now. John says it is good for me, and to sleep all I can.

Indeed he started the habit by making me lie down for an hour after each meal.

It is a very bad habit I am convinced, for you see I don't sleep.

And that cultivates deceit, for I don't tell them I'm awake—O no!

The fact is I am getting a little afraid of John.

He seems very queer sometimes, and even Jennie has an inexplicable look.

It strikes me occasionally, just as a scientific hypothesis—that perhaps it is the paper!

I have watched John when he did not know I was looking, and come into the room suddenly on the most innocent excuses, and I've caught him several times *looking at the paper!* And Jennie too. I caught Jennie with her hand on it once.

She didn't know I was in the room, and when I asked her in a quiet, a very quiet voice, with the most restrained manner possible, what she was doing with the paper—she turned around as if she had been caught stealing, and looked quite angry—asked me why I should frighten her so!

Then she said that the paper stained everything it touched, that she had found yellow smooches on all my clothes and John's, and she wished we would be more careful!

Did not that sound innocent? But I know she was studying that pattern, and I am determined that nobody shall find it out but myself!

Life is very much more exciting now than it used to be. You see I have something more to expect, to look forward to, to watch. I really do eat better, and am more quiet than I was.

John is so pleased to see me improve! He laughed a little the other day, and said I seemed to be flourishing in spite of my wallpaper.

I turned it off with a laugh. I had no intention of telling him it was *because* of the wallpaper—he would make fun of me. He might even want to take me away.

I don't want to leave now until I have found it out. There is a week more, and I think that will be enough.

I'm feeling ever so much better! I don't sleep much at night, for it is so interesting to watch developments; but I sleep a good deal in the daytime.

In the daytime it is tiresome and perplexing.

There are always new shoots on the fungus, and new shades of yellow all over it. I cannot keep count of them, though I have tried conscientiously.

It is the strangest yellow, that wallpaper! It makes me think of all the yellow things I ever saw—not beautiful ones like buttercups, but old foul, bad yellow things.

But there is something else about that paper—the smell! I noticed it the moment we came into the room, but with so much air and sun it was not bad. Now we have had a week of fog and rain, and whether the windows are open or not, the smell is here.

It creeps all over the house.

I find it hovering in the dining-room, skulking in the parlor, hiding in the hall, lying in wait for me on the stairs.

It gets into my hair.

Even when I go to ride, if I turn my head suddenly and surprise it—there is that smell!

Such a peculiar odor, too! I have spent hours in trying to analyze it, to find what it smelled like.

It is not bad—at first, and very gentle, but quite the subtlest, most enduring odor I ever met.

In this damp weather it is awful, I wake up in the night and find it hanging over me.

It used to disturb me at first. I thought seriously of burning the house—to reach the smell.

But now I am used to it. The only thing I can think of that it is like is the *color* of the paper! A yellow smell.

There is a very funny mark on this wall, low down, near the mopboard. A streak that runs round the room. It goes behind every piece of furniture, except the bed, a long, straight, even *smooch,* as if it had been rubbed over and over.

I wonder how it was done and who did it, and what they did it for. Round and round and round—round and round and round—it makes me dizzy!

I really have discovered something at last.

Through watching so much at night, when it changes so, I have finally found out.

The front pattern *does* move—and no wonder! The woman behind shakes it!

Sometimes I think there are a great many women behind, and sometimes only one, and she crawls around fast, and her crawling shakes it all over.

Then in the very bright spots she keeps still, and in the very shady spots she just takes hold of the bars and shakes them hard.

And she is all the time trying to climb through. But nobody could climb through that pattern—it strangles so; I think that is why it has so many heads.

They get through, and then the pattern strangles them off and turns them upside down, and makes their eyes white!

If those heads were covered or taken off it would not be half so bad.

I think that woman gets out in the daytime!

And I'll tell you why—privately—I've seen her!

I can see her out of every one of my windows!

It is the same woman, I know, for she is always creeping, and most women do not creep by daylight.

I see her in that long shaded lane, creeping up and down. I see her in those dark grape arbors, creeping all around the garden.

I see her on that long road under the trees, creeping along, and when a carriage comes she hides under the blackberry vines.

I don't blame her a bit. It must be very humiliating to be caught creeping by daylight!

I always lock the door when I creep by daylight. I can't do it at night, for I know John would suspect something at once.

And John is so queer now, that I don't want to irritate him. I wish he would take another room! Besides, I don't want anybody to get that woman out at night but myself.

I often wonder if I could see her out of all the windows at once.

But, turn as fast as I can, I can only see out of one at one time.

And though I always see her, she *may* be able to creep faster than I can turn!

I have watched her sometimes away off in the open country, creeping as fast as a cloud shadow in a high wind.

If only that top pattern could be gotten off from the under one! I mean to try it, little by little.

I have found out another funny thing, but I shan't tell it this time! It does not do to trust people too much.

There are only two more days to get this paper off, and I believe John is beginning to notice. I don't like the look in his eyes.

And I heard him ask Jennie a lot of professional questions about me. She had a very good report to give.

She said I slept a good deal in the daytime.

John knows I don't sleep very well at night, for all I'm so quiet!

He asked me all sorts of questions, too, and pretended to be very loving and kind.

As if I couldn't see through him!

Still, I don't wonder he acts so, sleeping under this paper for three months.

It only interests me, but I feel sure John and Jennie are secretly affected by it.

Hurrah! This is the last day, but it is enough. John to stay in town over night, and won't be out until this evening.

Jennie wanted to sleep with me—the sly thing! but I told her I should undoubtedly rest better for a night all alone.

That was clever, for really I wasn't alone a bit! As soon as it was moonlight and that poor thing began to crawl and shake the pattern, I got up and ran to help her.

I pulled and she shook, I shook and she pulled, and before morning we had peeled off yards of that paper.

A strip about as high as my head and half around the room.

And then when the sun came and that awful pattern began to laugh at me, I declared I would finish it to-day!

We go away to-morrow, and they are moving all my furniture down again to leave things as they were before.

Jennie looked at the wall in amazement, but I told her merrily that I did it out of pure spite at the vicious thing.

She laughed and said she wouldn't mind doing it herself, but I must not get tired.

How she betrayed herself that time!

But I am here, and no person touches this paper but me—not *alive!*

She tried to get me out of the room—it was too patent! But I said it was so quiet and empty and clean now that I believed I would lie down again and sleep all I could; and not to wake me even for dinner—I would call when I woke.

So now she is gone, and the servants are gone, and the things are gone, and there is nothing left but that great bedstead nailed down, with the canvas mattress we found on it.

We shall sleep downstairs to-night, and take the boat home to-morrow.

I quite enjoy the room, now it is bare again.

How those children did tear about here!

This bedstead is fairly gnawed!

But I must get to work.

I have locked the door and thrown the key down into the front path.

I don't want to go out, and I don't want to have anybody come in, till John comes.

I want to astonish him.

I've got a rope up here that even Jennie did not find. If that woman does get out, and tries to get away, I can tie her!

But I forgot I could not reach far without anything to stand on!

This bed will *not* move!

I tried to lift and push it until I was lame, and then I got so angry I bit off a little piece at one corner—but it hurt my teeth.

Then I peeled off all the paper I could reach standing on the floor. It sticks horribly and the pattern just enjoys it! All those strangled heads and bulbous eyes and waddling fungus growths just shriek with derision!

I am getting angry enough to do something desperate. To jump out of the window would be admirable exercise, but the bars are too strong even to try.

Besides I wouldn't do it. Of course not. I know well enough that a step like that is improper and might be misconstrued.

I don't like to *look* out of the windows even—there are so many of those creeping women, and they creep so fast.

I wonder if they all come out of that wallpaper as I did?

But I am securely fastened now by my well-hidden rope—you don't get *me* out in the road there!

I suppose I shall have to get back behind the pattern when it comes night, and that is hard!

It is so pleasant to be out in this great room and creep around as I please!

I don't want to go outside. I won't, even if Jennie asks me to.

For outside you have to creep on the ground, and everything is green instead of yellow.

But here I can creep smoothly on the floor, and my shoulder just fits in that long smooch around the wall, so I cannot lose my way.

Why there's John at the door!

It is no use, young man, you can't open it!

How he does call and pound!

Now he's crying for an axe.

It would be a shame to break down that beautiful door!

"John dear!" said I in the gentlest voice, "the key is down by the front steps, under a plantain leaf!"

That silenced him for a few moments.

Then he said—very quietly indeed, "Open the door, my darling!"

"I can't," said I. "The key is down by the front door under a plantain leaf!"

And then I said it again, several times, very gently and slowly, and said it so often that he had to go and see, and he got it of course, and came in. He stopped short by the door.

"What is the matter?" he cried. "For God's sake, what are you doing?"

I kept on creeping just the same, but I looked at him over my shoulder.

"I've got out at last," said I, "in spite of you and Jane. And I've pulled off most of the paper, so you can't put me back!"

Now why should that man have fainted? But he did, and right across my path by the wall, so that I had to creep over him every time!

The Singular Vote of Aut Tilbox

Sarah Pratt McLean Greene
(1856–1935)

During the time I spent at Amity I made every effort to ingratiate myself with the citizens of the place as the bearer of an honorable if not of a profoundly aristocratic name; but in the occasional brief notices taken of my existence, I was designated only as "that young man from Boston." Moreover, to gain any idea of the sublime scorn, the severe and overpowering ridicule, implied in those simple words, one should hear them as they fell from the lips of the Amity town oracle, the occupier of the armchair in the Amity country store, Colonel Sonorous B. Bacon. The Colonel's own pseudonym of "Snore," which might even be supposed to bring a smile to the features of the uninitiated, was regarded among his townsmen as a title of ponderous dignity and respect.

"That young man from Boston," said Colonel Snore—to whom my insignificant presence at the opposite end of the store had not been as yet on this occasion revealed—"that young man from Boston everdently has a towerin' opinion of himself. I consider it a dooty and a kindness to that young man to take him down a peg." To which the others of the Colonel's audience, unfortunately conscious of my presence, although they graciously forebore to make any audible assent, replied by an expressive silence.

This imputation of inordinate conceit, I found afterward, was solely attributable to the fact that, during my stay in Amity, a severe cold in the head caused me to have frequent recourse to some white linen pocket-handkerchiefs; while, as a still further taunt to this unmanly weakness on my part, the Colonel's own method of blowing his nose, by the unaided means of his thumb and forefinger, was brought, I now remember, into loud and frequent requisition.

Yet, despised and ridiculed as I was, I clung meekly to the ever-varying theatre of interest afforded me by the conduct of the Amity magnates, and so that I might occupy a humble seat in the auditorium of the country store, bore the Colonel's derisive shafts with silent resignation.

"It is a beautiful and a thrillin' sight, gentlemen," Colonel Snore began, seated now amid a transient company of drovers, his whole countenance glowing with a splendid consciousness of the occasion and of his own ability to shine. But here I was seized with the fatal impulse to sneeze. I drew out my despised pocket-handkerchief with a deprecating gesture. But the Colonel paused.

"Been to Boston lately?" he inquired of the group, with an expressive wink and a slight inclination of the thumb in my direction.

"Wa'al, yes, tol'able so," one answered.

"I hear they've been a-tryin' to get it incopperated as a city— eh?" the Colonel continued, indulging in a still more vastly facetious play of the eyebrows.

"Wa'al, yes, I believe they made it out some little time sence," replied the willing votary of this heartless wit.

"Glad to hear it!" exclaimed Colonel Snore, with loud emphasis—"glad to hear it! Let perseverance and virterous industry have their reward."

Having paused to crush me thus as a fleeting diversion, the Colonel now resumed that thread of his discourse, to which the pompous gravity of his tone had been so evidently adapted:

"It is a beautiful and a thrillin' sight, gentlemen, amidst the party strife which is devastatin' our country, the fraud and pussonal ambition ragin' in the capertols of our land, to turn for a moment to view the perlitical sittuation as it is here in our little country town of Amity. Yes, gentlemen, we may not be great, we may not be fastijous, we may not be yet incoppered as a city, but we can thank Heaven that there is yet *one* place in our land onblighted by the hand of perlitical corruption, and where patterotism is still a name.

"Not, gentlemen, but what we have had here in Amity some very closely contested elections, and on some occasions I do not deny to have witnessed no small display of party spirit; but this is owing not so much, gentlemen, to our discord as to our *u*quanimity. Sech is the *u*quanimity of our vote here in Amity that we have become distinguished, fur and wide, for our *ties*. And in our caukerses I have frequently heard it brought to a point of issoo, not to defeat this party or to carry that party, but 'Countrymen and fellercitizens, let us on this momenchous occasion nerve ourselves to the conflict, brace up our scattered cohorts, and do our durndest to av*i*de a tie!'

"As clost a perlitical contest, perhaps, gentlemen, as I have ever witnessed occurred here some year or more ago, when Jedge Marlborough and me, one and severally, competed ag'inst each other for the j'int office of Town Clark and Reegistrar of the town of Amity. Though often urged to it by my feller-citizens, I had always prev'ously refused to run, a lukertive business of my own—ownin'

perhaps the largest tobacco farm in the State, gentlemen—havin'
made it ompossible for me to engage to any extent in polertics.
But Beardsley come to me, and says he: 'Snore, the fate of the
Rerpublican party of the town of Amity is a-hangin' on your
hands. You and you only can afford to meet the Jedge on this campaign.' Jedge Marlborough bein', with perhaps one exception, gentlemen, the richest man in Amity. 'I have carried the Rerpublican
party on my shoulders for five years,' says Beardsley, 'and should
continnoo in it as my dooty and my priverlige. But my tobacco
crop has gone back on me this year, and I know my figger. I know
that I ain't competent to the Jedge.'

" 'Beardsley,' says I, 'at what figger do you place the impendin'
election of the town of Amity?'

" 'Snore,' says Beardsley, 'patterotism may rage high, and there's
no makin' percise calkerlations. I put it, Snore, at *two hunderd dollars.'*

" 'Beardsley,' says I, '*accept my note.'*

" 'Snore,' says Beardsley, 'that's patterotic, and it's munifercent;
but no, Snore, it won't do. There's got to be some degree of popplearity. Sence I foreclosed on Tim O'Rian I've lost my hold on
the Irish element. I thought o' runnin' Jones, but sence his darter
got the deestrict school away from Wright's darter there's been a
split in the party. No, Snore, the issoo lies with you and you only,
and you must meet the Jedge.'

" 'Beardsley,' says I, amusin' myself by takin' a last desprit measure, 'in considerin' a canderdate for any office, we must consider
his qualerfications *for* that office. My extensive business responser-
bilities and dooties as a man of property has not as yet give me no
time to pay much attention to the art of penmanship.'

" 'Snore,' says Beardsley, '*ef you can't write, you can talk.'*

"Wa'al, gentlemen, there didn't seem to be nothin' further to
be said. The caucus was held, and I was nommernated; and after

positively refusin' the nommernation, my onwillingness was declined, and I was acknowledged to be run, after the usual form.

"Gentlemen, there was various reasons why that campaign was
calkerlated to be a clost one. For more 'n a year young Hec Aspinwall, up on the mountain, simultaneous with Marl Junior
here—Jedge Marlborough's son—not to speak of our little Parson
Waters and an ondefinite number of others, had all been a-holdin'
court to my darter Fairbell. It's a singerler fact, gentlemen, that before I married the present Mrs. Bacon, although the town was full
of purty gals, lively and interestin' creeters, she was *the* one sought
after. And jest so it was with our Fairbell. By the time that gal got
to be sixteen years old she was so primmatoorly handsome and
smart, and so deuced fascernatin' in her ways, that her ma and
me—whose boodwar adjines the parlor—on Sunday nights in especial, almost despaired o' keepin' on her till she come o' age. But
on that p'int Mrs. Bacon was strong, Fairbell bein' our only child—
which Mrs. Bacon on one occasion regrettin', 'Mrs. Bacon,' says I,
'madam, a woman that has raised sech a darter as that has done
her dooty.'

"Of all the pursooers of my darter's affections I was inclined at
one time to think most fav'rably of Marl Junior as a well-ballasted
young man—though a member of the Dimmocracy—and carryin'
an old head for business. But Mrs. Bacon—and to me, gentlemen,
a woman's penetration in sech matters will never cease to be sur-
prisin'—Mrs. Bacon informed me that if Fairbell ever consented
to any of 'em, it would be our young Rerpublican, Hec Aspinwall.
'Your reasons, Mrs. Bacon,' says I, 'and her reasons?' 'They are
proberbly jest as foolish, Snore,' says Mrs. Bacon, resortin' to that
playful mood in which Mrs. Bacon and myself sometimes in-
dulges, 'as them for which I married you.'

"Wa'al, Hec *was* as handsome a dog as ever you see, as tall and
straight as a Norwejjan pine, with a black mustache a-swoopin'

down under as straight-cut a nose as ever adorned a statoote, but somehow it seemed as though Fairbell had fairly took a notion *ag'in him*. She had a good word for Marl or Waters or any o' the rest, but when it come to Hec, he was too big or too rude or somethin', and always a-flushin up at him as ef she was mad when he come in, until I swan I sometimes felt like takin' up on the young man's part. Howsumever, the dog was puffectly able to manage his own affairs, mind ye, and there's no knowin' what might 'a happened, ef it hadn't been for Mrs. Bacon's supernateral instinct as to how things stood; and in spite o' Marl's wooin' and Hec's threatenin' and little Waters's whinin', that onparalleled woman put her foot down strong that Fairbell shouldn't leave her father's house with *no* man till she come o' age.

"It chanced that Fairbell was jest a dawnin' into her eighteenth year, gentlemen, when I competed with the Jedge on the campaign before mentioned; and it appears to me that it was the very night of the caucus—a singerlarly beautiful and starlight night, gentle-men—that Marl and Hec and the rest on 'em was a-settin' around in the parlor afterwards, and Marl and Hec was givin' it to each other purty sharp on polertics, and a-gittin' oncomf'tably warm, teasin' Fairbell as to which she'd keep company with on some pertickler occasion, ontil by-and-by the gal flushes up and gives a sort of a 'Now I dare ye!' look to Hec, and says she, 'Of course I goes with the winnin' party!' and the minit she'd said it she give Hec the first sorry look that ever I see; but Hec stretches himself up, 'And so you shall, Fairbell,' says he. 'And so you shall, Fairbell,' says little Marl; and them two simultaneous riz, and went out.

"Gentlemen, in the campaign that follered, wherever I see fit to lend an old friend and constittuent a dollar, the Jedge lent him two. Where the Jedge lent two, Hec lent three. Where Hec lent three, Marl Junior lent four, leavin' in many sech cases a consid'able surplus of five dollars to be supplied by myself. Where I sought popplearity with the Irish element by a six months' release on a foreclosure, the Jedge sent a new image over to the Catholic church, say nothin' of attendin' papal services four weeks regerlar with his wife and darters. Where I obliged a neighbor by the temperrary loan of a hoe, the Jedge accomerdated with a spade, which, responded to by a plough on my part, the Jedge in turn reciprercated by a hoss-rake, until the Jedge's domains and mine was as fairly dernuded of all farmin' appurternances as though we'd been swep' over by the Old Testament deluge. But when Griggs came in one day to borrer my bell-crown, Mrs. Bacon declared that there *was* bounds, and that they had now been reached, and I was obliged to take Griggs outside, and compermise with him for a soft felt, to which, though somewhat worn, I have no hesertation in sayin', gentlemen, I had become pertickerlarly attached.

"By the fifth day of that campaign I see that all there was left for me was the honor, the other perrogatives bein' prev'ously more'n swallered up in the defence of my country. Howsumever, havin' once set out, I was not the man to flinch in my dooty; and as the Jedge hounded and anticerpated me, so there was no perlitical measure took by the Jedge but what I and my constittuents riz up to defeat it.

"Gentlemen, I wish the whole world might pause to witness an election like that which I am about to relate to you as havin' took place in our little country town of Amity.

"From a night unbroken by any incerdent, except for the continnual sound of cannonadin', and a slight skirmish between the Boys in Blue, headed by Hec Aspinwall, and the Boys in White, led on by Marl Junior—in which some was oncapacitated, but no serious loss to life or limb—the day rose calm and bright. Ere Phœbus had yet fully riz to light the orb of day, teams might 'a been seen a-wendin' their way from mountains and valleys toward the scene of interest. The wimmin stopped to the houses of their more centrerly located sisters to spend the day in them pursoots dear to the femernine heart, while the men congergated in and around the precincts of the Town-hall.

"By nine o'clock, gentlemen, I don't believe there was an able-bodied voter in the town of Amity but what had arrove punctual to the polls, while the lame and the halt and the blind from fur and near was a-bein' escorted thither in teams dispatched for the purpose by the reprersentatives of our respective factions; but I regard it as a stain upon our history, gentlemen, yes, as an infamous blot upon our history, that, in the ondue crowd and excitement of the hour, Jedge Marlborough was even known to employ the Amity town hearse. *And I wish that I might add, gentlemen, that his attentions was confined exclusively to the outside seat.*

"Gentlemen, it is not the practice at our elections to cast a hurried and onpremeditated vote, and then fly from the scene of action. Sech is not the brotherly feelin' which has always annermated the voters of the town of Amity. Many was the friendly discussions held that mornin' in and around the hoss-sheds and the Town-hall. Sech as had long been enermies was seen a-walkin' arm in arm, and sech as had never known each other was witnessed affectionertly reclinin' ag'inst the same fence rail. And I ventur' to say that not a vote had as yet been cast when it was announced that the *i*ysters was now ready, and our stomachs—which had only been sustained hitherto on a little weak cider, I do assure you, gentlemen—hastened to partake of them delicious varmints.

"Gentlemen, when I say that I am fond of *i*ysters, I speak warmly, but with limertations—with limertations. But the capacity displayed for *i*ysters by some of my constittuents that day, I do not hesertate to say, was thoroughly alarmin'. Gentlemen, I consider a quart bowl full of them delightful insects, well seasoned with a quantity of crackers, a most nourishin' compound, grateful and satisfyin' to the needs of man. But when it comes to two, three, four, and, yes, gentlemen, in some insternces, *six* bowls full, devoured by a single individooal, I am disposed to tremble for my country and my cause. Howsumever, I was determined not to flinch, and as often as a represrentative of my own party was borne over to partake of that mis'able cider dispensed by the constittuents of Jedge Marl, so often was some weak and totterin' member of the Dimmocracy led triumpherntly up to partake of Rerpublican *iys*ters. Everywhere Hec and Marl Junior was conspicuous a-cullin' detachments from the ranks of their respective enermies, and leadin' their scattered cohorts on to victory.

"I have stood in the thick of battle in defence of my country's cause, but, gentlemen, never have I witnessed a more thrillin' contest than that which I am now relatin' to you. Never, gentlemen, have I beheld sech an onparalleled display of patterotism. Of the supply of the enemy's ammernition in the shape of sech cider as I have above mentioned there could be no doubt. The only question was, would the supply of *i*ysters prove equal to sech an onexpected and onparalleled capacity. I am grateful to say, gentlemen, that it did; but I must not anticerpate.

"Perhaps the most curious incerdent connected with this eventful day, or, indeed, as ever occurred in all my perlitical experience, is what I shall reveal to you at the close of this narrative concerning the singerlar vote of Aut Tilbox. For the present I will only say that Aut is the derscendant of an ancient race which assumes to have suffered much pecunerrary loss through the war, bein' now some sixty years old, of a tall and corperlent phys*i*ke, and though a nomernal member of the Dimmocracy, has long, as to his practercal vote, been considered more'n waverin'. I had seen Aut on this eventful day led enticin'ly from *i*ysters to cider, and from cider back agin' to *i*ysters, ontil, irrespective of party issoo, I was about to interfere in the general cause of humanerty. But Hec assured me that he had known him to stand fur more on prev'ous

elections, and I watched his perceedin's at last in silence with a so-
licertude which was only exceeded by my amazement and cur'os-
ity. From *i*ysters to cider, and from cider back ag'in to *i*ysters, Aut
was winnin'ly and engagin'ly meandered by our respective factions, a prommernant figger in the general confusion, and one to
which I confess, gentlemen, my eyes had now become glued with
an onaccountable fascernation.

"In certain stages of his inebr'ancy Aut has a reppertation for
elerquence on-equalled by any one in our town. Yes, gentlemen,
and I think there is not a platform in our land which would have
been disgraced by his address delivered that day in the Town-hall
of Amity. But though speakin' most elerquently of patterotism and
dooty, and denouncin', with a voice of thunder, the ragin' sea of
perlitical corruption in our land, he give no hint as to which way
he was pussonally inclinin' to vote on this pertickerlar occasion,
ontil, jest as he was closin', Marl Junior was seen to press somethin'
affectionertly into his hand. 'When my eyes has closed on earthly
scenes,' then says Aut, 'and I hear the flusterin' of angels' wings, let
my last words be that I voted'—here Hec in passin' was seen still
more affectionertly to press somethin' into the speaker's hand—'let
my last words be,' says Aut, pausin' for a moment, and rollin' his
eyes up'ards, while a lingerin' smile played over his features, '*i*ysters,
*i*ysters, *i*ysters.'

"Aut descended, and was now almost despairingly by Hec and
Marl meandered back and forth ag'in, ontil I was compelled to observe that his symptoms grew still more elerquent, and he was only
with great differculty pervented from castin' a primmatoor and in-
erfectooal vote for the deceased Horace Greeley. 'Stay me not!'
cries Aut. 'He was the savior of his country, the institooter of a new
order, a martyr in the glo'rous cause of liberty, and, *above all, the pussonal friend of Aut Tilbox!'* And he endeavored wildly to reach the
polls, but was restrained, and on bein' told that the illustrious can-

derdate was dead, he retired into a corner, and for some moments was seen to weep onrestrainedly.

"He was again rescued by Hec and Marl, and led tremblin'ly back from *i*ysters to cider, and from cider back ag'in to *i*ysters; but it began to be everdent that his capacity was well-nigh reached. His elerquence was gone. He set harmlessly down on the hearth of the box-stove, which fortinitly contained no fire, and refused every inclernation to move. But when Marl whispered to him once more the accustomed invertation, a dangerous gleam shot from his closin' eyes: 'Young man,' says he, 'there is but one word left that I can hear, and that word is not a pleasant word, and that word is, *iysters and cider*, and woe be to him that speaks it!' And he riz up, and leanin' on the shoulders of his compatterots, disappeared temperrarily from the scene.

"It bein' now somewhat advanced in the afternoon a suggestion was made that we should perceed at once to the polls. But the brotherly feelin' which has always annermated the voters of the town of Amity, as I have said, gentlemen, has never permitted the castin' of a hurried and onpremeditated vote. I fear, however, that Williamston had been indulgin' somewhat too freely in the cider of the Dimmocracy, when, after some difficulty, he succeeded at length in reachin' the chair, and pounded an entirely onnecessary length of time on the counter perlimmernary to introducin' a bill. His tones, which at first was husky, grew clear and loud as he perceeded.

" 'I move,' says he, 'that an injunction be put upon the publercation, cirkerlation, or perusin' of any almanick save and exceptin Robert B. Thomas's old-fashioned, old farmer's, yaller-covered, ten-cent almanick! Gentlemen,' says he, 'I was induced last year to accept another almanick as a gift from an acquainternce. I took it home to my family as a instructor and a guide. Gentlemen, that almanick was the work of a incenderrary and a fiend. My wife and me was made to go to church on Saturday, and wondered to find the doors of the sanctooary closed ag'in us. We was made the scandal of our neighbors by washin' on Sunday, and bakin' in the middle of the week. Gentlemen, the moon in that almanick was seen at first quarter in perigee in the mornin', and fulled in apogee before night, besides bein' represented of a shape to draw tears from the eyes of science. December was set down as showery and January without a thaw. Moreover, in the back part of that almanick was receipts, among which was given one for removin' stains from the mouth after eatin' huckleberry pie. My wife and me innercently applied the mixter. Gentlemen, for days we was in torments, and our blistered burnin' mouths was closed to our family and friends. Gentlemen, shall not sech dastardly and inhuman perceedin's be stopped?' Here Williamston sunk exhausted into his chair, and the motion was put and carried by an overwhelmin' majority.

"Scarcely had Williamston been removed ere a member of my own party was brought triumpherntly forrerd by his compatterots and set upon the chair. His emotions was sech that the ruler sunk lifeless from his hands, and it was some moments before he could perceed. He begun in a fur-away dyin' tone that graduerly burst into a voice of thunder.

" 'I am tired,' says he, 'of party strife and perlitical intrigues. I am sick of campaigns and nommernations and 'lections and caukerses. I want to settle it once and forever by nommernatin' a good squar' hereddertary king. And I hereby move and nommernate that Colonel Sonorous B. Bacon be app'inted hereddertary king!'

"There is no knowin' what action might have been took in regard to my rash though well-meaning constittuent, had not our attention been diverted by the fact that the voters of the town of Amity was suddenly seen in a body wendin' their way towards the Deep Gully and Loud Western railroad tracks, which tracks, gentlemen, runs parallel with each other through the sand-gap, at a distance of some three or four rods from the Amity Town-hall. Soon I perceived that I was standin' alone by the deserted polls, and I turned and follered my compatterots to learn what might be the cause of this singerler conduct.

"Gentlemen, I have already narrated to you more than was my intention of the brotherly feelin', the friendly and am'able perceedin's, which was carried on in our little town of Amity durin' this important occasion, but I think I should fail in my dooty if I neglected to say that, as I j'ined my companions in the gap, it was everdent that the bettin' had been high and the stakes was about equal. For I beheld Jones settin' with his hoss and buggy on the Deep Gully railroad track, calmly awaitin' the arrival of the Loud Western train, with which, yes, gentlemen, with which it was his intention to run parallel in a race through the gap!

"As I gazed upon Jones, gentlemen, I cannot describe to you the emotions which temperrarily overcome me. I had expected much of my constittuents, but I was not prepared for sech a display of patterotism as this. I was about to rush forrerd to assure him that this was onnecessary, when the roar of the approachin' train was heard, and, calmly waitin' to git abreast of the Loud Western engine, Jones loosened the reins on his palpertatin' steed, and disappeared like a met'or up the track.

"Gentlemen, I have heard it said that there is a singerlarity about the hosses and waggins of the voters of Amity which would cause them to be easily distinguished anywhere on the face of the globe. And I will not deny that the back to the seat of Jones's buggy was formed of a mahogany pew door procured from the ruins of the old Presbyterian church, and upon which the figger 6, representin' the number of the pew to its former occupants, was still strikin'ly visible. Moreover, Jones's wife, bein' of an estheticky nature, had tacked around the ramparts of the buggy consid'rable of the old pulpit fringe, simerlarly procured from the ruins.

"But now, gentlemen, as I watched that figger 6 disappearin' up the track in a wavin' sea of fringe, and heard the clatterin' of Jones's hoss and buggy risin' even above the roar of the eng*i*ne, all lesser emotions was forgotten. I was compelled to lean upon a neighbor for support. But when the breathless excitement had died away, and it was announced, by sech as had stationed themselves to the ter-mernation of the gap, *a tie,* perlitical issoos was for the moment swallered up in our mutual despair. We grasped each other's hands in silence, and I don't believe, no, gentlemen, I don't believe there was a dry eye amongst the voters of the town of Amity.

"But the sun was fast westerin'. The polls was about to close. Realizin' this fact, the voters of Amity rushed permisc'ously toward the Town-hall. Leavin' our valiernt constittuents to defend for a moment our interests at the polls, Hec and I sped to the hoss-sheds, where Aut Tilbox was still loudly, sweetly sleepin'. We spoke to Aut in gentle and entreatin' accents, but he answered not. We shook and we threatened him, but the sound of his resoundin' slumbers was the only reply borne to our waitin' ears. There was a despairin' gleam in Hec's eye, and then an onaccountable flash of triermph. In less time than the words leaves my mouth Hec was exchangin' clo's with the unconscious Aut. Heights was equally tall, and corperlancy was supplied by means of a half sheaf of straw procured from a neighborin' waggin, and which was stuffed under the perdigious waistcoat Hec had now assumed. There was but one thing wantin': Aut's beard was of a peculiar yallowish tinge, growin' in perfusion from under his chin, his face bein' otherwise smooth. Hec's lightnin' eye fell upon the tail of Jedge Marlborough's hoss, standin' near. Yes, gentlemen, there was no denyin', that beard and that hoss's tail was of the same singerlar and onnatural color. Gentlemen, it was no sooner said than done! Marlborough's hoss stood without a tail—that is, gentlemen, without no tail to speak on. But a differculty arose on account of Hec's mustache: 'I half anticerpated this,' says he, and, groanin' drew a razor from his pocket. 'It's all for Fairbell,' says he. And 'It'll grow ag'in,' says he; and without another word that beautiful curvin' mustache fell to the earth. By means of some pine pitch the tail of Jedge Marlborough's hoss was quickly adjusted under the chin of my youthful constittuent; and then assumin' Aut's beaver hat as a last tetch, and thrustin' one arm akimbo, and steppin' out with that peculiar tread for which Aut is distinguished, and which I can only describe to you, gentlemen, as a kind of a hop and a skip, as though he was a-keepin' time to the insperation of invisible music, Hec wended his way towards the Town-hall.

"Gentlemen, sech was my emotions that I set weakly down on the nearest rail, and if my life had been the issoo at stake, for some moments I could not have riz. Positively, gentlemen, I could not have riz. Gentlemen, if the actual Aut Tilbox had rose up to take his place by the side of Hec he would not have been believed in. His identerty would have been questioned, and he would have been cast aside as an impostor. For, gentlemen, as my youthful constittuent wended his proud and amblin' and corperlant way towards the Town-hall, it could not be denied to my amazed and gaspin' vision that he was the Aut Tilboxest Aut Tilbox that ever I see! Gentlemen, he was Aut Tilboxer than Aut Tilbox himself!

"So the persumptive form of Aut entered the Town-hall, and marchin' towards the polls, and swingin' his Rerpublican ticket derfiantly aloft, he dropped it inter the box; and powerfully thrustin' to one side the wonder and exclamations of his disapp'inted compatterots, he was permitted, in the excitement of the moment, to disappear unfollered from the scene.

"Five minutes afterwards, as I was a-standin' with Hec, rehabertated in his own clo's, the loss of his mustache and a little griminess under the chin not bein' at sech a time made no account of, I was declared Town Clark and Reegistrar of the town of Amity by a majority, gentlemen—*by a majority of one!*

"I will not linger longer over the scenes which happened to the close of this eventful day. Serficient to say that when Jedge Marlborough's hoss was brought around to him, as he stood discoursin' loudly on the Town-hall steps after the election, and he observed the sittuation of that hoss's tail, his language was sech as I should hesertate, gentlemen, to describe in this narration. 'Anybody,' says Jedge Marlborough, in resoundin' tones—'anybody that'll disfigger and muterlate the tail of a noble animal like that, is not worthy of the name of Dimmocracy!' And the continuation of his language was simply petrifyin'. Howsumever, as I wended my way homewards that evenin' my thoughts was gratefulness and peace, which could not be disturbed even by observin' the constittuents of Jedge Marl hilar'ously burnin' me in effergy over in the shadder of the Hornpike woods.

"And on the following day, gentlemen, Fairbell Bacon and Hector Aspinwall was j'ined together in matrimony, to the residence of the bride's parents. The incerdents of yesterday was forgotten. The voters of the town of Amity with their wives gathered festive to my house, irrespective of perlitical differences. If little Parson Waters' eyes was tearful when he tied the knot, gentlemen, I do not consider it a thing to be onfeelin'ly commented on. And earnestly shakin' hands with Marl Junior, who stood somewhat pale in a corner, 'Marl,' says I, 'I wish that I had another darter like Fairbell for you, I do indeed.' 'Colonel,' says Marl, 'I wish you had, but that would be ompossible.'

"Fairbell and Hec have lived most happy together. Their house is, perhaps, with one exception, the finest reserdence in Amity, bein' pleasantly surrounded by piazzers, a fountain, and a cowpello, and, two weeks ago, an infant cherrib, which bears, gentlemen, the name of Sonorous Bacon Aspinwall.

"But some days after the 'lection Aut Tilbox was struttin' around in his proud and amblin' and corperlant way, makin' his boast of bein' diserfected with all existin' polertics, and of not havin' cast his vote for *no* party. On bein' overwhelmin'ly informed by the Dimmocracy that he had been seen on the prev'ous election to cast his vote for the Rerpublican canderdate, his denial and indignation knew no bounds. 'Then I was dragged into it when I was onsensible,' says he. 'It was intimerdation! It was intimerdation at the polls!' he cries. 'No,' says they; 'you walked in onassisted and of your own accord; and, more than that, Aut,' says they, 'you made a boast and a spectacle of it. You swung your Rerpublican ticket derfiantly in the air, Aut, and then dropped it into the box.' The number of witnesses was overwhelmin'. A sad and bedizzened look crept over Aut's face. He give them one last beseechin' gaze, and then turned and walked sorrerfully away.

"Gentlemen, it is safe to say that from that hour Aut Tilbox was a changed man. 'What is this mystery in science or in natur',' I have heard him say, 'that a man may, onknowin' to himself, commit sech desprit and onnatural deeds? It is solemn and myster'ous, and it bids us pause.' And Aut has forsook the ondue use of cider, and may be seen—yes, gentlemen, he may be seen on any Sunday, arrayed in his 'lection suit and beaver hat, quietly wendin' his way with Mrs. Tilbox down towards the Methodist meetin'-house."

Colonel Sonorous B. Bacon paused. Listening with rapt attention to his narrative I had long been struggling with the fatal impulse to sneeze. This desire, together with the thrilling close of the Colonel's recital, at length proved irresistible. Assuming as my last resort in this extremity an air of meek abstraction, I cautiously sought for my pocket-handkerchief. But the Colonel detected the movement. A slow and bitter smile, in which there was more than usual of withering contempt, overspread his features. Lifting his thumb and forefinger to his nose, he gave utterance to a blast which startled his audience from their seats and shook the dishes upon the grocery shelves. When the surcharged atmosphere had cleared a space, the Colonel sat calmly majestic in his chair, while I observed that every eye had become fastened upon me, the writhing object of his disdain.

"So they've got it incopperated as a city, eh?" continued Colonel Snore. "Have they nommernated a Mayor yet, I wonder? For everdently, gentlemen," said Colonel Snore, with the last severe thrust which his merciless sarcasm could give—"everdently we have here a canderdate!"

The Man without a Country

Edward Everett Hale

(1822–1909)

I suppose that very few casual readers of the "New York Herald" of August 13th observed, in an obscure corner, among the "Deaths," the announcement,

> "NOLAN. DIED, on board U. S. Corvette Levant,
> Lat. 2° 11' S., Long. 131° W., on the 11th of
> May, PHILIP NOLAN."

I happened to observe it, because I was stranded at the old Mission-House in Mackinac, waiting for a Lake-Superior steamer which did not choose to come, and I was devouring, to the very stubble, all the current literature I could get hold of, even down to the deaths and marriages in the "Herald." My memory for names and people is good, and the reader will see, as he goes on, that I had reason enough to remember Philip Nolan. There are hundreds of readers who would have paused at that announcement, if the officer of the Levant who reported it had chosen to make it thus:—"Died, May 11, THE MAN WITHOUT A COUNTRY."

For it was as "The Man without a Country" that poor Philip Nolan had generally been known by the officers who had him in charge during some fifty years, as, indeed, by all the men who sailed under them. I dare say there is many a man who has taken wine with him once a fortnight, in a three years' cruise, who never knew that his name was "Nolan," or whether the poor wretch had any name at all.

There can now be no possible harm in telling this poor creature's story. Reason enough there has been till now, ever since Madison's administration went out in 1817, for very strict secrecy, the secrecy of honor itself, among the gentlemen of the navy who have had Nolan in successive charge. And certainly it speaks well for the *esprit de corps* of the profession and the personal honor of its members, that to the press this man's story has been wholly unknown—and, I think, to the country at large also. I have reason to think, from some investigations I made in the Naval Archives when I was attached to the Bureau of Construction, that every official report relating to him was burned when Ross burned the public buildings at Washington. One of the Tuckers, or possibly one of the Watsons, had Nolan in charge at the end of the war; and when, on returning from his cruise, he reported at Washington to one of the Crowninshields—who was in the Navy Department when he came home—he found that the Department ignored the whole business. Whether they really knew nothing about it, or whether it was a *"Non mi ricordo,"* determined on as a piece of policy, I do not know. But this I do know, that since 1817, and possibly before, no naval officer has mentioned Nolan in his report of a cruise.

But, as I say, there is no need for secrecy any longer. And now the poor creature is dead, it seems to me worth while to tell a little of his story, by way of showing young Americans of to-day what it is to be

A MAN WITHOUT A COUNTRY

Philip Nolan was as fine a young officer as there was in the "Legion of the West," as the Western division of our army was then called. When Aaron Burr made his first dashing expedition down to New Orleans in 1805, at Fort Massac, or somewhere above on the river, he met, as the Devil would have it, this gay, dashing, bright young fellow, at some dinner-party, I think. Burr marked him, talked to him, walked with him, took him a day or two's voyage in his flat-boat, and, in short, fascinated him. For the next year, barrack-life was very tame to poor Nolan. He occasionally availed himself of the per-mission the great man had given him to write to him. Long, high-worded, stilted letters the poor boy wrote and rewrote and copied. But never a line did he have in reply from the gay deceiver. The other boys in the garrison sneered at him, because he sacrificed in this unrequited affection for a politician the time which they de-voted to Monongahela, sledge, and high-low-jack. Bourbon, euchre, and poker were still unknown. But one day Nolan had his revenge. This time Burr came down the river, not as an attorney seeking a place for his office, but as a disguised conqueror. He had defeated I know not how many district-attorneys; he had dined at I know not how many public dinners; he had been heralded in I know not how many Weekly Arguses; and it was rumored that he had an army be-hind him and an empire before him. It was a great day—his ar-rival—to poor Nolan. Burr had not been at the fort an hour before he sent for him. That evening he asked Nolan to take him out in his skiff, to show him a canebrake or a cotton-wood tree, as he said—really to seduce him; and by the time the sail was over, Nolan was enlisted body and soul. From that time, though he did not yet know it, he lived as A MAN WITHOUT A COUNTRY.

What Burr meant to do I know no more than you, dear reader. It is none of our business just now. Only, when the grand catastrophe came, and Jefferson and the House of Virginia of that day undertook to break on the wheel all the possible Clarences of the then House of York, by the great treason-trial at Richmond, some of the lesser fry in that distant Mississippi Valley, which was farther from us than Puget's Sound is to-day, introduced the like novelty on their provincial stage, and to while away the monotony of the summer at Fort Adams, got up, for *spectacles,* a string of court-martials on the officers there. One and another of the colonels and majors were tried, and, to fill out the list, little Nolan, against whom, Heaven knows, there was evidence enough—that he was sick of the service, had been willing to be false to it, and would have obeyed any order to march any-whither with any one who would follow him, had the order been signed, "By command of His Exc. A. Burr." The courts dragged on. The big flies escaped—rightly for all I know. Nolan was proved guilty enough, as I say; yet you and I would never have heard of him, reader, but that, when the president of the court asked him at the close whether he wished to say anything to show that he had always been faithful to the United States, he cried out, in a fit of frenzy—

"D— the United States! I wish I may never hear of the United States again!"

I suppose he did not know how the words shocked old Colonel Morgan, who was holding the court. Half the officers who sat in it had served through the Revolution, and their lives, not to say their necks, had been risked for the very idea which he so cavalierly cursed in his madness. He, on his part, had grown up in the West of those days, in the midst of "Spanish plot," "Orleans plot," and all the rest. He had been educated on a plantation where the finest company was a Spanish officer or a French merchant from Orleans. His education, such as it was, had been perfected in commercial expeditions to Vera Cruz, and I think he told me his father once hired an Englishman to be a private tutor for a winter on the plantation. He had spent half his youth with an older brother, hunting horses in Texas; and, in a word, to him "United States" was scarcely a reality. Yet he had been fed by "United States" for all the years since he had been in the army. He had sworn on his faith as a Christian to be true to "United States." It was "United States" which gave him the uniform he wore, and the sword by his side. Nay, my poor Nolan, it was only because "United States" had picked you out first as one of her own confidential men of honor that "A. Burr" cared for you a straw more than for the flat-boat men who sailed his ark for him. I do not excuse Nolan; I only explain to the reader why he damned his country, and wished he might never hear her name again.

He never did hear her name but once again. From that moment, September 23, 1807, till the day he died, May 11, 1863, he never heard her name again. For that half century and more he was a man without a country.

Old Morgan, as I said, was terribly shocked. If Nolan had compared George Washington to Benedict Arnold, or had cried, "God save King George," Morgan would not have felt worse. He called the court into his private room, and returned in fifteen minutes, with a face like a sheet, to say—

"Prisoner, hear the sentence of the Court. The Court decides, subject to the approval of the President, that you never hear the name of the United States again."

Nolan laughed. But nobody else laughed. Old Morgan was too solemn, and the whole room was hushed dead as night for a minute. Even Nolan lost his swagger in a moment. Then Morgan added—

"Mr. Marshal, take the prisoner to Orleans in an armed boat, and deliver him to the naval commander there."

The marshal gave his orders and the prisoner was taken out of court.

"Mr. Marshal," continued old Morgan, "see that no one mentions the United States to the prisoner. Mr. Marshal, make my respects to Lieutenant Mitchell at Orleans, and request him to order that no one shall mention the United States to the prisoner while he is on board ship. You will receive your written orders from the officer on duty here this evening. The court is adjourned without day."

I have always supposed that Colonel Morgan himself took the proceedings of the court to Washington city, and explained them to Mr. Jefferson. Certain it is that the President approved them— certain, that is, if I may believe the men who say they have seen his signature. Before the Nautilus got round from New Orleans to the Northern Atlantic coast with the prisoner on board, the sentence had been approved, and he was a man without a country.

The plan then adopted was substantially the same which was necessarily followed ever after. Perhaps it was suggested by the ne-cessity of sending him by water from Fort Adams and Orleans. The Secretary of the Navy—it must have been the first Crowninshield, though he is a man I do not remember—was requested to put Nolan on board a government vessel bound on a long cruise, and to direct that he should be only so far confined there as to make it cer-tain that he never saw or heard of the country. We had few long cruises then, and the navy was very much out of favor; and as almost all of this story is traditional, as I have explained, I do not know cer-tainly what his first cruise was. But the commander to whom he was intrusted—perhaps it was Tingey or Shaw, though I think it was one of the younger men—we are all old enough now—regulated the etiquette and the precautions of the affair, and according to his scheme they were carried out, I suppose, till Nolan died.

When I was second officer of the Intrepid, some thirty years after, I saw the original paper of instructions. I have been sorry ever since that I did not copy the whole of it. It ran, however, much in this way:—

"Washington," (with a date
which must have been late in 1807.)

"SIR—You will receive from Lt. Neale the person of
Philip Nolan, late a Lieutenant in the United States Army.

"This person on his trial by court-martial expressed
with an oath the wish that he might 'never hear of the
United States again.'

"The Court sentenced him to have his wish fulfilled.

"For the present, the execution of the order is intrusted by the President to this department.

"You will take the prisoner on board your ship, and keep
him there with such precautions as shall prevent his escape.

"You will provide him with such quarters, rations, and
clothing as would be proper for an officer of his late rank,
if he were a passenger on your vessel on the business of his
Government.

"The gentlemen on board will make any arrangements agreeable to themselves regarding his society. He is
to be exposed to no indignity of any kind, nor is he ever
unnecessarily to be reminded that he is a prisoner.

"But under no circumstances is he ever to hear of his
country or to see any information regarding it; and you
will especially caution all the officers under your command to take care, that, in the various indulgences which
may be granted, this rule, in which his punishment is involved, shall not be broken.

"It is the intention of the Government that he shall
never again see the country which he has disowned. Before the end of your cruise you will receive orders which
will give effect to this intention.

"Resp'y yours,

"W. SOUTHARD, for the Sec'y of the Navy."

If I had only preserved the whole of this paper, there would be no break in the beginning of my sketch of this story. For Captain Shaw, if it were he, handed it to his successor in the charge, and he to his, and I suppose the commander of the Levant has it to-day as his authority for keeping this man in this mild custody.

The rule adopted on board the ships on which I have met "the man without a country" was, I think, transmitted from the beginning. No mess liked to have him permanently because his presence cut off all talk of home or of the prospect of return, of politics or letters, of peace or of war—cut off more than half the talk men like to have at sea. But it was always thought too hard that he should never meet the rest of us, except to touch hats, and we finally sank into one system. He was not permitted to talk with the men, unless an officer was by. With officers he had unrestrained intercourse, as far as they and he chose. But he grew shy, though he had favorites: I was one. Then the captain always asked him to dinner on Monday. Every mess in succession took up the invitation in its turn. According to the size of the ship, you had him at your mess more or less often at dinner. His breakfast he ate in his own state-room— he always had a state-room—which was where a sentinel, or somebody on the watch, could see the door. And whatever else he ate or drank he ate or drank alone. Sometimes, when the marines or sailors had any special jollification, they were permitted to invite "Plain-Buttons," as they called him. Then Nolan was sent with some officer, and the men were forbidden to speak of home while he was there. I believe the theory was, that the sight of his punishment did them good. They called him "Plain-Buttons," because, while he always chose to wear a regulation army-uniform, he was not permitted to wear the army-button, for the reason that it bore either the initials or the insignia of the country he had disowned.

I remember, soon after I joined the navy, I was on shore with some of the older officers from our ship and from the Brandywine, which we had met at Alexandria. We had leave to make a party and go up to Cairo and the Pyramids. As we jogged along, (you went on donkeys then,) some of the gentlemen (we boys called them "Dons," but the phrase was long since changed) fell to talking about Nolan, and some one told the system which was adopted from the first about his books and other reading. As he was almost never permitted to go on shore, even though the vessel lay in port for months, his time, at the best, hung heavy; and everybody was permitted to lend him books, if they were not published in America and made no allusion to it. These were common enough in the old days, when people in the other hemisphere talked of the United States as little as we do of Paraguay. He had almost all the foreign papers that came into the ship, sooner or later; only somebody must go over them first, and cut out any advertisement or stray paragraph that alluded to America. This was a little cruel sometimes, when the back of what was cut out might be as innocent as Hesiod. Right in the midst of one of Napoleon's battles, or one of Canning's speeches, poor Nolan would find a great hole, because on the back of the page of that paper there had been an advertisement of a packet for New York, or a scrap from the President's message. I say this was the first time I ever heard of this plan, which afterwards I had enough, and more than enough, to do with. I remember it, because poor Phillips, who was of the party, as soon as the allusion to reading was made, told a story of something which happened at the Cape of Good Hope on Nolan's first voyage; and it is the only thing I ever knew of that voyage. They had touched at the Cape, and had done the civil thing with the English Admiral and the fleet, and then, leaving for a long cruise up the Indian Ocean, Phillips had borrowed a lot of English books from an officer, which, in those days, as indeed in these, was quite a windfall. Among them, as the Devil would order, was the "Lay of the Last Minstrel," which they had all of them heard of, but which

most of them had never seen. I think it could not have been published long. Well, nobody thought there could be any risk of anything national in that, though Phillips swore old Shaw had cut out
the "Tempest" from Shakspeare before he let Nolan have it, because he said "the Bermudas ought to be ours, and, by Jove, should
be one day." So Nolan was permitted to join the circle one afternoon when a lot of them sat on deck smoking and reading aloud.
People do not do such things so often now; but when I was young
we got rid of a great deal of time so. Well, so it happened that in
his turn Nolan took the book and read to the others; and he read
very well, as I know. Nobody in the circle knew a line of the
poem, only it was all magic and Border chivalry, and was ten thousand years ago. Poor Nolan read steadily through the fifth canto,
stopped a minute and drank something, and then began, without
a thought of what was coming—

> "Breathes there the man, with soul so dead,
> Who never to himself hath said,"—

It seems impossible to us that anybody ever heard this for the first
time; but all these fellows did then, and poor Nolan himself went
on, still unconsciously or mechanically—

> "This is my own, my native land!"

Then they all saw something was to pay; but he expected to get
through, I suppose, turned a little pale, but plunged on—

> "Whose heart hath ne'er within him burned,
> As home his footsteps he hath turned
>   From wandering on a foreign strand?—
> If such there breathe, go, mark him well."

By this time the men were all beside themselves, wishing there was any way to make him turn over two pages; but he had not quite presence of mind for that; he gagged a little, colored crimson, and staggered on—

> *"For him no minstrel raptures swell;*
> *High though his titles, proud his name,*
> *Boundless his wealth as wish can claim,*
> *Despite these titles, power, and pelf,*
> *The wretch, concentred all in self,"*—

and here the poor fellow choked, could not go on, but started up, swung the book into the sea, vanished into his state-room, "and by Jove," said Phillips, "we did not see him for two months again. And I had to make up some beggarly story to that English surgeon why I did not return his Walter Scott to him."

That story shows about the time when Nolan's braggadocio must have broken down. At first, they said, he took a very high tone, considered his imprisonment a mere farce, affected to enjoy the voyage, and all that; but Phillips said that after he came out of his state-room he never was the same man again. He never read aloud again, unless it was the Bible or Shakspeare, or something else he was sure of. But it was not that merely. He never entered in with the other young men exactly as a companion again. He was always shy afterwards, when I knew him—very seldom spoke, unless he was spoken to, except to a very few friends. He lighted up occasionally—I remember late in his life hearing him fairly eloquent on something which had been suggested to him by one of Fléchier's sermons—but generally he had the nervous, tired look of a heart-wounded man.

When Captain Shaw was coming home—if, as I say, it was Shaw—rather to the surprise of everybody they made one of the

Windward Islands, and lay off and on for nearly a week. The boys said the officers were sick of salt-junk, and meant to have turtle-soup before they came home. But after several days the Warren came to the same rendezvous; they exchanged signals; she sent to Phillips and these homeward-bound men letters and papers, and told them she was outward-bound, perhaps to the Mediterranean, and took poor Nolan and his traps on the boat back to try his second cruise. He looked very blank when he was told to get ready to join her. He had known enough of the signs of the sky to know that till that moment he was going "home." But this was a distinct evidence of something he had not thought of, perhaps—that there was no going home for him, even to a prison. And this was the first of some twenty such transfers, which brought him sooner or later into half our best vessels, but which kept him all his life at least some hundred miles from the country he had hoped he might never hear of again.

It may have been on that second cruise—it was once when he was up the Mediterranean—that Mrs. Graff, the celebrated Southern beauty of those days, danced with him. They had been lying a long time in the Bay of Naples, and the officers were very intimate in the English fleet, and there had been great festivities, and our men thought they must give a great ball on board the ship. How they ever did it on board the Warren I am sure I do not know. Perhaps it was not the Warren, or perhaps ladies did not take up so much room as they do now. They wanted to use Nolan's state-room for something, and they hated to do it without asking him to the ball; so the captain said they might ask him, if they would be responsible that he did not talk with the wrong people, "who would give him intelligence." So the dance went on, the finest party that had ever been known, I dare say; for I never heard of a man-of-war ball that was not. For ladies they had the family of the American consul, one or two travellers who had adventured so far,

and a nice bevy of English girls and matrons, perhaps Lady Hamil-
ton herself.

Well, different officers relieved each other in standing and talking with Nolan in a friendly way, so as to be sure that nobody else
spoke to him. The dancing went on with spirit, and after a while
even the fellows who took this honorary guard of Nolan ceased to
fear any *contre-temps*. Only when some English lady—Lady Hamil-
ton, as I said, perhaps—called for a set of "American dances," an odd
thing happened. Everybody then danced contra-dances. The black
band, nothing loath, conferred as to what "American dances" were,
and started off with "Virginia Reel," which they followed with
"Money-Musk," which, in its turn in those days, should have been
followed by "The Old Thirteen." But just as Dick, the leader, tapped
for his fiddles to begin, and bent forward, about to say, in true negro
state, " 'The Old Thirteen,' gentlemen and ladies!" as he had said
" 'Virginny Reel,' if you please!" and " 'Money-Musk,' if you please!"
the captain's boy tapped him on the shoulder, whispered to him, and
he did not announce the name of the dance; he merely bowed, began
on the air, and they all fell to—the officers teaching the English girls
the figure, but not telling them why it had no name.

But that is not the story I started to tell.—As the dancing went
on, Nolan and our fellows all got at ease, as I said—so much so,
that it seemed quite natural for him to bow to that splendid Mrs.
Graff, and say—

"I hope you have not forgotten me, Miss Rutledge. Shall I
have the honor of dancing?"

He did it so quickly, that Shubrick, who was by him, could not
hinder him. She laughed, and said—

"I am not Miss Rutledge any longer, Mr. Nolan; but I will
dance all the same," just nodded to Shubrick, as if to say he must
leave Mr. Nolan to her, and led him off to the place where the
dance was forming.

Nolan thought he had got his chance. He had known her at Philadelphia, and at other places had met her, and this was a God-send. You could not talk in contra-dances, as you do in cotillions, or even in the pauses of waltzing; but there were chances for tongues and sounds, as well as for eyes and blushes. He began with her travels, and Europe, and Vesuvius, and the French; and then, when they had worked down, and had that long talking-time at the bottom of the set, he said, boldly—a little pale, she said, as she told me the story, years after—

"And what do you hear from home, Mrs. Graff?"

And that splendid creature looked through him. Jove! how she must have looked through him!

"Home!! Mr. Nolan!!! I thought you were the man who never wanted to hear of home again!"—and she walked directly up the deck to her husband, and left poor Nolan alone, as he always was—He did not dance again.

I cannot give any history of him in order: nobody can now: and, indeed, I am not trying to. These are the traditions, which I sort out, as I believe them, from the myths which have been told about this man for forty years. The lies that have been told about him are legion. The fellows used to say he was the "Iron Mask"; and poor George Pons went to his grave in the belief that this was the author of "Junius," who was being punished for his celebrated libel on Thomas Jefferson. Pons was not very strong in the historical line. A happier story than either of these I have told is of the War. That came along soon after. I have heard this affair told in three or four ways—and, indeed, it may have happened more than once. But which ship it was on I cannot tell. However, in one, at least, of the great frigate-duels with the English, in which the navy was really baptized, it happened that a round shot from the enemy entered one of our ports square, and took right down the officer of the gun himself, and almost every man of the gun's crew. Now you may say what you choose about courage, but that is not a nice thing to see. But, as the men who were not killed picked themselves up, and as they and the surgeon's people were carrying off the bodies, there appeared Nolan, in his shirt-sleeves, with the rammer in his hand, and, just as if he had been the officer, told them off with authority—who should go to the cockpit with the wounded men, who should stay with him—perfectly cheery, and with that way which makes men feel sure all is right and is going to be right. And he finished loading the gun with his own hands, aimed it, and bade the men fire. And there he stayed, captain of that gun, keeping those fellows in spirits, till the enemy struck— sitting on the carriage while the gun was cooling, though he was exposed all the time—showing them easier ways to handle heavy shot—making the raw hands laugh at their own blunders—and when the gun cooled again, getting it loaded and fired twice as often as any other gun on the ship. The captain walked forward, by way of encouraging the men, and Nolan touched his hat and said—

"I am showing them how we do this in the artillery, Sir."

And this is the part of the story where all the legends agree: that the Commodore said—

"I see you do, and I thank you, Sir; and I shall never forget this day, Sir, and you never shall, Sir."

And after the whole thing was over, and he had the Englishman's sword, in the midst of the state and ceremony of the quarter-deck, he said—

"Where is Mr. Nolan? Ask Mr. Nolan to come here."

And when Nolan came, the captain said—

"Mr. Nolan, we are all very grateful to you to-day; you are one of us to-day; you will be named in the despatches."

And then the old man took off his own sword of ceremony, and gave it to Nolan, and made him put it on. The man told me this who saw it. Nolan cried like a baby, and well he might. He had not worn a sword since that infernal day at Fort Adams. But always afterwards, on occasions of ceremony, he wore that quaint old French sword of the Commodore's.

The captain did mention him in the despatches. It was always said he asked that he might be pardoned. He wrote a special letter to the Secretary of War. But nothing ever came of it. As I said, that was about the time when they began to ignore the whole transaction at Washington, and when Nolan's imprisonment began to carry itself on because there was nobody to stop it without any new orders from home.

I have heard it said that he was with Porter when he took possession of the Nukahiwa Islands. Not this Porter, you know, but old Porter, his father, Essex Porter—that is, the old Essex Porter, not this Essex. As an artillery officer, who had seen service in the West, Nolan knew more about fortifications, embrasures, ravelins, stockades, and all that, than any of them did; and he worked with a right good will in fixing that battery all right. I have always thought it was a pity Porter did not leave him in command there with Gamble. That would have settled all the question about his punishment. We should have kept the islands, and at this moment we should have one station in the Pacific Ocean. Our French friends, too, when they wanted this little watering-place, would have found it was preoccupied. But Madison and the Virginians, of course, flung all that away.

All that was near fifty years ago. If Nolan was thirty then, he must have been near eighty when he died. He looked sixty when he was forty. But he never seemed to me to change a hair afterwards. As I imagine his life, from what I have seen and heard of it, he must have been in every sea, and yet almost never on land. He must have known, in a formal way, more officers in our service than any man living knows. He told me once, with a grave smile, that no man in the world lived so methodical a life as he. "You know the boys say I am the Iron Mask, and you know how busy he was." He said it did not do for any one to try to read all the time, more than to do anything else all the time; but that he read just five hours a day. "Then," he said, "I keep up my note-books, writing in them at such and such hours from what I have been reading; and I include in these my scrap-books." These were very curious indeed. He had six or eight, of different subjects. There was one of History, one of Natural Science, one which he called "Odds and Ends." But they were not merely books of extracts from news-papers. They had bits of plants and ribbons, shells tied on, and carved scraps of bone and wood, which he had taught the men to cut for him, and they were beautifully illustrated. He drew ad-mirably. He had some of the funniest drawings there, and some of the most pathetic, that I have ever seen in my life. I wonder who will have Nolan's scrap-books.

Well, he said his reading and his notes were his profession, and that they took five hours and two hours respectively of each day. "Then," said he, "every man should have a diversion as well as a profession. My Natural History is my diversion." That took two hours a day more. The men used to bring him birds and fish, but on a long cruise he had to satisfy himself with centipedes and cockroaches and such small game. He was the only naturalist I ever met who knew anything about the habits of the house-fly and the mosquito. All those people can tell you whether they are *Lepi-doptera* or *Steptopotera;* but as for telling how you can get rid of them, or how they get away from you when you strike them— why, Linnæus knew as little of that as John Foy the idiot did. These nine hours made Nolan's regular daily "occupation." The rest of the time he talked or walked. Till he grew very old, he went aloft a great deal. He always kept up his exercise; and I never heard that he was ill. If any other man was ill, he was the kindest nurse in the world; and he knew more than half the surgeons do. Then if anybody was sick or died, or if the captain wanted him to on any other occasion, he was always ready to read prayers. I have remarked that he read beautifully.

My own acquaintance with Philip Nolan began six or eight years after the War, on my first voyage after I was appointed a midshipman. It was in the first days after our Slave-Trade treaty, while the Reigning House, which was still the House of Virginia, had still a sort of sentimentalism about the suppression of the horrors of the Middle Passage, and something was sometimes done that way. We were in the South Atlantic on that business. From the time I joined, I believe I thought Nolan was a sort of lay chaplain—a chaplain with a blue coat. I never asked about him. Everything in the ship was strange to me. I knew it was green to ask questions, and I suppose I thought there was a "Plain-Buttons" on every ship. We had him to dine in our mess once a week, and the caution was given that on that day nothing was to be said about home. But if they had told us not to say anything about the planet Mars or the Book of Deuteronomy, I should not have asked why; there were a great many things which seemed to me to have as little reason. I first came to understand anything about "the man without a country" one day when we overhauled a dirty little schooner which had slaves on board. An officer was sent to take charge of her, and, after a few minutes, he sent back his boat to ask that some one might be sent him who could speak Portuguese. We were all looking over the rail when the message came, and we all wished we could interpret, when the captain asked who spoke Portuguese. But none of the officers did; and just as the captain was sending forward to ask if any of the people could, Nolan stepped out and said he should be glad to interpret, if the captain wished, as he understood the language. The captain thanked him, fitted out another boat with him, and in this boat it was my luck to go.

When we got there, it was such a scene as you seldom see, and never want to. Nastiness beyond account, and chaos run loose in the midst of the nastiness. There were not a great many of the negroes; but by way of making what there were understand that they were free, Vaughan had had their hand-cuffs and ankle-cuffs knocked off, and, for convenience' sake, was putting them upon the rascals of the schooner's crew. The negroes were, most of them, out of the hold, and swarming all round the dirty deck, with a central throng surrounding Vaughan and addressing him in every dialect and *patois* of a dialect, from the Zulu click up to the Parisian of Beledeljereed.

As we came on deck, Vaughan looked down from a hogshead, on which he had mounted in desperation, and said—

"For God's love, is there anybody who can make these wretches understand something? The men gave them rum, and that did not quiet them. I knocked that big fellow down twice, and that did not soothe him. And then I talked Choctaw to all of them together; and I'll be hanged if they understood that as well as they understood the English."

Nolan said he could speak Portuguese, and one or two fine-looking Kroomen were dragged out, who, as it had been found already, had worked for the Portuguese on the coast at Fernando Po.

"Tell them they are free," said Vaughan; "and tell them that these rascals are to be hanged as soon as we can get rope enough."

Nolan "put that into Spanish,"*—that is, he explained it in such Portuguese as the Kroomen could understand, and they in turn to such of the negroes as could understand them. Then there was such a yell of delight, clinching of fists, leaping and dancing,

---

*The phrase is General Taylor's. When Santa Aña brought up his immense army at Buena Vista, he sent a flag of truce to invite Taylor to surrender. "Tell him to go to hell," said old Rough-and-Ready. "Bliss, put that into Spanish." "Perfect Bliss," as this accomplished officer, too early lost, was called, interpreted liberally, replying to the flag, in exquisite Castilian, "Say to General Santa Aña, that, if he wants us, he must come and take us." And this is the answer which has gone into history.

kissing of Nolan's feet, and a general rush made to the hogshead by way of spontaneous worship of Vaughan, as the *deus ex machina* of the occasion.

"Tell them," said Vaughan, well pleased, "that I will take them all to Cape Palmas."

This did not answer so well. Cape Palmas was practically as far from the homes of most of them as New Orleans or Rio Janeiro was; that is, they would be eternally separated from home there. And their interpreters, as we could understand, instantly said, "*Ah, non Palmas,*" and began to propose infinite other expedients in most voluble language. Vaughan was rather disappointed at this result of his liberality, and asked Nolan eagerly what they said. The drops stood on poor Nolan's white forehead, as he hushed the men down, and said—

"He says, 'Not Palmas.' He says, 'Take us home, take us to our own country, take us to our own house, take us to our own pickaninnies and our own women.' He says he has an old father and mother, who will die, if they do not see him. And this one says he left his people all sick, and paddled down to Fernando to beg the white doctor to come and help them, and that these devils caught him in the bay just in sight of home, and that he has never seen anybody from home since then. And this one says," choked out Nolan, "that he has not heard a word from his home in six months, while he has been locked up in an infernal barracoon."

Vaughan always said he grew gray himself while Nolan struggled through this interpretation. I, who did not understand anything of the passion involved in it, saw that the very elements were melting with fervent heat, and that something was to pay somewhere. Even the negroes themselves stopped howling, as they saw Nolan's agony, and Vaughan's almost equal agony of sympathy. As quick as he could get words, he said—

"Tell them yes, yes, yes; tell them they shall go to the Mountains of the Moon, if they will. If I sail the schooner through the Great White Desert, they shall go home!"

And after some fashion Nolan said so. And then they all fell to kissing him again, and wanted to rub his nose with theirs.

But he could not stand it long; and getting Vaughan to say he might go back, he beckoned me down into our boat. As we lay back in the stern-sheets and the men gave way, he said to me—"Youngster, let that show you what it is to be without a family, without a home, and without a country. And if you are ever tempted to say a word or to do a thing that shall put a bar between you and your family, your home, and your country, pray God in His mercy to take you that instant home to His own heaven. Stick by your family, boy; forget you have a self, while you do everything for them. Think of your home, boy; write and send, and talk about it. Let it be nearer and nearer to your thought, the farther you have to travel from it; and rush back to it, when you are free, as that poor black slave is doing now. And for your country, boy," and the words rattled in his throat, "and for that flag," and he pointed to the ship, "never dream a dream but of serving her as she bids you, though the service carry you through a thousand hells. No matter what happens to you, no matter who flatters you or who abuses you, never look at another flag, never let a night pass but you pray God to bless that flag. Remember, boy, that behind all these men you have to do with, behind officers, and government, and people even, there is the Country Herself, your Country, and that you belong to Her as you belong to your own mother. Stand by Her, boy, as you would stand by your mother, if those devils there had got hold of her to-day!"

I was frightened to death by his calm, hard passion; but I blundered out that I would, by all that was holy, and that I had never thought of doing anything else. He hardly seemed to hear me; but he did, almost in a whisper, say—"Oh, if anybody had said so to me when I was of your age!"

I think it was this half-confidence of his, which I never abused, for I never told this story till now, which afterward made us great friends. He was very kind to me. Often he sat up, or even got up, at night to walk the deck with me, when it was my watch. He explained to me a great deal of my mathematics, and I owe to him my taste for mathematics. He lent me books, and helped me about my reading. He never alluded so directly to his story again; but from one and another officer I have learned, in thirty years, what I am telling. When we parted from him in St. Thomas harbor, at the end of our cruise, I was more sorry than I can tell. I was very glad to meet him again in 1830; and later in life, when I thought I had some influence in Washington, I moved heaven and earth to have him discharged. But it was like getting a ghost out of prison. They pretended there was no such man, and never was such a man. They will say so at the Department now! Perhaps they do not know. It will not be the first thing in the service of which the Department appears to know nothing!

There is a story that Nolan met Burr once on one of our vessels, when a party of Americans came on board in the Mediterranean. But this I believe to be a lie; or, rather, it is a myth, *ben trovato,* involving a tremendous blowing-up with which he sunk Burr—asking him how he liked to be "without a country." But it is clear, from Burr's life, that nothing of the sort could have happened; and I mention this only as an illustration of the stories which get a-going where there is the least mystery at bottom.

So poor Philip Nolan had his wish fulfilled. I know but one fate more dreadful: it is the fate reserved for those men who shall have one day to exile themselves from their country because they have attempted her ruin, and shall have at the same time to see the prosperity and honor to which she rises when she has rid herself of them and their iniquities. The wish of poor Nolan, as we all learned to call him, not because his punishment was too great, but because his repentance was so clear, was precisely the wish of every Bragg and Beauregard who broke a soldier's oath two years ago, and of every Maury and Barron who broke a sailor's. I do not know how often they have repented. I do know that they have done all that in them lay that they might have no country—that all the honors, associations, memories, and hopes which belong to "country" might be broken up into little shreds and distributed to the winds. I know, too, that their punishment, as they vegetate through what is left of life to them in wretched Boulognes and Leicester Squares, where they are destined to upbraid each other till they die, will have all the agony of Nolan's, with the added pang that every one who sees them will see them to despise and to execrate them. They will have their wish, like him.

For him, poor fellow, he repented of his folly, and then, like a man, submitted to the fate he had asked for. He never intentionally added to the difficulty or delicacy of the charge of those who had him in hold. Accidents would happen; but they never happened from his fault. Lieutenant Truxton told me, that, when Texas was annexed, there was a careful discussion among the officers, whether they should get hold of Nolan's handsome set of maps, and cut Texas out of it—from the map of the world and the map of Mexico. The United States had been cut out when the atlas was bought for him. But it was voted, rightly enough, that to do this would be virtually to reveal to him what had happened, or, as Harry Cole said, to make him think Old Burr had succeeded. So it was from no fault of Nolan's that a great botch happened at my own table, when, for a short time, I was in command of the George Washington corvette, on the South American station. We were lying in the La Plata, and some of the officers, who had been on shore, and had just joined again, were entertaining us with accounts of their misadventures in riding the half-wild horses of

Buenos Ayres. Nolan was at table, and was in an unusually bright and talkative mood. Some story of a tumble reminded him of an adventure of his own, when he was catching wild horses in Texas with his brother Stephen, at a time when he must have been quite a boy. He told the story with a good deal of spirit—so much so, that the silence which often follows a good story hung over the table for an instant, to be broken by Nolan himself. For he asked, perfectly unconsciously—

"Pray, what has become of Texas? After the Mexicans got their independence, I thought that province of Texas would come forward very fast. It is really one of the finest regions on earth; it is the Italy of this continent. But I have not seen or heard a word of Texas for near twenty years."

There were two Texan officers at the table. The reason he had never heard of Texas was that Texas and her affairs had been painfully cut out of his newspapers since Austin began his settlements; so that, while he read of Honduras and Tamaulipas, and, till quite lately, of California, this virgin province, in which his brother had travelled so far, and, I believe, had died, had ceased to be to him. Waters and Williams, the two Texas men, looked grimly at each other and tried not to laugh. Edward Morris had his attention attracted by the third link in the chain of the captain's chandelier. Watrous was seized with a convulsion of sneezing. Nolan himself saw that something was to pay, he did not know what. And I, as master of the feast, had to say—

"Texas is out of the map, Mr. Nolan. Have you seen Captain Back's curious account of Sir Thomas Roe's Welcome?"

After that cruise I never saw Nolan again. I wrote to him at least twice a year, for in that voyage we became even confidentially intimate; but he never wrote to me. The other men tell me that in those fifteen years he *aged* very fast, as well he might indeed, but that he was still the same gentle, uncomplaining, silent sufferer that he ever was, bearing as best he could his self-appointed punish-ment—rather less social, perhaps, with new men whom he did not know, but more anxious, apparently, than ever to serve and be-friend and teach the boys, some of whom fairly seemed to worship him. And now it seems the dear old fellow is dead. He has found a home at last, and a country.

Since writing this, and while considering whether or not I would print it, as a warning to the young Nolans and Vallandighams and Tatnalls of to-day of what it is to throw away a country, I have re-ceived from Danforth, who is on board the Levant, a letter which gives an account of Nolan's last hours. It removes all my doubts about telling this story.

To understand the first words of the letter, the non-professional reader should remember that after 1817 the position of every officer who had Nolan in charge was one of the great-est delicacy. The Government had failed to renew the order of 1807 regarding him. What was a man to do? Should he let him go? What, then, if he were called to account by the Department for violating the order of 1807? Should he keep him? What, then, if Nolan should be liberated some day, and should bring an ac-tion for false imprisonment or kidnapping against every man who had had him in charge? I urged and pressed this upon Southard, and I have reason to think that other officers did the same thing. But the Secretary always said, as they so often do at Washington, that there were no special orders to give, and that we must act on our own judgment. That means, "If you succeed, you will be sustained; if you fail, you will be disavowed." Well, as Danforth says, all that is over now, though I do not know but I expose myself to a criminal prosecution on the evidence of the very revelation I am making.

Here is the letter:—

"*Levant,* 2° 2' S. @ 131° W.

"DEAR FRED—I try to find heart and life to tell you
that it is all over with dear old Nolan. I have been with
him on this voyage more than I ever was, and I can understand wholly now the way in which you used to speak
of the dear old fellow. I could see that he was not strong,
but I had no idea the end was so near. The doctor had
been watching him very carefully, and yesterday morning
came to me and told me that Nolan was not so well, and
had not left his state-room—a thing I never remember before. He had let the doctor come and see him as he lay
there—the first time the doctor had been in the state-
room—and he said he should like to see me. Oh, dear! do
you remember the mysteries we boys used to invent about
his room, in the old Intrepid days? Well, I went in, and
there, to be sure, the poor fellow lay in his berth, smiling
pleasantly as he gave me his hand, but looking very frail. I
could not help a glance round, which showed me what a
little shrine he had made of the box he was lying in. The
stars and stripes were triced up above and around a picture
of Washington, and he had painted a majestic eagle, with
lightnings blazing from his beak and his foot just clasping
the whole globe, which his wings overshadowed. The dear
old boy saw my glance, and said, with a sad smile, 'Here,
you see, I have a country!' And then he pointed to the
foot of his bed, where I had not seen before a great map
of the United States, as he had drawn it from memory, and
which he had there to look upon as he lay. Quaint, queer
old names were on it, in large letters: 'Indiana Territory,'
'Mississippi Territory,' and 'Louisiana Territory,' as I suppose our fathers learned such things: but the old fellow
had patched in Texas, too; he had carried his western

boundary all the way to the Pacific, but on that shore he had defined nothing.

" 'Oh, Danforth,' he said, 'I know I am dying. I cannot get home. Surely you will tell me something now?—Stop! stop! Do not speak till I say what I am sure you know, that there is not in this ship, that there is not in America—God bless her!—a more loyal man than I. There cannot be a man who loves the old flag as I do, or prays for it as I do, or hopes for it as I do. There are thirty-four stars in it now, Danforth. I thank God for that, though I do not know what their names are. There has never been one taken away: I thank God for that. I know by that, that there has never been any successful Burr. Oh, Danforth, Danforth,' he sighed out, 'how like a wretched night's dream a boy's idea of personal fame or of separate sovereignty seems, when one looks back on it after such a life as mine! But tell me—tell me something—tell me everything, Danforth, before I die!'

"Ingham, I swear to you that I felt like a monster that I had not told him everything before. Danger or no danger, delicacy or no delicacy, who was I, that I should have been acting the tyrant all this time over this dear, sainted old man, who had years ago expiated, in his whole manhood's life, the madness of a boy's treason? 'Mr. Nolan,' said I, 'I will tell you everything you ask about. Only, where shall I begin?'

"Oh, the blessed smile that crept over his white face! and he pressed my hand and said, 'God bless you!' 'Tell me their names,' he said, and he pointed to the stars on the flag. 'The last I know is Ohio. My father lived in Kentucky. But I have guessed Michigan and Indiana and Mississippi—that was where Fort Adams is—they make twenty.

But where are your other fourteen? You have not cut up any of the old ones, I hope?'

"Well, that was not a bad text, and I told him the names, in as good order as I could, and he bade me take down his beautiful map and draw them in as I best could with my pencil. He was wild with delight about Texas, told me how his brother died there; he had marked a gold cross near where he supposed his brother's grave was; and he had guessed at Texas. Then he was delighted as he saw California and Oregon;—that, he said, he had suspected partly, because he had never been permitted to land on that shore, though the ships were there so much. 'And the men,' said he, laughing, 'brought off a good deal besides furs.' Then he went back—heavens, how far!—to ask about the Chesapeake, and what was done to Barron for surrendering her to the Leopard, and whether Burr ever tried again—and he ground his teeth with the only passion he showed. But in a moment that was over, and he said, 'God forgive me, for I am sure I forgive him.' Then he asked about the old war—told me the true story of his serving the gun the day we took the Java—asked about dear old David Porter, as he called him. Then he settled down more quietly, and very happily, to hear me tell in an hour the history of fifty years.

"How I wished it had been somebody who knew something! But I did as well as I could. I told him of the English war. I told him about Fulton and the steamboat beginning. I told him about old Scott, and Jackson; told him all I could think of about the Mississippi, and New Orleans, and Texas, and his own old Kentucky. And do you think he asked who was in command of the "Legion of the West." I told him it was a very gallant officer, named Grant, and that, by our last news, he was about to establish his head-quarters at Vicksburg. Then, 'Where was Vicksburg?' I worked that out on the map; it was about a hundred miles, more or less, above his old Fort Adams; and I thought Fort Adams must be a ruin now. 'It must be at old Vick's plantation,' said he; 'well, that is a change!'

"I tell you, Ingham, it was a hard thing to condense the history of half a century into that talk with a sick man. And I do not now know what I told him—of emigration, and the means of it—of steamboats and railroads and telegraphs—of inventions and books and literature—of the colleges and West Point and the Naval School—but with the queerest interruptions that ever you heard. You see it was Robinson Crusoe asking all the accumulated questions of fifty-six years!

"I remember he asked, all of a sudden, who was President now; and when I told him, he asked if Old Abe was General Benjamin Lincoln's son. He said he met old General Lincoln, when he was quite a boy himself, at some Indian treaty. I said no, that Old Abe was a Kentuckian like himself, but I could not tell him of what family; he had worked up from the ranks. 'Good for him!' cried Nolan; 'I am glad of that. As I have brooded and wondered, I have thought our danger was in keeping up those regular successions in the first families.' Then I got talking about my visit to Washington. I told him of meeting the Oregon Congressman, Harding; I told him about the Smithsonian and the Exploring Expedition; I told him about the Capitol—and the statues for the pediment—and Crawford's Liberty—and Greenough's Washington: Ingham, I told him everything I could think of that would show the grandeur of his country and its prosperity; but I could not make up my mouth to tell him a word about this infernal Rebellion!

"And he drank it in, and enjoyed it as I cannot tell you. He grew more and more silent, yet I never thought he was tired or faint. I gave him a glass of water, but he just wet his lips, and told me not to go away. Then he asked me to bring the Presbyterian 'Book of Public Prayer,' which lay there, and said, with a smile, that it would open at the right place—and so it did. There was his double red mark down the page; and I knelt down and read, and he repeated with me—'For ourselves and our country, O gracious God, we thank Thee, that, notwithstanding our manifold transgressions of Thy holy laws, Thou hast continued to us Thy marvellous kindness,'—and so to the end of that thanksgiving. Then he turned to the end of the same book, and I read the words more familiar to me—'Most heartily we beseech Thee with Thy favor to behold and bless Thy servant, the President of the United States, and all others in authority'— and the rest of the Episcopal collect. 'Danforth,' said he, 'I have repeated those prayers night and morning, it is now fifty-five years.' And then he said he would go to sleep. He bent me down over him and kissed me; and he said, 'Look in my Bible, Danforth, when I am gone.' And I went away.

"But I had no thought it was the end. I thought he was tired and would sleep. I knew he was happy, and I wanted him to be alone.

"But in an hour, when the doctor went in gently, he found Nolan had breathed his life away with a smile. He had something pressed close to his lips. It was his father's badge of the Order of the Cincinnati.

"We looked in his Bible, and there was a slip of paper, at the place where he had marked the text—

" 'They desire a country, even a heavenly: wherefore God is not ashamed to be called their God: for he hath prepared for them a city.'

"On this slip of paper he had written—

" 'Bury me in the sea; it has been my home, and I love it. But will not some one set up a stone for my memory at Fort Adams or at Orleans, that my disgrace may not be more than I ought to bear? Say on it—

" '*In Memory of*
" 'Philip Nolan,
" '*Lieutenant in the Army of the United States.*

" 'He loved his country as no other man has loved her; but no man deserved less at her hands.' "

The Two Offers

Frances Harper
(1825–1911)

What is the matter with you, Laura, this morning? I have been watching you this hour, and in that time you have commenced a half-dozen letters and torn them all up. What matter of such grave moment is puzzling your dear little head, that you do not know how to decide?'

'Well, it is an important matter: I have two offers for marriage, and I do not know which to choose.'

'I should accept neither, or to say the least, not at present.'

'Why not?'

'Because I think a woman who is undecided between two offers has not love enough for either to make a choice; and in that very hesitation, indecision, she has a reason to pause and seriously reflect, lest her marriage, instead of being an affinity of souls or a union of hearts, should only be a mere matter of bargain and sale, or an affair of convenience and selfish interest.'

'But I consider them both very good offers, just such as many a girl would gladly receive. But to tell you the truth, I do not think that I regard either as a woman should the man she chooses for her husband. But then if I refuse, there is the risk of being an old maid, and that is not to be thought of.'

'Well, suppose there is? Is that the most dreadful fate that can befall a woman? Is there not more intense wretchedness in an ill-assorted marriage, more utter loneliness in a loveless home, than in the lot of the old maid who accepts her earthly mission as a gift from God and strives to walk the path of life with earnest and unfaltering steps?'

'Oh! what a little preacher you are. I really believe that you were cut out for an old maid—that when nature formed you she put in a double portion of intellect to make up for a deficiency of love; and yet you are kind and affectionate. But I do not think that you know anything of the grand, overmastering passion, or the deep necessity of woman's heart for loving.'

'Do you think so?' resumed the first speaker, and bending over her work she quietly applied herself to the knitting that had lain neglected by her side during this brief conversation. But as she did so, a shadow flitted over her pale and intellectual brow, a mist gathered in her eyes, and a slight quivering of the lips revealed a depth of feeling to which her companion was a stranger.

But before I proceed with my story, let me give you a slight history of the speakers. They were cousins who had met life under different auspices. Laura Lagrange was the only daughter of rich and indulgent parents who had spared no pains to make her an accomplished lady. Her cousin, Janette Alston, was the child of parents rich only in goodness and affection. Her father had been unfortunate in business and, dying before he could retrieve his fortunes, left his business in an embarrassed state. His widow was unacquainted with his business affairs, and when the estate was settled, hungry creditors had brought their claims and the lawyers had received their fees, she found herself homeless and almost penniless, and she, who had been sheltered in the warm clasp of loving arms, found them too powerless to shield her from the pitiless pelting storms of adversity. Year after year she struggled with poverty and wrestled with want, till her toilworn hands became too feeble to hold the shattered chords of existence, and her tear-dimmed eyes grew heavy with the slumber of death.

Her daughter had watched over her with untiring devotion, had closed her eyes in death and gone out into the busy, restless world, missing a precious tone from the voices of earth, a beloved step from the paths of life. Too self-reliant to depend on the charity of relations, she endeavored to support herself by her own exertions, and she had succeeded. Her path for a while was marked with struggle and trial, but instead of uselessly repining she met them bravely, and her life became not a thing of ease and indulgence, but of conquest, victory and accomplishments.

At the time when this conversation took place, the deep trials of her life had passed away. The achievements of her genius had won her a position in the literary world, where she shone as one of its bright particular stars. And with her fame came a competence of worldly means, which gave her leisure for improvement and the riper development of her rare talents. And she, that pale, intellectual woman, whose genius gave life and vivacity to the social circle and whose presence threw a halo of beauty and grace around the charmed atmosphere in which she moved, had at one period of her life known the mystic and solemn strength of an all-absorbing love. Years faded into the misty past had seen the kindling of her eye, the quick flushing of her cheek and the wild throbbing of her heart at tones of a voice long since hushed to the stillness of death. Deeply, wildly, passionately, she had loved. . . . This love quickened her talents, inspired her genius and threw over her life a tender and spiritual earnestness.

And then came a fearful shock, a mournful waking from that 'dream of beauty and delight.' A shadow fell around her path; it came between her and the object of her heart's worship. First a few cold words, estrangement, and then a painful separation: the old story of woman's pride. . . . And thus faded out from that young heart her bright, brief and saddened dream of life. Faint and spirit-broken, she turned from the scenes associated with the memory of the loved and lost. She tried to break the chain of sad associations that bound her to the mournful past; and so . . . her genius gathered strength from suffering, and wondrous power and brilliancy from the agony she hid within the desolate chambers of her soul . . . and turning, with an earnest and shattered spirit to life's duties and trials, she found a calmness and strength that she had only imagined in her dreams of poetry and song.

We will now pass over a period of ten years, and the cousins have met again. In that calm and lovely woman, in whose eyes is a depth of tenderness tempering the flashes of her genius, whose looks and tones are full of sympathy and love, we recognize the once smitten and stricken Janette Alston. The bloom of her girlhood had given way to a higher type of spiritual beauty, as if some unseen hand had been polishing and refining the temple in which her lovely spirit found its habitation. . . .

Never in the early flush of womanhood, when an absorbing love had lit up her eyes and glowed in her life, had she appeared so interesting as when, with a countenance which seemed overshadowed with a spiritual light, she bent over the deathbed of a young woman just lingering at the shadowy gates of the unseen land.

'Has he come?' faintly but eagerly exclaimed the dying woman. 'Oh! how I have longed for his coming, and even in death he forgets me.'

'Oh, do not say so, dear Laura. Some accident may have detained him,' said Janette to her cousin; for on that bed, from whence she will never rise, lies the once beautiful and light-hearted Laura Lagrange, the brightness of whose eyes had long since been dimmed with tears, and whose voice had become like a harp whose every chord is tuned to sadness—whose faintest thrill and loudest vibrations are but the variations of agony. A heavy hand was laid upon her once warm and bounding heart, and a voice came whispering through her soul that she must die. But to her the tidings was a message of deliverance—a voice hushing her wild sorrows to the calmness of resignation and hope.

Life had grown so weary upon her head—the future looked so hopeless—she had no wish to tread again the track where thorns had pierced her feet and clouds overcast her sky, and she hailed the coming of death's angel as the footsteps of a welcome friend. And yet, earth had one object so very dear to her weary heart. It was her absent and recreant husband; for, since that conversation [ten years earlier], she had accepted one of her offers and become a wife. But before she married she learned that great lesson of human experience and woman's life—to love the man who bowed at her shrine, a willing worshipper.

He had a pleasing address, raven hair, flashing eyes, a voice of thrilling sweetness and lips of persuasive eloquence; and being well versed in the ways of the world, he won his way to her heart and she became his bride, and he was proud of his prize. Vain and superficial in his character, he looked upon marriage not as a divine sacrament for the soul's development and human progression, but as the title deed that gave him possession of the woman he thought he loved. But alas for her, the laxity of his principles had rendered him unworthy of the deep and undying devotion of a pure-hearted woman. But, for a while, he hid from her his true character, and she blindly loved him, and for a short period was happy in the consciousness of being beloved. Though sometimes a vague unrest would fill her soul, when, overflowing with a sense of the good, the beautiful and the true, she would turn to him but find no response to the deep yearnings of her soul—no appreciation of life's highest realities, its solemn grandeur and significant importance. Their souls never met, and soon she found a void in her bosom that his earthborn love could not fill. He did not satisfy the wants of her mental and moral nature: between him and her there was no affinity of minds, no intercommunion of souls.

Talk as you will of woman's deep capacity for loving—of the strength of her affectional nature. I do not deny it. But will the mere possession of any human love fully satisfy all the demands of her whole being? You may paint her in poetry or fiction as a frail vine, clinging to her brother man for support and dying when deprived of it, and all this may sound well enough to please the imaginations of schoolgirls, or lovelorn maidens. But woman—the true woman—if you would render her happy, it needs more than the mere development of her affectional nature. Her conscience should be enlightened, her faith in the true and right established, and scope given to her heaven-endowed and God-given faculties. The true aim of female education should be, not a development of one or two, but all the faculties of the human soul, because no perfect womanhood is developed by imperfect culture. Intense love is often akin to intense suffering, and to trust the whole wealth of woman's nature on the frail bark of human love may often be like trusting a cargo of gold and precious gems to a bark that has never battled with the storm or buffeted the waves. Is it any wonder, then, that so many life-barks . . . are stranded on the shoals of existence, mournful beacons and solemn warnings for the thoughtless, to whom marriage is a careless and hasty rushing together of the affections? Alas, that an institution so fraught with good for humanity should be so perverted, and that state of life which should be filled with happiness become so replete with misery. And this was the fate of Laura Lagrange.

For a brief period after her marriage her life seemed like a bright and beautiful dream, full of hope and radiant with joy. And then there came a change: he found other attractions that lay beyond the pale of home influences. The gambling saloon had power to win him from her side; he had lived in an element of unhealthy and unhallowed excitements, and the society of a loving wife, the pleasures of a well-regulated home, were enjoyments too tame for one who had vitiated his tastes by the pleasures of sin. There were charmed houses of vice, built upon dead men's loves, where, amid a flow of song, laughter, wine and careless mirth, he would spend hour after hour, forgetting the cheek that was paling through his neglect, heedless of the tear-dimmed eyes peering anxiously into the darkness, waiting or watching his return.

The influence of old associations was upon him. In early life, home had been to him a place of ceilings and walls, not a true home built upon goodness, love and truth. It was a place where velvet carpets hushed his tread, where images of loveliness and beauty, invoked into being by painter's art and sculptor's skill, pleased the eye and gratified the taste, where magnificence surrounded his way and costly clothing adorned his person; but it was not the place for the true culture and right development of his soul. His father had been too much engrossed in making money and his mother in spending it, in striving to maintain a fashionable position in society and shining in the eyes of the world, to give the proper direction to the character of their wayward and impulsive son. His mother put beautiful robes upon his body but left ugly scars upon his soul; she pampered his appetite but starved his spirit. . . .

That parental authority which should have been preserved as a string of precious pearls, unbroken and unscattered, was simply the administration of chance. At one time obedience was enforced by authority, at another time by flattery and promises, and just as often it was not enforced. . . . His early associations were formed as chance directed, and from his want of home training, his character received a bias, his life a shade, which ran through every avenue of his existence and darkened all his future hours. . . .

Before a year of his married life had waned, his young wife had learned to wait and mourn his frequent and uncalled-for absence. More than once had she seen him come home from his midnight haunts, the bright intelligence of his eye displaced by the drunkard's stare, and his manly gait changed to the inebriate's stagger; and she was beginning to know the bitter agony that is compressed in the mournful words

'drunkard's wife.'

And then there came a bright but brief episode in her experience. The angel of life gave to her existence a deeper meaning and loftier significance: she sheltered in the warm clasp of her loving arms a dear babe, a precious child whose love filled every chamber of her heart. . . . How many lonely hours were beguiled by its winsome ways, its answering smiles and fond caresses! How exquisite and solemn was the feeling that thrilled her heart when she clasped the tiny hands together and taught her dear child to call God 'Our Father'!

What a blessing was that child! The father paused in his headlong career, awed by the strange beauty and precocious intellect of his child; and the mother's life had a better expression through her ministrations of love. And then there came hours of bitter anguish, shading the sunlight of her home and hushing the music of her heart. The angel of death bent over the couch of her child and beckoned it away. Closer and closer the mother strained her child to her wildly heaving breast and struggled with the heavy hand that lay upon its heart. Love and agony contended with death. . . .

But death was stronger than love and mightier than agony, and won the child for the land of crystal founts and deathless flowers, and the poor stricken mother sat down beneath the shadow of her mighty grief, feeling as if a great light had gone out from her soul and that the sunshine had suddenly faded around her path. She turned in her deep anguish to the father of her child, the loved and cherished dead. For a while his words were kind and tender, his heart seemed subdued and his tenderness fell upon her worn and weary heart like rain on perishing flowers, or cooling waters to lips all parched with thirst and scorched with fever. But the change was evanescent; the influence of unhallowed associations and evil habits had vitiated and poisoned the springs of his existence. They had bound him in their meshes, and he lacked the moral strength to break his fetters and stand erect in all the strength and dignity of a true manhood, making life's highest excellence his ideal and striving to gain it.

And yet moments of deep contrition would sweep over him, when he would resolve to abandon the wine cup forever, when he was ready to forswear the handling of another card, and he would try to break away from the associations that he felt were working his ruin. But when the hour of temptation came his strength was weakness, his earnest purposes were cobwebs, his well-meant resolutions ropes of sand—and thus passed year after year of the married life of Laura Lagrange. She tried to hide her agony from the public gaze, to smile when her heart was almost breaking. But year after year her voice grew fainter and sadder, her once light and bounding step grew slower and faltering.

Year after year she wrestled with agony and strove with despair, till the quick eyes of her brother read, in the paling of her cheek and the dimming eye, the secret anguish of her worn and weary spirit. On that wan, sad face he saw the death tokens, and he knew the dark wing of the mystic angel swept coldly around her path.

'Laura,' said her brother to her one day, 'you are not well, and I think you need our mother's tender care and nursing. You are daily losing strength, and if you will go I will accompany you.'

At first she hesitated; she shrank almost instinctively from presenting that pale, sad face to the loved ones at home. . . . But then a deep yearning for home sympathy woke within her a passionate longing for love's kind words, for tenderness and heart support, and she resolved to seek the home of her childhood and lay her weary head upon her mother's bosom, to be folded again in her loving arms, to lay that poor, bruised and aching heart where it might beat and throb closely to the loved ones at home.

A kind welcome awaited her. All that love and tenderness could devise was done to bring the bloom to her cheek and the light to her eye. But it was all in vain; hers was a disease that no medicine could cure, no earthly balm would heal. It was a slow wasting of the vital forces, the sickness of the soul. The unkindness and neglect of her husband lay like a leaden weight upon her heart. . . .

And where was he that had won her love and then cast it aside as a useless thing, who rifled her heart of its wealth and spread bitter ashes upon its broken altars? He was lingering away from her when the death damps were gathering on her brow, when his name was trembling on her lips! Lingering away! when she was watching his coming, though the death films were gathering before her eyes and earthly things were fading from her vision.

'I think I hear him now,' said the dying woman, 'surely that is his step,' but the sound died away in the distance.

Again she started from an uneasy slumber: 'That is his voice! I am so glad he has come.'

Tears gathered in the eyes of the sad watchers by that dying bed, for they knew that she was deceived. He had not returned. For her sake they wished his coming. Slowly the hours waned away, and then came the sad, soul-sickening thought that she was forgotten, forgotten in the last hour of human need, forgotten when the spirit, about to be dissolved, paused for the last time on the threshold of existence, a weary watcher at the gates of death.

'He has forgotten me,' again she faintly murmured, and the last tears she would ever shed on earth sprung to her mournful eyes, and . . . a few broken sentences issued from her pale and quivering lips. They were prayers for strength, and earnest pleading for him who had desolated her young life by turning its sunshine to shadows, its smiles to tears.

'He has forgotten me,' she murmured again, 'but I can bear it; the bitterness of death is passed, and soon I hope to exchange the shadows of death for the brightness of eternity, the rugged paths of life for the golden streets of glory, and the care and turmoils of earth for the peace and rest of heaven.'

Her voice grew fainter and fainter; they saw the shadows that never deceive flit over her pale and faded face and knew that the death angel waited to soothe their weary one to rest, to calm the throbbing of her bosom and cool the fever of her brain. And amid the silent hush of their grief the freed spirit, refined through suffering and brought into divine harmony through the spirit of the living Christ, passed over the dark waters of death as on a bridge of light, over whose radiant arches hovering angels bent. They parted the dark locks from her marble brow, closed the waxen lids over the once bright and laughing eye and left her to the dreamless slumber of the grave.

Her cousin turned from that deathbed a sadder and wiser woman. She resolved more earnestly than ever to make the world better by her example, gladder by her presence, and to kindle the fires of her genius on the altars of universal love and truth. She had a higher and better object in all her writings than the mere acquisition of gold or acquirement of fame. She felt that she had a high and holy mission on the battlefield of existence—that life was not given her to be frittered away in nonsense or wasted away in trifling pursuits. She would willingly espouse an unpopular cause, but not an unrighteous one.

In her the downtrodden slave found an earnest advocate; the flying fugitive remembered her kindness as he stepped cautiously through our Republic to gain his freedom in a monarchial land, having broken the chains on which the rust of centuries had gathered. Little children learned to name her with affection; the poor called her blessed as she broke her bread to the pale lips of hunger.

Her life was like a beautiful story, only it was clothed with the dignity of reality and invested with the sublimity of truth. True, she was an old maid; no husband brightened her life with his love or shaded it with his neglect. No children nestling lovingly in her arms called her mother. No one appended Mrs to her name.

She was indeed an old maid, not vainly striving to keep up an appearance of girlishness when 'departed' was written on her youth, not vainly pining at her loneliness and isolation. The world was full of warm, loving hearts, and her own beat in unison with them. Neither was she always sentimentally sighing for something to love; objects of affection were all around her, and the world was not so wealthy in love that it had no use for hers. In blessing others she made a life and benediction, and as old age descended peacefully and gently upon her, she had learned one of life's most precious lessons: that true happiness consists not so much in the fruition of our wishes as in the regulation of desires and the full development and right culture of our whole natures.

The Luck of Roaring Camp

Bret Harte

(1836–1902)

There was commotion in Roaring Camp. It could not have been a fight, for in 1850 that was not novel enough to have called together the entire settlement. The ditches and claims were not only deserted, but "Tuttle's grocery" had contributed its gamblers, who, it will be remembered, calmly continued their game the day that French Pete and Kanaka Joe shot each other to death over the bar in the front room. The whole camp was collected before a rude cabin on the outer edge of the clearing. Conversation was carried on in a low tone, but the name of a woman was frequently repeated. It was a name familiar enough in the camp—"Cherokee Sal."

Perhaps the less said of her the better. She was a coarse, and, it is to be feared, a very sinful woman. But at that time she was the only woman in Roaring Camp, and was just then lying in sore extremity, when she most needed the ministration of her own sex. Dissolute, abandoned, and irreclaimable, she was yet suffering a martyrdom hard enough to bear even when veiled by sympathizing womanhood, but now terrible in her loneliness. The primal curse had come to her in that original isolation which must have made the punishment of the first transgression so dreadful. It was, perhaps, part of the expiation of her sin, that, at a moment when she most lacked her sex's intuitive tenderness and care, she met only the half-contemptuous faces of her masculine associates. Yet a few of the spectators were, I think, touched by her sufferings. Sandy Tipton thought it was "rough on Sal," and, in the contemplation of her condition, for a moment rose superior to the fact that he had an ace and two bowers in his sleeve.

It will be seen, also, that the situation was novel. Deaths were by no means uncommon in Roaring Camp, but a birth was a new thing. People had been dismissed from the camp effectively, finally, and with no possibility of return; but this was the first time that anybody had been introduced *ab initio*. Hence the excitement.

"You go in there, Stumpy," said a prominent citizen known as "Kentuck," addressing one of the loungers. "Go in there, and see what you kin do. You've had experience in them things."

Perhaps there was a fitness in the selection. Stumpy, in other climes, had been the putative head of two families; in fact, it was owing to some legal informality in these proceedings that Roaring Camp—a city of refuge—was indebted to his company. The crowd approved the choice, and Stumpy was wise enough to bow to the majority. The door closed on the extempore surgeon and midwife, and Roaring Camp sat down outside, smoked its pipe, and awaited the issue.

The assemblage numbered about a hundred men. One or two of these were actual fugitives from justice, some were criminal, and all were reckless. Physically, they exhibited no indication of their past lives and character. The greatest scamp had a Raphael face, with a profusion of blond hair; Oakhurst, a gambler, had the melancholy air and intellectual abstraction of a Hamlet; the coolest and most courageous man was scarcely over five feet in height, with a soft voice and an embarrassed, timid manner. The term "roughs" applied to them was a distinction rather than a definition. Perhaps in the minor details of fingers, toes, ears, etc., the camp may have been deficient, but these slight omissions did not detract from their aggregate force. The strongest man had but three fingers on his right hand; the best shot had but one eye.

Such was the physical aspect of the men that were dispersed around the cabin. The camp lay in a triangular valley, between two hills and a river. The only outlet was a steep trail over the summit of a hill that faced the cabin, now illuminated by the rising moon. The suffering woman might have seen it from the rude bunk whereon she lay—seen it winding like a silver thread until it was lost in the stars above.

A fire of withered pine-boughs added sociability to the gathering. By degrees the natural levity of Roaring Camp returned. Bets were freely offered and taken regarding the result. Three to five that "Sal would get through with it"; even, that the child would survive; side bets as to the sex and complexion of the coming stranger. In the midst of an excited discussion an exclamation came from those nearest the door, and the camp stopped to listen. Above the swaying and moaning of the pines, the swift rush of the river, and the crackling of the fire rose a sharp, querulous cry—a cry unlike anything heard before in the camp. The pines stopped moaning, the river ceased to rush, and the fire to crackle. It seemed as if Nature had stopped to listen too.

The camp rose to its feet as one man! It was proposed to explode a barrel of gunpowder, but, in consideration of the situation of the mother, better counsels prevailed, and only a few revolvers were discharged; for, whether owing to the rude surgery of the camp, or some other reason, Cherokee Sal was sinking fast. Within an hour she had climbed, as it were, that rugged road that led to the stars, and so passed out of Roaring Camp, its sin and shame forever. I do not think that the announcement disturbed them much, except in speculation as to the fate of the child. "Can he live now?" was asked of Stumpy. The answer was doubtful. The only other being of Cherokee Sal's sex and maternal condition in the settlement was an ass. There was some conjecture as to fitness, but the experiment was tried. It was less problematical than the ancient treatment of Romulus and Remus, and apparently as successful.

When these details were completed, which exhausted another hour, the door was opened, and the anxious crowd of men who had already formed themselves into a queue, entered in single file. Beside the low bunk or shelf, on which the figure of the mother was starkly outlined below the blankets stood a pine table. On this a candle-box was placed, and within it, swathed in staring red flannel, lay the last arrival at Roaring Camp. Beside the candle-box was placed a hat. Its use was soon indicated. "Gentlemen," said Stumpy, with a singular mixture of authority and *ex officio* complacency—"Gentlemen will please pass in at the front door, round the table, and out at the back door. Them as wishes to contribute anything toward the orphan will find a hat handy." The first man entered with his hat on; he uncovered, however, as he looked about him, and so, unconsciously, set an example to the next. In such communities good and bad actions are catching. As the procession filed in, comments were audible—criticisms addressed, perhaps, rather to Stumpy, in the character of showman—"Is that him?" "mighty small specimen"; "hasn't more'n got the color"; "ain't bigger nor a derringer." The contributions were as characteristic: A silver tobacco-box; a doubloon; a navy revolver, silver mounted; a gold specimen; a very beautifully embroidered lady's handkerchief (from Oakhurst the gambler); a diamond breastpin; a diamond ring (suggested by the pin, with the remark from the giver that he "saw that pin and went two diamonds better"); a slung-shot; a Bible (contributor not detected); a golden spur; a silver teaspoon (the initials, I regret to say, were not the giver's); a pair of surgeon's shears; a lancet; a Bank of England note for £5; and about $200 in loose gold and silver coin. During these proceedings Stumpy maintained a silence as impassive as the dead on his left, a gravity as inscrutable as that of the newly born on his right. Only one incident occurred to break the monotony of the curious procession. As Kentuck bent over the candle-box half curiously, the child turned, and, in a spasm of pain, caught at his groping finger, and held it fast for a moment. Kentuck looked foolish and embarrassed. Something like a blush tried to assert itself in his weather-beaten cheek. "The d—d little cuss!" he said, as he extricated his finger, with, perhaps, more tenderness and care than he might have been deemed capable of showing. He held that finger a little apart from its fellows as he went out, and examined it curiously. The examination provoked the same original remark in regard to the child. In fact, he seemed to enjoy repeating it. "He rastled with my finger," he remarked to Tipton, holding up the member, "the d—d little cuss!"

It was four o'clock before the camp sought repose. A light burnt in the cabin where the watchers sat, for Stumpy did not go to bed that night. Nor did Kentuck. He drank quite freely, and related with great gusto his experience, invariably ending with his characteristic condemnation of the new-comer. It seemed to relieve him of any unjust implication of sentiment, and Kentuck had the weaknesses of the nobler sex. When everybody else had gone to bed, he walked down to the river, and whistled reflectingly. Then he walked up the gulch, past the cabin, still whistling with demonstrative unconcern. At a large redwood tree he paused and retraced his steps, and again passed the cabin. Half-way down to the river's bank he again paused, and then returned and knocked at the door. It was opened by Stumpy. "How goes it?" said Kentuck, looking past Stumpy toward the candle-box. "All serene," replied Stumpy. "Anything up?" "Nothing." There was a pause—an embarrassing one—Stumpy still holding the door. Then Kentuck had recourse to his finger, which he held up to Stumpy. "Rastled with it—the d—d little cuss," he said, and retired.

The next day Cherokee Sal had such rude sepulture as Roaring Camp afforded. After her body had been committed to the hillside, there was a formal meeting of the camp to discuss what should be done with her infant. A resolution to adopt it was unanimous and enthusiastic. But an animated discussion in regard to the manner and feasibility of providing for its wants at once sprang up. It was remarkable that the argument partook of none of those fierce personalities with which discussions were usually conducted at Roaring Camp. Tipton proposed that they should send the child to Red Dog—a distance of forty miles—where female attention could be procured. But the unlucky suggestion met with fierce and unanimous opposition. It was evident that no plan which entailed parting from their new acquisition would for a moment be entertained. "Besides," said Tom Ryder, "them fellows at Red Dog would swap it, and ring in somebody else on us." A disbelief in the honesty of other camps prevailed at Roaring Camp as in other places.

The introduction of a female nurse in the camp also met with objection. It was argued that no decent woman could be prevailed to accept Roaring Camp as her home, and the speaker urged that "they didn't want any more of the other kind." This unkind allusion to the defunct mother, harsh as it may seem, was the first spasm of propriety—the first symptom of the camp's regeneration. Stumpy advanced nothing. Perhaps he felt a certain delicacy in interfering with the selection of a possible successor in office. But when questioned, he averred stoutly that he and "Jinny"—the mammal before alluded to—could manage to rear the child. There was something original, independent, and heroic about the plan that pleased the camp. Stumpy was retained. Certain articles were sent for to Sacramento. "Mind," said the treasurer, as he pressed a bag of gold-dust into the expressman's hand, "the best that can be got—lace, you know, and filigree-work and frills—d—m the cost!"

Strange to say, the child thrived. Perhaps the invigorating climate of the mountain camp was compensation for material deficiencies. Nature took the foundling to her broader breast. In that rare atmosphere of the Sierra foot-hills—that air pungent with balsamic odor, that ethereal cordial at once bracing and exhilarating—he may have found food and nourishment, or a subtle chemistry that transmuted asses' milk to lime and phosphorus. Stumpy inclined to the belief that it was the latter and good nursing. "Me and that ass," he would say, "has been father and mother to him! Don't you," he would add, apostrophizing the helpless bundle before him, "never go back on us."

By the time he was a month old, the necessity of giving him a name became apparent. He had generally been known as "the Kid," "Stumpy's Boy," "the Cayote" (an allusion to his vocal powers), and even by Kentuck's endearing diminutive of "the d—d little cuss." But these were felt to be vague and unsatisfactory, and were at last dismissed under another influence. Gamblers and adventurers are generally superstitious, and Oakhurst one day declared that the baby had brought "the luck" to Roaring Camp. It was certain that of late they had been successful. "Luck" was the name agreed upon, with the prefix of Tommy for greater convenience. No allusion was made to the mother, and the father was unknown. "It's better," said the philosophical Oakhurst, "to take a fresh deal all round. Call him Luck, and start him fair." A day was accordingly set apart for the christening. What was meant by this ceremony the reader may imagine, who has already gathered some idea of the reckless irreverence of Roaring Camp. The master of ceremonies was one "Boston," a noted wag, and the occasion seemed to promise the greatest facetiousness. This ingenious satirist had spent two days in preparing a burlesque of the church service, with pointed local allusions. The choir was properly trained, and Sandy Tipton was to stand godfather. But after the procession had marched to the grove with music and banners, and the child had been deposited before a mock altar, Stumpy stepped before the expectant crowd. "It ain't my style to spoil fun, boys," said the little man, stoutly, eyeing the faces around him, "but it strikes me that this thing ain't exactly on the squar. It's playing it pretty low down on this yer baby to ring in fun on him that he ain't goin' to understand. And ef there's goin' to be any godfathers round, I'd like to see who's got any better rights than me." A silence followed Stumpy's speech. To the credit of all humorists be it said, that the first man to acknowledge its justice was the satirist, thus stopped of his fun. "But," said Stumpy, quickly following up his advantage, "we're here for a christening, and we'll have it. I proclaim you Thomas Luck, according to the laws of the United States and the State of California, so help me God." It was the first time that the name of the Deity had been uttered otherwise than profanely in the camp. The form of christening was perhaps even more ludicrous than the satirist had conceived; but, strangely enough, nobody saw it and nobody laughed. "Tommy" was christened as seriously as he would have been under a Christian roof, and cried and was comforted in as orthodox fashion.

And so the work of regeneration began in Roaring Camp. Almost imperceptibly a change came over the settlement. The cabin assigned to "Tommy Luck"—or "The Luck," as he was more frequently called—first showed signs of improvement. It was kept scrupulously clean and whitewashed. Then it was boarded, clothed, and papered. The rosewood cradle—packed eighty miles by mule—had, in Stumpy's way of putting it, "sorter killed the rest of the furniture." So the rehabilitation of the cabin became a necessity. The men who were in the habit of lounging in at Stumpy's to see "how The Luck got on" seemed to appreciate the change, and, in self-defence, the rival establishment of "Tuttle's grocery" bestirred itself, and imported a carpet and mirrors. The reflections of the latter on the appearance of Roaring Camp tended to produce stricter habits of personal cleanliness. Again, Stumpy imposed a kind of quarantine upon those who aspired to the honor and privilege of holding "The Luck." It was a cruel mortification to Kentuck—who, in the carelessness of a large nature and the habits of frontier life, had begun to regard all garments as a second cuticle, which, like a snake's, only sloughed off through decay—to be debarred this privilege from certain prudential reasons. Yet such was the subtle influence of innovation that he thereafter appeared regularly every afternoon in a clean shirt, and face still shining from his ablutions. Nor were moral and social sanitary laws neglected. "Tommy," who was supposed to spend his whole existence in a persistent attempt to repose, must not be disturbed by noise. The shouting and yelling which had gained the camp its infelicitous title were not permitted within hearing distance of Stumpy's. The men conversed in whispers, or smoked with Indian gravity. Profanity was tacitly given up in these sacred precincts, and throughout the camp a popular form of expletive, known as "D—n the luck!" and "Curse the luck!" was abandoned, as having a new personal bearing. Vocal music was not interdicted, being supposed to have a soothing, tranquilizing quality, and one song, sung by "Man-o'-War Jack," an English sailor, from her Majesty's Australian colonies, was quite popular as a lullaby. It was a lugubrious recital of the exploits of "the Arethusa, Seventy-four," in a muffled minor, ending with a prolonged dying fall at the burden of each verse, "On b-o-o-o-ard of the Arethusa." It was a fine sight to see Jack holding The Luck, rocking from side to side as if with the motion of a ship, and crooning forth this naval ditty. Either through the peculiar rocking of Jack or the length of his song—it contained ninety stanzas, and was continued with conscientious deliberation to the bitter end—the lullaby generally had the desired effect. At such times the men would lie at full length under the trees, in the soft summer twilight, smoking their pipes and drinking in the melodious utterances. An indistinct idea that this was pastoral happiness pervaded the camp. "This 'ere kind o' think," said the Cockney Simmons, meditatively reclining on his elbow, "is 'evingly." It reminded him of Greenwich.

On the long summer days The Luck was usually carried to the gulch from whence the golden store of Roaring Camp was taken. There, on a blanket spread over pine-boughs, he would lie while the men were working in the ditches below. Latterly, there was a rude attempt to decorate this bower with flowers and sweet-smelling shrubs, and generally some one would bring him a cluster of wild honeysuckles, azaleas, or the painted blossoms of Las Mariposas. The men had suddenly awakened to the fact that there were beauty and significance in these trifles, which they had so long trodden carelessly beneath their feet. A flake of glittering mica, a fragment of variegated quartz, a bright pebble from the bed of the creek, became beautiful to eyes thus cleared and strengthened, and were invariably put aside for "The Luck." It was wonderful how many treasures the woods and hillsides yielded that "would do for Tommy." Surrounded by playthings such as never child out of fairy-land had before, it is to be hoped that Tommy was content. He appeared to be securely happy, albeit there was an infantine gravity about him, a contemplative light in his round gray eyes that sometimes worried Stumpy. He was always tractable and quiet, and it is recorded that once, having crept beyond his "corral"—a hedge of tessellated pine-boughs, which surrounded his bed—he dropped over the bank on his head in the soft earth, and remained with his mottled legs in the air in that position for at least five minutes with unflinching gravity. He was extricated without a murmur. I hesitate to record the many other instances of his sagacity, which rest, unfortunately, upon the statements of prejudiced friends. Some of them were not without a tinge of superstition. "I crep' up the bank just now," said Kentuck one day, in a breathless state of excitement, "and dern my skin if he wasn't a talking to a jay-bird as was a sittin' on his lap. There they was, just as free and sociable as anything you please, a jawin' at each other just like two cherry-bums." Howbeit, whether creeping over the pine-boughs or lying lazily on his back blinking at the leaves above him, to him the birds sang, the squirrels chattered, and the flowers bloomed. Nature was his nurse and playfellow. For him she would let slip between the leaves golden shafts of sunlight that fell just within his grasp; she would send wandering breezes to visit him with the balm of bay and resinous gums; to him the tall red-woods nodded familiarly and sleepily, the bumble-bees buzzed, and the rooks cawed a slumbrous accompaniment.

Such was the golden summer of Roaring Camp. They were "flush times,"—and the Luck was with them. The claims had yielded enormously. The camp was jealous of its privileges and looked suspiciously on strangers. No encouragement was given to immigration, and, to make their seclusion more perfect, the land on either side of the mountain wall that surrounded the camp they duly preempted. This, and a reputation for singular proficiency with the revolver, kept the reserve of Roaring Camp inviolate. The expressman—their only connecting link with the surrounding world—sometimes told wonderful stories of the camp. He would say, "They've a street up there in 'Roaring,' that would lay over any street in Red Dog. They've got vines and flowers round their houses, and they wash themselves twice a day. But they're mighty rough on strangers, and they worship an Ingin baby."

With the prosperity of the camp came a desire for further improvement. It was proposed to build a hotel in the following spring, and to invite one or two decent families to reside there for the sake of "The Luck"—who might perhaps profit by female companionship. The sacrifice that this concession to the sex cost these men, who were fiercely sceptical in regard to its general virtue and usefulness, can only be accounted for by their affection for Tommy. A few still held out. But the resolve could not be carried into effect for three months, and the minority meekly yielded in the hope that something might turn up to prevent it. And it did.

The winter of 1851 will long be remembered in the foot-hills. The snow lay deep on the Sierras, and every mountain creek became a river, and every river a lake. Each gorge and gulch was transformed into a tumultuous watercourse that descended the hillsides, tearing down giant trees and scattering its drift and débris along the plain. Red Dog had been twice under water, and Roaring Camp had been forewarned. "Water put the gold into them gulches," said Stumpy. "It's been here once and will be here again!" And that night the North Fork suddenly leaped over its banks, and swept up the triangular valley of Roaring Camp.

In the confusion of rushing water, crashing trees, and crackling timber, and the darkness which seemed to flow with the water and blot out the fair valley, but little could be done to collect the scattered camp. When the morning broke, the cabin of Stumpy nearest the river-bank was gone. Higher up the gulch they found the body of its unlucky owner; but the pride, the hope, the joy, the Luck, of Roaring Camp had disappeared. They were returning with sad hearts, when a shout from the bank recalled them.

It was a relief-boat from down the river. They had picked up, they said, a man and an infant, nearly exhausted, about two miles below. Did anybody know them, and did they belong here?

It needed but a glance to show them Kentuck lying there, cruelly crushed and bruised, but still holding the Luck of Roaring

Camp in his arms. As they bent over the strangely assorted pair, they saw that the child was cold and pulseless. "He is dead," said one. Kentuck opened his eyes. "Dead?" he repeated feebly. "Yes, my man, and you are dying too." A smile lit the eyes of the expiring Kentuck. "Dying," he repeated, "he's a taking me with him—tell the boys I've got the Luck with me now"; and the strong man, clinging to the frail babe as a drowning man is said to cling to a straw, drifted away into the shadowy river that flows forever to the unknown sea.

The Minister's Black Veil

A PARABLE*

Nathaniel Hawthorne

(1804–1864)

⌒⌒⌒

T he sexton stood in the porch of Milford meeting-house, pulling lustily at the bell-rope. The old people of the village came stooping along the street. Children, with bright faces, tript merrily beside their parents, or mimicked a graver gait, in the conscious dignity of their Sunday clothes. Spruce bachelors looked sidelong at the pretty maidens, and fancied that the Sabbath sunshine made them prettier than on week-days. When the throng had mostly streamed into the porch, the sexton began to toll the bell, keeping his eye on the Reverend Mr. Hooper's door. The first glimpse of the clergyman's figure was the signal for the bell to cease its summons.

'But what has good Parson Hooper got upon his face?' cried the sexton in astonishment.

*Another clergyman in New England, Mr. Joseph Moody, of York, Maine, who died about eighty years since, made himself remarkable by the same eccentricity that is here related of the Reverend Mr. Hooper. In his case, however, the symbol had a different import. In early life he had accidentally killed a beloved friend; and from that day till the hour of his own death, he hid his face from men.

All within hearing immediately turned about, and beheld the semblance of Mr. Hooper, pacing slowly his meditative way towards the meeting-house. With one accord they started, expressing more wonder than if some strange minister were coming to dust the cushions of Mr. Hooper's pulpit.

'Are you sure it is our parson?' inquired Goodman Gray of the sexton.

'Of a certainty it is good Mr. Hooper,' replied the sexton. 'He was to have exchanged pulpits with Parson Shute of Westbury; but Parson Shute sent to excuse himself yesterday, being to preach a funeral sermon.'

The cause of so much amazement may appear sufficiently slight. Mr. Hooper, a gentlemanly person of about thirty, though still a bachelor, was dressed with due clerical neatness, as if a careful wife had starched his band, and brushed the weekly dust from his Sunday's garb. There was but one thing remarkable in his appearance. Swathed about his forehead, and hanging down over his face, so low as to be shaken by his breath, Mr. Hooper had on a black veil. On a nearer view, it seemed to consist of two folds of crape, which entirely concealed his features, except the mouth and chin, but probably did not intercept his sight, farther than to give a darkened aspect to all living and inanimate things. With this gloomy shade before him, good Mr. Hooper walked onward, at a slow and quiet pace, stooping somewhat, and looking on the ground, as is customary with abstracted men, yet nodding kindly to those of his parishioners who still waited on the meeting-house steps. But so wonder-struck were they, that his greeting hardly met with a return.

'I can't really feel as if good Mr. Hooper's face was behind that piece of crape,' said the sexton.

'I don't like it,' muttered an old woman, as she hobbled into the meeting-house. 'He has changed himself into something awful, only by hiding his face.'

'Our parson has gone mad!' cried Goodman Gray, following him across the threshold.

A rumor of some unaccountable phenomenon had preceded Mr. Hooper into the meeting-house, and set all the congregation astir. Few could refrain from twisting their heads towards the door; many stood upright, and turned directly about; while several little boys clambered upon the seats, and came down again with a terrible racket. There was a general bustle, a rustling of the women's gowns and shuffling of the men's feet, greatly at variance with that hushed repose which should attend the entrance of the minister. But Mr. Hooper appeared not to notice the perturbation of his people. He entered with an almost noiseless step, bent his head mildly to the pews on each side, and bowed as he passed his oldest parishioner, a white-haired great-grandsire, who occupied an arm-chair in the centre of the aisle. It was strange to observe, how slowly this venerable man became conscious of something singular in the appearance of his pastor. He seemed not fully to partake of the prevailing wonder, till Mr. Hooper had ascended the stairs, and showed himself in the pulpit, face to face with his congregation, except for the black veil. That mysterious emblem was never once withdrawn. It shook with his measured breath as he gave out the psalm; it threw its obscurity between him and the holy page, as he read the Scriptures; and while he prayed, the veil lay heavily on his uplifted countenance. Did he seek to hide it from the dread Being whom he was addressing?

Such was the effect of this simple piece of crape, that more than one woman of delicate nerves was forced to leave the meeting-house. Yet perhaps the pale-faced congregation was almost as fearful a sight to the minister, as his black veil to them.

Mr. Hooper had the reputation of a good preacher, but not an energetic one: he strove to win his people heavenward, by mild persuasive influences, rather than to drive them thither, by the thunders of the Word. The sermon which he now delivered, was marked by the same characteristics of style and manner, as the general series of his pulpit oratory. But there was something, either in the sentiment of the discourse itself, or in the imagination of the auditors, which made it greatly the most powerful effort that they had ever heard from their pastor's lips. It was tinged, rather more darkly than usual, with the gentle gloom of Mr. Hooper's temperament. The subject had reference to secret sin, and those sad mysteries which we hide from our nearest and dearest, and would fain conceal from our own consciousness, even forgetting that the Omniscient can detect them. A subtle power was breathed into his words. Each member of the congregation, the most innocent girl, and the man of hardened breast, felt as if the preacher had crept upon them, behind his awful veil, and discovered their hoarded iniquity of deed or thought. Many spread their clasped hands on their bosoms. There was nothing terrible in what Mr. Hooper said; at least, no violence; and yet, with every tremor of his melancholy voice, the hearers quaked. An unsought pathos came hand in hand with awe. So sensible were the audience of some unwonted attribute in their minister, that they longed for a breath of wind to blow aside the veil, almost believing that a stranger's visage would be discovered, though the form, gesture, and voice were those of Mr. Hooper.

At the close of the services, the people hurried out with indecorous confusion, eager to communicate their pent-up amazement, and conscious of lighter spirits, the moment they lost sight of the black veil. Some gathered in little circles, huddled closely together, with their mouths all whispering in the centre; some went homeward alone, wrapt in silent meditation; some talked loudly, and profaned the Sabbath-day with ostentatious laughter. A few shook their sagacious heads, intimating that they could penetrate the mystery; while one or two affirmed that there was no mystery at all, but only that Mr. Hooper's eyes were so weakened by the midnight lamp, as to require a shade. After a brief interval, forth came good Mr. Hooper also, in the rear of his flock. Turning his veiled face from one group to another, he paid due reverence to the hoary heads, saluted the middle-aged with kind dignity, as their friend and spiritual guide, greeted the young with mingled authority and love, and laid his hands on the little children's heads to bless them. Such was always his custom on the Sabbath-day. Strange and bewildered looks repaid him for his courtesy. None, as on former occasions, aspired to the honor of walking by their pastor's side. Old Squire Saunders, doubtless by an accidental lapse of memory, neglected to invite Mr. Hooper to his table, where the good clergyman had been wont to bless the food, almost every Sunday since his settlement. He returned, therefore, to the parsonage, and, at the moment of closing the door, was observed to look back upon the people, all of whom had their eyes fixed upon the minister. A sad smile gleamed faintly from beneath the black veil, and flickered about his mouth, glimmering as he disappeared.

'How strange,' said a lady, 'that a simple black veil, such as any woman might wear on her bonnet, should become such a terrible thing on Mr. Hooper's face!'

'Something must surely be amiss with Mr. Hooper's intellects,' observed her husband, the physician of the village. 'But the strangest part of the affair is the effect of this vagary, even on a sober-minded man like myself. The black veil, though it covers only our pastor's face, throws its influence over his whole person, and makes him ghost-like from head to foot. Do you not feel it so?'

'Truly do I,' replied the lady; 'and I would not be alone with him for the world. I wonder he is not afraid to be alone with himself!'

'Men sometimes are so,' said her husband.

The afternoon service was attended with similar circumstances. At its conclusion, the bell tolled for the funeral of a young lady. The relatives and friends were assembled in the house, and the more distant acquaintances stood about the door, speaking of the good qualities of the deceased, when their talk was interrupted by the appearance of Mr. Hooper, still covered with his black veil. It was now an appropriate emblem. The clergyman stepped into the room where the corpse was laid, and bent over the coffin, to take a last farewell of his deceased parishioner. As he stooped, the veil hung straight down from his forehead, so that, if her eye-lids had not been closed for ever, the dead maiden might have seen his face. Could Mr. Hooper be fearful of her glance, that he so hastily caught back the black veil? A person, who watched the interview between the dead and living, scrupled not to affirm, that, at that instant when the clergyman's features were disclosed, the corpse had slightly shuddered, rustling the shroud and muslin cap, though the countenance retained the composure of death. A superstitious old woman was the only witness of this prodigy. From the coffin, Mr. Hooper passed into the chamber of the mourners, and thence to the head of the staircase, to make the funeral prayer. It was a tender and heart-dissolving prayer, full of sorrow, yet so imbued with celestial hopes, that the music of a heavenly harp, swept by the fingers of the dead, seemed faintly to be heard among the saddest accents of the minister. The people trembled, though they but darkly understood him, when he prayed that they, and himself, and all of mortal race, might be ready, as he trusted this young maiden had been, for the dreadful hour that should snatch the veil from their faces. The bearers went heavily forth, and the mourners followed, saddening all the street, with the dead before them, and Mr. Hooper in his black veil behind.

'Why do you look back?' said one in the procession to his partner.

'I had a fancy,' replied she, 'that the minister and the maiden's spirit were walking hand in hand.'

'And so had I, at the same moment,' said the other.

That night, the handsomest couple in Milford village were to be joined in wedlock. Though reckoned a melancholy man, Mr. Hooper had a placid cheerfulness for such occasions, which often excited a sympathetic smile, where livelier merriment would have been thrown away. There was no quality of his disposition which made him more beloved than this. The company at the wedding awaited his arrival with impatience, trusting that the strange awe, which had gathered over him throughout the day, would now be dispelled. But such was not the result. When Mr. Hooper came, the first thing that their eyes rested on was the same horrible black veil, which had added deeper gloom to the funeral, and could portend nothing but evil to the wedding. Such was its immediate effect on the guests, that a cloud seemed to have rolled duskily from beneath the black crape, and dimmed the light of the candles. The bridal pair stood up before the minister. But the bride's cold fingers quivered in the tremulous hand of the bridegroom, and her deathlike paleness caused a whisper, that the maiden who had been buried a few hours before, was come from her grave to be married. If ever another wedding were so dismal, it was that famous one, where they tolled the wedding-knell. After performing the ceremony, Mr. Hooper raised a glass of wine to his lips, wishing happiness to the new-married couple, in a strain of mild pleasantry that ought to have brightened the features of the guests, like a cheerful gleam from the hearth. At that instant, catching a glimpse of his figure in the looking-glass, the black veil involved his own spirit in the horror with which it overwhelmed all others. His frame shuddered—his lips grew white—he spilt the untasted wine upon the carpet—and rushed forth into the darkness. For the Earth, too, had on her Black Veil.

The next day, the whole village of Milford talked of little else than Parson Hooper's black veil. That, and the mystery concealed behind it, supplied a topic for discussion between acquaintances meeting in the street, and good women gossiping at their open windows. It was the first item of news that the tavern-keeper told to his guests. The children babbled of it on their way to school. One imitative little imp covered his face with an old black handkerchief, thereby so affrighting his playmates, that the panic seized himself, and he well nigh lost his wits by his own waggery.

It was remarkable, that, of all the busy-bodies and impertinent people in the parish, not one ventured to put the plain question to Mr. Hooper, wherefore he did this thing. Hitherto, whenever there appeared the slightest call for such interference, he had never lacked advisers, nor shown himself averse to be guided by their judgment. If he erred at all, it was by so painful a degree of self-distrust, that even the mildest censure would lead him to consider an indifferent action as a crime. Yet, though so well acquainted with this amiable weakness, no individual among his parishioners chose to make the black veil a subject of friendly remonstrance. There was a feeling of dread, neither plainly confessed nor carefully concealed, which caused each to shift the responsibility upon another, till at length it was found expedient to send a deputation of the church, in order to deal with Mr. Hooper about the mystery, before it should grow into a scandal. Never did an embassy so ill discharge its duties. The minister received them with friendly courtesy, but became silent, after they were seated, leaving to his visiters the whole burthen of introducing their important business. The topic, it might be supposed, was obvious enough. There was the black veil, swathed round Mr. Hooper's forehead, and concealing every feature above his placid mouth, on which, at times, they could perceive the glimmering of a melancholy smile. But that piece of crape, to their imagination, seemed to hang down before his heart, the symbol of a fearful secret between him and them. Were the veil but cast aside, they might speak freely of it, but not till then. Thus they sat a considerable time, speechless, confused, and shrinking uneasily from Mr. Hooper's eye, which they felt to be fixed upon them with an invisible glance. Finally, the deputies returned abashed to their constituents, pronouncing the matter too weighty to be handled, except by a council of the churches, if, indeed, it might not require a general synod.

But there was one person in the village, unappalled by the awe with which the black veil had impressed all beside herself. When the deputies returned without an explanation, or even venturing to demand one, she, with the calm energy of her character, determined to chase away the strange cloud that appeared to be settling round Mr. Hooper, every moment more darkly than before. As his plighted wife, it should be her privilege to know what the black veil concealed. At the minister's first visit, therefore, she entered upon the subject with a direct simplicity, which made the task easier both for him and her. After he had seated himself, she fixed her eyes steadfastly upon the veil, but could discern nothing of the dreadful gloom that had so overawed the multitude: it was but a double fold of crape, hanging down from his forehead to his mouth, and slightly stirring with his breath.

'No,' said she aloud, and smiling, 'there is nothing terrible in this piece of crape, except that it hides a face which I am always glad to look upon. Come, good sir, let the sun shine from behind the cloud. First lay aside your black veil: then tell me why you put it on.'

Mr. Hooper's smile glimmered faintly.

'There is an hour to come,' said he, 'when all of us shall cast aside our veils. Take it not amiss, beloved friend, if I wear this piece of crape till then.'

'Your words are a mystery too,' returned the young lady. 'Take away the veil from them, at least.'

'Elizabeth, I will,' said he, 'so far as my vow may suffer me. Know, then, this veil is a type and a symbol, and I am bound to wear it ever, both in light and darkness, in solitude and before the gaze of multitudes, and as with strangers, so with my familiar friends. No mortal eye will see it withdrawn. This dismal shade must separate me from the world: even you, Elizabeth, can never come behind it!'

'What grievous affliction hath befallen you,' she earnestly inquired, 'that you should thus darken your eyes forever?'

'If it be a sign of mourning,' replied Mr. Hooper, 'I, perhaps, like most other mortals, have sorrows dark enough to be typified by a black veil.'

'But what if the world will not believe that it is the type of an innocent sorrow?' urged Elizabeth. 'Beloved and respected as you are, there may be whispers that you hide your face under the consciousness of secret sin. For the sake of your holy office, do away this scandal!'

The color rose into her cheeks, as she intimated the nature of the rumors that were already abroad in the village. But Mr. Hooper's mildness did not forsake him. He even smiled again— that same sad smile, which always appeared like a faint glimmering of light, proceeding from the obscurity beneath the veil.

'If I hide my face for sorrow, there is cause enough,' he merely replied; 'and if I cover it for secret sin, what mortal might not do the same?'

And with this gentle, but unconquerable obstinacy, did he resist all her entreaties. At length Elizabeth sat silent. For a few moments she appeared lost in thought, considering, probably, what new methods might be tried, to withdraw her lover from so dark a fantasy, which, if it had no other meaning, was perhaps a symptom of mental disease. Though of a firmer character than his own, the tears rolled down her cheeks. But, in an instant, as it were, a new feeling took the place of sorrow: her eyes were fixed insensibly on the black veil, when, like a sudden twilight in the air, its terrors fell around her. She arose, and stood trembling before him.

'And do you feel it then at last?' said he mournfully.

She made no reply, but covered her eyes with her hand, and turned to leave the room. He rushed forward and caught her arm.

'Have patience with me, Elizabeth!' cried he passionately. 'Do not desert me, though this veil must be between us here on earth. Be mine, and hereafter there shall be no veil over my face, no darkness between our souls! It is but a mortal veil—it is not for eternity! Oh! you know not how lonely I am, and how frightened to be alone behind my black veil. Do not leave me in this miserable obscurity for ever!'

'Lift the veil but once, and look me in the face,' said she.

'Never! It cannot be!' replied Mr. Hooper.

'Then, farewell!' said Elizabeth.

She withdrew her arm from his grasp, and slowly departed, pausing at the door, to give one long, shuddering gaze, that seemed almost to penetrate the mystery of the black veil. But, even amid his grief, Mr. Hooper smiled to think that only a material emblem had separated him from happiness, though the horrors which it shadowed forth, must be drawn darkly between the fondest of lovers.

From that time no attempts were made to remove Mr. Hooper's black veil, or, by a direct appeal, to discover the secret which it was supposed to hide. By persons who claimed a superiority to popular prejudice, it was reckoned merely an eccentric whim, such as often mingles with the sober actions of men otherwise rational, and tinges them all with its own semblance of insanity. But with the multitude, good Mr. Hooper was irreparably a bugbear. He could not walk the street with any peace of mind, so conscious was he that the gentle and timid would turn aside to avoid him, and that others would make it a point of hardihood to throw themselves in his way. The impertinence of the latter class compelled him to give up his customary walk, at sunset, to the burial ground; for when he leaned pensively over the gate, there would always be faces behind the grave-stones, peeping at his black veil. A fable went the rounds, that the stare of the dead people drove him thence. It grieved him, to the very depth of his kind heart, to observe how the children fled from his approach, breaking up their merriest sports, while his melancholy figure was yet afar off. Their instinctive dread caused him to feel, more strongly than aught else, that a preternatural horror was interwoven with the threads of the black crape. In truth, his own antipathy to the veil was known to be so great, that he never willingly passed before a mirror, nor stooped to drink at a still fountain, lest, in its peaceful bosom, he should be affrighted by himself. This was what gave plausibility to the whispers, that Mr. Hooper's conscience tortured him for some great crime, too horrible to be entirely concealed, or otherwise than so obscurely intimated. Thus, from beneath the black veil, there rolled a cloud into the sunshine, an ambiguity of sin or sorrow, which enveloped the poor minister, so that love or sympathy could never reach him. It was said, that ghost and fiend consorted with him there. With self-shudderings and outward terrors, he walked continually in its shadow, groping darkly within his own soul, or gazing through a medium that saddened the whole world. Even the lawless wind, it was believed, respected his dreadful secret, and never blew aside the veil. But still good Mr. Hooper sadly smiled, at the pale visages of the worldly throng as he passed by.

Among all its bad influences, the black veil had the one desirable effect, of making its wearer a very efficient clergyman. By the aid of his mysterious emblem—for there was no other apparent cause—he became a man of awful power, over souls that were in

agony for sin. His converts always regarded him with a dread peculiar to themselves, affirming, though but figuratively, that, before
he brought them to celestial light, they had been with him behind
the black veil. Its gloom, indeed, enabled him to sympathize with
all dark affections. Dying sinners cried aloud for Mr. Hooper, and
would not yield their breath till he appeared; though ever, as he
stooped to whisper consolation, they shuddered at the veiled face
so near their own. Such were the terrors of the black veil, even
when Death had bared his visage! Strangers came long distances to
attend service at his church, with the mere idle purpose of gazing
at his figure, because it was forbidden them to behold his face. But
many were made to quake ere they departed! Once, during Governor Belcher's administration, Mr. Hooper was appointed to
preach the election sermon. Covered with his black veil, he stood
before the chief magistrate, the council, and the representatives,
and wrought so deep an impression, that the legislative measures of
that year, were characterized by all the gloom and piety of our earliest ancestral sway.

In this manner Mr. Hooper spent a long life, irreproachable in
outward act, yet shrouded in dismal suspicions; kind and loving,
though unloved, and dimly feared; a man apart from men, shunned
in their health and joy, but ever summoned to their aid in mortal
anguish. As years wore on, shedding their snows above his sable
veil, he acquired a name throughout the New-England churches,
and they called him Father Hooper. Nearly all his parishioners,
who were of mature age when he was settled, had been borne
away by many a funeral: he had one congregation in the church,
and a more crowded one in the church-yard; and having wrought
so late into the evening, and done his work so well, it was now
good Father Hooper's turn to rest.

Several persons were visible by the shaded candlelight, in the
death-chamber of the old clergyman. Natural connections he had

none. But there was the decorously grave, though unmoved physician, seeking only to mitigate the last pangs of the patient whom he could not save. There were the deacons, and other eminently pious members of his church. There, also, was the Reverend Mr. Clark, of Westbury, a young and zealous divine, who had ridden in haste to pray by the bed-side of the expiring minister. There was the nurse, no hired handmaiden of death, but one whose calm affection had endured thus long, in secresy, in solitude, amid the chill of age, and would not perish, even at the dying hour. Who, but Elizabeth! And there lay the hoary head of good Father Hooper upon the death-pillow, with the black veil still swathed about his brow and reaching down over his face, so that each more difficult gasp of his faint breath caused it to stir. All through life that piece of crape had hung between him and the world: it had separated him from cheerful brotherhood and woman's love, and kept him in that saddest of all prisons, his own heart; and still it lay upon his face, as if to deepen the gloom of his darksome chamber, and shade him from the sunshine of eternity.

For some time previous, his mind had been confused, wavering doubtfully between the past and the present, and hovering forward, as it were, at intervals, into the indistinctness of the world to come. There had been feverish turns, which tossed him from side to side, and wore away what little strength he had. But in his most convulsive struggles, and in the wildest vagaries of his intellect, when no other thought retained its sober influence, he still showed an awful solicitude lest the black veil should slip aside. Even if his bewildered soul could have forgotten, there was a faithful woman at this pillow, who, with averted eyes, would have covered that aged face, which she had last beheld in the comeliness of manhood. At length the death-stricken old man lay quietly in the torpor of mental and bodily exhaustion, with an imperceptible pulse, and breath that grew fainter and fainter, except when a long, deep, and irregular inspiration seemed to prelude the flight of his spirit.

The minister of Westbury approached the bedside.

'Venerable Father Hooper,' said he, 'the moment of your release is at hand. Are you ready for the lifting of the veil, that shuts in time from eternity?'

Father Hooper at first replied merely by a feeble motion of his head; then, apprehensive, perhaps, that his meaning might be doubted, he exerted himself to speak.

'Yea,' said he, in faint accents, 'my soul hath a patient weariness until that veil be lifted.'

'And is it fitting,' resumed the Reverend Mr. Clark, 'that a man so given to prayer, of such a blameless example, holy in deed and thought, so far as mortal judgment may pronounce; is it fitting that a father in the church should leave a shadow on his memory, that may seem to blacken a life so pure? I pray you, my venerable brother, let not this thing be! Suffer us to be gladdened by your triumphant aspect, as you go to your reward. Before the veil of eternity be lifted, let me cast aside this black veil from your face!'

And thus speaking, the Reverend Mr. Clark bent forward to reveal the mystery of so many years. But, exerting a sudden energy, that made all the beholders stand aghast, Father Hooper snatched both his hands from beneath the bed-clothes, and pressed them strongly on the black veil, resolute to struggle, if the minister of Westbury would contend with a dying man.

'Never!' cried the veiled clergyman. "On earth, never!'

'Dark old man!' exclaimed the affrighted minister, 'with what horrible crime upon your soul are you now passing to the judgment?'

Father Hooper's breath heaved; it rattled in his throat; but, with a mighty effort, grasping forward with his hands, he caught hold of life, and held it back till he should speak. He even raised himself in bed; and there he sat, shivering with the arms of death around him, while the black veil hung down, awful, at that last moment, in the gathered terrors of a life-time. And yet the faint, sad smile, so often there, now seemed to glimmer from its obscurity, and linger on Father Hooper's lips.

'Why do you tremble at me alone?' cried he, turning his veiled face round the circle of pale spectators. 'Tremble also at each other! Have men avoided me, and women shown no pity, and children screamed and fled, only for my black veil? What, but the mystery which it obscurely typifies, has made this piece of crape so awful? When the friend shows his inmost heart to his friend; the lover to his best-beloved; when man does not vainly shrink from the eye of his Creator, loathsomely treasuring up the secret of his sin; then deem me a monster, for the symbol beneath which I have lived, and die! I look around me, and, lo! on every visage a Black Veil!'

While his auditors shrank from one another, in mutual affright, Father Hooper fell back upon his pillow, a veiled corpse, with a faint smile lingering on the lips. Still veiled, they laid him in his coffin, and a veiled corpse they bore him to the grave. The grass of many years has sprung up and withered on that grave, the burial-stone is moss-grown, and good Mr. Hooper's face is dust; but awful is still the thought, that it mouldered beneath the Black Veil!

The Legend of Sleepy Hollow

(Found among the Papers of the late Diedrich Knickerbocker)

Washington Irving

(1783–1859)

A pleasing land of drowsy head it was,
Of dreams that wave before the half-shut eye;
And of gay castles in the clouds that pass,
Forever flushing round a summer sky.

CASTLE OF INDOLENCE.

In the bosom of one of those spacious coves which indent the eastern shore of the Hudson, at that broad expansion of the river denominated by the ancient Dutch navigators the Tappaan Zee, and where they always prudently shortened sail, and implored the protection of St. Nicholas when they crossed, there lies a small market town or rural port, which by some is called Greensburgh, but which is more generally and properly known by the name of Tarry Town. This name was given, we are told, in former days, by the good housewives of the adjacent country, from the inveterate propensity of their husbands to linger about the village tavern on market days. Be that as it may, I do not vouch for the fact, but merely advert to it, for the sake of being precise and authentic. Not far from this village, perhaps about two miles, there is a little valley, or rather lap of land among high hills, which is one of the quietest places in the whole world. A small brook glides through it, with just murmur enough to lull one to repose, and the occasional whistle of a quail, or tapping of a woodpecker, is almost the only sound that ever breaks in upon the uniform tranquillity.

I recollect that when a stripling, my first exploit in squirrel shooting was in a grove of tall walnut trees that shades one side of the valley. I had wandered into it at noon time, when all nature is peculiarly quiet, and was startled by the roar of my own gun, as it broke the sabbath stillness around, and was prolonged and reverberated by the angry echoes. If ever I should wish for a retreat, whither I might steal from the world and its distractions, and dream quietly away the remnant of a troubled life, I know of none more promising than this little valley.

From the listless repose of the place, and the peculiar character of its inhabitants, who are descendants from the original Dutch settlers, this sequestered glen has long been known by the name of SLEEPY HOLLOW, and its rustic lads are called the Sleepy Hollow Boys throughout all the neighbouring country. A drowsy, dreamy influence seems to hang over the land, and to pervade the very atmosphere. Some say that the place was bewitched by a high German doctor during the early days of the settlement; others, that an old Indian chief, the prophet or wizard of his tribe, held his powwows there before the country was discovered by Master Hendrick Hudson. Certain it is, the place still continues under the sway of some witching power, that holds a spell over the minds of the good people, causing them to walk in a continual reverie. They are given to all kinds of marvellous beliefs; are subject to trances and visions, and frequently see strange sights, and hear music and voices in the air. The whole neighbourhood abounds with local tales, haunted spots, and twilight superstitions; stars shoot and meteors glare oftener across the valley than in any other part of the country, and the night mare, with her whole nine fold, seems to make it the favourite scene of her gambols.

The dominant spirit, however, that haunts this enchanted region, and seems to be commander in chief of all the powers of the air, is the apparition of a figure on horseback without a head. It is said by some to be the ghost of a Hessian trooper, whose head had been carried away by a cannon ball, in some nameless battle during the revolutionary war, and who is ever and anon seen by the country folk, hurrying along in the gloom of night, as if on the wings of the wind. His haunts are not confined to the valley, but extend at times to the adjacent roads, and especially to the vicinity of a church at no great distance. Indeed, certain of the most authentic historians of those parts, who have been careful in collecting and collating the floating facts concerning this spectre, allege, that the body of the trooper having been buried in the church yard, the ghost rides forth to the scene of battle in nightly quest of his head, and that the rushing speed with which he sometimes passes along the hollow, like a midnight blast, is owing to his being belated, and in a hurry to get back to the church yard before day break.

Such is the general purport of this legendary superstition, which has furnished materials for many a wild story in that region of shadows; and the spectre is known, at all the country firesides, by the name of The Headless Horseman of Sleepy Hollow.

It is remarkable, that the visionary propensity I have mentioned is not confined to the native inhabitants of the valley, but is unconsciously imbibed by every one who resides there for a time. However wide awake they may have been before they entered that sleepy region, they are sure, in a little time, to inhale the witching influence of the air, and begin to grow imaginative—to dream dreams, and see apparitions.

I mention this peaceful spot with all possible laud; for it is in such little retired Dutch valleys, found here and there embosomed in the great state of New York, that population, manners, and customs, remain fixed, while the great torrent of migration and improvement, which is making such incessant changes in other parts of this restless country, sweeps by them unobserved. They are like those little nooks of still water, which border a rapid stream, where we may see the straw and bubble riding quietly at anchor, or slowly revolving in their mimic harbour, undisturbed by the rush of the passing current. Though many years have elapsed since I trod the drowsy shades of Sleepy Hollow, yet I question whether I should not still find the same trees and the same families vegetating in its sheltered bosom.

In this by place of nature there abode, in a remote period of American history, that is to say, some thirty years since, a worthy wight of the name of Ichabod Crane, who sojourned, or, as he expressed it, "tarried," in Sleepy Hollow, for the purpose of instructing the children of the vicinity. He was a native of Connecticut, a state which supplies the Union with pioneers for the mind as well as for the forest, and sends forth yearly its legions of frontier woodmen and country schoolmasters. The cognomen of Crane was not inapplicable to his person. He was tall, but exceedingly lank, with narrow shoulders, long arms and legs, hands that dangled a mile out of his sleeves, feet that might have served for shovels, and his whole frame most loosely hung together. His head was small, and flat at top, with huge ears, large green glassy eyes, and a long snipe nose, so that it looked like a weathercock perched upon his spindle neck, to tell which way the wind blew. To see him striding along the profile of a hill on a windy day, with his clothes bagging and fluttering about him, one might have mistaken him for the genius of famine descending upon the earth, or some scarecrow eloped from a cornfield.

His school house was a low building of one large room, rudely constructed of logs; the windows partly glazed, and partly patched with leaves of old copy books. It was most ingeniously secured at

vacant hours, by a withe twisted in the handle of the door, and
stakes set against the window shutters; so that though a thief might
get in with perfect ease, he would find some embarrassment in
getting out; an idea most probably borrowed by the architect, Yost
Van Houten, from the mystery of an eelpot. The school house
stood in a rather lonely but pleasant situation, just at the foot of a
woody hill, with a brook running close by, and a formidable birch
tree growing at one end of it. From hence the low murmur of his
pupils' voices conning over their lessons, might be heard of a
drowsy summer's day, like the hum of a bee hive; interrupted now
and then by the authoritative voice of the master, in the tone of
menace or command, or peradventure, by the appalling sound of
the birch, as he urged some tardy loiterer along the flowery path
of knowledge. Truth to say, he was a conscientious man, and ever
bore in mind the golden maxim, "spare the rod and spoil the
child."—Ichabod Crane's scholars certainly were not spoiled.

I would not have it imagined, however, that he was one of
those cruel potentates of the school, who joy in the smart of their
subjects; on the contrary, he administered justice with discrimina-
tion rather than severity; taking the burthen off the backs of the
weak, and laying it on those of the strong. Your mere puny
stripling, that winced at the least flourish of the rod, was passed by
with indulgence; but the claims of justice were satisfied, by in-
flicting a double portion on some little, tough, wrong headed,
broad skirted Dutch urchin, who sulked and swelled and grew
dogged and sullen beneath the birch. All this he called "doing his
duty by their parents;" and he never inflicted a chastisement without following it by the assurance, so consolatory to the smarting
urchin, that "he would remember it and thank him for it the
longest day he had to live."

When school hours were over, he was even the companion
and playmate of the larger boys; and on holyday afternoons would

convoy some of the smaller ones home, who happened to have pretty sisters, or good housewives for mothers, noted for the comforts of the cupboard. Indeed, it behooved him to keep on good terms with his pupils. The revenue arising from his school was small, and would have been scarcely sufficient to furnish him with daily bread, for he was a huge feeder, and though lank, had the dilating powers of an Anaconda; but to help out his maintenance, he was, according to country custom in those parts, boarded and lodged at the houses of the farmers, whose children he instructed. With these he lived successively a week at a time, thus going the rounds of the neighbourhood, with all his worldly effects tied up in a cotton handkerchief.

That all this might not be too onerous on the purses of his rustic patrons, who are apt to consider the costs of schooling a grievous burthen, and schoolmasters as mere drones, he had various ways of rendering himself both useful and agreeable. He assisted the farmers occasionally in the lighter labours of their farms, helped to make hay, mended the fences, took the horses to water, drove the cows from pasture, and cut wood for the winter fire. He laid aside, too, all the dominant dignity and absolute sway, with which he lorded it in his little empire, the school, and became wonderfully gentle and ingratiating. He found favour in the eyes of the mothers, by petting the children, particularly the youngest, and like the lion bold, which whilome so magnanimously the lamb did hold, he would sit with a child on one knee, and rock a cradle with his foot, for whole hours together.

In addition to his other vocations, he was the singing master of the neighbourhood, and picked up many bright shillings by instructing the young folks in psalmody. It was a matter of no little vanity to him on Sundays, to take his station in front of the church gallery, with a band of chosen singers; where, in his own mind, he completely carried away the palm from the parson. Certain it is, his voice resounded far above all the rest of the congregation, and there are peculiar quavers still to be heard in that church, and which may even be heard half a mile off, quite to the opposite side of the mill pond, of a still Sunday morning, which are said to be legitimately descended from the nose of Ichabod Crane. Thus, by diverse little make shifts, in that ingenious way which is commonly denominated "by hook and by crook," the worthy pedagogue got on tolerably enough, and was thought, by all who understood nothing of the labour of headwork, to have a wonderfully easy life of it.

The schoolmaster is generally a man of some importance in the female circle of a rural neighbourhood, being considered a kind of idle gentleman like personage, of vastly superior taste and accomplishments to the rough country swains, and, indeed, inferior in learning only to the parson. His appearance, therefore, is apt to occasion some little stir at the tea table of a farm house, and the addition of a supernumerary dish of cakes or sweetmeats, or, peradventure, the parade of a silver tea pot. Our man of letters, therefore, was peculiarly happy in the smiles of all the country damsels. How he would figure among them in the church yard, between services on Sundays; gathering grapes for them from the wild vines that overrun the surrounding trees; reciting for their amusement all the epitaphs on the tombstones, or sauntering, with a whole bevy of them, along the banks of the adjacent mill pond; while the more bashful country bumpkins hung sheepishly back, envying his superior elegance and address.

From his half itinerant life, also, he was a kind of travelling gazette, carrying the whole budget of local gossip from house to house; so that his appearance was always greeted with satisfaction. He was, moreover, esteemed by the women as a man of great erudition, for he had read several books quite through, and was a perfect master of Cotton Mather's History of New England

Witchcraft, in which, by the way, he most firmly and potently believed.

He was, in fact, an odd mixture of small shrewdness and simple credulity. His appetite for the marvellous, and his powers of digesting it, were equally extraordinary; and both had been increased by his residence in this spell bound region. No tale was too gross or monstrous for his capacious swallow. It was often his delight, after his school was dismissed of an afternoon, to stretch himself on the rich bed of clover, bordering the little brook that whimpered by his school house, and there con over old Mather's direful tales, until the gathering dusk of evening made the printed page a mere mist before his eyes. Then, as he wended his way, by swamp and stream and awful woodland, to the farm house where he happened to be quartered, every sound of nature, at that witching hour, fluttered his excited imagination: the moan of the whip-poor-will from the hill side; the boding cry of the tree toad, that harbinger of storm; the dreary hooting of the screech owl; or the sudden rustling in the thicket, of birds frightened from their roost. The fire flies, too, which sparkled most vividly in the darkest places, now and then startled him, as one of uncommon brightness would stream across his path; and if, by chance, a huge blockhead of a beetle came winging his blundering flight against him, the poor varlet was ready to give up the ghost, with the idea that he was struck with a witch's token. His only resource on such occasions, either to drown thought, or drive away evil spirits, was to sing psalm tunes;—and the good people of Sleepy Hollow, as they sat by their doors of an evening, were often filled with awe, at hearing his nasal melody, "in linked sweetness long drawn out," floating from the distant hill, or along the dusky road.

Another of his sources of fearful pleasure was, to pass long winter evenings with the old Dutch wives, as they sat spinning by the fire, with a row of apples roasting and sputtering along the hearth, and listen to their marvellous tales of ghosts and goblins, and haunted fields and haunted brooks, and haunted bridges and haunted houses, and particularly of the headless horseman, or galloping Hessian of the Hollow, as they sometimes called him. He would delight them equally by his anecdotes of witchcraft, and of the direful omens and portentous sights and sounds in the air, which prevailed in the earlier times of Connecticut; and would frighten them wofully with speculations upon comets and shooting stars, and with the alarming fact that the world did absolutely turn round, and that they were half the time topsy-turvy!

But if there was a pleasure in all this, while snugly cuddling in the chimney corner of a chamber that was all of a ruddy glow from the crackling wood fire, and where, of course, no spectre dared to show its face, it was dearly purchased by the terrors of his subsequent walk homewards. What fearful shapes and shadows beset his path, amidst the dim and ghastly glare of a snowy night!—With what wistful look did he eye every trembling ray of light streaming across the waste fields from some distant window!—How often was he appalled by some shrub covered with snow, which like a sheeted spectre beset his very path!—How often did he shrink with curdling awe at the sound of his own steps on the frosty crust beneath his feet; and dread to look over his shoulder, lest he should behold some uncouth being tramping close behind him!—and how often was he thrown into complete dismay by some rushing blast, howling among the trees, in the idea that it was the gallopping Hessian on one of his nightly scourings.

All these, however, were mere terrors of the night, phantoms of the mind, that walk in darkness; and though he had seen many spectres in his time, and been more than once beset by Satan in diverse shapes, in his lonely perambulations, yet daylight put an end to all these evils; and he would have passed a pleasant life of it, in despite of the Devil and all his works, if his path had not been crossed by a being that causes more perplexity to mortal man, than ghosts, goblins, and the whole race of witches put together, and that was—a woman.

Among the musical disciples who assembled, one evening in each week, to receive his instructions in psalmody, was Katrina Van Tassel, the daughter and only child of a substantial Dutch farmer. She was a blooming lass of fresh eighteen; plump as a partridge; ripe and melting and rosy cheeked as one of her father's peaches, and universally famed, not merely for her beauty, but her vast expectations. She was withal a little of a coquette, as might be perceived even in her dress, which was a mixture of ancient and modern fashions, as most suited to set off her charms. She wore the ornaments of pure yellow gold, which her great great grandmother had brought over from Saardam; the tempting stomacher of the olden time, and withal a provokingly short petticoat, to display the prettiest foot and ankle in the country round.

Ichabod Crane had a soft and foolish heart toward the sex; and it is not to be wondered at, that so tempting a morsel soon found favour in his eyes, more especially after he had visited her in her paternal mansion. Old Baltus Van Tassel was a perfect picture of a thriving, contented, liberal hearted farmer. He seldom, it is true, sent either his eyes or his thoughts beyond the boundaries of his own farm; but within those every thing was snug, happy, and well conditioned. He was satisfied with his wealth, but not proud of it, and piqued himself upon the hearty abundance, rather than the style in which he lived. His strong hold was situated on the banks of the Hudson, in one of those green, sheltered, fertile nooks, in which the Dutch farmers are so fond of nestling. A great elm tree spread its broad branches over it, at the foot of which bubbled up a spring of the softest and sweetest water, in a little well, formed of a barrel, and then stole sparkling away through the grass, to a neighbouring brook, that babbled along among elders and dwarf willows. Hard by the farm house was a vast barn, that might have served for a church; every window and crevice of which seemed bursting forth with the treasures of the farm; the flail was busily resounding within it from morning to night; swallows and martins skimmed twittering about the eaves, and rows of pigeons, some with one eye turned up, as if watching the weather, some with their heads under their wings, or buried in their bosoms, and others, swelling, and cooing, and bowing about their dames, were enjoying the sunshine on the roof. Sleek unwieldy porkers were grunting in the repose and abundance of their pens, from whence sallied forth, now and then, troops of sucking pigs, as if to snuff the air. A stately squadron of snowy geese were riding in an adjoining pond, convoying whole fleets of ducks; regiments of turkeys were gobbling through the farm yard, and guinea fowls fretting about it like ill tempered housewives, with their peevish discontented cry. Before the barn door strutted the gallant cock, that pattern of a husband, a warrior, and a fine gentleman, clapping his burnished wings, and crowing in the pride and gladness of his heart—sometimes tearing up the earth with his feet, and then generously calling his ever hungry family of wives and children to enjoy the rich morsel which he had discovered.

The pedagogue's mouth watered, as he looked upon this sumptuous promise of luxurious winter fare. In his devouring mind's eye, he pictured to himself every roasting pig running about with a pudding in his belly, and an apple in his mouth; the pigeons were snugly put to bed in a comfortable pie, and tucked in with a coverlet of crust; the geese were swimming in their own gravy; and the ducks pairing cosily in dishes, like snug married couples, with a decent competency of onion sauce; in the porkers he saw carved out the future sleek side of bacon, and juicy relishing ham; not a turkey, but he beheld daintily trussed up, with its gizzard under its wing, and, peradventure, a necklace of savoury sausages; and even bright chanticleer himself lay sprawling on his back, in a side dish, with uplifted claws, as if craving that quarter, which his chivalrous spirit disdained to ask while living.

As the enraptured Ichabod fancied all this, and as he rolled his great green eyes over the fat meadow lands, the rich fields of wheat, of rye, of buckwheat, and Indian corn, and the orchards burthened with ruddy fruit, which surrounded the warm tenement of Van Tassel, his heart yearned after the damsel who was to inherit these domains, and his imagination expanded with the idea, how they might be readily turned into cash, and the money invested in immense tracts of wild land, and shingle palaces in the wilderness. Nay, his busy fancy already realized his hopes, and presented to him the blooming Katrina, with a whole family of children, mounted on the top of a waggon loaded with household trumpery, with pots and kettles dangling beneath; and he beheld himself bestriding a pacing mare, with a colt at her heels, setting out for Kentucky, Tennessee, or the Lord knows where!

When he entered the house, the conquest of his heart was complete. It was one of those spacious farm houses, with high ridged, but lowly sloping roofs, built in the style handed down from the first Dutch settlers. The low, projecting eaves formed a piazza along the front, capable of being closed up in bad weather. Under this were hung flails, harness, various utensils of husbandry, and nets for fishing in the neighbouring river. Benches were built along the sides for summer use; and a great spinning wheel at one end, and a churn at the other, showed the various uses to which this important porch might be devoted. From this piazza the wondering Ichabod entered the hall, which formed the centre of the mansion, and the place of usual residence. Here, rows of resplendent pewter, ranged on a long dresser, dazzled his eyes. In one cor-

ner stood a huge bag of wool ready to be spun; in another a quantity of linsey-woolsey just from the loom; ears of Indian corn, and
strings of dried apples and peaches, hung in gay festoons along the
walls, mingled with the gaud of red peppers; and a door left ajar,
gave him a peep into the best parlour, where the claw footed
chairs, and dark mahogany tables, shone like mirrors; andirons,
with their accompanying shovel and tongs, glistened from their
covert of asparagus tops; mock oranges and conch shells decorated
the mantelpiece; strings of various coloured birds' eggs were suspended above it; a great ostrich egg was hung from the centre of
the room, and a corner cupboard, knowingly left open, displayed
immense treasures of old silver and well mended china.

From the moment Ichabod laid his eyes upon these regions of
delight, the peace of his mind was at an end, and his only study was
how to gain the affections of the peerless daughter of Van Tassel.
In this enterprize, however, he had more real difficulties than generally fell to the lot of a knight errant of yore, who seldom had any
thing but giants, enchanters, fiery dragons, and such like easily
conquered adversaries, to contend with; and had to make his way
merely through gates of iron and brass, and walls of adamant, to the
castle keep, where the lady of his heart was confined; all which he
achieved as easily as a man would carve his way to the centre of a
Christmas pie, and then the lady gave him her hand as a matter of
course. Ichabod, on the contrary, had to win his way to the heart
of a country coquette, beset with a labyrinth of whims and
caprices, which were for ever presenting new difficulties and im-
pediments, and he had to encounter a host of fearful adversaries of
real flesh and blood, the numerous rustic admirers, who beset
every portal to her heart, keeping a watchful and angry eye upon
each other, but ready to fly out in the common cause against any
new competitor.

Among these, the most formidable, was a burly, roaring, roystering blade, of the name of Abraham, or, according to the Dutch abbreviation, Brom Van Brunt, the hero of the country round, which rung with his feats of strength and hardihood. He was broad shouldered and double jointed, with short curly black hair, and a bluff, but not unpleasant countenance, having a mingled air of fun and arrogance. From his Herculean frame and great powers of limb, he had received the nick name of BROM BONES, by which he was universally known. He was famed for great knowledge and skill in horsemanship, being as dexterous on horseback as a Tartar. He was foremost at all races and cock fights, and with the ascendancy which bodily strength acquires in rustic life, was the umpire in all disputes, setting his hat on one side, and giving his decisions with an air and tone admitting of no gainsay or appeal. He was always ready for either a fight or a frolick; but had more mischief than ill will in his composition; and with all his overbearing roughness, there was a strong dash of waggish good humour at bottom. He had three or four boon companions, who regarded him as their model, and at the head of whom he scoured the country, attending every scene of feud or merriment for miles round. In cold weather he was distinguished by a fur cap, surmounted with a flaunting fox's tail, and when the folks at a country gathering descried this well known crest at a distance, whisking about among a squad of hard riders, they always stood by for a squall. Sometimes his crew would be heard dashing along past the farm houses at midnight, with whoop and halloo, like a troop of Don Cossacks, and the old dames, startled out of their sleep, would listen for a moment till the hurry scurry had clattered by, and then exclaim, "aye, there goes Brom Bones and his gang!" The neighbours looked upon him with a mixture of awe, admiration, and good will; and when any mad cap prank, or rustic brawl, occurred in the vicinity, always shook their heads, and warranted Brom Bones was at the bottom of it.

This rantipole hero had for some time singled out the blooming Katrina for the object of his uncouth gallantries, and though
his amorous toyings were something like the gentle caresses and
endearments of a bear, yet it was whispered that she did not altogether discourage his hopes. Certain it is, his advances were signals
for rival candidates to retire, who felt no inclination to cross a lion
in his amours; insomuch, that when his horse was seen tied to Van
Tassel's paling, of a Sunday night, (a sure sign that his master was
courting, or, as it is termed, "sparking," within,) all other suitors
passed by in despair, and carried the war into other quarters.

Such was the formidable rival with whom Ichabod Crane had
to contend, and, considering all things, a stouter man than he
would have shrunk from the competition, and a wiser man would
have despaired. He had, however, a happy mixture of pliability and
perseverance in his nature; he was in form and spirit like a supple
jack—yielding, but tough; though he bent, he never broke; and
though he bowed beneath the slightest pressure, yet, the moment
it was away—jerk!—he was as erect, and carried his head as high
as ever.

To have taken the field openly against his rival, would have
been madness; for he was not a man to be thwarted in his amours,
any more than that stormy lover, Achilles. Ichabod, therefore, made
his advances in a quiet and gently insinuating manner. Under cover
of his character of singing master, he made frequent visits at the
farm house; not that he had any thing to apprehend from the
meddlesome interference of parents, which is so often a stumbling
block in the path of lovers. Balt Van Tassel was an easy indulgent
soul; he loved his daughter better even than his pipe, and like a reasonable man, and an excellent father, let her have her way in every
thing. His notable little wife too, had enough to do to attend to
her housekeeping and manage her poultry, for, as she sagely observed, ducks and geese are foolish things, and must be looked

after, but girls can take care of themselves. Thus while the busy dame bustled about the house, or plied her spinning wheel at one end of the piazza, honest Balt would sit smoking his evening pipe at the other, watching the achievements of a little wooden warrior, who, armed with a sword in each hand, was most valiantly fighting the wind on the pinnacle of the barn. In the mean time, Ichabod would carry on his suit with the daughter by the side of the spring under the great elm, or sauntering along in the twilight, that hour so favourable to the lover's eloquence.

I profess not to know how women's hearts are wooed and won. To me they have always been matters of riddle and admiration. Some seem to have but one vulnerable point, or door of access; while others have a thousand avenues, and may be captured in a thousand different ways. It is a great triumph of skill to gain the former, but a still greater proof of generalship to maintain possession of the latter, for a man must battle for his fortress at every door and window. He who wins a thousand common hearts, is therefore entitled to some renown; but he who keeps undisputed sway over the heart of a coquette, is indeed a hero. Certain it is, this was not the case with the redoutable Brom Bones; and from the moment Ichabod Crane made his advances, the interests of the former evidently declined; his horse was no longer seen tied at the palings on Sunday nights, and a deadly feud gradually arose between him and the preceptor of Sleepy Hollow.

Brom, who had a degree of rough chivalry in his nature, would fain have carried matters to open warfare, and have settled their pretensions to the lady, according to the mode of those most concise and simple reasoners, the knights errant of yore—by single combat; but Ichabod was too conscious of the superior might of his adversary to enter the lists against him; he had overheard a boast of Bones, that he would "double the schoolmaster up, and lay him on a shelf of his own school house;" and he was too wary to give him an opportunity. There was something extremely provoking in this obstinately pacific system; it left Brom no alternative but to draw upon the funds of rustic waggery in his disposition, and to play off boorish practical jokes upon his rival. Ichabod became the object of whimsical persecution to Bones, and his gang of rough riders. They harried his hitherto peaceful domains; smoked out his singing school, by stopping up the chimney; broke into the school house at night, in spite of its formidable fastenings of withe and window stakes, and turned every thing topsy-turvy, so that the poor schoolmaster began to think all the witches in the country held their meetings there. But what was still more annoying, Brom took all opportunities of turning him into ridicule in presence of his mistress, and had a scoundrel dog, whom he taught to whine in the most ludicrous manner, and introduced as a rival of Ichabod's, to instruct her in psalmody.

In this way, matters went on for some time, without producing any material effect on the relative situations of the contending powers. On a fine autumnal afternoon, Ichabod, in pensive mood, sat enthroned on the lofty stool from whence he usually watched all the concerns of his little literary realm. In his hand he swayed a ferule, that sceptre of despotic power; the birch of justice reposed on three nails, behind the throne, a constant terror to evil doers; while on the desk before him might be seen sundry contraband articles and prohibited weapons, detected upon the persons of idle urchins, such as half munched apples, popguns, whirligigs, fly cages, and whole legions of rampant little paper game cocks. Apparently there had been some appalling act of justice recently inflicted, for his scholars were all busily intent upon their books, or slyly whispering behind them with one eye kept upon the master; and a kind of buzzing stillness reigned throughout the school room. It was suddenly interrupted by the appearance of a negro in tow cloth jacket and trowsers, a round crowned fragment of a hat, like the cap of Mercury, and mounted on the back of a ragged, wild, half broken colt, which he managed with a rope by way of halter. He came clattering up to the school door with an invitation to Ichabod to attend a merry making, or "quilting frolick," to be held that evening at Mynheer Van Tassel's, and having delivered his message with that air of importance, and effort at fine language, which a negro is apt to display on petty embassies of the kind, he dashed over the brook, and was seen scampering away up the hollow, full of the importance and hurry of his mission.

All was now bustle and hubbub in the late quiet school room. The scholars were hurried through their lessons, without stopping at trifles; those who were nimble, skipped over half with impunity, and those who were tardy, had a smart application now and then in the rear, to quicken their speed, or help them over a tall word. Books were flung aside, without being put away on the shelves; inkstands were overturned, benches thrown down, and the whole school was turned loose an hour before the usual time; bursting forth like a legion of young imps, yelping and racketing about the green, in joy at their early emancipation.

The gallant Ichabod now spent at least an extra half hour at his toilet, brushing and furbishing up his best, and indeed only suit of rusty black, and arranging his looks by a bit of broken looking glass, that hung up in the school house. That he might make his appearance before his mistress in the true style of a cavalier, he borrowed a horse from the farmer with whom he was domiciliated, a choleric old Dutchman, of the name of Hans Van Ripper, and thus gallantly mounted, issued forth like a knight errant in quest of adventures. But it is meet I should, in the true spirit of romantic story, give some account of the looks and equipments of my hero and his steed. The animal he bestrode was a broken down plough horse, that had outlived almost every thing but his viciousness. He was gaunt and shagged, with a ewe neck and a head like a hammer; his rusty mane and tail were tangled and knotted with burrs; one eye had lost its pupil, and was glaring and spectral, but the other had the gleam of a genuine devil in it. Still he must have had fire and mettle in his day, if we may judge from the name he bore of Gunpowder. He had, in fact, been a favourite steed of his master's, the cholerick Van Ripper, who was a furious rider, and had infused, very probably, some of his own spirit into the animal, for, old and broken down as he looked, there was more of the lurking devil in him than in any young filly in the country.

Ichabod was a suitable figure for such a steed. He rode with short stirrups, which brought his knees nearly up to the pommel of the saddle; his sharp elbows stuck out like grasshoppers'; he carried his whip perpendicularly in his hand, like a sceptre, and as his horse jogged on, the motion of his arms was not unlike the flapping of a pair of wings. A small wool hat rested on the top of his nose, for so his scanty strip of forehead might be called, and the skirts of his black coat fluttered out almost to the horse's tail. Such was the appearance of Ichabod and his steed, as they shambled out of the gate of Hans Van Ripper, and it was altogether such an apparition as is seldom to be met with in broad day light.

It was, as I have said, a fine autumnal day, the sky was clear and serene, and nature wore that rich and golden livery which we always associate with the idea of abundance. The forests had put on their sober brown and yellow, while some trees of the tenderer kind had been nipped by the frosts into brilliant dyes of orange, purple, and scarlet. Streaming files of wild ducks began to make their appearance high in the air; the bark of the squirrel might be heard from the groves of beech and hickory nuts, and the pensive whistle of the quail at intervals from the neighbouring stubble field.

The small birds were taking their farewell banquets. In the fullness of their revelry, they fluttered, chirping and frolicking, from bush to bush, and tree to tree, capricious from the very profusion and variety around them. There was the honest cock robin, the favourite game of stripling sportsmen, with its loud querulous note; and the twittering blackbirds flying in sable clouds; and the golden winged woodpecker, with his crimson crest, his broad black gorget, and splendid plumage; and the cedar bird, with its red tipt wings and yellow tipt tail, and its little monteiro cap of feathers; and the blue jay, that noisy coxcomb, in his gay light blue coat and white under clothes, screaming and chattering, nodding, and bobbing, and bowing, and pretending to be on good terms with every songster of the grove.

As Ichabod jogged slowly on his way, his eye, ever open to every symptom of culinary abundance, ranged with delight over the treasures of jolly autumn. On all sides he beheld vast store of apples, some hanging in oppressive opulence on the trees, some gathered into baskets and barrels for the market, others heaped up in rich piles for the cider press. Further on he beheld great fields of Indian corn, with its golden ears peeping from their leafy coverts, and holding out the promise of cakes and hasty pudding; and the yellow pumpkins lying beneath them, turning up their fair round bellies to the sun, and giving ample prospects of the most luxurious of pies; and anon he passed the fragrant buckwheat fields, breathing the odour of the bee hive, and as he beheld them, soft anticipations stole over his mind of dainty slap jacks, well buttered, and garnished with honey or treacle, by the delicate little dimpled hand of Katrina Van Tassel.

Thus feeding his mind with many sweet thoughts and "sugared suppositions," he journeyed along the sides of a range of hills which look out upon some of the goodliest scenes of the mighty Hudson. The sun gradually wheeled his broad disk down into the west. The wide bosom of the Tappaan Zee lay motionless and glassy, excepting that here and there a gentle undulation waved and prolonged the blue shadow of the distant mountain: a few amber clouds floated in the sky, without a breath of air to move them. The horizon was of a fine golden tint, changing gradually into a pure apple green, and from that into the deep blue of the mid-heaven. A slanting ray lingered on the woody crests of the precipices that over-hung some parts of the river, giving greater depth to the dark grey and purple of their rocky sides. A sloop was loitering in the distance, dropping slowly down with the tide, her sail hanging uselessly against the mast, and as the reflection of the sky gleamed along the still water, it seemed as if the vessel was suspended in the air.

It was toward evening that Ichabod arrived at the castle of the Heer Van Tassel, which he found thronged with the pride and flower of the adjacent country. Old farmers, a spare, leathern faced race, in homespun coats and breeches, blue stockings, huge shoes and magnificent pewter buckles. Their brisk withered little dames in close crimped caps, long waisted short gowns, homespun petti-coats, with scissors and pincushions, and gay calico pockets, hang-ing on the outside. Buxom lasses, almost as antiquated as their mothers, excepting where a straw hat, a fine ribband, or perhaps a white frock, gave symptoms of city innovation. The sons, in short square skirted coats with rows of stupendous brass buttons, and their hair generally queued in the fashion of the times, especially if they could procure an eel skin for the purpose, it being esteemed throughout the country as a potent nourisher and strengthener of the hair.

Brom Bones, however, was the hero of the scene, having come to the gathering on his favourite steed Daredevil, a creature, like himself, full of mettle and mischief, and which no one but himself could manage. He was in fact noted for preferring vicious animals, given to all kinds of tricks, which kept the rider in constant risk of his neck, for he held a tractable well broken horse as unworthy of a lad of spirit.

Fain would I pause to dwell upon the world of charms that burst upon the enraptured gaze of my hero, as he entered the state parlour of Van Tassel's mansion. Not those of the bevy of buxom lasses, with their luxurious display of red and white: but the ample charms of a genuine Dutch country tea table, in the sumptuous time of autumn. Such heaped up platters of cakes of various and almost indescribable kinds, known only to experienced Dutch housewives. There was the doughty dough nut, the tenderer oly koek, and the crisp and crumbling cruller; sweet cakes and short cakes, ginger cakes and honey cakes, and the whole family of cakes. And then there were apple pies and peach pies and pumpkin pies; besides slices of ham and smoked beef; and moreover delectable dishes of preserved plums, and peaches, and pears, and quinces; not to mention broiled shad and roasted chickens; together with bowls of milk and cream, all mingled higgledy-piggledy, pretty much as I have enumerated them, with the motherly tea pot sending up its clouds of vapour from the midst—Heaven bless the mark! I want breath and time to discuss this banquet as its deserves, and am too eager to get on with my story. Happily, Ichabod Crane was not in so great a hurry as his historian, but did ample justice to every dainty.

He was a kind and thankful creature, whose heart dilated in proportion as his skin was filled with good cheer, and whose spirits rose with eating, as some men's do with drink. He could not help, too, rolling his large eyes round him as he ate, and chuckling with the possibility that he might one day be lord of all this scene of almost unimaginable luxury and splendour. Then, he thought, how soon he'd turn his back upon the old school house; snap his fingers in the face of Hans Van Ripper, and every other niggardly patron, and kick any itinerant pedagogue out of doors that should dare to call him comrade!

Old Baltus Van Tassel moved about among his guests with a

face dilated with content and good humour, round and jolly as the harvest moon. His hospitable attentions were brief, but expressive, being confined to a shake of the hand, a slap on the shoulder, a loud laugh, and a pressing invitation to "fall to, and help themselves."

And now the sound of the music from the common room or hall, summoned to the dance. The musician was an old grey headed negro, who had been the itinerant orchestra of the neighbourhood for more than half a century. His instrument was as old and battered as himself. The greater part of the time he scraped away on two or three strings, accompanying every movement of the bow with a motion of the head; bowing almost to the ground, and stamping with his foot whenever a fresh couple were to start.

Ichabod prided himself upon his dancing as much as upon his vocal powers. Not a limb, not a fibre about him was idle, and to have seen his loosely hung frame in full motion, and clattering about the room, you would have thought Saint Vitus himself, that blessed patron of the dance, was figuring before you in person. He was the admiration of all the negroes, who, having gathered, of all ages and sizes, from the farm and the neighbourhood, stood forming a pyramid of shining black faces at every door and window, gazing with delight at the scene, rolling their white eye balls, and showing grinning rows of ivory from ear to ear. How could the flogger of urchins be otherwise than animated and joyous; the lady of his heart was his partner in the dance; and smiling graciously in reply to all his amorous oglings, while Brom Bones, sorely smitten with love and jealousy, sat brooding by himself in one corner.

When the dance was at an end, Ichabod was attracted to a knot of the sager folks, who, with old Van Tassel, sat smoking at one end of the piazza, gossiping over former times, and drawling out long stories about the war.

This neighbourhood, at the time of which I am speaking, was

one of those highly favoured places which abound with chronicle and great men. The British and American line had run near it during the war; it had, therefore, been the scene of marauding, and been infested with refugees, cow boys, and all kinds of border chivalry. Just sufficient time had elapsed to enable each story teller to dress up his tale with a little becoming fiction, and in the indistinctness of his recollection, to make himself the hero of every exploit.

There was the story of Doffue Martling, a large, blue bearded Dutchman, who had nearly taken a British frigate with an old iron nine pounder from a mud breastwork, only that his gun burst at the sixth discharge. And there was an old gentleman who shall be nameless, being too rich a mynheer to be lightly mentioned, who in the battle of Whiteplains, being an excellent master of defence, parried a musket ball with a small sword, insomuch that he absolutely felt it whiz round the blade, and glance off at the hilt: in proof of which, he was ready at any time to show the sword, with the hilt a little bent. There were several more who had been equally great in the field, not one of whom but was persuaded that he had a considerable hand in bringing the war to a happy termination.

But all these were nothing to the tales of ghosts and apparitions that succeeded. The neighbourhood is rich in legendary treasures of the kind. Local tales and superstitions thrive best in these sheltered, long settled retreats; but are trampled under foot, by the shifting throng that forms the population of most of our country places. Besides, there is no encouragement for ghosts in most of our villages, for they have scarce had time to finish their first nap, and turn themselves in their graves, before their surviving friends have travelled away from the neighbourhood, so that when they turn out of a night to walk the rounds, they have no acquaintance left to call upon. This is perhaps the reason why we so seldom hear of ghosts except in our long established Dutch communities.

The immediate cause, however, of the prevalence of supernatural stories in these parts, was doubtless owing to the vicinity of Sleepy Hollow. There was a contagion in the very air that blew from that haunted region; it breathed forth an atmosphere of dreams and fancies infecting all the land. Several of the Sleepy Hollow people were present at Van Tassel's, and, as usual, were doling out their wild and wonderful legends. Many dismal tales were told about funeral trains, and mournful cries and wailings heard and seen about the great tree where the unfortunate Major André was taken, and which stood in the neighbourhood. Some mention was made also of the woman in white, that haunted the dark glen at Raven Rock, and was often heard to shriek on winter nights before a storm, having perished there in the snow. The chief part of the stories, however, turned upon the favourite spectre of Sleepy Hollow, the headless horseman, who had been heard several times of late, patroling the country; and it was said, tethered his horse nightly among the graves in the church yard.

The sequestered situation of this church seems always to have made it a favourite haunt of troubled spirits. It stands on a knoll, surrounded by locust trees and lofty elms, from among which its decent, whitewashed walls shine modestly forth, like Christian purity, beaming through the shades of retirement. A gentle slope descends from it to a silver sheet of water, bordered by high trees, between which, peeps may be caught at the blue hills of the Hudson. To look upon its grass grown yard, where the sunbeams seem to sleep so quietly, one would think that there at least the dead might rest in peace. On one side of the church extends a wide woody dell, along which raves a large brook among broken rocks and trunks of fallen trees. Over a deep black part of the stream, not far from the church, was formerly thrown a wooden bridge;

the road that led to it, and the bridge itself, were thickly shaded by overhanging trees, which cast a gloom about it, even in the day time; but occasioned a fearful darkness at night. Such was one of the favourite haunts of the headless horseman, and the place where he was most frequently encountered. The tale was told of old Brouwer, a most heretical disbeliever in ghosts, how he met the horseman returning from his foray into Sleepy Hollow, and was obliged to get up behind him; how they gallopped over bush and brake, over hill and swamp, until they reached the bridge, when the horseman suddenly turned into a skeleton, threw old Brouwer into the brook, and sprang away over the tree tops with a clap of thunder.

This story was immediately matched by a thrice marvellous adventure of Brom Bones, who made light of the gallopping Hessian as an arrant jockey. He affirmed, that on returning one night from the neighbouring village of Sing-Sing, he had been overtaken by this midnight trooper; that he had offered to race with him for a bowl of punch, and should have won it too, for Daredevil beat the goblin horse all hollow, but just as they came to the church bridge, the Hessian bolted, and vanished in a flash of fire.

All these tales, told in that drowsy under tone with which men talk in the dark, the countenances of the listeners only now and then receiving a casual gleam from the glare of a pipe, sunk deep in the mind of Ichabod. He repaid them in kind with large extracts from his invaluable author, Cotton Mather, and added many very marvellous events that had taken place in his native state of Connecticut, and fearful sights which he had seen in his nightly walks about Sleepy Hollow.

The revel now gradually broke up. The old farmers gathered together their families in their wagons, and were heard for some time rattling along the hollow roads, and over the distant hills. Some of the damsels, mounted on pillions behind their favourite swains, and their light hearted laughter mingling with the clatter of hoofs, echoed along the silent woodlands, sounding fainter and fainter until they gradually died away—and the late scene of noise and frolick was all silent and deserted. Ichabod only lingered behind, according to the custom of country lovers, to have a tête-a-tête with the heiress; fully convinced that he was now on the high road to success. What passed at this interview I will not pretend to say, for in fact I do not know. Something, however, I fear me, must have gone wrong, for he certainly sallied forth, after no very great interval, with an air quite desolate and chopfallen—Oh these women! these women! Could that girl have been playing off any of her coquettish tricks?—Was her encouragement of the poor pedagogue all a mere sham to secure her conquest of his rival?— Heaven only knows, not I!—Let it suffice to say, Ichabod stole forth with the air of one who had been sacking a hen roost, rather than a fair lady's heart. Without looking to the right or left to notice the scene of rural wealth, on which he had so often gloated, he went straight to the stable, and with several hearty cuffs and kicks, roused his steed most uncourteously from the comfortable quarters in which he was soundly sleeping, dreaming of mountains of corn and oats, and whole valleys of timothy and clover.

It was the very witching time of night that Ichabod, heavy hearted and crest fallen, pursued his travel homewards, along the sides of the lofty hills which rise above Tarry Town, and which he had traversed so cheerily in the afternoon. The hour was as dismal as himself. Far below him the Tappaan Zee spread its dusky and indistinct waste of waters, with here and there the tall mast of a sloop, riding quietly at anchor under the land. In the dead hush of midnight, he could even hear the barking of the watch dog from the opposite shore of the Hudson; but it was so vague and faint as only to give an idea of his distance from this faithful companion of man. Now and then, too, the long drawn crowing of a cock, accidentally awakened, would sound far, far off, from some farm house away among the hills—but it was like a dreaming sound in his ear. No signs of life occurred near him, but occasionally the melancholy chirp of a cricket, or perhaps the guttural twang of a bull frog, from a neighbouring marsh, as if sleeping uncomfortably, and turning suddenly in his bed.

All the stories of ghosts and goblins that he had heard in the afternoon, now came crowding upon his recollection. The night grew darker and darker; the stars seemed to sink deeper in the sky, and driving clouds occasionally hid them from his sight. He had never felt so lonely and dismal. He was, moreover, approaching the very place where many of the scenes of the ghost stories had been laid. In the centre of the road stood an enormous tulip tree, which towered like a giant above all the other trees of the neighbourhood, and formed a kind of land mark. Its limbs were gnarled, and fantastic, large enough to form trunks for ordinary trees, twisting down almost to the earth, and rising again into the air. It was connected with the tragical story of the unfortunate André, who had been taken prisoner hard by; and was universally known by the name of Major André's tree. The common people regarded it with a mixture of respect and superstition, partly out of sympathy for the fate of its ill starred namesake, and partly from the tales of strange sights, and doleful lamentations, told concerning it.

As Ichabod approached this fearful tree, he began to whistle; he thought his whistle was answered: it was but a blast sweeping sharply through the dry branches. As he approached a little nearer, he thought he saw something white, hanging in the midst of the tree: he paused and ceased whistling; but on looking more narrowly, perceived that it was a place where the tree had been scathed by lightning, and the white wood laid bare. Suddenly he heard a groan—his teeth chattered, and his knees smote against the saddle: it was but the rubbing of one huge bough upon another, as they were swayed about by the breeze. He passed the tree in safety, but new perils lay before him.

About two hundred yards from the tree, a small brook crossed the road, and ran into a marshy and thickly wooded glen, known by the name of Wiley's Swamp. A few rough logs, laid side by side, served for a bridge over this stream. On that side of the road where the brook entered the wood, a group of oaks and chestnuts, matted thick with wild grape vines, threw a cavernous gloom over it. To pass this bridge, was the severest trial. It was at this identical spot that the unfortunate André was captured, and under the covert of those chestnuts and vines were the sturdy yeomen concealed who surprised him. This has ever since been considered a haunted stream, and fearful are the feelings of the schoolboy who has to pass it alone after dark.

As he approached the stream, his heart began to thump; he, however, summoned up all his resolution, gave his horse half a score of kicks in the ribs, and attempted to dash briskly across the bridge; but instead of starting forward, the perverse old animal made a lateral movement, and ran broadside against the fence. Ichabod, whose fears increased with the delay, jerked the reins on the other side, and kicked lustily with the contrary foot: it was all in vain; his steed started, it is true, but it was only to plunge to the opposite side of the road into a thicket of brambles and alder bushes. The schoolmaster now bestowed both whip and heel upon the starvelling ribs of old Gunpowder, who dashed forward, snuffling and snorting, but came to a stand just by the bridge with a suddenness that had nearly sent his rider sprawling over his head. Just at this moment a plashy tramp by the side of the bridge caught the sensitive ear of Ichabod. In the dark shadow of the grove, on the margin of the brook, he beheld something huge, misshapen, black and towering. It stirred not, but seemed gathered up in the gloom, like some gigantic monster ready to spring upon the traveller.

The hair of the affrighted pedagogue rose upon his head with terror. What was to be done? To turn and fly was now too late; and besides, what chance was there of escaping ghost or goblin, if such it was, which could ride upon the wings of the wind? Summoning up, therefore, a show of courage, he demanded in stammering accents—"who are you?" He received no reply. He repeated his demand in a still more agitated voice.—Still there was no answer. Once more he cudgelled the sides of the inflexible Gunpowder, and shutting his eyes, broke forth with involuntary fervour into a psalm tune. Just then the shadowy object of alarm put itself in motion, and with a scramble and a bound, stood at once in the middle of the road. Though the night was dark and dismal, yet the form of the unknown might now in some degree be ascertained. He appeared to be a horseman of large dimensions, and mounted on a black horse of powerful frame. He made no offer of molestation or sociability, but kept aloof on one side of the road, jogging along on the blind side of old Gunpowder, who had now got over his fright and waywardness.

Ichabod, who had no relish for this strange midnight companion, and bethought himself of the adventure of Brom Bones with the gallopping Hessian, now quickened his steed, in hopes of leaving him behind. The stranger, however, quickened his horse to an equal pace; Ichabod pulled up, and fell into a walk, thinking to lag behind—the other did the same. His heart began to sink within him; he endeavoured to resume his psalm tune, but his parched tongue clove to the roof of his mouth, and he could not utter a stave. There was something in the moody and dogged silence of this pertinacious companion, that was mysterious and appalling. It was soon fearfully accounted for. On mounting a rising ground, which brought the figure of his fellow traveller in relief against the sky, gigantic in height, and muffled in a cloak, Ichabod was horror struck, on perceiving that he was headless! but his horror was still

more increased, on observing, that the head, which should have
rested on his shoulders, was carried before him on the pommel of
the saddle! His terror rose to desperation; he rained a shower of
kicks and blows upon Gunpowder, hoping, by a sudden movement, to give his companion the slip—but the spectre started full
jump with him. Away, then, they dashed, through thick and thin;
stones flying, and sparks flashing, at every bound. Ichabod's flimsy
garments fluttered in the air, as he stretched his long lank body
away over his horse's head, in the eagerness of his flight.

They had now reached the road which turns off to Sleepy
Hollow; but Gunpowder, who seemed possessed with a demon,
instead of keeping up it, made an opposite turn, and plunged headlong down hill to the left. This road leads through a sandy hollow
shaded by trees for about a quarter of a mile, where it crosses the
bridge famous in goblin story, and just beyond swells the green
knoll on which stands the whitewashed church.

As yet the panic of the steed had given his unskilful rider an
apparent advantage in the chase, but just as he had got half way
through the hollow, the girths of the saddle gave way, and he felt it
slipping from under him; he seized it by the pommel, and endeavoured to hold it firm, but in vain; and had just time to save himself by clasping old Gunpowder round the neck, when the saddle
fell to the earth, and he heard it trampled under foot by his pursuer. For a moment the terror of Hans Van Ripper's wrath passed
across his mind—for it was his Sunday saddle; but this was no time
for petty fears: the goblin was hard on his haunches; and (unskilful
rider that he was!) he had much ado to maintain his seat; sometimes slipping on one side, sometimes on another, and sometimes
jolted on the high ridge of his horse's back bone, with a violence
that he verily feared would cleave him asunder.

An opening in the trees now cheered him with the hopes that
the Church Bridge was at hand. The wavering reflection of a sil-

ver star in the bosom of the brook told him that he was not mistaken. He saw the walls of the church dimly glaring under the trees beyond. He recollected the place where Brom Bones' ghostly competitor had disappeared. "If I can but reach that bridge," thought Ichabod, "I am safe." Just then he heard the black steed panting and blowing close behind him; he even fancied that he felt his hot breath. Another convulsive kick in the ribs, and old Gunpowder sprung upon the bridge; he thundered over the resounding planks; he gained the opposite side, and now Ichabod cast a look behind to see if his pursuer should vanish, according to rule, in a flash of fire and brimstone. Just then he saw the goblin rising in his stirrups, and in the very act of hurling his head at him. Ichabod endeavoured to dodge the horrible missile, but too late. It encountered his cranium with a tremendous crash—he was tumbled headlong into the dust, and Gunpowder, the black steed, and the goblin rider, passed by like a whirlwind. ——

The next morning the old horse was found without his saddle, and with the bridle under his feet, soberly cropping the grass at his master's gate. Ichabod did not make his appearance at breakfast—dinner hour came, but no Ichabod. The boys assembled at the school house, and strolled idly about the banks of the brook; but no schoolmaster. Hans Van Ripper now began to feel some uneasiness about the fate of poor Ichabod, and his saddle. An inquiry was set on foot, and after diligent investigation they came upon his traces. In one part of the road leading to the church, was found the saddle trampled in the dirt; the tracks of horses' hoofs deeply dented in the road, and evidently at furious speed, were traced to the bridge, beyond which, on the bank of a broad part of the brook, where the water ran deep and black, was found the hat of the unfortunate Ichabod, and close beside it a shattered pumpkin.

The brook was searched, but the body of the schoolmaster was not to be discovered. Hans Van Ripper, as executor of his estate, examined the bundle which contained all his worldy effects. They consisted of two shirts and a half; two stocks for the neck; a pair or two of worsted stockings; an old pair of corduroy small clothes; a rusty razor; a book of psalm tunes, full of dog's ears; and a broken pitch pipe. As to the books and furniture of the schoolhouse, they belonged to the community, excepting Cotton Mather's History of Witchcraft, a New England Almanack, and a book of dreams and fortune telling, in which last was a sheet of foolscap much scribbled and blotted, in several fruitless attempts to make a copy of verses in honour of the heiress of Van Tassel. These magic books and the poetic scrawl were forthwith consigned to the flames by Hans Van Ripper, who from that time forward determined to send his children no more to school, observing, that he never knew any good come of this same reading and writing. Whatever money the schoolmaster possessed, and he had received his quarter's pay but a day or two before, he must have had about his person at the time of his disappearance.

The mysterious event caused much speculation at the Church on the following Sunday. Knots of gazers and gossips were collected in the church yard, at the bridge, and at the spot where the hat and pumpkin had been found. The stories of Brouwer, of Bones, and a whole budget of others, were called to mind; and when they had diligently considered them all, and compared them with the symptoms of the present case, they shook their heads, and came to the conclusion, that Ichabod had been carried off by the gallopping Hessian. As he was a bachelor, and in nobody's debt, nobody troubled his head any more about him, the school was removed to a different quarter of the hollow, and another pedagogue reigned in his stead.

It is true, an old farmer, who had been down to New York on a visit several years after, and from whom this account of the ghostly adventure was received, brought home the intelligence that

Ichabod Crane was still alive; that he had left the neighbourhood partly through fear of the goblin and Hans Van Ripper, and partly in mortification at having been suddenly dismissed by the heiress; that he had changed his quarters to a distant part of the country; had kept school and studied law at the same time; had been admitted to the bar, turned politician, electioneered, written for the newspapers, and finally had been made a Justice of the Ten Pound Court. Brom Bones too, who, shortly after his rival's disappearance, conducted the blooming Katrina in triumph to the altar, was observed to look exceedingly knowing whenever the story of Ichabod was related, and always burst into a hearty laugh at the mention of the pumpkin; which led some to suspect that he knew more about the matter than he chose to tell.

The old country wives, however, who are the best judges of these matters, maintain to this day, that Ichabod was spirited away by supernatural means; and it is a favourite story often told about the neighbourhood round the winter evening fire. The bridge became more than ever an object of superstitious awe, and that may be the reason why the road has been altered of late years, so as to approach the church by the border of the millpond. The school house being deserted, soon fell to decay, and was reported to be haunted by the ghost of the unfortunate pedagogue; and the plough boy, loitering homeward of a still summer evening, has often fancied his voice at a distance, chanting a melancholy psalm tune among the tranquil solitudes of Sleepy Hollow.

The Sage-brush Hen

Thomas A. Janvier
(1849–1913)

S he blew in one day on Hill's coach from Santa Fé— Hill ran
the coach that year the end of the track was at Palomitas, it
being shorter going up that way to Pueblo and Denver and
Leadville than round by the Atchison and changing at El Moro to
the Narrow Gauge—and, being up on the box with Hill, she was
so all over dust that Cherry sung out to him, "Where'd you get
your sage-brush hen from?" And the name stuck.

More folks in Palomitas had names that had tumbled to 'em
like that than the kind that had come regular. And even when they
sounded regular you never could be dead sure they was. Regular
names used to get lost pretty often coming across the Plains in
those days—more'n a few finding it better, about as they got to the
Missouri, to leave behind what they'd been called by back East and
draw something new from the pack. Making a change like that was
apt to be wholesomer, and often saved talk.

Hill said the Hen was more fun coming across from Santa Fé
than a basketful of monkeys; and she was all the funnier, he said,
because when he picked her up at the Fonda she looked like as if

butter wouldn't melt in her mouth and started in with her monkey-shines so sort of quiet and demure. Along with her, waiting at the Fonda, was an old gent with spectacles who turned out to be a mine-sharp—one of them fellows the government sends out to the Territory to write up serious in books all the fool stories prospectors and such unload on 'em: the kind that needs to be led, and 'll eat out of your hand. The Hen and the old gent and Hill had the box seat, the Hen in between; and she was that particular about her skirts climbing up, and about making room after she got there, that Hill said he sized her up himself for an officer's wife going East.

Except to say thank you, and talk polite that way, she didn't open her head till they'd got clear of the town and were going slow in that first bit of bad road among the sand-hills; and it was the old gent speaking to her—telling her it was a fine day, and he hoped she liked it—that set her stamps a-going a little then. She allowed the weather was about what it ought to be, and said she was much obliged and it suited her; and then she got her tongue in behind her teeth again as if she meant to keep it there—till the old gent took a fresh start by asking her if she'd been in the Territory long. She said polite she hadn't, and was quiet for a minute. Then she got out her pocket-handkerchief and put it up to her eyes and said she'd been in it longer'n she wanted, and was glad she was going away. Hill said her talking that way made him feel kind of curious himself; but he didn't have no need to ask questions—the old gent saving him that trouble by going for her sort of fatherly and pumping away at her till he got the whole thing.

It come out scrappy, like as might be expected, Hill said; and so natural-sounding he thought he must be asleep and dreaming—he knowing pretty well what was going on in the Territory, and she telling about doings that was news to him and the kind he'd been sure to hear a lot of if they'd ever really come off. Hill said he wished he could tell it all as she did—speaking low, and ketching her breath in the worst parts, and mopping at her eyes with her pocket-handkerchief—but he couldn't; and all he could say about it was it was better'n any theatre show he'd ever seen. The nubs of it was, he said, that she said her husband had taken out a troop from Fort Wingate against the Apaches (Hill knew blame well up there in the Navajo country was no place to look for Apaches) and the troop had been ambushed in a cañon in the Zuni Mountains (which made the story still tougher) and every man of 'em, along with her "dear Captain," as she called him, had lost his hair. "His loved remains are where those fierce creatures left them," she said. "I have not even the sad solace of properly burying his precious bones!" And she cried.

The old gent was quite broke up, Hill said, and took a-hold of her hand fatherly—she was a powerful fine-looking woman—and said she had his sympathy; and when she eased up on her crying so she could talk she said she was much obliged—and felt it all the more, she said, because he looked like a young uncle of hers who'd brought her up, her father being dead, till she was married East to her dear Captain and had come out to the Territory with him to his doom.

Hill said it all went so smooth he took it down himself at first—but he got his wind while she was crying, and he asked her what her Captain's name was, and what was his regiment; telling her he hadn't heard of any trouble up around Wingate, and it was news to him Apaches was in those parts. She gave him a dig in the ribs with her elbow—as much as to tell him he wasn't to ask no such questions—and said back to him her dear husband was Captain Chiswick of the Twelfth Cavalry; and it had been a big comedown for him, she said, when he got his commission in the Regulars, after he'd been a Volunteer brigadier-general in the war.

Hill knew right enough there wasn't no Twelfth Cavalry

nowhere, and he knew the boys at Wingate were A and F troops of the Fourth; but he ketched on to the way she was giving it to the old gent—and so *he* give *her* a dig in the ribs, and said he'd known Captain Chiswick intimate, and he was as good a fellow as ever was, and it was a blame pity he was killed. She give him a dig back again, at that—and was less particular about making room on his side.

The old gent took it all in, just as it come along; and after she'd finished up about the Apaches killing her dear Captain he wanted to know where she was heading for—because if she was going home East, he said, he was going East himself and could give her a father's care.

She said back to him, pleasant-like, that a young man like him couldn't well be fathering an old lady like her, though it was obliging of him to offer; but, anyway, she wasn't going straight back East, because she had to wait a while at Palomitas for a remittance she was expecting to pay her way through—and she wasn't any too sure about it, she said, whether she'd get her remittance; or, if she did get it, when it would come. Everything bad always got down on you at once, she said; and just as the cruel savages had slain her dear Captain along come the news the bank East he'd put his money in had broke the worst kind. Her financial difficulties wasn't a patch on the trouble her sorrowing heart was giving her, she said; but she allowed they added what she called pangs of bitterness to her deeper pain.

The old gent—he wasn't a fool clean through—asked her what was the matter with her government transportation; she having a right to transportation, being an officer's widow going home. Hill said he gave her a nudge at that, as much as to say the old gent had her. She didn't faze a bit, though. It was her government transportation she was waiting for, she cracked back to him smooth and natural; but such things had to go all the way to Washington to be settled, she said, and then come West again—Hill said he 'most snickered out at that—and she'd known cases when red tape had got in the way and transportation hadn't been allowed at all. Then she sighed terrible, and said it might be a long, long while before she could get home again to her little boy—who was all there was left her in the world. Her little Willy was being took care of by his grandmother, she said, and he was just his father's own handsome self over again—and she got out her pocket-handkerchief and jammed it up to her eyes.

Her left hand was lying in her lap, sort of casual, and the old gent got a-hold of it and said he didn't know how to tell her how sorry he was for her. Talking from behind her pocket-handkerchief, she said such sympathy was precious; and then she went on, kind of pitiful, saying she s'posed her little Willy'd have forgot all about her before she'd get back to him—and she cried some more. Hill said she did it so well he was half took in himself for a minute, and felt so bad he went to licking and swearing at his mules.

After a while she took a brace—getting down her pocket-handkerchief, and calling in the hand the old gent was a-holding—and said she must be brave, like her dear Captain 'd always been, so he'd see when he was a-looking at her from heaven she was doing the square thing. And as to having to wait around before she went East, she said, in one way it didn't make any matter—seeing she'd be well cared for and comfortable at Palomitas staying in the house of the Baptist minister, who'd married her aunt.

Hill said when she went to talking about Baptist ministers and aunts in Palomitas he shook so laughing inside he 'most fell off the box. Except the Mexican padre who belonged there—the one that made a record, and Bishop Lamy had to bounce—and sometimes the French one from San Juan, who was a good fellow and hadn't a fly on him anywhere, there wasn't a fire-escape ever showed himself in Palomitas; and as to the ladies of the town—well, the ladies wasn't just what you'd call the aunt kind. It's a cold fact that that year when the end of the track stuck there Palomitas was about the cussedest town there was in the whole Territory—and so it was no more'n natural Hill should pretty near bust himself trying to hold in his laughing when the Hen took to talking so offhand about Palomitas and Baptist ministers and aunts. She felt how he was shaking, and jammed him hard with her elbow to keep him from letting his laugh out and giving her away.

Hill said they'd got along to Pojuaque by the time the Hen had finished telling about herself, and the fix she was in because she had to wait along with her aunt in Palomitas till her transportation come from Washington—and she just sick to get East and grab her little Willy in her arms. And the old gent was that interested in it all, Hill said, it was a sight to see how he went on.

At Pojuaque the coach always made a noon stop, and the team was changed and the passengers eat lunch at old man Bouquet's. He was a Frenchman, old man Bouquet was; but he'd been in the Territory from 'way back, and he'd got a nice garden round his house and fixed things up French style. His strongest hold was his wine-making. He made a first-class drink, as drinks of that sort go; and, for its kind, it was pretty strong. As his cooking was first class too, Hill's passengers—and the other folks that stopped for grub there—always wanted to make a good long halt.

The old gent, Hill said, knew how to talk French, and that made old man Bouquet extra obliging—and he set up a rattling good lunch and fetched out some of the wine he said he was in the habit of keeping for himself, seeing he'd got somebody in the house for once who really knew the difference between good and bad. He fixed up a table out in the garden—where he'd a queer tree, all growed together, he thought a heap of—and set down with 'em himself; and Hill said it was one of the pleasantest lunches he'd eat in all his life.

The Hen and the old gent got friendlier and friendlier—she being more cheerful when she'd been lunching a while, and getting to talking so comical she kept 'em all on a full laugh. Now and then, though, she'd pull up sudden and kind of back away—making out she didn't want it to show so much—and get her pocket-handkerchief to her eyes and snuffle; and then she'd pull herself together sort of conspicuous, and say she didn't want to spoil the party, but she couldn't help thinking how long it was likely to be before she'd see her little boy. And then the old gent would say that such tender motherliness did her credit, and hers was a sweet nature, and he'd hold her hand till she took it away.

Hill said the time passed so pleasant he forgot how it was going, and when he happened to think to look at his watch he found he'd have to everlastingly hustle his mules to get over to Palomitas in time to ketch the Denver train. He went off in a tearing hurry to hitch up, and old man Bouquet went along to help him—the old gent saying he guessed he and Mrs. Chiswick would stay setting where they was, it being cool and comfortable in the garden, till the team was put to. They set so solid, Hill said, they didn't hear him when he sung out to 'em he was ready; and he said he let his mouth go wide open and yelled like h—ll. (Hill always talked that careless way. He didn't mean no harm by it. He said it was just a habit he'd got into driving mules.) They not coming, he went to hurry 'em, he said—and as he come up behind 'em the Hen was stuffing something into her frock, and the old gent was saying: "I want you to get quickly to your dear infant, my daughter. You can return at your convenience my trifling loan. And now I will give you a fatherly kiss—"

But he didn't, Hill said—because the Hen heard Hill's boots on the gravel and faced round so quick she spoiled his chance. He seemed a little jolted, Hill said; but the Hen was so cool, and talked so pleasant and natural about the good lunch they'd been having, and what a fine afternoon it was, he braced up and got to talking easy too.

Then they all broke for the coach, and got away across the Tesuque River and on through the sand-hills—with Hill cutting away at his mules and using words to 'em fit to blister their hides, and when they fetched the Cañada they were about up again to schedule time. After the Mexican who kept the Santa Cruz post office had made the mess he always did with the mail matter, and had got the cussing he always got from Hill, they started off again—coming slow through that bit of extra-heavy road along by the Rio Grande, but getting to the deepo at Palomitas to ketch the Denver train.

All the way over from Pojuaque, Hill said, he could see out of the corner of his eye the old gent was nudging up to the Hen with his shoulder, friendly and sociable; and he said he noticed the Hen was a good deal less particular about making room. The old gent flushed up and got into a regular temper, Hill said, when Cherry sung out as they pulled into the deepo platform, "Where'd you get your sage-brush hen from?"—and that way give her what stuck fast for her name.

As it turned out, they might have kept on lunching as long as they'd a mind to at Pojuaque; and Hill might have let his mules take it easy, without tiring himself swearing at 'em, on a dead walk—there being a washout in the Comanche Cañon, up above the Embudo, that held the train. It wasn't much of a washout, the conductor said; but he said he guessed all hands would be more comfortable waiting at Palomitas, where there were things doing, than they would be setting still in the cañon while the track gang finished their job—and he said he reckoned the train wouldn't start for about three hours.

The Hen and the old gent was standing on the deepo platform, where they'd landed from the coach; and Hill said as he was taking his mails across to the express-car he heard him asking her once more if she hadn't better come right along East to her lonely babe; and promising to take a father's care of her all the way. The Hen seemed to be in two minds about it for a minute, Hill said; and then she thanked him, sweet as sugar, for his goodness to her in her time of trouble; and told him it would be a real comfort to go East with such a kind escort to take care of her—but she said it wouldn't work, because she was expected in Palomitas, and not stopping there would be disappointing to her dear uncle and aunt.

It was after sundown, and getting duskish, while they were talking; and she said she must be getting along. The old gent said he'd like to go with her; but she said he mustn't think of it, as it was only a step to the parsonage and she knew the way. While he was keeping on telling her she really must let him see her safe with her relatives, up come Santa Fé Charley—and Charley sung out: "Hello, old girl—so you've got here! I was looking for you on the coach, and I thought you hadn't come."

Hill said he began to shake with laughter, as he was sure it would be a dead give-away for her—Santa Fé being the dealer at the Forest Queen, and about the toughest tough there was in town. Charley didn't look tough, though. He always dressed toney, all in black, with a long frock coat and a black felt hat—so he looked like he'd just come off Fifth Avenue—and a white tie. It helped him in his business, sometimes, dressing that way.

Hill said the Hen give a little jump when he sung out to her, but she didn't turn a hair. "Dear Uncle Charley, I am *so* glad to see you!" she said—and went right on, speaking to the old gent: "This is my uncle, the Baptist minister, sir, come to take me to the parsonage to my dear aunt. It's almost funny to have so young an uncle. Aunt's young too—you see, grandfather married a second time. We're more like sister and brother—being so near of an age; and he always will talk to me free and easy, like he always did—

though I tell him now he's a minister it don't sound well." And then she whipped round to Charley, so quick he hadn't time to get a word in edgewise, and said to him: "I hope Aunt Jane's well, and didn't have to go up to Denver—as she said she might in her last letter—to look after Cousin Mary. And I hope you've finished the painting she said was going on at the parsonage—so you can take me in there till my transportation comes and I can start East. This kind gentleman, who's going up on to-night's train, has been offering—and it's just as good of him, even if I can't go—to escort me home to my dear baby; and he's been just full of sympathy over my dear husband Captain Chiswick's loss."

Hill said he never knew anybody take cards as quick as Santa Fé took the cards the Hen was giving him. "I'm very happy to meet you, sir," he said to the old gent; "and most grateful to you for your kindness to my poor niece Rachel in her distress. We have been sorrowing over her during Captain Chiswick's long and painful illness—"

"My dear Captain had been sick for three months, and got out of his bed to go and be killed with his men by those dreadful Apaches," the Hen cut in.

"—and when, the news came of the massacre," Charley went right on, as cool as an iced drink, "our hearts almost broke for her. Captain Chiswick was a splendid gentleman, sir; one of the finest officers ever sent out to this Territory. His loss is a bad thing for the Service; but it is a worse thing for my poor niece—left forsaken with her sweet babes. They are noble children, sir; worthy of their noble sire!"

"Oh, Uncle Charley!" said the Hen. "Didn't you get my letter telling you my little Jane died of croup? I've only my little Willy, now!" And she kind of gagged.

"My poor child! My poor child!" said Santa Fé. "I did not know that death had winged a double dart at you like that—your letter never came." And then he said to the old gent: "The mail service in this Territory, sir, is just about as bad as it can be. The government ought to be ashamed!"

Hill said while they was giving it and taking it that way he 'most choked—particular as the old gent took it all down whole.

Hill said the three of 'em was sort of quiet and sorrowful for a minute, and then Santa Fé said: "It is too bad, Rachel, but your aunt Jane did have to go up to Denver yesterday—a despatch came saying Cousin Mary's taken worse. And the parsonage is in such a mess still with the painters that I've moved over to the Forest Queen Hotel. But you can come there too—it's kept by an officer's widow, you know, and is most quiet and respectable—and you'll be 'most as comfortable waiting there till your transportation comes along as you would be if I could take you home."

Hill said hearing the Forest Queen talked about as quiet and respectable, and old Tenderfoot Sal, who kept it, called an officer's widow, so set him to shaking he had to get to where there was a keg of railroad spikes and set down on it and hold his sides with both hands.

Santa Fé turned to the old gent, Hill said—talking as polite as a Pullman conductor—and told him since he'd been so kind to his unhappy niece he hoped he'd come along with 'em to the hotel too—where he'd be more comfortable, Santa Fé said, getting something to eat and drink than he would be kicking around the deepo waiting till they'd filled in the washout and the train could start.

Hill said the Hen gave Santa Fé a queer sort of look at that, as much as to ask him if he was dead sure he had the cards for that lead. Santa Fé gave her a look back again, as much as to say he knew what was and what wasn't on the table; and then he went on to the old gent, speaking pleasant, telling him likely it might be a little bit noisy over at the hotel—doing her best, he said, Mrs.

Major Rogers couldn't help having noise sometimes, things being so rough and tumble out there on the frontier; but he had a private room for his study, where he wrote his sermons, he said, and got into it by a side door—and so he guessed things wouldn't be too bad.

That seemed to make the Hen easy, Hill said; and away the three of 'em went together to the Forest Queen. Hill knew it was straight enough about the private room and the side door—Santa Fé had it to do business in for himself, on the quiet, when he didn't have to deal; and Hill'd known of a good many folks who'd gone in that private room by that side door and hadn't come out again till Santa Fé'd scooped their pile. But it wasn't no business of his, he said; and he said he was glad to get shut of 'em so he might get the chance to let out the laughing that fairly was hurting his insides.

As they were going away from the deepo, Hill said, he heard Santa Fé telling the old gent he was sorry it was getting so dark— as he'd like to take him round so he could see the parsonage, and the new church they'd just finished building and was going to put an organ in as soon as they'd raised more funds; but it wasn't worth while going out of their way, he said, because they wouldn't show to no sort advantage with the light so bad. As the only church in Palomitas was the Mexican mud one about two hundred years old, and as the nearest thing to a parsonage was the padre's house that Denver Jones had rented and had his faro-bank in, Hill said he guessed Charley acted sensible in not trying to show the old gent around that part of the town.

Hill said after he'd got his supper he thought he'd come down to the deepo and sort of wait around there; on the chance he'd ketch on—when the old gent come over to the train—to what Santa Fé and the Hen'd been putting upon him. Sure enough, he did.

Along about ten o'clock a starting order come down to the

agent—the track gang by that time having the washout so near fixed it would be fit by the time the train got there to go across— and the agent sent word over to the Forest Queen to the old gent, who was the only Pullman passenger, he'd better be coming along.

In five minutes or so he showed up. He wasn't in the best shape, Hill said, and Santa Fé and the Hen each of 'em was giving him an arm; though what he seemed to need more'n arms, Hill said, was legs—the ones he had not being in first-class order and working bad. But he didn't make no exhibition of himself, and talked right enough—only that he spoke sort of short and scrappy—and the three of 'em was as friendly together as friendly could be. Hill said he didn't think it was any hurt to listen, things being the way they were, and he edged up close to 'em—while they stood waiting for the porter to light up the Pullman—and though he couldn't quite make sense of all they was saying he did get on to enough of it to size up pretty close how they'd put the old gent through.

"Although it is for my struggling church, a weak blade of grass in the desert," Santa Fé was saying when Hill got the range of 'em, "I cannot but regret having taken from you your splendid contri- bution to our parish fund in so unusual, I might almost say in so unseemly a way. That I have returned to you a sufficient sum to enable you to prosecute your journey to its conclusion places you under no obligation to me. Indeed, I could not have done less— considering the very liberal loan that you have made to my poor niece to enable her to return quickly to her helpless babe. As I hardly need tell you, that loan will be returned promptly—as soon as Mrs. Captain Chiswick gets East and is able to disentangle her affairs."

"Indeed it will," the Hen put in. "My generous benefactor shall be squared with if I have to sell my clothes!"

"Mustn't think of such a thing. Catch cold," the old gent said. "Pleasure's all mine to assist such a noble woman in her unmerited distress. And now I shall have happiness, and same time sorrow, to give her fatherly kiss for farewell."

The Hen edged away a little, Hill said, and Santa Fé shortened his grip a little on the old gent's arm—so his fatherly kissing missed fire. But he didn't seem to notice, and said to Santa Fé: "Never knew a minister know cards like you. Wonderful! And wonderful luck what you held. Played cards a good deal myself. Never could play like you!"

Santa Fé steadied the old gent, Hill said, and said to him in a kind of explaining way: "As I told you, my dear sir, in my wild college days—before I got light on my sinful path and headed for the ministry—I was reckoned something out of the common as a card-player, and what the profane call luck used to be with me all the time. Of course, since I humbly—but, I trust, helpfully—took to being a worker in the vineyard, I have not touched those devil's picture-books; nor should I have touched them to-night but for my hope that a little game would help to while away your time of tedious waiting. As for playing for money, that would have been quite impossible if it had not been for my niece's suggestion that my winnings—in case such came to me—should be added to our meagre parish fund. I trust that I have not done wrong in yielding to my impulse. At least I have to sustain me the knowledge that if you, my dear sir, are somewhat the worse, my impoverished church is much the better for our friendly game of chance."

Hill said hearing Santa Fé Charley talking about chance in any game where he had the dealing was so funny it was better'n going to the circus. But the old gent took it right enough—and the Hen added on: "Yes, Uncle Charley can get the organ he's been wanting so badly for his church, now. And I'm sure we'll all think of how we owe its sweet music to you every time we hear it played!"—and she edged up to him again, so he could hold her hand. "It must make you very, very happy, sir," she kept on, speaking kind of low and gentle, but not coming as close as he wanted her, "to go about the world doing such generous-hearted good deeds! I'm sure I'd like to thank you enough—only there isn't any fit words to thank you in—for your noble-hearted generous goodness to me!"

The old gent hauled away on her hand, Hill said, trying to get her closer, and said back to her: "Words quite unnecessary. Old man's heart filled with pleasure obliging such dear child. Never mind about words. Accept old man's fatherly kiss, like daughter, for good-bye."

But he missed it that time too, Hill said—and Hill said, speaking in his careless cuss-word way, it was pretty d—n rough on him what poor luck in fatherly kisses he seemed to have—because just then the train-conductor swung his lantern and sung out, "All aboard!"

That ended things. Before the old gent knew what had got him, Santa Fé and the Hen had boosted him up the steps on to the platform of the Pullman—where the Pullman conductor got a grip on him just in time to save him from spilling—and then the train pulled out: with the Pullman conductor keeping him steady, and he throwing back good-bye kisses to the Hen with both hands.

Hill said the Hen and Santa Fé kept quiet till the hind lights showed beyond the end of the deepo platform: and then the Hen grabbed Santa Fé round the neck and just hung on to him—so full of laugh she was limp—while they both roared. And Hill said he roared too. It was the most comical bit of business, he said, he'd tumbled to in all his born days!

It wasn't until the train got clear round the curve above the station, Hill said, that Charley and the Hen could pull 'emselves together so they could talk. Then the Hen let a-go of Santa Fé's neck and said comical—speaking kind of precise and toney, like as if she was an officer's wife sure enough: "You'd better return to your study, dear Uncle Charles, and finish writing that sermon you said we'd interrupt you in about caring for the sheep as well as the lambs!"

And then they went off together yelling, Hill said, over to the Forest Queen.

A White Heron

Sarah Orne Jewett
(1849–1909)

I

The woods were already filled with shadows one June evening, just before eight o'clock, though a bright sunset still glimmered faintly among the trunks of the trees. A little girl was driving home her cow, a plodding, dilatory, provoking creature in her behavior, but a valued companion for all that. They were going away from the western light, and striking deep into the dark woods, but their feet were familiar with the path, and it was no matter whether their eyes could see it or not.

There was hardly a night the summer through when the old cow could be found waiting at the pasture bars; on the contrary, it was her greatest pleasure to hide herself away among the high huckleberry bushes, and though she wore a loud bell she had made the discovery that if one stood perfectly still it would not ring. So Sylvia had to hunt for her until she found her, and call Co'! Co'! with never an answering Moo, until her childish patience was quite spent. If the creature had not given good milk and plenty of it, the case would have seemed very different to her owners. Besides, Sylvia had all the time there was, and very little use to make of it. Sometimes in pleasant weather it was a consolation to look upon the cow's pranks as an intelligent attempt to play hide and seek, and as the child had no playmates she lent herself to this amusement with a good deal of zest. Though this chase had been so long that the wary animal herself had given an unusual signal of her whereabouts, Sylvia had only laughed when she came upon Mistress Moolly at the swamp-side, and urged her affectionately homeward with a twig of birch leaves. The old cow was not inclined to wander farther, she even turned in the right direction for once as they left the pasture, and stepped along the road at a good pace. She was quite ready to be milked now, and seldom stopped to browse. Sylvia wondered what her grandmother would say because they were so late. It was a great while since she had left home at half-past five o'clock, but everybody knew the difficulty of making this errand a short one. Mrs. Tilley had chased the hornéd torment too many summer evenings herself to blame any one else for lingering, and was only thankful as she waited that she had Sylvia, nowadays, to give such valuable assistance. The good woman suspected that Sylvia loitered occasionally on her own account; there never was such a child for straying about out-of-doors since the world was made! Everybody said that it was a good change for a little maid who had tried to grow for eight years in a crowded manufacturing town, but, as for Sylvia herself, it seemed as if she never had been alive at all before she came to live at the farm. She thought often with wistful compassion of a wretched dry geranium that belonged to a town neighbor.

" 'Afraid of folks,' " old Mrs. Tilley said to herself, with a smile, after she had made the unlikely choice of Sylvia from her daughter's houseful of children, and was returning to the farm. " 'Afraid of folks,' they said! I guess she won't be troubled no great with 'em up to the old place!" When they reached the door of the lonely house and stopped to unlock it, and the cat came to purr loudly, and rub against them, a deserted pussy, indeed, but fat with young robins, Sylvia whispered that this was a beautiful place to live in, and she never should wish to go home.

The companions followed the shady wood-road, the cow taking slow steps, and the child very fast ones. The cow stopped long at the brook to drink, as if the pasture were not half a swamp, and Sylvia stood still and waited, letting her bare feet cool themselves in the shoal water, while the great twilight moths struck softly against her. She waded on through the brook as the cow moved away, and listened to the thrushes with a heart that beat fast with pleasure. There was a stirring in the great boughs overhead. They were full of little birds and beasts that seemed to be wide-awake, and going about their world, or else saying good-night to each other in sleepy twitters. Sylvia herself felt sleepy as she walked along. However, it was not much farther to the house, and the air was soft and sweet. She was not often in the woods so late as this, and it made her feel as if she were a part of the gray shadows and the moving leaves. She was just thinking how long it seemed since she first came to the farm a year ago, and wondering if everything went on in the noisy town just the same as when she was there; the thought of the great red-faced boy who used to chase and frighten her made her hurry along the path to escape from the shadow of the trees.

Suddenly this little woods-girl is horror-stricken to hear a clear whistle not very far away. Not a bird's whistle, which would have a sort of friendliness, but a boy's whistle, determined, and somewhat aggressive. Sylvia left the cow to whatever sad fate might await her, and stepped discreetly aside into the bushes, but she was just too late. The enemy had discovered her, and called out in a very cheerful and persuasive tone, "Halloa, little girl, how far is it to the road?" and trembling Sylvia answered almost inaudibly, "A good ways."

She did not dare to look boldly at the tall young man, who carried a gun over his shoulder, but she came out of her bush and again followed the cow, while he walked alongside.

"I have been hunting for some birds," the stranger said kindly, "and I have lost my way, and need a friend very much. Don't be afraid," he added gallantly. "Speak up and tell me what your name is, and whether you think I can spend the night at your house, and go out gunning early in the morning."

Sylvia was more alarmed than before. Would not her grandmother consider her much to blame? But who could have foreseen such an accident as this? It did not appear to be her fault, and she hung her head as if the stem of it were broken, but managed to answer "Sylvy," with much effort when her companion again asked her name.

Mrs. Tilley was standing in the doorway when the trio came into view. The cow gave a loud moo by way of explanation.

"Yes, you'd better speak up for yourself, you old trial! Where'd she tucked herself away this time, Sylvy?" Sylvia kept an awed silence; she knew by instinct that her grandmother did not comprehend the gravity of the situation. She must be mistaking the stranger for one of the farmer-lads of the region.

The young man stood his gun beside the door, and dropped a heavy game-bag beside it; then he bade Mrs. Tilley good-evening, and repeated his wayfarer's story, and asked if he could have a night's lodging.

"Put me anywhere you like," he said. "I must be off early in the morning, before day; but I am very hungry, indeed. You can give me some milk at any rate, that's plain."

"Dear sakes, yes," responded the hostess, whose long slumbering hospitality seemed to be easily awakened. "You might fare better if you went out to the main road a mile or so, but you're welcome to what we've got. I'll milk right off, and you make yourself at home. You can sleep on husks or feathers," she proffered graciously. "I raised them all myself. There's good pasturing for geese just below here towards the ma'sh. Now step round and set a plate for the gentleman, Sylvy!" And Sylvia promptly stepped. She was glad to have something to do, and she was hungry herself.

It was a surprise to find so clean and comfortable a little dwelling in this New England wilderness. The young man had known the horrors of its most primitive housekeeping, and the dreary squalor of that level of society which does not rebel at the companionship of hens. This was the best thrift of an old-fashioned farmstead, though on such a small scale that it seemed like a hermitage. He listened eagerly to the old woman's quaint talk, he watched Sylvia's pale face and shining gray eyes with ever growing enthusiasm, and insisted that this was the best supper he had eaten for a month; then, afterward, the new-made friends sat down in the doorway together while the moon came up.

Soon it would be berry-time, and Sylvia was a great help at picking. The cow was a good milker, though a plaguy thing to keep track of, the hostess gossiped frankly, adding presently that she had buried four children, so Sylvia's mother, and a son (who might be dead) in California were all the children she had left. "Dan, my boy, was a great hand to go gunning," she explained sadly. "I never wanted for pa'tridges or gray squer'ls while he was to home. He's been a great wand'rer, I expect, and he's no hand to write letters. There, I don't blame him, I'd ha' seen the world myself if it had been so I could.

"Sylvy takes after him," the grandmother continued affectionately, after a minute's pause. "There ain't a foot o' ground she don't know her way over, and the wild creatur's counts her one o' themselves. Squer'ls she'll tame to come an' feed right out o' her hands, and all sorts o' birds. Last winter she got the jay-birds to bangeing here, and I believe she'd 'a' scanted herself of her own meals to have plenty to throw out amongst 'em, if I hadn't kep' watch. Anything but crows, I tell her, I'm willin' to help support—though Dan he went an' tamed one o' them that did seem to have reason same as folks. It was round here a good spell after he went away. Dan an' his father they didn't hitch—but he never held up his head ag'in after Dan had dared him an' gone off."

The guest did not notice this hint of family sorrows in his eager interest in something else.

"So Sylvy knows all about birds, does she?" he exclaimed, as he looked round at the little girl who sat, very demure but increasingly sleepy, in the moonlight. "I am making a collection of birds myself. I have been at it ever since I was a boy." (Mrs. Tilley smiled.) "There are two or three very rare ones I have been hunting for these five years. I mean to get them on my own ground if they can be found."

"Do you cage 'em up?" asked Mrs. Tilley doubtfully, in response to this enthusiastic announcement.

"Oh, no, they're stuffed and preserved, dozens and dozens of them," said the ornithologist, "and I have shot or snared every one myself. I caught a glimpse of a white heron three miles from here on Saturday, and I have followed it in this direction. They have never been found in this district at all. The little white heron, it is," and he turned again to look at Sylvia with the hope of discovering that the rare bird was one of her acquaintances.

But Sylvia was watching a hop-toad in the narrow footpath.

"You would know the heron if you saw it," the stranger continued eagerly. "A queer tall white bird with soft feathers and long thin legs. And it would have a nest perhaps in the top of a high tree, made of sticks, something like a hawk's nest."

Sylvia's heart gave a wild beat; she knew that strange white bird, and had once stolen softly near where it stood in some bright green swamp grass, away over at the other side of the woods. There was an open place where the sunshine always seemed strangely yellow and hot, where tall, nodding rushes grew, and her grandmother had warned her that she might sink in the soft black mud underneath and never be heard of more. Not far beyond were the salt marshes and beyond those was the sea, the sea which Sylvia wondered and dreamed about, but never had looked upon, though its great voice could often be heard above the noise of the woods on stormy nights.

"I can't think of anything I should like so much as to find that heron's nest," the handsome stranger was saying. "I would give ten dollars to anybody who could show it to me," he added desperately, "and I mean to spend my whole vacation hunting for it if need be. Perhaps it was only migrating, or had been chased out of its own region by some bird of prey."

Mrs. Tilley gave amazed attention to all this, but Sylvia still watched the toad, not divining, as she might have done at some calmer time, that the creature wished to get to its hole under the doorstep, and was much hindered by the unusual spectators at that hour of the evening. No amount of thought, that night, could decide how many wished-for treasures the ten dollars, so lightly spoken of, would buy.

The next day the young sportsman hovered about the woods, and Sylvia kept him company, having lost her first fear of the friendly lad, who proved to be most kind and sympathetic. He told her many things about the birds and what they knew and where they lived and what they did with themselves. And he gave her a jackknife, which she thought as great a treasure as if she were a desert-islander. All day long he did not once make her troubled or afraid

except when he brought down some unsuspecting singing creature from its bough. Sylvia would have liked him vastly better
without his gun; she could not understand why he killed the very
birds he seemed to like so much. But as the day waned, Sylvia still
watched the young man with loving admiration. She had never
seen anybody so charming and delightful; the woman's heart,
asleep in the child, was vaguely thrilled by a dream of love. Some
premonition of that great power stirred and swayed these young
foresters who traversed the solemn woodlands with soft-footed
silent care. They stopped to listen to a bird's song; they pressed forward again eagerly, parting the branches—speaking to each other
rarely and in whispers; the young man going first and Sylvia following, fascinated, a few steps behind, with her gray eyes dark with
excitement.

She grieved because the longed-for white heron was elusive,
but she did not lead the guest, she only followed, and there was no
such thing as speaking first. The sound of her own unquestioned
voice would have terrified her—it was hard enough to answer yes
or no when there was need of that. At last evening began to fall,
and they drove the cow home together, and Sylvia smiled with
pleasure when they came to the place where she heard the whistle and was afraid only the night before.

II

Half a mile from home, at the farther edge of the woods, where
the land was highest, a great pine-tree stood, the last of its gener-
ation. Whether it was left for a boundary mark, or for what reason,
no one could say; the woodchoppers who had felled its mates were
dead and gone long ago, and a whole forest of sturdy trees, pines
and oaks and maples, had grown again. But the stately head of this

old pine towered above them all and made a landmark for sea and shore miles and miles away. Sylvia knew it well. She had always believed that whoever climbed to the top of it could see the ocean; and the little girl had often laid her hand on the great rough trunk and looked up wistfully at those dark boughs that the wind always stirred, no matter how hot and still the air might be below. Now she thought of the tree with a new excitement, for why, if one climbed it at break of day, could not one see all the world, and easily discover from whence the white heron flew, and mark the place, and find the hidden nest?

What a spirit of adventure, what wild ambition! What fancied triumph and delight and glory for the later morning when she could make known the secret! It was almost too real and too great for the childish heart to bear.

All night the door of the little house stood open and the whippoorwills came and sang upon the very step. The young sportsman and his old hostess were sound asleep, but Sylvia's great design kept her broad awake and watching. She forgot to think of sleep. The short summer night seemed as long as the winter darkness, and at last when the whippoorwills ceased, and she was afraid the morning would after all come too soon, she stole out of the house and followed the pasture path through the woods, hastening toward the open ground beyond, listening with a sense of comfort and companionship to the drowsy twitter of a half-awakened bird, whose perch she had jarred in passing. Alas, if the great wave of human interest which flooded for the first time this dull little life should sweep away the satisfactions of an existence heart to heart with nature and the dumb life of the forest!

There was the huge tree asleep yet in the paling moonlight, and small and hopeful Sylvia began with utmost bravery to mount to the top of it, with tingling, eager blood coursing the channels of her whole frame, with her bare feet and fingers, that pinched and held like bird's claws to the monstrous ladder reaching up, up, almost to the sky itself. First she must mount the white oak tree that grew alongside, where she was almost lost among the dark branches and the green leaves heavy and wet with dew; a bird fluttered off its nest, and a red squirrel ran to and fro and scolded pettishly at the harmless housebreaker. Sylvia felt her way easily. She had often climbed there, and knew that higher still one of the oak's upper branches chafed against the pine trunk, just where its lower boughs were set close together. There, when she made the dangerous pass from one tree to the other, the great enterprise would really begin.

She crept out along the swaying oak limb at last, and took the daring step across into the old pine-tree. The way was harder than she thought; she must reach far and hold fast, the sharp dry twigs caught and held her and scratched her like angry talons, the pitch made her thin little fingers clumsy and stiff as she went round and round the tree's great stem, higher and higher upward. The sparrows and robins in the woods below were beginning to wake and twitter to the dawn, yet it seemed much lighter there aloft in the pine-tree, and the child knew she must hurry if her project were to be of any use.

The tree seemed to lengthen itself out as she went up, and to reach farther and farther upward. It was like a great main-mast to the voyaging earth; it must truly have been amazed that morning through all its ponderous frame as it felt this determined spark of human spirit creeping and climbing from higher branch to branch. Who knows how steadily the least twigs held themselves to advantage this light, weak creature on her way! The old pine must have loved his new dependent. More than all the hawks, and bats, and moths, and even the sweet-voiced thrushes, was the brave, beating heart of the solitary gray-eyed child. And the tree stood still and held away the winds that June morning while the dawn grew bright in the east.

Sylvia's face was like a pale star, if one had seen it from the ground, when the last thorny bough was past, and she stood trembling and tired but wholly triumphant, high in the tree-top. Yes, there was the sea with the dawning sun making a golden dazzle over it, and toward that glorious east flew two hawks with slow-moving pinions. How low they looked in the air from that height when before one had only seen them far up, and dark against the blue sky. Their gray feathers were as soft as moths; they seemed only a little way from the tree, and Sylvia felt as if she too could go flying away among the clouds. Westward, the woodlands and farms reached miles and miles into the distance; here and there were church steeples, and white villages; truly it was a vast and awesome world.

The birds sang louder and louder. At last the sun came up bewilderingly bright. Sylvia could see the white sails of ships out at sea, and the clouds that were purple and rose-colored and yellow at first began to fade away. Where was the white heron's nest in the sea of green branches, and was this wonderful sight and pageant of the world the only reward for having climbed to such a giddy height? Now look down again, Sylvia, where the green marsh is set among the shining birches and dark hemlocks; there where you saw the white heron once you will see him again; look, look! a white spot of him like a single floating feather comes up from the dead hemlock and grows larger, and rises, and comes close at last, and goes by the landmark pine with steady sweep of wing and outstretched slender neck and crested head. And wait! wait! do not move a foot or a finger, little girl, do not send an arrow of light and consciousness from your two eager eyes, for the heron has perched on a pine bough not far beyond yours, and cries back to his mate on the nest, and plumes his feathers for the new day!

The child gives a long sigh a minute later when a company of shouting cat-birds comes also to the tree, and vexed by their fluttering and lawlessness the solemn heron goes away. She knows his secret now, the wild, light, slender bird that floats and wavers, and goes back like an arrow presently to his home in the green world beneath. Then Sylvia, well satisfied, makes her perilous way down again, not daring to look far below the branch she stands on, ready to cry sometimes because her fingers ache and her lamed feet slip. Wondering over and over again what the stranger would say to her, and what he would think when she told him how to find his way straight to the heron's nest.

"Sylvy, Sylvy!" called the busy old grandmother again and again, but nobody answered, and the small husk bed was empty, and Sylvia had disappeared.

The guest waked from a dream, and remembering his day's pleasure hurried to dress himself that it might sooner begin. He was sure from the way the shy little girl looked once or twice yesterday that she had at least seen the white heron, and now she must really be persuaded to tell. Here she comes now, paler than ever, and her worn old frock is torn and tattered, and smeared with pine pitch. The grandmother and the sportsman stand in the door together and question her, and the splendid moment has come to speak of the dead hemlock-tree by the green marsh.

But Sylvia does not speak after all, though the old grandmother fretfully rebukes her, and the young man's kind appealing eyes are looking straight in her own. He can make them rich with money; he has promised it, and they are poor now. He is so well worth making happy, and he waits to hear the story she can tell.

No, she must keep silence! What is it that suddenly forbids her and makes her dumb? Has she been nine years growing and now, when the great world for the first time puts out a hand to her, must she thrust it aside for a bird's sake? The murmur of the pine's green branches is in her ears, she remembers how the white heron

came flying through the golden air and how they watched the sea
and the morning together, and Sylvia cannot speak; she cannot tell
the heron's secret and give its life away.

Dear loyalty, that suffered a sharp pang as the guest went away disappointed later in the day, that could have served and followed him
and loved him as a dog loves! Many a night Sylvia heard the echo
of his whistle haunting the pasture path as she came home with
the loitering cow. She forgot even her sorrow at the sharp report
of his gun and the sight of thrushes and sparrows dropping silent
to the ground, their songs hushed and their pretty feathers stained
and wet with blood. Were the birds better friends than their hunter
might have been—who can tell? Whatever treasures were lost to
her, woodlands and summer-time, remember! Bring your gifts and
graces and tell your secrets to this lonely country child!

The Little Convent Girl

Grace King
(1852–1932)

⌒⌒⌒

She was coming down on the boat from Cincinnati, the little convent girl. Two sisters had brought her aboard. They gave her in charge of the captain, got her a state-room, saw that the new little trunk was put into it, hung the new little satchel up on the wall, showed her how to bolt the door at night, shook hands with her for good-by (good-bys have really no significance for sisters), and left her there. After a while the bells all rang, and the boat, in the awkward elephantine fashion of boats, got into midstream. The chambermaid found her sitting on the chair in the state-room where the sisters had left her, and showed her how to sit on a chair in the saloon. And there she sat until the captain came and hunted her up for supper. She could not do anything of herself; she had to be initiated into everything by some one else.

She was known on the boat only as "the little convent girl." Her name, of course, was registered in the clerk's office, but on a steamboat no one thinks of consulting the clerk's ledger. It is always the little widow, the fat madam, the tall colonel, the parson, etc. The captain, who pronounced by the letter, always called her the little *convent* girl. She was the beau-ideal of the little convent girl. She never raised her eyes except when spoken to. Of course she never spoke first, even to the chambermaid, and when she did speak it was in the wee, shy, furtive voice one might imagine a just-budding violet to have; and she walked with such soft, easy, carefully calculated steps that one naturally felt the penalties that must have secured them—penalties dictated by a black code of deportment.

She was dressed in deep mourning. Her black straw hat was trimmed with stiff new crape, and her stiff new bombazine dress had crape collar and cuffs. She wore her hair in two long plaits fastened around her head tight and fast. Her hair had a strong inclination to curl, but that had been taken out of it as austerely as the noise out of her footfalls. Her hair was as black as her dress; her eyes, when one saw them, seemed blacker than either, on account of the bluishness of the white surrounding the pupil. Her eyelashes were almost as thick as the black veil which the sisters had fastened around her hat with an extra pin the very last thing before leaving. She had a round little face, and a tiny pointed chin; her mouth was slightly protuberant from the teeth, over which she tried to keep her lips well shut, the effort giving them a pathetic little forced expression. Her complexion was sallow, a pale sallow, the complexion of a brunette bleached in darkened rooms. The only color about her was a blue taffeta ribbon from which a large silver medal of the Virgin hung over the place where a breastpin should have been. She was so little, so little, although she was eighteen, as the sisters told the captain; otherwise they would not have permitted her to travel all the way to New Orleans alone.

Unless the captain or the clerk remembered to fetch her out in front, she would sit all day in the cabin, in the same place, crocheting lace, her spool of thread and box of patterns in her lap, on the handkerchief spread to save her new dress. Never leaning back—oh, no! always straight and stiff, as if the conventual back board were there within call. She would eat only convent fare at first, notwithstanding the importunities of the waiters, and the jocularities of the captain, and particularly of the clerk. Every one knows the fund of humor possessed by a steamboat clerk, and what a field for display the table at meal-times affords. On Friday she fasted rigidly, and she never began to eat, or finished, without a little Latin movement of the lips and a sign of the cross. And always at six o'clock of the evening she remembered the angelus, although there was no church bell to remind her of it.

She was in mourning for her father, the sisters told the captain, and she was going to New Orleans to her mother. She had not seen her mother since she was an infant, on account of some disagreement between the parents, in consequence of which the father had brought her to Cincinnati, and placed her in the convent. There she had been for twelve years, only going to her father for vacations and holidays. So long as the father lived he would never let the child have any communication with her mother. Now that he was dead all that was changed, and the first thing that the girl herself wanted to do was to go to her mother.

The mother superior had arranged it all with the mother of the girl, who was to come personally to the boat in New Orleans, and receive her child from the captain, presenting a letter from the mother superior, a facsimile of which the sisters gave the captain.

It is a long voyage from Cincinnati to New Orleans, the rivers doing their best to make it interminable, embroidering themselves *ad libitum* all over the country. Every five miles, and sometimes oftener, the boat would stop to put off or take on freight, if not both. The little convent girl, sitting in the cabin, had her terrible frights at first from the hideous noises attendant on these landings—the whistles, the ringings of the bells, the running to and fro, the shouting. Every time she thought it was shipwreck, death, judg-

ment, purgatory; and her sins! her sins! She would drop her crochet, and clutch her prayer-beads from her pocket, and relax the
constraint over her lips, which would go to rattling off prayers with
the velocity of a relaxed windlass. That was at first, before the captain took to fetching her out in front to see the boat make a landing. Then she got to liking it so much that she would stay all day
just where the captain put her, going inside only for her meals. She
forgot herself at times so much that she would draw her chair a little closer to the railing, and put up her veil, actually, to see better.
No one ever usurped her place, quite in front, or intruded upon
her either with word or look; for every one learned to know her
shyness, and began to feel a personal interest in her, and all wanted
the little convent girl to see everything that she possibly could.

And it was worth seeing—the balancing and *chasséeing* and
waltzing of the cumbersome old boat to make a landing. It seemed
to be always attended with the difficulty and the improbability of
a new enterprise; and the relief when it did sidle up anywhere
within rope-throw's of the spot aimed at! And the roustabout
throwing the rope from the perilous end of the dangling gang-
plank! And the dangling roustabouts hanging like drops of water
from it—dropping sometimes twenty feet to the land, and not infrequently into the river itself. And then what a rolling of barrels,
and shouldering of sacks, and singing of Jim Crow songs, and pacing of Jim Crow steps; and black skins glistening through torn
shirts, and white teeth gleaming through red lips, and laughing, and
talking and—bewildering! entrancing! Surely the little convent
girl in her convent walls never dreamed of so much unpunished
noise and movement in the world!

The first time she heard the mate—it must have been like the
first time woman ever heard man—curse and swear, she turned
pale, and ran quickly, quickly into the saloon, and—came out
again? No, indeed! not with all the soul she had to save, and all the

other sins on her conscience. She shook her head resolutely, and was not seen in her chair on deck again until the captain not only reassured her, but guaranteed his reassurance. And after that, whenever the boat was about to make a landing, the mate would first glance up to the guards, and if the little convent girl was sitting there he would change his invective to sarcasm, and politely request the colored gentlemen not to hurry themselves—on no account whatever; to take their time about shoving out the plank; to send the rope ashore by post-office—write him when it got there; begging them not to strain their backs; calling them mister, colonel, major, general, prince, and your royal highness, which was vastly amusing. At night, however, or when the little convent girl was not there, language flowed in its natural curve, the mate swearing like a pagan to make up for lost time.

The captain forgot himself one day: it was when the boat ran aground in the most unexpected manner and place, and he went to work to express his opinion, as only steamboat captains can, of the pilot, mate, engineer, crew, boat, river, country, and the world in general, ringing the bell, first to back, then to head, shouting himself hoarser than his own whistle—when he chanced to see the little black figure hurrying through the chaos on the deck; and the captain stuck as fast aground in midstream as the boat had done.

In the evening the little convent girl would be taken on the upper deck, and going up the steep stairs there was such confusion, to keep the black skirts well over the stiff white petticoats; and, coming down, such blushing when suspicion would cross the unprepared face that a rim of white stocking might be visible; and the thin feet, laced so tightly in the glossy new leather boots, would cling to each successive step as if they could never, never make another venture; and then one boot would (there is but that word) hesitate out, and feel and feel around, and have such a pause of helpless agony as if indeed the next step must have been wilfully removed, or was nowhere to be found on the wide, wide earth.

It was a miracle that the pilot ever got her up into the pilot-house; but pilots have a lonely time, and do not hesitate even at miracles when there is a chance for company. He would place a box for her to climb to the tall bench behind the wheel, and he would arrange the cushions, and open a window here to let in air, and shut one there to cut off a draft, as if there could be no tenderer consideration in life for him than her comfort. And he would talk of the river to her, explain the chart, pointing out eddies, whirlpools, shoals, depths, new beds, old beds, cut-offs, caving banks, and making banks, as exquisitely and respectfully as if she had been the River Commission.

It was his opinion that there was as great a river as the Mississippi flowing directly under it—an underself of a river, as much a counterpart of the other as the second story of a house is of the first; in fact, he said they were navigating through the upper story. Whirlpools were holes in the floor of the upper river, so to speak; eddies were rifts and cracks. And deep under the earth, hurrying toward the subterranean stream, were other streams, small and great, but all deep, hurrying to and from that great mother-stream underneath, just as the small and great overground streams hurry to and from their mother Mississippi. It was almost more than the little convent girl could take in: at least such was the expression of her eyes; for they opened as all eyes have to open at pilot stories. And he knew as much of astronomy as he did of hydrology, could call the stars by name, and define the shapes of the constellations; and she, who had studied astronomy at the convent, was charmed to find that what she had learned was all true. It was in the pilot-house, one night, that she forgot herself for the first time in her life, and stayed up until after nine o'clock. Although she appeared almost intoxicated at the wild pleasure, she was immediately overwhelmed at the wickedness of it, and observed much more rigidity of conduct thereafter. The engineer, the boiler-men, the firemen, the stokers, they all knew when the little convent girl was up in the pilot-house: the speaking-tube became so mild and gentle.

With all the delays of river and boat, however, there is an end to the journey from Cincinnati to New Orleans. The latter city, which at one time to the impatient seemed at the terminus of the never, began, all of a sudden, one day to make its nearingness felt; and from that period every other interest paled before the interest in the immanence of arrival into port, and the whole boat was seized with a panic of preparation, the little convent girl with the others. Although so immaculate was she in person and effects that she might have been struck with a landing, as some good people might be struck with death, at any moment without fear of results, her trunk was packed and repacked, her satchel arranged and rearranged, and, the last day, her hair was brushed and plaited and smoothed over and over again until the very last glimmer of a curl disappeared. Her dress was whisked, as if for microscopic inspection; her face was washed; and her finger-nails were scrubbed with the hard convent nail-brush, until the disciplined little tips ached with a pristine soreness. And still there were hours to wait, and still the boat added up delays. But she arrived at last, after all, with not more than the usual and expected difference between the actual and the advertised time of arrival.

There was extra blowing and extra ringing, shouting, commanding, rushing up the gangway and rushing down the gangway. The clerks, sitting behind tables on the first deck, were plied, in the twinkling of an eye, with estimates, receipts, charges, countercharges, claims, reclaims, demands, questions, accusations, threats, all at topmost voices. None but steamboat clerks could have stood it. And there were throngs composed of individuals every one of whom wanted to see the captain first and at once: and those who could not get to him shouted over the heads of the others; and as usual he lost his temper and politeness, and began to do what he termed "hustle."

"Captain! Captain!" a voice called him to where a hand plucked his sleeve, and a letter was thrust toward him. "The cross, and the name of the convent." He recognized the envelop of the mother superior. He read the duplicate of the letter given by the sisters. He looked at the woman—the mother—casually, then again and again.

The little convent girl saw him coming, leading some one toward her. She rose. The captain took her hand first, before the other greeting, "Good-by, my dear," he said. He tried to add something else, but seemed undetermined what. "Be a good little girl—" It was evidently all he could think of. Nodding to the woman behind him, he turned on his heel, and left.

One of the deck-hands was sent to fetch her trunk. He walked out behind them, through the cabin, and the crowd on deck, down the stairs, and out over the gangway. The little convent girl and her mother went with hands tightly clasped. She did not turn her eyes to the right or left, or once (what all passengers do) look backward at the boat which, however slowly, had carried her surely over dangers that she wot not of. All looked at her as she passed. All wanted to say good-by to the little convent girl, to see the mother who had been deprived of her so long. Some expressed surprise in a whistle; some in other ways. All exclaimed audibly, or to themselves, "Colored!"

It takes about a month to make the round trip from New Orleans to Cincinnati and back, counting five days' stoppage in New Orleans. It was a month to a day when the steamboat came puffing and blowing up to the wharf again, like a stout dowager after too long a walk; and the same scene of confusion was enacted, as it had been enacted twelve times a year, at almost the same wharf for twenty years; and the same calm, a death calmness by contrast, followed as usual the next morning.

The decks were quiet and clean; one cargo had just been delivered, part of another stood ready on the levee to be shipped. The captain was there waiting for his business to begin, the clerk was in his office getting his books ready, the voice of the mate could be heard below, mustering the old crew out and a new crew in; for if steamboat crews have a single principle—and there are those who deny them any—it is never to ship twice in succession on the same boat. It was too early yet for any but roustabouts, marketers, and church-goers; so early that even the river was still partly mist-covered; only in places could the swift, dark current be seen rolling swiftly along.

"Captain!" A hand plucked at his elbow, as if not confident that the mere calling would secure attention. The captain turned. The mother of the little convent girl stood there, and she held the little convent girl by the hand. "I have brought her to see you," the woman said. "You were so kind—and she is so quiet, so still, all the time, I thought it would do her a pleasure."

She spoke with an accent, and with embarrassment; otherwise one would have said that she was bold and assured enough.

"She don't go nowhere, she don't do nothing but make her crochet and her prayers, so I thought I would bring her for a little visit of 'How d' ye do' to you."

There was, perhaps, some inflection in the woman's voice that might have made known, or at least awakened, the suspicion of some latent hope or intention, had the captain's ear been fine enough to detect it. There might have been something in the little convent girl's face, had his eye been more sensitive—a trifle paler, maybe, the lips a little tighter drawn, the blue ribbon a shade

faded. He may have noticed that, but— And the visit of "How d'
ye do" came to an end.

They walked down the stairway, the woman in front, the little
convent girl—her hand released to shake hands with the captain—
following, across the bared deck, out to the gangway, over to the
middle of it. No one was looking, no one saw more than a flutter
of white petticoats, a show of white stockings, as the little convent
girl went under the water.

The roustabout dived, as the roustabouts always do, after the
drowning, even at the risk of their good-for-nothing lives. The
mate himself jumped overboard; but she had gone down in a
whirlpool. Perhaps, as the pilot had told her whirlpools always did,
it may have carried her through to the underground river, to that
vast, hidden, dark Mississippi that flows beneath the one we see;
for her body was never found.

Bartleby the Scrivener

Herman Melville

(1819–1891)

I am a rather elderly man. The nature of my avocations for the last thirty years has brought me into more than ordinary contact with what would seem an interesting and somewhat singular set of men, of whom, as yet, nothing that I know of has ever been written—I mean the law-copyists, or scriveners. I have known very many of them, professionally and privately, and, if I pleased, could relate divers histories at which good-natured gentlemen might smile and sentimental souls might weep. But I waive the biographies of all other scriveners for a few passages in the life of Bartleby, who was a scrivener, the strangest I ever saw or heard of. While of other law-copyists I might write the complete life, of Bartleby nothing of that sort can be done. I believe that no materials exist for a full and satisfactory biography of this man. It is an irreparable loss to literature. Bartleby was one of those beings of whom nothing is ascertainable except from the original sources, and, in his case, those are very small. What my own astonished eyes saw of Bartleby, *that* is all I know of him, except, indeed, one vague report, which will appear in the sequel.

Ere introducing the scrivener as he first appeared to me, it is fit I make some mention of myself, my employees, my business, my chambers and general surroundings, because some such description is indispensable to an adequate understanding of the chief character about to be presented. *Imprimis:* I am a man who, from his youth upwards, has been filled with a profound conviction that the easiest way of life is the best. Hence, though I belong to a profession proverbially energetic and nervous even to turbulence at times, yet nothing of that sort have I ever suffered to invade my peace. I am one of those unambitious lawyers who never addresses a jury or in any way draws down public applause, but, in the cool tranquillity of a snug retreat, do a snug business among rich men's bonds, and mortgages, and title deeds. All who know me consider me an eminently *safe* man. The late John Jacob Astor, a personage little given to poetic enthusiasm, had no hesitation in pronouncing my first grand point to be prudence, my next, method. I do not speak it in vanity, but simply record the fact that I was not unemployed in my profession by the late John Jacob Astor, a name which, I admit, I love to repeat, for it hath a rounded and orbicular sound to it, and rings like unto bullion. I will freely add that I was not insensible to the late John Jacob Astor's good opinion.

Some time prior to the period at which this little history begins my avocations had been largely increased. The good old office, now extinct in the State of New York, of a Master in Chancery, had been conferred upon me. It was not a very arduous office, but very pleasantly remunerative. I seldom lose my temper, much more seldom indulge in dangerous indignation at wrongs and outrages, but I must be permitted to be rash here and declare that I consider the sudden and violent abrogation of the office of Master in Chancery, by the new Constitution, as a —— premature act, inasmuch as I had counted upon a life lease of the profits, whereas I only received those of a few short years. But this is by the way.

My chambers were upstairs, at No. — Wall Street. At one end they looked upon the white wall of the interior of a spacious sky-light shaft, penetrating the building from top to bottom.

This view might have been considered rather tame than other-wise, deficient in what landscape painters call "life." But, if so, the view from the other end of my chambers offered at least a con-trast, if nothing more. In that direction, my windows commanded an unobstructed view of a lofty brick wall, black by age and ever-lasting shade, which wall required no spyglass to bring out its lurk-ing beauties, but, for the benefit of all nearsighted spectators, was pushed up to within ten feet of my windowpanes. Owing to the great height of the surrounding buildings, and my chambers' being on the second floor, the interval between this wall and mine not a little resembled a huge square cistern.

At the period just preceding the advent of Bartleby, I had two persons as copyists in my employment, and a promising lad as an office boy. First, Turkey; second, Nippers; third, Ginger Nut. These may seem names the like of which are not usually found in the Di-rectory. In truth, they were nicknames, mutually conferred upon each other by my three clerks, and were deemed expressive of their respective persons or characters. Turkey was a short, pursy Eng-lishman, of about my own age—that is, somewhere not far from sixty. In the morning, one might say, his face was of a fine florid hue, but after twelve o'clock, meridian—his dinner hour—it blazed like a grate full of Christmas coals; and continued blazing— but, as it were, with a gradual wane—till six o'clock, P.M., or there-abouts; after which I saw no more of the proprietor of the face, which, gaining its meridian with the sun, seemed to set with it, to rise, culminate, and decline the following day, with the like regu-larity and undiminished glory. There are many singular coincidences I have known in the course of my life, not the least among which was the fact, that, exactly when Turkey displayed his fullest beams from his red and radiant countenance, just then, too, at that critical moment, began the daily period when I considered his business capacities as seriously disturbed for the remainder of the twenty-four hours. Not that he was absolutely idle or averse to business then; far from it. The difficulty was, he was apt to be altogether too energetic. There was a strange, inflamed, flurried, flighty recklessness of activity about him. He would be incautious in dipping his pen into his inkstand. All his blots upon my documents were dropped there after twelve o'clock, meridian. Indeed, not only would he be reckless and sadly given to making blots in the afternoon, but some days he went further and was rather noisy. At such times, too, his face flamed with augmented blazonry, as if cannel coal had been heaped on anthracite. He made an unpleasant racket with his chair; spilled his sandbox; in mending his pens, impatiently split them all to pieces and threw them on the floor in a sudden passion; stood up and leaned over his table, boxing his papers about in a most indecorous manner, very sad to behold in an elderly man like him. Nevertheless, as he was in many ways a most valuable person to me, and all the time before twelve o'clock, meridian, was the quickest, steadiest creature, too, accomplishing a great deal of work in a style not easily to be matched—for these reasons I was willing to overlook his eccentricities, though indeed, occasionally, I remonstrated with him. I did this very gently, however, because, though the civilest, nay, the blandest and most reverential of men in the morning, yet, in the afternoon he was disposed, upon provocation, to be slightly rash with his tongue— in fact, insolent. Now, valuing his morning services as I did, and resolved not to lose them—yet, at the same time, made uncomfortable by his inflamed ways after twelve o'clock—and being a man of peace, unwilling by my admonitions to call forth unseemly retorts from him, I took upon me one Saturday noon (he was always worse on Saturdays) to hint to him, very kindly, that perhaps, now that he was growing old, it might be well to abridge his labors; in short, he need not come to my chambers after twelve o'clock, but, dinner over, had best go home to his lodgings and rest himself till teatime. But no; he insisted upon his afternoon devotions. His countenance became intolerably fervid, as he oratorically assured me—gesticulating with a long ruler at the other end of the room—that if his services in the morning were useful, how indispensable, then, in the afternoon?

"With submission, sir," said Turkey, on this occasion, "I consider myself your right-hand man. In the morning I but marshal and deploy my columns, but in the afternoon I put myself at their head, and gallantly charge the foe, thus"—and he made a violent thrust with the ruler.

"But the blots, Turkey," intimated I.

"True; but, with submission, sir, behold these hairs! I am getting old. Surely, sir, a blot or two of a warm afternoon is not to be severely urged against gray hairs. Old age—even if it blot the page—is honourable. With submission, sir, we *both* are getting old."

This appeal to my fellow feeling was hardly to be resisted. At all events, I saw that go he would not. So I made up my mind to let him stay, resolving, nevertheless, to see to it that, during the afternoon, he had to do with my less important papers.

Nippers, the second on my list, was a whiskered, sallow, and upon the whole rather piratical-looking young man of about five and twenty. I always deemed him the victim of two evil powers—ambition and indigestion. The ambition was evinced by a certain impatience of the duties of a mere copyist, an unwarrantable usurpation of strictly professional affairs, such as the original drawing up of legal documents. The indigestion seemed betokened in an occasional nervous testiness and grinning irritability, causing the

teeth to audibly grind together over mistakes committed in copying; unnecessary maledictions, hissed rather than spoken, in the heat
of business; and especially by a continual discontent with the height
of the table where he worked. Though of a very ingenious me-
chanical turn, Nippers could never get this table to suit him. He put
chips under it, blocks of various sorts, bits of pasteboard, and at last
went so far as to attempt an exquisite adjustment by final pieces of
folded blotting paper. But no invention would answer. If, for the
sake of easing his back, he brought the table lid at a sharp angle well
up toward his chin, and wrote there like a man using the steep roof
of a Dutch house for his desk, then he declared that it stopped the
circulation in his arms. If now he lowered the table to his waist-
bands and stooped over it in writing, then there was a sore aching
in his back. In short, the truth of the matter was Nippers knew not
what he wanted. Or, if he wanted anything, it was to be rid of a
scrivener's table altogether. Among the manifestations of his diseased ambition was a fondness he had for receiving visits from certain ambiguous-looking fellows in seedy coats, whom he called his
clients. Indeed, I was aware that not only was he, at times, considerable of a ward politician, but he occasionally did a little business
at the Justices' courts, and was not unknown on the steps of the
Tombs. I have good reason to believe, however, that one individual
who called upon him at my chambers, and who, with a grand air,
he insisted was his client, was no other than a dun, and the alleged
title deed, a bill. But, with all his failings, and the annoyances he
caused me, Nippers, like his compatriot Turkey, was a very useful
man to me; wrote a neat, swift hand; and, when he chose, was not
deficient in a gentlemanly sort of deportment. Added to this, he always dressed in a gentlemanly sort of way, and so, incidentally, reflected credit upon my chambers. Whereas, with respect to Turkey,
I had much ado to keep him from being a reproach to me. His
clothes were apt to look oily, and smell of eating houses. He wore

his pantaloons very loose and baggy in summer. His coats were ex-ecrable, his hat not to be handled. But while the hat was a thing of indifference to me, inasmuch as his natural civility and deference, as a dependent Englishman, always led him to doff it the moment he entered the room, yet his coat was another matter. Concerning his coats, I reasoned with him, but with no effect. The truth was, I sup-pose, that a man with so small an income could not afford to sport such a lustrous face and a lustrous coat at one and the same time. As Nippers once observed, Turkey's money went chiefly for red ink. One winter day, I presented Turkey with a highly respectable-looking coat of my own—a padded gray coat of a most comfort-able warmth, and which buttoned straight up from the knee to the neck. I thought Turkey would appreciate the favor and abate his rashness and obstreperousness of afternoons. But no; I verily believe that buttoning himself up in so downy and blanket-like a coat had a pernicious effect upon him—upon the same principle that too much oats are bad for horses. In fact, precisely as a rash, restive horse is said to feel his oats, so Turkey felt his coat. It made him insolent. He was a man whom prosperity harmed.

Though, concerning the self-indulgent habits of Turkey, I had my own private surmises, yet, touching Nippers, I was well per-suaded that, whatever might be his faults in other respects, he was, at least, a temperate young man. But indeed, nature herself seemed to have been his vintner, and, at his birth, charged him so thor-oughly with an irritable, brandy-like disposition that all subsequent potations were needless. When I consider how, amid the stillness of my chambers, Nippers would sometimes impatiently rise from his seat, and, stooping over his table, spread his arms wide apart, seize the whole desk, and move it, and jerk it, with a grim, grinding mo-tion on the floor, as if the table were a perverse voluntary agent, intent on thwarting and vexing him, I plainly perceive that, for Nippers, brandy-and-water were altogether superfluous.

It was fortunate for me that, owing to its peculiar cause—indigestion—the irritability and consequent nervousness of Nippers were mainly observable in the morning, while in the afternoon he was comparatively mild. So that, Turkey's paroxysms only coming on about twelve o'clock, I never had to do with their eccentricities at one time. Their fits relieved each other, like guards. When Nippers's was on, Turkey's was off; and vice versa. This was a good natural arrangement, under the circumstances.

Ginger Nut, the third on my list, was a lad some twelve years old. His father was a carman, ambitious of seeing his son on the bench instead of a cart before he died. So he sent him to my office, as student at law, errand boy, cleaner and sweeper, at the rate of one dollar a week. He had a little desk to himself, but he did not use it much. Upon inspection, the drawer exhibited a great array of the shells of various sorts of nuts. Indeed, to this quick-witted youth, the whole noble science of the law was contained in a nutshell. Not the least among the employments of Ginger Nut, as well as one which he discharged with the most alacrity, was his duty as cake and apple purveyor for Turkey and Nippers. Copying law papers being proverbially a dry, husky sort of business, my two scriveners were fain to moisten their mouths very often with Spitzenbergs, to be had at the numerous stalls nigh the Custom House and Post Office. Also, they sent Ginger Nut very frequently for that peculiar cake—small, flat, round, and very spicy—after which he had been named by them. Of a cold morning, when business was but dull, Turkey would gobble up scores of these cakes, as if they were mere wafers—indeed, they sell them at the rate of six or eight for a penny—the scrape of his pen blending with the crunching of the crisp particles in his mouth. Of all the fiery afternoon blunders and flurried rashnesses of Turkey was his once moistening a ginger cake between his lips and clapping it on to a mortgage for a seal. I came within an ace of dismissing him then. But he mollified me by making an Oriental bow, and saying:

"With submission, sir, it was generous of me to find you in stationery on my own account."

Now my original business—that of a conveyancer and title hunter, and drawer-up of recondite documents of all sorts—was considerably increased by receiving the Master's office. There was now great work for scriveners. Not only must I push the clerks already with me, but I must have additional help.

In answer to my advertisement, a motionless young man one morning stood upon my office threshold, the door being open, for it was summer. I can see that figure now—pallidly neat, pitiably respectable, incurably forlorn! It was Bartleby.

After a few words touching his qualifications, I engaged him, glad to have among my corps of copyists a man of so singularly sedate an aspect, which I thought might operate beneficially upon the flighty temper of Turkey and the fiery one of Nippers.

I should have stated before that ground-glass folding doors divided my premises into two parts, one of which was occupied by my scriveners, the other by myself. According to my humor, I threw open these doors or closed them. I resolved to assign Bartleby a corner by the folding doors, but on my side of them, so as to have this quiet man within easy call, in case any trifling thing was to be done. I placed his desk close up to a small side window in that part of the room, a window which originally had afforded a lateral view of certain grimy back yards and bricks, but which, owing to subsequent erections, commanded at present no view at all, though it gave some light. Within three feet of the panes was a wall, and the light came down from far above, between two lofty buildings, as from a very small opening in a dome. Still further to a satisfactory arrangement, I procured a high green folding screen, which might entirely isolate Bartleby from my sight, though not remove him from my voice. And thus, in a manner, privacy and society were conjoined.

At first, Bartleby did an extraordinary quantity of writing. As if long famishing for something to copy, he seemed to gorge himself on my documents. There was no pause for digestion. He ran a day and night line, copying by sunlight and by candlelight. I should have been quite delighted with his application, had he been cheerfully industrious. But he wrote on silently, palely, mechanically.

It is, of course, an indispensable part of a scrivener's business to verify the accuracy of his copy, word by word. Where there are two or more scriveners in an office, they assist each other in this examination, one reading from the copy, the other holding the original. It is a very dull, wearisome, and lethargic affair. I can readily imagine that, to some sanguine temperaments, it would be altogether intolerable. For example, I cannot credit that the mettlesome poet, Byron, would have contentedly sat down with Bartleby to examine a law document of, say five hundred pages, closely written in a crimpy hand.

Now and then, in the haste of business, it had been my habit to assist in comparing some brief document myself, calling Turkey or Nippers for this purpose. One object I had in placing Bartleby so handy to me behind the screen was to avail myself of his services on such trivial occasions. It was on the third day, I think, of his being with me, and before any necessity had arisen for having his own writing examined, that, being much hurried to complete a small affair I had in hand, I abruptly called to Bartleby. In my haste and natural expectancy of instant compliance, I sat with my head bent over the original on my desk, and my right hand sideways, and somewhat nervously extended with the copy, so that, immediately upon emerging from his retreat, Bartleby might snatch it and proceed to business without the least delay.

In this very attitude did I sit when I called to him, rapidly stating what it was I wanted him to do—namely, to examine a small paper with me. Imagine my surprise, nay, my consternation, when, without moving from his privacy, Bartleby, in a singularly mild, firm voice, replied, "I would prefer not to."

I sat a while in perfect silence, rallying my stunned faculties. Immediately it occurred to me that my ears had deceived me, or Bartleby had entirely misunderstood my meaning. I repeated my request in the clearest tone I could assume; but in quite as clear a one came the previous reply, "I would prefer not to."

"Prefer not to," echoed I, rising in high excitement, and crossing the room with a stride. "What do you mean? Are you moonstruck? I want you to help me compare this sheet here—take it," and I thrust it towards him.

"I would prefer not to," said he.

I looked at him steadfastly. His face was leanly composed; his gray eye dimly calm. Not a wrinkle of agitation rippled him. Had there been the least uneasiness, anger, impatience, or impertinence in his manner; in other words, had there been anything ordinarily human about him, doubtless I should have violently dismissed him from the premises. But as it was I should have as soon thought of turning my pale plaster-of-Paris bust of Cicero out of doors. I stood gazing at him a while, as he went on with his own writing, and then reseated myself at my desk. This is very strange, thought I. What had one best do? But my business hurried me. I concluded to forget the matter for the present, reserving it for my future leisure. So calling Nippers from the other room, the paper was speedily examined.

A few days after this, Bartleby concluded four lengthy documents, being quadruplicates of a week's testimony taken before me in my High Court of Chancery. It became necessary to examine them. It was an important suit, and great accuracy was imperative. Having all things arranged, I called Turkey, Nippers, and Ginger

Nut from the next room, meaning to place the four copies in the hands of my four clerks, while I should read from the original. Accordingly, Turkey, Nippers, and Ginger Nut had taken their seats in a row, each with his document in his hand, when I called to Bartleby to join this interesting group.

"Bartleby! quick, I am waiting."

I heard a slow scrape of his chair legs on the uncarpeted floor, and soon he appeared standing at the entrance of his hermitage.

"What is wanted?" said he, mildly.

"The copies, the copies," said I, hurriedly. "We are going to examine them. There"—and I held towards him the fourth quadruplicate.

"I would prefer not to," he said, and gently disappeared behind the screen.

For a few moments I was turned into a pillar of salt, standing at the head of my seated column of clerks. Recovering myself, I advanced towards the screen and demanded the reason for such extraordinary conduct.

"*Why* do you refuse?"

"I would prefer not to."

With any other man I should have flown outright into a dreadful passion, scorned all further words, and thrust him ignominiously from my presence. But there was something about Bartleby that not only strangely disarmed me, but, in a wonderful manner, touched and disconcerted me. I began to reason with him.

"These are your own copies we are about to examine. It is labor saving to you, because one examination will answer for your four papers. It is common usage. Every copyist is bound to help examine his copy. Is it not so? Will you not speak? Answer!"

"I prefer not to," he replied in a flutelike tone. It seemed to me that, while I had been addressing him, he carefully revolved every statement that I made; fully comprehended the meaning; could not gainsay the irresistible conclusion; but, at the same time, some paramount consideration prevailed with him to reply as he did.

"You are decided, then, not to comply with my request—a request made according to common usage and common sense?"

He briefly gave me to understand that on that point my judgment was sound. Yes: his decision was irreversible.

It is not seldom the case that, when a man is browbeaten in some unprecedented and violently unreasonable way, he begins to stagger in his own plainest faith. He begins, as it were, vaguely to surmise that, wonderful as it may be, all the justice and all the reason is on the other side. Accordingly, if any disinterested persons are present, he turns to them for some reinforcement for his own faltering mind.

"Turkey," said I, "what do you think of this? Am I not right?"

"With submission, sir," said Turkey, in his blandest tone, "I think that you are."

"Nippers," said I, "what do *you* think of it?"

"I think I should kick him out of the office."

(The reader of nice perceptions will here perceive that, it being morning, Turkey's answer is couched in polite and tranquil terms, but Nippers replies in ill-tempered ones. Or, to repeat a previous sentence, Nippers's ugly mood was on duty, and Turkey's off.)

"Ginger Nut," said I, willing to enlist the smallest suffrage in my behalf, 'what do *you* think of it?"

"I think, sir, he's a little *luny*," replied Ginger Nut, with a grin.

"You hear what they say," said I, turning towards the screen, "come forth and do your duty."

But he vouchsafed no reply. I pondered a moment in sore perplexity. But once more business hurried me. I determined again to postpone the consideration of this dilemma to my future leisure. With a little trouble we made out to examine the papers without Bartleby, though at every page or two Turkey deferentially dropped his opinion that this proceeding was quite out of the common; while Nippers, twitching in his chair with a dyspeptic nervousness, ground out between his set teeth occasional hissing maledictions against the stubborn oaf behind the screen. And for his (Nippers's) part, this was the first and the last time he would do another man's business without pay.

Meanwhile Bartleby sat in his hermitage, oblivious to everything but his own peculiar business there.

Some days passed, the scrivener being employed upon another lengthy work. His late remarkable conduct led me to regard his ways narrowly. I observed that he never went to dinner; indeed, that he never went anywhere. As yet I had never, of my personal knowledge, known him to be outside of my office. He was a perpetual sentry in the corner. At about eleven o'clock, though, in the morning, I noticed that Ginger Nut would advance towards the opening in Bartleby's screen, as if silently beckoned thither by a gesture invisible to me where I sat. The boy would then leave the office jingling a few pence, and reappear with a handful of gingernuts, which he delivered in the hermitage, receiving two of the cakes for his trouble.

He lives, then, on gingernuts, thought I; never eats a dinner, properly speaking; he must be a vegetarian, then; but no, he never eats even vegetables, he eats nothing but gingernuts. My mind then ran on in reveries concerning the probable effects upon the human constitution of living entirely on gingernuts. Gingernuts are so called because they contain ginger as one of their peculiar constituents, and the final flavoring one. Now, what was ginger? A hot, spicy thing. Was Bartleby hot and spicy? Not at all. Ginger, then, had no effect upon Bartleby. Probably he preferred it should have none.

Nothing so aggravates an earnest person as a passive resistance. If the individual so resisted be of a not inhumane temper, and the resisting one perfectly harmless in his passivity, then, in the better moods of the former, he will endeavour charitably to construe to his imagination what proves impossible to be solved by his judgment. Even so, for the most part, I regarded Bartleby and his ways. Poor fellow! thought I, he means no mischief; it is plain he intends no insolence; his aspect sufficiently evinces that his eccentricities are involuntary. He is useful to me. I can get along with him. If I turn him away, the chances are he will fall in with some less indulgent employer, and then he will be rudely treated, and perhaps driven forth miserably to starve. Yes. Here I can cheaply purchase a delicious self-approval. To befriend Bartleby, to humor him in his strange willfulness, will cost me little or nothing, while I lay up in my soul what will eventually prove a sweet morsel for my conscience. But this mood was not invariable with me. The passiveness of Bartleby sometimes irritated me. I felt strangely goaded on to encounter him in new opposition—to elicit some angry spark from him answerable to my own. But, indeed, I might as well have essayed to strike fire with my knuckles against a bit of Windsor soap. But one afternoon the evil impulse in me mastered me, and the following little scene ensued:

"Bartleby," said I, "when those papers are all copied, I will compare them with you."

"I would prefer not to."

"How? Surely you do not mean to persist in that mulish vagary?"

No answer.

I threw open the folding doors near by, and, turning upon Turkey and Nippers, exclaimed:

"Bartleby a second time says he won't examine his papers. What do you think of it, Turkey?"

It was afternoon, be it remembered. Turkey sat glowing like a brass boiler, his bald head steaming, his hands reeling among his blotted papers.

"Think of it?" roared Turkey. "I think I'll just step behind his screen and black his eyes for him!"

So saying, Turkey rose to his feet and threw his arms into a pugilistic position. He was hurrying away to make good his promise when I detained him, alarmed at the effect of incautiously rousing Turkey's combativeness after dinner.

"Sit down, Turkey," said I, "and hear what Nippers has to say. What do you think of it, Nippers? Would I not be justified in immediately dismissing Bartleby?"

"Excuse me, that is for you to decide, sir. I think his conduct quite unusual, and indeed, unjust, as regards Turkey and myself. But it may only be a passing whim."

"Ah," exclaimed I, "you have strangely changed your mind, then—you speak very gently of him now."

"All beer," cried Turkey; "gentleness is effects of beer—Nippers and I dined together today. You see how gentle *I* am, sir. Shall I go and black his eyes?"

"You refer to Bartleby, I suppose. No, not today, Turkey," I replied; "pray, put up your fists."

I closed the doors and again advanced towards Bartleby. I felt additional incentives tempting me to my fate. I burned to be rebelled against again. I remembered that Bartleby never left the office.

"Bartleby," said I, "Ginger Nut is away; just step around to the Post Office, won't you? (it was but a three minutes' walk), and see if there is anything for me."

"I would prefer not to."

"You *will* not?"

"I *prefer* not."

I staggered to my desk and sat there in a deep study. My blind inveteracy returned. Was there any other thing in which I could procure myself to be ignominiously repulsed by this lean, penniless wight?—my hired clerk? What added thing is there, perfectly reasonable, that he will be sure to refuse to do?

"Bartleby!"

No answer.

"Bartleby," in a louder tone.

No answer.

"Bartleby," I roared.

Like a very ghost, agreeably to the laws of magical invocation, at the third summons he appeared at the entrance of his hermitage.

"Go to the next room, and tell Nippers to come to me."

"I prefer not to," he respectfully and slowly said, and mildly disappeared.

"Very good, Bartleby," said I, in a quiet sort of serenely severe self-possessed tone, intimating the unalterable purpose of some terrible retribution very close at hand. At the moment I half intended something of the kind. But upon the whole, as it was drawing towards my dinner hour, I thought it best to put on my hat and walk home for the day, suffering much from perplexity and distress of mind.

Shall I acknowledge it? The conclusion of this whole business was that it soon became a fixed fact of my chambers, that a pale young scrivener by the name of Bartleby had a desk there; that he copied for me at the usual rate of four cents a folio (one hundred words); but he was permanently exempt from examining the work done by him, that duty being transferred to Turkey and Nippers, out of compliment, doubtless, to their superior acuteness; moreover, said Bartleby was never, on any account, to be dispatched on the most trivial errand of any sort; and that even if entreated to take upon him such a matter, it was generally understood that he would "prefer not to"—in other words, that he would refuse point-blank.

As days passed on, I became considerably reconciled to Bartleby.

His steadiness, his freedom from all dissipation, his incessant industry (except when he chose to throw himself into a standing reverie behind his screen), his great stillness, his unalterableness of demeanor under all circumstances, made him a valuable acquisition. One prime thing was this—*he was always there*—first in the morning, continually through the day, and the last at night. I had a singular confidence in his honesty. I felt my most precious papers perfectly safe in his hands. Sometimes, to be sure, I could not, for the very soul of me, avoid falling into sudden spasmodic passions with him. For it was exceeding difficult to bear in mind all the time those strange peculiarities, privileges, and unheard-of exemptions, forming the tacit stipulations on Bartleby's part under which he remained in my office. Now and then, in the eagerness of dispatching pressing business, I would inadvertently summon Bartleby, in a short, rapid tone, to put his finger, say, on the incipient tie of a bit of red tape with which I was about compressing some papers. Of course, from behind the screen the usual answer, "I prefer not to," was sure to come; and then, how could a human creature, with the common infirmities of our nature, refrain from bitterly exclaiming upon such perverseness—such unreasonableness? However, every added repulse of this sort which I received only tended to lessen the probability of my repeating the inadvertence.

Here it must be said that, according to the custom of most legal gentlemen occupying chambers in densely populated law buildings, there were several keys to my door. One was kept by a woman residing in the attic, which person weekly scrubbed and daily swept and dusted my apartments. Another was kept by Turkey for convenience' sake. The third I sometimes carried in my own pocket. The fourth I knew not who had.

Now, one Sunday morning I happened to go to Trinity Church, to hear a celebrated preacher, and finding myself rather early on the ground I thought I would walk round to my chambers for a while. Luckily I had my key with me, but upon applying it to the lock, I found it resisted by something inserted from the inside. Quite surprised, I called out, when to my consternation a key was turned from within, and, thrusting his lean visage at me, and holding the door ajar, the apparition of Bartleby appeared, in his shirt sleeves, and otherwise in a strangely tattered deshabille, saying quietly that he was sorry, but he was deeply engaged just then, and—preferred not admitting me at present. In a brief word or two, he moreover added, that perhaps I had better walk round the block two or three times, and by that time he would probably have concluded his affairs.

Now, the utterly unsurmised appearance of Bartleby, tenanting my law chambers of a Sunday morning, with his cadaverously gentlemanly *nonchalance,* yet withal firm and self-possessed, had such a strange effect upon me that incontinently I slunk away from my own door and did as desired. But not without sundry twinges of impotent rebellion against the mild effrontery of this unaccountable scrivener. Indeed, it was his wonderful mildness, chiefly, which not only disarmed me but unmanned me, as it were. For I consider that one, for the time, is sort of unmanned when he tranquilly permits his hired clerk to dictate to him and order him away from his own premises. Furthermore, I was full of uneasiness as to what Bartleby could possibly be doing in my office in his shirt sleeves, and in an otherwise dismantled condition, of a Sunday morning. Was anything amiss going on? Nay, that was out of the question. It was not to be thought of for a moment that Bartleby was an immoral person. But what could he be doing there?—copying? Nay again, whatever might be his eccentricities, Bartleby was an eminently decorous person. He would be the last man to sit down to his desk in any state approaching to nudity. Besides, it was Sunday; and there was something about Bartleby that forbade the supposition that he would by any secular occupation violate the proprieties of the day.

Nevertheless, my mind was not pacified, and full of a restless curiosity, at last I returned to the door. Without hindrance I inserted my key, opened it, and entered. Bartleby was not to be seen. I looked round anxiously, peeped behind his screen, but it was very plain that he was gone. Upon more closely examining the place, I surmised that for an indefinite period Bartleby must have ate, dressed, and slept in my office, and that, too, without plate, mirror, or bed. The cushioned seat of a rickety old sofa in one corner bore the faint impress of a lean, reclining form. Rolled away under his desk I found a blanket; under the empty grate, a blacking box and brush; on a chair, a tin basin, with soap and a ragged towel; in a newspaper a few crumbs of gingernuts and a morsel of cheese. Yes, thought I, it is evident enough that Bartleby has been making his home here, keeping bachelor's hall all by himself. Immediately then the thought came sweeping across me, what miserable friendlessness and loneliness are here revealed. His poverty is great, but his solitude, how horrible! Think of it. Of a Sunday, Wall Street is deserted as Petra, and every night of every day it is an emptiness. This building, too, which of weekdays hums with industry and life, at nightfall echoes with sheer vacancy, and all through Sunday is forlorn. And here Bartleby makes his home, sole spectator of a solitude which he has seen all populous—a sort of innocent and transformed Marius brooding among the ruins of Carthage!

For the first time in my life a feeling of overpowering stinging melancholy seized me. Before, I had never experienced aught but a not unpleasing sadness. The bond of a common humanity now drew me irresistibly to gloom. A fraternal melancholy! For both I and Bartleby were sons of Adam. I remembered the bright silks and sparkling faces I had seen that day, in gala trim, swanlike sailing down the Mississippi of Broadway; and I contrasted them with the pallid copyist, and thought to myself, Ah, happiness courts the light, so we deem the world is gay, but misery hides aloof, so we deem that misery there is none. These sad fancyings—chimeras, doubtless, of a sick and silly brain—led on to other and more special thoughts, concerning the eccentricities of Bartleby. Presentiments of strange discoveries hovered round me. The scrivener's pale form appeared to me laid out, among uncaring strangers in its shivering winding sheet.

Suddenly I was attracted by Bartleby's closed desk, the key in open sight left in the lock.

I mean no mischief, seek the gratification of no heartless curiosity, thought I; besides, the desk is mine, and its contents, too, so I will make bold to look within. Everything was methodically arranged, the papers smoothly placed. The pigeonholes were deep, and removing the files of documents, I groped into their recesses. Presently I felt something there, and dragged it out. It was an old bandanna handkerchief, heavy and knotted. I opened it, and saw it was a savings bank.

I now recalled all the quiet mysteries which I had noted in the man. I remembered that he never spoke but to answer; that, though at intervals he had considerable time to himself, yet I had never seen him reading—no, not even a newspaper; that for long periods he would stand looking out, at his pale window behind the screen, upon the dead brick wall; I was quite sure he never visited any refectory or eating house, while his pale face clearly indicated that he never drank beer like Turkey, or tea and coffee even, like other men; that he never went anywhere in particular that I could learn; never went out for a walk, unless, indeed, that was the case at present; that he had declined telling who he was, or whence he came, or whether he had any relatives in the world; that though so thin and pale, he never complained of ill health. And more than all I remembered a certain unconscious air of pallid—how shall I call it?—of pallid haughtiness, say, or rather an austere reserve about him, which had positively awed me into my tame compliance with his eccentricities, when I had feared to ask him to do the slightest incidental thing for me, even though I might know, from his long-continued motionlessness, that behind his screen he must be standing in one of those dead-wall reveries of his.

Revolving all these things, and coupling them with the recently discovered fact that he made my office his constant abiding place and home, and not forgetful of his morbid moodiness—revolving all these things, a prudential feeling began to steal over me. My first emotions had been those of pure melancholy and sincerest pity; but just in proportion as the forlornness of Bartleby grew and grew to my imagination, did that same melancholy merge into fear, that pity into repulsion. So true it is, and so terrible too, that up to a certain point the thought or sight of misery enlists our best affections; but, in certain special cases, beyond that point it does not. They err who would assert that invariably this is owing to the inherent selfishness of the human heart. It rather proceeds from a certain hopelessness of remedying excessive and organic ill. To a sensitive being, pity is not seldom pain. And when at last it is perceived that such pity cannot lead to effectual succor, common sense bids the soul be rid of it. What I saw that morning persuaded me that the scrivener was the victim of innate and incurable disorder. I might give alms to his body, but his body did not pain him—it was his soul that suffered, and his soul I could not reach.

I did not accomplish the purpose of going to Trinity Church that morning. Somehow, the things I had seen disqualified me for the time from churchgoing. I walked homeward, thinking what I would do with Bartleby. Finally, I resolved upon this—I would put certain calm questions to him the next morning, touching his history, etc., and if he declined to answer them openly and unreservedly (and I supposed he would prefer not), then to give him a twenty-dollar bill over and above whatever I might owe him, and tell him his services were no longer required; but that if in any other way I could assist him, I would be happy to do so, especially if he desired to return to his native place, wherever that might be, I would willingly help to defray the expenses. Moreover, if, after reaching home, he found himself at any time in want of aid, a letter from him would be sure of a reply.

The next morning came.

"Bartleby," said I, gently calling to him behind his screen.

No reply.

"Bartleby," said I, in a still gentler tone, "come here; I am not going to ask you to do anything you would prefer not to do—I simply wish to speak to you."

Upon this he noiselessly slid into view.

"Will you tell me, Bartleby, where you were born?"

"I would prefer not to."

"Will you tell me *anything* about yourself?"

"I would prefer not to."

"But what reasonable objection can you have to speak to me? I feel friendly towards you."

He did not look at me while I spoke, but kept his glance fixed upon my bust of Cicero, which, as I then sat, was directly behind me, some six inches above my head.

"What is your answer, Bartleby?" said I, after waiting a considerable time for a reply, during which his countenance remained immovable, only there was the faintest conceivable tremor of the white attenuated mouth.

"At present I prefer to give no answer," he said, and retired into his hermitage.

It was rather weak in me I confess, but his manner, on this occasion, nettled me. Not only did there seem to lurk in it a certain calm disdain, but his perverseness seemed ungrateful, considering the undeniable good usage and indulgence he had received from me.

Again I sat ruminating what I should do. Mortified as I was at his behavior, and resolved as I had been to dismiss him when I entered my office, nevertheless I strangely felt something superstitious knocking at my heart, and forbidding me to carry out my purpose, and denouncing me for a villain if I dared to breathe one bitter word against this forlornest of mankind. At last, familiarly drawing my chair behind his screen, I sat down and said: "Bartleby, never mind, then, about revealing your history; but let me entreat you, as a friend, to comply as far as may be with the usages of this office. Say now, you will help to examine papers tomorrow or next day: in short, say now, that in a day or two you will begin to be a little reasonable:—say so, Bartleby."

"At present I would prefer not to be a little reasonable," was his mildly cadaverous reply.

Just then the folding doors opened and Nippers approached. He seemed suffering from an unusually bad night's rest, induced by severer indigestion than common. He overheard those final words of Bartleby.

"*Prefer not,* eh?" gritted Nippers—"I'd *prefer* him, if I were you, sir," addressing me—"I'd *prefer* him; I'd give him preferences, the stubborn mule! What is it, sir, pray, that he *prefers* not to do now?"

Bartleby moved not a limb.

"Mr. Nippers," said I, "I'd prefer that you would withdraw for the present."

Somehow, of late, I had got into the way of involuntarily using this word "prefer" upon all sorts of not exactly suitable occasions. And I trembled to think that my contact with the scrivener had already and seriously affected me in a mental way. And what further and deeper aberration might it not yet produce? This apprehension had not been without efficacy in determining me to summary measures.

As Nippers, looking very sour and sulky, was departing, Turkey blandly and deferentially approached.

"With submission, sir," said he, "yesterday I was thinking about Bartleby here, and I think that if he would but prefer to take a quart of good ale every day, it would do much towards mending him, and enabling him to assist in examining his papers."

"So you have got the word, too," said I, slightly excited.

"With submission, what word, sir?" asked Turkey, respectfully crowding himself into the contracted space behind the screen, and by so doing making me jostle the scrivener. "What word, sir?"

"I would prefer to be left alone here," said Bartleby, as if offended at being mobbed in his privacy.

"*That's* the word, Turkey," said I—"*that's* it."

"Oh, *prefer?* oh yes—queer word. I never use it myself. But, sir, as I was saying, if he would but prefer——"

"Turkey," interrupted I, "you will please withdraw."

"Oh certainly, sir, if you prefer that I should."

As he opened the folding door to retire, Nippers at his desk caught a glimpse of me, and asked whether I would prefer to have a certain paper copied on blue paper or white. He did not in the least roguishly accent the word prefer. It was plain that it involuntarily rolled from his tongue. I thought to myself, surely I must get rid of a demented man, who already has in some degree turned the tongues, if not the heads, of myself and clerks. But I thought it prudent not to break the dismission at once.

The next day I noticed that Bartleby did nothing but stand at his window in his dead-wall reverie. Upon asking him why he did not write, he said that he had decided upon doing no more writing.

"Why, how now? what next?" exclaimed I, "do no more writing?"

"No more."

"And what is the reason?"

"Do you not see the reason for yourself?" he indifferently replied.

I looked steadfastly at him, and perceived that his eyes looked dull and glazed. Instantly it occurred to me that his unexampled diligence in copying by his dim window for the first few weeks of his stay with me might have temporarily impaired his vision.

I was touched. I said something in condolence with him. I hinted that of course he did wisely in abstaining from writing for a while; and urged him to embrace that opportunity of taking wholesome exercise in the open air. This, however, he did not do. A few days after this, my other clerks being absent, and being in a great hurry to dispatch certain letters by the mail, I thought that having nothing else earthly to do, Bartleby would surely be less inflexible than usual, and carry these letters to the Post Office. But he blankly declined. So, much to my inconvenience, I went myself.

Still added days went by. Whether Bartleby's eyes improved or not, I could not say. To all appearance, I thought they did. But when I asked him if they did, he vouchsafed no answer. At all events, he would do no copying. At last, in reply to my urgings, he informed me that he had permanently given up copying.

"What!" exclaimed I; "suppose your eyes should get entirely well—better than ever before—would you not copy then?"

"I have given up copying," he answered, and slid aside.

He remained as ever, a fixture in my chamber. Nay—if that were possible—he became still more of a fixture than before. What was to be done? He would do nothing in the office; why should he stay there? In plain fact, he had now become a millstone to me, not only useless as a necklace, but afflictive to bear. Yet I was sorry for him. I speak less than truth when I say that, on his own account, he occasioned me uneasiness. If he would but have named a single relative or friend, I would instantly have written and urged their taking the poor fellow away to some convenient retreat. But he seemed alone, absolutely alone in the universe. A bit of wreck in the mid-Atlantic. At length, necessities connected with my business tyrannized over all other considerations. Decently as I could, I told Bartleby that in six days' time he must unconditionally leave the office. I warned him to take measures, in the interval, for procuring some other abode. I offered to assist him in this endeavour, if he himself would but take the first step towards a removal. "And when you finally quit me, Bartleby," added I, "I shall see that you go not away entirely unprovided. Six days from this hour, remember."

At the expiration of that period, I peeped behind the screen, and lo! Bartleby was there.

I buttoned up my coat, balanced myself, advanced slowly towards him, touched his shoulder, and said, "The time has come; you must quit this place; I am sorry for you; here is money; but you must go."

"I would prefer not," he replied, with his back still towards me.

"You *must*."

He remained silent.

Now I had an unbounded confidence in this man's common honesty. He had frequently restored to me sixpences and shillings carelessly dropped upon the floor, for I am apt to be very reckless in such shirt-button affairs. The proceeding, then, which followed will not be deemed extraordinary.

"Bartleby," said I, "I owe you twelve dollars on account; here are thirty-two; the odd twenty are yours—Will you take it?" and I handed the bills towards him.

But he made no motion.

"I will leave them here, then," putting them under a weight on the table. Then taking my hat and cane and going to the door, I tranquilly turned and added—"After you have removed your things from these offices, Bartleby, you will of course lock the door—since everyone is now gone for the day but you—and if you please, slip your key underneath the mat, so that I may have it in the morning. I shall not see you again; so good-bye to you. If, hereafter, in your new place of abode, I can be of any service to you, do not fail to advise me by letter. Good-bye, Bartleby, and fare you well."

But he answered not a word; like the last column of some ruined temple, he remained standing mute and solitary in the middle of the otherwise deserted room.

As I walked home in a pensive mood, my vanity got the better of my pity. I could not but highly plume myself on my masterly management in getting rid of Bartleby. Masterly I call it, and such it must appear to any dispassionate thinker. The beauty of my procedure seemed to consist in its perfect quietness. There was no vulgar bullying, no bravado of any sort, no choleric hectoring and striding to and fro across the apartment, jerking out vehement commands for Bartleby to bundle himself off with his beggarly traps. Nothing of the kind. Without loudly bidding Bartleby depart—as an inferior genius might have done—I *assumed* the ground that depart he must, and upon that assumption built all I had to say. The more I thought over my procedure, the more I was charmed with it. Nevertheless, next morning, upon awakening, I had my doubts—I had somehow slept off the fumes of vanity. One of the coolest and wisest hours a man has is just after he awakes in the morning. My procedure seemed as sagacious as ever—but only in theory. How it would prove in practice—there was the rub. It was truly a beautiful thought to have assumed Bartleby's departure; but, after all, that assumption was simply my own, and none of Bartleby's. The great point was, not whether I had assumed that he would quit me, but whether he would prefer so to do. He was more a man of preferences than assumptions.

After breakfast, I walked downtown, arguing the probabilities pro and con. One moment I thought it would prove a miserable failure, and Bartleby would be found all alive at my office as usual; the next moment it seemed certain that I should find his chair empty. And so I kept veering about. At the corner of Broadway and Canal Street, I saw quite an excited group of people standing in earnest conversation.

"I'll take odds he doesn't," said a voice as I passed.

"Doesn't go?—done!" said I, "put up your money."

I was instinctively putting my hand in my pocket to produce my own, when I remembered that this was an election day. The words I had overheard bore no reference to Bartleby but to the success or nonsuccess of some candidate for the mayoralty. In my intent frame of mind, I had, as it were, imagined that all Broadway shared in my excitement, and were debating the same question with me. I passed on, very thankful that the uproar of the street screened my momentary absent-mindedness.

As I had intended, I was earlier than usual at my office door. I stood listening for a moment. All was still. He must be gone. I tried the knob. The door was locked. Yes, my procedure had worked to a charm; he indeed must be vanished. Yet a certain melancholy mixed with this: I was almost sorry for my brilliant success. I was fumbling under the doormat for the key, which Bartleby was to have left there for me, when accidentally my knee knocked against a panel, producing a summoning sound, and in response a voice came to me from within—"Not yet; I am occupied."

It was Bartleby.

I was thunderstruck. For an instant I stood like the man who, pipe in mouth, was killed one cloudless afternoon long ago in Virginia by summer lightning; at his own warm open window he was killed, and remained leaning out there upon the dreamy afternoon, till someone touched him, when he fell.

"Not gone!" I murmured at last. But again obeying that wondrous ascendency which the inscrutable scrivener had over me, and from which ascendency, for all my chafing, I could not completely escape, I slowly went downstairs and out into the street, and while walking round the block considered what I should next do in this unheard-of perplexity. Turn the man out by an actual thrusting I could not; to drive him away by calling him hard names would not do; calling in the police was an unpleasant idea; and yet, permit him to enjoy his cadaverous triumph over me—this, too, I could not think of. What was to be done? or, if nothing could be done, was there anything further that I could *assume* in the matter? Yes, as before I had prospectively assumed that Bartleby would depart, so now I might retrospectively assume that departed he was. In the legitimate carrying out of this assumption I might enter my office in a great hurry, and, pretending not to see Bartleby at all, walk straight against him as if he were air. Such a proceeding would in a singular degree have the appearance of a home thrust. It was hardly possible that Bartleby could withstand such an application of the doctrine of assumptions. But upon second thoughts the success of the plan seemed rather dubious. I resolved to argue the matter over with him again.

"Bartleby," said I, entering the office, with a quietly severe expression, "I am seriously displeased. I am pained, Bartleby. I had thought better of you. I had imagined you of such a gentlemanly organization that in any delicate dilemma a slight hint would suffice—in short, an assumption. But it appears I am deceived. Why," I added, unaffectedly starting, "you have not even touched that money yet," pointing to it, just where I had left it the evening previous.

He answered nothing.

"Will you, or will you not, quit me?" I now demanded in a sudden passion, advancing close to him.

"I would prefer *not* to quit you," he replied, gently emphasizing the *not*.

"What earthly right have you to stay here? Do you pay any rent? Do you pay my taxes? Or is this property yours?"

He answered nothing.

"Are you ready to go on and write now? Are your eyes recovered? Could you copy a small paper for me this morning? or help examine a few lines? or step round to the Post Office? In a word, will you do anything at all to give a coloring to your refusal to depart the premises?"

He silently retired into his hermitage.

I was now in such a state of nervous resentment that I thought it but prudent to check myself at present from further demonstrations. Bartleby and I were alone. I remembered the tragedy of the unfortunate Adams and the still more unfortunate Colt in the solitary office of the latter; and how poor Colt, being dreadfully incensed by Adams, and imprudently permitting himself to get wildly excited, was at unawares hurried into his fatal act—an act which certainly no man could possibly deplore more than the actor himself. Often it had occurred to me in my ponderings upon the subject that had that altercation taken place in the public street, or at a private residence, it would not have terminated as it did. It was the circumstance of being alone in a solitary office, upstairs, of a building entirely unhallowed by humanizing domestic associations—an uncarpeted office, doubtless, of a dusty, haggard sort of appearance—this it must have been which greatly helped to enhance the irritable desperation of the hapless Colt.

But when this old Adam of resentment rose in me and tempted me concerning Bartleby, I grappled him and threw him. How? Why, simply by recalling the divine injunction: "A new commandment give I unto you, that ye love one another." Yes, this it was that saved me. Aside from higher considerations, charity often operates as a vastly wise and prudent principle—a great safeguard to its possessor. Men have committed murder for jealousy's sake, and anger's sake, and hatred's sake, and selfishness' sake, and spiritual pride's sake; but no man that ever I heard of ever committed a diabolical murder for sweet charity's sake. Mere self-interest, then, if no better motive can be enlisted, should, especially with high-tempered men, prompt all beings to charity and philanthropy. At any rate, upon the occasion in question, I strove to drown my exasperated feelings towards the scrivener by benevolently construing his conduct. Poor fellow, poor fellow! thought I, he don't mean anything, and besides, he has seen hard times, and ought to be indulged.

I endeavoured, also, immediately to occupy myself, and at the same time to comfort my despondency. I tried to fancy that in the course of the morning, at such time as might prove agreeable to him, Bartleby, of his own free accord, would emerge from his hermitage and take up some decided line of march in the direction of the door. But no. Half-past twelve o'clock came; Turkey began to glow in the face, overturn his inkstand, and become generally obstreperous; Nippers abated down into quietude and courtesy; Ginger Nut munched his noon apple; and Bartleby remained standing at his window in one of his profoundest dead-wall reveries. Will it be credited? Ought I to acknowledge it? That afternoon I left the office without saying one further word to him.

Some days now passed during which, at leisure intervals, I looked a little into "Edwards on the Will," and "Priestley on Necessity." Under the circumstances, those books induced a salutary feeling. Gradually I slid into the persuasion that these troubles of mine touching the scrivener had been all predestinated from eternity, and Bartleby was billeted upon me for some mysterious purpose of an all-wise Providence, which it was not for a mere mortal like me to fathom. Yes, Bartleby, stay there behind your screen, thought I; I shall persecute you no more; you are harmless and noiseless as any of these old chairs; in short, I never feel so private as when I know you are here. At last I see it, I feel it; I penetrate to the predestinated purpose of my life. I am content. Others may have loftier parts to enact, but my mission in this world, Bartleby, is to furnish you with office room for such period as you may see fit to remain.

I believe that this wise and blessed frame of mind would have continued with me had it not been for the unsolicited and uncharitable remarks obtruded upon me by my professional friends who visited the rooms. But thus it often is that the constant friction of illiberal minds wears out at last the best resolves of the more generous. Though, to be sure, when I reflected upon it it was not strange that people entering my office should be struck by the peculiar aspect of the unaccountable Bartleby, and so be tempted to throw out some sinister observations concerning him. Sometimes an attorney having business with me, and calling at my office, and finding no one but the scrivener there, would undertake to obtain some sort of precise information from him touching my whereabouts; but without heeding his idle talk, Bartleby would remain standing immovable in the middle of the room. So, after contemplating him in that position for a time, the attorney would depart no wiser than he came.

Also, when a reference was going on, and the room full of lawyers and witnesses, and business driving fast, some deeply-occupied legal gentleman present, seeing Bartleby wholly unemployed, would request him to run round to his (the legal gentleman's) office and fetch some papers for him. Thereupon Bartleby would tranquilly decline, and yet remain idle as before. Then the lawyer would give a great stare, and turn to me. And what could I say? At last I was made aware that all through the circle of my professional acquaintance a whisper of wonder was running round, having reference to the strange creature I kept at my office. This worried me very much. And as the idea came upon me of his possibly turning out a longlived man, and keep occupying my chambers, and denying my authority; and perplexing my visitors; and scandalizing my professional reputation; and casting a general gloom over the premises; keeping soul and body together to the last upon his savings (for doubtless he spent but half a dime a day), and in the end perhaps outlive me, and claim possession of my office by right of his perpetual occupancy—as all these dark anticipations crowded upon me more and more, and my friends continually intruded their relentless remarks upon the apparition in my room, a great change was wrought in me. I resolved to gather all my faculties together and forever rid me of this intolerable incubus.

Ere revolving any complicated project, however, adapted to this end, I first simply suggested to Bartleby the propriety of his permanent departure. In a calm and serious tone, I commended the idea to his careful and mature consideration. But, having taken three days to meditate upon it, he apprised me that his original determination remained the same; in short, that he still preferred to abide with me.

What shall I do? I now said to myself, buttoning up my coat to the last button. What shall I do? what ought I to do? what does conscience say I *should* do with this man, or, rather, ghost. Rid myself of him, I must; go, he shall. But how? You will not thrust him, the poor, pale, passive mortal—you will not thrust such a helpless creature out of your door? you will not dishonor yourself by such cruelty? No, I will not, I cannot do that. Rather would I let him live and die here, and then mason up his remains in the wall. What, then, will you do? For all your coaxing, he will not budge. Bribes he leaves under your own paperweight on your table; in short, it is quite plain that he prefers to cling to you.

Then something severe, something unusual, must be done. What! surely you will not have him collared by a constable, and commit his innocent pallor to the common jail? And upon what ground could you procure such a thing to be done?—a vagrant, is he? What! he a vagrant, a wanderer, who refuses to budge? It is because he will *not* be a vagrant, then, that you seek to count him *as* a vagrant. That is too absurd. No visible means of support: there I have him. Wrong again: for indubitably he *does* support himself, and that is the only unanswerable proof that any man can show of his possessing the means so to do. No more, then. Since he will not quit me, I must quit him. I will change my offices; I will move elsewhere, and give him fair notice that if I find him on my new premises I will then proceed against him as a common trespasser.

Acting accordingly, next day I thus addressed him: "I find these chambers too far from the City Hall; the air is unwholesome. In a word, I propose to remove my offices next week, and shall no longer require your services. I tell you this now, in order that you may seek another place."

He made no reply, and nothing more was said.

On the appointed day I engaged carts and men, proceeded to my chambers, and, having but little furniture, everything was removed in a few hours. Throughout, the scrivener remained standing behind the screen, which I directed to be removed the last thing. It was withdrawn; and, being folded up like a huge folio, left him the motionless occupant of a naked room. I stood in the entry watching him a moment, while something from within me upbraided me.

I re-entered, with my hand in my pocket—and—and my heart in my mouth.

"Good-bye, Bartleby; I am going—good-bye; and God some way bless you; and take that," slipping something in his hand. But it dropped upon the floor, and then—strange to say—I tore myself from him whom I had so longed to be rid of.

Established in my new quarters, for a day or two I kept the

door locked, and started at every footfall in the passages. When I returned to my rooms after any little absence, I would pause at the threshold for an instant and attentively listen ere applying my key. But these fears were needless. Bartleby never came nigh me.

I thought all was going well, when a perturbed-looking stranger visited me, inquiring whether I was the person who had recently occupied rooms at No. — Wall Street.

Full of forebodings, I replied that I was.

"Then, sir," said the stranger, who proved a lawyer, "you are responsible for the man you left there. He refuses to do any copying; he refuses to do anything; he says he prefers not to; and he refuses to quit the premises."

"I am very sorry, sir," said I, with assumed tranquillity, but an inward tremor, "but, really, the man you allude to is nothing to me—he is no relation or apprentice of mine, that you should hold me responsible for him."

"In mercy's name, who is he?"

"I certainly cannot inform you. I know nothing about him. Formerly I employed him as a copyist; but he has done nothing for me now for some time past."

"I shall settle him, then—good morning, sir."

Several days passed, and I heard nothing more; and, though I often felt a charitable prompting to call at the place and see poor Bartleby, yet a certain squeamishness, of I know not what, withheld me.

All is over with him, by this time, thought I at last, when, through another week, no further intelligence reached me. But, coming to my room the day after, I found several persons waiting at my door in a high state of nervous excitement.

"That's the man—here he comes," cried the foremost one, whom I recognized as the lawyer who had previously called upon me alone.

"You must take him away, sir, at once," cried a portly person among them, advancing upon me, and whom I knew to be the landlord of No. — Wall Street. "These gentlemen, my tenants, cannot stand it any longer; Mr. B——," pointing to the lawyer, "has turned him out of his room, and he now persists in haunting the building generally, sitting upon the banisters of the stairs by day, and sleeping in the entry by night. Everybody is concerned; clients are leaving the offices; some fears are entertained of a mob; something you must do, and that without delay."

Aghast at this torrent, I fell back before it, and would fain have locked myself in my new quarters. In vain I persisted that Bartleby was nothing to me—no more than to any one else. In vain—I was the last person known to have anything to do with him, and they held me to the terrible account. Fearful, then, of being exposed in the papers (as one person present obscurely threatened), I considered the matter, and at length said that if the lawyer would give me a confidential interview with the scrivener, in his (the lawyer's) own room, I would, that afternoon, strive my best to rid them of the nuisance they complained of.

Going upstairs to my old haunt, there was Bartleby silently sitting upon the banister at the landing.

"What are you doing here, Bartleby?" said I.

"Sitting upon the banister," he mildly replied.

I motioned him into the lawyer's room, who then left us.

"Bartleby," said I, "are you aware that you are the cause of great tribulation to me, by persisting in occupying the entry after being dismissed from the office?"

No answer.

"Now one of two things must take place. Either you must do something, or something must be done to you. Now what sort of business would you like to engage in? Would you like to re-engage in copying for someone?"

"No; I would prefer not to make any change."

"Would you like a clerkship in a dry-goods store?"

"There is too much confinement about that. No, I would not like a clerkship; but I am not particular."

"Too much confinement," I cried; "why you keep yourself confined all the time!"

"I would prefer not to take a clerkship," he rejoined, as if to settle that little item at once.

"How would a bartender's business suit you? There is no trying of the eyesight in that."

"I would not like it at all; though, as I said before, I am not particular."

His unwonted wordiness inspirited me. I returned to the charge.

"Well, then, would you like to travel through the country collecting bills for the merchants? That would improve your health."

"No, I would prefer to be doing something else."

"How, then, would going as a companion to Europe, to entertain some young gentleman with your conversation—how would that suit you?"

"Not at all. It does not strike me that there is anything definite about that. I like to be stationary. But I am not particular."

"Stationary you shall be, then," I cried, now losing all patience, and, for the first time in all my exasperating connection with him, fairly flying into a passion. "If you do not go away from these premises before night, I shall feel bound—indeed, I *am* bound—to—to—to quit the premises myself!" I rather absurdly concluded, knowing not with what possible threat to try to frighten his immobility into compliance. Despairing of all further efforts, I was precipitately leaving him, when a final thought occurred to me—one which had not been wholly unindulged before.

"Bartleby," said I, in the kindest tone I could assume under such exciting circumstances, "will you go home with me now—

not to my office, but my dwelling—and remain there till we can conclude upon some convenient arrangement for you at our leisure? Come, let us start now, right away."

"No; at present I would prefer not to make any change at all."

I answered nothing, but, effectually dodging everyone by the suddenness and rapidity of my flight, rushed from the building, ran up Wall Street towards Broadway, and, jumping into the first omnibus, was soon removed from pursuit. As soon as tranquillity returned, I distinctly perceived that I had now done all that I possibly could, both in respect to the demands of the landlord and his tenants, and with regard to my own desire and sense of duty, to benefit Bartleby, and shield him from rude persecution. I now strove to be entirely carefree and quiescent, and my conscience justified me in the attempt, though, indeed, it was not so successful as I could have wished. So fearful was I of being again hunted out by the incensed landlord and his exasperated tenants, that, surrendering my business to Nippers for a few days, I drove about the upper part of the town and through the suburbs in my rockaway; crossed over to Jersey City and Hoboken, and paid fugitive visits to Manhattanville and Astoria. In fact, I almost lived in my rockaway for the time.

When again I entered my office, lo, a note from the landlord lay upon the desk. I opened it with trembling hands. It informed me that the writer had sent to the police, and had Bartleby removed to the Tombs as a vagrant. Moreover, since I knew more about him than anyone else, he wished me to appear at that place and make a suitable statement of the facts. These tidings had a conflicting effect upon me. At first I was indignant, but at last almost approved. The landlord's energetic, summary disposition had led him to adopt a procedure which I do not think I would have decided upon myself; and yet, as a last resort, under such peculiar circumstances, it seemed the only plan.

As I afterwards learned, the poor scrivener, when told that he must be conducted to the Tombs, offered not the slightest obstacle, but, in his pale, unmoving way, silently acquiesced.

Some of the compassionate and curious bystanders joined the party, and headed by one of the constables arm in arm with Bartleby, the silent procession filed its way through all the noise, and heat, and joy of the roaring thoroughfares at noon.

The same day I received the note, I went to the Tombs, or, to speak more properly, the Halls of Justice. Seeking the right officer, I stated the purpose of my call, and was informed that the individual I described was indeed within. I then assured the functionary that Bartleby was a perfectly honest man, and greatly to be compassionated, however unaccountably eccentric. I narrated all I knew, and closed by suggesting the idea of letting him remain in as indulgent confinement as possible till something less harsh might be done—though, indeed, I hardly knew what. At all events, if nothing else could be decided upon, the almshouse must receive him. I then begged to have an interview.

Being under no disgraceful charge, and quite serene and harmless in all his ways, they had permitted him freely to wander about the prison, and, especially, in the inclosed grass-platted yards thereof. And so I found him there, standing all alone in the quietest of the yards, his face towards a high wall, while all around, from the narrow slits of the jail windows, I thought I saw peering out upon him the eyes of murderers and thieves.

"Bartleby!"

"I know you," he said, without looking round—"and I want nothing to say to you."

"It was not I that brought you here, Bartleby," said I, keenly pained at his implied suspicion. "And, to you, this should not be so vile a place. Nothing reproachful attaches to you by being here. And see, it is not so sad a place as one might think. Look, there is the sky, and here is the grass."

"I know where I am," he replied, but would say nothing more, and so I left him.

As I entered the corridor again, a broad meatlike man in an apron accosted me, and, jerking his thumb over his shoulder, said— "Is that your friend?"

"Yes."

"Does he want to starve? If he does, let him live on the prison fare, that's all."

"Who are you?" asked I, not knowing what to make of such an unofficially speaking person in such a place.

"I am the grubman. Such gentlemen as have friends here hire me to provide them with something good to eat."

"Is this so?" said I, turning to the turnkey.

He said it was.

"Well, then," said I, slipping some silver into the grubman's hands (for so they called him), "I want you to give particular attention to my friend there; let him have the best dinner you can get. And you must be as polite to him as possible."

"Introduce me, will you?" said the grubman, looking at me with an expression which seemed to say he was all impatience for an opportunity to give a specimen of his breeding.

Thinking it would prove of benefit to the scrivener, I acquiesced, and, asking the grubman his name, went up with him to Bartleby.

"Bartleby, this is a friend; you will find him very useful to you."

"Your sarvant, sir, your sarvant," said the grubman, making a low salutation behind his apron. "Hope you find it pleasant here, sir; nice grounds—cool apartments—hope you'll stay with us some time—try to make it agreeable. What will you have for dinner today?"

"I prefer not to dine today," said Bartleby, turning away. "It would disagree with me; I am unused to dinners." So saying, he slowly moved to the other side of the inclosure and took up a position fronting the dead-wall.

"How's this?" said the grubman, addressing me with a stare of astonishment. "He's odd, ain't he?"

"I think he is a little deranged," said I, sadly.

"Deranged? deranged is it? Well, now, upon my word, I thought that friend of yourn was a gentleman forger; they are always pale and genteel-like, them forgers. I can't help pity 'em— can't help it, sir. Did you know Monroe Edwards?" he added, touchingly, and paused. Then, laying his hand piteously on my shoulder, sighed, "He died of consumption at Sing-Sing. So you weren't acquainted with Monroe?"

"No, I was never socially acquainted with any forgers. But I cannot stop longer. Look to my friend yonder. You will not lose by it. I will see you again."

Some few days after this, I again obtained admission to the Tombs, and went through the corridors in quest of Bartleby; but without finding him.

"I saw him coming from his cell not long ago," said a turnkey, "maybe he's gone to loiter in the yards."

So I went in that direction.

"Are you looking for the silent man?" said another turnkey, passing me. "Yonder he lies—sleeping in the yard there. 'Tis not twenty minutes since I saw him lie down."

The yard was entirely quiet. It was not accessible to the common prisoners. The surrounding walls, of amazing thickness, kept off all sounds behind them. The Egyptian character of the masonry weighed upon me with its gloom. But a soft imprisoned turf grew under foot. The heart of the eternal pyramids, it seemed, wherein, by some strange magic, through the clefts, grass-seed, dropped by birds, had sprung.

Strangely huddled at the base of the wall, his knees drawn up and lying on his side, his head touching the cold stones, I saw the wasted Bartleby. But nothing stirred. I paused, then went close up to him, stooped over, and saw that his dim eyes were open; otherwise he seemed profoundly sleeping. Something prompted me to touch him. I felt his hand, when a tingling shiver ran up my arm and down my spine to my feet.

The round face of the grubman peered upon me now. "His dinner is ready. Won't he dine today, either? Or does he live without dining?"

"Lives without dining," said I, and closed the eyes.

"Eh!—He's asleep, ain't he?"

"With kings and counselors," murmured I.

There would seem little need for proceeding further in this history. Imagination will readily supply the meager recital of poor Bartleby's interment. But, ere parting with the reader, let me say that if this little narrative has sufficiently interested him to awaken curiosity as to who Bartleby was, and what manner of life he led prior to the present narrator's making his acquaintance, I can only reply that in such curiosity I fully share, but am wholly unable to gratify it. Yet here I hardly know whether I should divulge one little item of rumor which came to my ear a few months after the scrivener's decease. Upon what basis it rested I could never ascertain, and hence how true it is I cannot now tell. But, inasmuch as this vague report has not been without a certain suggestive interest to me, however sad, it may prove the same with some others, and so I will briefly mention it. The report was this: that Bartleby had been a subordinate clerk in the Dead Letter Office at Washington, from which he had been suddenly removed by a change in the administration. When I think over this rumor, hardly can I express the emotions which seize me. Dead letters! does it not sound like dead men? Conceive a man by nature and misfortune prone to a pallid hopelessness, can any business seem more fitted to heighten it than that of continually handling these dead letters, and assorting them for the flames? For by the cartload they are annually burned. Sometimes from out the folded paper the pale clerk takes a ring—the finger it was meant for, perhaps, molders in the grave; a bank note sent in swiftest charity—he whom it would relieve nor eats nor hungers any more; pardon for those who died despairing; hope for those who died unhoping; good tidings for those who died stifled by unrelieved calamities. On errands of life, these letters speed to death.

Ah, Bartleby! Ah, humanity!

The Dancin' Party at Harrison's Cove

Mary N. Murfree
(1850–1922)

Fur ye see, Mis' Darley, them Harrison folks over yander ter the Cove hev determined on a dancin' party."

The drawling tones fell unheeded on old Mr. Kenyon's ear, as he sat on the broad hotel piazza of the New Helvetia Springs, and gazed with meditative eyes at the fair August sky. An early moon was riding, clear and full, over this wild spur of the Alleghanies; the stars were few and very faint; even the great Scorpio lurked, vaguely outlined, above the wooded ranges; and the white mist, that filled the long, deep, narrow valley between the parallel lines of mountains, shimmered with opalescent gleams.

All the world of the watering-place had converged to that focus, the ball-room, and the cool, moonlit piazzas were nearly deserted. The fell determination of the "Harrison folks" to give a dancing party made no impression on the preoccupied old gentleman. Another voice broke his reverie—a soft, clear, well-modulated voice—and he started and turned his head as his own name was called, and his niece, Mrs. Darley, came to the window.

"Uncle Ambrose—are you there? So glad! I was afraid you were down at the summer-house, where I hear the children singing. Do come here a moment, please. This is Mrs. Johns, who brings the Indian peaches to sell—you know the Indian peaches?"

Mr. Kenyon knew the Indian peaches, the dark crimson fruit streaked with still darker lines, and full of blood-red juice, which he had meditatively munched that very afternoon. Mr. Kenyon knew the Indian peaches right well. He wondered, however, what had brought Mrs. Johns back in so short a time, for although the principal industry of the mountain people about the New Helvetia Springs is selling fruit to the summer sojourners, it is not customary to come twice on the same day, nor to appear at all after nightfall.

Mrs. Darley proceeded to explain.

"Mrs. Johns's husband is ill and wants us to send him some medicine."

Mr. Kenyon rose, threw away the stump of his cigar, and entered the room. "How long has he been ill, Mrs. Johns?" he asked, dismally.

Mr. Kenyon always spoke lugubriously, and he was a dismal-looking old man. Not more cheerful was Mrs. Johns; she was tall and lank, and with such a face as one never sees except in these mountains—elongated, sallow, thin, with pathetic, deeply sunken eyes, and high cheek-bones, and so settled an expression of hopeless melancholy that it must be that naught but care and suffering had been her lot; holding out wasted hands to the years as they pass—holding them out always, and always empty. She wore a shabby, faded calico, and spoke with the peculiar expressionless drawl of the mountaineer. She was a wonderful contrast to Mrs. Darley, all furbelows and flounces, with her fresh, smooth face and soft hair, and plump, round arms half-revealed by the flowing sleeves of her thin, black dress. Mrs. Darley was in mourning, and therefore did not affect the ballroom. At this moment, on benevolent thoughts intent, she was engaged in uncorking sundry small phials, gazing inquiringly at their labels, and shaking their contents.

In reply to Mr. Kenyon's question, Mrs. Johns, sitting on the extreme edge of a chair and fanning herself with a pink calico sunbonnet, talked about her husband, and a misery in his side and in his back, and how he felt it "a-comin' on nigh on ter a week ago." Mr. Kenyon expressed sympathy, and was surprised by the announcement that Mrs. Johns considered her husband's illness "a blessin', 'kase ef he war able ter git out'n his bed, he 'lowed ter go down ter Harrison's Cove ter the dancin' party, 'kase Rick Pearson war a-goin' ter be thar, an' hed said ez how none o' the Johnses should come."

"What, Rick Pearson, that terrible outlaw!" exclaimed Mrs. Darley, with wide open blue eyes. She had read in the newspapers sundry thrilling accounts of a noted horse thief and outlaw, who with a gang of kindred spirits defied justice and roamed certain sparsely-populated mountainous counties at his own wild will, and she was not altogether without a feeling of fear as she heard of his proximity to the New Helvetia Springs—not fear for life or limb, because she was practical-minded enough to reflect that the sojourners and employés of the watering-place would far outnumber the outlaw's troop, but fear that a pair of shiny bay ponies, Castor and Pollux, would fall victims to the crafty wiles of the expert horse thief.

"I think I have heard something of a difficulty between your people and Rick Pearson," said old Mr. Kenyon. "Has a peace never been patched up between them?"

"No-o," drawled Mrs. Johns; "same as it always war. My old man 'll never believe but what Rick Pearson stole that thar bay filly we lost 'bout five year ago. But I don't believe he done it; plenty other folks around is ez mean ez Rick, leastways mos' ez mean; plenty mean enough ter steal a horse, ennyhow. Rick *say* he never tuk the filly; say he war a-goin' ter shoot off the nex' man's head ez say so. Rick say he'd ruther give two bay fillies than hev a man say he tuk a horse ez he never tuk. Rick say ez how he kin stand up ter what he does do, but it's these hyar lies on him what kills him out. But ye know, Mis' Darley, ye know yerself, he never give nobody two bay fillies in this world, an' what's more he 's never goin' ter. My old man an' my boy Kossute talks on 'bout that thar bay filly like she war stole yestiddy, an' 't war five year ago an' better; an' when they hearn ez how Rick Pearson hed showed that red head o' his'n on this hyar mounting las' week, they war fightin' mad, an' would hev lit out fur the gang sure, 'ceptin' they hed been gone down the mounting fur two days. An' my son Kossute, he sent Rick word that he had better keep out'n gunshot o' these hyar woods; that he didn't want no better mark than that red head o' his'n, an' he could hit it two mile off. An' Rick Pearson, he sent Kossute word that he would kill him fur his sass the very nex' time he see him, an' ef he don't want a bullet in that pumpkin head o' his'n he hed better keep away from that dancin' party what the Harrisons hev laid off ter give, 'kase Rick say he's a-goin' ter it hisself, an' is a-goin' ter dance too; he ain't been invited, Mis' Darley, but Rick don't keer fur that. He is a-goin' ennyhow, an' he say ez how he ain't a-goin' ter let Kossute come, 'count o' Kossute's sass an' the fuss they've all made 'bout that bay filly that war stole five year ago—'t war five year an' better. But Rick say ez how he is goin', fur all he ain't got no invite, an' is a-goin' ter dance too, 'kase you know, Mis' Darley, it's a-goin' ter be a dancin' party; the Harrisons hev determined on that. Them gals of theirn air mos' crazed 'bout a dancin' party. They ain't been a bit of account sence they went ter Cheatham's Cross-Roads ter see thar gran'mother, an' picked up all them queer new notions. So the Harrisons hev determined on a dancin' party; an' Rick say ez how he is goin' ter dance too; but Jule, *she* say ez how she know thar ain't a gal on the mounting ez would dance with him; but I ain't so sure 'bout that, Mis' Darley; gals air cur'ous critters, ye know yerself; thar's no sort o' countin' on 'em; they'll do one thing one time, an' another thing nex' time; ye can't put no dependence in 'em. But Jule say ef he kin git Mandy Tyler ter dance with him, it's the mos' he kin do, an' the gang'll be no whar. Mebbe he kin git Mandy ter dance with him, 'kase the other boys say ez how none o' them is a-goin' ter ax her ter dance, 'count of the trick she played on 'em down ter the Wilkins settlemint—las' month, war it? no, 't war two month ago, an' better; but the boys ain't forgot how scandalous she done 'em, an' none of 'em is a-goin' ter ax her ter dance."

"Why, what did she do?" exclaimed Mrs. Darley, surprised. "She came here to sell peaches one day, and I thought her such a nice, pretty, well-behaved girl."

"Waal, she hev got mighty quiet say-nuthin' sort'n ways, Mis' Darley, but that thar gal do behave *rediculous*. Down thar ter the Wilkins settlemint—ye know it's 'bout two mile or two mile 'n a half from hyar—waal, all the gals walked down thar ter the party an hour by sun, but when the boys went down they tuk thar horses, ter give the gals a ride home behind 'em. Waal, every boy axed his gal ter ride while the party war goin' on, an' when 't war all over they all set out fur ter come home. Waal, this hyar Mandy Tyler is a mighty *favorite* 'mongst the boys—they ain't got no sense, ye know, Mis' Darley—an' stiddier one of 'em axin' her ter ride home, thar war five of 'em axed her ter ride, ef ye'll believe me, an' what do ye think she done, Mis' Darley? She tole all five of 'em yes; an' when the party war over, she war the last ter go, an' when she started out'n the door, thar war all five of them boys a-standin' thar waitin' fur her, an' every one a-holdin' his horse by the bridle, an' none of 'em knowed who the others war a-waitin' fur. An' this hyar Mandy Tyler, when she got ter the door an' seen 'em all a-standin' thar, never said one word, jest walked right through 'mongst 'em, an' set out fur the mounting on foot with all them five boys a-followin' an' a-leadin' thar horses an' a-quarrelin' enough ter take off each others' heads 'bout which one war a-goin' ter ride with her; which none of 'em did, Mis' Darley, fur I hearn ez how the whole lay-out footed it all the way ter New Helveshy. An' thar would hev been a fight 'mongst 'em, 'ceptin' her brother, Jacob Tyler, went along with 'em, an' tried ter keep the peace atwixt 'em. An' Mis' Darley, all them married folks down thar at the party—them folks in the Wilkins settlemint is the biggest fools, sure—when all them married folks come out ter the door, an' see the way Mandy Tyler hed treated them boys, they jest hollered and laffed an' thought it war mighty smart an' funny in Mandy; but she never say a word till she kem up the mounting, an' I never hearn ez how she say ennything then. An' now the boys all say none of 'em is a-goin' ter ax her ter dance, ter pay her back fur them fool airs of hern. But Kossute say he 'll dance with her ef none the rest will. Kossute he thought 't war all mighty funny too—he's sech a fool 'bout gals, Kossute is—but Jule, she thought ez how 't war scandalous."

Mrs. Darley listened in amused surprise; that these mountain wilds could sustain a first-class coquette was an idea that had not hitherto entered her mind; however, "that thar Mandy" seemed, in Mrs. Johns's opinion at least, to merit the unenviable distinction, and the party at Wilkins settlement and the prospective gayety of Harrison's Cove awakened the same sentiments in her heart and mind as do the more ambitious germans and kettledrums of the lowland cities in the heart and mind of Mrs. Grundy. Human nature is the same everywhere, and the Wilkins settlement is a microcosm. The metropolitan centres, stripped of the civilization of wealth, fashion, and culture, would present only the bare skeleton of humanity outlined in Mrs. Johns's talk of Harrison's Cove, the Wilkins settlement, the enmities and scandals and sorrows and misfortunes of the mountain ridge. As the absurd resemblance developed, Mrs. Darley could not forbear a smile. Mrs. Johns looked up with a momentary expression of surprise; the story presented no humorous phase to her perceptions, but she too smiled a little as she repeated, "Scandalous, ain't it?" and proceeded in the same lack-lustre tone as before.

"Yes—Kossute say ez how he'll dance with her ef none the rest will, fur Kossute say ez how he hev laid off ter dance, Mis' Darley; an' when I ax him what he thinks will become of his soul ef he dances, he say the devil may crack away at it, an' ef he kin hit it he's welcome. Fur soul or no soul he's a-goin' ter dance. Kossute is a-fixin' of hisself this very minit ter go; but I am verily afeard the boy'll be slaughtered, Mis' Darley, 'kase thar is goin' ter be a fight, an' ye never in all yer life hearn sech sass ez Kossute and Rick Pearson done sent word ter each other."

Mr. Kenyon expressed some surprise that she should fear for so young a fellow as Kossuth. "Surely," he said, "the man is not brute enough to injure a mere boy; your son is a mere boy."

"That's so," Mrs. Johns drawled. "Kossute ain't more 'n twenty year old, an' Rick Pearson is double that ef he is a day; but ye see it's the fire-arms ez makes Kossute more 'n a match fur him, 'kase Kossute is the best shot on the mounting, an' Rick knows that in a shootin' fight Kossute's better able ter take keer of hisself an' hurt somebody else nor ennybody. Kossute's more likely ter hurt Rick nor Rick is ter hurt him in a shootin' fight; but ef Rick didn't hurt him, an' he war ter shoot Rick, the gang would tear him ter pieces in a minit; and 'mongst 'em I'm actually afeard they'll slaughter the boy."

Mr. Kenyon looked even graver than was his wont upon receiving this information, but said no more; and after giving Mrs.

Johns the febrifuge she wished for her husband, he returned to his
seat on the piazza.

Mrs. Darley watched him with some little indignation as he
proceeded to light a fresh cigar. "How cold and unsympathetic
uncle Ambrose is," she said to herself. And after condoling effu-
sively with Mrs. Johns on her apprehensions for her son's safety, she
returned to the gossips in the hotel parlor, and Mrs. Johns, with her
pink calico sun-bonnet on her head, went her way in the brilliant
summer moonlight.

The clear lustre shone white upon all the dark woods and
chasms and flashing waters that lay between the New Helvetia
Springs and the wide, deep ravine called Harrison's Cove, where
from a rude log hut the vibrations of a violin, and the quick throb
of dancing feet, already mingled with the impetuous rush of a
mountain stream close by and the weird night-sounds of the
hills—the cry of birds among the tall trees, the stir of the wind, the
monotonous chanting of frogs at the water side, the long, drowsy
drone of the nocturnal insects, the sudden faint blast of a distant
hunter's horn, and the far baying of hounds.

Mr. Harrison had four marriageable daughters, and had arrived
at the conclusion that something must be done for the girls; for,
strange as it may seem, the prudent father exists even among the
"mounting folks." Men there realize the importance of providing
suitable homes for their daughters as men do elsewhere, and the
eligible youth is as highly esteemed in those wilds as is the much
scarcer animal at a fashionable watering-place. Thus it was that Mr.
Harrison had "determined on a dancin' party." True, he stood in
bodily fear of the judgment day and the circuit-rider; but the
dancing party was a rarity eminently calculated to please the young
hunters of the settlements round about, so he swallowed his
qualms, to be indulged at a more convenient season, and threw
himself into the vortex of preparation with an ardor very gratify-

ing to the four young ladies, who had become imbued with so-phistication at Cheatham's Cross-Roads.

Not so Mrs. Harrison; she almost expected the house to fall and crush them, as a judgment on the wickedness of a dancing party; for so heinous a sin, in the estimation of the greater part of the mountain people, had not been committed among them for many a day. Such trifles as killing a man in a quarrel, or on suspicion of stealing a horse, or wash-tub, or anything that came handy, of course, does not count; but a dancing party! Mrs. Harrison could only hold her idle hands, and dread the heavy penalty that must surely follow so terrible a crime.

It certainly had not the gay and lightsome aspect supposed to be characteristic of such a scene of sin: the awkward young mountaineers clogged heavily about in their uncouth clothes and rough shoes, with the stolid-looking, lack-lustre maids of the hill, to the violin's monotonous iteration of The Chicken in the Bread-Trough, or The Rabbit in the Pea-Patch—all their grave faces as grave as ever. The music now and then changed suddenly to one of those wild, melancholy strains sometimes heard in old-fashioned dancing tunes, and the strange pathetic cadences seemed more attuned to the rhythmical dash of the waters rushing over their stone barricades out in the moonlight yonder, or to the plaintive sighs of the winds among the great dark arches of the primeval forests, than to the movement of the heavy, coarse feet dancing a solemn measure in the little log cabin in Harrison's Cove. The elders, sitting in rush-bottomed chairs close to the walls, and looking on at the merriment, well-pleased despite their religious doubts, were somewhat more lively; every now and then a guffaw mingled with the violin's resonant strains and the dancers' well-marked pace; the women talked to each other with somewhat more animation than was their wont, under the stress of the unusual excitement of a dancing party, and from out the shed-room adjoining came an anticipative odor of more substantial sin than the fiddle or the grave jiggling up and down the rough floor. A little more cider too, and a very bad article of illegally-distilled whiskey, were ever and anon circulated among the pious abstainers from the dance; but the sinful votaries of Terpsichore could brook no pause nor delay, and jogged up and down quite intoxicated with the mirthfulness of the plaintive old airs and the pleasure of other motion than following the plow or hoeing the corn.

And the moon smiled right royally on her dominion: on the long, dark ranges of mountains and mist-filled valleys between; on the woods and streams, and on all the half-dormant creatures either amongst the shadow-flecked foliage or under the crystal waters; on the long, white, sandy road winding in and out through the forest; on the frowning crags of the wild ravine; on the little bridge at the entrance of the gorge, across which a party of eight men, heavily armed and gallantly mounted, rode swiftly and disappeared amid the gloom of the shadows.

The sound of the galloping of horses broke suddenly on the music and the noise of the dancing; a moment's interval, and the door gently opened and the gigantic form of Rick Pearson appeared in the aperture. He was dressed, like the other mountaineers, in a coarse suit of brown jeans somewhat the worse for wear, the trowsers stuffed in the legs of his heavy boots; he wore an old soft felt hat, which he did not remove immediately on entering, and a pair of formidable pistols at his belt conspicuously challenged attention. He had auburn hair, and a long full beard of a lighter tint reaching almost to his waist; his complexion was much tanned by the sun, and roughened by exposure to the inclement mountain weather; his eyes were brown, deep-set, and from under his heavy brows they looked out with quick, sharp glances, and occasionally with a roguish twinkle; the expression of his countenance was rather good-humored—a sort of imperious good-humor, however—the expression of a man accustomed to have his own way and not to be trifled with, but able to afford some amiability since his power is undisputed.

He stepped slowly into the apartment, placed his gun against the wall, turned, and solemnly gazed at the dancing, while his followers trooped in and obeyed his example. As the eight guns, one by one, rattled against the wall, there was a startled silence among the pious elders of the assemblage, and a sudden disappearance of the animation that had characterized their intercourse during the evening. Mrs. Harrison, who by reason of flurry and a housewifely pride in the still unrevealed treasures of the shed-room had wellnigh forgotten her fears, felt that the anticipated judgment had even now descended, and in what terrible and unexpected guise! The men turned the quids of tobacco in their cheeks and looked at each other in uncertainty; but the dancers bestowed not a glance upon the newcomers, and the musician in the corner, with his eyes half-closed, his head bent low upon the instrument, his hard, horny hand moving the bow back and forth over the strings of the crazy old fiddle, was utterly rapt by his own melody. At the supreme moment when the great red beard had appeared portentously in the doorway and fear had frozen the heart of Mrs. Harrison within her at the ill-omened apparition, the host was in the shed-room filling a broken-nosed pitcher from the cider-barrel. When he re-entered, and caught sight of the grave sunburned face with its long red beard and sharp brown eyes, he too was dismayed for an instant, and stood silent at the opposite door with the pitcher in his hand. The pleasure and the possible profit of the dancing party, for which he had expended so much of his scanty store of this world's goods and risked the eternal treasures laid up in heaven, were a mere phantasm; for, with Rick Pearson among them, in an ill frame of mind and at odds with half the men in the room, there would certainly be a fight, and in all probability one would be killed, and the dancing party at Harrison's Cove would be a text for the bloody-minded sermons of the circuit-rider for all time to come. However, the father of four marriageable daughters is apt to become crafty and worldly-wise; only for a moment did he stand in indecision; then, catching suddenly the small brown eyes, he held up the pitcher with a grin of invitation. "Rick!" he called out above the scraping of the violin and the clatter of the dancing feet, "slip round hyar ef ye kin, I've got somethin' for ye;" and he shook the pitcher significantly.

Not that Mr. Harrison would for a moment have thought of Rick Pearson in a matrimonial point of view, for even the sophistication of the Cross-Roads had not yet brought him to the state of mind to consider such a half loaf as this better than no bread, but he felt it imperative from every point of view to keep that set of young mountaineers dancing in peace and quiet, and their guns idle and out of mischief against the wall. The great red beard disappeared and reappeared at intervals, as Rick Pearson slipped along the gun-lined wall to join his host and the cider-pitcher, and after he had disposed of the refreshment, in which the gang shared, he relapsed into silently watching the dancing and meditating a participation in that festivity.

Now, it so happened that the only young girl unprovided with a partner was "that thar Mandy Tyler," of Wilkins settlement renown; the young men had rigidly adhered to their resolution to ignore her in their invitations to dance, and she had been sitting since the beginning of the festivities, quite neglected, among the married people, looking on at the amusement which she had been debarred sharing by that unpopular bit of coquetry at Wilkins settlement. Nothing of disappointment or mortification was expressed in her countenance; she felt the slight of course—even a "mounting" woman is susceptible of the sting of wounded pride; all her long-anticipated enjoyment had come to naught by this in-

fliction of penance for her ill-timed jest at the expense of those
five young fellows dancing with their triumphant partners and be-
stowing upon her not even a glance; but she looked the express
image of immobility as she sat in her clean pink calico, so carefully
gotten up for the occasion, her short black hair curling about her
ears, and watched the unending reel with slow, dark eyes. Rick's
glance fell upon her, and without further hesitation he strode over
to where she was sitting and proffered his hand for the dance. She
did not reply immediately, but looked timidly about her at the
shocked pious ones on either side, who were ready but for mortal
fear to aver that "dancin' ennyhow air bad enough, the Lord
knows, but dancin' with a horse thief air jest scandalous!" Then, for
there is something of defiance to established law and prejudice in
the born flirt everywhere, with a sudden daring spirit shining in
her brightening eyes, she responded, "Don't keer ef I do," with a
dimpling half-laugh; and the next minute the two outlaws were
flying down the middle together.

While Rick was according grave attention to the intricacies of
the mazy dance and keeping punctilious time to the scraping of
the old fiddle, finding it all a much more difficult feat than galloping from the Cross-Roads to the "Snake's Mouth" on some
other man's horse with the sheriff hard at his heels, the solitary figure of a tall gaunt man had followed the long winding path leading deep into the woods, and now began the steep descent to
Harrison's Cove. Of what was old Mr. Kenyon thinking, as he
walked on in the mingled shadow and sheen? Of St. Augustin and
his Forty Monks, probably, and what they found in Britain. The
young men of his acquaintance would gladly have laid you any
odds that he could think of nothing but his antique hobby, the ancient church. Mr. Kenyon was the most prominent man in St. Martin's church in the city of B———, not excepting the rector. He was
a lay-reader, and officiated upon occasions of "clerical sore-throat,"

as the profane denominate the ministerial summer exodus from heated cities. This summer, however, Mr. Kenyon's own health had succumbed, and he was having a little "sore-throat" in the mountains on his own account. Very devout was Mr. Kenyon. Many people wondered that he had never taken orders. Many people warmly congratulated themselves that he never had; for drier sermons than those he selected were surely never heard, and a shuddering imagination shrinks appalled from the problematic mental drought of his ideal original discourse. But he was an integrant part of St. Martin's; much of his piety, materialized into contributions, was built up in its walls and shone before men in the costliness of its decorations. Indeed, the ancient name had been conferred upon the building as a sort of tribute to Mr. Kenyon's well-known enthusiasm concerning apostolic succession and kindred doctrines.

Dull and dismal was Mr. Kenyon, and therefore it may be considered a little strange that he should be a notable favorite with men. They were of many different types, but with one invariable bond of union: they had all at one time served as soldiers; for the war, now ten years passed by, its bitterness almost forgotten, had left some traces that time can never obliterate. What a friend was the droning old churchman in those days of battle and bloodshed and suffering and death! Not a man sat within the walls of St. Martin's who had not received some signal benefit from the hand stretched forth to impress the claims of certain ante-Augustin British clergy to consideration and credibility; not a man who did not remember stricken fields where a good Samaritan went about under shot and shell, succoring the wounded and comforting the dying; not a man who did not applaud the indomitable spirit and courage that cut his way from surrender and safety, through solid barriers of enemies, to deliver the orders on which the fate of an army depended; not a man whose memory did not harbor fatiguing recollections of long, dull sermons read for the souls' health of the soldiery. And through it all—by the camp-fires at night, on the long white country-roads in the sunshiny mornings; in the mountains and the morasses; in hilarious advance and in cheerless retreat; in the heats of summer and by the side of frozen rivers, the ancient British clergy went through it all. And, whether the old churchman's premises and reasoning were false, whether his tracings of the succession were faulty, whether he dropped a link here or took in one there, he had caught the spirit of those staunch old martyrs, if not their falling churchly mantle.

The mountaineers about the New Helvetia Springs supposed that Mr. Kenyon was a regularly ordained preacher, and that the sermons which they had heard him read were, to use the vernacular, out of his own head. For many of them were accustomed on Sunday mornings to occupy humble back benches in the ball-room, where on week-day evenings the butterflies sojourning at New Helvetia danced, and on the Sabbath metaphorically beat their breasts, and literally avowed that they were "miserable sinners," following Mr. Kenyon's lugubrious lead.

The conclusion of the mountaineers was not unnatural, therefore, and when the door of Mr. Harrison's house opened and another uninvited guest entered, the music suddenly ceased. The half-closed eyes of the fiddler had fallen upon Mr. Kenyon at the threshold, and, supposing him a clergyman, he immediately imagined that the man of God had come all the way from New Helvetia Springs to stop the dancing and snatch the revelers from the jaws of hell. The rapturous bow paused shuddering on the string, the dancing feet were palsied, the pious about the walls were racking their slow brains to excuse their apparent conniving at sin and bargaining with Satan, and Mr. Harrison felt that this was indeed an unlucky party and it would undoubtedly be dispersed by the direct interposition of Providence before the shed-room was opened

and the supper eaten. As to his soul—poor man! these constantly
recurring social anxieties were making him callous to immortality;
this life was about to prove too much for him, for the fortitude and
tact even of a father of four marriageable young ladies has a limit.
Mr. Kenyon, too, seemed dumb as he hesitated in the door-way,
but when the host, partially recovering himself, came forward and
offered a chair, he said with one of his dismal smiles that he hoped
Mr. Harrison had no objection to his coming in and looking at the
dancing for a while. "Don't let me interrupt the young people, I
beg," he added, as he seated himself. The astounded silence was unbroken for a few moments. To be sure he was not a circuit-rider,
but even the sophistication of Cheatham's Cross-Roads had never
heard of a preacher who did not object to dancing. Mr. Harrison
could not believe his ears, and asked for a more explicit expression
of opinion.

"Ye say ye don't keer ef the boys an' gals dance?" he inquired.
"Ye don't think it's sinful?"

And after Mr. Kenyon's reply, in which the astonished "mounting folks" caught only the surprising statement that dancing if
properly conducted was an innocent, cheerful, and healthful
amusement, supplemented by something about dancing in the fear
of the Lord, and that in all charity he was disposed to consider ob-
jections to such harmless recreations a tithing of mint and anise
and cummin, whereby might ensue a neglect of weightier matters
of the law; that clean hands and clean hearts—hands clean of blood
and ill-gotten goods, and hearts free from falsehood and cruel
intention—these were the things well-pleasing to God—after his
somewhat prolix reply, the gayety recommenced. The fiddle qua-
vered tremulously at first, but soon resounded with its former vigorous tones, and the joy of the dance was again exemplified in the
grave joggling back and forth.

Meanwhile Mr. Harrison sat beside this strange new guest and asked him questions concerning his church, being instantly, it is needless to say, informed of its great antiquity, of the journeying of St. Augustin and his Forty Monks to Britain, of the church they found already planted there, of its retreat to the hills of Wales under its oppressors' tyranny, of many cognate themes, side issues of the main branch of the subject, into which the talk naturally drifted, the like of which Mr. Harrison had never heard in all his days. And as he watched the figures dancing to the violin's strains, and beheld as in a mental vision the solemn gyrations of those renowned Forty Monks to the monotone of old Mr. Kenyon's voice, he abstractedly hoped that the double dance would continue without interference till a peaceable dawn.

His hopes were vain. It so chanced that Kossuth Johns, who had by no means relinquished all idea of dancing at Harrison's Cove and defying Rick Pearson, had hitherto been detained by his mother's persistent entreaties, some necessary attentions to his father, and the many trials which beset a man dressing for a party who has very few clothes, and those very old and worn. Jule, his sister-in-law, had been most kind and complaisant, putting on a button here, sewing up a slit there, darning a refractory elbow, and lending him the one bright ribbon she possessed as a neck-tie. But all these things take time, and the moon did not light Kossuth down the gorge until she was shining almost vertically from the sky, and the Harrison Cove people and the Forty Monks were dancing together in high feather. The ecclesiastic dance halted suddenly, and a watchful light gleamed in old Mr. Kenyon's eyes as he became silent and the boy stepped into the room. The moonlight and the lamp-light fell mingled on the calm, inexpressive features and tall, slender form of the young mountaineer. "Hy 're, Kossute!" A cheerful greeting from many voices met him. The next moment the music ceased once again, and the dancing came to a standstill, for as the name fell on Pearson's ear he turned, glanced sharply toward the door, and drawing one of his pistols from his belt advanced to the middle of the room. The men fell back; so did the frightened women, without screaming, however, for that indication of feminine sensibility had not yet penetrated to Cheatham's Cross-Roads, to say nothing of the mountains.

"I told ye that ye warn't ter come hyar," said Rick Pearson imperiously, "and ye've got ter go home ter yer mammy, right off, or ye'll never git thar no more, youngster."

"I've come hyar ter put *you* out, ye cussed red-headed horse thief!" retorted Kossuth, angrily; "ye hed better tell me whar that thar bay filly is, or light out, one."

It is not the habit in the mountains to parley long on these occasions. Kossuth had raised his gun to his shoulder as Rick, with his pistol cocked, advanced a step nearer. The outlaw's weapon was struck upward by a quick, strong hand, the little log cabin was filled with flash, roar, and smoke, and the stars looked in through a hole in the roof from which Rick's bullet had sent the shingles flying. He turned in mortal terror and caught the hand that had struck his pistol—in mortal terror, for Kossuth was the crack shot of the mountains and he felt he was a dead man. The room was somewhat obscured by smoke, but as he turned upon the man who had disarmed him, for the force of the blow had thrown the pistol to the floor, he saw that the other hand was over the muzzle of young Johns's gun, and Kossuth was swearing loudly that by the Lord Almighty if he didn't take it off he would shoot it off.

"My young friend," Mr. Kenyon began, with the calmness appropriate to a devout member of the one catholic and apostolic church; but then, the old Adam suddenly getting the upper-hand, he shouted out in irate tones, "If you don't stop that noise, I'll break your head! Well, Mr. Pearson," he continued, as he stood between the combatants, one hand still over the muzzle of young

Johns's gun, the other, lean and sinewy, holding Pearson's power-ful right arm with a vise-like grip, "well, Mr. Pearson, you are not so good a soldier as you used to be; you didn't fight boys in the old times."

Rick Pearson's enraged expression suddenly gave way to a sur-prised recognition. "Ye may drag me through hell an' beat me with a soot-bag ef hyar ain't the old fightin' preacher agin!" he cried.

"I have only one thing to say to you," said Mr. Kenyon. "You must go. I will not have you here shooting boys and breaking up a party."

Rick demurred. "See hyar, now," he said, "ye've got no business meddlin'."

"You must go," Mr. Kenyon reiterated.

"Preachin's yer business," Rick continued; " 'pears like ye don't 'tend to it, though."

"You must go."

"S'pose I say I won't," said Rick, good-humoredly; "I s'pose ye'd say ye'd make me."

"You must go," repeated Mr. Kenyon. "I am going to take the boy home with me, but I intend to see you off first."

Mr. Kenyon had prevented the hot-headed Kossuth from fir-ing by keeping his hand persistently over the muzzle of the gun; and young Johns had feared to try to wrench it away lest it should discharge in the effort. Had it done so, Mr. Kenyon would have been in sweet converse with the Forty Monks in about a minute and a quarter. Kossuth had finally let go the gun, and made fran-tic attempts to borrow a weapon from some of his friends, but the stern authoritative mandate of the belligerent peacemaker had pre-vented them from gratifying him, and he now stood empty-handed beside Mr. Kenyon, who had shouldered the old rifle in an absent-minded manner, although still retaining his powerful grasp on the arm of the outlaw.

"Waal, parson," said Rick at length, "I'll go, jest ter pleasure you-uns. Ye see, I ain't forgot Shiloh."

"I am not talking about Shiloh now," said the old man. "You must get off at once—all of you," indicating the gang, who had been so whelmed in astonishment that they had not lifted a finger to aid their chief.

"Ye say ye'll take that—that"—Rick looked hard at Kossuth while he racked his brains for an injurious epithet—"that sassy child home ter his mammy?"

"Come, I am tired of this talk," said Mr. Kenyon; "you must go."

Rick walked heavily to the door and out into the moonlight. "Them was good old times," he said to Mr. Kenyon, with a regretful cadence in his peculiar drawl; "good old times, them War days. I wish they was back agin—I wish they was back agin. I ain't forgot Shiloh yit, though, and I ain't a-goin' ter. But I'll tell ye one thing, parson," he added, his mind reverting from ten years ago to the scene just past, as he unhitched his horse and carefully examined the saddle-girth and stirrups, "ye're a mighty queer preacher, ye air, a-sittin' up an' lookin' at sinners dance an' then gittin' in a fight that don't consarn ye—ye're a mighty queer preacher! Ye ought ter be in my gang, that whar *ye* ought ter be," he exclaimed with a guffaw, as he put his foot in the stirrup; "ye've got a damned deal too much grit fur a preacher. But I ain't forgot Shiloh yit, an' I don't mean ter, nuther."

A shout of laughter from the gang, an oath or two, the quick tread of horses' hoofs pressing into a gallop, and the outlaw's troop were speeding along the narrow paths that led deep into the vistas of the moonlit summer woods.

As the old churchman, with the boy at his side and the gun still on his shoulder, ascended the rocky, precipitous slope on the opposite side of the ravine above the foaming waters of the wild mountain stream, he said but little of admonition to his companion; with the disappearance of the flame and smoke and the dangerous ruffian his martial spirit had cooled; the last words of the outlaw, the highest praise Rick Pearson could accord to the highest qualities Rick Pearson could imagine—he had grit enough to belong to the gang—had smitten a tender conscience. He, at his age, using none of the means rightfully at his command, the gentle suasion of religion, must needs rush between armed men, wrench their weapons from their hands, threatening with such violence that an outlaw and desperado, recognizing a parallel of his own belligerent and lawless spirit, should say that he ought to belong to the gang! And the heaviest scourge of the sin-laden conscience was the perception that, so far as the unsubdued old Adam went, he ought indeed.

He was not so tortured, though, that he did not think of others. He paused on reaching the summit of the ascent, and looked back at the little house nestling in the ravine, the lamp-light streaming through its open doors and windows across the path among the laurel bushes, where Rick's gang had hitched their horses.

"I wonder," said the old man, "if they are quiet and peaceable again; can you hear the music and dancing?"

"Not now," said Kossuth. Then, after a moment, "Now, I kin," he added, as the wind brought to their ears the oft-told tale of the rabbit's gallopade in the pea-patch. "They're a-dancin' now, and all right agin."

As they walked along, Mr. Kenyon's racked conscience might have been in a slight degree comforted had he known that he was in some sort a revelation to the impressible lad at his side, that Kossuth had begun dimly to comprehend that a Christian may be a man of spirit also, and that bravado does not constitute bravery. Now that the heat of anger was over, the young fellow was glad that the fearless interposition of the warlike peace-maker had prevented any killing, " 'kase ef the old man hedn't hung on ter my gun like he done, I 'd have been a murderer like he said, an' Rick would hev been dead. An' the bay filly ain't sech a killin' matter nohow; ef it war the roan three-year-old now, 't would be different."

The Lady of Shalott

Elizabeth Stuart Phelps

(1844–1911)

I
t is not generally known that the Lady of Shalott lived last
summer in an attic, at the east end of South Street.

The wee-est, thinnest, whitest little lady! And yet the
brightest, stillest, and ah, such a smiling little lady!

If you had held her up by the window—for she could not hold
up herself—she would have hung like a porcelain transparency in
your hands. And if you had said, laying her gently down, and giving the tears a smart dash, that they should not fall on her lifted
face, "Poor child!" the Lady of Shalott would have said, "Oh,
don't!" and smiled. And you would have smiled yourself, for very
surprise that she should outdo you; and between the two there
would have been so much smiling done that one would have fairly
thought that it was a delightful thing to live last summer in an attic
at the east end of South Street.

This, perhaps, was the more natural in the Lady of Shalott because she had never lived anywhere else.

When the Lady of Shalott was five years old, her mother threw
her down-stairs one day, by mistake, instead of the whisky-jug.

This is a fact which I think Mr. Tennyson has omitted to mention in his poem.

They picked the Lady of Shalott up and put her on the bed; and there she lay from that day until last summer, unless, as I said, somebody had occasion to use her for a transparency.

The mother and the jug both went down the stairs together a few years after, and never came up at all; and that was a great convenience, for the Lady of Shalott's palace in the attic was not large, and they took up much unnecessary room.

Since that the Lady of Shalott had lived with her sister, Sary Jane.

Sary Jane made nankeen vests, at sixteen and three-quarter cents a dozen.

Sary Jane had red hair, and crooked shoulders, and a voice so much like the snap of a rat-trap which she sometimes set on the stairs, that the Lady of Shalott could seldom tell which was which until she had thought about it a little while. When there was a rat caught, she was apt to ask, "What?" and when Sary Jane spoke she more often than not said, "There 's another!"

Her crooked shoulders Sary Jane had acquired from sitting under the eaves of the palace to sew. That physiological problem was simple. There was not room enough under the eaves to sit straight.

Sary Jane's red hair was the result of sitting in the sun on July noons under those eaves, to see to thread her needle. There was no question about that. The Lady of Shalott had settled it in her own mind, past dispute. Sary Jane's hair had been—what was it? brown? once. Sary Jane was slowly taking fire. Who would not, to sit in the sun in that palace? The only matter of surprise to the Lady of Shalott was that the palace itself did not smoke. Sometimes, when Sary Jane hit the rafters, she was sure that she saw sparks.

As for Sary Jane's voice, when one knew that she made nankeen vests at sixteen and three-quarter cents a dozen, *that* was a matter of no surprise. It never surprised the Lady of Shalott.

But Sary Jane was very cross; there was no denying that; very cross.

And the palace. Let me tell you about the palace. It measured just twelve by nine feet. It would have been seven feet post—if there had been a post in the middle of it. From the centre it sloped away to the windows, where Sary Jane had just room enough to sit crooked under the eaves at work. There were two windows and a loose scuttle to the palace. The scuttle let in the snow in winter and the sun in summer, and the rain and wind at all times. It was quite a diversion to the Lady of Shalott to see how many different ways of doing a disagreeable thing seemed to be practicable to that scuttle. Besides the bed on which the Lady of Shalott lay, there was a stove in the palace, two chairs, a very ragged rag-mat, a shelf, with two notched cups and plates upon it, one pewter teaspoon, and a looking-glass. On washing-days Sary Jane climbed upon the chair and hung her clothes out through the scuttle on the roof; or else she ran a little rope from one of the windows to the other for a drying-rope. It would have been more exact to have said on washing-nights; for Sary Jane always did her washing after dark. The reason was evident. If the rest of us were in the habit of wearing all the clothes we had, like Sary Jane, I have little doubt that we should do the same.

I should mention that there was no sink in the Lady of Shalott's palace; no water. There was a dirty hydrant in the yard, four flights below, which supplied the Lady of Shalott and all her neighbors. The Lady of Shalott kept her coal under the bed; her flour, a pound at a time, in a paper parcel, on the shelf, with the teacups and the pewter spoon. If she had anything else to keep, it went out through the palace scuttle and lay on the roof. The Lady of Shalott's palace opened directly upon a precipice. The lessor of the house called it a flight of stairs. When Sary Jane went up and down, she went sideways to preserve her balance. There were no banisters to the precipice. The entry was dark. Some dozen or twenty of the Lady of Shalott's neighbors patronized the precipice, and about once a week a baby patronized the rat-trap, instead. Once, when there was a fire-alarm, the precipice was very serviceable. Four women and an old man went over. With one exception (she was eighteen, and could bear a broken collar-bone), they will not, I am informed, go over again.

The Lady of Shalott paid one dollar a week for the rent of her palace.

But then there was a looking-glass in the palace. I think I noticed it. It hung on the slope of the rafters, just opposite the Lady of Shalott's window—for she considered that her window at which Sary Jane did not make nankeen vests at sixteen and three-quarter cents a dozen.

Now, because the looking-glass was opposite the window at which Sary Jane did *not* make vests, and because the rafters sloped, and because the bed lay almost between the looking-glass and the window, the Lady of Shalott was happy. And because, to the patient heart that is a seeker after happiness "the little more, and how much it is!" (and the little less, what worlds away!) the Lady of Shalott was proud as well as happy. The looking-glass measured in inches ten by six. I think that the Lady of Shalott would have experienced rather a touch of mortification than of envy if she had known that there was a mirror in a house just around the corner measuring almost as many feet. But that was one of the advantages of being the Lady of Shalott. She never parsed life in the comparative degree.

I suppose that one must go through a process of education to understand what comfort there may be in a ten by six inch looking-glass. All the world came for the Lady of Shalott into her little looking-glass—the joy of it, the anguish of it, the hope and fear of it, the health and hurt—ten by six inches of it exactly.

"It is next best to not having been thrown down-stairs yourself!" said the Lady of Shalott.

To tell the truth, it sometimes occurred to her that there was a monotony about the world. A garret window like her own, for instance, would fill her sight if she did not tip the glass a little. Children sat in it, and did not play. They made lean faces at her. They were locked in for the day, and were hungry. She could not help knowing how hungry they were, and so tipped the glass. Then there was the trap-door in the sidewalk. She became occasionally tired of that trap-door. Seven people lived under the sidewalk; and when they lifted and slammed the trap, coming in and out, they reminded her of something which Sary Jane bought her once, when she was a very little child, at Christmas time—long ago, when rents were cheaper and flour low. It was a monkey, with whiskers and a calico jacket, who jumped out of a box when the cover was lifted; and then you crushed him down and hasped him in. Sometimes she wished she had never had that monkey, he was so much like the people coming out of the sidewalk.

In fact, there was a monotony about all the people in the Lady of Shalott's looking-glass. If their faces were not dirty, their hands were. If they had hats they went without shoes. If they did not sit in the sun with their heads on their knees, they lay in the mud with their heads on a jug.

"Their faces look blue!" she said to Sary Jane.

"No wonder!" snapped Sary Jane.

"Why?" asked the Lady of Shalott.

"Wonder is we ain't all dead!" barked Sary Jane.

"But we ain't, you know," said the Lady of Shalott, after some thought.

The people in the Lady of Shalott's glass died, however,

sometimes—often in the summer; more often last summer, when the attic smoked continually, and she mistook Sary Jane's voice for the rat-trap every day.

The people were jostled into pine boxes (in the glass), and carried away (in the glass) by twilight, in a cart. Three of the monkeys from the spring-box in the sidewalk went, in one week, out into foul, purple twilight, away from the looking-glass, in carts.

"I'm glad of that, poor things!" said the Lady of Shalott, for she had always felt a kind of sorrow for the monkeys. Principally, I think, because they had no glass.

When the monkeys had gone, the sickly twilight folded itself up, over the spring-box, into great feathers, like the feathers of a wing. That was pleasant. The Lady of Shalott could almost put out her fingers and stroke it, it hung so near, and was so clear, and brought such a peacefulness into the looking glass.

"Sary Jane, dear, it's very pleasant," said the Lady of Shalott. Sary Jane said, it was very dangerous, the Lord knew, and bit her threads off.

"And Sary Jane, dear!" added the Lady of Shalott, "I see so many other pleasant things."

"The more fool you!" said Sary Jane.

But she wondered about it that day over her tenth nankeen vest. What, for example, *could* the Lady of Shalott see?

"Waves!" said the Lady of Shalott, suddenly, as if she had been asked the question. Sary Jane jumped. She said, "Nonsense!" For the Lady of Shalott had only seen the little wash-tub full of dingy water on Sunday nights, and the dirty little hydrant (in the glass) spouting dingy jets. She would not have known a wave if she had seen it.

"But I see waves," said the Lady of Shalott. She felt sure of it. They ran up and down across the glass. They had green faces and gray hair. They threw back their hands, like cool people resting, and it seemed unaccountable, at the east end of South Street last summer, that anything, anywhere, if only a wave in a looking-glass, could be cool or at rest. Besides this, they kept their faces clean. Therefore the Lady of Shalott took pleasure in watching them run up and down across the glass. That a thing could be clean, and green, and white, was only less a wonder than cool and rest last summer in South Street.

"Sary Jane, dear," said the Lady of Shalott, one day, "how hot *is* it up here?"

"Hot as Hell!" said Sary Jane.

"I thought it was a little warm," said the Lady of Shalott. "Sary Jane, dear? Isn't the yard down there a little—dirty?"

Sary Jane put down her needles and looked out of the blazing, blindless window. It had always been a subject of satisfaction, to Sary Jane somewhere down below her lean shoulders and in the very teeth of the rat-trap, that the Lady of Shalott could not see out of that window. So she winked at the window, as if she would caution it to hold its burning tongue, and said never a word.

"Sary Jane, dear," said the Lady of Shalott, once more, "had you ever thought that perhaps I was a little—weaker—than I was—once?"

"I guess you can stand it if I can!" said the rat-trap.

"Oh, yes, dear," said the Lady of Shalott. "I can stand it if you can."

"Well, then!" said Sary Jane. But she sat and winked at the bald window, and the window held its burning tongue.

It grew hot in South Street. It grew very hot in South Street. The lean children, in the attic opposite, fell sick, and sat no longer in the window making faces, in the Lady of Shalott's glass.

Two more monkeys from the spring-box were carried away one ugly twilight in a cart. The purple wing that hung over the spring-box lifted to let them pass; and then fell, as if it had brushed them away.

"It has such a soft color!" said the Lady of Shalott, smiling.

"So has nightshade!" said Sary Jane.

One day a beautiful thing happened. One could scarcely understand how a beautiful thing *could* happen at the east end of South
Street. The Lady of Shalott herself did not entirely understand.

"It is all the glass," she said.

She was lying very still when she said it. She had folded her
hands, which were hot, to keep them quiet, too. She had closed her
eyes, which ached, to close away the glare of the noon. At once she
opened them, and said:—

"It is the glass."

Sary Jane stood in the glass. Now Sary Jane, she well knew, was
not in the room that noon. She had gone out to see what she
could find for dinner. She had five cents to spend on dinner. Yet
Sary Jane stood in the glass. And in the glass, ah! what a beautiful
thing!

"Flowers!" cried the Lady of Shalott aloud. But she had never
seen flowers. But neither had she seen waves. So she said, "They
come as the waves come;" and knew them, and lay smiling. Ah!
what a beautiful, beautiful thing!

Sary Jane's hair was fiery and tumbled (in the glass), as if she
had walked fast and far. Sary Jane (in the glass) was winking, as she
had winked at the blazing window; as if she said to what she held
in her arms, Don't tell! And in her arms (in the glass), where the
waves were—oh! beautiful, beautiful! The Lady of Shalott lay
whispering: "Beautiful, beautiful!" She did not know what else to
do. She dared not stir. Sary Jane's lean arms (in the glass) were full
of silver bells; they hung out of a soft green shadow, like a church
tower; they nodded to and fro: when they shook, they shook out
sweetness.

"Will they ring?" asked the Lady of Shalott of the little glass.

I doubt, in my own mind, if you or I, being in South Street, and seeing a lily of the valley (in a ten by six inch looking-glass) for the very first time, would have asked so sensible a question.

"Try 'em and see," said the looking-glass. Was it the looking-glass? Or the rat-trap? Or was it—

Oh, the beautiful thing! That the glass should have nothing to do with it, after all! That Sary Jane, in flesh and blood, and tumbled hair, and trembling, lean arms, should stand and shake an armful of church towers and silver bells down into the Lady of Shalott's little puzzled face and burning hands!

And that the Lady of Shalott should think that she must have got into the glass herself, by a blunder—as the only explanation possible of such a beautiful thing!

"No, it isn't glass-dreams," said Sary Jane, winking at the church towers, where they made a solemn green shadow against the Lady of Shalott's poor cheek. "Smell 'em, and see! You can 'most stand the yard with them round. Smell 'em and see! It ain't the glass; it's the Flower Charity."

"The what?" asked the Lady of Shalott, slowly.

"The Flower Charity. Heaven bless it!"

"Heaven bless it!" said the Lady of Shalott. But she said nothing more.

She laid her cheek over into the shadow of the leaves. "And there'll be more," said Sary Jane, hunting for her wax. "There'll be more, whenever I can call for 'em—bless it!"

"Heaven bless it!" said the Lady of Shalott again.

"But I only got a lemon for dinner," said Sary Jane.

"Heaven bless it!" said the Lady of Shalott, with her face hidden under the leaves. But I don't think that she meant the lemon, though Sary Jane did.

"They *do* ring," said the Lady of Shalott, by and by. She drew the tip of her thin fingers across the tip of the tiny bells. "I thought they would."

"Humph!" said Sary Jane, squeezing her lemon under her work-box. "I never see your beat for glass-dreams. What do they say? Come, now!"

Now the Lady of Shalott knew very well what they said. Very well! But she only drew the tips of her poor fingers over the tips of the silver bells. Never mind! It was not necessary to tell Sary Jane.

But it grew hot in South Street. It grew very hot in South Street. Even the Flower Charity (bless it!) could not sweeten the dreadfulness of that yard. Even the purple wing above the spring-box fell heavily upon the Lady of Shalott's strained eyes, across the glass. Even the gray-haired waves ceased running up and down and throwing back their hands before her; they sat still, in heaps upon a blistering beach, and gasped for breath. The Lady of Shalott herself gasped sometimes, in watching them.

One day she said: "There's a man in them."

"A *what* in *which?*" buzzed Sary Jane. "Oh! There's a man across the yard, I suppose you mean. Among them young ones, yonder. I wish he'd stop 'em throwing stones, plague on 'em! See him, don't you?"

"I don't see the children," said the Lady of Shalott, a little troubled. Her glass had shown her so many things strangely since the days grew hot. "But I see a man, and he walks upon the waves. See, see!"

The Lady of Shalott tried to pull herself up on the elbow of her calico night-dress, to see.

"That's one of them Hospital doctors," said Sary Jane, looking out of the blazing window. "I've seen him round before. Don't know what business he's got down here; but I've seen him. He's talking to them boys now, about the stones. There! He'd better! If they don't look out, they'll hit"—

"Oh the glass! the glass!"

The Hospital Doctor stood still; so did Sary Jane, half risen from her chair; so did the very South Street boys, gaping in the gutter, with their hands full of stones—such a cry rang out from the palace window.

"Oh, the glass! the glass! the glass!"

In a twinkling the South Street boys were at the mercy of the South Street police; and the Hospital Doctor, bounding over a beachful of shattered, scattered waves, stood, out of breath, beside the Lady of Shalott's bed.

"Oh the little less and what worlds away."

The Lady of Shalott lay quite still in her brown calico night-gown [I cannot learn, by the way, that Bulfinch's studious and in general trustworthy researches have put him in possession of this point. Indeed, I feel justified in asserting that Mr. Bulfinch never so much as *intimated* that the Lady of Shalott wore a brown calico night-dress]—the Lady of Shalott lay quite still, and her lips turned blue.

"Are you very much hurt? Where were you struck? I heard the cry, and came. Can you tell me where the blow was?"

But then the Doctor saw the glass, broken and blown in a thousand glittering sparks across the palace floor: and then the Lady of Shalott gave him a little blue smile.

"It's not me. Never mind, I wish it was. I'd rather it was me than the glass. Oh, my glass! My glass! But never mind. I suppose there'll be some other—pleasant thing."

"Were you so fond of the glass?" asked the Doctor, taking one of the two chairs that Sary Jane brought him, and looking sorrow-fully about the room. What other "pleasant thing" could even the Lady of Shalott discover in that room last summer, at the east end of South Street?

"How long have you lain here?" asked the sorrowful Doctor, suddenly.

"Since I can remember, sir," said the Lady of Shalott, with that blue smile. "But then I have always had my glass."

"Ah!" said the Doctor, "the Lady of Shalott!"

"Sir?" said the Lady of Shalott.

"Where is the pain?" asked the Doctor, gently, with his finger on the Lady of Shalott's pulse.

The Lady of Shalott touched the shoulders of her brown calico night-dress, smiling.

"And what did you see in your glass?" asked the Doctor, once more, stooping to examine "the pain."

The Lady of Shalott tried to tell him, but felt confused. So she only said that there were waves and a purple wing, and that they were broken now, and lay upon the floor.

"Purple wings?" asked the Doctor.

"Over the sidewalk," nodded the Lady of Shalott. "It comes up at night."

"Oh!" said the Doctor, "the malaria. No wonder!"

"And what about the waves?" asked the Doctor, talking while he touched and tried the little brown calico shoulders. "I have a little girl of my own down by the waves this summer. She—I suppose she is no older than you!"

"I am seventeen, sir," said the Lady of Shalott. "Do they have green faces and white hair? Does she see them run up and down? I never saw any waves, sir, but those in my glass. I am very glad to know your little girl is by the waves."

"Where *you* ought to be," said the Doctor, half under his breath. "It is cruel, cruel!"

"What is cruel?" asked the Lady of Shalott, looking up into the Doctor's face.

The little brown calico night-dress swam suddenly before the Doctor's eyes. He got up and walked across the room. As he walked he stepped upon the pieces of the broken glass.

"Oh, don't!" cried the Lady of Shalott. But then she thought that perhaps she had hurt the Doctor's feelings; so she smiled, and said, "Never mind."

"Her case could be cured," said the Doctor, still under his breath, to Sary Jane. "The case could be cured yet. It is cruel!"

"Sir," said Sary Jane—she lifted her sharp face sharply out of billows of nankeen vests—"it may be because I make vests at six-teen and three-quarter cents a dozen, sir: but I say before God there's *something* cruel *somewhere*. Look at her. Look at me. Look at them stairs. Just see that scuttle, will you? Just feel the sun in t' these windows. Look at the rent we pay for this 'ere oven. What do you s'pose the merkiry is up here? Look at them pisen fogs arisin' out over the sidewalk. Look at the dead as have died in the Devil in this street this week. Then look out here!"

Sary Jane drew the Doctor to the blazing, blindless window, out of which the Lady of Shalott had never looked.

"Now talk of curin' *her!*" said Sary Jane.

The Doctor turned away from the window, with a sudden white face.

"The Board of Health"—

"Don't talk to *me* about the Board of Health!" said Sary Jane.

"I'll talk to *them,*" said the Doctor. "I did not know matters were so bad. They shall be attended to directly. To-morrow I leave town"—He stopped, looking down at the Lady of Shalott, think-ing of the little lady by the waves, whom he would see to-morrow, hardly knowing what to say. "But something shall be done at once. Meantime, there's the Hospital."

"She tried Horspital long ago," said Sary Jane. "They said they couldn't do nothing. What's the use? Don't bother her. Let her be."

"Yes, let me be," said the Lady of Shalott, faintly. "The glass is broken."

"But something must be done!" urged the Doctor, hurrying away. "I will attend to the matter directly, directly."

He spoke in a busy doctor's busy way. Undoubtedly he thought that he should attend to the matter directly.

"You have flowers here, I see." He lifted, in hurrying away, a spray of lilies that lay upon the bed, freshly sent to the Lady of Shalott that morning.

"They ring," said the Lady of Shalott, softly. "Can you hear? '*Bless*—it! *Bless*—it!' Ah, yes, they ring!"

"Bless what?" asked the Doctor, half out of the door.

"The Flower Charity," said the Lady of Shalott.

"*Amen!*" said the Doctor. "But I'll attend to it directly." And he was quite out of the door, and the door was shut.

"Sary Jane, dear?" said the Lady of Shalott, a few minutes after.

"Well!" said Sary Jane.

"The glass is broken," said the Lady of Shalott.

"Should think I might know that!" said Sary Jane, who was down upon her knees sweeping shining pieces away into a pasteboard dust-pan.

"Sary Jane, dear?" said the Lady of Shalott again.

"Dear, dear!" echoed Sary Jane, tossing purple feathers out of the window and seeming, to the eyes of the Lady of Shalott, to have the spray of green waves upon her hands. "There they go!"

"Yes, there they go," said the Lady of Shalott. But she said no more till night.

It was a hot night for South Street. It was a very hot night for even South Street. The lean children in the attic opposite cried savagely, like lean cubs. The monkeys from the spring-box came out and sat upon the lid for air. Dirty people lay around the dirty hydrant; and the purple wing stretched itself a little in a quiet way to cover them.

"Sary Jane, dear?" said the Lady of Shalott, at night. "The glass is broken. And, Sary Jane, dear, I am afraid I *can't* stand it as well as you can."

Sary Jane gave the Lady of Shalott a sharp look, and put away her nankeen vests. She came to the bed.

"It isn't time to stop sewing, is it?" asked the Lady of Shalott, in faint surprise. Sary Jane only said:—

"Nonsense! That man will be back again yet. He'll look after ye, maybe. Nonsense!"

"Yes," said the Lady of Shalott, "he will come back again. But my glass is broken."

"Nonsense!" said Sary Jane. But she did not go back to her sewing. She sat down on the edge of the bed, by the Lady of Shalott; and it grew dark.

"Perhaps they'll do something about the yards; who knows?" said Sary Jane.

"But my glass is broken," said the Lady of Shalott.

"Sary Jane, dear!" said the Lady of Shalott. "He is walking on the waves."

"Nonsense!" said Sary Jane. For it was quite, quite dark.

"Sary Jane, dear!" said the Lady of Shalott. "Not that man. But there *is* a Man, and he is walking on the waves."

The Lady of Shalott raised herself upon her calico night-dress sleeve. She looked at the wall where the ten by six inch looking-glass had hung.

"Sary Jane, dear!" said the Lady of Shalott. "I am glad that girl is down by the waves. I am very glad. But the glass is broken."

Two days after, the Board of Health at the foot of the precipice which the lessor called a flight of stairs, the one that led into the Lady of Shalott's palace, were met and stopped by another board.

"*This* one's got the right of way, gentlemen!" said something at the brink of the precipice, which sounded so much like a rat-trap that the Board of Health looked down by instinct at its individual and collective feet, to see if they were in danger, and dared not by instinct stir a step.

The board which had the right of way was a pine board, and

the Lady of Shalott lay on it, in her brown calico night-dress, with Sary Jane's old shawl across her feet. The Flower Charity (Heaven bless it!) had half-covered the old shawl with silver bells, and solemn green shadows, like the shadows of church towers. And it was a comfort to Sary Jane to know that these were the only bells which tolled for the Lady of Shalott, and that no other church shadow fell upon her burial.

"Gentlemen," said the Hospital Doctor, "we're too late, I see. But you'd better go on."

The gentlemen of the Board of Health went on; and the Lady of Shalott went on.

The Lady of Shalott went out into the cart that had carried away the monkeys from the spring-box, and the purple wing lifted to let her pass; then fell again, as if it had brushed her away.

The Board of Health went up the precipice, and stood by the window out of which the Lady of Shalott had never looked.

They sent orders to the scavenger, and orders to the Water Board, and how many other orders nobody knows; and they sprinkled themselves with camphor, and they went their ways.

And the board that had the Right of Way went its way, too. And Sary Jane folded up the shawl, which she could not afford to lose, and came home, and made nankeen vests at sixteen and three-quarter cents a dozen in the window out of which the Lady of Shalott had never looked.

The Tell-Tale Heart

Edgar Allan Poe

(1809–1849)

True!—nervous—very, very dreadfully nervous I had been and am; but why *will* you say that I am mad? The disease had sharpened my senses—not destroyed—not dulled them. Above all was the sense of hearing acute. I heard all things in the heaven and in the earth. I heard many things in hell. How, then, am I mad? Hearken! and observe how healthily—how calmly I can tell you the whole story.

It is impossible to say how first the idea entered my brain; but once conceived, it haunted me day and night. Object there was none. Passion there was none. I loved the old man. He had never wronged me. He had never given me insult. For his gold I had no desire. I think it was his eye! yes, it was this! One of his eyes resembled that of a vulture—a pale blue eye, with a film over it. Whenever it fell upon me, my blood ran cold; and so by degrees—very gradually—I made up my mind to take the life of the old man, and thus rid myself of the eye for ever.

Now this is the point. You fancy me mad. Madmen know nothing. But you should have seen *me*. You should have seen how wisely I proceeded—with what caution—with what foresight—with what dissimulation I went to work! I was never kinder to the old man than during the whole week before I killed him. And every night, about midnight, I turned the latch of his door and opened it—oh, so gently! And then, when I had made an opening sufficient for my head, I put in a dark lantern, all closed, closed, so that no light shone out, and then I thrust in my head. Oh, you would have laughed to see how cunningly I thrust it in! I moved it slowly—very, very slowly, so that I might not disturb the old man's sleep. It took me an hour to place my whole head within the opening so far that I could see him as he lay upon his bed. Ha!—would a madman have been so wise as this? And then, when my head was well in the room, I undid the lantern cautiously—oh, so cautiously—cautiously (for the hinges creaked)—I undid it just so much that a single ray fell upon the vulture eye. And this I did for seven long nights—every night just at midnight—but I found the eye closed; and so it was impossible to do the work; for it was not the old man who vexed me, but his Evil Eye. And every morning, when the day broke, I went boldly into the chamber, and spoke courageously to him, calling him by name in a hearty tone, and inquiring how he had passed the night. So you see he would have been a very profound old man, indeed, to suspect that every night, just at twelve, I looked in upon him while he slept.

Upon the eighth night I was more than usually cautious in opening the door. A watch's minute hand moves more quickly than did mine. Never before that night had I *felt* the extent of my own powers—of my sagacity. I could scarcely contain my feelings of triumph. To think that there I was, opening the door, little by little, and he not even to dream of my secret deeds or thoughts. I fairly chuckled at the idea; and perhaps he heard me; for he moved on the bed suddenly, as if startled. Now you may think that I drew back—but no. His room was as black as pitch with the thick darkness (for the shutters were close fastened, through fear of robbers), and so I knew that he could not see the opening of the door, and I kept pushing it on steadily, steadily.

I had my head in, and was about to open the lantern, when my thumb slipped on the tin fastening, and the old man sprang up in the bed, crying out—"Who's there?"

I kept quite still and said nothing. For a whole hour I did not move a muscle, and in the meantime I did not hear him lie down. He was still sitting up in the bed listening;—just as I have done, night after night, hearkening to the death watches in the wall.

Presently I heard a slight groan, and I knew it was the groan of mortal terror. It was not a groan of pain or of grief—oh, no!— it was the low stifled sound that arises from the bottom of the soul when overcharged with awe. I knew the sound well. Many a night, just at midnight, when all the world slept, it has welled up from my own bosom, deepening, with its dreadful echo, the terrors that distracted me. I say I knew it well. I knew what the old man felt, and pitied him, although I chuckled at heart. I knew that he had been lying awake ever since the first slight noise, when he had turned in bed. His fears had been ever since growing upon him. He had been trying to fancy them causeless, but could not. He had been saying to himself—"It is nothing but the wind in the chimney— it is only a mouse crossing the floor," or "it is merely a cricket which has made a single chirp." Yes, he had been trying to comfort himself with these suppositions; but he had found all in vain. *All in vain;* because Death, in approaching him, had stalked with his black shadow before him, and enveloped the victim. And it was the mournful influence of the unperceived shadow that caused him to feel—although he neither saw nor heard—to *feel* the presence of my head within the room.

When I had waited a long time, very patiently, without hearing him lie down, I resolved to open a little—a very, very little crevice in the lantern. So I opened it—you cannot imagine how stealthily, stealthily—until, at length, a single dim ray, like the thread of the spider, shot from out the crevice and full upon the vulture eye.

It was open—wide, wide open—and I grew furious as I gazed upon it. I saw it with perfect distinctness—all a dull blue, with a hideous veil over it that chilled the very marrow in my bones; but I could see nothing else of the old man's face or person: for I had directed the ray as if by instinct, precisely upon the damned spot.

And now have I not told you that what you mistake for madness is but over-acuteness of the senses?—now, I say, there came to my ears a low, dull, quick sound, such as a watch makes when enveloped in cotton. I knew *that* sound well too. It was the beating of the old man's heart. It increased my fury, as the beating of a drum stimulates the soldier into courage.

But even yet I refrained and kept still. I scarcely breathed. I held the lantern motionless. I tried how steadily I could maintain the ray upon the eye. Meantime the hellish tattoo of the heart increased. It grew quicker and quicker, and louder and louder every instant. The old man's terror *must* have been extreme! It grew louder, I say, louder every moment!—do you mark me well? I have told you that I am nervous: so I am. And now at the dead hour of the night, amid the dreadful silence of that old house, so strange a noise as this excited me to uncontrollable terror. Yet, for some minutes longer I refrained and stood still. But the beating grew louder, louder! I thought the heart must burst. And now a new anxiety seized me—the sound would be heard by a neighbor! The old man's hour had come! With a loud yell, I threw open the lantern and leaped into the room. He shrieked once—once only. In an instant I dragged him to the floor, and pulled the heavy bed over him. I then smiled gaily, to find the deed so far done. But, for many minutes, the heart beat on with a muffled sound. This, however, did not vex me; it would not be heard through the wall. At length it ceased. The old man was dead. I removed the bed and examined the corpse. Yes, he was stone, stone dead. I placed my hand upon the heart and held it there many minutes. There was no pulsation. He was stone dead. His eye would trouble me no more.

If still you think me mad, you will think so no longer when I describe the wise precautions I took for the concealment of the body. The night waned, and I worked hastily, but in silence. First of all I dismembered the corpse. I cut off the head and the arms and the legs.

I then took up three planks from the flooring of the chamber, and deposited all between the scantlings. I then replaced the boards so cleverly, so cunningly, that no human eye—not even *his*—could have detected any thing wrong. There was nothing to wash out—no stain of any kind—no blood-spot whatever. I had been too wary for that. A tub had caught all—ha! ha!

When I had made an end of these labors, it was four o'clock—still dark as midnight. As the bell sounded the hour, there came a knocking at the street door. I went down to open it with a light heart—for what had I *now* to fear? There entered three men, who introduced themselves, with perfect suavity, as officers of the police. A shriek had been heard by a neighbor during the night; suspicion of foul play had been aroused; information had been lodged at the police office, and they (the officers) had been deputed to search the premises.

I smiled—for *what* had I to fear? I bade the gentlemen welcome. The shriek, I said, was my own in a dream. The old man, I mentioned, was absent in the country. I took my visitors all over the house. I bade them search—search *well*. I led them, at length, to *his* chamber. I showed them his treasures, secure, undisturbed. In the enthusiasm of my confidence, I brought chairs into the room, and desired them *here* to rest from their fatigues, while I myself, in the wild audacity of my perfect triumph, placed my own seat upon the very spot beneath which reposed the corpse of the victim.

The officers were satisfied. My *manner* had convinced them. I was singularly at ease. They sat, and while I answered cheerily, they chatted familiar things. But, ere long, I felt myself getting pale and wished them gone. My head ached, and I fancied a ringing in my ears: but still they sat and still chatted. The ringing became more distinct:—it continued and became more distinct: I talked more freely to get rid of the feeling: but it continued and gained definitiveness—until, at length, I found that the noise was *not* within my ears.

No doubt I now grew *very* pale;—but I talked more fluently, and with a heightened voice. Yet the sound increased—and what could I do? It was *a low, dull, quick sound—much such a sound as a watch makes when enveloped in cotton.* I gasped for breath—and yet the officers heard it not. I talked more quickly—more vehemently; but the noise steadily increased. I arose and argued about trifles, in a high key and with violent gesticulations, but the noise steadily increased. Why *would* they not be gone? I paced the floor to and fro with heavy strides, as if excited to fury by the observation of the men—but the noise steadily increased. Oh God! what *could* I do? I foamed—I raved—I swore! I swung the chair upon which I had been sitting, and grated it upon the boards, but the noise arose over all and continually increased. It grew louder—louder—*louder!* And still the men chatted pleasantly, and smiled. Was it possible they heard not? Almighty God!—no, no! They heard!—they suspected!—they *knew!*—they were making a mockery of my horror!—this I thought, and this I think. But any thing was better than this agony! Any thing was more tolerable than this derision!

I could bear those hypocritical smiles no longer! I felt that I must scream or die!—and now—again!—hark! louder! louder! louder! *louder!*—

"Villains!" I shrieked, "dissemble no more! I admit the deed!— tear up the planks!—here, here!—it is the beating of his hideous heart!"

The Lady, or the Tiger?

Frank R. Stockton

(1834–1902)

In the very olden time there lived a semibarbaric king, whose
ideas, though somewhat polished and sharpened by the pro-
gressiveness of distant Latin neighbors, were still large, florid,
and untrammelled, as became the half of him which was barbaric.
He was a man of exuberant fancy, and, withal, of an authority so
irresistible that, at his will, he turned his varied fancies into facts.
He was greatly given to self-communing; and when he and himself agreed upon anything, the thing was done. When every member of his domestic and political systems moved smoothly in its
appointed course, his nature was bland and genial; but whenever
there was a little hitch, and some of his orbs got out of their or-
bits, he was blander and more genial still, for nothing pleased him
so much as to make the crooked straight, and crush down uneven
places.

Among the borrowed notions by which his barbarism had become semified was that of the public arena, in which, by exhibi-
tions of manly and beastly valor, the minds of his subjects were
refined and cultured.

But even here the exuberant and barbaric fancy asserted itself. The arena of the king was built not to give the people an opportunity of hearing the rhapsodies of dying gladiators, nor to enable them to view the inevitable conclusion of a conflict between religious opinions and hungry jaws, but for purposes far better adapted to widen and develop the mental energies of the people. This vast amphitheatre, with its encircling galleries, its mysterious vaults, and its unseen passages, was an agent of poetic justice, in which crime was punished, or virtue rewarded, by the decrees of an impartial and incorruptible chance.

When a subject was accused of a crime of sufficient importance to interest the king, public notice was given that on an appointed day the fate of the accused person would be decided in the king's arena—a structure which well deserved its name; for, although its form and plan were borrowed from afar, its purpose emanated solely from the brain of this man, who, every barleycorn a king, knew no tradition to which he owed more allegiance than pleased his fancy, and who ingrafted on every adopted form of human thought and action the rich growth of his barbaric idealism.

When all the people had assembled in the galleries, and the king, surrounded by his court, sat high up on his throne of royal state on one side of the arena, he gave a signal, a door beneath him opened, and the accused subject stepped out into the amphitheatre. Directly opposite him, on the other side of the enclosed space, were two doors, exactly alike and side by side. It was the duty and the privilege of the person on trial to walk directly to these doors and open one of them. He could open either door he pleased: he was subject to no guidance or influence but that of the aforementioned impartial and incorruptible chance. If he opened the one, there came out of it a hungry tiger, the fiercest and most cruel that could be procured, which immediately sprang upon him and tore him to pieces, as a punishment for his guilt. The moment that the case of the criminal was thus decided, doleful iron bells were clanged, great wails went up from the hired mourners posted on the outer rim of the arena, and the vast audience, with bowed heads and downcast hearts, wended slowly their homeward way, mourning greatly that one so young and fair, or so old and respected, should have merited so dire a fate.

But if the accused person opened the other door, there came forth from it a lady, the most suitable to his years and station that his majesty could select among his fair subjects; and to this lady he was immediately married, as a reward of his innocence. It mattered not that he might already possess a wife and family, or that his affections might be engaged upon an object of his own selection: the king allowed no such subordinate arrangements to interfere with his great scheme of retribution and reward. The exercises, as in the other instance, took place immediately, and in the arena. Another door opened beneath the king, and a priest, followed by a band of choristers, and dancing maidens blowing joyous airs on golden horns and treading an epithalamic measure, advanced to where the pair stood side by side; and the wedding was promptly and cheerily solemnized. Then the gay brass bells rang forth their merry peals, the people shouted glad hurrahs, and the innocent man, preceded by children strewing flowers on his path, led his bride to his home.

This was the king's semibarbaric method of administering justice. Its perfect fairness is obvious. The criminal could not know out of which door would come the lady: he opened either he pleased, without having the slightest idea whether, in the next instant, he was to be devoured or married. On some occasions the tiger came out of one door, and on some out of the other. The decisions of this tribunal were not only fair, they were positively determinate: the accused person was instantly punished if he found himself guilty; and if innocent, he was rewarded on the spot, whether he liked it or not. There was no escape from the judgments of the king's arena.

The institution was a very popular one. When the people gathered together on one of the great trial-days, they never knew whether they were to witness a bloody slaughter or a hilarious wedding. This element of uncertainty lent an interest to the occasion which it could not otherwise have attained. Thus the masses were entertained and pleased, and the thinking part of the community could bring no charge of unfairness against this plan; for did not the accused person have the whole matter in his own hands?

This semibarbaric king had a daughter as blooming as his most florid fancies, and with a soul as fervent and imperious as his own. As is usual in such cases, she was the apple of his eye, and was loved by him above all humanity. Among his courtiers was a young man of that fineness of blood and lowness of station common to the conventional heroes of romance who love royal maidens. This royal maiden was well satisfied with her lover, for he was handsome and brave to a degree unsurpassed in all this kingdom; and she loved him with an ardor that had enough of barbarism in it to make it exceedingly warm and strong. This love-affair moved on happily for many months, until one day the king happened to discover its existence. He did not hesitate nor waver in regard to his duty in the premises. The youth was immediately cast into prison, and a day was appointed for his trial in the king's arena. This, of course, was an especially important occasion; and his Majesty, as well as all the people, was greatly interested in the workings and development of this trial. Never before had such a case occurred; never before had a subject dared to love the daughter of a king. In after-years such things became commonplace enough; but then they were, in no slight degree, novel and startling.

The tiger-cages of the kingdom were searched for the most

savage and relentless beasts, from which the fiercest monster might
be selected for the arena; and the ranks of maiden youth and
beauty throughout the land were carefully surveyed by competent
judges, in order that the young man might have a fitting bride in
case fate did not determine for him a different destiny. Of course
everybody knew that the deed with which the accused was
charged had been done. He had loved the princess, and neither he,
she, nor any one else thought of denying the fact; but the king
would not think of allowing any fact of this kind to interfere with
the workings of the tribunal, in which he took such great delight
and satisfaction. No matter how the affair turned out, the youth
would be disposed of; and the king would take an æsthetic pleasure in watching the course of events, which would determine
whether or not the young man had done wrong in allowing himself to love the princess.

The appointed day arrived. From far and near the people gathered, and thronged the great galleries of the arena; and crowds, unable to gain admittance, massed themselves against its outside walls.
The king and his court were in their places, opposite the twin
doors—those fateful portals, so terrible in their similarity.

All was ready. The signal was given. A door beneath the royal
party opened, and the lover of the princess walked into the arena.
Tall, beautiful, fair, his appearance was greeted with a low hum of
admiration and anxiety. Half the audience had not known so grand
a youth had lived among them. No wonder the princess loved
him! What a terrible thing for him to be there!

As the youth advanced into the arena, he turned, as the custom was, to bow to the king: but he did not think at all of that
royal personage; his eyes were fixed upon the princess, who sat to
the right of her father. Had it not been for the moiety of barbarism
in her nature it is probable that lady would not have been there;
but her intense and fervid soul would not allow her to be absent

on an occasion in which she was so terribly interested. From the moment that the decree had gone forth that her lover should decide his fate in the king's arena, she had thought of nothing, night or day, but this great event and the various subjects connected with it. Possessed of more power, influence, and force of character than any one who had ever before been interested in such a case, she had done what no other person had done—she had possessed herself of the secret of the doors. She knew in which of the two rooms that lay behind those doors stood the cage of the tiger, with its open front, and in which waited the lady. Through these thick doors, heavily curtained with skins on the inside, it was impossible that any noise or suggestion should come from within to the person who should approach to raise the latch of one of them; but gold, and the power of a woman's will, had brought the secret to the princess.

And not only did she know in which room stood the lady ready to emerge, all blushing and radiant, should her door be opened, but she knew who the lady was. It was one of the fairest and loveliest of the damsels of the court who had been selected as the reward of the accused youth, should he be proved innocent of the crime of aspiring to one so far above him; and the princess hated her. Often had she seen, or imagined that she had seen, this fair creature throwing glances of admiration upon the person of her lover, and sometimes she thought these glances were perceived and even returned. Now and then she had seen them talking together; it was but for a moment or two, but much can be said in a brief space; it may have been on most unimportant topics, but how could she know that? The girl was lovely, but she had dared to raise her eyes to the loved one of the princess; and, with all the intensity of the savage blood transmitted to her through long lines of wholly barbaric ancestors, she hated the woman who blushed and trembled behind that silent door.

When her lover turned and looked at her, and his eye met hers as she sat there paler and whiter than any one in the vast ocean of anxious faces about her, he saw, by that power of quick perception which is given to those whose souls are one, that she knew behind which door crouched the tiger, and behind which stood the lady. He had expected her to know it. He understood her nature, and his soul was assured that she would never rest until she had made plain to herself this thing, hidden to all other lookers-on, even to the king. The only hope for the youth in which there was any element of certainty was based upon the success of the princess in discovering this mystery; and the moment he looked upon her, he saw she had succeeded, as in his soul he knew she would succeed.

Then it was that his quick and anxious glance asked the question, "Which?" It was as plain to her as if he shouted it from where he stood. There was not an instant to be lost. The question was asked in a flash; it must be answered in another.

Her right arm lay on the cushioned parapet before her. She raised her hand, and made a slight, quick movement toward the right. No one but her lover saw her. Every eye but his was fixed on the man in the arena.

He turned, and with a firm and rapid step he walked across the empty space. Every heart stopped beating, every breath was held, every eye was fixed immovably upon that man. Without the slightest hesitation, he went to the door on the right, and opened it.

Now, the point of the story is this: Did the tiger come out of that door, or did the lady?

The more we reflect upon this question the harder it is to answer. It involves a study of the human heart which leads us through devious mazes of passion, out of which it is difficult to find our way. Think of it, fair reader, not as if the decision of the question depended upon yourself, but upon that hot-blooded, semibarbaric princess, her soul at a white heat beneath the combined fires of despair and jealousy. She had lost him, but who should have him?

How often, in her waking hours and in her dreams, had she started in wild horror and covered her face with her hands as she thought of her lover opening the door on the other side of which waited the cruel fangs of the tiger!

But how much oftener had she seen him at the other door! How in her grievous reveries had she gnashed her teeth and torn her hair when she saw his start of rapturous delight as he opened the door of the lady! How her soul had burned in agony when she had seen him rush to meet that woman, with her flushing cheek and sparkling eye of triumph; when she had seen him lead her forth, his whole frame kindled with the joy of recovered life; when she had heard the glad shouts from the multitude, and the wild ringing of the happy bells; when she had seen the priest, with his joyous followers, advance to the couple, and make them man and wife before her very eyes; and when she had seen them walk away together upon their path of flowers, followed by the tremendous shouts of the hilarious multitude, in which her one despairing shriek was lost and drowned!

Would it not be better for him to die at once, and go to wait for her in the blessed regions of semibarbaric futurity?

And yet, that awful tiger, those shrieks, that blood!

Her decision had been indicated in an instant, but it had been made after days and nights of anguished deliberation. She had known she would be asked, she had decided what she would answer, and, without the slightest hesitation, she had moved her hand to the right.

The question of her decision is one not to be lightly considered, and it is not for me to presume to set myself up as the one person able to answer it. And so I leave it with all of you: Which came out of the opened door—the lady, or the tiger?

The Tea Rose

Harriet Beecher Stowe
(1811–1896)

There it stood, in its little green vase, on a light ebony stand, in the window of the drawing-room. The rich satin curtains, with their costly fringes, swept down on either side of it, and around it glittered every rare and fanciful trifle which wealth can offer to luxury; and yet that simple rose was the fairest of them all. So pure it looked, its white leaves just touched with that delicious creamy tint peculiar to its kind; its cup so full, so perfect; its head bending as if it were sinking and melting away in its own richness—Oh, when did ever man make anything to equal the living, perfect flower?

But the sunlight that streamed through the window revealed something fairer than the rose. Reclined on an ottoman, in a deep recess, and intently engaged with a book, rested what seemed the counterpart of that so lovely flower. That cheek so pale, that fair forehead so spiritual, that countenance so full of high thought, those long, downcast lashes, and the expression of the beautiful mouth, sorrowful, yet subdued and sweet—it seemed like the picture of a dream.

"Florence! Florence!" echoed a merry and musical voice, in a sweet, impatient tone. Turn your head, reader, and you will see a light and sparkling maiden, the very model of some little willful elf, born of mischief and motion, with a dancing eye, a foot that scarcely seems to touch the carpet, and a smile so multiplied by dimples that it seems like a thousand smiles at once. "Come, Florence, I say," said the little sprite, "put down that wise, good, and excellent volume, and descend from your cloud, and talk with a poor little mortal."

The fair apparition, thus adjured, obeyed; and, looking up, revealed just such eyes as you expected to see beneath such lids—eyes deep, pathetic, and rich as a strain of sad music.

"I say, cousin," said the "bright ladye," "I have been thinking what you are to do with your pet rose when you go to New York, as, to our consternation, you are determined to do; you know it would be a sad pity to leave it with such a scatterbrain as I am. I do love flowers, that is a fact; that is, I like a regular bouquet, cut off and tied up, to carry to a party; but as to all this tending and fussing, which is needful to keep them growing, I have no gifts in that line."

"Make yourself easy as to that, Kate," said Florence, with a smile; "I have no intention of calling upon your talents; I have an asylum in view for my favorite."

"Oh, then you know just what I was going to say. Mrs. Marshall, I presume, has been speaking to you; she was here yesterday, and I was quite pathetic upon the subject, telling her the loss your favorite would sustain, and so forth; and she said how delighted she would be to have it in her greenhouse, it is in such a fine state now, so full of buds. I told her I knew you would like to give it to her, you are so fond of Mrs. Marshall, you know."

"Now Kate, I am sorry, but I have otherwise engaged it."

"Whom can it be to? you have so few intimates here."

"Oh, it is only one of my odd fancies."

"But do tell me, Florence."

"Well, cousin, you know the little pale girl to whom we give sewing."

"What! little Mary Stephens? How absurd! Florence, this is just another of your motherly, old-maidish ways—dressing dolls for poor children, making bonnets and knitting socks for all the little dirty babies in the region round about. I do believe you have made more calls in those two vile, ill-smelling alleys back of our house, than ever you have in Chestnut Street, though you know everybody is half dying to see you; and now, to crown all, you must give this choice little bijou to a seamstress girl, when one of your most intimate friends, in your own class, would value it so highly. What in the world can people in their circumstances want of flowers?"

"Just the same as I do," replied Florence calmly. "Have you not noticed that the little girl never comes here without looking wistfully at the opening buds? And don't you remember, the other morning, she asked me so prettily if I would let her mother come and see it, she was so fond of flowers?"

"But, Florence, only think of this rare flower standing on a table with ham, eggs, cheese, and flour, and stifled in that close little room where Mrs. Stephens and her daughter manage to wash, iron, cook, and nobody knows what besides."

"Well, Kate, and if I were obliged to live in one coarse room, and wash, and iron, and cook, as you say—if I had to spend every moment of my time in toil, with no prospect from my window but a brick wall and dirty lane—such a flower as this would be untold enjoyment to me."

"Pshaw! Florence—all sentiment: poor people have no time to be sentimental. Besides, I don't believe it will grow with them; it is a greenhouse flower, and used to delicate living."

"Oh, as to that, a flower never inquires whether its owner is rich or poor; and Mrs. Stephens, whatever else she has not, has sunshine of as good quality as this that streams through our window. The beautiful things that God makes are his gift to all alike. You will see that my fair rose will be as well and cheerful in Mrs. Stephens's room as in ours."

"Well, after all, how odd! When one gives to poor people, one wants to give them something useful—a bushel of potatoes, a ham, and such things."

"Why, certainly, potatoes and ham must be supplied; but, having ministered to the first and most craving wants, why not add any other little pleasures or gratifications we may have it in our power to bestow? I know there are many of the poor who have fine feeling and a keen sense of the beautiful, which rusts out and dies because they are too hard pressed to procure it any gratification. Poor Mrs. Stephens, for example: I know she would enjoy birds, and flowers, and music as much as I do. I have seen her eye light up as she looked on these things in our drawing-room, and yet not one beautiful thing can she command. From necessity, her room, her clothing, all she has, must be coarse and plain. You should have seen the almost rapture she and Mary felt when I offered them my rose."

"Dear me! all this may be true, but I never thought of it before. I never thought that these hard-working people had any ideas of taste!"

"Then why do you see the geranium or rose so carefully nursed in the old cracked teapot in the poorest room, or the morning-glory planted in a box and twined about the window? Do not these show that the human heart yearns for the beautiful in all ranks of life? You remember, Kate, how our washerwoman sat up a whole night, after a hard day's work, to make her first baby a pretty dress to be baptized in."

"Yes, and I remember how I laughed at you for making such a tasteful little cap for it."

"Well, Katy, I think the look of perfect delight with which the poor mother regarded her baby in its new dress and cap was something quite worth creating: I do believe she could not have felt more grateful if I had sent her a barrel of flour."

"Well, I never thought before of giving anything to the poor but what they really needed, and I have always been willing to do that when I could without going far out of my way."

"Well, cousin, if our Heavenly Father gave to us after this mode, we should have only coarse, shapeless piles of provisions lying about the world, instead of all this beautiful variety of trees, and fruits, and flowers."

"Well, well, cousin, I suppose you are right—but have mercy on my poor head; it is too small to hold so many new ideas all at once—so go on your own way." And the little lady began practicing a waltzing step before the glass with great satisfaction.

It was a very small room, lighted by only one window. There was no carpet on the floor; there was a clean, but coarsely covered bed in one corner; a cupboard, with a few dishes and plates, in the other; a chest of drawers; and before the window stood a small cherry stand, quite new, and, indeed, it was the only article in the room that seemed so.

A pale, sickly-looking woman of about forty was leaning back in her rocking-chair, her eyes closed and her lips compressed as if in pain. She rocked backward and forward a few minutes, pressed her hand hard upon her eyes, and then languidly resumed her fine stitching, on which she had been busy since morning. The door opened, and a slender little girl of about twelve years of age entered, her large blue eyes dilated and radiant with delight as she bore in the vase with the rose-tree in it.

"Oh, see, mother, see! Here is one in full bloom, and two more half out, and ever so many more pretty buds peeping out of the green leaves."

The poor woman's face brightened as she looked, first on the rose and then on her sickly child, on whose face she had not seen so bright a color for months.

"God bless her!" she exclaimed unconsciously.

"Miss Florence—yes, I knew you would feel so, mother. Does it not make your head feel better to see such a beautiful flower? Now, you will not look so longingly at the flowers in the market, for we have a rose that is handsomer than any of them. Why, it seems to me it is worth as much to us as our whole little garden used to be. Only see how many buds there are! Just count them, and only smell the flower! Now, where shall we set it up?" And Mary skipped about, placing her flower first in one position and then in another, and walking off to see the effect, till her mother gently reminded her that the rose-tree could not preserve its beauty without sunlight.

"Oh yes, truly," said Mary; "well, then, it must stand here on our new stand. How glad I am that we have such a handsome new stand for it! it will look so much better." And Mrs. Stephens laid down her work, and folded a piece of newspaper, on which the treasure was duly deposited.

"There," said Mary, watching the arrangement eagerly, "that will do—no, for it does not show both the opening buds; a little farther around—a little more; there, that is right;" and then Mary walked around to view the rose in various positions, after which she urged her mother to go with her to the outside, and see how it looked there. "How kind it was in Miss Florence to think of giving this to us!" said Mary; "though she had done so much for us, and given us so many things, yet this seems the best of all, because it seems as if she thought of us, and knew just how we felt and so few do that, you know, mother."

What a bright afternoon that little gift made in that little room! How much faster Mary's fingers flew the livelong day as she sat sewing by her mother! and Mrs. Stephens, in the happiness of her child, almost forgot that she had a headache, and thought, as she sipped her evening cup of tea, that she felt stronger than she had for some time.

That rose! its sweet influence died not with the first day. Through all the long, cold winter, the watching, tending, cherishing that flower awakened a thousand pleasant trains of thought, that beguiled the sameness and weariness of their life. Every day the fair, growing thing put forth some fresh beauty—a leaf, a bud, a new shoot, and constantly awakened fresh enjoyment in its possessors. As it stood in the window, the passer-by would sometimes stop and gaze, attracted by its beauty, and then proud and happy was Mary; nor did even the serious and careworn widow notice with indifference this tribute to the beauty of their favorite.

But little did Florence think, when she bestowed the gift, that there twined about it an invisible thread that reached far and brightly into the web of her destiny.

One cold afternoon in early spring, a tall and graceful gentleman called at the lowly room to pay for the making of some linen by the inmates. He was a stranger and wayfarer recommended through the charity of some of Mrs. Stephens's patrons. As he turned to go, his eye rested admiringly on the rose-tree; and he stopped to gaze at it.

"How beautiful!" said he.

"Yes," said little Mary; "and it was given to us by a lady as sweet and beautiful as that is."

"Ah," said the stranger, turning upon her a pair of bright dark eyes, pleased and rather struck by the communication; "and how came she to give it to you, my little girl?"

"Oh, because we are poor and mother is sick, and we never

can have anything pretty. We used to have a garden once; and we loved flowers so much, and Miss Florence found it out, and so she gave us this."

"Florence!" echoed the stranger.

"Yes, Miss Florence l'Estrange—a beautiful lady. They say she was from foreign parts; but she speaks English just like other ladies, only sweeter."

"Is she here now? is she in this city?" said the gentleman eagerly.

"No; she left some months ago," said the widow, noticing the shade of disappointment on his face. "But," said she, "you can find out all about her at her aunt's, Mrs. Carlysle's, No 10 —— Street."

A short time after, Florence received a letter in a handwriting that made her tremble. During the many early years of her life spent in France she had well learned to know that writing—had loved as a woman like her loves only once; but there had been obstacles of parents and friends, long separation, long suspense, till, after anxious years, she had believed the ocean had closed over that hand and heart; and it was this that had touched with such pensive sorrow the lines in her lovely face.

But this letter told that he was living—that he had traced her, even as a hidden streamlet may be traced, by the freshness, the verdure of heart, which her deeds of kindness had left wherever she had passed. Thus much said, our readers need no help in finishing my story for themselves.

The Celebrated Jumping Frog of Calaveras County

Mark Twain

(1835–1910)

In compliance with the request of a friend of mine, who wrote me from the East, I called on good-natured, garrulous old Simon Wheeler, and inquired after my friend's friend, *Leonidas W.* Smiley, as requested to do, and I hereunto append the result. I have a lurking suspicion that *Leonidas W.* Smiley is a myth; that my friend never knew such a personage; and that he only conjectured that, if I asked old Wheeler about him, it would remind him of his infamous *Jim* Smiley, and he would go to work and bore me nearly to death with some infernal reminiscence of him as long and tedious as it should be useless to me. If that was the design, it certainly succeeded.

I found Simon Wheeler dozing comfortably by the bar-room stove of the old, dilapidated tavern in the ancient mining camp of Angel's, and I noticed that he was fat and bald-headed, and had an expression of winning gentleness and simplicity upon his tranquil countenance. He roused up and gave me good-day. I told him a friend of mine had commissioned me to make some inquiries about a cherished companion of his boyhood named *Leonidas W. Smiley*—*Rev. Leonidas W.* Smiley—a young minister of the Gospel, who he had heard was at one time a resident of Angel's Camp. I added that, if Mr. Wheeler could tell me any thing about this Rev. Leonidas W. Smiley, I would feel under many obligations to him.

Simon Wheeler backed me into a corner and blockaded me there with his chair, and then sat down and reeled off the monotonous narrative which follows this paragraph. He never smiled, he never frowned, he never changed his voice from the gentle-flowing key to which he tuned his initial sentence, he never betrayed the slightest suspicion of enthusiasm; but all through the interminable narrative there ran a vein of impressive earnestness and sincerity, which showed me plainly that, so far from his imagining that there was any thing ridiculous or funny about his story, he regarded it as a really important matter, and admired its two heroes as men of transcendent genius in *finesse*. To me, the spectacle of a man drifting serenely along through such a queer yarn without ever smiling, was exquisitely absurd. As I said before, I asked him to tell me what he knew of Rev. Leonidas W. Smiley, and he replied as follows. I let him go on in his own way, and never interrupted him once:

There was a feller here once by the name of *Jim* Smiley, in the winter of '49—or may be it was the spring of '50—I don't recollect exactly, somehow, though what makes me think it was one or the other is because I remember the big flume wasn't finished when he first came to the camp; but any way, he was the curiosest man about always betting on any thing that turned up you ever see, if he could get any body to bet on the other side; and if he couldn't, he'd change sides. Any way that suited the other man would suit him—any way just so's he got a bet, *he* was satisfied. But still he was lucky, uncommon lucky; he most always come out winner. He was always ready and laying for a chance; there couldn't be no solitry thing mentioned but that feller'd offer to bet on it, and take any side you please, as I was just telling you. If there was a horse-race, you'd find him flush, or you'd find him busted at the end of it; if there was a dog-fight, he'd bet on it; if there was a cat-fight, he'd bet on it; if there was a chicken-fight, he'd bet on it; why, if there was two birds setting on a fence, he would bet you which one would fly first; or if there was a camp-meeting, he would be there reg'lar, to bet on Parson Walker, which he judged to be the best exhorter about here, and so he was, too, and a good man. If he even seen a straddle-bug start to go anywheres, he would bet you how long it would take him to get wherever he was going to, and if you took him up, he would foller that straddle-bug to Mexico but what he would find out where he was bound for and how long he was on the road. Lots of the boys here has seen that Smiley, and can tell you about him. Why, it never made no difference to *him*—he'd bet on *any* thing—the dangdest feller. Parson Walker's wife laid very sick once, for a good while, and it seemed as if they warn't going to save her; but one morning he come in, and Smiley asked how she was, and he said she was considerable better—thank the Lord for his inf'nit mercy—and coming on so smart that, with the blessing of Prov'dence, she'd get well yet; and Smiley, before he thought, says, "Well, I'll risk two-and-a-half that she don't, any way."

Thish-yer Smiley had a mare—the boys called her the fifteen-minute nag, but that was only in fun, you know, because of course she was faster than that—and he used to win money on that horse, for all she was so slow and always had the asthma, or the distemper, or the consumption, or something of that kind. They used to give her two or three hundred yards start, and then pass her under way; but always at the fag-end of the race she'd get excited and desperate-like, and come cavorting and straddling up, and scattering her legs around limber, sometimes in the air, and sometimes out to one side amongst the fences, and kicking up m-o-r-e dust, and raising m-o-r-e racket with her coughing and sneezing and blowing her nose—and always fetch up at the stand just about a neck ahead, as near as you could cipher it down.

And he had a little small bull pup, that to look at him you'd think he wan't worth a cent, but to set around and look ornery, and lay for a chance to steal something. But as soon as money was up on him, he was a different dog; his under-jaw'd begin to stick out like the fo'castle of a steamboat, and his teeth would uncover, and shine savage like the furnaces. And a dog might tackle him, and bully-rag him, and bite him, and throw him over his shoulder two or three times, and Andrew Jackson—which was the name of the pup—Andrew Jackson would never let on but what *he* was satisfied, and hadn't expected nothing else—and the bets being doubled and doubled on the other side all the time, till the money was all up; and then all of a sudden he would grab that other dog just by the j'int of his hind leg and freeze to it—not chaw, you understand, but only just grip and hang on till they throwed up the sponge, if it was a year. Smiley always come out winner on that pup, till he harnessed a dog once that didn't have no hind legs, because they'd been sawed off by a circular saw, and when the thing had gone along far enough, and the money was all up, and he come to make a snatch for his pet holt, he saw in a minute how he'd been imposed on, and how the other dog had him in the door, so to speak, and he 'peared surprised, and then he looked sorter discouraged-like, and didn't try no more to win the fight, and so he got shucked out bad. He give Smiley a look, as much as to say his heart was broke, and it was *his* fault, for putting up a dog that hadn't no hind legs for him to take holt of, which was his main dependence in a fight, and then he limped off a piece and laid down and died. It was a good pup, was that Andrew Jackson,

and would have made a name for hisself if he'd lived, for the stuff
was in him, and he had genius—I know it, because he hadn't had
no opportunities to speak of, and it don't stand to reason that a dog
could make such a fight as he could under them circumstances, if
he hadn't no talent. It always makes me feel sorry when I think of
that last fight of his'n, and the way it turned out.

Well, thish-yer Smiley had rat-tarriers, and chicken cocks, and
tom-cats, and all them kind of things, till you couldn't rest, and you
couldn't fetch nothing for him to bet on but he'd match you. He
ketched a frog one day, and took him home, and said he cal'klated
to edercate him; and so he never done nothing for three months
but set in his back yard and learn that frog to jump. And you bet
you he *did* learn him, too. He'd give him a little punch behind, and
the next minute you'd see that frog whirling in the air like a
doughnut—see him turn one summerset, or may be a couple, if he
got a good start, and come down flat-footed and all right, like a
cat. He got him up so in the matter of cetching flies, and kept him
in practice so constant, that he'd nail a fly every time as far as he
could see him. Smiley said all a frog wanted was education, and he
could do most any thing—and I believe him. Why, I've seen him
set Dan'l Webster down here on this floor—Dan'l Webster was the
name of the frog—and sing out, "Flies, Dan'l, flies!" and quicker'n
you could wink, he'd spring straight up, and snake a fly off'n the
counter there, and flop down on the floor again as solid as a gob
of mud, and fall to scratching the side of his head with his hind
foot as indifferent as if he hadn't no idea he'd been doin' any
more'n any frog might do. You never see a frog so modest and
straightfor'ard as he was, for all he was so gifted. And when it come
to fair and square jumping on a dead level, he could get over more
ground at one straddle than any animal of his breed you ever see.
Jumping on a dead level was his strong suit, you understand; and
when it come to that, Smiley would ante up money on him as

long as he had a red. Smiley was monstrous proud of his frog, and well he might be, for fellers that had traveled and been everywheres, all said he laid over any frog that ever *they* see.

Well, Smiley kept the beast in a little lattice box, and he used to fetch him down town sometimes and lay for a bet. One day a feller—a stranger in the camp, he was—come across him with his box, and says:

"What might it be that you've got in the box?"

And Smiley says, sorter indifferent like, "It might be a parrot, or it might be a canary, may be, but it an't—it's only just a frog."

And the feller took it, and looked at it careful, and turned it round this way and that, and says, "H'm—so 'tis. Well, what's *he* good for?"

"Well," Smiley says, easy and careless, "He's good enough for *one* thing, I should judge—he can outjump ary frog in Calaveras county."

The feller took the box again, and took another long, particular look, and give it back to Smiley, and says, very deliberate, "Well, I don't see no p'ints about that frog that's any better'n any other frog."

"May be you don't," Smiley says. "May be you understand frogs, and may be you don't understand 'em; may be you've had experience, and may be you an't only a amature, as it were. Anyways, I've got *my* opinion, and I'll risk forty dollars that he can outjump any frog in Calaveras county."

And the feller studied a minute, and then says, kinder sad like, "Well, I'm only a stranger here, and I an't got no frog; but if I had a frog, I'd bet you."

And then Smiley says, "That's all right—that's all right—if you'll hold my box a minute, I'll go and get you a frog." And so the feller took the box, and put up his forty dollars along with Smiley's, and set down to wait.

So he set there a good while thinking and thinking to hisself, and then he got the frog out and prized his mouth open and took a teaspoon and filled him full of quail shot—filled him pretty near up to his chin—and set him on the floor. Smiley he went to the swamp and slopped around in the mud for a long time, and finally he ketched a frog, and fetched him in, and give him to this feller, and says:

"Now, if you're ready, set him alongside of Dan'l, with his forepaws just even with Dan'l's, and I'll give the word." Then he says, "One—two—three—jump!" and him and the feller touched up the frogs from behind, and the new frog hopped off, but Dan'l give a heave, and hysted up his shoulders—so—like a Frenchman, but it wan't no use—he couldn't budge; he was planted as solid as an anvil, and he couldn't no more stir than if he was anchored out. Smiley was a good deal surprised, and he was disgusted too, but he didn't have no idea what the matter was, of course.

The feller took the money and started away; and when he was going out at the door, he sorter jerked his thumb over his shoulder—this way—at Dan'l, and says again, very deliberate, "Well, I don't see no p'ints about that frog that's any better'n any other frog."

Smiley he stood scratching his head and looking down at Dan'l a long time, and at last he says, "I do wonder what in the nation that frog throw'd off for—I wonder if there an't something the matter with him—he 'pears to look mighty baggy, somehow." And he ketched Dan'l by the nap of the neck, and lifted him up and says, "Why, blame my cats, if he don't weigh five pound!" and turned him upside down, and he belched out a double handful of shot. And then he see how it was, and he was the maddest man— he set the frog down and took out after that feller, but he never ketched him. And——

[Here Simon Wheeler heard his name called from the front yard, and got up to see what was wanted.] And turning to me as he moved away, he said: "Just set where you are, stranger, and rest easy—I an't going to be gone a second."

But, by your leave, I did not think that a continuation of the history of the enterprising vagabond *Jim* Smiley would be likely to afford me much information concerning the Rev. *Leonidas W.* Smiley, and so I started away.

At the door I met the sociable Wheeler returning, and he buttonholed me and recommenced:

"Well, thish-yer Smiley had a yaller one-eyed cow that didn't have no tail, only jest a short stump like a bannanner, and——"

"Oh! hang Smiley and his afflicted cow!" I muttered, good-naturedly, and bidding the old gentleman good-day, I departed.

A New England Nun

Mary E. Wilkins-Freeman
(1852–1930)

It was late in the afternoon, and the light was waning. There was a difference in the look of the tree shadows out in the yard. Somewhere in the distance cows were lowing and a little bell was tinkling; now and then a farm-wagon tilted by, and the dust flew; some blue-shirted laborers with shovels over their shoulders plodded past; little swarms of flies were dancing up and down before the people's faces in the soft air. There seemed to be a gentle stir arising over everything for the mere sake of subsidence—a very premonition of rest and hush and night.

This soft diurnal commotion was over Louisa Ellis also. She had been peacefully sewing at her sitting-room window all the afternoon. Now she quilted her needle carefully into her work, which she folded precisely, and laid in a basket with her thimble and thread and scissors. Louisa Ellis could not remember that ever in her life she had mislaid one of these little feminine appurtenances, which had become, from long use and constant association, a very part of her personality.

Louisa tied a green apron round her waist, and got out a flat straw hat with a green ribbon. Then she went into the garden with a little blue crockery bowl, to pick some currants for her tea. After the currants were picked she sat on the back door-step and stemmed them, collecting the stems carefully in her apron, and afterwards throwing them into the hen-coop. She looked sharply at the grass beside the step to see if any had fallen there.

Louisa was slow and still in her movements; it took her a long time to prepare her tea; but when ready it was set forth with as much grace as if she had been a veritable guest to her own self. The little square table stood exactly in the centre of the kitchen, and was covered with a starched linen cloth whose border pattern of flowers glistened. Louisa had a damask napkin on her tea-tray, where were arranged a cut-glass tumbler full of teaspoons, a silver cream-pitcher, a china sugar-bowl, and one pink china cup and saucer. Louisa used china every day—something which none of her neighbors did. They whispered about it among themselves. Their daily tables were laid with common crockery, their sets of best china stayed in the parlor closet, and Louisa Ellis was no richer nor better bred than they. Still she would use the china. She had for her supper a glass dish full of sugared currants, a plate of little cakes, and one of light white biscuits. Also a leaf or two of lettuce, which she cut up daintily. Louisa was very fond of lettuce, which she raised to perfection in her little garden. She ate quite heartily, though in a delicate, pecking way; it seemed almost surprising that any considerable bulk of the food should vanish.

After tea she filled a plate with nicely baked thin corn-cakes, and carried them out into the back-yard.

"Caesar!" she called. "Caesar! Caesar!"

There was a little rush, and the clank of a chain, and a large yellow-and-white dog appeared at the door of his tiny hut, which was half hidden among the tall grasses and flowers. Louisa patted him and gave him the corn-cakes. Then she returned to the house and washed the tea-things, polishing the china carefully. The twilight had deepened; the chorus of the frogs floated in at the open window wonderfully loud and shrill, and once in a while a long sharp drone from a tree-toad pierced it. Louisa took off her green gingham apron, disclosing a shorter one of pink-and-white print. She lighted her lamp, and sat down again with her sewing.

In about half an hour Joe Dagget came. She heard his heavy step on the walk, and rose and took off her pink-and-white apron. Under that was still another—white linen with a little cambric edging on the bottom; that was Louisa's company apron. She never wore it without her calico sewing apron over it unless she had a guest. She had barely folded the pink-and-white one with methodical haste and laid it in a table-drawer when the door opened and Joe Dagget entered.

He seemed to fill up the whole room. A little yellow canary that had been asleep in his green cage at the south window woke up and fluttered wildly, beating his little yellow wings against the wires. He always did so when Joe Dagget came into the room.

"Good-evening," said Louisa. She extended her hand with a kind of solemn cordiality.

"Good-evening, Louisa," returned the man, in a loud voice.

She placed a chair for him, and they sat facing each other, with the table between them. He sat bolt-upright, toeing out his heavy feet squarely, glancing with a good-humored uneasiness around the room. She sat gently erect, folding her slender hands in her white-linen lap.

"Been a pleasant day," remarked Dagget.

"Real pleasant," Louisa assented, softly. "Have you been haying?" she asked, after a little while.

"Yes, I've been haying all day, down in the ten-acre lot. Pretty hot work."

"It must be."

"Yes, it's pretty hot work in the sun."

"Is your mother well to-day?"

"Yes, mother's pretty well."

"I suppose Lily Dyer's with her now?"

Dagget colored. "Yes, she's with her," he answered, slowly.

He was not very young, but there was a boyish look about his large face. Louisa was not quite as old as he, her face was fairer and smoother, but she gave people the impression of being older.

"I suppose she's a good deal of help to your mother," she said, further.

"I guess she is; I don't know how mother'd get along without her," said Dagget, with a sort of embarrassed warmth.

"She looks like a real capable girl. She's pretty-looking too," remarked Louisa.

"Yes, she is pretty fair-looking."

Presently Dagget began fingering the books on the table. There was a square red autograph album, and a Young Lady's Gift-Book which had belonged to Louisa's mother. He took them up one after the other and opened them; then laid them down again, the album on the Gift-Book.

Louisa kept eying them with mild uneasiness. Finally she rose and changed the position of the books, putting the album underneath. That was the way they had been arranged in the first place.

Dagget gave an awkward little laugh. "Now what difference did it make which book was on top?" said he.

Louisa looked at him with a deprecating smile. "I always keep them that way," murmured she.

"You do beat everything," said Dagget, trying to laugh again. His large face was flushed.

He remained about an hour longer, then rose to take leave. Going out, he stumbled over a rug, and trying to recover himself, hit Louisa's work-basket on the table, and knocked it on the floor.

He looked at Louisa, then at the rolling spools; he ducked himself awkwardly toward them, but she stopped him. "Never mind," said she; "I'll pick them up after you're gone."

She spoke with a mild stiffness. Either she was a little disturbed, or his nervousness affected her, and made her seem constrained in her effort to reassure him.

When Joe Dagget was outside he drew in the sweet evening air with a sigh, and felt much as an innocent and perfectly well-intentioned bear might after his exit from a china shop.

Louisa, on her part, felt much as the kind-hearted, long-suffering owner of the china shop might have done after the exit of the bear.

She tied on the pink, then the green apron, picked up all the scattered treasures and replaced them in her work-basket, and straightened the rug. Then she set the lamp on the floor, and began sharply examining the carpet. She even rubbed her fingers over it, and looked at them.

"He's tracked in a good deal of dust," she murmured. "I thought he must have."

Louisa got a dust-pan and brush, and swept Joe Dagget's track carefully.

If he could have known it, it would have increased his perplexity and uneasiness, although it would not have disturbed his loyalty in the least. He came twice a week to see Louisa Ellis, and every time, sitting there in her delicately sweet room, he felt as if surrounded by a hedge of lace. He was afraid to stir lest he should put a clumsy foot or hand through the fairy web, and he had always the consciousness that Louisa was watching fearfully lest he should.

Still the lace and Louisa commanded perforce his perfect respect and patience and loyalty. They were to be married in a month, after a singular courtship which had lasted for a matter of fifteen years. For fourteen out of the fifteen years the two had not once seen each other, and they had seldom exchanged letters. Joe had been all those years in Australia, where he had gone to make his fortune, and where he had stayed until he made it. He would have stayed fifty years if it had taken so long, and come home feeble and tottering, or never come home at all, to marry Louisa.

But the fortune had been made in the fourteen years, and he had come home now to marry the woman who had been patiently and unquestioningly waiting for him all that time.

Shortly after they were engaged he had announced to Louisa his determination to strike out into new fields, and secure a competency before they should be married. She had listened and assented with the sweet serenity which never failed her, not even when her lover set forth on that long and uncertain journey. Joe, buoyed up as he was by his sturdy determination, broke down a little at the last, but Louisa kissed him with a mild blush, and said good-by.

"It won't be for long," poor Joe had said, huskily; but it was for fourteen years.

In that length of time much had happened. Louisa's mother and brother had died, and she was all alone in the world. But greatest happening of all—a subtle happening which both were too simple to understand—Louisa's feet had turned into a path, smooth maybe under a calm, serene sky, but so straight and unswerving that it could only meet a check at her grave, and so narrow that there was no room for any one at her side.

Louisa's first emotion when Joe Dagget came home (he had not apprised her of his coming) was consternation, although she would not admit it to herself, and he never dreamed of it. Fifteen years ago she had been in love with him—at least she considered herself to be. Just at that time, gently acquiescing with and falling into the natural drift of girlhood, she had seen marriage ahead as a reasonable feature and a probable desirability of life. She had listened with calm docility to her mother's views upon the subject. Her mother was remarkable for her cool sense and sweet, even temperament. She talked wisely to her daughter when Joe Dagget presented himself, and Louisa accepted him with no hesitation. He was the first lover she had ever had.

She had been faithful to him all these years. She had never dreamed of the possibility of marrying any one else. Her life, especially for the last seven years, had been full of a pleasant peace, she had never felt discontented nor impatient over her lover's absence; still she had always looked forward to his return and their marriage as the inevitable conclusion of things. However, she had fallen into a way of placing it so far in the future that it was almost equal to placing it over the boundaries of another life.

When Joe came she had been expecting him, and expecting to be married, for fourteen years, but she was as much surprised and taken aback as if she had never thought of it.

Joe's consternation came later. He eyed Louisa with an instant confirmation of his old admiration. She had changed but little. She still kept her pretty manner and soft grace, and was, he considered, every whit as attractive as ever. As for himself, his stent was done; he had turned his face away from fortune-seeking, and the old winds of romance whistled as loud and sweet as ever through his ears. All the song which he had been wont to hear in them was Louisa; he had for a long time a loyal belief that he heard it still, but finally it seemed to him that although the winds sang always that one song, it had another name. But for Louisa the wind had never more than murmured; now it had gone down, and everything was still. She listened for a little while with half-wistful attention; then she turned quietly away and went to work on her wedding-clothes.

Joe had made some extensive and quite magnificent alterations in his house. It was the old homestead; the newly-married couple would live there, for Joe could not desert his mother, who refused to leave her old home. So Louisa must leave hers. Every morning, rising and going about among her neat maidenly possessions, she felt as one looking her last upon the faces of dear friends. It was true that in a measure she could take them with her, but, robbed of their old environments, they would appear in such new guises that they would almost cease to be themselves. Then there were some peculiar features of her happy solitary life which she would probably be obliged to relinquish altogether. Sterner tasks than these graceful but half-needless ones would probably devolve upon her. There would be a large house to care for; there would be company to entertain; there would be Joe's rigorous and feeble old mother to wait upon; and it would be contrary to all thrifty village traditions for her to keep more than one servant. Louisa had a little still, and she used to occupy herself pleasantly in summer weather with distilling the sweet and aromatic essences from roses and peppermint and spearmint. By-and-by her still must be laid away. Her store of essences was already considerable, and there would be no time for her to distil for the mere pleasure of it. Then Joe's mother would think it foolishness; she had already hinted her opinion in the matter. Louisa dearly loved to sew a linen seam, not always for use, but for the simple, mild pleasure which she took in it. She would have been loath to confess how more than once she had ripped a seam for the mere delight of sewing it together again. Sitting at her window during long sweet afternoons, drawing her needle gently through the dainty fabric, she was peace itself. But there was small chance of such foolish comfort in the future. Joe's mother, domineering, shrewd old matron that she was even in her old age, and very likely even Joe himself, with his honest masculine rudeness, would laugh and frown down all these pretty but senseless old maiden ways.

Louisa had almost the enthusiasm of an artist over the mere order and cleanliness of her solitary home. She had throbs of genuine triumph at the sight of the window-panes which she had polished until they shone like jewels. She gloated gently over her orderly bureau-drawers, with their exquisitely folded contents redolent with lavender and sweet clover and very purity. Could she be sure of the endurance of even this? She had visions, so startling that she half repudiated them as indelicate, of coarse masculine belongings strewn about in endless litter; of dust and disorder arising necessarily from a coarse masculine presence in the midst of all this delicate harmony.

Among her forebodings of disturbance, not the least was with regard to Caesar. Caesar was a veritable hermit of a dog. For the greater part of his life he had dwelt in his secluded hut, shut out from the society of his kind and all innocent canine joys. Never had Caesar since his early youth watched at a woodchuck's hole; never had he known the delights of a stray bone at a neighbor's kitchen door. And it was all on account of a sin committed when hardly out of his puppyhood. No one knew the possible depth of remorse of which this mild-visaged, altogether innocent-looking old dog might be capable; but whether or not he had encountered remorse, he had encountered a full measure of righteous retribution. Old Caesar seldom lifted up his voice in a growl or a bark; he was fat and sleepy; there were yellow rings which looked like spectacles around his dim old eyes; but there was a neighbor who bore on his hand the imprint of several of Caesar's sharp white youthful teeth, and for that he had lived at the end of a chain, all alone in a little hut, for fourteen years. The neighbor, who was choleric and smarting with the pain of his wound, had demanded either Caesar's death or complete ostracism. So Louisa's brother, to whom the dog had belonged, had built him his little kennel and tied him up. It was now fourteen years since, in a flood of youthful spirits, he had inflicted that memorable bite, and with the exception of short excursions, always at the end of the chain, under the strict guardianship of his master or Louisa, the old dog had remained a close prisoner. It is doubtful if, with his limited ambition, he took much pride in the fact, but it is certain that he was possessed of considerable cheap fame. He was regarded by all the children in the village and by many adults as a very monster of ferocity. St. George's dragon could hardly have surpassed in evil repute Louisa Ellis's old yellow dog. Mothers charged their children with solemn emphasis not to go too near to him, and the children listened and believed greedily, with a fascinated appetite for terror, and ran by Louisa's house stealthily, with many sidelong and backward glances at the terrible dog. If perchance he sounded a hoarse bark, there was a panic. Wayfarers chancing into Louisa's yard eyed him with respect, and inquired if the chain were stout. Caesar at large might have seemed a very ordinary dog, and excited no comment whatever; chained, his reputation overshadowed him, so that he lost his own proper outlines and looked darkly vague and enormous. Joe Dagget, however, with his good-humored sense and shrewdness, saw him as he was. He strode valiantly up to him and patted him on the head, in spite of Louisa's soft clamor of warning, and even attempted to set him loose. Louisa grew so alarmed that he desisted, but kept announcing his opinion in the matter quite forcibly at intervals. "There ain't a better-natured dog in town," he would say, "and it's downright cruel to keep him tied up there. Some day I'm going to take him out."

Louisa had very little hope that he would not, one of these days, when their interests and possessions should be more completely fused in one. She pictured to herself Caesar on the rampage through the quiet and unguarded village. She saw innocent children bleeding in his path. She was herself very fond of the old dog, because he had belonged to her dead brother, and he was always very gentle with her; still she had great faith in his ferocity. She always warned people not to go too near him. She fed him on ascetic fare of corn-mush and cakes, and never fired his dangerous temper with heating and sanguinary diet of flesh and bones. Louisa looked at the old dog munching his simple fare, and thought of her approaching marriage and trembled. Still no anticipation of disorder and confusion in lieu of sweet peace and harmony, no forebodings of Caesar on the rampage, no wild fluttering of her little yellow canary, were sufficient to turn her a hair's-breadth. Joe Dagget had been fond of her and working for her all these years. It was not for her, whatever came to pass, to prove untrue and break his heart. She put the exquisite little stitches into her wedding-garments, and the time went on until it was only a week before her wedding-day. It was a Tuesday evening, and the wedding was to be a week from Wednesday.

There was a full moon that night. About nine o'clock Louisa strolled down the road a little way. There were harvest-fields on either hand, bordered by low stone walls. Luxuriant clumps of bushes grew beside the wall, and trees—wild cherry and old apple-trees—at intervals. Presently Louisa sat down on the wall and looked about her with mildly sorrowful reflectiveness. Tall shrubs of blueberry and meadow-sweet, all woven together and tangled with blackberry vines and horsebriers, shut her in on either side. She had a little clear space between them. Opposite her, on the other side of the road, was a spreading tree; the moon shone between its boughs, and the leaves twinkled like silver. The road was bespread with a beautiful shifting dapple of silver and shadow; the air was full of a mysterious sweetness. "I wonder if it's wild grapes?" murmured Louisa. She sat there some time. She was just thinking of rising, when she heard footsteps and low voices, and remained quiet. It was a lonely place, and she felt a little timid. She

A NEW ENGLAND NUN

thought she would keep still in the shadow and let the persons, whoever they might be, pass her.

But just before they reached her the voices ceased, and the footsteps. She understood that their owners had also found seats upon the stone wall. She was wondering if she could not steal away unobserved, when a voice broke the stillness. It was Joe Dagget's. She sat still and listened.

The voice was announced by a loud sigh, which was as familiar as itself. "Well," said Dagget, "you've made up your mind, then, I suppose?"

"Yes," returned another voice; "I'm going day after to-morrow."

"That's Lily Dyer," thought Louisa to herself. The voice embodied itself in her mind. She saw a girl tall and full-figured, with a firm, fair face, looking fairer and firmer in the moonlight, her strong yellow hair braided in a close knot. A girl full of a calm rustic strength and bloom, with a masterful way which might have beseemed a princess. Lily Dyer was a favorite with the village folk; she had just the qualities to arouse the admiration. She was good and handsome and smart. Louisa had often heard her praises sounded.

"Well," said Joe Dagget, "I ain't got a word to say."

"I don't know what you could say," returned Lily Dyer.

"Not a word to say," repeated Joe, drawing out the words heavily. Then there was a silence. "I ain't sorry," he began at last, "that that happened yesterday—that we kind of let on how we felt to each other. I guess it's just as well we knew. Of course I can't do anything any different. I'm going right on an' get married next week. I ain't going back on a woman that's waited for me fourteen years, an' break her heart."

"If you should jilt her to-morrow, I wouldn't have you," spoke up the girl, with sudden vehemence.

"Well, I ain't going to give you the chance," said he; "but I don't believe you would, either."

"You'd see I wouldn't. Honor's honor, an' right's right. An' I'd never think anything of any man that went against 'em for me or any other girl; you'd find that out, Joe Dagget."

"Well, you'll find out fast enough that I ain't going against 'em for you or any other girl," returned he. Their voices sounded almost as if they were angry with each other. Louisa was listening eagerly.

"I'm sorry you feel as if you must go away," said Joe, "but I don't know but it's best."

"Of course it's best. I hope you and I have got common-sense."

"Well, I suppose you're right." Suddenly Joe's voice got an undertone of tenderness. "Say, Lily," said he, "I'll get along well enough myself, but I can't bear to think—You don't suppose you're going to fret much over it?"

"I guess you'll find out I sha'n't fret much over a married man."

"Well, I hope you won't—I hope you won't, Lily. God knows I do. And—I hope—one of these days—you'll—come across somebody else—"

"I don't see any reason why I shouldn't." Suddenly her tone changed. She spoke in a sweet, clear voice, so loud that she could have been heard across the street. "No, Joe Dagget," said she, "I'll never marry any other man as long as I live. I've got good sense, an' I ain't going to break my heart nor make a fool of myself; but I'm never going to be married, you can be sure of that. I ain't that sort of a girl to feel this way twice."

Louisa heard an exclamation and a soft commotion behind the bushes; then Lily spoke again—the voice sounded as if she had risen. "This must be put a stop to," said she. "We've stayed here long enough. I'm going home."

Louisa sat there in a daze, listening to their retreating steps. After a while she got up and slunk softly home herself. The next day she did her housework methodically; that was as much a matter of course as breathing; but she did not sew on her wedding-clothes. She sat at her window and meditated. In the evening Joe came. Louisa Ellis had never known that she had any diplomacy in her, but when she came to look for it that night she found it, although meek of its kind, among her little feminine weapons. Even now she could hardly believe that she had heard aright, and that she would not do Joe a terrible injury should she break her troth-plight. She wanted to sound him without betraying too soon her own inclinations in the matter. She did it successfully, and they finally came to an understanding; but it was a difficult thing, for he was as afraid of betraying himself as she.

She never mentioned Lily Dyer. She simply said that while she had no cause of complaint against him, she had lived so long in one way that she shrank from making a change.

"Well, I never shrank, Louisa," said Dagget. "I'm going to be honest enough to say that I think maybe it's better this way; but if you'd wanted to keep on, I'd have stuck to you till my dying day. I hope you know that."

"Yes, I do," said she.

That night, she and Joe parted more tenderly than they had done for a long time. Standing in the door, holding each other's hands, a last great wave of regretful memory swept over them.

"Well, this ain't the way we've thought it was all going to end, is it, Louisa?" said Joe.

She shook her head. There was a little quiver on her placid face.

"You let me know if there's ever anything I can do for you," said he. "I ain't ever going to forget you, Louisa." Then he kissed her, and went down the path.

Louisa, all alone by herself that night, wept a little, she hardly knew why; but the next morning, on waking, she felt like a queen who, after fearing lest her domain be wrested away from her, sees it firmly insured in her possession.

Now the tall weeds and grasses might cluster around Caesar's little hermit hut, the snow might fall on its roof year in and year out, but he never would go on a rampage through the unguarded village. Now the little canary might turn itself into a peaceful yellow ball night after night, and have no need to wake and flutter with wild terror against its bars. Louisa could sew linen seams, and distil roses, and dust and polish and fold away in lavender, as long as she listed. That afternoon she sat with her needle-work at the window, and felt fairly steeped in peace. Lily Dyer, tall and erect and blooming, went past; but she felt no qualm. If Louisa Ellis had sold her birthright she did not know it, the taste of the pottage was so delicious, and had been her sole satisfaction for so long. Serenity and placid narrowness had become to her as the birthright itself. She gazed ahead through a long reach of future days strung together like pearls in a rosary, every one like the others, and all smooth and flawless and innocent, and her heart went up in thankfulness. Outside was the fervid summer afternoon; the air was filled with the sounds of the busy harvest of men and birds and bees; there were halloos, metallic clatterings, sweet calls, and long hummings. Louisa sat, prayerfully numbering her days, like an uncloistered nun.

"Miss Grief"

Constance Fenimore Woolson
(1840–1894)

A conceited fool" is a not uncommon expression. Now, I know that I am not a fool, but I also know that I am conceited. But, candidly, can it be helped if one happens to be young, well and strong, passably good looking, with some money that one has inherited and more that one has earned—in all, enough to make life comfortable—and if upon this foundation rests also the pleasant superstructure of a literary success? The success is deserved, I think: certainly it was not lightly gained. Yet even with this I fully appreciate its rarity. Thus, I find myself very well entertained in life: I have all I wish in the way of society, and a deep, though of course carefully concealed, satisfaction in my own little fame; which fame I foster by a gentle system of non-interference. I know that I am spoken of as "that quiet young fellow who writes those delightful little studies of society, you know"; and I live up to that definition.

A year ago I was in Rome, and enjoying life particularly. I had a large number of my acquaintances there, both American and English, and no day passed without its invitation. Of course I understood it: it is seldom that you find a literary man who is good tempered, well dressed, sufficiently provided with money, and amiably obedient to all the rules and requirements of "society." "When found, make a note of it"; and the note was generally an invitation.

One evening, upon returning to my lodgings, my man Simpson informed me that a person had called in the afternoon, and upon learning that I was absent had left not a card, but her name— "Miss Grief." The title lingered—Miss Grief! "Grief has not so far visited me here," I said to myself, dismissing Simpson and seeking my little balcony for a final smoke, "and she shall not now. I shall take care to be 'not at home' to her if she continues to call." And then I fell to thinking of Isabel Abercrombie, in whose society I had spent that and many evenings: they were golden thoughts.

The next day there was an excursion; it was late when I reached my rooms, and again Simpson informed me that Miss Grief had called.

"Is she coming continuously?" I said, half to myself.

"Yes, sir; she mentioned that she should call again."

"How does she look?"

"Well, sir, a lady, but not so prosperous as she was, I should say," answered Simpson, discreetly.

"Young?"

"No, sir."

"Alone?"

"A maid with her, sir."

But once outside in my little high-up balcony with my cigar, I again forgot Miss Grief and whatever she might represent. Who would not forget in that moonlight, with Isabel Abercrombie's face to remember?

The stranger came a third time, and I was absent; then she let two days pass, and began again. It grew to be a regular dialogue between Simpson and myself when I came in at night: "Grief today?"

"Yes, sir."

"What time?"

"Four, sir."

"Happy the man," I thought, "who can keep her confined to a particular hour!"

But I should not have treated my visitor so cavalierly if I had not felt sure that she was eccentric and unconventional—qualities extremely tiresome in a woman no longer young or attractive. If she were not eccentric, she would not have persisted in coming to my door day after day in this silent way, without stating her errand, leaving a note, or presenting her credentials in any shape. I made up my mind that she had something to sell—a bit of carving or some intaglio supposed to be antique. It was known that I had a fancy for oddities. I said to myself, "She has read or heard of my 'Old Gold' story, or else 'The Buried God,' and she thinks me an idealizing ignoramus upon whom she can impose. Her sepulchral name is at least not Italian; probably she is a sharp countrywoman of mine, turning, by means of the present æsthetic craze, an honest penny when she can."

She had called seven times during a period of two weeks without seeing me, when one day I happened to be at home in the afternoon, owing to a pouring rain and a fit of doubt concerning Miss Abercrombie. For I had constructed a careful theory of that young lady's characteristics in my own mind, and she had lived up to it delightfully until the previous evening, when with one word she had blown it to atoms and taken flight, leaving me standing, as it were, on a desolate shore, with nothing but a handful of mistaken inductions wherewith to console myself. I do not know a more exasperating frame of mind, at least for a constructor of theories. I could not write, and so I took up a French novel (I model myself a little on Balzac). I had been turning over its pages but a few moments when Simpson knocked, and, entering softly, said, with just a shadow of a smile on his well-trained face, "Miss Grief." I briefly consigned Miss Grief to all the Furies, and then, as he still lingered—perhaps not knowing where they resided—I asked where the visitor was.

"Outside, sir—in the hall. I told her I would see if you were at home."

"She must be unpleasantly wet if she had no carriage."

"No carriage, sir: they always come on foot. I think she *is* a little damp, sir."

"Well, let her in: but I don't want the maid. I may as well see her now, I suppose, and end the affair."

"Yes, sir."

I did not put down my book. My visitor should have a hearing, but not much more: she had sacrificed her womanly claims by her persistent attacks upon my door. Presently Simpson ushered her in. "Miss Grief," he said, and then went out, closing the curtain behind him.

A woman—yes, a lady—but shabby, unattractive, and more than middle-aged.

I rose, bowed slightly, and then dropped into my chair again, still keeping the book in my hand. "Miss Grief?" I said interrogatively as I indicated a seat with my eyebrows.

"Not Grief," she answered—"Crief: my name is Crief."

She sat down, and I saw that she held a small flat box.

"Not carving, then," I thought—"probably old lace, something that belonged to Tullia or Lucrezia Borgia." But, as she did not speak, I found myself obliged to begin: "You have been here, I think, once or twice before?"

"Seven times; this is the eighth."

A silence.

"I am often out; indeed, I may say that I am never in," I remarked carelessly.

"Yes; you have many friends."

"—Who will perhaps buy old lace," I mentally added. But this time I too remained silent; why should I trouble myself to draw her out? She had sought me; let her advance her idea, whatever it was, now that entrance was gained.

But Miss Grief (I preferred to call her so) did not look as though she could advance anything; her black gown, damp with rain, seemed to retreat fearfully to her thin self, while her thin self retreated as far as possible from me, from the chair, from everything. Her eyes were cast down; an old-fashioned lace veil with a heavy border shaded her face. She looked at the floor, and I looked at her.

I grew a little impatient, but I made up my mind that I would continue silent and see how long a time she would consider necessary to give due effect to her little pantomime. Comedy? Or was it tragedy? I suppose full five minutes passed thus in our double silence; and that is a long time when two persons are sitting opposite each other alone in a small still room.

At last my visitor, without raising her eyes, said slowly, "You are very happy, are you not, with youth, health, friends, riches, fame?"

It was a singular beginning. Her voice was clear, low, and very sweet as she thus enumerated my advantages one by one in a list. I was attracted by it, but repelled by her words, which seemed to me flattery both dull and bold.

"Thanks," I said, "for your kindness, but I fear it is undeserved. I seldom discuss myself even when with my friends."

"I am your friend," replied Miss Grief. Then, after a moment, she added slowly, "I have read every word you have written."

I curled the edges of my book indifferently; I am not a fop, I hope, but—others have said the same.

"What is more, I know much of it by heart," continued my visitor. "Wait: I will show you"; and then, without pause, she began to repeat something of mine word for word, just as I had written it. On she went, and I—listened. I intended interrupting her after a moment, but I did not, because she was reciting so well, and also because I felt a desire gaining upon me to see what she would make of a certain conversation which I knew was coming—a conversation between two of my characters which was, to say the least, sphinx-like, and somewhat incandescent as well. What won me a little, too, was the fact that the scene she was reciting (it was hardly more than that, though called a story) was secretly my favorite among all the sketches from my pen which a gracious public has received with favor. I never said so, but it was; and I had always felt a wondering annoyance that the aforesaid public, while kindly praising beyond their worth other attempts of mine, had never noticed the higher purpose of this little shaft, aimed not at the balconies and lighted windows of society, but straight up toward the distant stars. So she went on, and presently reached the conversation: my two people began to talk. She had raised her eyes now, and was looking at me soberly as she gave the words of the woman, quiet, gentle, cold, and the replies of the man, bitter, hot, and scathing. Her very voice changed, and took, though always sweetly, the different tones required, while no point of meaning, however small, no breath of delicate emphasis which I had meant, but which the dull types could not give, escaped an appreciative and full, almost overfull, recognition which startled me. For she had understood me—understood me almost better than I had understood myself. It seemed to me that while I had labored to interpret, partially, a psychological riddle, she, coming after, had comprehended its bearings better than I had, though confining herself strictly to my own words and emphasis. The scene ended (and it ended rather suddenly), she dropped her eyes, and moved her hand nervously to and fro over the box she held; her gloves were old and shabby, her hands small.

I was secretly much surprised by what I had heard, but my ill humor was deep-seated that day, and I still felt sure, besides, that the box contained something which I was expected to buy.

"You recite remarkably well," I said carelessly, "and I am much flattered also by your appreciation of my attempt. But it is not, I presume, to that alone that I owe the pleasure of this visit?"

"Yes," she answered, still looking down, "it is, for if you had not written that scene I should not have sought you. Your other sketches are interiors—exquisitely painted and delicately finished, but of small scope. *This* is a sketch in a few bold, masterly lines—work of entirely different spirit and purpose."

I was nettled by her insight. "You have bestowed so much of your kind attention upon me that I feel your debtor," I said, conventionally. "It may be that there is something I can do for you—connected, possibly, with that little box?"

It was impertinent, but it was true; for she answered, "Yes."

I smiled, but her eyes were cast down and she did not see the smile.

"What I have to show you is a manuscript," she said after a pause which I did not break; "it is a drama. I thought that perhaps you would read it."

"An authoress! This is worse than old lace," I said to myself in dismay.—Then, aloud, "My opinion would be worth nothing, Miss Crief."

"Not in a business way, I know. But it might be—an assistance personally." Her voice had sunk to a whisper; outside, the rain was pouring steadily down. She was a very depressing object to me as she sat there with her box.

"I hardly think I have the time at present—" I began.

She had raised her eyes and was looking at me; then, when I paused, she rose and came suddenly toward my chair. "Yes, you will read it," she said with her hand on my arm—"you will read it.

Look at this room; look at yourself; look at all you have. Then look at me, and have pity."

I had risen, for she held my arm, and her damp skirt was brushing my knees.

Her large dark eyes looked intently into mine as she went on: "I have no shame in asking. Why should I have? It is my last endeavor; but a calm and well-considered one. If you refuse I shall go away, knowing that Fate has willed it so. And I shall be content."

"She is mad," I thought. But she did not look so, and she had spoken quietly, even gently. "Sit down," I said, moving away from her. I felt as if I had been magnetized; but it was only the nearness of her eyes to mine, and their intensity. I drew forward a chair, but she remained standing.

"I cannot," she said in the same sweet, gentle tone, "unless you promise."

"Very well, I promise; only sit down."

As I took her arm to lead her to the chair, I perceived that she was trembling, but her face continued unmoved.

"You do not, of course, wish me to look at your manuscript now?" I said, temporizing; "it would be much better to leave it. Give me your address, and I will return it to you with my written opinion; though, I repeat, the latter will be of no use to you. It is the opinion of an editor or publisher that you want."

"It shall be as you please. And I will go in a moment," said Miss Grief, pressing her palms together, as if trying to control the tremor that had seized her slight frame.

She looked so pallid that I thought of offering her a glass of wine; then I remembered that if I did it might be a bait to bring her here again, and this I was desirous to prevent. She rose while the thought was passing through my mind. Her pasteboard box lay on the chair she had first occupied; she took it, wrote an address on the cover, laid it down, and then, bowing with a little air of formality, drew her black shawl round her shoulders and turned toward the door.

I followed, after touching the bell. "You will hear from me by letter," I said.

Simpson opened the door, and I caught a glimpse of the maid, who was waiting in the anteroom. She was an old woman, shorter than her mistress, equally thin, and dressed like her in rusty black. As the door opened she turned toward it a pair of small dim, blue eyes with a look of furtive suspense. Simpson dropped the curtain, shutting me into the inner room; he had no intention of allowing me to accompany my visitor further. But I had the curiosity to go to a bay window in an angle from whence I could command the street door, and presently I saw them issue forth in the rain and walk away side by side, the mistress, being the taller, holding the umbrella: probably there was not much difference in rank between persons so poor and forlorn as these.

It grew dark. I was invited out for the evening, and I knew that if I should go I should meet Miss Abercrombie. I said to myself that I would not go. I got out my paper for writing, I made my preparations for a quiet evening at home with myself; but it was of no use. It all ended slavishly in my going. At the last allowable moment I presented myself, and—as a punishment for my vacillation, I suppose—I never passed a more disagreeable evening. I drove homeward in a murky temper; it was foggy without, and very foggy within. What Isabel really was, now that she had broken through my elaborately built theories, I was not able to decide. There was, to tell the truth, a certain young Englishman—But that is part from this story.

I reached home, went up to my rooms, and had a supper. It was to console myself; I am obliged to console myself scientifically once in a while. I was walking up and down afterward, smoking and feeling somewhat better, when my eye fell upon the pasteboard box. I took it up; on the cover was written an address which showed that my visitor must have walked a long distance in order to see me: "A. Crief."—"A Grief," I thought; "and so she is. I positively believe she has brought all this trouble upon me: she has the evil eye." I took out the manuscript and looked at it. It was in the form of a little volume, and clearly written; on the cover was the word "Armor" in German text, and, underneath, a pen–and–ink sketch of a helmet, breastplate, and shield.

"Grief certainly needs armor," I said to myself, sitting down by the table and turning over the pages. "I may as well look over the thing now; I could not be in a worse mood." And then I began to read.

Early the next morning Simpson took a note from me to the given address, returning with the following reply: "No; I prefer to come to you; at four; A. CRIEF." These words, with their three semicolons, were written in pencil upon a piece of coarse printing paper, but the handwriting was as clear and delicate as that of the manuscript in ink.

"What sort of a place was it, Simpson?"

"Very poor, sir, but I did not go all the way up. The elder person came down, sir, took the note, and requested me to wait where I was."

"You had no chance, then, to make inquiries?" I said, knowing full well that he had emptied the entire neighborhood of any information it might possess concerning these two lodgers.

"Well, sir, you know how these foreigners will talk, whether one wants to hear or not. But it seems that these two persons have been there but a few weeks; they live alone, and are uncommonly silent and reserved. The people round there call them something that signifies 'the Madames American, thin and dumb.' "

At four the "Madames American" arrived; it was raining again, and they came on foot under their old umbrella. The maid waited in the anteroom, and Miss Grief was ushered into my bachelor's parlor. I had thought that I should meet her with great deference; but she looked so forlorn that my deference changed to pity. It was the woman that impressed me then, more than the writer—the fragile, nerveless body more than the inspired mind. For it was inspired: I had set up half the night over her drama, and had felt thrilled through and through more than once by its earnestness, passion, and power.

No one could have been more surprised than I was to find myself thus enthusiastic. I thought I had outgrown that sort of thing. And one would have supposed, too (I myself should have supposed so the day before), that the faults of the drama, which were many and prominent, would have chilled any liking I might have felt, I being a writer myself, and therefore critical; for writers are as apt to make much of the "how," rather than the "what," as painters, who, it is well known, prefer an exquisitely rendered representation of a commonplace theme to an imperfectly executed picture of even the most striking subject. But in this case, on the contrary, the scattered rays of splendor in Miss Grief's drama had made me forget the dark spots, which were numerous and disfiguring; or, rather, the splendor had made me anxious to have the spots removed. And this also was a philanthropic state very unusual with me. Regarding unsuccessful writers, my motto had been "Væ victis!"

My visitor took a seat and folded her hands; I could see, in spite of her quiet manner, that she was in breathless suspense. It seemed so pitiful that she should be trembling there before me— a woman so much older than I was, a woman who possessed the divine spark of genius, which I was by no means sure (in spite of my success) had been granted to me—that I felt as if I ought to go down on my knees before her, and entreat her to take her proper place of supremacy at once. But there! one does not go down on one's knees, combustively, as it were, before a woman over fifty, plain in feature, thin, dejected, and ill dressed. I contented myself with taking her hands (in their miserable old gloves) in mine, while I said cordially, "Miss Crief, your drama seems to me full of original power. It has roused my enthusiasm: I sat up half the night reading it."

The hands I held shook, but something (perhaps a shame for having evaded the knees business) made me tighten my hold and bestow upon her also a reassuring smile. She looked at me for a moment, and then, suddenly and noiselessly, tears rose and rolled down her cheeks. I dropped her hands and retreated. I had not thought her tearful: on the contrary, her voice and face had seemed rigidly controlled. But now here she was bending herself over the side of the chair with her head resting on her arms, not sobbing aloud, but her whole frame shaken by the strength of her emotion. I rushed for a glass of wine; I pressed her to take it. I did not quite know what to do, but, putting myself in her place, I decided to praise the drama; and praise it I did. I do not know when I have used so many adjectives. She raised her head and began to wipe her eyes.

"Do take the wine," I said, interrupting myself in my cataract of language.

'I dare not," she answered; then added humbly, "that is, unless you have a biscuit here or a bit of bread."

I found some biscuits; she ate two, and then slowly drank the wine, while I resumed my verbal Niagara. Under its influence— and that of the wine too, perhaps—she began to show new life. It was not that she looked radiant—she could not—but simply that she looked warm. I now perceived what had been the principal discomfort of her appearance heretofore: it was that she had looked all the time as if suffering from cold.

At last I could think of nothing more to say, and stopped. I

really admired the drama, but I thought I had exerted myself sufficiently as an anti-hysteric, and that adjectives enough, for the
present at least, had been administered. She had put down her
empty wineglass, and was resting her hands on the broad cushioned arms of her chair with, for a thin person, a sort of expanded
content.

"You must pardon my tears," she said, smiling; "it was the re-
vulsion of feeling. My life was at a low ebb: if your sentence had
been against me, it would have been my end."

"Your end?"

"Yes, the end of my life; I should have destroyed myself."

"Then you would have been a weak as well as wicked
woman," I said in a tone of disgust. I do hate sensationalism.

"Oh no, you know nothing about it. I should have destroyed
only this poor worn tenement of clay. But I can well understand
how *you* would look upon it. Regarding the desirableness of life,
the prince and the beggar may have different opinions. We will say
no more of it, but talk of the drama instead." As she spoke the word
"drama" a triumphant brightness came into her eyes.

I took the manuscript from a drawer and sat down beside her.
"I suppose you know that there are faults," I said, expecting ready
acquiescence.

"I was not aware that there were any," was her gentle reply.

Here was a beginning! After all my interest in her—and, I may
say under the circumstances, my kindness—she received me in this
way! However, my belief in her genius was too sincere to be altered by her whimsies; so I persevered. "Let us go over it together,"
I said. "Shall I read it to you, or will you read it to me?"

"I will not read it, but recite it."

"That will never do; you will recite it so well that we shall see
only the good points, and what we have to concern ourselves with
now is the bad ones."

"I will recite it," she repeated.

"Now, Miss Crief," I said bluntly, "for what purpose did you come to me? Certainly not merely to recite: I am no stage manager. In plain English, was it not your idea that I might help you in obtaining a publisher?"

"Yes, yes," she answered, looking at me apprehensively, all her old manner returning.

I followed up my advantage, opened the little paper volume and began. I first took the drama line by line, and spoke of the faults of expression and structure; then I turned back and touched upon two or three glaring impossibilities in the plot. "Your absorbed interest in the motive of the whole no doubt made you forget these blemishes," I said apologetically.

But, to my surprise, I found that she did not see the blemishes— that she appreciated nothing I had said, comprehended nothing. Such unaccountable obtuseness puzzled me. I began again, going over the whole with even greater minuteness and care. I worked hard: the perspiration stood in beads upon my forehead as I struggled with her—what shall I call it—obstinacy? But it was not exactly obstinacy. She simply could not see the faults of her own work, any more than a blind man can see the smoke that dims a patch of blue sky. When I had finished my task the second time, she still remained as gently impassive as before. I leaned back in my chair exhausted, and looked at her.

Even then she did not seem to comprehend (whether she agreed with it or not) what I must be thinking. "It is such a heaven to me that you like it!" she murmured dreamily, breaking the silence. Then, with more animation, "And *now* you will let me recite it?"

I was too weary to oppose her; she threw aside her shawl and bonnet, and, standing in the center of the room, began.

And she carried me along with her: all the strong passages were doubly strong when spoken, and the faults, which seemed nothing to her, were made by her earnestness to seem nothing to me, at least for that moment. When it was ended, she stood looking at me with a triumphant smile.

"Yes," I said, "I like it, and you see that I do. But I like it because my taste is peculiar. To me originality and force are everything—perhaps because I have them not to any marked degree myself—but the world at large will not overlook as I do your absolutely barbarous shortcomings on account of them. Will you trust me to go over the drama and correct it at my pleasure?" This was a vast deal for me to offer; I was surprised at myself.

"No," she answered softly, still smiling. "There shall not be so much as a comma altered." Then she sat down and fell into a reverie as though she were alone.

"Have you written anything else?" I said after a while, when I had become tired of the silence.

"Yes."

"Can I see it? Or is it *them?*"

"It is *them.* Yes, you can see all."

"I will call upon you for the purpose."

"No, you must not," she said, coming back to the present nervously. "I prefer to come to you."

At this moment Simpson entered to light the room, and busied himself rather longer than was necessary over the task. When he finally went out, I saw that my visitor's manner had sunk into its former depression: the presence of the servant seemed to have chilled her.

"When did you say I might come?" I repeated, ignoring her refusal.

"I did not say it. It would be impossible."

"Well, then, when will you come here?" There was, I fear, a trace of fatigue in my tone.

"At your good pleasure, sir," she answered humbly.

My chivalry was touched by this: after all, she was a woman. "Come tomorrow," I said. "By the way, come and dine with me then; why not?" I was curious to see what she would reply.

"Why not, indeed? Yes, I will come. I am forty-three: I might have been your mother."

This was not quite true, as I am over thirty; but I look young, while she—Well, I had thought her over fifty. "I can hardly call you 'mother,' but we might compromise upon 'aunt,' " I said, laughing. "Aunt what?"

"My name is Aaronna," she gravely answered. "My father was much disappointed that I was not a boy, and gave me as nearly as possible the name he had prepared—Aaron."

"Then come and dine with me tomorrow, and bring with you the other manuscripts, Aaronna," I said, amused at the quaint sound of the name. On the whole, I did not like "aunt."

"I will come," she answered.

It was twilight and still raining, but she refused all offers of escort or carriage, departing with her maid, as she had come, under the brown umbrella. The next day we had the dinner. Simpson was astonished—and more than astonished, grieved—when I told him that he was to dine with the maid; but he could not complain in words, since my own guest, the mistress, was hardly more attractive. When our preparations were complete, I could not help laughing: the two prim little tables, one in the parlor and one in the anteroom, and Simpson disapprovingly going back and forth between them, were irresistible.

I greeted my guest hilariously when she arrived, and, fortunately, her manner was not quite so depressed as usual: I could never have accorded myself with a tearful mood. I had thought that perhaps she would make, for the occasion, some change in her attire; I have never known a woman who had not some scrap of finery, however small, in reserve for that unexpected occasion of which she is ever dreaming. But no: Miss Grief wore the same black gown, unadorned and unaltered. I was glad that there was no rain that day, so that the skirt did not at least look so damp and rheumatic.

She ate quietly, almost furtively, yet with a good appetite, and she did not refuse the wine. Then, when the meal was over and Simpson had removed the dishes, I asked for the new manuscripts. She gave me an old green copybook filled with short poems, and a prose sketch by itself; I lit a cigar and sat down at my desk to look them over.

"Perhaps you will try a cigarette?" I suggested, more for amusement than anything else, for there was not a shade of Bohemianism about her; her whole appearance was puritanical.

"I have not yet succeeded in learning to smoke."

"You have tried?" I said, turning round.

"Yes: Serana and I tried, but we did not succeed."

"Serena is your maid?"

"She lives with me."

I was seized with inward laughter, and began hastily to look over her manuscripts with my back toward her, so that she might not see it. A vision had risen before me of those two forlorn women, alone in their room with locked doors, patiently trying to acquire the smoker's art.

But my attention was soon absorbed by the papers before me. Such a fantastic collection of words, lines, and epithets I had never before seen, or even in dreams imagined. In truth, they were like the work of dreams: they were *Kubla Khan,* only more so. Here and there was radiance like the flash of a diamond, but each poem, almost each verse and line, was marred by some fault or lack which seemed wilful perversity, like the work of an evil sprite. It was like a case of jeweller's wares set before you, with each ring unfinished, each bracelet too large or too small for its purpose, each breastpin without its fastening, each necklace purposely broken. I turned the pages, marvelling. When about half an hour had passed, and I was leaning back for a moment to light another cigar, I glanced toward my visitor. She was behind me, in an easy chair before my small fire, and she was—fast asleep! In the relaxation of her unconsciousness I was struck anew by the poverty her appearance expressed; her feet were visible, and I saw the miserable worn old shoes which hitherto she had kept concealed.

After looking at her for a moment, I returned to my task and took up the prose story; in prose she must be more reasonable. She was less fantastic perhaps, but hardly more reasonable. The story was that of a profligate and commonplace man forced by two of his friends, in order not to break the heart of a dying girl who loves him, to live up to a high imaginary ideal of himself which her pure but mistaken mind has formed. He has a handsome face and sweet voice, and repeats what they tell him. Her long, slow decline and happy death, and his own inward ennui and profound wariness of the rôle he has to play, made the vivid points of the story. So far, well enough, but here was the trouble: through the whole narrative moved another character, a physician of tender heart and exquisite mercy, who practiced murder as a fine art, and was regarded (by the author) as a second Messiah! This was monstrous. I read it through twice, and threw it down; then, fatigued, I turned round and leaned back, waiting for her to wake. I could see her profile against the dark hue of the easy chair.

Presently she seemed to feel my gaze, for she stirred, then opened her eyes. "I have been asleep," she said, rising hurriedly.

"No harm in that, Aaronna."

But she was deeply embarrassed and troubled, much more so than the occasion required; so much so, indeed, that I turned the conversation back upon the manuscripts as a diversion. "I cannot stand that doctor of yours," I said, indicating the prose story; "no one would. You must cut him out."

Her self-possession returned as if by magic. "Certainly not," she answered haughtily.

"Oh, if you do not care—I had labored under the impression that you were anxious these things should find a purchaser."

"I am, I am," she said, her manner changing to deep humility with wonderful rapidity. With such alternations of feeling as this sweeping over her like great waves, no wonder she was old before her time.

"Then you must take out that doctor."

"I am willing, but do not know how," she answered, pressing her hands together helplessly. "In my mind he belongs to the story so closely that he cannot be separated from it."

Here Simpson entered, bringing a note for me: it was a line from Mrs. Abercrombie inviting me for that evening—an unexpected gathering, and therefore likely to be all the more agreeable. My heart bounded in spite of me; I forgot Miss Grief and her manuscripts for the moment as completely as though they had never existed. But, bodily, being still in the same room with her, her speech brought me back to the present.

"You have had good news?" she said.

"Oh no, nothing especial—merely an invitation."

"But good news also," she repeated. "And now, as for me, I must go."

Not supposing that she would stay much later in any case, I had that morning ordered a carriage to come for her at about that hour. I told her this. She made no reply beyond putting on her bonnet and shawl.

"You will hear from me soon," I said; "I shall do all I can for you."

She had reached the door, but before opening it she stopped, turned and extended her hand. "You are good," she said: "I give you thanks. Do not think me ungrateful or envious. It is only that you are young, and I am so—so old." Then she opened the door and passed through the anteroom without pause, her maid accompanying her and Simpson with gladness lighting the way. They were gone. I dressed hastily and went out—to continue my studies in psychology.

Time passed; I was busy, amused and perhaps a little excited (sometimes psychology is exciting). But, though much occupied with my own affairs, I did not altogether neglect my self-imposed task regarding Miss Grief. I began by sending her prose story to a friend, the editor of a monthly magazine, with a letter making a strong plea for its admittance. It should have a chance first on its own merits. Then I forwarded the drama to a publisher, also an acquaintance, a man with a taste for phantasms and a soul above mere common popularity, as his own coffers knew to their cost. This done, I waited with conscience clear.

Four weeks passed. During this waiting period I heard nothing from Miss Grief. At last one morning came a letter from my editor. "The story has force, but I cannot stand that doctor," he wrote. "Let her cut him out, and I might print it." Just what I myself had said. The package lay there on my table, travel worn and grimed; a returned manuscript is, I think, the most melancholy object on earth. I decided to wait, before writing to Aaronna, until the second letter was received. A week later it came. "Armor" was declined. The publisher had been "impressed" by the power displayed in certain passages, but the "impossibilities of the plot" rendered it "unavailable for publication"—in fact, would "bury it in ridicule" if brought before the public, a public "lamentably" fond of amusement, "seeking it, undaunted, even in the cannon's mouth." I doubt if he knew himself what he meant. But one thing, at any rate, was clear: "Armor" was declined.

Now, I am, as I have remarked before, a little obstinate. I was determined that Miss Grief's work should be received. I would alter and improve it myself, without letting her know: the end justified the means. Surely the sieve of my own good taste, whose mesh had been pronounced so fine and delicate, would serve for two. I began; and utterly failed.

I set to work first upon "Armor." I amended, altered, left out, put in, pieced, condensed, lengthened; I did my best, and all to no avail. I could not succeed in completing anything that satisfied me, or that approached, in truth, Miss Grief's own work just as it stood. I suppose I went over that manuscript twenty times: I covered sheets of paper with my copies. But the obstinate drama refused to be corrected; as it was it must stand or fall.

Wearied and annoyed, I threw it aside and took up the prose story: that would be easier. But, to my surprise, I found that that apparently gentle "doctor" would not out: he was so closely interwoven with every part of the tale that to take him out was like taking out one especial figure in a carpet: that is, impossible, unless you unravel the whole. At last I did unravel the whole, and then the story was no longer good, or Aaronna's: it was weak, and mine. All this took time, for of course I had much to do in connection with my own life and tasks. But, though slowly and at my leisure, I really did try my best as regarded Miss Grief, and without success. I was forced at last to make up my mind that either my own powers were not equal to the task, or else that her perversities were as essential a part of her work as her inspirations, and not to be separated from it. Once during this period I showed two of the short poems to Isabel, withholding of course the writer's name. "They were written by a woman,'" I explained.

"Her mind must have been disordered, poor thing!" Isabel said in her gentle way when she returned them—"at least, judging by these. They are hopelessly mixed and vague."

Now, they were not vague so much as vast. But I knew that I could not make Isabel comprehend it, and (so complex a creature is man) I do not know that I wanted her to comprehend it. These were the only ones in the whole collection that I would have shown her, and I was rather glad that she did not like even these. Not that poor Aaronna's poems were evil: they were simply unrestrained, large, vast, like the skies or the wind. Isabel was bounded on all sides, like a violet in a garden bed. And I liked her so.

One afternoon, about the time when I was beginning to see that I could not "improve" Miss Grief, I came upon the maid. I was driving, and she had stopped on the crossing to let the carriage pass. I recognized her at a glance (by her general forlornness), and called to the driver to stop. "How is Miss Grief?" I said. "I have been intending to write to her for some time."

"And your note, when it comes," answered the old woman on the crosswalk fiercely, "she shall not see."

"What?"

"I say she shall not see it. Your patronizing face shows that you have no good news, and you shall not rack and stab her any more on *this* earth, please God, while I have authority."

"Who has racked or stabbed her, Serena?"

"Serena, indeed! Rubbish! I'm no Serena: I'm her aunt. And as to who has racked and stabbed her, I say you, *you*—YOU literary men!" She had put her old head inside my carriage, and flung out these words at me in a shrill, menacing tone. "But she shall die in peace in spite of you," she continued. "Vampires! you take her ideas and fatten on them, and leave her to starve. You know you do—*you* who have had her poor manuscripts these months and months!"

"Is she ill?" I asked in real concern, gathering that much at least from the incoherent tirade.

"She is dying," answered the desolate old creature, her voice softening and her dim eyes filling with tears.

"Oh, I trust not. Perhaps something can be done. Can I help you in any way?"

"In all ways if you would," she said, breaking down and beginning to sob weakly, with her head resting on the sill of the carriage window. "Oh, what have we not been through together, we two! Piece by piece I have sold all."

I am goodhearted enough, but I don't like to have old women weeping across my carriage door. I suggested, therefore, that she should come inside and let me take her home. Her shabby old skirt was soon beside me, and, following her directions, the driver turned down one of the most wretched quarters of the city, the abode of poverty, crowded and unclean. Here, in a large bare chamber up many flights of stairs, I found Miss Grief.

As I entered I was startled: I thought she was dead. There seemed no life present until she opened her eyes, and even then they rested upon us vaguely, as though she did not know who we were. But as I approached a light came into them: she recognized me, and this sudden revivification, this return of the soul to the almost deserted body, was the most wonderful thing I ever saw. "You have good news of the drama?" she whispered as I bent over her: "tell me. I *know* you have good news."

What was I to answer? Pray, what would you have answered, puritan?

'Yes, I have good news, Aaronna," I said. "The drama will appear." (And who knows? Perhaps it will in some other world.)

She smiled, and her now brilliant eyes did not leave my face.

"He knows I'm your aunt: I told him," said the old woman, coming to the bedside.

'Did you?" whispered Miss Grief, still gazing at me with a smile. "Then please, dear Aunt Martha, give me something to eat."

Aunt Martha hurried across the room, and I followed her. "It's the first time she's asked for food in weeks," she said in a husky tone.

She opened a cupboard door vaguely, but I could see nothing within. "What have you for her?" I asked with some impatience, though in a low voice.

"Please God, nothing!" answered the poor old woman, hiding her reply and her tears behind the broad cupboard door. "I was going out to get a little something when I met you."

"Good Heavens! is it money you need? Here, take this and send; or go yourself in the carriage waiting below."

She hurried out breathless, and I went back to the bedside, much disturbed by what I had seen and heard. But Miss Grief's eyes were full of life, and as I sat down beside her she whispered earnestly, "Tell me."

And I did tell her—a romance invented for the occasion. I venture to say that none of my published sketches could compare with it. As for the lie involved, it will stand among my few good deeds, I know, at the judgment bar.

And she was satisfied. "I have never known what it was," she whispered, "to be fully happy until now." She closed her eyes, and when the lids fell I again thought that she had passed away. But no, there was still pulsation in her small, thin wrist. As she perceived my touch she smiled. "Yes, I am happy," she said again, though without audible sound.

The old aunt returned; food was prepared, and she took some. I myself went out after wine that should be rich and pure. She rallied a little, but I did not leave her: her eyes dwelt upon me and compelled me to stay, or rather my conscience compelled me. It was a damp night, and I had a little fire made. The wine, fruit, flowers, and candles I had ordered made the bare place for the time being bright and fragrant. Aunt Martha dozed in her chair from sheer fatigue—she had watched many nights—but Miss Grief was awake, and I sat beside her.

"I make you my executor," she murmured, "as to the drama.

But my other manuscripts place, when I am gone, under my head, and let them be buried with me. They are not many—those you have and these. See!"

I followed her gesture, and saw under her pillows the edges of two more copybooks like the one I had. "Do not look at them— my poor dead children!" she said tenderly. "Let them depart with me—unread, as I have been."

Later she whispered, "Did you wonder why I came to you? It was the contrast. You were young—strong—rich—praised— loved—successful: all that I was not. I wanted to look at you—and imagine how it would feel. You had success—but I had the greater power. Tell me, did I not have it?"

"Yes, Aaronna."

"It is all in the past now. But I am satisfied."

After another pause she said with a faint smile. "Do you re- member when I fell asleep in your parlor? It was the good and rich food. It was so long since I had had food like that!"

I took her hand and held it, conscience stricken, but now she hardly seemed to perceive my touch. "And the smoking?" she whispered. "Do you remember how you laughed? I saw it. But I had heard that smoking soothed—that one was no longer tired and hungry—with a cigar."

In little whispers of this sort, separated by long rests and pauses, the night passed. Once she asked if her aunt was asleep, and when I answered in the affirmative she said, "Help her to return home— to America: the drama will pay for it. I ought never to have brought her away."

I promised, and she resumed her bright-eyed silence.

I think she did not speak again. Toward morning the change came, and soon after sunrise, with her old aunt kneeling by her side, she passed away.

All was arranged as she had wished. Her manuscripts, covered with violets, formed her pillow. No one followed her to the grave save her aunt and myself; I thought she would prefer it so. Her name was not "Crief," after all, but "Moncrief"; I saw it written out by Aunt Martha for the coffin plate, as follows: "Aaronna Moncrief, aged forty-three years, two months, and eight days."

I never knew more of her history than is written here. If there was more that I might have learned, it remained unlearned, for I did not ask.

And the drama? I keep it here in this locked case. I could have had it published at my own expense; but I think that now she knows its faults herself, perhaps, and would not like it.

I keep it; and, once in a while, I read it over—not as a *memento mori* exactly, but rather as a memento of my own good fortune, for which I should continually give thanks. The want of one grain made all her work void, and that one grain was given to me. She, with the greater power, failed—I, with the less, succeeded. But no praise is due to me for that. When I die "Armor" is to be destroyed unread: not even Isabel is to see it. For women will misunderstand each other; and, dear and precious to me as my sweet wife is, I could not bear that she or anyone should cast so much as a thought of scorn upon the memory of the writer, upon my poor dead, "un-available," unaccepted "Miss Grief."

About the Authors

Louisa May Alcott (1832-1888) was born into a progressive New England family with ties to the American Transcendentalist movement. Although best known as the author of *Little Women* (1868), *Little Men* (1871), and other children's classics, she aspired throughout her life to be read as a writer of serious socially and culturally informed fiction. Her novels *Moods* (1863) and *Work* (1873) are realistic explorations of the role of women in nineteenth-century American society, and the stories she collected as *Hospital Sketches* (1863) were drawn from her brief experience as a nurse during the American Civil War. She also wrote many Gothic thrillers, which were later collected in various anthologies.

Thomas Bailey Aldrich (1836-1907) was a journalist and poet who first gained renown with the publication of his verse collection *The Bells* (1855). Much of his fiction is informed by the history and personalities of his native New England, including his semi-autobiographical novel *The Story of a Bad Boy* (1870) and the romance *Prudence Palfrey* (1874). Aldrich showed a flair for humor and social comedy in his novel *The Queen of Sheba* (1877) and especially the stories collected in *Marjorie Daw and Other People* (1873). He served as the editor of the *Atlantic Monthly* between 1881 and 1890.

Ambrose Bierce (1842-1914?) was born into an Ohio farming family, and was wounded in action while serving in the Union Army during the American Civil War. After the war, he moved to San Francisco and embarked on a career as a journalist. As an editor of and contributor to the *Argonaut*, and especially William Randolph Hearst's San Francisco *Examiner*, Bierce earned a reputation as a caustic commentator and merciless critic of people and events of the day. His acerbic wit extended to his short fiction and sketches, collected in *Tales of Soldiers and Civilians* (1891), *Can Such Things Be?* (1893), and *Fantastic Fables* (1899), among other volumes. Bierce's tales of the Civil War and the American Southwest are some of the most powerful examples of grim realism in American literature.

George Washington Cable (1844-1925) was born and raised in New Orleans and his earliest fiction is steeped in the history and customs of Louisiana's Creole culture. His story collection, *Old Creole Days* (1879), and his novels, *The Grandissimes* (1880) and *Madame Delphine* (1881), were considered controversial by the Creole population but established his reputation nationally as a writer with a skill for local color and language, as well as an interest in race relations. Even after he moved with his family to Massachusetts in 1885, Cable continued to address themes that distinguished him as a southern writer. His novel, *John March, Southerner* (1894), explored the social and moral challenges faced by an aristocratic southern family. *The Cavalier* (1901) grew out of his experiences as a Confederate soldier in the American Civil War.

Kate Chopin (1851-1904) did not begin writing until she was thirty-nine years old, by which time she was already a mother of six and a widow. She quickly amassed a distinguished body of fiction, notably the novel *At Fault* (1890) and the short stories collected in *Bayou Folk* (1894) and *A Night in Acadie* (1897). Much of her writing is steeped in the Creole and Acadian culture of Louisiana, where she spent most of her married life, and is renowned for its bold treatment of controversial themes including race relations, the role of women in modern American society, and social and domestic problems. Her novel, *The Awakening* (1899), is one of the most highly regarded American novels of the nineteenth century and a landmark of feminist writing.

Stephen Crane (1871-1900) was acclaimed a prodigy with the publication of his seminal Civil War novel, *The Red Badge of Courage* (1895), when he was only twenty-four years old. Prior to its publication, Crane had worked most-ly as a journalist in New York City, where his experience of the poverty, squalor, and grim realities of modern urban life inspired his first novel *Maggie: A Girl of the Streets* (1893). He also produced the poetry collections *The Black Riders and Other Lines* (1895) and *War is Kind* (1900), the short story collection *The Open Boat and Other Tales of Adventure* (1898), and sketches of small-town life collected as *Whilomville Stories* (1900). Crane died of tuberculosis in Germany while working on a comic novel, *The O'Ruddy*.

Rebecca Harding Davis (1831-1910) achieved instant renown in 1861 with the publication of her first work of fiction, "Life in the Iron Mills." Although born into a comfortably middle-class family, she brought an authenticity to her portrayal of the working class and their victimization by industrialization, making the story a classic of nineteenth-century American realism. Her interest in social and political reform extends to much of her writing, including *Waiting for the Verdict* (1868), concerned with the plight of emancipated slaves; *John Andross* (1874), a study of political corruption; and *Earthen Pitchers* (1873-74), a novel of women in the workplace. She married L. Clarke Davis in 1863; her children include the prolific journalist Richard Harding Davis.

John W. De Forest (1826-1906) was born in Connecticut to an upper-mid-dle-class family and traveled abroad extensively as a young man. His early books were non-fiction, including the historical *History of the Indians of Connecticut from the Earliest Known Period to 1850* (1851). His work as a nov-elist reflects his immersion in American history: *Witching Times* (1856-1857) dramatized events of the Salem Witch Trials. *Miss Ravenel's Conversion from Secession to Loyalty* (1867), based on his his experiences in the American Civil War, is regarded the first novel in the English language from a writer with firsthand experience of battle. *The Bloody Chasm* (1881) was also concerned with the Civil War. Although admired for the blunt and often cynical realism of his fiction, De Forest incorporated melodramatic and romantic elements into his novels *Seacliff* (1859), *Overland* (1871), and *The Wetherel Affair* (1873).

Philander Deming (1829-1915) spent most of his early years in the foothills of the Adirondack Mountains in New York. Upon graduating from the University of Vermont, he moved to Albany, and secured work as legislative reporter for the *New York Times*. After a series of rejections for his essays, he submitted his story "Lost" to the *Atlantic Monthly*, which published it in 1873. It was the first of what would prove several collections worth of short stories based on the people and geography of his native Adirondack region. The stories collected in *Adirondack Stories* (1880) and *Tompkins, and Other Folks: Stories of the Hudson and the Adirondacks* (1885) are memorable for their local color and sympathetic treatment of simple people whose lives and experiences have the potential for drama and tragedy.

Paul Laurence Dunbar (1872-1906) was the child of former slaves and is best known as a writer of verse that limned the Black experience in the American South both before and after the Civil War. His first volume of poetry was *Oak and Ivy* (1893). Although criticized by some for their lyricism and stereotypical depictions of plantation life, Dunbar's poems earned the admiration of William Dean Howells and other leading literary figures. His other poetry collections include *Lyrics of Lowly Life* (1896), *Majors and Minors* (1896), and *Lyrics of Love and Laughter* (1903). Much of Dunbar's writing shows a sensitivity to racial issues that influenced American social and political thought in the nineteenth century, including the stories collected in *The Strength of Gideon and Other Stories* (1900) and *In Old Plantation Days* (1903).

Alice Dunbar-Nelson (1875-1935), a descendant of African, Native American, and European ancestry, spent much of her early years in New Orleans. Her early short fiction, collected in *Violets and Other Tales* (1895) and *The Goodness of St. Rocque and Other Stories* (1899), is memorable not only for its local Louisiana color and romantic Creole inflections, but also for its concern with racial, gender, and religious issues. She was married to the poet Paul Laurence Dunbar between 1898 and 1906. In her later years, Dunbar-Nelson served as a school administrator and parole officer, and crusaded tirelessly for racial and feminist causes.

Mary Hallock Foote (1847-1938) was born into a Quaker family based in upstate New York. She studied art and design in the hope of becoming an illustrator before marrying a mining engineer and moving west. Her experiences in California, Colorado, and Idaho inspired many of her stories and illustrations. Many of her stories are traditional westerns filled with character types and incidents of frontier days. Her books include *The Led-Horse Claim* (1883), *In Exile and Other Stories* (1894), *Coeur d'Alene* (1894), *The Cup of Trembling and Other Stories* (1895), and *Little Fig-tree Stories* (1900).

Hamlin Garland (1860-1940) spent much of the first two decades of his life in Wisconsin, Iowa, Minnesota, and the Dakota Territory. His short fiction, the best of which was collected in *Main-Travelled Roads* (1891) and *Prairie Folks* (1893), is rich with portraiture of settlers of the plains and prairies and unflinchingly realistic in its depiction of the economic and physical hardships of frontier life. His novels *Jason Edwards: Average Man, A Spoil of Office,* and *Member of the Third House,* all published in 1892, are politically liberal tales concerned with oppressive economic laws, government corruption, and legislative reform. His novel *Captain of the Grayhorse Troop* (1902) and collection *Book of the American Indian* (1923) are sympathetic to the plight of Native Americans. His biography, *A Daughter of the Middle Border* (1921), was a winner of the Pulitzer Prize.

Charlotte Perkins Gilman (1860-1935) was a distant relative of abolitionist Harriet Beecher Stowe. Her most famous story, "The Yellow Wallpaper," about the suffocating limitations in the lives of American women at the end of the nineteenth century, grew out of her own struggle with depression and its treatment. Published in 1892, the notoriety of this story has all but eclipsed her hundreds of other distinguished short stories. A champion of female independence in the home and workplace, she authored a number of sociological studies touching on the subject, including *Women and Economics* (1898), *The Home* (1904), and *Man-Made World* (1911). *Herland* (1915), a speculative fantasy about a society created and governed exclusively by women, is one of several utopian novels she wrote encompassing feminist themes.

Sarah Pratt McLean Greene (1856-1935) was educated at Mount Holyoke Seminary and taught school in Connecticut before writing *Cape Cod Folks* (1882), a novel loosely based on friends, family, and the life she knew. The book, published under her maiden name, caused local controversy for its realistic, thinly-disguised portraits of actual people, but it established her reputation as a perceptive and talented regional writer. Other stories set in New England, including *Towhead: The Story of a Girl* (1883) and *Some Other Folks* (1883), followed shortly after. Her other novels include *Last Chance Junction* (1889), *Vesty of the Basins* (1889), and *Winslow Plain* (1902).

Edward Everett Hale (1822-1909) was a lineal descendant of Revolutionary War hero Nathan Hale and a member of a prominent New England family with pre-Revolutionary War roots. A liberal theologian and a patriot, he wrote prolifically, both fiction and non-fiction. He is best known for his story "The Man without a Country," which was published in the *Atlantic Monthly* in 1853 and so popular that it merited book publication two years later. His other fiction includes the Utopian satire *Sybaris and Other Homes* (1869), *Ten Times One is Ten* (1871), and *The Fortunes of Rachel* (1884). He also wrote two autobiographical volumes, *A New England Boyhood* (1893) and *Memories of a Hundred Years* (1902), and the highly regarded historical biography, *Franklin in France* (1887-1888).

Frances Harper (1825-1911) was the daughter of freeborn Black parents. She was a precocious writer who published her first volume of poetry, *Forest Leaves,* when she was sixteen years old. She became involved in the abolitionist movement and the Underground Railroad, and soon thereafter, she became a well-known public speaker aligned with anti-slavery and civil rights organizations. Harper achieved her greatest notoriety as poet with her collection *Poems on Miscellaneous Subjects* (1854), which contained a number of poems on anti-slavery themes and was reprinted many times during her life. Although she wrote only a handful of short stories, her oft-reprinted "The Two Offers" (1959) is thought to be the first short story published by a Black woman in America. Her novel, *Iola Leroy; or Shadows Uplifted* (1892), bears the same distinction.

Bret Harte (1836-1902) was born Francis Brett Harte and showed an early proficiency at writing, publishing several poems before he was a teenager. He moved with his family to California in 1854 and held a variety of odd jobs, all of which would contribute to his picaresque tales of the West and its people. In 1868, he became the first editor of the influential *Overland Monthly,* which published many of his colorful stories and sketches. *The Luck of Roaring Camp and Other Sketches* (1870), his best-known collection of short fiction, is considered an important volume for introducing the American West to the popular imagination. His fiction has been collected in a number of volumes, including *Mrs. Skaggs' Husbands* (1873), *Tales of the Argonauts* (1875), and *Some Other People* (1892). He also wrote the novels *Gabriel Conroy* (1876) and *Jeff Briggs' Love Story* (1880), and the plays *Two Men of Sandy Bar* (1876) and *Ah Sin* (1877).

Nathaniel Hawthorne (1804-1864) was born into a family with Puritan roots and lived most of his life in Massachusetts. He began publishing in 1928, and eventually collected his short stories into two volumes, *Twice-told Tales* (1837) and *Mosses from an Old Manse* (1849), which were praised for their richly symbolic depiction of America as a moral landscape that challenged and confronted its settlers and citizens. His first true novel, *The Scarlet Letter* (1849), an allegorical treatment of intolerance and hypocrisy in Puritan times, extends themes and approaches in his short fiction and is regarded a masterpiece of American literature. Hawthorne's other novels include *The House of the Seven Gables* (1851), *The Blithedale Romance* (1852), and *The Marble Faun* (1860).

Washington Irving (1783-1859) was born in New York City and began writing as an avocation while pursuing a career in law and business. He contributed to the humorous periodical *Salmagundi* between 1807 and 1808, and under the pseudonym Diedrich Knickerbocker wrote a best-selling comic *History of New York* (1809). In 1818, he turned to writing professionally. His story collection *The Sketch Book of Geoffrey Crayon* (1819-1820), which contains the classics "Rip Van Winkle," "The Legend of Sleepy Hollow," and other tales and sketches that adapt traditional European story forms for American characters and settings, is recognized as an important book for the development of the modern short story. Irving is best known as a writer who celebrated New York State and especially the Hudson River Valley and its people in *Bracebridge Hall* (1822), *Tales of a Traveller* (1824), and other writings.

Thomas A. Janvier (1849-1913) began working as a journalist in 1871 on Philadelphia newspapers. After years of travel in the American southwest,

Mexico, France, and England, he wrote *The Mexican Guide* (1886), a travel book drawn from his firsthand experience of the country. He is best remembered as a writer on the bohemian subculture and artist enclaves of Greenwich Village in nineteenth-century New York. The tales collected in *Color Studies* (1885) are vivid snapshots of their time and place, distinguished for their local color, flamboyant characters, and romance. Janvier published many stories in *Harper's* magazine, and a number of them were collected in *Stories of Old New Spain* (1891) and *The Uncle of an Angel and Other Stories* (1891). He also wrote many books on the history and culture of New York, notably *In Old New York* (1894).

Sarah Orne Jewett (1849-1909) was born into a New England family with pre-revolutionary roots and fortunes tied to shipbuilding. She began writing while a teenager and published a collection of sketches and stories, *Deephaven,* in 1877. Although much of her writing is set in rural towns and features sympathetic and humorous portraits of traditional New England types, it is unconventional in its elaboration of the domestic tensions and political and social concerns that motivate her characters. Her novel *A Country Doctor* (1884), a progressive tale of a female country doctor, is representative of the feminist concerns that inform her writing. Her short fiction is collected in *A White Heron and Other Stories* (1886), and in her acclaimed volume *The Country of Pointed Firs* (1896).

Grace King (1852-1932) was born in New Orleans to a family that suffered financial setbacks as a result of the Civil War. Her fiction is dominated by her familiarity with southern life during the Reconstruction and her unapologetic self-identification as a southern writer. She wrote her first published story, "Monsieur Motte" (1885), in direct reaction to George Washington Cable and other writers whose fiction romanticized the antebellum South. Issues of gender and race, and exquisite exercises in local color, permeate the stories she collected in *Tales of a Time and Place* (1892) and *Balcony Stories* (1893). Her novel *The Pleasant Ways of St. Medard* (1916) is regarded a classic of Reconstruction fiction. She also wrote the historical chronicle *New Orleans: The Place and the People* (1895), and the autobiographical *Memories of a Southern Woman of Letters* (1932).

Herman Melville (1819-1891) was descended from families that had fought in the American Revolution and grew up in a merchant family. In 1839, unable to find gainful employment, he shipped out as a sailor and spent most of the next five years at sea. His experiences were the inspiration for his first two books, *Typee: A Peep at Polynesian Life* (1846) and *Omoo* (1847). Melville wrote of life at sea in a number of other novels and stories, but never so brilliantly as in *Moby-Dick* (1851). A blend of realistic narrative, visionary allegory, and metaphysical speculation, the book was a commercial flop when published but eventually secured Melville's reputation in the twentieth century as a leading figure in American letters. Melville's novels *Pierre; or, The Ambiguities* (1852) and *The Confidence Man* (1857), as well as the stories collected in *The Piazza Tales* (1856), are recognized today as some of the most challenging fiction written in America in the nineteenth century.

Mary N. Murfree (1850-1922) was born in Murfreesboro, Tennessee, a town named for her distinguished family, and spent most of her life in Tennessee. Concerned that the work of a female writer would not be treated seriously, she submitted most of her fiction under the pseudonym Charles Egbert Craddock. Most of her short stories are swatches of local color steeped in the manner and mores of Cumberland Mountain folks and told in Appalachian dialect. Her short fiction was collected in numerous volumes, including *In the Tennessee Mountains* (1884) and *The Raid of the Guerilla and Other Stories* (1912). She also wrote *Where the Battle Was Fought* (1884) and *The Storm Centre* (1895), both novels on the American Civil War, and two novels concerned with the colonial Southwest, *A Spectre of Power* (1903) and *The Amulet* (1906).

Elizabeth Stuart Phelps (1844-1911), was named for her mother and raised in a minister's household in Boston. She began publishing fiction for young readers while a teenager and continued into her adult writing career, starting with *Ellen's Idol* (1864) and including the Gypsy Breynton series, a forerunner of the fiction of Louisa May Alcott, Laura Ingalls Wilder, and other writers for young-adult readers. Like these novels, her fiction for adult readers is shaped by her Christian beliefs, especially her best-selling novel of the afterlife, *The Gates Ajar* (1868), and its two sequels, *Beyond the Gates* (1883) and *The Gates Between* (1887). Phelps was a social crusader and feminist, and several of her stories collected in *Songs of the Silent World* (1891) juxtapose the romance of classic fairy tales to the grim reality of modern life for her heroines.

Edgar Allan Poe (1809-1849) is generally acknowledged one of the most important writers in the English language in the nineteenth century. He published his first collection of poetry, *Tamerlane and Other Poems,* in 1827, but it was his contest-winning first short story, "Ms. Found in a Bottle," published in 1833, that introduced him to literary society. Poe's short stories, many narrated by monomaniacal and psychologically distressed protagonists, form a bridge between the classic Gothic and the modern tale of suspense and horror. He also wrote many darkly amusing satires, and is credited with writing the first tale of modern detection, "Murders in the Rue Morgue," in 1841. His short stories are considered masterpieces of construction, and inspired many essays in which he codified the unities that governed the writing of short fiction. His best-known poem, "The Raven" (1845), also gave rise to his essay "The Philosophy of Composition" (1846), a landmark of theory on poetics. Poe was one of the leading critics of his day, and reviews and essays he wrote for *Burton's Gentleman's Magazine, The New York Mirror, Godey's Lady's Book,* and other periodicals, are among his most respected work.

Frank R. Stockton (1834-1902) was a prolific writer of short stories and novels who spent most of his life in Philadelphia. He served as an editor of *St. Nicholas* magazine for young readers, contributing stories and sketches which were later collected in *Ting-a-Ling* (1870) and *The Floating Prince and Other Fairy Tales* (1881). His writing for adults is notable for its wit and wry humor and includes the short story collections *The Lady, or the Tiger* (1884), the episodic domestic comedy *Rudder Grange* (1879), and its sequels *The Rudder Grangers Abroad* (1891) and *Pomona's Travels* (1894). Stockton incorporated fantastic themes and premises into much of his writing, and his tales *The Great Stone of Sardis* (1898), *A Vizier of the Two Horned Alexander* (1899), and *The Great War Syndicate* (1899) are regarded as important early contributions to modern fantasy and science fiction.

Harriet Beecher Stowe (1811-1896) was the child of a New England Calvinist minister and her family acquainted her early with theological and social causes. She began writing after she was already a mother of six to supplement family income. In the 1830s, she became acquainted with the Underground Railroad and the growing abolitionist movement. Her passionate anti-slavery writings eventually led her to publish *Uncle Tom's Cabin* (1852), a melodramatic treatment of plantation life, whose popularity as an abolitionist text is linked to events that sparked the American Civil War. The book's renown has overshadowed much of Stowe's other writing, which includes the novels *Pink and White Tyranny* (1871) and *We and Our Neighbors* (1875), and the rustic short stories collected in *Oldtown Folks* (1869) and *Sam Lawson's Oldtown Fireside Stories* (1872).

Mark Twain (1835-1910) was born Samuel Langhorne Clemens and spent his early life in towns along the Mississippi River, which figures prominently in his writing. His early books, including *The Innocents Abroad* (1869) and *Roughing It* (1872), were blends of fiction and non-fiction admired for their perceptive, frequently satirical presentations of modern American values. His true skills as a storyteller emerged in his short stories and novels, many of which are told in the vernacular of the rural South and feature some of the most engaging and memorable characters in American literature. His classic novel *The Adventures of Huckleberry Finn* (1885) is considered by many to be the quintessential novel of the nineteenth-century American experience. Twain's many other well-known works include *The Adventures of Tom Sawyer* (1876), *The Prince and the Pauper* (1882), *Life on the Mississippi* (1883), and *A Connecticut Yankee in King Arthur's Court* (1889).

Mary E. Wilkins-Freeman (1852-1930) was born in Massachusetts and spent most of her life in New England. She began publishing stories for children and adults readers in 1881, and was soon known as a prolific writer of short stories, novels, plays, essays, and poems. Her stories, considered highwater marks of New England regionalist writing, often featured heroines who reflected her own early personal situation living as an unmarried woman in a patriarchal society in transition from a tradition-bound to modern era. They have been collected in *A Humble Romance and Other Stories* (1887), *A New England Nun and Other Stories* (1891), and other volumes. Her novels include *Pembroke* (1894) and *The Shoulders of Atlas* (1908). She was inducted into the American Academy of Letters in 1926.

Constance Fenimore Woolson (1840–1894) was born in New Hampshire, but moved to Europe in 1879 and was a close friend and confidante of Henry James before her suicide in 1894. Her earliest sketches and stories were collected in *Castle Nowhere: Lake Country Sketches* (1875) and *Rodman the Keeper: Southern Sketches* (1880). Her best known story, "Miss Grief," published in 1880 but never collected in her lifetime, is a representative tale in which she considers the professional lives of women and the conflict between art and commercialism. Her novels include *Anne* (1882), *For the Major* (1883), *East Angels* (1886), and the posthumously published *Horace Chase* (1894).